Reap the Harvest

Born in Gainsborough, Lincolnshire, Margaret Dickinson moved to the coast at the age of seven and so began her love for the sea and the Lincolnshire landscape.

Her ambition to be a writer began early and she had her first novel published at the age of twenty-five. This was followed by ten further titles, including *Plough the Furrow* and *Sow the Seed*, the first two books in her Lincolnshire trilogy. Married with two daughters, Margaret Dickinson combines a busy working life with her writing career.

Margaret Dickinson

Reap the Harvest

PAN BOOKS

First published 1996 by Pan Books
and simultaneously by Macmillan

This edition published 2001 by Pan Books
an imprint of Macmillan Publishers Ltd
25 Eccleston Place, London SW1W 9NF
Basingstoke and Oxford
www.macmillan.com

Associated companies throughout the world

ISBN 0 330 34479 X

5 7 9 8 6 4

A CIP catalogue record for this book is available from
the British Library.

Typeset by CentraCet Limited, Cambridge
Printed and bound in Great Britain

For Dennis, Mandy and Zoë

Acknowledgements

My special thanks to Ruth Walker, Museum Assistant at Lincolnshire County Council's Church Farm Museum, Skegness, on which 'Brumbys' Farm' is modelled, for all her interest and help in my research.

I am also deeply grateful to those who so generously gave me their time and expertise and also shared their memories with me; Caroline and Gwyn Morris; Renée Bradford; Linda and Terry Allaway; Pauline Griggs; my sister and her husband, Robena and Fred Hill, and all the staff at Skegness Library for their ever cheerful and friendly responses to all my 'difficult questions'.

To all of you, my love, my gratitude and my thanks. Your kind interest is a constant source of inspiration.

M.D.
Skegness, 1996

Part One

One

LINCOLNSHIRE, JANUARY 1953

'So this is ya bastard.'

Ella Hilton scowled at the old woman standing in the doorway, hands on hips, looking down at her. Beside her, she heard her mother draw in a deep breath and the hand, resting on her shoulder, stiffened as Kate snapped back, 'Well, if that's the way you greet your granddaughter the first time you meet her, Mam, we'll turn right round and be off back the way we came.'

Shocked, Ella gaped up at her mother; Kate Hilton rarely lost her temper, but she was angry now.

The woman still stood there, barring their way into the house. 'I told you ten years ago I didn't want you here, or ya bastard, and I still don't. Nothing's changed.'

The young girl clenched her fists. Even at ten years old, Ella knew what the name meant; she had heard it often enough shouted after her in the playground.

'Oh I see,' Kate was saying. 'So I can't even come back for my grandad's funeral? Well, Mam, no one's going to stop me; not even you. We'll stay at Rookery Farm . . .'

'With the Elands? You'll do no such thing. I'll not have you staying there – with them.'

Ella felt the anger drain out of her mother now as Kate said, sadly, 'The family feud still going on, is it? Can't you ever forget or forgive anyone, Mam?'

With a sniff, the older woman turned away. Sighing, her mother gave Ella a gentle push, but the girl held on to the door frame, refusing to enter. 'No, Mum,' she whispered. 'Let's go home. I don't like it here and . . .' Her wide eyes followed the rigid back of the woman and the unspoken words hung in the air, '. . . and I don't like her.'

Kate, once more the gentle mother Ella knew, said, 'It's all right. Come along,' and she urged the reluctant child through the back scullery and into the warm kitchen of the farmhouse.

'Sit in the chair near the range, Ella, and warm your hands. Poor child's perished,' Kate explained. 'The train was freezing. I thought me dad might have met us at the station.'

The woman thumped her rolling pin down on to the pastry. 'Ya dad's too busy with the ploughing to be meeting trains.'

Ella perched herself on the wooden seat of the spindly chair at one side of the huge black range. Logs crackled in the grate and the kettle on the hob gently puffed steam from its spout. The warmth hit her cold cheeks, making them burn. Flexing her white fingers, she stretched out her hands towards the glow. Tiredness swept over her in waves; like the waves she had heard distantly as they had walked along the lonely lane following the line of sand-dunes all the way from the town to this remote farmhouse.

They had walked for miles, it seemed to Ella, whose legs had begun to grow tired. 'Can't we wait for a bus, Mum?'

Kate had smiled. 'You'd wait a long time, love. They don't come out this far.'

'No buses!' the girl had exclaimed, her skipping stilled for a horrified moment. To their right the fields, brown and flat, stretched westwards as far as the distant horizon with only a lonely farm, or a line of trees here and there, to break the monotony.

Then Ella was skipping again, taking little running jumps and stretching her neck, trying to see over the sand-dunes. 'Where's the sea, Mum? You said we were coming to the seaside. I've never seen the sea.'

'Beyond the dunes and across the marsh, love,' Kate had answered, waving her hand absently to the left. 'You can go and look at it later.'

Now, sitting in the kitchen that must once have been her mother's home, Ella looked about her at the peg rug on the hearth, the brick walls painted red, the pots and pans lining the shelves and a ham hanging from a hook in the ceiling. Then her gaze came back to the woman standing behind the scrubbed table peeling and coring apples and laying the slices in a pastry-lined, circular tin.

Ella studied her. So this woman, who had called her that dreadful name, was her grandmother.

Although old in the girl's eyes, Esther Godfrey's hair was thick and still a luxuriant auburn colour though there were strands of grey at her temples. It was piled high on the top of her head and two combs thrust into its thickness held it in place. Only the curls on her forehead and escaping tendrils softened the severe style. Her skin, though tanned through working outside in all weathers, was smooth and remarkably unlined for a grandmother. The woman's green eyes glanced up briefly and for a moment met Ella's blue gaze. 'Dun't stare, Missy. It's rude. And stop kicking ya Grandpa's chair; ya'll scratch it.'

Unflinching, Ella glared back, deliberately widening her eyes but she stopped swinging her legs; not in obedience but because it was Grandpa Godfrey's chair. Ella loved her Grandpa Godfrey. He visited them in Lincoln three or four times a year and had done so for as long as Ella could remember, but her grandmother had never once come with him. Ella had known about her, of course; had listened as

Kate always asked, 'How's me Mam?' but the young girl knew too that her mother and her grandmother had quarrelled years ago. Now, today, she had witnessed for herself the depth of bitterness between them. Ella put her head on one side and stared at Esther Godfrey, pondering what could possibly have caused a quarrel so dreadful that a mother did not ever want to see her daughter? The girl's gaze flickered towards Kate and for one awful moment Ella imagined how devastated she would feel if, for some reason, she were never to see her own mother again.

Her grandmother's voice interrupted her wandering thoughts. 'Wipe ya chin, Missy. Ya've got summat on ya face. Just here . . .' The woman touched her own cheek, leaving a dab of flour.

Ella stuck out her chin, thrusting the tiny port-wine stain on her left jawline towards the woman. 'It's a birthmark. I can't rub it off.'

Kate's voice came softly. 'Don't you remember, Mam?'

For a moment the older woman looked startled and stared at Kate, her mouth slightly open. She glanced back, just once, at Ella and then dropped her gaze.

'Can I mash a pot of tea, Mam?' Kate said, as if trying to change the subject. 'I'm parched. We've had nothing since leaving Lincoln.'

Esther's shoulders lifted in a shrug. 'Ya know where everything is,' she said, neither granting permission nor withholding it.

'Is he – is he still here?' Kate asked as she moved between the shelves along one wall and the table, laying cups and saucers and spooning tea into the brown pot. Esther nodded and jerked her head towards a door leading out of the kitchen further into the house.

'In his room,' was her only reply.

Seeing Kate move towards the door, Ella jumped up.

'No, love, you stay here . . .'

'I'm coming with you . . .' she began.

'Do as ya mother tells ya,' the older woman snapped, but Ella took no notice and moved towards her mother.

'It's all right, Mam,' Kate said swiftly. 'She can come with me.'

'Lid's off,' Esther said bluntly, mystifying the young girl even more. Ella watched her mother's eyes widen and saw her swallow hard, hesitating for a moment, but then she took Ella's hand, opened the door and together they stepped out of the kitchen and into a living room.

Heavy blue velvet curtains shut out most of the light and Ella had only a shadowy impression of dark, solid furniture and the gleam of fleshy green leaves on a plant standing in a blue and white pot on the plush-clothed table. Not wanting to disturb the solemn tick of the grandfather clock in one corner, the girl found herself tip-toeing across the room and into the small hall beyond.

Immediately before them was another door, but Kate paused, her hand on the knob, and looked down again at Ella. 'You wait here love, just a minute 'til I see how he looks.'

Her mother opened the door and disappeared into the room leaving Ella standing in the cold, dingy hall. She stood first on one foot then on the other. The minutes passed and Ella became impatient. She pressed her ear to the door but she couldn't hear anything. Holding her breath, Ella slowly pushed the door open.

In the centre of the room was a black iron bedstead with a black and white striped mattress. There were no bedclothes on the bed and on top of the bare mattress lay a coffin with brass handles. The lid stood on its end against the wall and her mother was leaning over the coffin almost as if she were talking to someone.

Ella bit her lip, her whispered 'Mum!' echoing in the silent room. When Kate half-turned round, Ella saw, with a shock, that there were tears in her eyes. Although Kate brushed them away quickly with the back of her hand, the child-like gesture disconcerted the young girl. Ella tiptoed into the room. 'What's the matter, Mum?' she whispered.

Her mother put out her arm to draw her closer. 'Don't be frightened, love. He looks real peaceful.'

'Let me see.'

'I don't think . . .' Kate began.

'Please, Mum.'

As her mother lifted her up, Ella looked down at the man lying in the coffin. 'Is that your grandad?' she whispered.

Pressing her lips together, Kate nodded.

Like a figure lying on a cathedral tomb, smooth and marble cold, his hands rested upon his chest, fingers curling in natural repose. He was dressed in a long, white nightshirt, his head on an embroidered pillow.

Ella shuddered. 'Let me down . . .' and her mother's hold loosened and Ella was standing on the floor again, the silent, lifeless figure gone from her view.

'Go back to Nannie,' her mother said absently. 'I'll be back in a minute.'

Determined not to go back into the kitchen without her mother, Ella waited in the hall. She glanced up the narrow stairs and then began to climb, pausing to listen every time a step creaked. She reached the top and stood on the tiny landing between two doors. Glancing just once over her shoulder, she lifted the latch, pushed open the door to her left and stepped into what was obviously her grandparents' bedroom, for in the corner on a stand was Grandpa Godfrey's best Sunday suit.

Like the rooms downstairs, the furniture was old, but solid and lovingly polished to a rich dark mahogany colour. A picture of the Virgin and Child was the only ornament on the stark, white walls. Ella ran her fingers along the multicoloured patchwork quilt covering the iron bedstead and her feet made no sound on the thick peg rug at the side of the bed. In the far corner, a green-patterned bowl, huge jug and soap-dish stood on a marble wash-stand.

Ella's darting glance came to rest on a line of silver-framed photographs on the pink-painted mantelpiece above the fire-grate. She tiptoed forward and bent closer to look at them. One was of a little girl with long flowing hair; that must be her own mother, Kate, as a child. She knew now, since meeting Esther Godfrey, that Kate had inherited her hair colouring from her own mother, but where did Ella's own colour come from then?

'Such a pretty strawberry blonde,' the hairdresser always said as she trimmed Ella's tightly curling hair. 'But I do wish you'd let her grow it a bit longer, Kate. It's so pretty . . .'

'It's not my fault,' Kate would laugh. 'There I was thinking I'd get a little girl I could dress up in pretty dresses with long, golden curls, a bit like Alice in Wonderland, and what do I get . . .?' By this time Ella would be laughing with her mother, knowing what was coming next but knowing, too, that it was gentle, loving teasing. 'A tomboy with short hair who'd spend her life in trousers and shorts given half a chance.'

Ella's wandering thoughts came back to the pictures in front of her. There was another of a young woman in a uniform. That was definitely her mother, because Ella knew she had been in the WAAFs in the last war. Kate's two best friends from those days – Mavis and Isobel – still visited them quite often and they were Ella's godmothers too.

Another photograph showed a small child with straight, mousey hair and a sulky face. Perhaps that was her mother's younger sister, Lilian. Ella couldn't be sure, for her aunt lived away and they had never met.

The last photograph stood at the very back of the shelf, half-obscured by a letter propped in front of it. Curious, Ella pushed the envelope to one side and found herself looking at a fading, sepia photograph of a young man in uniform. He was standing stiffly, as if he was hardly daring to breathe and in his eyes there was a look of – not exactly fear, Ella decided, he just looked sort of – lost. The girl frowned thoughtfully and put her head on one side, pondering. He looked strangely familiar, but she knew it wasn't her Grandpa Godfrey as a young man because the man in the photograph had black curly hair and dark eyes whereas Jonathan Godfrey had fair hair, turning grey now. He was not very tall either, certainly not as tall as Grandpa . . .

'What are you doing in here, Missy? Nosing into things that dun't concern ya?'

The voice made her jump and she swivelled round to see her grandmother standing in the doorway. Ella had been so intent upon the family pictures that she had not heard footsteps mounting the stairs.

The excuse came easily to her lips for although it had not been the initial reason she had ventured upstairs, it was now the truth. 'I wanted the lav, Nannie. I can't find it.'

The woman gave a snort of laughter. 'We dun't have such fancy things as an indoor lav in the country, Missy. It's outside.'

'So's ours at home. It's across the back yard,' Ella said and began to cross towards her grandmother and the door, making no apology for having been caught in Esther's bedroom.

'And dun't call me "Nannie"' Esther said. 'Meks me sound like a goat. You call me Grannie.'

Ella stared at her and then suddenly the young girl's face broke into an impish grin. Her blue eyes danced with mischief. 'All right – Gran.'

It was a half-way concession without being complete capitulation.

Her grandmother's green eyes flashed fire. 'Grannie.'

Boldly, the girl's gaze never faltered. 'Gran,' she said, calmly but decisively.

The battle of wills had begun.

Two

Her grandmother's strong fingers were digging into Ella's shoulder as she found herself being propelled down the narrow stairs, through the living room, kitchen and scullery and out of the back door. Turning to the right towards smaller brick buildings attached to the main house, they passed one door and came to a second. Esther flung this open.

It was nothing like the lav across the yard back home in Lincoln. There, it was a proper flush toilet with a chain to pull; here, it was a wooden bench fitted against the wall with a hole in the centre. Dangling from a hook on the wall a loop of string held squares of neatly torn newspaper. Ella wrinkled her nose at the sour smell in the gloomy, confined space, the only light coming from the draughty gaps above and below the wooden door. Perched on the seat, her feet swinging above the rough-set cobbles of the floor, Ella shuddered and was glad to jump down, yank up her knickers and push open the door. It crashed back against the brick wall.

'What are you doing, child? Ya'll have the door off its hinges.'

Blinking in the sudden light, Ella saw her grandmother coming across the yard from the barn. The girl breathed deeply in the fresh air. 'It pongs in there.'

Esther sucked her tongue against her teeth in a sound of exasperation and pointed towards the back door. 'Into the scullery with you and wash ya hands.'

Pushing up the sleeves of her jumper, Ella frowned. In the deep sink there was a white, enamel bowl and on the window-sill, a dish and soap. But where were the taps? To the side of the sink, there was a huge sort of spout and a big handle, but there were no taps.

Ella opened her mouth and shouted, 'Mum. Mum!'

But it was her grandmother who appeared again in the doorway to the kitchen. '*Now* what's the matter?'

'Where are the taps?'

They glared at each other once more. 'Taps? What do ya think this is? A posh hotel? Work the pump, child.'

Ella blinked. Pump? What on earth did this old woman mean? What pump?

'Dear, oh dear. What has your mother been doing? Dun't you know anything?'

Impatiently, the woman pushed past Ella and grasped the big handle. She worked it up and down and water splashed from the spout into the bowl. 'There, see how to do it?'

The girl said nothing, but plunged her hands into the bowl, only to pull them out again quickly.

'Ugh! It's cold.' She twisted her head round and looked up at her grandmother resentfully.

'Course it's cold. None of ya namby-pamby ways here, Missy. We always wash in cold water, night and morning.'

Thinking with longing of the steaming hot water gushing from the taps at home, Ella stared up at her grandmother. 'You don't *bath* in cold water, do you?' she asked incredulously, although she was beginning to think that anything might be possible in this place.

'Bath night's on a Friday night in a tin bath on the hearth in the kitchen. Every drop of hot water comes from the side boiler in the range.'

Ella gawped at her again, trying to imagine bathing in

the kitchen in front of the fire instead of in the white enamelled bath at home.

'It seems,' Esther Godfrey remarked drily, 'that you've been spoilt by city life, Missy. You've a lot to learn . . .'

'I don't think I want . . .' Ella began and then the sound of hob-nailed boots in the yard made her glance out of the scullery window. Suddenly everything was all right, for coming across the yard was someone she knew – knew very well – and loved dearly.

'Grandpa. Grandpa!' she cried, and, shaking the icy droplets from her hands, she ran out of the back door.

'Just a minute,' her grandmother began, 'you haven't finished washing your hands properly . . .'

But Ella was gone, scampering across the yard towards the tall man whose blue eyes crinkled with laughter when he saw her. Knowing her grandmother must still be watching, Ella flung her arms wide in greeting, inviting him to catch her and swing her up into his arms.

'My, you're getting a big girl,' Jonathan Godfrey said, pretending to puff and pant under her weight.

Casting a sly glance back towards where her grandmother stood, hands on hips, watching, Ella wound her arms around her grandfather's neck and pressed her cheek close to his bristly face. Seeing the frown on her grandmother's face, Ella was triumphant.

'Have you given Kate her letter, Esther?' Grandpa Godfrey said as he pulled off his cap, unwound the long woollen scarf from his neck and kissed Kate's cheek in greeting.

'Letter? For me?'

Ella saw her mother's puzzled expression. 'Why should a letter for me come here? I haven't lived here for years.'

With a work-worn hand, the purple veins standing out

against the tanned skin, he swept back the untidy lock of greying hair that fell across his forehead and shrugged. 'Well, it did. Last week. I was going to send it on to you, but knowing you'd be coming for the funeral . . . Where is it, Esther?'

'On the mantelpiece in me bedroom.'

A few moments later Jonathan was handing it to Kate.

'Who's it from, Mum?'

'I . . .' Her mother's fingers were trembling. She was staring, mesmerized, at the envelope in her hand.

'Open it, Mum,' Ella urged, hopping up and down. 'Who's it from?'

'Be still, child. Leave ya mother be . . .' her grandmother began.

'Come outside with me, Ella,' Grandpa Godfrey said.

'But I want to know . . .'

'Come along. Put your coat on.' Though his voice was gentle, his hand on her shoulder was firm and would allow no argument. 'We'll go and feed the pigs.'

'Mum . . .?' Ella began again, but her mother was not listening. Instead Kate was now hurrying towards the door leading into the privacy of the living room, everyone else in the kitchen forgotten . . .

'Where are we going, Mum? Are we going home now?'

They were walking back the way they had come along the lane, but this time towards the town. Ella, never still, skipped and danced and hopped beside her mother. The late January day was blustery and cold. The icy wind stung the girl's cheeks.

'No. We're going to Rookery Farm.'

'Who lives there, then?'

Her mother's voice was soft. 'Uncle Danny.'

Ella stopped her skipping and stood still for a moment, her eyes shining, a grin stretching her wide mouth. 'Uncle Danny?' she squeaked with delight. 'Really?'

Her mother nodded. Before they had gone very far, Kate said, 'This way, Ella,' and they turned to the left off the coast road, taking a lane leading inland. Ahead of them in the distance, Ella could see tall chimneys poking skywards from a clump of trees.

'Is that it? Is that where Uncle Danny and Aunty Rose live?'

Kate smiled. 'No, love. That's the old squire's place. It's empty now, I think.'

'Why?' Ella jumped over a puddle at the side of the lane and back again, but the heels of her sturdy, lace-up shoes caught the edge and spattered her grey knee-length socks with muddy water.

'Oh, darling.' Kate sighed. 'Do walk properly.'

Ella came and walked sedately beside her mother for a few moments. 'Why's the house empty, Mum?'

'The squire died a few years back and his son lives in London.'

Ella, skipping once more, glanced across the expanse of open fields all around her. Shuddering, she pulled her scarf closer around her neck and muttered, 'Don't blame him.'

She felt her mother look at her. 'Don't you like it here, Ella? It's our home.'

'No, it isn't. Lincoln's our home.'

'Well, yes, I suppose so. But our roots are here. This is where all our family are . . .'

'Aunty Peggy's our family,' Ella retorted stoutly. She and her mother lived with Peggy Godfrey, Grandpa Godfrey's sister, in a terraced house in Lincoln; it was the only home Ella had ever known. '*She* wants us,' the young girl added pointedly. 'Gran doesn't.'

She heard her mother sigh and looked up to see the expression in Kate's green eyes that said, You're too sharp for your own good sometimes, young Ella Hilton. It was what Aunty Peggy often said to her when she asked too many questions. 'Is that why we've never been here before?' the girl persisted now. 'Because you and Gran quarrelled?'

Kate looked away again, her glance roaming over the flat fields all around them. 'I suppose so.'

'What was it about?'

'It's a long story, love.'

'Tell me?'

'Not now. We're getting near Rookery Farm.'

To their right, Ella saw a long, low farmhouse with white-washed walls surrounded by buildings, sheds and barns. Her mother was bending towards her. 'You're not to ask awkward questions when we get there, Ella. D'you hear?'

'Why?' The girl's candid blue eyes demanded an explanation.

'Because . . . Oh I can't explain it all now.'

'Tell me!'

'No, not now.' Her mother was firm as she said again, 'When you're older, I'll explain everything.'

'Promise?'

'I promise.'

Ella Hilton was an intelligent child with an understanding and perception which sometimes exceeded her years. But at this moment she was beginning to feel, disturbingly, that there was a great deal she did not know or understand about her own family. As soon as another thought came into her head, it came out of her mouth. 'That old man in the coffin? Your grandfather . . .'

'He was always so good to me,' Kate murmured, tears

in her voice. She seemed to be thinking aloud, not really talking to Ella so much as reminiscing to herself.

Ella tugged at her mother's sleeve. 'He's not – he can't be – that old woman's father.'

Kate stopped and stared at her daughter. 'Old woman . . .?' Laughter bubbled up inside Kate, banishing for a moment her melancholy memories. Child-like, she clapped her hand over her mouth. 'Oh Ella, she'd box your ears if she heard you call her that. My mother, Esther Godfrey, an old woman!'

Ella was laughing too, dancing around her mother in the lane. She watched Kate take a deep breath, revelling in the breeze ruffling her long, shoulder-length auburn hair; saw her close her eyes and lift her face to the sky, a small smile curving her mouth.

'Oh, it's so good to be back,' Kate murmured. 'I hadn't realised just how much I missed this place.'

Ella's laughter died. She was suddenly, uncomfortably, aware that back here in the place she still called 'home', her mother did not share her feeling of belonging in the city. To Ella, these wide open spaces and glowering grey skies were awesome and lonely.

'I don't like it here,' she muttered as Kate pushed open the farmyard gate and two sheepdogs near the back door of the house began barking. 'I don't like that tiny bedroom I had to sleep in last night. I bumped my head on that sloping ceiling and it was all – all creaky in the night.'

Kate laughed. 'It's only the wind. There's nothing to hurt you.'

'There was a funny rustling in the roof,' Ella insisted.

'Only birds, I expect,' her mother murmured.

'Well, I want to go home.'

'Don't you want to see Uncle Danny and Aunty Rose again?' Kate paused, her hand resting on the gate. Even though Ella had never visited Fleethaven Point before, she knew Danny and Rosie Eland. Like Grandpa Godfrey, they visited Kate and her daughter in Lincoln, usually at the beginning of December when they came to the city to do their Christmas shopping. It was a time she looked forward to, when the tiny terraced house was filled with laughter and presents.

Ella was quiet for a moment, torn between wanting to see them again and her desire to leave this place. 'Well, yes . . .' she began, trying to weigh her dislike of these windswept fields against the pleasure of seeing the Elands. Then her expression brightened. 'Will Rob be here?'

'Rob? Why, yes, I expect so.'

The smile on the girl's face was impish now. 'Good. He's about my age, isn't he? But I've never met him.'

'No, you haven't. I was forgetting that,' Kate said, smiling as she added, 'They've always left him at home with his grandma so they could do their shopping in peace.'

Ella was marching eagerly through the farmyard gate now but as the dogs came loping towards them, she hesitated once more. The two animals bounded around them, wagging their tails in welcome and shaking their long black and white coats. Ella began to sneeze. 'Do something, Mum. You know I – atishoo – don't like dogs.'

The back door of the farmhouse opened and as Ella heard a squeal of delight, she looked up to see Rosie running towards them, her arms stretched wide in welcome. 'Kate, oh, Katie, and little Ella, too.'

Ella frowned momentarily at hearing herself described as 'little' when already she came up to her mother's shoulder. But then finding herself clasped against the woman's soft bosom and her face showered with kisses, she couldn't help smiling. At least Aunty Rosie's welcome was better than her grandmother's.

'Hello, Rosie,' her mother was saying and submitted to being clasped in a bear-hug too.

Rosie Eland was plump, but not fat. Her hair was a fluffy cloud of shoulder-length blonde curls, swept back from her face by two combs on either side of her head, with a huge roll curl on the top. She wore a paisley patterned wrap-over apron and the sleeves of her blouse were rolled up above her elbows. Her blue eyes sparkled with her obvious delight at seeing them and her smooth skin shone with sweat. 'I was up to me elbows in soap suds in the wash-house, when I heard the dogs barking and came to see what all the racket was about. Oh, it's so lovely to see you and Ella. Come on in. I knew you'd come. I told Danny so . . .' Rosie chattered on. '"Kate will come for her grandad's funeral", I told him, "whatever her mam ses, she'll come". I was right, wasn't I, Katie? I knew you wouldn't stay away from poor old Will Benson's funeral. Eh, but it's good to have you back home after all these years, even if the reason for you coming is a sad one.'

Rosie Eland linked her arm through Kate's and, putting her other arm about Ella's shoulders, she urged again, 'Come along in. I've got the kettle on and we'll mek a pot of tea and have a good old gossip before the boys come home.'

Ella hung back a little and, feeling her reluctance, Rosie said, 'What is it, love? Don't you want to come in?'

'It's the dogs, Rosie . . .' Kate began.

'Oh don't be afraid of Bunty and Bess. They mek a lot of noise, but they won't hurt you . . .'

'I'm not afraid,' the young girl said stoutly, 'but they make me sneeze.'

Rosie looked puzzled until Kate explained. 'She has

some sort of allergy to dogs and horses.' Her voice dropped so that Ella scarcely heard. 'I think it's hereditary.'

Rosie stared at Kate and then blinked. 'Oh. Oh, I see.' But even to the ten-year-old girl, it was obvious that Rosie did not quite see. Then she said, 'Wait a minute, I'll tie them up near the barn. They'll be well out of your way then.'

The two dogs followed her reluctantly, their tails drooping, and submitted to being tied to a ring in the wall of the barn. Soulfully they eyed the visitors until Ella said, 'Oh, I'm sorry. Poor things. Let them go, Aunty Rosie . . .'

Rosie put her arm about the girl's shoulders once more and hugged her. 'Don't worry, love. They'll be all right just while you're here. Fancy you sneezing your head off every time you come near animals. And there I was just going to show you some pretty little kittens our cat's just had.'

'Oh, cats don't bother me, just dogs and horses.'

'Really? Oh, well then, come and look at them while me and yar mam have a good old chin-wag.'

Near the back door of the farmhouse, set to one side, was a long triangular-shaped chicken coop. Rosie lifted one of the lids and there, nestling in a bed of straw, was a tabby cat with four kittens, who were crawling around the straw, mewling blindly.

'They're not ever so pretty yet,' Rosie said. 'Not until they gets their eyes open.'

The mother cat was licking one of her offspring so furiously that she rolled it over on the straw. Ella knelt in front of the coop, so fascinated by the little family that she hardly noticed Rosie and her mother move away and go into the house.

Ella lost track of how long she stayed there, stroking the mother cat's head and watching her suckle her four kittens, purring loudly. She heard the click of the farm gate and looked up to see her uncle Danny limping across the yard. His left leg was held stiffly, as if he could not bend it, and he swung it outwards as he walked. Ella knew he had been injured during the war when the bomber in which he had been a rear gunner had crashed.

'It's a miracle he wasn't killed,' her mother had explained when Ella had once asked about Uncle Danny's 'poorly leg'. 'The whole rear turret of the plane fell off and landed in a tree. That tree saved his life.'

As he crossed the yard towards her, Ella scrambled up, but at that moment her mother appeared in the doorway. Ella hesitated, seeing the look that passed between the two adults, a slow smile curving both their mouths. They moved towards each other, into each other's arms. Whenever they met, Ella thought, it was always the same; the look, the smile, and then the embrace that seemed to last for a long time, her mother resting her head on Danny's shoulder, and he, his hand stroking her hair, murmuring softly, 'Katie,' before they pulled back and looked into each other's eyes. And it never seemed to matter who was there at the time, they made no attempt to hide their obvious affection for each other.

Then, as always, Danny turned to Ella and held out his arms. Now she ran to him to be swung up into the air and round and round until she laughed and squealed that she was dizzy.

Pretending breathlessness, Danny panted as he set her on the ground once more. 'My, you're getting heavy and so tall too. She's nearly as tall as our Rob, and he's like a streak of pump water.'

Kate smiled. 'Where is he, anyway?'

'On the marsh or in the dunes, just like we used to be, Katie,' he said softly. 'He nearly lives out there when he can get out of doing his fair share of the work.'

Kate laughed, her head thrown back, her hair ruffled. 'We used to do our share of disappearing at milking time . . .'

Ella looked up at them, her glance going from one to the other. 'Were you friends then? When you were my age?'

They looked down at her, startled by her question, almost as if, for a moment, they had forgotten she was there.

'Oh yes, Ella love,' Danny began, 'we were friends all right . . .' Suddenly, there was the noise of rubber tyres skidding on the loose gravel at the edge of the lane and they all turned to see a boy, a few months older than Ella, riding his bicycle at breakneck speed into the farmyard, narrowly missing the gatepost. The brakes squealed as the bike slithered to a halt a few feet from them.

'Talk of the Devil,' Danny murmured. 'Here he is.'

It was like looking at a much younger version of her Uncle Danny; the same black curly hair, the same wide grin and laughing, cheeky, brown eyes.

At her side, Ella heard her mother gasp. Kate was gaping at the boy and her face was suddenly, strangely, pale. 'Heavens! He's the spitting image of you and – and . . .' Her voice faded away and Ella saw the glance that passed between her mother and Danny.

Slowly the man nodded. 'I know. I'm not going to be allowed to forget who my father was, am I, Katie? Not while young Rob's around?'

Kate shook her head, her gaze coming back to rest on the boy.

Curious, Ella stared at him too. So this, she thought, was Rob Eland. Ella watched as the boy propped his bicycle against the barn wall and walked towards them, a swagger in every step.

'One of these days,' Danny was saying to his son, 'you'll come such a cropper off that bike.'

But the boy's grin only widened, the brown eyes full of mischievous daring.

Danny put his arm about Ella's thin shoulders, drawing her forward. 'This is Ella, Rob, and her mam . . .' Again the swift glance flew between the two adults, before he added, 'yar aunty Kate.'

Ella was still staring at Rob. He was slightly taller than she was and just as thin, but, she guessed, wiry and strong. His short, coal black curly hair glistened wetly and even though it was a wintry January day, he wore only a sleeveless pullover over his shirt, short trousers and knee-length grey socks that were apparently permanently wrinkled around his ankles.

'Hello,' he nodded towards Kate and then his gaze met Ella's fixed stare.

'Rob, show Ella around the farm while I have a talk with her mam,' Danny said.

There was a fleeting expression of irritation on the boy's face, but Ella noticed that he hid it valiantly from his father. As Danny turned away, he put his arm around Kate's waist and led her into the house. Ella watched Rob's brown eyes darken as he stared after them. Then his gaze flickered briefly towards Ella, an unspoken question in their depths, then back again to the doorway through which the adults had disappeared. She saw him lift his shoulders fractionally, shrugging off something he could not understand.

'Come on, then,' he muttered, and marched ahead of her towards a line of brick buildings, kicking a stone as he went, sending it rattling across the cobbles of the yard. 'We've got a calf in here. Like to see it?'

Ella nodded.

He showed her all round the farm; the huge sow with her litter of seven piglets. 'One died,' he told Ella, 'but she's rearing the rest.'

Then he took her to a low wall at the bottom of the yard overlooking the vast expanse of flat fields, the newly ploughed brown furrows stretching straight true to the horizon. 'We farm all this.' He waved his hand seeming to encompass all the land as far as they could see. Showing off, Ella thought, just like a boy.

'As far as that line of trees. See? Then it's your grandmother's farm.' He turned round to look at her and there was a definite note of admiration in his voice as he added, 'She *owns* all her farm.'

'Don't you?'

He shook his head. 'We're only tenants of part of the old squire's estate.'

Ella stared at him and her eyes grew large with surprise as he went on. 'She's great, your grannie. I like going to Brumbys' Farm. We often go over and help 'em out at harvest time. And your grandpa, Mester Godfrey, he's a whiz with engines and stuff. Me dad's good, but he always ses himself he's not a patch on your grandpa.'

Ella swelled with pride because she loved her Grandpa Godfrey dearly, but as for her grandmother . . . 'You actually *like* her?' The words were spoken before she could stop them escaping her lips.

Rob blinked. 'Yeah, 'course I do. We're great pals, me an' her.' The grin widened, showing a perfect, even line of white teeth. 'She calls me "Boy".' There was pride in his voice. To him, her nickname for him was an endearment.

'Well, I don't like her. I think she's a horrible old woman.'

He gaped at her for a moment. 'You're a right little spitfire, aren't ya? I bet *she* puts you in ya place.'

'Ella, Ella, where are you?' It was her mother's voice calling.

'Race you back,' she challenged him, turned and began to run.

She heard the pounding of his boots behind her and as they rounded the corner of the farmhouse and saw the three grown-ups in the yard – Kate, Danny and now Rosie too – they were neck and neck. Ella, taking the inside line, nearer the corner, gained a few valuable strides and she reached the adults first, slowing down as she passed them and turning to grin triumphantly at the boy behind her.

'I'll get you next time,' he stabbed his finger at her, but Ella only threw back her head and laughed aloud. 'I'll beat you any day, Rob Eland.'

As they joined the adults, Ella heard Danny say softly to her mother, 'My, that takes us back a bit, dun't it, Katie? I could never keep up with you, could I?'

Kate smiled down at her daughter and ruffled her short curls. 'She takes after me in some things, right enough. But she's a lot of me mam in her too.'

Ella looked up at her mother, her blue eyes sparking anger. 'Don't you say I'm like *her*,' she spat, and she turned and marched away without even bidding Danny, Rosie and young Rob 'goodbye'.

Faintly, she heard her mother sigh and say, 'See what I mean . . .?'

Without waiting for her mother, Ella walked out of the farmyard and up the lane, deliberately keeping her gaze straight ahead.

Three

The funeral on the following day was at a village called Suddaby, some thirteen or so miles inland from the coast.

'I promised him he'd be buried between 'em,' Esther Godfrey informed her family, 'so that's where he's going. But I 'spect it'll set all the tongues wagging again.'

'Oh, come, Esther love,' Jonathan Godfrey said in his deep voice, his gentle smile creasing the lines around his eyes. 'It's all so long ago. No one will remember now . . .'

'Huh, dun't you believe it,' Esther countered. 'Village folk have got long memories, 'specially when it's a nice bit o' scandal. 'Sides,' she added, resentment in her tone. 'They've got a more recent juicy morsel. Like grandmother, like granddaughter, ain't it?' Esther pursed her lips and glanced briefly at Kate, but when her glance came to rest on Ella, the young girl was surprised to see the hard expression in the older woman's eyes soften. 'Aye, an' you an' me are the innocents in it all, ain't we, Missy?'

Ella opened her mouth to ask what she meant, but one glance at her mother's face, flaming red with embarrassment, was enough to make the girl bite back her searching question.

The mourners travelled in a convoy of cars behind the hearse, a huge black gleaming vehicle with glass windows, the coffin covered with three wreaths; one from Esther, one from Kate and Ella and one with a card which read 'From all the Eland Family'.

As the vehicles drew to a halt outside the gate of the tiny church, there were only two more people who were still strangers to Ella. One was helped out of the car driven by Danny and bringing Rosie and Rob too. She was an older lady, with a gentle, rather sad, face, Ella thought. Her grey hair, white at the temples, was pulled back from her face into a round bun at the nape of her neck. She was very stout and waddled a little as she walked, as if her legs hurt her. Her round face had hardly any wrinkles, except for a few faint lines around her eyes, though the fold of fat under her jawline made it look as if she had two chins. Her smile as she came towards Ella and her mother was gentle, and, to Ella's amazement, loving.

'Oh, Kate, my little Kate.' Her fat arms enveloped Kate and then she bent towards Ella. 'And this is Ella. What pretty hair . . .' She reached out and touched the girl's curls. Usually Ella would have drawn back from such a display from a stranger, but she knew instinctively that this woman's affection was genuine and that to rebuff her gesture would hurt her.

And if anyone knew what that felt like, then Ella Hilton did. So she smiled at the woman and submitted to being hugged to the ample bosom.

'This is Mrs Eland, Ella. Rob's grandma,' Kate said.

'Oh, call me, Grandma Eland, love,' the large woman said, 'everyone else does.'

The other stranger was waiting for the funeral party in the church porch. A tall, thin woman, with short, dull-coloured hair. She wore glasses on her thin nose and her mouth was so pinched that she scarcely seemed to have any lips at all.

'Well now, fancy her coming,' Ella heard her grandmother murmur as they walked up the pathway towards the church.

'Who is it, Mum?' the curious girl whispered.

A wry smile twitched at the corner of Kate's mouth. 'Someone I thought you'd never meet, Ella. My sister – your aunty Lilian.'

Ella watched, wide-eyed, as her grandmother greeted the woman. 'So, you found time to come to yar grandad's funeral, then?'

The thin woman sniffed and leaned forward to kiss Esther, though the action was one of duty rather than of affection. 'Hello, Mother,' she said stiffly.

The stranger was greeted by each member of the family in turn.

'This *is* a surprise, Lilian,' Ella heard her mother say. 'How are you?'

'I'm very well, thank you, Kate.' The polite enquiry was not reciprocated and then Ella found herself standing before the woman looking up into the coldest eyes she had ever seen. She was holding out her slim fingers towards Ella. 'And I suppose *this* is your – er – daughter. How do you do, Danielle?'

Ella was hardly ever called by her full name, not even by her teachers at school, so it was quite a shock to hear it used so formally and, it seemed somehow, with deliberate emphasis.

That shock appeared to be shared by her mother, for she heard Kate gasp. Above the girl's head, the two sisters glared at each other until Jonathan Godfrey said gently, 'Come along, it's time we were going in.'

Putting his arm around Esther, he led her forward to enter the church behind the coffin leaving the other members of the family to arrange themselves and follow. With obvious reluctance, Kate and Lilian walked beside each other and Ella found her hand being taken by the large, kindly Grandma Eland. 'You walk with me, lovey. Yar mam's got to sit up the front. But you sit with me and young Rob.'

Once again a brief look of disgust crossed the boy's face and Ella grinned inwardly. Boys of his age didn't like being made to sit with girls, but there was not a thing he could do about it.

After the service in the church the party moved into the graveyard, making their way amongst the gravestones towards the place where a deep hole had been dug between two identical existing headstones. Standing, shivering, between the large lady and Rob Eland, Ella read the two inscriptions whilst the vicar in a monotone rattled through the words of the interment. '. . . Ashes to ashes . . .' flowed over Ella's head as her mind dwelt on the words on the two simple white marble headstones.

To the left of the newly dug grave, the inscription read: 'In loving memory of Rebecca Benson, beloved wife of William Benson, departed this life 30th March 1919, aged 62 years. Her reward is in Heaven.'

That must be the old man's wife, Ella thought. What a long time ago it was since she had died. She did quick mental arithmetic; it was over thirty years. But then she knew her great-grandfather had been over ninety.

Her glance went to the grave on the other side of the hole. 'In loving memory of Constance Everatt who fell asleep 9th June 1893, aged nineteen years. The Lord giveth and the Lord taketh away.'

She felt sad to think that someone should die so young. She imagined it could be Will and Rebecca's daughter, but her name was funny – not Benson. Everatt? It was not a surname Ella knew and yet the girl was buried so close to

Will and with a headstone to match the one at the head of where Will's wife lay.

The vicar's voice faded away and the grown-ups were beginning to move away from the side of the grave. Ella pointed at the headstone on the right and asked, 'Who's the girl who died young?'

In the silence her voice sounded shrill and intrusive. The moment she had spoken, Ella knew she had said the wrong thing. At her side Grandma Eland squeezed her hand and bent towards her to whisper softly, 'It's some relation of your . . .'

'Children should be seen and not heard,' Esther snapped, though her forbidding gaze was not on her inquisitive granddaughter but on Grandma Eland. Ella looked up to see the large woman's cheeks turn pink. She was biting her lip and even though Ella whispered again, 'Who? Who is it?' Grandma Eland shook her head and muttered, 'I'd best say no more, love.'

Esther, tucking her arm through her husband's, turned away, pausing only to glance towards Kate and add, 'Can't you control your . . .'

Ella held her breath. In the stillness it seemed as if everyone present was waiting and listening. Then she saw her grandpa place his hand over Esther's where it rested on his arm. 'Steady on, love,' he said quietly. 'Think about the child. You should know how it feels.' Esther's gaze swivelled swiftly, her mouth open to utter a sharp retort. But meeting his concerned, loving eyes, that gentled his censure, instead, a small smile played on her mouth and she gave a tiny nod as if understanding exactly what he meant. Ella saw her grandmother glance briefly at the grave of the young girl and then she looked again at Ella, who returned her stare, though knowing her own face was growing red. The girl dipped her head to the left; it was a self-conscious habit, though she was scarcely aware of it herself, to hide the tiny birthmark on her jawline.

Surprisingly, the older woman's eyes softened as she seemed to be seeing her granddaughter properly for the first time. She took her hand from Jonathan's arm and held it out towards Ella. 'Come and walk with me an' yar grandpa,' she said. Suddenly, like the sun appearing from behind a black cloud, Esther Godfrey smiled.

Feeling Grandma Eland release her hand and give her a gentle push, Ella moved forward to walk between Esther and Jonathan.

'Well,' her grandmother remarked. 'We're the oldest now, Jonathan. Head of the family . . .' she snorted with wry laughter and above Ella's head glanced at her husband. 'For what that's worth.'

Ella heard Jonathan's deep chuckle, but her head was turned to look up at Esther. The broad-brimmed hat almost hid her grandmother's lovely hair; only the wisps of grey at the temples were visible. The black tailored coat hugged her slim figure and she marched along with sprightly, determined steps as if eager to get back to her farm and its never-ending work.

'The farm's my mother's life,' Ella had often heard her mother say to Peggy, even before she had met Esther Godfrey. 'That and, of course, Dad.'

And Peggy would smile and say softly, 'I think if it came to a contest, though, my brother would win, Kate.'

'Without a doubt,' Kate would laugh. 'Hands down.'

Now as she walked along between them, their conversation flowing above her head, Ella could feel the affection between the couple. The ten-year-old girl could sense, though perhaps not rationalise, that these two people were all in all to each other and, suddenly, she felt left out, an intruder between them.

Her grandpa said, 'Perhaps Rob will take you on the beach when we get back, Ella.'

She shrugged. 'I don't think he'll want to.'

'Course he'll take you,' Esther said sharply. 'If *I* ask him.'

Ella saw the look that passed between the adults. 'She'll be all right with him,' her grandmother murmured, 'Rob's a good lad. Can't do any harm . . .' There was a strange melancholy in her voice and she sighed as she added, 'Not this time.'

Jonathan nodded and then his work-roughened, yet still gentle, fingers rested briefly on her curls. 'You listen to what Rob tells you, Ella. He knows the sea and its moods. The beach can be a dangerous place if the mists come up suddenly.'

She heard her grandmother's stifled laughter and her murmured, 'Oh, you rogue!' Then they reached out towards each other and, behind Ella's back, held hands like a young courting couple. Perceptively, Ella guessed her grandfather's words had revived a secret memory that brought an impish smile to Esther Godfrey's mouth and excluded the young girl walking between them even more. Tired of feeling an interloper, she ducked under the loop of their joined hands, saying, 'I'll wait for Mum.'

But when she turned back to look for Kate, she saw her mother and Danny walking together.

'It'll be all right for me to borrow your car on Saturday afternoon, then?' Kate was asking.

'Of course ya can. Where are you going?'

Kate tapped his nose playfully. 'Ask no questions . . .'

'. . . told no lies,' they both finished, laughing together, their heads bent towards each other, almost touching.

'I thought you were going back tomorrow?' he said, probing again.

Kate's eyes sparkled suddenly. 'There's been a change of plan and don't ask me why, because I'm not telling you.'

'Oh, Mum,' Ella complained petulantly. 'We're not staying here any longer, are we?'

'Hey.' Danny looked down at her, feigning an expression of hurt pride. 'Don't you want to stay here with us?'

Candidly the girl said, 'If we could stay with *you*, yes.' Her glance flickered meaningfully towards her grandmother.

Danny raised his eyebrows and his mouth rounded in a silent 'oh'.

'Run and find Rob, there's a good girl,' Kate said, and turned back to talk to Danny.

Ella glanced about her. Behind them, Rosie was helping Grandma Eland down the pathway back towards the waiting cars. As for her aunty Lilian, she had preceded all of them from the churchyard and was walking swiftly along the road towards a brand new car parked a little way beyond the church. The thin shoulders were hunched as she hurried along, as if she couldn't wait to get away from this place. Ella felt ignored by everyone and she was annoyed now to think that she must spend yet another night in the horrible little room. It was no better than an attic.

'Where is Rob?' she demanded in a loud voice. Her mother and Danny turned to look at her, staring at her as if, in the space of a few moments, they had completely forgotten she was still there.

'Oh – er . . .' Danny glanced about. 'I don't know. He was here a minute ago . . .'

Behind them they heard the rustle of leaves and the smack of wood on wood and Ella turned to see the boy flinging a stick up into a tree.

Ella turned and was jumping and skipping over the graves to reach him.

'Ella – Ella, don't do that!' Kate called.

Then she heard her grandmother's sharp voice. 'Danielle Hilton! Come back here this instant.'

But Ella pretended not to hear and ran on.

Four

'Never seen the sea!' The boy couldn't believe it.

'So what?' Ella retorted defensively. 'You ever seen the city?'

'Course I have.'

'Have you been to the very top of the tower of the cathedral, then?'

He stared at her, shook his head, then smirked. 'Bet you haven't.'

'Yes, I have. So there.'

'When?'

'Last summer, with Mum.'

'I bet,' he scoffed.

'Ask her. Go on, then, ask her.' She gripped his arm and, fury lending her strength, she dragged him towards where her mother and Danny were at the kitchen table pouring out cups of tea and handing them round.

'I thought our Lilian might have come back to the house,' Kate was murmurmg.

'Couldn't get away fast enough, could she?' Danny replied. 'It's a shame for ya mam and dad.'

'Mum, just tell him, will you, we went up the cathedral tower last summer. He doesn't believe me. Tell him, Mum.'

Kate smiled. 'Yes, Rob. Right to the very top.'

'There, I told you so,' Ella said triumphantly. 'I *never* tell lies.'

'I'm pleased to hear it, Missy,' remarked her grandmother, coming into the kitchen at that moment. 'Mind ya never do. Now then, off you go, the pair of you, and give us old 'uns a bit o' peace. Rob, tek Ella on the beach, will ya?' And when the boy looked disgruntled at once again being asked to 'look after' Ella, her grandmother, with an impish smile on her mouth, added, 'Time we educated this townie, ain't it?'

As the boy laughed with her at Ella's expense, Esther ruffled his black hair. 'Off ya go then, Boy.'

Ella caught her uncle Danny's eye and, giving her a broad wink, he said, 'Well, if Ella's a "townie", I reckon we're a load o' country bumpkins.'

She gave him a swift, grateful smile and, grabbing a sausage roll from the table piled high with ham and tongue, pastries and cakes, and stuffing it into her mouth, followed Rob out of the back door.

The wind whistled through the elder trees as they climbed the dunes. Pushing their way through the bushes, Ella drew her hand back quickly. 'Ouch!'

The boy looked round. 'That's a buckthorn. They've got very sharp prickles.'

She glowered at him, 'You might have said,' she muttered, but he only grinned and went on ahead.

There was a sudden rustle in the thick grass and a blur of grey fur scurried over her feet and bounded down the sandy slope. Ella screamed. 'What was it?'

'Only a rabbit. The sandhills are full of 'em.'

Hugging her arms around herself, her eyes darting to left and right, they climbed to the top of the dunes. She stood and looked about her whilst Rob pointed westwards. 'There's yar grannie's farm and all her land right to the river and beyond. That's our place over there . . .' She followed the line of his finger and saw the long low farmhouse and the farm buildings clustered around it.

'And those chimneys ya can just see above the trees, that's the Grange. And right over there,' he pointed to the south-west now, 'that's Souters' Farm, but it's a bit far away to see it properly from here. My best mate, Jimmy, lives there.'

'Mum said that big house is empty now,' Ella murmured.

'That's right, but I'm going to live there one day.'

'Now who's bragging?'

He turned his dark brown eyes upon her, his face serious. 'Oh, I aren't bragging, Townie. I mean it.'

Conditioned to crueller taunts, Ella laughed. 'All right, Country Bumpkin. I believe you.'

Still not content that she really did believe him, Rob added, 'I aren't ever going to leave here. I'm going to be a farmer like me dad, and one day I'm going to buy the Grange and live in it.'

He was gazing out across the flat wintry fields, a small smile playing on his mouth. He wasn't being arrogant, she realized. He loved this place, his home, the land and if it was his ambition to live in the big house, then at this moment she could believe he would make it come true.

'Fleethaven Point's over there.' He gestured, much closer now, to their left. 'We'll come back that way.' He swivelled round and she followed. Now they faced east-ward, but even yet she could not see the sea. Before them lay a flat expanse of marshland, a sea of green grass through which tiny rivulets meandered secretly, lying in wait for the unwary. The vast openness unnerved the city girl, used to noise and bustle and people. At home, even at night, there was always the distant hum of a passing vehicle, whilst here, in the tiny bedroom with its sloping roof, there was only the wind whistling around the remote farmhouse and a disconcerting rustling of birds – or worse

– in the roof. Ella shivered. She felt vulnerable and knew, alone, she would soon get completely lost. But Rob, her guide, knew every inch of this marsh. It was his playground. Grudgingly she had to acknowledge that what her gran had said was true; while she was with Rob Eland, she was safe.

'Come on,' he urged her. 'The sea's beyond that second line of dunes. This part of the coastline keeps getting built up by the currents sweeping the sand down the coast and because we're at the mouth of the Wash it settles here.'

She listened, amazed at his knowledge. As they crossed the marsh, jumping the streams, he paused every so often to point out a plant or a gull soaring above them. 'That's a black-headed gull and that's a common gull and that's a great black-backed gull.' There seemed to be a flock of birds wheeling above their heads now.

'How can you tell the difference?' she asked. 'They all look alike to me.'

''S easy. The common gull has a grey back and no red spot on its beak, unlike the others. The black-backed gull, like its name, is black right across its back and wingspan. And there's a red dot on its beak. I wish we'd got me dad's binoculars with us. You'd see it then. He's got some massive binoculars.' Rob laughed, the sound bouncing on the breeze. 'First time I used 'em, it brought everythin' that close, I thought a gull was diving straight at me.'

'And I suppose,' she said sarcastically, 'the black-headed gull has a black head.'

'How very clever of you,' he mocked her cheerfully in return. 'Right, close ya eyes now.'

'What for?'

'I'll take you to the top and then you can open 'em and see the sea.'

She did as he bid and felt him grasp her elbow to steer

her up to the top of the dune. Now she could hear the waves plainly.

'Right, stand still. Now – open ya eyes.'

She gasped at the sight of the vast expanse of grey water. Huge breakers came rolling towards the shore, their tips foaming white even before they reached their final roll to come crashing on to the sand.

Ella took a step backwards. 'I'm not going in that lot!'

Rob laughed. 'You should see it when the wind's in the right direction. We get some magnificent rollers then.' He stretched up his hand skywards. 'Big as a house sometimes, they are.'

Ella shuddered.

'Ya dun't get owt like that in the town, d'ya?' he goaded.

She turned to go back, but he said, 'Come on, let's go right to the edge.'

She hesitated a moment too long, looking doubtfully at the angry sea, suddenly afraid of its power. It looked as if it could engulf her and sweep her away . . .

Slyly he said, 'Scaredy cat. I dare ya.'

That did it.

Suddenly, she found herself running across the sand towards the waves, with Rob pounding after her.

They played 'catch me if you can' with the waves until Ella failed to skip out of the way quickly enough and the swiftly flowing wave caught the toes of her brown leather shoes.

'That'll ruin yar shoes. Now you're for it.'

Ella shrugged. 'Mum'll just sigh and say, "Oh, Ella," but she'll not get mad.'

'Mebbe not. But yar grannie will,' Rob reminded her.

Ella snorted. 'I don't care what *she* says.'

The boy stared at her. 'Well, you ought to. She's nice, your gran.' And with that, he turned and marched away from her along the beach, leaving Ella staring after him.

She caught up with him as he skirted round the land that formed the Point itself. As she drew level he gestured towards a long promontory of land jutting out into the sea as it swirled around the Point, and said, 'That's the Spit. Yar gran loves that place. She walks right along the bank and stands at the very end, just watching the sea and the sky.'

It was obvious that her grandmother figured largely in his life, as if her very presence in this place touched the lives of all those who lived here.

'Come on, I'll show you where both my grandmas live in the cottages over there.'

They were following the curve of the coastline and coming to the triangular piece of land which lay between the marsh, the mouth of the river and the sea. They came first to a dilapidated building, only half-standing, the rest crumbling into ruin.

'What's that place, then?'

'Oh, that was the pub, the Seagull. It was bombed in the war. My grandad Eland was killed in it.'

'Oh how awful!'

'Me grandma Eland lives on her own in that cottage second from the far end, and me grandad and grandma Maine live in this end cottage.' Rob was indicating a line of four cottages in front of which lay a stretch of grass and then the river which flowed into the sea and helped to form the Point which gave the place its name. He turned and looked at her. 'Where's your other gran live, then?'

'Eh? Oh – I haven't got one.'

'Ya must have. Ya dad's mam. Everybody's got two.'

Ella shook her head. 'Well, I haven't.'

He was leaning closer. 'Ain't you got a dad?'

'He was in the war.' It was the answer she always gave, trusting to luck that it wasn't really a lie. Nearly all the men had been in the war at the time she had been born; there was every chance he really had been in one of the services, whoever he was, she always thought bitterly, but would say no more. From her curt answer, she allowed people to guess for themselves what might have happened to him. Deliberately changing the subject, she put her head on one side and said, 'Well, *I* like *your* gran. Shall we swap? I'll have yours and you can have mine.'

He laughed, but insisted, 'She's all right, your gran, when ya get to know her.'

He turned and led her towards where the road rose steeply over a natural bank and dipped down the other side.

'Oh,' Ella said, as she stood on the top of the rise. 'I know where we are now. This is the road back to town, isn't it?'

'Yeah. Come on, we'd best be getting back.'

They ran down the incline and, only a short distance along the lane, they turned into the gate of Brumbys' Farm.

Her grandmother met them at the back door. 'Just look at your shoes, Missy.'

'It weren't her fault, Missus. She didn't know the salt water would mark 'em.'

'Don't try and mek excuses, Boy. She should have known better.'

Unabashed by Esther's tirade, Rob said, 'She can't help being a townie, Missus.'

He grinned up at Esther Godfrey and she, despite her

irritation, had to smile. 'You young rogue! Why is it I can never stay mad at you for many minutes? You soon have me laughing in spite of mesen.' She pulled the door wider open and, with one last, despairing glance at Ella's shoes where the sea water had left an uneven white line of salt across the toes, she sighed and said, 'Come on in and get those wet shoes off. Mebbe yar grandpa can get the stain off.' She tutted disapprovingly as the two youngsters trooped past her into the living room where the other adults were still gathered.

Ella's glance went at once to her mother. She was sitting beside Danny, her head inclined towards him listening to him, her gaze upon his face, a small smile playing on her gentle mouth. He must have said something which amused them both, for they laughed softly, swaying towards each other, their heads, for a second even closer, almost touching. By her side, Ella was aware that Rob was staring at his father too, a puzzled frown creasing his young forehead. They hadn't even noticed them enter the room until Esther said, 'She's ruined her good shoes, Kate. She'd be to her bed with no supper if I had owt to do wi' it.'

Kate looked up and held her hand out to Ella, drawing her closer. Glancing down at her daughter's feet, she sighed and said, 'Oh, Ella . . .'

Behind her, Ella heard Rob stifle a giggle as her mother, predictable as ever, had said exactly what Ella had said she would.

The girl grinned at her mother, love for her gentleness flowing through her. 'I'm sorry, Mum. Honest. I didn't know it would make such a mark. I thought it'd just dry off like when I get them wet in a puddle.'

'The sea's different to rainwater puddles, love,' Danny explained. 'It's the salt.'

'Tek 'em off.' Esther spoke again. 'Put them near the

range. When they're dry, we'll see what we can do. And if you go on the beach again, wear some rubber boots.'

'Yes, Gran,' the child said, feigning meekness and dropped her chin so that none of the adults should see the mischief in her eyes.

'Grannie!' came the sharp reminder above her bowed head.

Ella said nothing.

'We'd better be going.' Grandma Eland levered herself up from the low chair beside the fire. Her right cheek was red with the warmth from the fire. She moved awkwardly across the room towards Esther. 'I'm real sorry about ya dad, Esther.'

Ella watched as her grandmother, standing by the door, said stiffly, 'Thank you, Beth.' The two women stared at each other and then, suddenly, Esther put out her hand and touched the other's arm. She said again, 'Thank you, Beth, for coming,' and this time there was a wealth of difference in her tone that was obvious even to the ten-year-old girl, who watched the exchange. Beth Eland nodded and patted Esther's hand and then moved on out of the room to leave, Esther following her. Those left in the room heard the murmur of their voices.

'I'll never understand those two,' Ella heard Danny say. 'Long as I live, I won't.'

'I don't think they understand themselves,' Kate said pensively. 'But there's so much between them, Danny. So much they can't forget, yet they always come together when there's trouble.'

'Aye, they do,' he said, his voice dropping so that it was almost inaudible even to Ella's sharp ears.

'What, Mum? What are you talking about?' Ella touched her mother's arm, to attract her attention. 'What about Gran and Grandma Eland?'

'Never you mind, Missy,' her grandmother said sharply as she came back into the room. 'Really, Kate, I have never met a child who asks so many impertinent questions.'

Unseen by her grandmother, Ella grinned cheekily at her mother and heard her uncle Danny try valiantly to smother his laughter.

Five

'I don't want to stay here any longer. I hate it here. Please, Mum, can't we go home today?'

'Ella, darling,' Kate tried to placate her daughter, 'it's only another two nights. Just until Sunday evening.'

The girl glowered at her mother. 'You promise?'

Kate sighed. 'I promise.'

'But why have we got to stay longer?'

Suddenly, there was a light in her mother's eyes and with a nervous gesture, she touched her lips with the tips of her fingers. 'There's – there's someone I have to meet tomorrow . . .'

'Who?' Ella asked, and, with sudden intuition, she put her head on one side and added, 'It's to do with that letter you had, isn't it?'

Kate's cheeks were pink as she nodded. 'It was from someone I knew in the war.'

'Like Aunty Mave and Aunty Isobel, you mean?'

'Yes – yes, like them – well – sort of, except with this – person, we – we haven't seen each other since then.'

'Can I come with you?'

'No, darling, not this time. Maybe another time.'

'I'm not stopping here on my own with *her*.'

Kate sighed again. 'Well, I'm borrowing Uncle Danny's car.'

'Is he going with you?'

Kate shook her head. 'No, but I have to drive a few

miles up the coast. Maybe you could stay the afternoon at Rookery Farm – with Rob.'

Ella thought for a moment, then grinned mischievously. Rob wouldn't like that. 'All right, then. I'll go there.'

That evening as night closed in around Brumbys' Farm, the wind seemed to batter against the farmhouse, rattling the windows and blowing in under the back door, lifting the mat.

'I hate gales,' Esther complained, and for once Ella found herself in agreement with her grandmother. 'It always reminds me—' The older woman stopped and Ella saw her glance across at Kate, before she turned away and poked vigorously at the glowing coals in the range grate, making the sparks fly and the flames spurt. 'Well,' she muttered lamely, 'I just hate wind, ya know I do.'

'You're not the only one,' Kate said, and nodded towards Ella sitting huddled in a chair, her arms around herself, her knees drawn up. Esther's eyes softened and she held out her hand. 'Come and sit by the fire, Missy, and let's forget about the storm out there.'

'Where's Grandpa?' Ella asked.

Esther shuddered. 'Outside mekin' sure the cows are safely in the byre. We dun't want 'em wandering about in this lot. And I think he's tying the tarpaulin over his beloved tractor an' all, in case we get a downpour.' She cast an anxious glance towards the back door. 'He should be back in a minute and then we can shut the storm out. I know.' She smiled suddenly. 'We'll roast some chestnuts. You'd like that, wouldn't you?'

'I – dunno,' Ella glanced at her mother for reassurance.

'I don't think she's ever had any, Mam.'

'Not had roast chestnuts? Well, I never did. Have you taught the poor child nothing, Kate Hilton?'

Kate laughed. 'They're not so easy to come by in the city, Mam.'

Esther snorted with laughter as she disappeared into the pantry and returned a few moments later with a bowl of shiny brown nuts. Kneeling before the range, the dancing firelight illuminated her face in its soft glow, making her seem, for a moment, much younger than her years. Ella caught a fleeting sight of the lovely girl her grandmother must once have been, glimpsed the young woman her grandfather must have fallen in love with; the smooth dark skin, rosy in the firelight's glow, green sparkling eyes and beautiful auburn hair.

'Now, we take the fire tongs, see. Grasp a chestnut . . .' As she spoke Esther carried out the action, operating the claws of the tongs to clasp a nut then lifting it carefully towards the bars of the grate where she balanced it close to the coals. 'When the skin begins to blister and split, we turn it round.'

Fascinated, Ella watched.

'Now,' said her grandmother, holding out the tongs towards her, 'you try.'

The girl took the tongs and squeezed the handles to open the claws. After several attempts she managed to grasp a chestnut and slowly she moved it towards the fire, gritting her teeth in concentration. Steadily, she placed it on the bar of the fire.

'Well done, darling,' Kate said, clapping her hands and Ella glanced up to see her grandmother nod approval. A warm glow, that was nothing to do with the heat of the fire, spread through the young girl.

At that moment the back door opened as Jonathan

came in. The storm seemed to rage into the house, lifting the peg rug in the scullery and blowing a cold draught round Ella's legs even as she sat by the fire in the kitchen.

'Shut the door quickly,' Esther called to him, 'and come into the warm. We're roasting chestnuts.'

Jonathan came into the room rubbing his cold hands, seeming to fill the shadowy kitchen with his presence. 'It's a rough old lot out there. I've never heard the sea so plainly as you can tonight. Let's hope they don't have to launch the lifeboat . . .'

Ella saw her mother's eyes widen and she stared up at Jonathan. 'Dad, is Danny still in the lifeboat crew?'

He shook his head. 'No, love. When he came back after the war with his leg wound, it was decided he couldn't really be a part of the crew any more. But he's still a launcher.'

Ella saw her mother shudder. 'That's bad enough on a night like this,' Kate murmured.

'Yar dad sometimes takes his tractor up to help launch, an' all,' Esther said, and Ella could detect a note of disapproval in her grandmother's voice, but her grandpa only smiled his slow, gentle smile.

'Well, in a small community we all have to do our bit.'

The conversation ranged on over the girl's head; she was feeling drowsy now and, tucking her legs under her, she leant her head against the wooden Windsor chair.

Her grandmother's voice broke into her dreams, 'You goin' to eat these chestnuts, Missy?' and Ella raised her head.

She reached out to take the nut, peeled to reveal a creamy kernel. 'Careful, it's hot,' Esther warned her.

Ella blew on the nut and then carefully bit into it, it was crunchy and sweet. 'Ooh it's nice.'

'A few more, and then it's your bedtime.'

Ella glanced fearfully across at her mother. 'Are you coming up?'

Before Kate could answer, Esther broke in, 'Dun't be such a baby! You're a big girl now to be wanting your mam to take you up to bed. When I was your age I was having to look after me younger cousins.'

Ella's sharp mind latched on to the last word. 'Cousins?' she asked. 'Not brothers and sisters?'

'No,' Esther said shortly, and poked the fire again, stabbing a burning log resting on top of the bed of red-hot coals so viciously that sparks shot up the flue, casting eerie, dancing shadows about the darkened room, lit only by an oil lamp standing on the table. But Ella's concentration was on her grandmother. 'That old man who died – he was your dad, wasn't he?'

Esther nodded.

'Didn't you live with him and your mam, then?'

Slowly Esther turned to face her granddaughter and in the glow from the firelight they stared at each other, each one weighing up the other, perhaps really seeing one another for the first time. In the shadows, Jonathan and Kate were silent, watching the scene almost, it seemed, holding their breath. Outside the wind battered against the farmhouse, whistled around the buildings and rattled the roof tiles, but in the warm kitchen it was cosy and safe.

Esther reached out and gently touched the faint birthmark on Ella's jawline shaped like two tiny finger marks. 'Oh, Missy.' In the firelight, Esther's face was suddenly filled with a gentle sadness, a compassion, as she whispered, 'You're more like me than you could ever know.'

Ella waited, holding her breath, but suddenly, the spell was broken as Esther seemed to shake herself and snatch her hand away as if she was suddenly angry at herself for almost being led into giving too much away, into becoming, for a few minutes, soft and gentle and human. She got to her feet. 'Time you were in bed, child,' she said sharply, 'Kate . . .'

'Yes, Mam,' Kate said meekly and cast a wry grin at her daughter. 'Come on, darling, I'll come up with you.' And though Esther tut-tutted in disgust, Kate went upstairs with Ella and did not leave her until she had been reassured that the noise really was only the wind whipping across the open, flat land.

The following day, the last day of January, was a Saturday.

Hugging her coat around her against the blustery wind, Ella stood in the yard at Rookery Farm watching her mother climb into Uncle Danny's car. It was small and green, with a sloping back and huge bulbous headlights.

Danny was holding the door and bending forward, pointing out all the instruments to Kate. 'Do be careful, Kate. It'll be very rough along the coast road with these gales,' he was saying, almost shouting above the racket the wind was making. 'Try to get back before it gets dark, if you can. The shipping forecast reckons it's going to get even worse by tonight.'

Ella saw her mother pull a face expressing doubt. 'I will be back tonight, but I don't know whether I can make it before dark. I've a fair way to go up the coast.'

Danny looked at her. 'Any good me asking just where and why?'

Kate's laughter bounced over the wind, her eyes sparkling. 'Not a scrap. But I might tell you when I get back.'

Listening, Ella thought, it's a real secret if she's not even telling Uncle Danny.

'Well, be careful, then,' Danny said again as he shut the door.

Kate wound down the window. 'Be a good girl, Ella, won't you? Go back to Grannie's at tea-time.'

'She can stay here for her tea, if she wants,' Danny put in, but Kate shook her head. 'She'd better go back there, thanks all the same.'

Ella opened her mouth to argue – she would much prefer to stay at Rookery Farm until her mother came back – but as Kate pressed the starter and the engine burst into life, her protests were drowned in the noise.

'Mum!' Ella ran forward, her fingers grasped the door of the car. Suddenly, she was filled with a terrible foreboding. 'Mum, please let me come with you. Don't leave me here.'

'You'll be all right, darling. Stay with Uncle Danny and Aunty Rosie – and Rob—'

'No, Mum, let me come. Please.'

'Darling, I can't,' Kate said. 'I'm sorry.' She revved the engine and let in the clutch.

'Please, Mum—'

As it moved, Ella felt Danny grasp her round the waist and her grip was prised loose.

He held her until the vehicle had turned out of the farmyard gate and, once in the lane, began to gather speed. As he released his hold, Ella sped towards the gate.

'Mum! Mum!' she shouted after it, but the car drew away and all Ella could see was her mother's arm sticking out of the window waving to her.

The young girl stood a forlorn, lonely figure in the lane, the cold wind snatching at her coat, whipping around her legs. She watched the car turn left at the end of the lane and move along the coast road towards Lynthorpe. Her gaze followed it until, passing behind a clump of trees, it was lost from her sight.

'Oh, Mum, please come back,' Ella whispered. 'Please don't leave me here . . .'

Six

As dusk began to close in, Rob took her back to Brumbys' Farm.

Ella had not enjoyed her afternoon; the feeling of apprehension just would not go away, not even when Aunty Rosie fed her with scones topped with raspberry jam and cream.

'I'm off to play with Jimmy,' Rob had announced.

'Oh no you're not,' Danny said. 'You stay here and look after Ella.'

'Aw, Dad . . .'

'Can't I come too?' she suggested, but Rob said moodily, 'We dun't play with girls.'

'What about Jimmy's sister, Janice? You play with her then, don't you?' Rob's mother said.

Rob shrugged. 'Not if we can get rid of her. She just tags along, that's all.'

Rosie smiled at Ella. 'Boys!'

But Rob did not stay moody for long and later he showed her how to make a bow and arrow and they played 'Robin Hood' in the big barn.

'Can I see the kittens again?' she asked, and when he lifted the lid of the coop, she gasped. In only two days they had altered. Little balls of fluff, they were crawling all over their mother. For a fleeting moment her worry was banished. 'Oh aren't they pretty?' Ella cried, forgetting her desire not to appear 'girlish' in front of Rob. 'I do like the black and white one. Look, all its little paws are white.'

As if determined to keep them so, the mother cat licked at the kitten who wriggled and twisted to get out of the way. Ella giggled as she tickled the mother cat under her chin and the animal closed her eyes and purred, a high-pitched whirring sound of ecstasy.

'Look, that one's eyes are just beginning to open,' Rob pointed. 'They'll not be ready to leave the mother cat for a few weeks yet, but me mam ses we've enough cats about the place now, so we've got to find homes for them. Would yar mam let you have one, d'you think?'

Ella's eyes clouded and she shook her head. 'No. She says it wouldn't be fair for us to have a pet where we live. It might get run over.' The picture of a neighbour's cat she had seen lying squashed in the middle of the street made her shudder afresh.

'We'll tek the short cut,' Rob told her as they set off from Rookery Farm as dusk was blown in by the still raging gales.

They crossed the lane opposite the farm gate and climbed a stile into the first field. Rob pointed and put his mouth close to her ear so that she could hear him above the wind whipping around them. 'It'd be even shorter if we could go straight across the middle of the field to Brumbys' Farm, but we'd better go round the edge.' The field was ploughed in deep, straight furrows. 'Else you'll get yar shoes all muddy.' He grinned. 'We got into enough trouble about your shoes from your grannie last time, didn't we? You really ought to get some boots for when you're here.'

The wind gusted across the wide open space, catching Ella's breath and almost lifting her off her feet. Heavy clouds scudded across the sky and huge spots of rain were icy on her face.

'Come on, it's going to chuck it down in a minute,' he warned and Ella trudged after the boy leading the way round the grass verge of the field.

Never mind him and his 'boots for next time', she thought morosely. There won't be a next time if I have anything to do with it. The minute Mum comes back, I'm off home.

'Careful, dun't fall in,' he warned as they came to a bridge made out of two planks over a water-filled dyke. Gingerly, she walked across, placing her feet as if walking on a slippery tightrope. The wind buffeting her as she balanced precariously above the murky dyke water didn't help and when she jumped the last pace on to the bank, she let out her breath in relief. The next field was a meadow, the grass short and springy, and they ran across the middle towards a hole in the hedge at the end of the orchard in the front of Brumbys' Farm.

'There you are,' was the greeting from her grandmother emerging from the cowshed. 'Come along in out o' this lot.' She nodded angrily at the darkening sky. 'I'm leaving the cows in the shed again tonight. Poor things, they dun't like this weather any more'n I do. I wish yar mam'd hurry up and get back 'afore dark.' And Ella saw her glance up the lane as if willing the car to appear.

As Rob turned to go, Esther shouted after him, 'You go straight home, Boy. It's not fit for man nor beast to be out.'

'I'm just off to mek sure the old 'uns are all right at the Point, Missus.'

Esther pretended to shake her fist at him, but she was smiling as she said, 'Cheeky young rogue! I'll give you "old 'uns", indeed. Is that what you call me an' all?'

The boy's grin widened. 'Who me, Missus? I wouldn't dare!' With a cheery wave he was gone.

They stood in the yard and watched the boy as he reached the lane, turned to the right and broke into a run, blown along by the wind.

'He's a good lad,' Esther murmured to no one in particular.

'I know his gran and his other grandma live in the cottages, but who else lives at the Point?' Ella asked, suddenly curious.

As they entered the back door and Esther leant her weight against it to close it against the wind, she said, 'The two Harris boys live in the very end cottage, next door to his grandma Eland.'

Ella's eyes widened. 'Boys? Two boys live on their own?'

'Eh?' For a moment Esther stared at her, a puzzled frown on her forehead. Then she laughed. 'Oh, they're boys to me, but let's think, they'll both be pushing fifty-odd now.'

'Fifty!' Ella squeaked. 'Why, that's *ancient*.'

'Oh, thank you very much, seein' as I'm nearly sixty.'

'Are you really?' Ella said, with her usual candid honesty. 'Well, you don't look it.'

Esther stood, hands on hips, her head on one side. 'You trying to flannel me, Missy?'

Suddenly, Ella grinned impishly and, mocking Rob's words, said, 'Who me, Gran? I wouldn't dare!'

If it were possible, the gales seemed to get worse. They raged around the farmhouse, battering the back door, rattling the tiles and whistling around the farm buildings. By eight o'clock when Kate had still not returned even the placid Jonathan was obviously agitated. He went out every few minutes to the gate to look up the lane, watching for the headlights. 'Maybe she's broken down somewhere.'

'I don't know what she wanted to go tearing off in this weather for, anyway.' Esther's anxiety took the form of irritation. She turned and looked sharply at Ella. 'Do you know, Missy?'

Ella shook her head. She felt close to tears, yet she was determined not to cry in front of her grandmother. But her fear was growing with every passing minute that her mother did not return.

'Oh, do stop running out to the gate,' Esther snapped at her husband. 'It won't mek her come any quicker.'

He tried to smile. 'I know, love, but I can't seem to settle until I know she's safely back.'

Ella saw her grandmother reach out and touch her husband's arm by way of silent apology for her sharpness. Understanding, he patted her hand. Ella bit her lip and then felt his gaze upon her. She looked into his eyes, her own equally as troubled.

'I know what we'll do to take our minds off the weather,' he said brightly, but it was a forced brightness and they all knew it. He came towards the warmth of the range. 'Get the draughts board out, Esther. I'll beat Ella at draughts till her mam gets back.'

Esther snorted with a sudden spurt of wry laughter. 'Oh, very appropriate on a night like this.' But she went upstairs and found the checkered board and the pieces.

Ella sat on the peg rug in front of the range and set up the board ready for play.

Suddenly she looked up at her grandfather as he sat in the Windsor chair. 'Grandpa, what's that noise?'

Ella's sharp hearing had caught a different sound above the noise of the wind.

'What noise, love? I don't hear anything.'

'Listen . . .' Esther stood still near the table. For a breathless moment they all strained to hear, then Esther sprang towards the window and dragged back the curtain, peering out into the wild night.

'Oh no!' Her hand still clutching the curtain, her eyes wide with panic, she turned to look at Jonathan. 'It's the sea!' she gasped.

'What?' Jonathan was up and out of his chair, hurrying towards the back door. Esther turned and followed him. Ella scrambled to her feet and went to the window. As her grandmother had done, she pulled back the curtain and peered out into the night. In the dim light cast by the oil lamp and filtering through the window, Ella could see a brown swirl of water raging around the farmhouse. She dropped the curtain and ran to the back door. Channelled between the farm buildings, a wave of water came roaring towards the house.

'Shut the door,' Esther screamed and, as the torrent came towards them, Jonathan slammed the back door and leant against it. They heard the water slap against it. Ella saw her grandparents stare at each other in helpless horror, and then silently they watched as the water began to seep in under the door, first in tiny rivulets and then spreading relentlessly towards their feet.

Esther clutched Jonathan's arm. 'A boat. We need a boat. Where can we get a boat?'

'Esther, take the child and go upstairs.'

'But we have to get out – we have to get away.'

'Esther, you'll be safe upstairs, but the folks at the Point – I have to go . . .'

'No.' She clung to him trying to prevent him going. 'You'll be drowned!'

Gently, Jonathan tried to release himself from her grasp. 'Esther. The water will be much deeper the other side of the Hump and they're only in cottages. This side, we'll be all right. It'll spread out over the fields, but Beth and the others . . .'

'Not her. Not Beth Eland!' There was a wealth of bitterness in Esther's tone. 'I won't lose you an' all because of her. I won't have it happen again. Not again.' Holding on to his coat, she was babbling now, incoherently. Ella listened with growing terror.

Jonathan prised Esther's fingers loose and planted a swift kiss on her forehead, promising, 'I'll be careful, love.' Then he opened the back door. The water flooded into the house swirling icily around their feet, threatening to bowl them over with its force.

'Don't go, Jonathan. Please . . .'

His hand on the door, he turned back. 'Go upstairs, Esther. Just – for once – do as I say.'

He went out and though he tried to pull the door shut after him, against the flowing water, it was now impossible. The wind shrieked into the house and, above its noise, Ella cried, 'Gran, Gran, what about Mum?'

Through the gloom, Esther stared at her and then she closed her eyes and threw back her head. 'Oh, Katie, me little Katie,' she wailed and at the grief-stricken tone in the older woman's voice, the girl shook with dread.

Esther opened her arms wide and Ella, hesitating only a moment, splashed through the murky water towards her.

Terrified, grandmother and granddaughter clung together whilst the sea flowed relentlessly into the house.

'Come on, we'd better do as he said and get oursens upstairs.' Her grandmother gently released Ella's arms from about her waist but they still clung to each other as they paddled back into the kitchen where Esther took down a candle in a pink holder from the shelf and lit it.

Ella was shivering both with cold and fear. 'Gran, it's up to my ankles already.'

'I know, lass. It's getting deeper every minute.'

The girl's voice rose with hysteria. 'Will it get right up to the roof? Rob said there's waves as big as a house sometimes . . .' In her mind was a picture of that vast expanse of grey water whipped by the gales into a seething, vengeful torrent that would flow endlessly across the marsh, over the sand dunes, into their farmhouse and on and on across the fields. There was nothing to stop it.

'No, no, course it won't. Ya heard what ya grandpa said?'

Esther, after her brief moment of terror, seemed once more in control of her fear, but the girl's voice still trembled. 'I didn't understand what he meant.'

'The water won't come very deep into our house.'

Ella shuddered again, feeling the icy water creeping up and up her legs. 'Are you sure?'

'Course I am. Stands to reason. The land's flat out there, ain't it?' Esther waved her hand towards the kitchen window facing out across the fields. 'When it settles, it'll find its own level. It's only – only the other side the Hump, y'know, the bank in the road, where it'll get deeper – a lot deeper . . .' Her fear for Jonathan was back and she stopped mid-sentence.

'But how far will the water go across the fields?' Ella's voice was high-pitched with dread.

Esther shook her head. 'I don't know, lass. If only the wind would stop . . .'

As if hearing her words, the wind dropped for a moment and they heard clearly the waves slapping against the old walls of the farmhouse. Then the gale roared once more, blowing in through the open back door and rippling the black water all around them.

'If only ya grandpa hadn't gone out in it,' Esther muttered. 'But that's him all over.' She gave a huge sigh and seemed to pull herself together. 'Eh, what am I standing here for? What am I thinking of? Go upstairs, Ella, and take ya wet shoes and socks off.'

'What about you? Aren't you coming up?' The upstairs, far from seeming a sanctuary, looking black and cold and lonely.

'I'm going to try and save some o' me things. Do as I tell you and then you can come back down here and carry some bits up. But don't get in the water again.'

Ella felt her way upstairs and into the big bedroom where her mother slept.

She was sobbing silently to herself, crying inside. 'Oh, Mum, please come back. Come home – now!'

While Esther waded about in the water downstairs, Ella, with shaking fingers and trying to gulp back her tears, lit the candle on top of the big chest standing in one corner of the large bedroom and went into the small, narrow bedroom where she slept, leading off the larger room. The gale was even louder here, howling only just outside the sloping ceiling. Snatching a clean pair of socks she went back into the big room and shut the door. Her teeth began to chatter as she pulled off her drenched shoes and socks and, picking up a towel from the rail on the wash-stand, rubbed her legs and pulled on the dry pair. Then she found her slippers and went to the window. Could she see the road to Rookery Farm from here? Were there car headlights? But the world outside her window was like a black void. Not a light twinkled anywhere. She shuddered again, gripping the curtain tightly, overwhelmed by a fierce longing to be back in the city with the glow of the street lamps just outside her window, the sound of traffic on the main road at the top of the street, doors banging and the sound of voices. But now there was only the sound of the roaring wind and the rushing water below and that awful, interminable blackness.

'Mum, oh, Mum, where are you?' she whispered aloud and felt sick with fear. What if she never came back? What if . . . ?

She turned from the window, went out of the room and down the stairs again to where the water was already up to the first step.

Standing there in the darkness, the tempest raging outside, Ella tried to swallow her fear. 'Gran,' she called croakily and then louder, 'Gran?'

For a dreadful moment she could hear nothing except the storm. 'Gran,' she shouted, panic rising in her voice, 'where are you?'

'Here,' came her grandmother's voice from the kitchen or pantry, Ella could not be sure which. 'Stay there . . .'

Ella stood on the stairs, straining to hear her grandmother splashing about in the water, muttering crossly at the invasion of her home. With something to do, Esther seemed calmer. Now she was angry: at the sea, at Jonathan for going out, maybe, even at Ella for being an extra responsibility. The girl watched the flickering light from the oil lamp as her grandmother took it from room to room, deciding what she could carry upstairs, trying to salvage as many of her belongings as she could. Ella wished she could go to her gran; she needed to be with someone, she didn't like being left alone in the dark and the cold watching the water rising, rising . . .

But for once, the girl did as her grandmother had told her and stayed where she was. The water was lapping over the first stair and encroaching upon the second by the time Esther appeared again carrying a heavy, low-seated chair from the front parlour, its legs already wet. She lugged it, step by step, up the stairs. 'Out the way, Missy,' she ordered as Ella stepped backwards up the stairs with each step that Esther took. Next she salvaged an odd assortment of items; an embroidered fire-screen, a footstool, the huge family Bible . . .

'Oh, heck! What am I doing?' Esther swept the hair back from her forehead with the back of her hand. 'I aren't thinking straight. Food. We ought to take some food up. Stand there and you can carry it up as I bring it to the stairs. Don't get in the water again, Missy. There's enough of us getting soaking wet already.' As she moved away into the darkness, Ella heard her mutter, 'I wish he'd come back.'

So do I, Ella thought fervently. And Mum.

Esther was back, thrusting dishes and tins into her hands. 'Look sharp, Missy. Mek ya'sen useful. Tek these up and put 'em in one of the rooms. Anywhere, it dun't matter.'

After several journeys to and from the pantry, Esther came to the stairs carrying a small lamp. 'I've left the big one burning on the kitchen table for yar grandpa to see by when he comes back. I'd got this little one in the pantry. It'll do us for upstairs.'

She pulled herself up out of the water and paused a moment, leaning against the wall, obviously feeling suddenly exhausted by her efforts. 'I'd best get me stockings off, an' me skirt. By heck, that water's perishing. I dun't reckon me feet'll ever feel warm again. I've brought me rubber boots from the scullery if I need to go paddling again, but they're wet inside now. They were already floating afore I thought about 'em.' She gave a click of annoyance and began to climb the stairs.

Ella took one last look at the black water in the hall. Floating on the surface, swollen and ruined, was the cardboard draughts board.

She turned away and, keeping close to her, followed her grandmother. She held the lamp whilst Esther, panting and shaking with cold, pulled off her stockings, dried her legs and pulled on a clean pair. Suddenly, above the noise of the gale, they heard a loud banging from below and for a moment they stared at each other in the flickering lamplight.

'Is that ya grandpa?' Esther said. 'Oh, I hope to goodness it is.'

Heedless of the fact that she had just put on dry clothes, Esther rushed down the stairs. 'I'm coming, I'm coming.'

Left to carry the lamp, this time Ella followed her down and, tucking her skirt up into her knickers, stepped once more into the water; now it was up to her knees. The intense cold was a shock, but she waded through the scum-covered water sending waves rippling out to splash against the walls. As she passed through the living room, everything looked so odd, half-submerged in the water, rugs floating just beneath the surface, wrapping themselves against her legs like some creature from the deep.

'Gran,' she called, her voice quavering. 'Wait for me . . .'

Now she could hear voices, a commotion near the back door, and reaching the doorway from the kitchen into the scullery, she saw three figures struggling together in the darkness.

'Here, lean on me, Beth. That's it,' came her grandmother's voice.

'Esther – oh, Esther,' Rob's grandma cried, her bulk swaying against Esther, her fat arms clawing for support. 'I thought I was going to drown. He saved me. Jonathan saved me life.'

'Ya safe now, Beth. Come along.'

Quickly, Ella turned back and put the lamp in the centre

of the kitchen table, pushing her grandpa's wooden chair, floating in the water, out of her way. She splashed back into the scullery and, skirting round her grandmother still struggling to bring Beth into the kitchen and towards the stairs, Ella reached her grandpa who was leaning against the door frame, his eyes closed, his breathing laboured and rasping. He was drenched, wet through from head to foot.

Ella tugged at his sleeve. 'Grandpa, where's Mum? Have you heard where Mum is?'

He coughed painfully, bent almost double, unable to take another step, shivering uncontrollably. He shook his head and his voice was hoarse. 'No. Nothing.'

He put his arm around the girl's shoulders, the water from his clothes soaking quickly through her wool jumper and chilling her shoulders, but she put her small arms around him and tried to help him into the house. Staggering like drunks, the young girl scarcely able to keep her balance under his weight, they reached the foot of the stairs, but Jonathan was unable to find the energy to climb. From above, Ella could hear her grandmother's voice. 'Get out o' them wet things, Beth. Wrap ya'sen in blankets.'

'Gran!' the girl called up. 'Gran, come and help me with Grandpa.'

In a moment her grandmother was rushing down the stairs and taking hold of him, easing his weight from Ella on to herself.

He rested his head against her shoulder. 'Oh, Esther, I – I got bowled over once by the waves. I – I thought I'd had it. I thought of you – knew what it would mean to you if – if . . .' He left the sentence unfinished but Ella saw him raise his head and look searchingly straight into Esther's eyes. 'I wouldn't hurt you for the world, my love,' he said softly. A spasm of coughing seized him, but he struggled between coughs to say, 'But I had to go. I couldn't leave folks there in trouble. Please, try to understand.'

Esther stared at him for a moment and then slowly she nodded. 'Yes, I know, Jonathan,' she said quietly. She sighed deeply and a small, wry smile twitched the corner of her mouth. 'You and your blasted conscience . . .' She left the sentence unfinished and said instead, 'Come on, let's get you upstairs. Ya'll catch ya death.' Though she gently chided him, the anger was gone from her tone; she was too thankful to have him back with her.

Somehow between them they got him upstairs and into his own room. For the next half-hour Esther went between the two, helping first her husband then Beth, asking questions all the time.

'What about the Maines and the Harris boys?'

'They've – they've gone to Rookery Farm. But poor Beth couldn't make it any further. They'll tell Danny she's safe here. He'll be frantic.'

'How far's the water gone? Mebbe Rookery Farm's got it as well.'

'I should think it has,' Jonathan said grimly, as his breathing became a little easier. 'God knows how far it's gone.'

Hovering outside the bedroom doors on the tiny landing, Ella's question came again. 'Mum? What about Mum?' But no one knew how to answer her.

'Get into bed with you, Jonathan,' she heard her grandmother say briskly. 'I'll fetch the bricks up from the range oven. Lucky I'd put 'em in already to warm the child's bed. But she'll not mind.'

'Oh, don't let Ella be cold. She'll feel it more . . .' even from outside the door, Ella heard his teeth chatter suddenly, '. . . than us.'

She raised her voice and shouted to him. 'No, I won't, Grandpa, you have the bricks. Shall I get them, Gran?'

'No, no, you stay where you are.' The bedroom door opened. 'Ya can come in now and sit with yar grandpa whilst I fetch 'em.'

Esther crossed into the other room to say, 'You all right, Beth? I'll bring a brick up. Get into the bed and keep warm.' Then as her grandmother went down the stairs into the black water, Ella once more stripped off her soaking footwear and crept under the quilt on her grandparents' bed pressing herself against her grandpa through the covers, trying to warm him.

Jonathan was lying back against the pillows, his eyes closed, his breathing a rasping noise. A few moments later her grandmother returned with the two bricks wrapped in pieces of blanket and pushed them beneath the covers, one at his feet, and the other half-way up the bed.

'I've got another couple for Beth. The water's not got up to the fire in the range yet. I can boil the kettle and make us all a hot drink. I'll put a tot of whisky in 'em to warm us.'

Jonathan did not answer; it seemed to be taking all his energy to concentrate on dragging in the next breath. Ella and her grandmother exchanged a worried glance.

'You go and snuggle in beside Grandma Eland,' her grandmother's tone was unusually gentle, 'and I'll bring you both a nice cup of something warm.'

The girl shivered. 'Don't stay down there too long, else you'll get a chill.'

'Me, Missy?' Her grandmother raised a small smile, but it was forced. 'Not me! I'm tough as owd boots, lass.'

There was a ghost of a smile on Ella's mouth and in this moment for the first time she saw what it was that Rob so admired about her grandmother. In the midst of the drama, after that first initial shock, she was strong and determined once more. Not even the might of the sea invading her home could intimidate Esther Godfrey for long.

'Oh, me pigs! What about me pigs? They'll all be drowned,' Esther said suddenly as she handed mugs of steaming liquid first to Grandma Eland and then to Jonathan and Ella.

'Esther love, they'll have to take their chance. I really can't . . .'

'No, no. You stay there, you're not moving again. I'll go . . .'

'No, Esther . . .' But she was not listening.

'Wait for me, Gran. I'm coming with you.' Ella quickly swallowed the hot milk that tasted odd but warmed her and put the mug down. 'I'm coming with you.'

'You stay there,' her grandmother began, starting down the stairs. As the girl followed, she snapped, 'Do as I say, Missy.'

'No. I'm coming to help you.'

In the fitful light, they glared at each other. 'You get back upstairs. I dun't want you catching cold an' all.'

Suddenly, Ella grinned cheekily. 'Who me, Gran? Not me . . .' And adopting the Lincolnshire dialect so strong in her grandmother's speech, Ella mimicked, 'Not me. Ah'm tough as owd boots, an' all!'

'Eh, ya saucy minx,' her grandmother said, but suddenly, amidst all the chaos the two were laughing. 'Oh, very well then. Wait there 'til I get you a pair of rubber boots from the scullery, if they've not floated away, an' all.'

Ella waited on the step just above the water. Bet she

doesn't come back, she thought, but then she heard her grandmother wading through the water towards her.

'Here you are. Put these on. There was an old pair on the rack. They're dry.'

The boots were too big and chafed the back of her knees if she tried to bend her legs, but Ella made no complaint. Holding hands, they waded through the house to the back door and peered out. The black water rose and fell but there were no longer huge, swollen waves gushing towards them. Above the noise of the wind, they could hear the frightened cows lowing piteously from the cowshed.

'Poor beggars!' her grandmother muttered. 'Still, it shouldn't be too deep in there. I think the brick floor's built up a bit higher. It's the pigs I'm bothered about. Lady, and the two gilts.'

Ella said, 'Lady?'

'The sow,' Esther said and added, 'Well, Missy, are ya ready?'

Clenching her teeth together to stop them chattering, Ella said, 'Yes, Gran.'

Holding on to each other they waded out into the yard. The wind plucked at them and the sea swirled around them, threatening to bowl them over and plunge them beneath the black surface. The water slapped over the top of Ella's boots and ran, like ice, down her legs.

'Hang on to me, Missy. Dun't let go, whatever ya do,' her grandmother shouted above the noise of the wind. Ella made no reply, concentrating on keeping her balance, dreadfully afraid of falling down.

They reached the sty and Esther pulled open the top half of the stable-type door. 'Can you see 'em?'

The girl peered into the gloom. 'No – I – oh, there's something floating . . .'

'Oh, damn it!' her grandmother muttered. 'We're too late.'

Then out of the darkness came a snuffling grunt, and the water splashed against the door. 'It's Lady,' Esther said joyfully. She unlatched the door and dragged it open, stretching out her hands in the darkness to feel the bristly back of the huge sow. 'Come on, old girl. Grab hold of her ear, Ella, and let's take her back to the house.'

'The – the house?'

'I can't leave her out here. If the water comes any higher, she'll drown too. It's only 'cos she's such a big pig . . .'

The animal was struggling to escape, but Ella grasped her ear and keeping her between them, they shuffled back towards the house, the pig grunting and squealing in protest.

They pushed her in through the back door.

Taking a moment's respite, Esther looked down at the pig standing in the middle of her kitchen, grunting gently, the water up to its belly. 'Well, I never thought I'd be trying to get a pig up me stairs, but that's where she'll have to go, into the little bedroom.'

'In my room? With me?' Ella was wide-eyed.

'Why ever not?' Then her grandmother chuckled at the sight of Ella's mortified face. 'I'm only teasing you, Missy. You bring ya things out of there and snuggle in with Grandma Eland. It'll be warmer for you in the big bedroom anyway.'

Ella, suddenly sober again, said, 'Gran, what do you think will have happened to Mum?'

Gently, Esther said, 'Ya grandpa thinks she'll have stayed in the town – in Lynthorpe – that she'll be quite safe.'

'But what if the town's flooded too?' the girl asked.

'Oh, there'll be no floods there, Missy,' her grandmother said confidently. 'It'll only be us got a surge come up the river 'cos of the high tides at this time of the year and with the wind to drive it . . .'

'Are you sure?'

'Course I am. Ya Grandpa ses so.'

Comforted now by the confidence in her grandmother's voice and trusting her grandpa's knowledge, she tried to bury the worry about her mother and concentrate on heaving and pushing the huge pink sow up the staircase of Brumbys' Farm.

What Ella did not, at that moment, know – what none of them knew – was that, far from being the only place affected by the floods, Fleethaven Point had in fact suffered very little in comparison with the tragedy the long night was bringing to others. Unknown to the small community at the Point, struggling in the stormy night with their own problems, all down the east coast of Lincolnshire, and even further south, the sea had ravaged the land in the worst flooding within living memory. A north-westerly gale, with gusts approaching hurricane proportions, had swelled the southward flow of the flood tide down the east coast; crashing through promenades, bearing aloft huge tons of concrete like bits of flotsam; ripping gaps hundreds of yards long through the sea defences; tearing aside the dunes, dredging up tons of sand and spewing it into towns and villages; flinging chalets and caravans into heaps of splintered matchwood; rending whole roofs from bungalows and floating them away; rushing into homes, engulfing families caught unawares; without warning and without mercy.

And somewhere, out there, was Kate Hilton.

Seven

'Gran, there's a boat coming. Someone's coming in a boat.'

She rushed downstairs, praying fervently to herself as she went. 'Oh, let it be Mum. Oh, please let it be Mum!'

Snuggled up to the comforting bulk of Grandma Eland during the night, Ella had slept fitfully, waking every so often from a nightmare of crashing waves battering against the house. Each time, she lay listening to Grandma Eland's gentle snoring beside her, while outside the storm still raged. Once she tiptoed out on to the landing to peer down the stairs, irrationally afraid that the water might be rising steadily to engulf them all. Sometimes when she woke, Grandma Eland was awake too and they whispered together.

'Do you think Mum's all right?' she asked, more than once, in the darkness.

The fat arms came around her, hugging her close. 'Course she will be. She'll've taken the car back to our Danny and be safely at Rookery Farm. You'll see.'

They were all trying to reassure her; but were they sure themselves or just saying it to calm her fears? And their own.

In cold light of dawn, that first grey lightening of the darkness, Ella had woken to the sound of snuffling and grunting from the other side of the door into the small bedroom, and the place beside her in the bed, though rumpled, was empty. She swung her legs to the floor and, barefoot, padded to the window. Drawing back the curtains she looked out on to a grey lake. There were no surging waves now. The wind, still strong though no longer gale-force, merely rippled the surface of the water. She could see now that the floodwater extended to a line just beyond the far bank of the river; beyond that, she could see the brown earth of the fields. She pressed her face to the window trying to see Rookery Farm and though she could see the buildings she could not be sure from this distance whether the water had reached the farm or not.

She dressed hurriedly, shivering in the cold, finding her thickest jumper and warmest socks. Then she went out onto the landing. She knocked on the bedroom door opposite and when there was no answer she pushed open the door and peeped inside.

There was no one in the room.

A moment's absurd fear swept through her that her grandparents, and Grandma Eland, had gone in the night and she was now entirely alone; marooned in an empty house. She swallowed such a foolish thought.

She went into her grandparents' room and went to the window. Maybe she could see Rookery Farm from here . . .

It was then that she saw the boat.

On the step just above the water stood the pair of rubber boots she had worn last night. Struggling into them, ignoring the damp insides and holding up her skirt, she stepped carefully down into the water, surprised at the cold which penetrated even the thick rubber of the boots. She could hear the splashing of water as someone moved about. Slowly she waded out of the hall and into the living room; then through that and stopped at the kitchen door. 'Gran?' In the kitchen her grandmother and Grandma Eland were lifting chairs out of the water and on to the table.

'You stay upstairs, Missy,' her grandmother snapped. 'I dun't want you getting soaking wet again. The range fire's out now and there's no way I can relight it.' Ella saw the older woman cast an angry, resentful glance at the cold fire-grate.

Ella ignored her grandmother's scolding and said, 'Gran, there's someone coming in a boat.'

Esther looked at her. 'Really?' And she began to wade towards the back door, with Grandma Eland close behind her and Ella following, asking, 'It'll be Mum coming back. I'm sure it's Mum coming. Where's Grandpa? Is he all right this morning?'

Esther sniffed with disapproval. 'Silly man. He's got a bit of a cough through getting chilled but he's gone out again to see to the cows.'

The three of them stood together in the murky sea water at the open back door watching a little rowing boat being manoeuvred from the lane, or at least where the lane should be, through the farmyard gate and towards the back door of the house.

'It's Uncle Danny and Rob.' Ella's sharp eyes recognized them first. 'But – but I can't see Mum. Maybe she's stopped at Rookery Farm and they've come to take me to her . . .'

At that moment Jonathan emerged from the cowshed. Hitching his thigh boots up as far as he could, he began to wade towards the boat. He shouted a greeting. 'Morning, Harbour Master, what time's the tide go out?'

They heard Danny's laughter drifting towards them. 'Glad you can joke about it.' And as the boat floated closer, he called, 'You all right, Missus, and the young 'un?'

'As well as can be expected,' Esther replied tartly, but she was smiling even if a little wryly. Danny pulled in the oars and he and Rob sat in the boat as it floated near the back door.

'What about you, Mam?'

Grandma Eland's face beamed. 'If it hadn't been for that man there,' she nodded towards Jonathan, 'I wouldn't be standing here at all.'

'How's things with you, Danny?' Jonathan asked, swiftly turning the attention away from himself, but Ella noticed that his voice was still husky and his breathing difficult.

'We're okay. The surge came in over the headland and up the river and that's why you've got it. It was too sudden, too fast for the river to cope with the volume. It's come into our yard, but not into the house. So, we've come to fetch all of you to Rookery Farm,' he said, his glance going from one to the other.

Without waiting for her husband's opinion, Esther said sharply, 'I aren't leaving me farm and no one's going to make me.'

'Now, wait a minute, Esther—' Jonathan began, but she rounded on him. 'I'm not going and that's flat!'

'Well, what about Ella, then?'

Esther did not answer Danny's question, but instead asked, 'Is Kate with you? Is she back?'

The colour drained from Danny's face and his mouth gagged open. 'Kate?' he said hoarsely. 'Isn't she here? With you?'

Esther shook her head.

Fear shot through Ella like a knife and her knees began to tremble, but she could say nothing, ask nothing. She just stared and stared at Danny.

'I thought—' he was stumbling over the words. 'When she didn't bring the car back I thought – I thought she must have come straight home and – and that she'd bring it back next day . . .'

'She'll be in Lynthorpe. She'll be in the town,' Jonathan said and, trying to raise their hopes, added, 'She's probably the lucky one, keeping her feet dry.'

But in Danny's eyes there was no laughter. 'She – she went up the coast, didn't she?'

In the boat, Rob, solemn and white-faced, sat beside his father. Ella began to cry, not caring now who saw her.

Her gaze never leaving Danny's face, Esther said quietly, 'There's more, isn't there, Danny? Come on, out with it.'

It was then that Danny began to tell them of the awful news bulletins that were coming over the wireless.

'This . . .' he waved his hand to encompass the floodwater all around, 'this is nothing compared to what's happened further north. We heard the news on our portable this morning. The whole of the Lincolnshire coast and, I think, Norfolk and Kent coastlines too, are devastated by flooding. The sea's gone as far as two miles inland in some parts and this morning's high tide's been nearly as bad. We've just been up to the Hump and stood on the top . . .' He glanced at Rob, sitting in the boat beside him. But the boy was pale, his eyes large and stricken. 'I've never seen rollers like it out to sea. I felt sea-sick just looking at 'em. Forty foot high, I reckon they must be.'

Esther gasped, 'You mean we're goin' to get more?'

Danny shook his head. 'Not here, I don't reckon. At least, no more than you've got now, but maybe that's why the water's not going down at all yet. It's still coming in.'

'What about the cottages at the Point?' Jonathan asked.

'Still standing – just – but it's a good job they all got out when they did, else . . .' Danny cleared his throat and said instead, 'But the pub's gone altogether now.'

Ella remembered Rob pointing out the crumbling ruins of a building that had been bombed in the war. His grandad Eland had been killed there, he'd said. Ella shuddered suddenly. And last night, his grandma Eland might have been drowned in her home if Grandpa Godfrey hadn't rescued her.

But where was her mum? Had anybody been there to rescue her?

Noticing Ella shiver, Esther said, 'Go on in, child. There's no need for you . . .'

'No,' the girl said. 'I've got to hear it.' Then realizing her tone had been brusque, almost rude, she looked up swiftly at her grandmother, adding softly so that only Esther, and not the others, should hear. 'Please, Gran. I *must*!'

Their attention was drawn back to Danny as, haltingly, he was saying the words they most dreaded to hear. 'There's – there's been people drowned in some places . . .'

They were all staring at each other now in horror, trying to take in the enormity of the destruction that had swept their county's coastline.

'What about the town?'

'I don't know. Later today I'm going to go up past the Grange and out that way and see if I can get news.'

Ella moved forward. 'Are you going to try and find Mum, Uncle Danny?'

The man looked at her and even the young girl could see the depth of suffering that was suddenly naked in his eyes. 'Yes,' he said hoarsely. 'That's why I'm going.'

There was silence and then he looked back at Esther again and said, 'At least let me take the child back home where it's warm and dry.'

'No,' her grandmother said firmly. 'She stays here. With me.'

From the tone in her grandmother's voice, Ella knew argument would be futile.

Over the next day or so, news filtered through gradually regarding the extent of the flooding; how the relentless waves had rolled inland, taking lives, destroying homes and livelihoods in one powerful, ruthless invasion. All the coastal holiday resorts of the county had suffered a terrible battering and now an army of mechanical vehicles moved in to fill up the breaches. Lorry load after lorry load of slag and stone was trundled hour after hour to the stricken coast and men worked day and night to hold back the sea.

With growing horror the people of Fleethaven Point heard of the devastation and counted themselves fortunate in comparison.

Yet they were not unscathed, for still there was no news of Kate Hilton.

Eight

By Thursday the water was gone from the house leaving a carpet of sand and sludge that Esther attacked with resentment. 'How dare it?' she muttered. 'I've loved the sea, ever since I first came here as a young lass, and *this* is what it does to me!'

Jonathan had nailed a thick strip of rubber on to a piece of wood and in turn attached it to a broom handle; a 'squee-gee' he called it, and showed Esther how to push it along the floor to sweep away the thick, muddy silt left by the sea.

On Saturday, exactly a week after the floods had come, for the first time Ella awoke to look out of her window and see that the water had finally soaked away leaving only puddles here and there and overflowing dykes as a reminder.

Now, she thought, Mum will come home. She must.

Pulling on the pair of rubber boots she had virtually claimed as her own, Ella went out into the yard, where Jonathan had all the rugs from the ground floor of the house spread about. He was carrying buckets of water from the pump and swilling them over Esther's peg rugs trying to wash away the sand and mud.

'I don't think I'm doing much good with these.' He glanced ruefully at Ella. He set the bucket down on the ground and bent double, resting his hands on his knees, as a fit of coughing racked him.

Ella went up to him. 'You shouldn't be doing this, Grandpa. You should be indoors resting.'

Jonathan took a deep breath and stood up slowly. He was smiling. 'You sound like your grannie.'

Her smile flickered briefly and then died. 'Grandpa, can I go to Rookery Farm now the water's gone?'

'Well . . .' He hesitated, doubtful, and then glanced about him. Then he looked down again at the girl. 'I suppose so, if you promise to keep to the lane. No going into the fields, mind. Why do you want to go?'

'I want to be there when Mum comes back. She'll come back today, now the water's gone. I know she will.' The words came out in a rush, tumbling over themselves in her eagerness; an excitement that hid her deep-rooted anxiety.

Jonathan touched her unruly curls with a tender gesture and his voice was husky as he said, 'Yes, love, of course she will. Off you go then, but tell your grannie first where you're going.'

'I will.'

As she left the yard and turned into the lane, trudging along in her over-large boots, the young girl felt the anxiety of the last few days lift a little. Today Mum would come back. She must have stayed somewhere in town and not been able to get home because of the floodwater.

But Uncle Danny had been into town and back by the road leading past the Grange inland, a niggling little voice reminded her. Why hadn't Mum come that way then? Perhaps she hadn't got back as far as Lynthorpe, Ella continued to argue inside her head. Perhaps she was still somewhere where the water had only just gone, like here at the Point. But today, she would come home.

She must find Uncle Danny. Perhaps he had some news.

*

'I've tried everything I can think of.' Danny stood facing Ella, her own anxiety mirrored in his face. He swept his hand up into his hair and grasped a handful, almost as if he would pull it out by the roots. His feeling of dread was every bit as great as Ella's and just as obvious. Behind him, Rosie fiddled with the corner of her apron, her troubled eyes going from one to the other.

'He's been up into town every day since the floods came,' she put in. 'And Rob's there now, asking round. You know, to see if anyone . . .' Her voice faded away and she cast an anxious glance at her husband, afraid perhaps her tongue might say too much.

They were standing in the warm kitchen at Rookery Farm and now, from the corner near the range, seated in a rocking chair with a shawl around her shoulders, came Grandma Eland's gentle voice.

'Come here, lovey, and sit with me. Rosie, get the child some hot soup. She can't have had anything warm inside her for days. If Esther weren't so stubborn . . .'

'Now, Mam,' Danny turned, forcing a laugh, 'dun't you start.' But he put his hand on Ella's thin shoulder and urged her towards the fire.

Moments later she was sipping at thick vegetable soup, not really hungry but not wanting to refuse their kindness, when the back door was flung open and Rob burst into the kitchen.

'Dad – Dad . . .' His face was red, his eyes wide and his coat flying open. As always, his socks were wrinkled around his ankles.

He did not see Ella sitting in the corner beside the range before he blurted out, 'Dad, they've found your car.'

The four people in the room stared at him and then the boy became aware of Ella's white face, her eyes, wide with terror, staring at him.

'Oh, heck,' she heard him mutter. 'I – I didn't know you was here.'

Danny was the first to speak, his voice a hoarse, strangled, whisper. 'Kate? What about Kate?'

The boy dragged his gaze away from Ella's face back to his father's. 'They – Sergeant Darby wouldn't tell me.'

'You – you went to the police station?'

Rob nodded. 'I thought they might be the people most likely to know owt. He – he said I was to ask you and the mester . . .' Rob jerked his head in the vague direction of Brumbys' Farm, 'to go an' see them. He – he wouldn't tell me any more,' he added again, leaving the listeners well aware, as Rob himself had been, that there was more to tell.

Under his breath, Ella heard Danny say, 'Oh – my – God!' and he passed his hand across his forehead and up into his hair again.

Swiftly, Rosie was at his side, touching his arm. 'Go straight away, love, and find out. Get the—' She clapped her hand to her mouth to stop the words she had been going to say – 'get the car out'. The phrase had come automatically to her lips before she had stopped to think. But, of course, their car was not here.

Ella was staring at Danny, biting her lower lip to still its trembling, swallowing the lump of fear rising in her throat and threatening to choke her. Tears prickled behind her eyes and she blinked rapidly to stop them falling. Not yet, she told herself fiercely, don't let them see you cry again; at least, not yet.

They had indeed found Danny's car. They presumed it had been travelling along the coast road some miles north of Lynthorpe where it ran along an embankment just below the sand-dunes. Then the sea had broken through, ripping aside the sand and vegetation, bearing aloft anything in its path and hurling the car over and over, plunging it down the bank until it had come to rest upside down in a deep dyke, where it lay undiscovered until the floodwater had subsided.

And they had found Kate.

She had been trapped inside and possibly, from the bruising on her head, knocked unconscious. 'From the position we found the car, we think she was coming back towards home,' the kindly policeman told them. 'Do you know why she was travelling on that particular road and at that time in the evening?'

Ella saw her grandparents exchange a glance. Her grandpa's voice came huskily. 'We think she was going to meet someone that afternoon, but she didn't say who it was or where exactly she was going.'

'So you don't know whether she actually met whoever it was, or not?'

Grandpa Godfrey shook his head and sighed sadly, 'Maybe we'll never know now.'

The policeman's sympathetic gaze came to rest on the young, white-faced girl. He seemed to guess, without being told, who she was, for he squatted down in front of her and held out his huge hands towards her. 'Your mum, was it, love?' and when Ella nodded, he added, 'She could hardly have known what was happening. She wouldn't have suffered . . .'

But the sensitivc child thought differently, and for many nights to come and even intermittently through the years, her nightmares would he haunted by the thought of her mother trapped in the car, alone and hurt, with the water rising relentlessly . . .

Of course they would not let her see her mother, not

even when they brought her back to the local chapel of rest at the undertakers' whilst a funeral was arranged. Danny and her grandfather had been obliged to identify the body and though they had tried to prevent Esther seeing her, their efforts had been in vain.

'I'll see me daughter and no one's goin' to stop me, not even you, Jonathan.' So she had gone, resolutely walking into town alone to the undertakers', forbidding anyone to accompany her.

She came back white-faced and sat down in the wooden Windsor chair near the range, her hands clutching the arms until the knuckles showed white just staring into the fire, yet her eyes were glazed, unseeing. She forgot the house and clearing up the mess left by the sea, she ignored the needs of her farm and the animals; she didn't even seem to realize her granddaughter was still there, needing her, at this moment, more than anyone or anything else. She sat like that for so long that Jonathan became concerned.

'If only she would cry – let it out,' Ella overheard him telling Danny. Perhaps more than any of them, though only young, Ella knew how her grandmother was feeling, for she felt the same. The grief was so deep, too deep for tears. There was a misery locked away inside that would not, could not find release. It was like a solid, aching mass of suffering in the pit of her stomach. She could not reach her grandmother and the older woman could not comfort the girl. So alike were they that they were both tormented in the same way and yet could not help each other.

For once Jonathan could do nothing with Esther; trying to cope with his own personal grief over Kate, whom he had loved since her childhood – and still suffering from the effects of his drenching in the cold floodwater – took all his energy. He was exhausted and devastated himself.

And then Beth Eland came to the farm.

Ella watched in astonishment as Beth came waddling into the house, heaving her heavy frame into the kitchen and coming to stand in front of Esther. Jonathan stood by the door, like Ella just watching and waiting.

The girl had gathered that there was some long-standing family feud between Esther and Rob's grandmother. What was it she had overheard her mother say to Uncle Danny at that old man's funeral? 'There's so much between them, Danny,' Kate had said. 'So much they can't forget, yet they always come together when there's trouble.'

And so now, in the greatest trouble that Ella could ever imagine happening, here was Grandma Beth Eland coming to Esther to try to help her.

'Well, lass . . .' Beth began, and Ella felt an hysterical giggle rise suddenly inside her. To hear these two old women call each other 'lass' would have been so funny if the reason for it were not so tragic. '. . . this won't do. It won't do at all, Esther.'

There was silence as Beth paused but there was no response. Beth tried again. 'Come along, Esther. The bairn needs you now. She's grieving. Much as we all loved Kate, and you know we did, her little lass has lost everything – everything. Ella needs to know you love her, Esther.'

Still, there was no answer and the thought came unbidden into Ella's mind. She can't say she loves me, because she doesn't. She doesn't love me, I know she doesn't love me and she never will, not like Mum loved me. No one could. The tears prickled at the back of her eyelids, but would not fall.

Ella saw Beth glance across towards Jonathan just once as if in mute apology for what she was about to do, for what she felt compelled to do. Then she leant over Esther, resting her hands on the arms of the chair, trying to force Esther to look up at her, to meet her gaze. Her voice was sharp. 'Where are you burying her, Esther? Next to her own father? Or out at Suddaby beside yar dad – and yar mam?'

Esther's head snapped up and her eyes focused, staring straight into Beth's dark brown, troubled gaze. Her voice was full of harsh bitterness. 'Aye, I'll tek her out to Suddaby all right. But I'll put her beside *my* mother. Two of a kind, they'd be, wouldn't they? Both brought bastards into the world! I spent all me young life, never allowed to forget what I was. And now, I've to face it all again.' With an almost violent gesture she flung out her hand towards Ella.

The girl heard her grandfather gasp. 'Esther, how can you say such a thing?' He was staring at his wife, a strange expression on his face; a mixture of anger, disgust and, yes, pity too. 'How *can* you?' His voice dropped to a hoarse whisper.

Esther stood up with a swift, angry movement. 'Oh, I can. I can,' she almost screamed at him and then suddenly, the floodgates of her tears broke open and she gave a howl of such misery that no one present was left in doubt any longer as to the depth of her suffering at the death of her daughter. Anger, resentment, bitterness, all the tumult of emotions were there, yet deep down Esther was heart-broken. She raised her arms to Beth who took her into her warm embrace. 'How – could she – do it to me? To me?' she wept against the other woman's shoulder.

Beth made no reply now, but rocked her like a child, only murmuring, 'There, there, lass. Let it come. Let it all come out.'

As release came to her grandmother, Ella too broke down and turned blindly to her grandfather, who picked her up in his strong, comforting arms and carried her out-side towards the warm dryness of the loft above the barn.

'We'll leave them alone for a while, Ella love. You and me, we'll go up here and we can have a little talk.'

They didn't say much for some time until Ella's sobs had subsided. He set her down in the warm, prickly hay and lowered himself to sit beside her, wrapping his arms around her to still the shivering that came more from her distress than from the cold. She snuggled into his chest and he stroked her hair, saying nothing until at last she raised her head and asked, 'What did she mean about her own mother?'

'Oh, Ella,' he sighed. 'It's a long, long story. Things that happened so many years ago now, yet your grannie can't forget, nor, I'm afraid, quite forgive.'

'To do with my mum, you mean?'

'Well, partly, love, yes,' he said gently.

She hiccuped and sniffed, brushing the back of her hand across her swollen eyes. Her grandfather fished into his pocket and pulled out a clean handkerchief and she blew her nose hard.

'What?' she asked again.

He sighed. 'I can't tell you it all, love, not now. It's really something your grannie ought to tell you about when you're older.'

Ella stared at him through the gloom of the hayloft. 'That's what Mum . . .' Her voice trembled afresh at the mention of her beloved mother who was lost to her for ever now. 'That's what Mum always said when I asked questions. "I'll tell you when you're older," she always said. But—' The tears spouted again. 'She won't be here now to tell me, will she?' Ella laid her head against his shoulder and wept again.

At the funeral neither Ella nor her grandmother cried; they refused to do so. They set their faces against a show of emotion, each with her jaw clamped firmly shut against the lump burning in her throat.

They did not take Kate to Suddaby. She was buried in the churchyard in Lynthorpe.

Ella travelled in the leading funeral car, sitting between her grandparents, feeling overawed and lost amidst all the black clothes and sad-faced people. She wished she could have been allowed to travel in the third car bringing Peggy Godfrey and Mavis and Isobel, her mother's friends from her days in the WAAF just before Ella herself had been born. All three were Ella's godmothers; she and her mother lived with Aunty Peggy, and Mavis and Isobel had visited often. Aunty Mavis was married with three children of her own, all several years younger than Ella, but Aunty Isobel had made a career in the service and was now quite a high-ranking officer. She was in her smart blue uniform today.

Ella would even have preferred riding in the second car, carrying the Eland family, to sitting in silence between a stiff-faced Esther and Jonathan whose own grief seemed today overwhelming, though he held Ella's hand, clutching it tightly. She sensed that today he needed her comfort more than she had need of his.

As the slow procession drew to a halt outside the church gate, Ella glanced up at her grandmother who returned her gaze. Today, of all days, Ella thought, I must be a good girl and not annoy Gran, if only for Mum. For a moment they stared at each other and then Esther, almost as if able to read Ella's thoughts, gave a slight nod, for once approving of the way the young girl was conducting herself.

The service was taken by a vicar who had known Kate well in her childhood and therefore the address he gave was personal and full of loving memories of the woman they had all lost. His words brought comfort, but the worst moment of all was when they stood in the draughty, windswept churchyard and watched the coffin being lowered into the ground. The vision of the old man lying in his coffin danced before Ella's eyes and merged to become her lovely mum, lying in the deep darkness of the ground, her eyes closed, her face alabaster white, her hands neatly folded; so still and silent for ever. The girl shuddered and a soft moan escaped her lips. It was the final parting, the last goodbye, and Ella found herself clutching not only her grandpa's hand, but in that terrible moment she reached out and grasped her grandmother's too.

She heard a sob and glanced up to look at her grandmother. But Esther was dry-eyed, staring down at the coffin.

Beyond her the Eland family stood huddled together and, with a shock, Ella saw that it was her uncle Danny, supported by Rosie and his mother, who was sobbing as if his heart would break.

Ella had never, ever, in her life seen a man cry and the sight of Danny Eland crying openly and unashamedly at her mother's graveside was to be engraved in her memory for ever.

Nine

Back at Rookery Farm it was a little easier. There seemed to be a sense of relief that the time they had all dreaded – the funeral – was at least over. But now there was the future to face without Kate and that wasn't going to be much easier.

'We should be at home,' Esther said, as she allowed herself to be ushered into the front parlour at Rookery Farm by Beth, her reluctance obvious for everyone to see.

'Now, Esther, I know it goes against the grain for you to accept help . . .'

Esther shot her a look, but Beth only smiled. 'But you can hardly put on a spread at your place with the house in the state the flood's left you.' She shook her head. 'At least we've been spared that. This is little enough we can do to help. Besides,' Beth's voice dropped low, 'we need to do something, Esther. We're grieving for her too, y'know. Why Danny, he's beside hissen. I dun't think he'll ever get over it – not properly.'

Ella saw a long look pass between the two elderly women. Then Esther nodded and whispered, 'I know, Beth, I know.'

Suddenly she seemed to become aware of Ella listening to every word being spoken and she said, quite sharply, 'Go and ask if you can help yar aunty Rosie, Missy.'

And as if to take some of the edge from her grandmother's voice, Beth Eland smiled at Ella and added, 'She'd be glad of your help, lovey.'

In the huge farmhouse kitchen, Peggy Godfrey, Mavis and Isobel were already supposedly 'helping' Rosie, though only Peggy was buttering rounds of bread to make sandwiches. Isobel stood near the sink lighting a cigarette with fingers that trembled and Mavis was leaning against the dresser, her arms folded around herself, at least as far round as her arms would reach. Mavis was large and comfortable and jolly; except that today, she was not jolly.

As Ella entered, she felt their gaze all come to rest on her and, in turn, she returned their stares. Peggy dropped the knife she was holding and came round the table to gather Ella into her arms. Ella hugged her in return, comforted by the waft of the flowery perfume Peggy always wore. It reminded her sharply of her home, for it was the scent that lingered on the landing outside Peggy's bedroom door. As always, Peggy was smartly dressed, though black did not really suit her pale, rather thin, face. And her make-up, usually so carefully applied, was a little blotchy. Peggy straightened up, and, resting her hands lightly on the girl's shoulders, looked down into Ella's upturned face.

'You all right, Ella?' she asked softly.

Peggy's kindness threatened to overwhelm her but Ella nodded and asked, 'Am I going back with you, Aunty Peggy? Am I going home?'

There was a silence in the kitchen, only the ticking of the clock on the mantelpiece and the hiss of the kettle on the hob broke the silence.

'I – I don't know, love. We'll talk about it later.' She turned back to her buttering.

'Hello, pet.' Rosie smiled brightly as she emerged from the pantry carrying out cups, saucers and plates, fruit cake and pastries.

'Gran said I was to come and help,' Ella said.

'Well, you can carry things through to the parlour, if you like. Start with these plates and then come back for the other things. I'll put everything I want you to take through here, look, on the corner of the kitchen table.'

'Aunty Peg.' Ella moved closer to the table and took hold of the plates.

'Mmm?' The knife flashed across the rounds of bread, smearing a film of butter across each one.

'Who was the man standing under the trees in the churchyard?'

The knife was still, suspended in mid-air. Peggy looked up and stared at her, but the question came from Isobel: 'What man, Ella?'

Ella glanced round the three faces now watching her, though Rosie, still bustling between kitchen and pantry, was ignoring the conversation.

'While we were at the – the grave, there was a tall man standing under the trees near the fence. He was still there when we came away. I think . . .' Ella hesitated. She had first noticed the man when she had looked away from Uncle Danny, whose tears had disconcerted her; embarrassed, she had turned her gaze away but not back to the coffin now lying at the bottom of the deep pit – she hadn't wanted to look at that either. And so her gaze had wandered and gone beyond the black-clad figures surrounding the grave, only to see the motionless figure of the tall man standing beneath the dripping trees watching them, his head bowed as if he too were taking part in the ceremony but did not like to approach too close.

'Go on,' Peggy urged.

'I think after we left he – he walked over to – to the grave. When we were walking down the path, I looked back again.' She lowered her gaze, not wanting to admit that she had not wanted to leave her mother lying in the half-frozen earth.

'What did he look like?' Mavis put in.

Ella screwed up her face, trying to recapture the picture in her mind. 'He'd got a long black coat on and he'd got curly fair hair, I think, but he was in the shadows under the trees. I couldn't see him ever so well. He just stood there with his hands in his pockets. He never moved, not till we'd gone, but he was watching us all the time.'

'One of the undertaker's men, I expect, just standing ready but keeping a respectful distance,' Peggy suggested, resuming her sandwich-making.

Ella saw Isobel and Mavis exchange a look.

'You don't think . . .' Isobel began but Mavis put her forefinger warningly to her lips and glanced meaningfully at Ella.

'Take those plates through for Rosie, Ella love,' Peggy said. Although Ella picked up the plates and left the kitchen, once in the passage leading to the front room, she paused and stood listening.

'You don't think,' Isobel was saying again, 'it was *him*?'

'How could it have been? How would he know about Kate's death?' Mavis answered.

'Well, Danny said that she'd gone off that afternoon to meet someone. She wouldn't say who. It was all very mysterious. Perhaps . . .'

At that moment Ella heard Rosie's footsteps tapping across the tiled floor of the kitchen towards the door. 'I'll just take these through,' Ella heard her say and the girl was obliged to move quickly into the front room before Rosie caught her eavesdropping. She scuttled into the parlour and dumped the plates on to the table and turned to hurry back to hear more.

'Careful with those plates, Missy. Don't go breaking Rosie's best china.'

'No, Gran,' she called back as she rushed to the kitchen, arriving in time to hear Isobel say, 'He was the only one she was really close to at that time. You know he was.'

Again Rosie was coming up behind her and as Ella stepped into the kitchen both Isobel and Mavis fell silent. Ella picked up two saucers, the two cups balancing on the top and turned away again. Once out of the kitchen, she hovered again near the door.

'Maybe we ought to try and find him anyway, for the kid's sake?' Isobel was saying.

'Do you really think so?' Mavis's tone was doubtful. 'He – he never knew about her, did he?'

'Mmm.' Isobel drew deeply on her cigarette. 'You have a point there, Mave.' There was a pause and then Isobel added, 'Poor little scrap. What'll happen to her now?'

In the passage, Ella stood perfectly still, holding her breath, waiting for the answer.

'I suppose she'll stay here with Kate's mother, won't she?'

Ella gasped and did not realize the cups and saucers had slid from her grasp until the crash at her feet and a jagged piece of porcelain hitting her leg made her jump and cry out. From all directions, grown-ups came hurrying.

'Oh, lovey, have you hurt yourself?'

'Whatever are you doing, child? I told you to be careful.' This from her grandmother.

Tears blinded her. She wouldn't live in Brumbys' Farm where the wind battered at the house and the sea invaded it. She wouldn't stay here with this horrible woman who did not, and never would, love her.

With a sob, Ella ran back through the kitchen, dragged

open the back door and raced across the yard towards the barn. She heard them calling her but she ran on.

It was Rob who found her a little later burrowed beneath the straw in the loft above the big barn at Rookery Farm. He said nothing but sat down beside her, wriggling into the straw to make himself a little nest too.

He held out a plate towards her. 'I've brought you some sandwiches. Thought you'd be hungry.'

She shook her head, clenching her teeth together stubbornly, though her stomach was now rumbling with emptiness.

'Oh, well, I'll eat 'em, then.' He picked one up and took a huge bite, munching with deliberate pleasure.

She reached out swiftly and grabbed one, stuffing it into her mouth. What would her grandmother say if she could see her now, she thought with glee. The plate wobbled and two sandwiches fell into the straw. 'Butterfingers.' Rob grinned, picked them carefully out of the straw and put them back on to the plate.

The two youngsters ate in silence in the deepening gloom of the hayloft.

'Oh, I almost forgot,' he said airily. 'They want you back at the house. Yar grandpa and grannie are leaving soon.'

'I'm not going back with her.'

'Well, you can't stay up here for ever.'

'I'm going back to Lincoln with Aunty Peggy or – or with . . .' She bit her lip, half wanting to confide in Rob and yet years of covering up the bald truth made her hesitate still. She wanted to blurt out, Have they said any more about the man in the churchyard? Have they said who he was? The thoughts were burning inside her head.

Was he – could he have been my father? Instead, she sat silently, digging her hands into the prickly straw and gripping handfuls of it in frustration.

'I don't reckon you're goin' back to Lincoln. They've been arguing half the afternoon.'

'Who?'

'All on 'em. Even your aunty Peg and – er – Isobel and Mavis, is it?'

'Yes.'

'Well, them an' all. And me dad and mum. Even my grandma put her two penn'orth in till your grannie told her to mind her own business and stay out of her affairs. Dun't tek 'em long to get back to their feudin', does it?'

'Your grandma was good when we first got the news, though,' Ella said in a small voice. There was another pause then she asked, 'What did Aunty Peggy say? Did she say I could go back with her?'

She heard the straw rustle as he moved. 'Er, well, not exactly. See, she – they all agreed that with her not bein' married and going out to work ev'ry day, well, she won't be at home to look after you—'

'I bet she never said that,' Ella defended Peggy hotly. 'I bet that was *her* – Gran.'

'No, as a matter of fact, it was your grandpa who said it wouldn't be fair on either Peg or you.'

Another silence.

'And Aunty Isobel and Aunty Mavis? What did they say?'

'We-ell, er . . .' He hesitated and then asked, 'Which is the posh one in uniform who smokes?'

'Isobel.'

'She said she can't take you 'cos she's still in the forces.'

'Are you sure they didn't say any more? I mean, about anybody else?'

He stared at her through the gloom. 'Who else is there?'

There was a pause until, in a small voice, she said, 'No one, I suppose.'

At his next words, her hopes leapt. 'But the other one, she said you could go to her. "Won't notice her among my rowdy three," she said.'

Oh, good old Aunty Mavis. Ella scrambled up. 'That's it then. I'll go with Aunty Mavis.'

But her hopes were short-lived. As she entered the kitchen with Rob behind her, her grandmother's voice was the first to greet her.

'There you are. Go and get yar coat. We must be off home now.'

In front of them all, ranged around the big room, Ella faced her grandmother. 'I'm not staying here. I want to go home with Aunty Mavis.' She glanced beyond her grandmother and caught Mavis's glance. 'I can, can't I, Aunty Mave?'

'Well . . .'

In a voice that would tolerate no argument, either from Ella or from anyone else, Esther said, 'You'll do nothing of the sort, Missy. You're coming home with me. You're my responsibility now.'

Ten

The storms raged on for days. Not the elements now, but the tempest between Ella and her grandmother.

'I won't live here in this God-forsaken place.'

'Mind your language, Missy.'

'I don't belong here. *You* don't want me. You don't love me.'

'Don't be so silly, child. You're my flesh and blood. It's my duty to look after you.'

Ella stared at her, waiting, willing her grandmother to say the words she so desperately needed to hear from her. But Esther turned away and poked the fire vigorously, muttering only, 'We're stuck with each other, Missy, so you'd best get used to it.'

Ella swallowed the lump of disappointment that rose in her throat and hardened her resolve. 'Well, I don't like it here,' she said, stubbornly determined not to be cowed. 'I want to go back to Lincoln.'

'There's nowhere for you to go back to.' Esther's words were harsh, but sadly, the truth; even Ella had to acknowledge that fact now.

Peggy, with troubled eyes, had quietly explained that she, a single woman with a full-time job, could not look after a ten-year-old properly. 'Maybe they'll let you come in the holidays and spend a few days with me,' she added, and had touched Ella's cheek gently. 'When I can get time off work.'

The girl had nodded, clenching her teeth together, willing herself not to cry, not in front of Peggy, not in front of anyone and certainly she would never, ever, let her grandmother see her tears.

Even Mavis, in the end, had reluctantly admitted that it would be best if Ella went to live with her grandparents. 'I – I'm not sure what the law is, pet. Your grannie will have, what do they call it, custody of you?'

It sounded as if she were going to prison and to Ella that's exactly what it felt like.

The only occasion when the girl had felt a surge of hope had been when Jonathan had said quietly one supper time, 'It's another very high tide again this weekend, Esther. We ought to go inland. Maybe we could go to Peg's for a few days.'

'Oh, Grandpa, yes!'

'We're not going anywhere, Jonathan. I'm not leaving my farm to the mercy of the sea or to looters. If the flood comes again, then we'll be in it again.'

And Ella's brief spark of hope was snuffed out.

Only two weeks after her mother's funeral, all their belongings from Lincoln, pathetically few it seemed, arrived on a removal van to be dumped in the corner of the big bedroom upstairs where Ella now slept. Kate's clothes, her precious sewing machine and a square, polished box. Ella tried to lift the lid, but the box was locked and there was no key. Perhaps it had been in her mother's handbag; that would have been with her in the car . . . Ella shuddered and pushed the box away from her.

With tears prickling her eyelids, she fingered her mother's favourite dress, held a warm, woolly cardigan to her cheek. Kate's perfume still lingered and in the privacy of her bedroom, Ella buried her face in its softness, breathing in the closeness of her mother and wept bitter, lonely tears. Then she ran her hands over the smooth lid of the sewing machine with which Kate had earned their keep as a dressmaker, using the front parlour as a workroom in the terraced house in Lincoln. Ella gave a gulp. Never again would she hear the whir of the machine from the front room where pins and paper patterns and lengths of fabric littered every surface, even the floor; or hear her mother's merry laughter as she talked with her customers who called for fittings. She had thought the house they lived in was theirs or at least that it belonged to both her mother and Aunty Peggy, but now it seemed that they had only been lodgers: the house belonged solely to Peggy Godfrey.

Ella could still not quite believe that Peggy really did not want her to live with her and she clung to the thought that it was all Esther Godfrey's fault. Her grandmother didn't want her, Ella thought, not really, but she saw it as her duty to look after her daughter's orphan; her bastard orphan.

So it seemed she would have to stay at Brumbys' Farm at least for the present, but she clung to the vow she had flung in a final fury at her grandmother, 'One day I'll run away . . .'

'Where would you run to?' had been the disparaging answer, whilst poor Jonathan had stood helplessly between them.

'Anywhere. Anywhere away from here. Away from you!'

'How? There's no buses out here.'

'Then I'll *walk* if I have to!' Ella had set her firm jaw in a hard, determined line.

For a moment she saw her grandmother looking at her strangely, nodding slowly. 'Aye, Missy, I believe you would, an' all.' Her tone then had been soft, wondering, and Ella had seen the look that passed between her grandparents.

'More like me than I care to admit,' Esther had said quietly.

Jonathan had spread his hands and shrugged his shoulders in a gesture of helplessness, beaten by the wilful strength of the two with whom he must now share his home.

About three weeks after Kate's funeral, Rob arrived at Brumbys' Farm one morning, carrying the black and white kitten, now a fluffy, wriggling ball of mischief with wide open eyes.

'I've asked yar grannie if you can have a kitten and she said yes.'

'She did?' Ella was startled for a moment.

'Well, why shouldn't she? A cat's no trouble to keep on a farm and, besides, I told her I thought it'd be company for you.'

'Oh.' For a moment the disappointment that the kindness had not come from her grandmother was acute. For the first time since the dreadful news about her mother had reached them, Ella's smile was genuine as she took the wriggling little kitten into her arms. Its tiny claws sticking through her jumper, the kitten climbed up Ella's chest and nuzzled her neck, licking her with its rough tongue and greeting her with a high-pitched, frantic purring.

'Is it a boy or a girl?'

'Boy.'

'Oh, he's lovely. What's his name?'

'Hasn't got one. You can call him what you like.'

Ella wrinkled her brow. 'I don't know what sort of name you call a cat.'

'Well, there's – um – er – well, anything really.'

'Let's ask Grandpa. He's swilling out the cowshed.'

As they walked towards the building, Rob said, 'How's things in the house? I mean, all the muck the sea left.'

'Oh, we've about got it clean but a lot of her things are ruined. She keeps setting me on to wash the floors and the walls.' Ella grinned again and mimicked her grandmother's Lincolnshire dialect to perfection. 'Ses it's time Ah made mesen useful.'

Rob laughed. 'Mind she dun't hear you. She'll clip your ear.'

Ella grinned again. Strangely, she didn't resent being set to work. At the moment it kept her busy, gave her something to do and stopped her thinking about her mother quite so much.

Only at night in the big, lonely bedroom, did she bury her head beneath the covers so that no one should hear and sob herself to sleep.

'She's thrown out all her peg rugs,' she went on to tell Rob now. 'Grandpa tried to wash them but he couldn't get the sand and mud out. Everywhere's so damp and the walls are all drying out white. It's the salt water, Grandpa says. And all the wallpaper's peeling off right up the wall, even higher than the water actually came.'

The boy nodded, but could think of nothing to say. The flood had caused far more tragedy to this family than a bit of peeling wallpaper and ruined rugs. It would be a long time before the house recovered from its soaking, but even longer for the pain of their terrible loss to ease.

'Grandpa, look. Rob's brought me a kitten. Isn't he lovely?'

Jonathan straightened up and pressed his hand to his back as if to ease an ache. Then he came to them and reached out his work-worn fingers to tickle the kitten under its chin. The kitten clutched his forefinger with its tiny paws and nibbled at it with its sharp teeth, but the action was playful not vicious, and Jonathan did not withdraw his fingers in pain.

'Can you think of a name, Grandpa? He hasn't got one and I don't know what to call a cat. Mum . . .' Her voice shook a little. 'Mum always said we couldn't have one in a town 'cos of it getting run over.'

'Quite right too,' Jonathan said. 'Now then, let's think about it.'

After several suggestions, the name Ella liked was Tibby but her grandmother's first words were, 'No sneaking him indoors, Missy. He'll sleep in the barn and mek 'issen useful.'

Ella heard Rob, still at her side, quickly stifle a giggle and turn it into a cough. Esther glanced at him sharply, but went on, 'We dun't have pets on a farm. He can earn his keep by keeping the rats and mice down.'

'Rats!' Ella's eyes widened. 'Are there rats in the barn?'

Her grandmother's expression was scathing. 'Course there are. What do you expect on a farm where there's meal?'

As the two youngsters went outside again into the yard, Ella whispered, 'What's she mean "meal"? What meal?'

'It's stuff we feed the animals on, the pigs, an' that.'

Ella looked down at the kitten in her arms. The little thing was still purring loudly. 'He's not big enough to catch rats yet, is he?'

'No,' Rob said, and, understanding Esther's command better than Ella did, added, 'No, but he'll grow.'

*

The police brought back the items found in the car. In a kind and sympathetic gesture someone had dried and cleaned everything. When Esther laid them out on the kitchen table, Ella picked up Kate's handbag and hugged it to her chest. Somehow the handbag, more than anything else, symbolized her mother. She had carried it everywhere and the contents in its voluminous depths represented Kate's life: the keys to their home in Lincoln, her identity card, an old ration book, a handkerchief, a packet of sewing needles, a diary, a nail-file, lipstick and powder compact; and, lastly, a letter. The pages had been separated and dried out and then carefully replaced in the envelope. Ella glanced at it, but the writing was illegible, the ink running in blue blotches all over the pages.

Ella put everything back into the bag and snapped shut the fastener. She gave a little sigh: the only thing she had hoped to find was not there. The key to the wooden box was not, as she had thought it might be, in her mother's handbag.

She looked up to find her grandparents standing on the other side of the table watching her.

Esther's voice was surprisingly gentle. 'There's a big blanket box in your room. I'll clear it out and ya can put all ya mam's things in there.'

Tears sprang to Ella's eyes but she bit her lip and nodded.

Jonathan cleared his throat. 'Ella, we – your grannie and I – we thought we'd ride out to – er – where it happened. Now, don't come if you don't want to.'

But Ella was nodding firmly, pressing her lips together to stop the tears yet determined. 'I want to come, Grandpa.'

Slowly he nodded and his voice was hoarse as he said, 'All right then, love.' He cleared his throat, turned to his wife and said more strongly, 'Dick Souter's offered to lend us his car.'

'Heavens!' The expression on Esther's face was comical. 'You do surprise me. They've never had much time for us. Well . . .' she put her head on one side and gave a small, wry smile, 'me, really.'

Jonathan lifted his shoulders in a small shrug. 'People can be extraordinarily kind when there's real trouble.'

'Mmm,' Esther nodded and there was a faraway look in her eyes. Then she seemed to shake herself and asked, 'That reminds me, how's Beth?'

Ella saw the startled look in her grandfather's eyes and there was an incredulous note in his voice as he repeated, 'Beth?'

'Yes, Beth. And dun't look at me like that.'

'She's all right, but Danny was saying yesterday that they don't think she'll go back to live at the Point. The cottages are a mess.'

'They'd clean,' Esther said and sniffed with impatience to think that someone would not take the trouble and effort. She had worked tirelessly to restore the farmhouse from the ravages of the sea-water and was scathing of anyone else without her energy and devotion to home and land.

Ella, listening to the exchange, saw her grandfather smile fondly at his wife. 'Enid and Walter Maine, and the Harris boys, they'll go back to their homes, of course, but Danny and Rosie want Beth to live at Rookery Farm. They've plenty of room there and there's no reason for Beth to go on living on her own at the Point. Besides, she only rented the cottage from the old squire's estate, didn't she?'

Esther nodded.

'There you are, then.'

Esther shrugged. 'I'm surprised, that's all. She's so many memories in that little cottage.' Her voice dropped so that Ella had to strain to hear the words. 'It's where Matthew lived, an' all.'

'Ah well,' Jonathan said gently. 'She'll carry her memories with her, won't she?'

'Aye, I 'spect she will.' Esther sighed. 'Good and bad.' And she raised her eyes to look directly into her husband's steady gaze, while Ella's puzzled glance went from one to the other and back again.

On Sunday morning, Jonathan drove the Souters' old Morris Eight into the yard.

'Good grief!' Esther exclaimed, staring at the mud-spattered exterior, at the running board hanging half-off on one side, at the cracked window, at the chicken feathers littering the back seat. 'Those Souters are a mucky lot.'

'Now, now, Esther,' Jonathan admonished gently. 'They've been kind enough to lend us the car.'

'Mebbe so, but will it get us there?' Esther muttered as she opened the door and brushed the torn leather of the seat. 'Dust that seat afore you sit down, Missy,' she added to Ella, who was climbing into the back.

No one said much above the noise of the engine as Jonathan drove along the coast road, through Lynthorpe and northwards.

'Oh, look,' Ella heard her grandmother exclaim. 'Just look!'

Where the sea had broken through the sand-dunes, ripping aside the sand and vegetation, the land was a sea of mud made worse by the lorries, jeeps, tractors, bulldozers and all manner of mechanical diggers working with fanatical urgency to fill in the breach. Temporary walls of sandbags, hastily built by the troops drafted in during the hours immediately following the storms, kept the sea at bay whilst the frenzied work to build a more permanent sea wall went on.

As Jonathan drew the car on to the side of the road, well out of the way of the contractors' vehicles, and switched off the engine, Ella leaned forward and asked, 'Grandpa, what's that noise?'

Above the sounds of the traffic came a steady, rhythmic 'thud-thud-thud'.

'It'll be the pile-driver.'

'Whatever's that?' Esther asked.

'They're sinking groynes – breakwaters to us – into the sand.'

'Why?'

'The tides bring the sand down the coast. It'll build up the level of the beach and, hopefully, be a natural sea defence.'

'And in the meantime?' Esther asked sceptically.

'They're also building a sea wall. Just look at the lorries bringing stuff in.'

In silence they sat watching the stream of tip lorries piled high with Derbyshire stone, slag, gravel, rubble, sand; anything it seemed that would shore up the coastline against the next high tides.

They drove on through a village where people dressed in boots, thick coats and with scarves around their heads were digging away the sand piled high against their front doors. In some places they could see a huge tube going in through ground floor windows attached to a machine on the outside.

'They're driers loaned by the army, I think. We could maybe get one, if you like, Esther. It'd help dry the walls out.'

They drove out of the village and on to the coast road again, running along an embankment with a sand-dune above them on their right. On their left the ground fell away to the fields below. They came to the place where the avalanche of water had swept Danny's car away on that dreadful night.

Again Jonathan parked the car and this time they got out and climbed the bank on the seaward side of the road.

'It's like the marsh at home,' Esther said, surprise in her voice. 'Only they've built between the two lines of sand-dunes.'

Though the flood waters had gone, below them the ground looked drenched. Directly in front of them only one bungalow remained standing forlornly amongst the piles of debris that were the only remains of shattered homes, demolished to matchwood in a few horrific moments by the might of the sea. They watched as a party of men in rubber boots, armed with spades, splashed through pools of water and began digging amongst the rubble.

'What are they doing, Grandpa?' Ella asked in a small voice. 'They're not looking for – for people, are they?'

His arm came about her shoulder and his voice was husky as he said, 'No, love, but I expect they're looking for their possessions, things they hadn't time to take with them.'

Beside them Esther gave a snort of disbelief. Her lips tight, she nodded towards the searchers. 'Looters, more like.'

But Jonathan shook his head. 'No, Esther, I've read about it in the paper. The authorities have organized officially supervised parties to search.'

'I shouldn't think there's much to find now,' Esther murmured, and now there was real sympathy in her voice.

Just below where they were standing, washed up against the bank was a chair and, close by, a sodden, mud-stained length of material – someone's curtains.

'I wonder if they all got out?' Jonathan said.

'If it came as fast as it did with us,' Esther said, 'I doubt they had chance.'

'Perhaps they got some sort of warning herc . . .' Jonathan murmured but his tone held little hope. 'Look, that far line of sand-dunes has almost gone.'

Ella lifted her eyes and looked towards the sea. In places, the sand-dunes had been completely swept away and she could even see the waves of the sea beyond. Only parts of the dunes had been left, little clumps of sand and trees, left standing like tiny islands in the ocean, and in the gaps between were the inevitable sandbags.

'It's like the war all over again, sandbags everywhere,' Esther muttered.

Jonathan sighed. 'When you have an enemy as mighty as the sea, it's like a war.'

They turned back down the bank and stood at the side of the road looking westward now. Even on this side, pools of water still lay in the fields and the dykes were full and overflowing. Mud and sand, sea-grass and bushes torn from the sand-hills were strewn everywhere.

'They'll be years getting this land to grow owt,' Ella heard her grandmother murmur and as if their previous conversation had triggered her memory, she added, 'It's as bad as France in nineteen-nineteen . . .'

Jonathan nodded. 'Well, there's no trenches, but I know what you mean. It's certainly grim.'

'What's that over there?' Ella pointed. Two fields away from where they were standing on the embankment, there were three or four mounds lying on the sodden ground.

'Dead sheep,' Esther said.

Ella gasped. 'Do – do you mean they – they were drowned? Couldn't they get away?'

Her grandmother shook her head. 'The water came so fast.' She pointed to a field to the left. 'There's dead cattle in that one. Look.'

Ella shuddered. Her poor mother had died out here, drowned along with the cattle and sheep. She pushed her hands into the pockets of her school mac and said in a small voice, 'Do you know – where . . .?'

Jonathan pointed below them to a place near a foot-bridge made out of sleepers across a dyke. 'The car was found down there, just near that little bridge.'

The three of them stood in silence just staring at the spot where Kate had died. Then Jonathan, putting an arm about each of them, said, 'Come on, let's go home.'

Climbing back into the car Ella realized finally that there was no chance of going back. Her mother was dead; she had seen where it had happened.

Her grandmother was her closest relative and, from now on, Brumbys' Farm was her only home.

But one day, she silently repeated the promise to herself, one day I'll run away.

Eleven

As the new girl at the school in Lynthorpe, Ella was, for a time, the object of everyone's interest.

'Ella, come and play "I sent a letter . . ."' In the playground, Alison Clark grabbed her arm and dragged her towards where the girls in her class were organizing themselves into a ring.

'You can be first, Ella.' The ring formed and Ella, taking her handkerchief from her pocket as the 'letter', stood on the outside ready to run round as the others chanted, 'I sent a letter to my love and on the way I dropped it . . .'

'Who you sending a letter to, Ella? Have you got a boyfriend?'

The ring broke formation as the others clustered around her. Ella shook her head. 'I don't know any boys here yet. At least, only one.'

'Who?'

'Rob Eland.'

The gasp rippled around the gathering and there was almost unanimous awe in their voices as they said, 'Rob? Rob Eland?'

Ella nodded. 'I've come to live with my gran at the Point and he lives near.'

They were staring at her now.

'Is he your boyfriend? 'Cos you'll have Janice Souter after you if he is.'

Ella stared at the girl. 'Why?'

'She likes him, that's why.'

'It's scrawled all over the lavvy doors. "JS loves RE true." Haven't you seen it?'

Maybe she had, Ella thought, but trying to decipher all the scratchings on the insides of the doors in the girls' lavatories would take a week and a half.

She had been going to say, 'No. Our families know each other, that's all,' but then her impish sense of mischief came bubbling up and, returning the stares of the other girls, instead she said, 'Well, we'll have to see about that, won't we?'

'Ooh-er, you're in for it,' Alison said and cast a gleeful glance towards a girl in the far corner of the playground who, every so often, jumped up, craning her neck to look over the hedge. 'That's her. That's Janice. See what she's doing?'

Ella shook her head.

'The boys are playing football in the field.' Alison nodded in the direction of the playing field beyond the hedge surrounding the playground. 'Rob's ever so good at football an' she's watching him.'

One of the girls from the group had run over to Janice and was now pulling on her arm and talking urgently to her. Then she pointed back towards where Ella was standing. The girl called Janice stared across the playground at Ella and then, slowly, she began to walk towards her.

'So, you're the new girl, a' ya?' Janice was standing before her, and though Ella was tall for her ten years, the other girl topped her by two inches. Freckles peppered her nose and high cheekbones and her long ginger hair was pulled back into a pony tail. Grey eyes stared directly in Ella's.

Facing her squarely, Ella said boldly, 'And you're Janice

Souter.' She was a striking-looking girl, even at this rather gangly, awkward age; one day she would be really pretty.

Janice blinked and Ella guessed she was not used to being outfaced. This was only Ella's second day at the town's primary school and yet already she had gleaned that Janice Souter was a ring-leader in the class in which Ella had been placed.

'She walks to school with Rob, Janice,' Alison volunteered and then stood back to watch the effect her piece of information was having.

Her gaze never leaving Ella's face, Janice said, 'You reckon he's ya boyfriend then, do ya?'

Someone in the group laughed. 'Her? Get a boyfriend? With that mark on her face?'

Ella felt her face turn red, but Janice ignored the jibe. Defiantly, Ella lifted her chin and answered Janice's question. 'Not really. I don't like him much.'

Now a surprised gasp rippled amongst the listeners. 'Dun't like him much? She must be blind – or daft.'

'He's the best-looking boy in the school, ain't he, Janice?'

Janice Souter was still watching Ella, her grey eyes narrowing slightly, a calculating look crossing her young face. 'You live at Brumbys' Farm, with ya gran, dun't ya?' Ella nodded and Janice went on, 'Rob comes to Brumbys' Farm a lot, dun't he?'

Ella shrugged. 'My gran likes him.' Janice was not to know, but that very fact was no recommendation to Ella.

'Well, she would do. They're related, aren't they?'

This was news to Ella. 'How?'

The other girl shrugged. 'When me mam heard about yourn getting drowneded in the floods,' Ella bit her lip but remained silent as the girl went on, 'me mam said, "Oh, them Hiltons and Elands and Godfreys, all muddled up together, they are."'

Ella shook her head. 'I don't know anything about that.'

Janice leant closer. 'So you see, he can't be ya boyfriend even if you wanted him to be.'

Ella lifted her shoulders again. She couldn't quite understand all this talk of boyfriends and girlfriends, but said stoutly, 'Well, I don't.'

'That's all right then. See, he's our Jimmy's best mate. He's in the same class.' Janice moved to her side and, linking her arm through Ella's, said, 'You can be my friend, Ella Hilton, 'cos we live at the next farm to you – and Rob.' She turned back to face the rest of the girls hovering around them. 'You hear? Ella's *my* friend.'

The girls gave faint smiles but said nothing, the taunts, it seemed, silenced.

At the end of afternoon school, Ella once more found herself the centre of attention. Outside the school gate a group of girls from her class encircled her: Alison and several others, whose names Ella did not yet know. But there was no sign of Janice.

'She's walking home with Rob, I 'spect.' Alison Clark's knowledge about other people's affairs seemed endless. She came close to Ella. 'See, she's older than all of us. She's nearly eleven.'

'She was ever so ill when she was six and missed a lot of school, so she's 'ad to be put down a class,' another informant volunteered.

Someone else sniggered. 'Naw, she's just thick, is Janice Souter. Her brother Jimmy's the same. He shouldn't still be at this school.'

'You'd better not let her hear you say that, Gillian, else she'll wallop ya.'

'Janice Souter dun't frighten me,' the other girl said boldly, but, Ella noticed, she had turned an uncomfortable shade of pink.

The group came to the crossroads where they were to part company, dispersing to various parts of the town or to take the lane leading out towards the Point.

When her grandpa had brought her to school that morning he had shown her the way to go home. 'Don't come home by the coast road yet, Ella. Come from inland, down past Rookery Farm. Rob and the Souter children should come this way, so you'll have some company. All right?'

She had nodded, although the wind blustering across the vast expanse of open fields all around her had made her shudder, feeling vulnerable and afraid. It would be dusk when she left school. What if she got lost?

'I'll watch out for you,' Grandpa had promised as he left her at the school gate. But now she found herself walking down the lane completely alone, except for the seagulls wheeling and screeching above her. Black clouds, threatening rain, were building up to the north behind her and the wind blew her along.

'Oy!' She heard a shout behind her. Turning, she saw a boy on a bicycle pedalling towards her. She stood waiting, but as he came nearer she could see it was not Rob. The boy, with spiky, carroty hair and a face almost completely covered with freckles, swerved his bike around her and continued to encircle her like a dog rounding up sheep.

'You're the new girl, in't ya? Me sister ses ya're in her class.'

Suddenly, she knew who the boy must be; Jimmy Souter, Janice's brother and Rob's 'best mate'.

Ella started to walk again and Jimmy Souter kept pace with her. 'Our Janice is walking home with Rob,' he gestured behind them with his head and grinned confidently, 'but he'll get fed up of her in a bit and come after me.'

He circled her again. 'Cat got ya tongue?'

She glared at him, but continued walking in silence.

'We're getting a telly soon.'

'A what?'

'Oh, ya can talk, then? A telly. Y'know, a television.'

She'd seen them in the big stores in Lincoln, but had never watched a programme. She didn't know anyone who actually owned one.

'We're getting one in time for the Coronation in June. It's going to be on.'

Ella eyed him. Was this boyish boasting or the truth?

They had reached the point in the road where she turned to the left to go towards the coast, past Rookery Farm and home, whereas Jimmy's home lay straight on. He scuffed his feet on the ground and swung his leg over his bicycle, swivelling it around across the road to bar her way.

'Did ya mam get drowned in the floods?'

Unable to speak, her eyes downcast, Ella nodded.

'Why've you come to live with your *gran*, then? Ain't ya got a dad?'

'He was in the war.' Again, the trusted answer.

There was a smirk on Jimmy Souter's face. 'Me mam ses you ain't got a dad, that you've never 'ad a dad. Ya mam weren't married . . .'

Ella clenched her fists and her eyes narrowed.

'So ya know what that makes *you*, dun't ya?'

She stepped forward and thrust her face towards Jimmy. 'Shut your gob else I'll shut it for you.'

Jimmy grinned at her, 'You wouldn't dare.'

Before the words were out, Ella had swung her right fist and caught him on the mouth.

'Ow!' Jimmy yelped, and reeled backwards. The bicycle toppled over and he fell on top of it, amidst pedals, handlebars and spinning wheels. Putting his hand to his mouth, he stared at Ella in surprise. 'Ya little bugger!' he said, swearing like an adult, but strangely, a note of respect had crept into his tone. Blood was now seeping from the inside of his lip, cut by his own teeth. 'I'll tell me mam of you, Ella Hilton.'

At that moment they heard a shout and Ella turned to see Rob Eland racing towards them on his bicycle. Some distance behind him was Janice, running to try to keep up with him. There was a squeak of brakes as he slid to a halt and stood looking down at Jimmy.

'You fall off, Jimmy?'

'Naw, she hit me.'

'Wha . . .?' Rob glanced at Ella in amazement and then back to Jimmy.

At that moment, Janice came up, panting and red-faced. 'Ya might 'ave waited, Rob.' She too stood looking down at her brother. 'W'as up wi' you, then?'

''Er,' he pointed an accusing finger at Ella. 'That's what's up.'

Ella was silent, but inside, she was sighing. Bang goes Janice's friendliness, she thought.

Rob had laid his own bicycle down on the grass verge and was now attempting to disentangle Jimmy.

'She hit me,' he said petulantly, to his sister. 'On the mouth. Look.'

To Ella's astonishment, Janice grinned at the boy still dabbing gingerly at his mouth. 'Serves ya right. 'Spect you said summat 'orrible, as usual.'

Jimmy looked shamefaced for a moment. 'She needn't 'ave hit me,' he muttered.

'Did ya hit her back?'

'I dun't hit girls.'

'Ya hit me when it suits ya.'

'That's different. You're me sister. 'Sides, I'll tell our mam and she'll go an' see the Missus at Brumbys' Farm.'

Rob heaved Jimmy to his feet and handed him his bike and then went to pick up his own. 'Come on, Ella, I'll give you a cross-bar. Hang on to the middle part of the handlebars.'

She hoisted herself on to the narrow bar of his bicycle and, wobbling a little at first under their combined weight, they set off down the road towards Rookery Farm.

She glanced back to see Jimmy mounting his bicycle and pedalling towards his own home, whilst Janice was left standing at the crossroads staring after Rob and Ella.

As they bowled along, close by her left ear, Rob said, 'You ought to ask ya grandpa to get you a bike.'

'Can't ride one,' she muttered.

The bicycle wobbled. 'Eh?' His tone was shocked. 'Can't . . . ? Crikey! I dun't know, Ella Hilton – never seen the sea and can't ride a bike.'

She turned her head to grin at him and found his face close to hers. 'You'll have to teach me, then, won't you?'

The bike wobbled dangerously now so that Rob put his feet to the ground and slithered to a halt a short distance from the gate into the yard of Rookery Farm. He held the bicycle whilst she slid off the cross-bar.

'See ya,' he began, and made to turn away. Ella nodded but made no move. 'That girl . . .' she began.

He looked at her. 'Who? Janice?'

Ella nodded. 'Is she your girlfriend?'

'Girlfriend? I ain't got no girlfriend.'

'Well, she thinks you have.'

'Jimmy's me best mate, that's all. She reckons she can tag along with us any time she likes.' His expression was mournful. 'We have the devil's own job to give her the slip.'

'So she's not your girlfriend then?'

'Don't be daft. All girls are soppy.' He turned his bicycle round and pedalled away. Now he sat upright on his saddle, not holding the handlebars at all but pushing his hands into the pockets of his trousers and steering the bicycle with his knees. He called back once, 'See ya in the morning. Dun't be late . . .' and then rode down the lane to the farmyard gate, his shrill whistling piercing the deepening dusk of the winter's afternoon.

Ella crossed the lane and mounted the stile into the field to take the short cut towards Brumbys' Farm. The water-logged ground squelched underfoot as she skirted the field and came to the footbridge, only just visible above the overflowing dyke.

Gingerly, she stepped on to the slippery planking. Holding her breath she inched her way across feeling the plank bouncing a little when she reached the middle. The water lapped over the edge and soaked her shoes. She stood still, fear suddenly immobilizing her. Her legs seemed to be rigid and she swayed slightly as if she might lose her balance and topple into the black water in the dyke, clogged with grass and reeds and debris. Ella bit her lip and then took a deep breath, willing her stubborn limbs to move. Somehow, she reached the other side and clambered up the bank. Skirting the meadow, she squeezed through a hole in the hedge into the orchard at Brumbys' Farm.

*

'Where on earth have you been, Missy? Ya grandpa's been fussing like a mother hen, running out to the gate every few minutes to watch for ya.'

'I came across the fields from Rookery . . .'

'The fields?' Her grandmother's voice rose. 'A' ya daft, girl?'

'I – what do you mean?'

'Dun't ya know better than to come across them fields just after the flood? The dykes must be full and the ground sodden.' There was a pause as her eyes went to Ella's soaking shoes, the wet creeping up her socks. 'Ya could have slipped in and drowned, you silly girl. Go on, up to bed with you this instant. And dun't you go across that way again till the ground's dried out. You hear me, Missy?'

Remembering her sudden fear in the middle of the plank footbridge and knowing her grandmother was right, she said, meekly, 'I'm sorry, Gran.'

'So ya should be,' was the only reply. Esther Godfrey shook her head. 'I dun't know what I'm going to do with you. Ya'll be the death of me!'

Ella bent to stroke Tibby's back as the kitten lapped delicately at a saucer of milk on the hearth, then she looked up. 'Gran, are we related to the Eland family?'

The knife Esther was holding to chop vegetables clattered to the floor. The woman's green eyes stared at her. 'What? Who's been telling you that? Has *she* said summat?'

Wide-eyed, Ella stared back. 'Who? Janice?'

'No – no, I didn't mean her – I meant – oh, never mind. Who's been saying that?'

'Janice Souter.'

Esther gave a snort. 'Oh, I might a' known. That's come from 'er mother. Nosy old beezum, she is.'

Ella stifled a giggle as her grandmother wagged her finger and said, 'You tek no notice of anything that girl ses, you hear me? It's none of their business.'

'But are we, Gran?' the girl persisted.

'It's nowt for you to worry yasen about, Missy, and get that cat out of this house now.'

'Aw, Gran, let him have a drink of milk in the scullery. It's so cold out there and he's so tiny . . .'

'He's to sleep in the barn.' Her grandmother was firm, but her tone was softer now. The girl knew that Esther respected her concern for the animal's welfare. 'Here,' her grandmother was saying, 'here's an old piece of blanket. Mek him a warm bed in the straw. You can take the saucer of milk out with you.'

Feigning meekness, Ella said, 'Yes, Gran,' and avoided Esther's penetrating gaze. She picked up the kitten, who, cross at being disturbed from his lapping, mewed plaintively.

'I'm only taking you to bed, Tibby.' She buried her face in the kitten's soft fur and whispered, 'Just be good. I've got an idea for later.'

In the blackness of the barn she burrowed a nest for the kitten and wrapped the blanket around him. Tibby purred and played peekaboo from beneath the blanket, his bright green eyes glowing in the dusk.

'I'll be back for you later. Now, just stay there.'

Back in the house, her grandmother was standing at the kitchen table, her hands on her hips, her mouth pursed as she surveyed her sewing machine. 'Ruined!' she muttered angrily, as Ella came into the kitchen. 'What can I have been thinking of to leave it on the floor?'

Jonathan eased his aching limbs up from the Windsor chair at the side of the hearth and came to stand beside Esther, putting his arm about her shoulders. 'The flood came so fast, love. There was no time to think.'

'Yes, but I always keep it on the little table under the window in the living room. What on earth possessed me to leave it on the *floor*?'

'You often do, Esther, when you're in the middle of making something. You know you do. You pile all the material, all the pieces you've cut out, on to the table and you leave the machine on the floor.'

Ella saw her grandmother look at him and then nod. 'Yes, you're right. So I do. But I hadn't been making anything just before the flood came, now had I?'

'No,' then Jonathan reminded her gently, 'but you had the tea after your father's funeral in there, and the little table was used to put things on.'

'Oh, aye, of course.' She sighed, remembering. 'I just forgot to lift it back up.'

'Normally it wouldn't have mattered, now would it?' he said reasonably.

Esther pulled a wry face. 'No, no it wouldn't.' She turned back to look down at the sewing machine plastered with mud and sand, its moving parts rusted solid by the salt water. 'But why, oh, why, did I have to leave it on the floor that night of all nights?' she moaned.

Ella watched her grandmother run her fingers lovingly over the wooden lid of the machine. 'It was the only kindly gesture me aunt Hannah ever made to me,' she murmured more to herself than to the other two. 'I got the shock of me life when she left it to me when she died instead of her own daughters. All me young life I'd never known anything from her but cuffs and knocks and work, work and more work. Mind you,' her smile was a wry twist on her mouth, 'I suppose I ought to be grateful to her. At least she made me a survivor.'

'I think,' Jonathan said slowly, 'you would have survived, Aunt Hannah or no Aunt Hannah. It's a cruel world for a youngster on her own with no parents . . .'

Their eyes turned towards Ella and Jonathan's voice dropped so low that she could scarcely hear his next words. 'But you had the spirit of survival in you, Esther, and, thank the Good Lord, so has she.' He smiled down at Ella with tenderness in his blue eyes and, tightening his arm about his wife's shoulder, added, teasing gently, 'Only trouble is, trying to live with the pair of you.'

Esther laughed and, for a moment, some of the bitterness and sadness left her face, making her look young again.

Ella moved forward to stand on the opposite side of the table.

'Gran . . .' As Esther met her steady gaze, the young girl took a deep breath and, though her voice wobbled a little, she said, 'You – you can have Mum's machine if you like. It – it was amongst all the things they brought from ho— from Lincoln.'

Esther's eyes softened and as she and Jonathan stood looking down into her upturned face, Ella glanced from one to the other and back again.

'Your mum would want you to have her machine one day, love.'

Ella shrugged. 'I can't use it. I don't know how.'

Esther's eyes widened. 'Do you mean to tell me yar mam didn't teach you to sew?'

The girl shook her head. 'She never had the time, Gran. She was always too busy sewing for other people. It was her job.'

Her grandmother tut-tutted and said, 'Well, in that case, Missy, it's high time you learnt.'

Jonathan nodded. 'Use Kate's machine for a while, Esther. Machines should be used anyway. It doesn't do them any good to be stood idle.'

Esther gave a snort, 'Like people.'

'And in the meantime, love, I'll take your machine out to the shed and take it to bits. Maybe I can clean it all up and get it working again. But it'll take a while. It'll be a fiddly job. I should have looked at it sooner . . .' He swept his hand through his hair in a gesture of tiredness. 'But there's been so much to see to.'

'I saw it as soon as the water went and knew it'd be ruined.' Esther sighed, still annoyed with herself.

'I'm sure I'll be able to do something with it, love,' Jonathan tried to reassure her.

'Of course you will.' Esther smiled fondly at him, her confidence in his ability boundless. 'And you'll love doing it, won't you?' She tapped his cheek almost coquettishly. 'You and your machines.'

'Well, it's not quite my usual size. I'm more used to tractors and such.'

Kate's sewing machine was carried down the narrow stairs and set carefully on the living-room table. The three of them stood looking at it and Ella felt a lump in her throat. The machine had been such an important part of Kate's life – of their lives in Lincoln – that it was almost as if her mother were there in the room. Now, mirroring her grandmother's action of a few moments ago with her own old machine, Ella reached out and ran her hand over the polished curve of the wooden lid.

Tears blinded her and rather than let them see her cry, Ella turned and ran from the room and the house. She heard her grandmother speak her name but Jonathan said,

'Let her go, love, she needs to be on her own . . .' and then she was out of earshot.

In the darkness of the barn she hugged the little kitten to her, her tears wetting its silky fur. Waiting until she heard her grandparents come out of the house and go towards the cowshed for evening milking, Ella slipped back into the house and up the stairs to her bedroom, the kitten hidden beneath her cardigan.

With Tibby snuggled under the bedclothes beside her, that night was the first since her mother's death that Ella did not sob herself to sleep.

Twelve

Early the following morning, before it was properly light, Ella awoke to hear the sound of raised voices in the front garden just below her window.

'And who gave you leave to push ya way through me hedge at this time of the morning, Aggie Souter?'

'It's that girl of yourn. Ya daughter's bastard ya've teken in. She's hit our Jimmy and made 'is mouth bleed. All swollen up, it is, this morning. She needs a good hiding, Esther Hilton.'

'Me name's Esther Godfrey and has been for a long time, Aggie Souter, and I'll thank you to remember it.'

'Aye, an' I could tell 'em a thing about you, an' all, Esther Hilton,' the woman persisted. 'Couldn't I just! Ya no better than ya should be. Why, I remember—'

'Pot calling kettle black, is it, Aggie? If it's the past ya want to rake up then I'll start an' all. Only five months from your wedding day to the day young Jimmy was born, wasn't it?'

'Ya've a wicked tongue on you, Esther Hilton, an' no mistake. Seems the young 'un teks after you, an' all, from what our Jimmy ses. Telled 'im to shut 'is gob else she'd shut it for 'im. Very ladylike, I must say.'

Ella pressed her face closer to the window. Hilton? Why did the woman keep calling her grandmother Esther Hilton? That was Ella's own name, hers and her mother's and, presumably, her father's, but it wasn't her grandmother's. So why . . .?

Mrs Souter was going now, back the way she had come through the hole in the hedge and across the fields to the west, yet the two women were still shouting after each other.

'. . . little bugger wants a good hiding . . .'

'. . . you mind your business, an' I'll mind mine . . .'

As the sound of voices died away, Ella strained her ears to listen for her grandmother coming back into the house, for the door to bang and her footsteps mount the stairs . . . She dressed hurriedly in her school clothes and tiptoed downstairs. There was no one in the house and when she opened the back door it was to hear the angry clattering of pails and churns from the cowshed.

Ella tore back upstairs, fished the kitten out from the bottom of the bed and put him outside the back door. His fur fluffy from sleep, Tibby eyed her indignantly and tried to slip back into the house.

'No, no, you'll have to stay outside. You'll get me into more bother and it sounds as if I'm going to be in enough already this morning.'

'You've had that cat in your bed, Ella Hilton. When I changed the sheets I found cat hairs all over them, so don't try to deny it.'

Ella faced her grandmother and nodded. There was no use denying it; besides, to do so would not even cross her mind. She was often disobedient and wilful, but she was never untruthful. Faced with one of her sins being found out, Ella would face up openly, admit it and take her punishment. She was surprised, however, that this was the only wrong-doing with which she was being accused. So far nothing had been said about Jimmy Souter and it had been two days since the boy's mother had stormed into Brumbys' Farm.

'He – he keeps me company, Gran.'

'A cat's place is in the barn, not in your bed.'

'Aw, Esther, don't be too hard on the child.' Jonathan, from the chair by the range, lowered his paper. 'The little kitten's doing no harm.'

'Tain't healthy,' Esther retorted. 'Besides, Ella disobeyed me deliberately.'

Ella could see her grandfather struggling to make his expression disapproving. 'Well, now, Ella, you shouldn't have done that. You must always do what your grannie tells you.'

'Yes, Grandpa,' she said meekly, but her eyes were full of mischief as she met his gaze.

'Off to bed with you now,' her grandmother said. 'And no more sneaking that cat upstairs.'

As she bade them goodnight in turn, and left the kitchen, Ella lingered in the living room through which she had to pass to reach the stairs, to listen.

'You're too hard on the child, Esther love.'

'She's got to be made to behave herself. She's a wilful little tyke. Not a bit like her mam . . .' For a moment, Esther's voice was low and full of sadness as she recalled fond memories. 'Kate was always biddable, but this one . . .!' There followed a click of exasperation and a sigh.

'I wonder, then,' Jonathan said pointedly, 'who she takes after.'

She heard her grandmother give a snort of laughter. 'You rogue!' she heard Esther say affectionately and then she added, 'Aye, you're right though. Aggie Souter said as much, an' all. And I have to admit, I can see a lot of mesen in the little lass.'

'Then you should be able to understand her, Esther, especially as she, too, has been left without parents,' he said gently.

At that moment, Ella heard one of them make a movement towards the door into the room where she was standing eavesdropping and the girl scuttled across the room into the hall and up the stairs.

Alone in her bedroom, Ella sat up in the bed, hugging her knees and staring into the darkness, thinking about her grandmother. She was a funny woman, the girl thought. One minute she was in a temper, her green eyes flashing, her voice harsh, the next she was laughing and teasing, but mainly, the girl acknowledged, the latter mood was with Jonathan or Rob; never with her. And why was she taking on so about the kitten and yet had said not a word about her thumping Jimmy Souter?

Ella sighed, trying to understand her grandmother and to sort out her own feelings about the woman. She had vowed to dislike her – no, stronger than that, to hate her! But with each passing day, she found it more difficult and often found herself wishing that she could be on the receiving end of one of Esther's magnificent smiles, when her whole face lit up and her eyes twinkled with merriment and love. Oh, how Ella wished her grandmother would smile at her like that.

She buried herself beneath the covers and, missing the warmth of Tibby's furry little body, fell asleep scheming as to how she might get the kitten back into her room without her grandmother finding out.

The day the head teacher called Ella out of class, the girl's heart thumped: she must be in trouble. Maybe Jimmy Souter had told the teacher about her hitting him.

'Now, dear,' the headmistress began as she opened the door of her office and ushered the girl in. Ella stepped into the room dominated by a huge desk standing in the centre on a square of carpet. Along the walls were bookshelves, a long table and a green metal filing cabinet. The headmistress drew Ella towards the table where there was a pile of toys and books. 'These have been sent by kind people all over the country to the schools in this area for children who were in the floods.' Her voice, which Ella knew could be sharply authoritative, was now softly sympathetic. 'In this school, there are only a few pupils whose homes were affected, so your teacher and I thought you should have first choice.' Gently, she urged Ella forward. 'Have a look, dear, and if there's anything you'd like . . .'

Ella's gaze wandered over the items; dolls and teddy bears, books and jigsaw puzzles, a puppet, toy cars and boats . . . And then she saw it: a board and a small wooden box. She reached out with fingers that trembled suddenly.

'What is it, dear?'

'We . . .' Her voice shook, 'Grandpa and me – we were playing draughts when – when the sea came. The board – it was on the floor and – and the water spoilt it.'

The headmistress pulled out the folded board and opened it up. The black and yellow squares danced before Ella's eyes as she relived the moment again just before the sea had come gushing into their home.

'Do you want it, dear?' the woman was asking and Ella, unable to speak, nodded.

She carried it carefully all the way home, and no one, not even Jimmy Souter, asked where she had got it. Maybe, Ella thought shrewdly, the other children had been told while I was out of the classroom. She could imagine her class teacher saying, 'Now, Ella Hilton has gone to choose a toy sent for the flood victims. As you all know, Ella's mother was drowned in the flood . . .' And now no one would dare to question her.

'Look, Grandpa, look what they gave me at school.'

She laid the box and the board on the kitchen table and opened it up. 'I was allowed to choose a toy, Grandpa, and I picked this because you lost yours.'

Her grandparents exchanged a look and her grandpa laid his hand on her curls. 'Now, wasn't that kind of people to send things.'

Esther murmured, 'They say all sorts of things have been sent to folks further up the coast who've lost everything. Food, clothes, toys – even furniture.'

Jonathan's deep voice said, 'There are some good people in the world trying to do what they can to help out in a tragedy.'

The symbol of a stranger's kindness lay on the table, a thoughtful gesture to ease the pain of the child's loss.

But nothing and no one could bring back her beloved mother.

Thirteen

'Kill a pig? Why? We've only got one now . . .' Ella's eyes widened in horror, a suspicion growing suddenly. 'You don't mean – oh, you can't mean – *Lady*?'

'We have to eat, Missy,' Esther said with exasperation.

'But you can't, I mean, not Lady. You saved her – took her into the house. You can't mean it!'

Since giving over her bedroom to Lady at the time of the flood, Ella had become quite fond of the huge bristly pink sow and she could not understand how her grandmother could treat an animal with such concern one moment and be planning to kill it the next. Why, Ella had seen her tickling the sow behind her ears and scratching her back, the animal snuffling pleasurably.

'How can you—?'

'Don't be so silly,' Esther cut in impatiently. 'That's what farming's all about.'

'Come with me, Ella.' Her grandpa took hold of her hand and was leading her towards the line of buildings to one side of the farmyard.

'Where are we going?'

'To see Lady.'

'No!' she said vehemently, but he held her hand firmly, though gently, not allowing her to pull free.

'I want to talk to you.'

'Well, I don't want to listen. I won't listen.'

'Now, now, that's not like my little girl.'

Ella pouted but said no more.

They came to the sty and Ella, standing on tiptoe, could just see into the dim interior. Jonathan leant his arms on the half-open door. 'Now then, old girl,' he said softly to the sow, who came waddling to the door, snuffling and grunting, and stood looking up at them with bright, beady eyes.

'It's time you understood farming ways, Ella. I know you've been brought up in a town . . .' As Ella opened her mouth to protest, her grandpa raised his hand to silence her. 'It's not your fault. I'm not criticizing you. After all, I was born and brought up in Lincoln too.'

She looked up at him. 'Were you? I didn't know.'

He nodded. 'I worked in an engineering works building traction engines. Farming's been your grannie's whole life, and mine, since I married her. But it took me a long time to learn country ways. We care for our livestock. We'd never willingly cause them suffering, but they're raised for a purpose. To provide food for us and for others. We grow crops, we keep cattle for milk or for their meat and we raise pigs either to sell on or to kill for ourselves.'

Ella could not prevent her lower lip from trembling, 'But, Grandpa – Lady!'

'I know, and don't think we don't care. We both do. She's a lovely old sow and we've had her a long time. She's given us lots of fine, healthy young piglets, over the years, but she's past her best for breeding now, so . . .' Jonathan sighed. 'I'm sorry, love. But you're old enough now to start to understand. The flood's hit us hard. The land that was under water, the authorities have advised us not to touch it for at least a year else they say we're in danger of ruining it for ten years or maybe even longer. So, all that land has just got to be left doing nothing until the salt's gone. The trees in the orchard, we'll lose most of them, I reckon, when the salt gets down to the deep roots and you know we lost the other two pigs we had?'

Ella nodded. They had been found floating in the sty, too small to keep their heads above the water like Lady.

'Well, two of the cows have got mastitis, that's a disease of the udders, through standing in that perishing water. And the other four, well, their milk yield's dropped.'

Ella stared at her grandfather, struggling with an inner conflict. He was treating her like a grown-up, trying patiently to explain the situation to her. The girl grappled with her tender instincts, trying to force her reasoning – her grandfather's sound reasoning – to triumph.

The following morning at breakfast, Esther said, 'We really must get this pig killed and put away, Jonathan. There's not many months left with an R in.'

Ella swallowed the sick, nervous feeling rising in her throat and tried to stop the spoonful of porridge, suspended in mid-air, trembling. She stared from one to the other, puzzlement on her face. A small smile was twitching at the corner of her grandpa's mouth.

'And dun't you laugh at me.' Esther was wagging her forefinger at him, but there was a twinkle in her green eyes. 'We should have got it done afore Christmas, but – well we didn't, what with me dad and then . . .' The sparkle was gone as she remembered. Esther cleared her throat and added firmly, 'Well, we didn't and that's that.' She turned and bustled into the pantry to fetch more fresh milk. Ella leaned forward and whispered, 'Grandpa, what's she mean about an R in the month?'

Jonathan glanced at the pantry door and leaned towards

her, his voice scarcely above a whisper. 'It's an old superstition that if you kill a pig in a month when there's no R in the spelling, the meat won't keep.'

'And doesn't it?' she asked reasonably.

'Oho, I wouldn't dare risk it to find out, love.' He was still chuckling as he levered himself up and moved towards the door from the kitchen into the scullery. Reaching up to the peg behind the door he pulled on his scarf and cap. Then he winked at Ella. 'But seeing as how we're into March already, we'd better get a move on.' He raised his voice and called to Esther, 'I'll go and ask Danny if he can come and help us, shall I?'

Esther appeared in the pantry doorway, carrying a large jug of milk. 'Please. He's the best man I know hereabouts for the killing. Quick and clean . . .' Her gaze came to rest upon Ella and she added, quietly, 'We try to be as humane as we can. I would never let any animal suffer unnecessarily, if I could help it.'

The girl returned her grandmother's steady gaze and knew she was speaking the truth. Although she sighed inwardly, slowly the girl nodded, accepting the inevitable. She nodded and mumbled, 'Grandpa explained it all to me.'

Esther's eyes widened and her gaze went from one to the other. 'Oh.'

Jonathan smiled and nodded. 'We went to have a look at Lady and had a little chat, didn't we, love?'

Ella nodded.

'And do you understand now?'

The girl gave the question serious, almost adult, consideration. 'I understand why, Gran, but I still don't like it.'

Her grandmother nodded. 'Well, that's a fair and sensible answer. Don't run away with the idea I enjoy it, 'cos

I don't, but, well, it's the way it has to be.' More briskly she added, 'And I'll be needing your help, Missy,' Esther said, placing the jug on the table and sitting down to her own breakfast.

Ella's eyes widened and her grandmother laughed. 'Oh, it's all right, you needn't watch the killing if you're squeamish.'

Needled, the girl stuck out her chin and said defiantly, 'I'm not. I'll be there.' As she dropped her glance to her bowl and resumed her meal, Ella was conscious of her grandmother's amused smile.

I'll show her, the girl thought.

But Lady's squealing almost broke Ella's resolve and it was only the thought of how foolish she would look in front of them all, her grandparents, Uncle Danny and Rob too, if she turned and ran away. So she stood, holding her breath, as Danny went into the sty. Through the open door she saw him stand behind the sow and place a rope in its mouth, twitching it up tightly round the pig's nose. Then he drove the animal out of the sty and towards a hook in the wall near the wash-house. Looping the end of the rope round the hook, he pulled it tight. It was then that Lady let out such a high-pitched squeal that Ella jumped and bit her lip to stop herself crying out too. Her grandmother, standing just behind her, rested her hands on the girl's shoulders.

Ella saw Danny, holding a tool like a gun in his hand, glance at her and then look up at her grandmother. Above the squealing he shouted, 'Hadn't Ella better go?' but from behind her, Esther shouted back, 'No, she'll have to learn.'

He gave a slight shrug and turned his attention back to the job in hand.

'Right, hold her . . .' Danny said and he held the humane killer close to the sow's forehead. There was a noise and the pig slumped sideways to the ground and was silent. Grandpa Godfrey and Rob held the limbs still and the long, sharp knife flashed in Danny's hand. Ella held her breath, her body rigid. The knife slid deeply into the soft folds of flesh between the sow's front legs and was drawn quickly upwards to her chin. Ella shut her eyes, screwing up her face.

Now all she could hear was scuffling as the men and the boy struggled with the awkward thirty-stone lump. Ella risked opening one eye, squinting fearfully. 'Is – is she dead, Gran?' she whispered.

'Yes. I told you Danny was quick, didn't I now?'

Ella nodded, her gaze held by the sight of the blood pouring from the slit in the animal's throat. Her grandfather was working the front leg to pump the blood out. Then they heaved the pig into a large rectangular wooden tub.

Ella pointed. 'Why've they left that long chain in the bottom of the tub under the pig?'

'They use that to slough all the bristles off. You'll see in a minute,' Esther said.

Now Danny was lifting buckets full of near-boiling water from the copper in the wash-house and pouring it over the carcass. Standing one on either side of the tub, Danny and Jonathan each picked up one end of the chain and worked it backwards and forwards under the pig, gradually moving it along. Ella watched as they turned the carcass over and repeated the action. Jonathan bent down and, with a metal scraper, began to clean all the bristles from the pig's skin. Then together, he and Danny lifted it on to the cratch, a low wooden bench with barrow-like handles at each end, and swilled water over the carcass.

With sharp knives they shaved off all the remaining whiskers even on her tail and inside her ears.

Ella winced as she watched Danny cut off the head, but to her surprise, once that was done, she found she ceased to think of the pig as Lady and was now fascinated by all that was happening.

Danny put a stretcher between the back legs to hold them wide open and hoisted the whole carcass up by its back legs onto a tripod of poles, just clear of the cratch beneath. He slit open the pig's belly and all the insides, red and slimy, came tumbling out, but instead of throwing them away, he placed them carefully into huge brown pancheons which her grandmother had carried out from the pantry.

'You can help me with all that later,' Esther said, close by her ear. 'I'll show you how to clean and turn some of the intestines to make sausage skins.'

The two men and Rob were hoisting the pig even higher and stretching the gaping slit wider open.

'Right, Missus. We'll leave her like that for now but I'll be back tonight. Can I give you a hand to carry this lot into the pantry?'

'No, Danny, we'll manage for a while now, thanks. I'll get you a beer afore you go.'

Danny's mouth widened in a smile. 'Home-made, Missus?'

'Of course.' Esther smiled back, pretending to bristle with indignation that he should suggest that she would offer him anything else but her own home-brew. Ella saw her grandmother wink at Rob. 'And a little drop for you, eh, Boy? If ya do a man's work, ya deserve a man's reward.'

And Rob's grin seemed to stretch right across his thin face.

'Do you use all that?' Ella watched as the pancheons were carried carefully into the pantry and set on the red tiled gantry.

'Every bit.' Her grandmother laughed. 'We always say we use everything but the squeal.'

'What's Uncle Danny coming back tonight for?'

'To cut the carcass up, once it's cooled, into hams and flitches. Then he'll put it all in that big tub again with salt and we leave it in the little barn for about a month to cure.'

'Won't the rats and mice eat it?'

'Not if your little cat does his job.'

Ella's eyes widened and she stared at Esther, who laughed and said, 'I'm only teasing. He's not really big enough yet. No, we'll cover it over with a wire-meshed frame.'

Ella nodded, relieved that poor little Tibby would not be expected to stand guard.

'Can I watch Uncle Danny tonight?'

'My, my, we are changing our tune.'

The girl shrugged. 'It wasn't as bad as I thought except just the bit where Uncle Danny – did it.'

'Maybe you've more farming in your blood than you know, Missy.'

Ella looked up at her grandmother, half expecting, half hoping to see, for once, her grandmother smiling down at her. But Esther was turning away. 'Well, I can't stand here idling all day, there's work to be done and a lot of it over the next couple of days. I'd best be gettin' a move on. Rosie'll come over tomorrow to give us a hand. Come on, Missy, there's plenty for you to do an' all. Get yarsen an apron out of that drawer and—'

Rob appeared at the back door. 'Missus, me dad ses I've to ask ya. Can I have the bladder to blow up for a football?'

'Aye, course ya can, Boy.'

His face beamed. 'Aw thanks, Missus.' And he was off and running across the yard, his work, for the moment, done.

'Now then, Missy,' came her grandmother's voice again. 'Don't stand there day-dreaming, let's set you to work . . .'

The following morning, Rosie arrived. 'Hello, love,' she said to Ella. 'You going to help us, then?'

Wrapped in a copious white apron, her hands scrubbed to pink cleanliness, Ella was standing at the kitchen table. 'What are we going to do today?' she asked, and Rosie smiled.

'We'll be making sausages.'

Ella nodded. 'I cleaned the skins last night. Gran showed me how to turn them inside out and scrape them with a spoon. They're in a bucket of salt water in the pantry now.' This morning, laid out in the pantry were bowls and dishes with all the different meat sorted and graded ready for use. They had all worked late into the night the previous evening, even Ella had not been told, 'Off to bed with ya.'

Outside in the small barn the previous evening, she had watched Danny cut up the carcass and rub salt into all the huge joints of meat. When at last he stood up and eased his aching back, she had skipped around him as he crossed the yard towards the house. 'Is that it? Have you finished?'

'Yes, all done, for now at any rate. D'ya reckon ya know how to kill a pig then, young Ella?' and she had giggled at his teasing as he opened the back door and they went into the house.

'Well,' he said to Esther, still busy at her kitchen table,

'ya'll soon have some pretty pictures up there now, Missus,' and he had nodded towards the hooks in the ceiling awaiting the hams and flitches which would be hung there once the joints had been cured.

'Aye, thanks to you, Danny,' Esther had said. 'Ya've done a grand job as usual. There'll be a chine for ya.'

'Thanks, Missus. That's good of you. But only if ya can spare it. We know ya've lost ya other two pigs.'

Esther had smiled and flapped her hand saying, 'Go on with you, it's nothing.'

'What else are we making?' Ella asked Rosie now.

Rosie wrinkled her smooth forehead and ticked off the items on her fingers, 'Haslet, brawn and pork-pies, though I'll leave them to ya gran. I can't make hot water pastry like ya gran does.

'What's that, Rosie?' Esther said, coming out of the pantry at that moment.

'I'm just telling Ella, no one makes pastry for the pies like you.'

'Oh, I don't know,' Esther said, modestly, and then glanced at Rosie, a strange look in her eyes. 'Danny's mam, she's always been a good hand wi' pastry.'

Rosie smiled and said softly, 'She'd be glad to hear you say that, Missus.'

'Aye well . . .' Esther sniffed and turned away back into the pantry.

For the rest of the morning, as they worked, Rosie's bright chatter filled the kitchen. Ella rinsed the sausage skins whilst Rosie prepared the meat to fill them. 'I always used to love coming here at pig-killing even as a youngster. You used to let us turn the mincer handle.'

'I'll set young Rob on that if he comes this afternoon,' Esther promised.

'Oh, he'll be here.' Rosie laughed.

'And then the two of them can take pig's cheer round the neighbours.'

Rosie's eyes clouded. 'Aye,' she said softly. 'Me an' Kate used to do that.' Her busy hands were idle for a moment, but then she seemed to shake herself and her nimble fingers were once more chopping up the pig's trotters.

Rob arrived just in time for a mid-day snack of scraps – bits of meat and fat baked crisp and piled on rounds of toast.

'By heck! You know how to time it, Boy,' Esther teased him and ruffled his black, curly hair.

'I came to show Ella what to do.'

Ella saw her grandmother glance at her. 'Oh, she's doing quite nicely for a townie!' and the older woman and the boy exchanged a grin at Ella's expense, but far from being offended, the girl felt a warm glow spread through her. Though it was said in an off-hand way, it was the closest she had come, yet, to a compliment from her grandmother. Then the older woman spoilt it by adding, 'At least it's keeping her out of mischief.'

After dinner, the two youngsters were dispatched with plates of pig's fry to the neighbours.

'That one's for Rosie's mam and dad in the cottages at the Point,' Esther pointed in turn to each plate containing pieces of liver, kidney, heart, sweetbread and bits of pork all covered with a piece of something that looked, to Ella, like a lacy white doily.

'What is it?'

'It's a sort of fatty skin, the skirt, we call it,' Esther said.

'Skin? It doesn't look like skin. It's too pretty.' The girl leaned closer touching it with curious fingers; it felt smooth and slightly greasy.

'Get ya fingers off, Missy,' her grandmother said, tapped the back of Ella's hand sharply and then continued telling her which plate was to be taken where. 'That one's for the Harris boys.'

'And that one,' her gran was pointing to the third plate, 'is for the Souters.'

Ella met her gaze. 'I'm not taking that one.'

'Oh, yes, you are, Missy.' The green eyes met the challenge steadily. 'And while you're about it, ya can say ya sorry to Missis for hitting young Jimmy.'

'I—' Ella began but, feeling a sharp nudge in the back from Rob, she thought better of it and clamped her jaw shut.

As they left the house, carrying the three plates, Esther shouted after them, 'And don't forget to tell 'em not to wash the plates.'

Ella glanced at Rob in surprise. '*Not* to wash the plates?'

Rob nodded. 'S'posed to be bad luck.'

Having delivered the two plates to the cottages at the Point, they were half-way along the lane leading inland from the coast road, past Rookery Farm and coming nearer to Souters' Farm, when Ella said, 'I don't want to go there.'

He sighed. 'You'd do better to get it over with. Ya gran'll find out if you *don't* go.'

Ella was silent, knowing what he said was more than likely true: her gran had a way of finding out things. She sighed. 'All right, then.'

Her knees were trembling as Rob banged on the back door of the Souters' farmhouse and stood back, leaving Ella standing waiting for the door to open, the plate of pig's cheer held out in front of her.

The door flew open and a woman stood there: a fat, blowsy-looking woman, with straight grey hair that looked as if it needed washing. A dirty pinny covered a dress with a frayed hem. 'Who on earth's banging like that? Has another war started?'

But Ella recognized the shrill voice as the one she had overheard in the front garden at Brumbys' Farm; this was Mrs Souter.

'Er, Gran sent this for you, Mrs Souter, and—'

'Yar gran? Who . . . ?' The puzzled expression cleared. 'Oh-ah, I know who *you* are.' The woman's mouth was open as if she were about to say more, but forestalling her, Ella said quickly, 'I'm sorry for hitting Jimmy, Missis, but he called me a rude name and he shouldn't have.'

The woman's mouth dropped open to reveal yellow, uneven teeth and, fleetingly, Ella wondered where on earth Janice got her good looks from; it was difficult to believe she had inherited her prettiness from this woman.

'Well! Well, I don't know.' Mrs Souter took the proffered plate and said again, 'Well, I don't know. I'll say this for you, young 'un, ya're honest,' and added, muttering, though Ella's sharp ears caught her words, 'It's more'n I can say for me own.' Louder, she said, 'Do you want to come in for a bite?' She pulled the door wider open, inviting them to step inside.

Ella shook her head and said politely, 'Thank you, but we'd better be getting back.'

The woman nodded and said, 'Well then, thank yar gran, won't ya?'

'Gran said, don't wash the plate.'

The woman gave a cackle of laughter. 'Oh, I knows not to do that, young 'un.'

Walking back through the Souters' farmyard, Ella looked about her and wrinkled her nose. Cow dung littered the cobbles of the yard and wisps of straw blew across the surface. An old tractor, rusty with neglect, stood near the barn wall, grass and nettles grown up around it.

Ella nodded towards it. 'Grandpa would like to get his hands into that.'

Rob laughed. 'He'd have a double-duck fit if he saw it in that state.' He leant towards her and whispered, 'They're a right scruffy lot, the Souters. It's a wonder they haven't been turned out ages ago. But the landlord lives up in London and doesn't care much about what's going on down here just so long as he keeps getting the rents paid on time.'

They walked back down the lane and as they passed a large square building, Ella said, 'Is that the place that's empty?'

'Yeah, the Grange. It's where the old landlord, Squire Marshall, used to live. He's dead now. It's his son who's the present landlord.'

'Why doesn't anyone live there now?'

'I told you, he lives in London. He's not bothered.'

'It looks – lonely.'

'Well, it won't always be, 'cos one day I'll live there. Come on,' he said, tiring of her questions. 'I'll race you back.'

Ella took a last glance at the house standing forlorn and lost amongst overgrown gardens. She shuddered. She couldn't understand anyone wanting to live in a big, deserted house like that, miles from anywhere. And once again she was filled with longing for the cosy, noisy terraced house in Lincoln; the house she still thought of as home.

Fourteen

'What are you looking for, love?'

Ella emerged from the disused stable into the sunshine of the July day and sneezed three times in quick succession.

'This.' She held out a shrimping net. 'Me and Janice are going shrimping. Rob says cats love cooked shrimps. We're going to catch some and cook them for Tibby.'

Jonathan touched the dusty, torn net. 'Why, fancy you finding that,' he murmured and his eyes misted over. 'I made that for your mam when she was little. It's years old. I'm surprised it hasn't fallen to pieces.'

'The net's all torn, but Rob says his dad's got some old fishing net he won't mind cutting up.'

Jonathan nodded, his gaze still on the old shrimping net. 'From the days when his dad was a fisherman off the Point.'

'I can have it, can't I, Grandpa?'

'Eh? Oh, yes, of course you can, love.'

Carrying the shrimping net, she squeezed through the hole in the hedge and made her way across the meadow; if it could be called that now, as her grandmother remarked resentfully, after the ravages of the flood this meadow's crop of hay was going to be of little use. But once across the plank footbridge over the dyke, in the next field where the salt sea-water had not reached, the grass was high, lush and green and almost ready for harvesting. As she ran, Ella left a flattened pathway through the crop until she climbed over the stile and jumped down into the lane leading to Rookery Farm.

'Uncle Danny, Uncle Danny,' Ella called, skipping across the yard, her skimpy cotton print dress above her knees. 'Please will you mend this for me?'

Ella had found her niche at school, had won a small circle of friends, though mainly because she was under the protection of Janice Souter. They played together after school and at weekends, often, at Janice's suggestion, tagging along after Rob and Jimmy; at least, they did when Ella could escape from the never-ending chores her grandmother set her.

'Ya can wash the walls down in the kitchen again, Missy. The salt's still drying out. I don't know when we'll ever get this place right,' she muttered crossly.

'We could have the walls rendered with some special stuff to seal it, Esther, if you like,' Jonathan said.

'I've tried repapering in the front rooms, but the salt just comes through again as fast as I do it. The paper won't seem to stick. It's all hanging off again near the floor already.'

'It'll be a long time before we get things back to normal,' Jonathan said, and Ella heard his voice drop as he added, 'if ever.' She knew he was thinking about her mother and bent her head to hide the sudden tears that threatened, pretending to concentrate on her scrubbing.

'What have you got there, Ella?' Danny was asking her now.

'It's a shrimping net Grandpa made for Mum years ago, he said.'

Danny reached out to take the net from her. The girl was surprised and a little embarrassed to see that his hands were trembling. He held it for several moments until Ella asked, tentatively, 'Could you mend it for me, Uncle Danny, please?'

She saw him jump physically, as if she had dragged him down the years from his memories back to the present.

'Of course.' His voice was a little husky, but he was smiling now. 'Leave it with me. You run and play.'

'Where's Rob?'

'Gone to the Souters, I reckon.'

In the lane once more, she skipped towards the Grange, its tall chimneys peeping out from a clump of trees, and the road leading to the Souters' farm. The day was hot and humid, the heat bouncing off the lane under her feet, the sun brilliant in an almost cloudless sky. Even the breeze which normally blew off the sea seemed to be taking a rest today.

As she reached the wrought-iron gate, Ella paused, thinking she heard the sound of laughter from the undergrowth. She pushed at the heavy gate. It opened reluctantly, squeaking protestingly. She heard a rustle in the bushes that lined the driveway. She stopped, holding her breath. But now there was stillness, the only sound the fluttering of a bird high in the treetops.

She walked slowly up the curving driveway, stopping every so often to listen, fancying she heard another sound like the crack of a twig. She glanced from side to side but there was nothing and no one.

Just as she reached the curve in the driveway which brought the big house into view, a stick hurtled across the path in front of her and at the same time a blood-curdling yell sounded as Jimmy Souter came crashing out of the bushes, waving a home-made bow and arrow.

'I've caught the Sheriff of Nottingham. I've got you now, Sheriff. You'll not escape back to your castle . . .'

Jimmy cupped his hands around his mouth and, as he made a sound like an owl, Ella heard someone trampling through the undergrowth and Rob leapt on to the driveway, with Janice, panting, a few yards behind him. He stopped when he saw Ella and stared. Then he grinned. 'Hello. Come to play Robin Hood with us?'

'Ya can play with us if ya like,' Jimmy Souter volunteered generously.

'She can't be Maid Marian. I'm Maid Marian,' Janice put in swiftly, smoothing back her hair with a preening action. 'You can be Will Scarlet, Ella, or Friar Tuck.'

'No, no, she's got to be the Sheriff of Nottingham, else she can't play,' Jimmy said, 'and I've just captured her – him. He's Robin Hood,' he pointed at Rob, 'and I'm Little John.'

'Oh, I don't mind,' Ella said airily. She glanced to her left and saw that her way was clear along a path leading in amongst the trees. 'I'll be the Sheriff, if you like. But first – you'll have to catch me . . .'

And she was away, running amongst the bushes, weaving her way through the trees before any of the other three had realized what she was doing. She laughed to herself as their shouts followed her and she heard them come crashing after her.

She ran on and suddenly coming out of the trees, she found herself on the edge of what had once been a huge lawn, smooth and well kept. But now it was overgrown, the grass long and unkempt. In front of her, across the open expanse of grass, was the house.

She stopped and gazed up at the building. There was no sound of the others following her; they must have lost her trail. She waded through the long grass, so thick it was almost like pushing her legs through water. The old house rose above her, majestic yet so lonely and forgotten. Birds fluttered in and out of a broken first-floor window and ivy crawled, unrestrained, over the walls, suffocating the windows. A sudden sadness gripped Ella's throat. What a beautiful house this must have been once and what a waste to see it falling into decay. For a fleeting moment she understood Rob's vow to live here one day.

Her child's mind could not visualize the adult Rob; could not even imagine herself grown. But she could see the house loved and cared for, the lawns smooth and the borders luxuriant with flowers. She could even picture Rob and herself running across the lawn . . .

A sudden sound from amongst the trees made her glance about for a hiding place. Set at the edge of the lawn and where the wooded area began, was a summer house, the wooden boards rotting and broken, the door standing open, drunkenly half-on, half-off its hinges.

Ella bounded back through the grass towards it and pushed at the door. It scraped on the floor but yielded when she put her shoulder against it. The inside was dim and musty, littered with old tennis rackets with broken strings, a tennis net rolled up loosely and a collection of long-handled mallets. Everywhere was covered with a thick dust and Ella pinched her nose to try to stop herself sneezing.

She hid behind the door as she heard the voices of the other three youngsters coming closer.

'Where's she gone?'

'There she is, in the grass. Look, it's moving. Let's get her!' This from Janice.

'Dun't be daft. There's no track. She'd have made a track through grass that high.'

'What about the summer house?'

Ella shrank back against the wall, but the rustling of their feet through the grass came closer and she heard the rasp of the door as it was pushed open and a shaft of sunlight crept across the floor.

The dust tickled her nose and Ella could no longer hold back the sneeze. The two boys were upon her dragging her out and Ella screwed up her eyes against the bright light.

'Back to the forest, Robin. We've caught the Sheriff of Nottingham.'

Hustled along by the two boys, their strong young fingers digging into her thin arms, Ella gritted her teeth and set her jaw against making any sound of complaint.

Janice skipped along beside them. 'Let me hold her – him – too. I want to capture the Sheriff too.'

'If *you're* Maid Marian, you wouldn't be chasing the Sheriff, now would you? You'd be back at the glade, cooking or summat,' her brother said scathingly.

Janice sniffed. 'Tuck'd be doing that.'

'Yeah, but we ain't got no one to be Friar Tuck, a' we?'

'Well, we just pretend we have,' Janice spread her hands. 'I ain't sitting in the middle of the wood waiting whilst you lot play.'

Ella said nothing whilst they argued. She wasn't bothered one way or the other whether she joined in their game or not, but anything was preferable to going home; cleaning out the chicken hut was next on her list of tasks.

The 'glade' was an area in the middle of the copse on the outskirts of the grounds where the boys had trodden all the undergrowth flat to make it their meeting place for Robin Hood and his Merry Men. To one side, amongst some thick bushes, they had constructed a den, entered by crawling under the bushes and then standing up in the centre.

'Tie him up,' Janice said. 'Ya can use the belt off me dress.'

'Robin wouldn't have had something like that—' Rob began.

'Yes, he would. Maid Marian would have had a sort of braid belt on. I've seen pictures.'

'I'll do it,' Rob said. 'You go and keep watch if any of his men come after him, looking for him.'

Joining in the spirit of the game, making it up as they went along, Janice obeyed and went to the edge of the clearing, climbing on to the lowest branch of a tree as a look-out. Jimmy, too, staff at the ready, patrolled the perimeter of the area.

Ella giggled and whispered softly to Rob, who was busily tying her hands together. 'I don't think Maid Marian would climb trees, but don't tell her I said so.'

Rob grinned at her, his dark eyes twinkling. 'She's not my idea of Maid Marian. But she will insist that's who she wants to be. Can't think why. She'd have much more fun pretending to be one of the Men.'

'Maid Marian was Robin's girlfriend,' Ella said slyly.

Rob pulled a face. 'She'll be lucky! What you doing here anyway?'

'I found a shrimping net in the old stable. Your dad's going to mend it for me. Then I can come shrimping too.'

'We can't get rid of you pair, can we?' Rob said, but he was laughing and Ella giggled too.

'What you two laughing about?' Jimmy demanded, moving closer. 'You ain't supposed to be laughing with the prisoner, Robin.'

Rob put his mouth close to Ella's ear. 'Teks it all so serious, does Jimmy,' and Ella laughed again.

''Sides,' Jimmy was saying again, 'it's time I was Robin for a bit. You said I could.'

Rob shrugged good-naturedly. 'I dun't mind. Be who ya like.'

'I'll be Maid Marian then,' Ella teased Jimmy, knowing that her suggestion would not please him.

Jimmy prodded his finger towards the birthmark on Ella's face. 'Maid Marian wouldn't be a scar-face,' he sneered.

At once Ella's good nature vanished. 'If you're going to be horrible, Jimmy Souter, then I'm off home. Undo my hands, Rob.'

Janice slithered down the tree and jumped to the ground. 'Aw, don't go, Ella. They run off an' leave me if I'm on me own.' She glanced round the other three, from Ella's angry, red face, to Rob's embarrassed expression and then her gaze came to rest on her brother. 'I 'eard what ya said.' Suddenly Janice raised her hand and clouted him across the back of his head with the flat of her hand. 'I'll tell our mam.'

Without waiting for Rob to untie her hands Ella began to run, out of the clearing and through the trees back towards the driveway. They caught up with her at the big gate.

'Aw, don't be like that Ella. Come back and play,' Rob said.

'Leave me alone,' she snapped and carried on walking, the other three following her down the lane and away from the Grange. Awkwardly, Ella climbed over the stile into the meadow thinking the others would tire of trailing after her, but they climbed over too.

'Who's come across the field trampling all the grass down?' Rob said.

Ella felt her face growing red.

'It's 'er. She did it,' Jimmy jeered, pointing at Ella. 'Look at her face. You did it, didn't you?'

Ella glanced at Rob, who said quietly, 'You shouldn't

have done that, Ella. It makes it more difficult for the reaper to cut it.'

'She dun't know any better. She's only a townie,' Jimmy scoffed. 'Townie! Townie!'

Through gritted teeth, she muttered, 'Untie my hands, Rob. Now!'

'Don't you dare, Rob Eland, she only wants to clobber me again,' Jimmy said.

Walking round the edge of the field they came to the plank bridge across the dyke. Rob went across first and stood watching from the opposite bank whilst Ella stepped on to the two wooden planks. She was half-way across, looking down and watching where she carefully placed her feet, when she heard a scuffle behind her and then Rob shouted, 'No, Jimmy, don't!'

Ella looked up to see Rob starting forward towards her and at the same moment she felt a hand push her in the back. Ella lost her balance and, with her hands tied, there was no way she could save herself from falling. Rob, reaching out to her, was a split second too late to catch her.

She fell sideways into the dyke, amongst the thickly growing nettles and into a foot of stagnant water in the bottom of the dyke. She let out a yell of shock as she fell and then as the nettles stung every exposed part of her – face, arms and bare legs – she cried out again.

Ignoring the stings, Rob jumped down into the dyke beside her, his feet splashing into the water. He reached down and pulled her upright and then pulled her up the bank. All the time the nettles grabbed at them, leaving their sting.

On the bank, he untied Ella's hands at once, but it was too late now. He glared at Jimmy. 'That was a rotten thing to do.'

Jimmy shrugged. 'Me? I didn't do anything. I was crossing behind her, that's all. I never touched her, did I, our Janice?' He turned on his sister and his look dared her to disagree.

But Janice was not intimidated. 'Oh yes, you did. Now I *shall* tell Mam.'

'Don't you dare,' he pointed at her, 'else I'll tell her it was you, not the cat, that knocked her best teapot off the table last week.'

Janice stuck her tongue out at her brother. 'See 'f I care.'

'We'd better tek Ella home,' Rob said, glancing from one to the other of the Souter children. '*All* of us.'

'You going to tell?' Jimmy sneered, prodding Ella. 'Tell-tale tit, ya tongue will split . . .'

'Come on.' Rob took Ella by the arm.

As they walked around the edge of the meadow, Rob leading the way, Ella felt the cold flap of her wet clothes against her back and looking down at the state of Rob's boots, knew that her back must be covered in evil-smelling, black mud. And all the while the nettle stings throbbed.

'Gran'll kill me,' Ella muttered.

Fifteen

'*Now* what have you done, Missy?'

Her grandmother was standing in the middle of the yard, hands on hips. 'Just look at ya shoes. Ruined! You naughty child. Ya'll be the death of me!' With a swift movement Esther moved forward and before Ella could move, her grandmother had delivered a stinging slap to the back of the girl's leg. Esther's hand, now covered with the black mud, swung Ella round none too gently, and she saw, for the first time, the slime covering the girl's back.

'What on earth were you doing?'

'Missus—' Rob began.

'Be quiet, Boy, I'm asking her. Well?'

The fearsome green gaze bored into her and though her eyes smarted with tears and her face, arms and legs throbbed with the pain of the nettle stings – and now from Esther's smack too – Ella set her jaw and refused to cry. She returned her grandmother's stare doggedly.

'I fell in the dyke coming across the planks.'

'Then you should be more careful. Can't you even walk across a bridge without tipplin' into this muck?'

'Missus—' Rob began again, but Esther was moving away towards the wash-house.

'Strip ya clothes off. It's a cold bath for you, me girl.'

'Come on,' Ella heard Rob mutter to the Souter children. 'We'd better go.' They turned and as they moved away, Rob said, 'You should have owned up, Jimmy. You should have told the truth.'

'I – I thought she'd tell.'

'Obviously she's *not* a tell-tale, is she?'

Then they were out of earshot and Ella was left standing in the middle of the yard under the burning sun, whilst her grandmother brought the tin bath from the wash-house, placed it under the pump in the yard and half-filled it with cold water.

'Do as I told you, get them things off. Though how I'm to get that stain out o' ya dress, I dun't know. Right, now in you get.'

Ella glanced round.

'They've gone. There's no one to see you.'

And Ella was obliged to step into the tin bath and wash herself in the middle of the yard. The cold water soothed her nettle stings, but even when Esther saw the extent of the white blisters covering Ella's arms, legs and even her face, all she said was, 'Teach you to be more careful.' She turned away and went back into the house, saying over her shoulder, 'Up to ya bed and stay there!'

Her body was a mass of stings, throbbing, pulsating, *hurting*. She buried her head beneath the covers and let the tears come. Tears of pain, humiliation – and anger. Then she felt a hand tugging back the sheet and she clutched it more tightly to her. She didn't want anyone to see her tears. Then a gentle voice said, 'Come on, love. It's Grandpa . . .' Reluctantly, she emerged from underneath the sheet and with a sob allowed herself to be enfolded into his arms.

'There, there. Tell me what happened.'

She was silent, still not wanting to tell the truth. She

was not sure what her grandfather would do. He might go to the Souters and that would only cause more trouble. Something similar had once happened back home in Lincoln. A group of children had been playing snowballs on the way home and she had thrown one at a bigger boy. In retaliation, he had grabbed her and rubbed snow into her face. When she had arrived home her eye had been swollen and her mother, demanding to know who had done it, had immediately marched round to the boy's home and created such a commotion that the boy had never spoken to Ella again and had turned some of her former friends against her too.

From that time onwards, young though she was, Ella had determined to fight her own battles; telling grown-ups only made matters worse.

'I – I—' she began now, her burning cheek against his chest, so close she could hear the beat of his heart in her ear. 'We were playing. I fell off the little bridge into the dyke.'

'I see,' he said quietly, and held her tightly, rocking her and stroking her short curly hair, but she wasn't sure, by the tone of his voice, whether he believed her.

Gently he eased her away from him. 'Let's have a look at all these nettle stings. Poor little lass. I bet they're hurting, aren't they?'

She bit her lip and nodded. They heard voices in the front garden, just below the open window of her bedroom. Her grandfather stood up and looked out. 'It's Rob, talking to your grannie. I'd better go down and see what he wants.'

When her grandfather had left the bedroom, Ella got out of bed and went to the window, kneeling down, so that she could peep just over the sill and look down on them below without being seen.

At the bottom of the orchard, just near the hole in the hedge, she could see Rob talking to her grandmother and waving his arm, gesturing behind him, back towards the direction of the dyke.

'Oh, no,' she groaned aloud, 'he's telling her what happened.' She pulled a face to herself. 'Now Jimmy'll really have it in for me.'

Rob seemed to be handing a bundle of something to Esther, but from here, Ella could not see what it was. As her grandmother turned and began to walk back towards the house, Ella bobbed down quickly out of sight lest Esther should look up and see her there.

When, a few moments later, she heard her grandmother's voice in the hall and heard her footsteps on the stairs, she hopped back into bed.

'I know, I know, Jonathan.' The sound of Esther's voice preceded her and then she was there, standing over the bed, a bundle of huge green leaves in her hands.

She stood looking down at Ella for a few moments and, returning her gaze, the girl thought the older woman seemed to be struggling to find the right words.

'Rob's just told me what happened. I'm sorry I smacked you, lass, on top of the stings an' all. But you should have told me ya'sen.'

Her gaze never leaving Esther's face, Ella sat up slowly. She couldn't remember ever having heard a grown-up apologize to a child before. She stared in amazement at her grandmother. She was a funny woman, the girl thought, not for the first time. Sharp almost to the point of unkindness at times, unable to show any affection for her grand-daughter, and yet here she was standing in front of Ella, admitting she had been hasty and wrong and saying sorry.

Well, if Esther Godfrey could be honest enough to

apologize, Ella Hilton was not one to bear a grudge. For a moment she forgot her discomfort and smiled suddenly at her grandmother.

'That's all right, Gran,' she said, disarmingly. 'You weren't to know. I don't like telling tales, you see. I once told Mum about something that had happened – but – but it only made it worse next day at school.'

Esther sat down on the bed and they looked at each other. 'Tell me about it?' Her voice was unusually gentle.

Suddenly, the young girl was overwhelmed with a feeling of warmth, of cosy intimacy. There were just the two of them in the bedroom, and her grandmother was actually sitting there, listening to her; taking notice of her.

So, she blurted out the whole story of the snowball incident, and at the end, Esther touched Ella's cheek where the nettle stings were now making her face look swollen and said softly, 'So you don't want me to go and see Mrs Souter?'

'Oh, no, Gran.' Her eyes were wide with a new fear. 'Please, *please* don't.'

Esther nodded. She was still holding the huge green leaves and as Ella's gaze dropped, she shook them a little so that they quivered. 'Rob brought these for you.'

Ella giggled. 'What are they? Flowers?'

Esther smiled too. 'No. They're dock leaves. If you rub them on a nettle sting, it's supposed to take away the pain.'

Ella grimaced. 'We'll need a lot, Gran,' she said, and pushed back the bedclothes to show the white blemishes covering her arms and legs.

Esther looked down at the mass of stings and Ella could see that her grandmother was imagining the pain she was suffering. 'Aw, lass, I am sorry. What a naughty boy that Jimmy Souter is. If it's one thing I can't abide, it's an untruthful child.'

'You won't go there, though, will you? Promise, Gran?'

Esther sighed but said, 'I promise.'

Ella relaxed. What was it her mum had always said? 'Me mam always keeps her word. Good or bad she never relents. She's got a will of iron.'

Esther crushed the leaves in her hands and began to smooth them over Ella's arms and legs. 'I don't know whether it will soothe this lot, but it's worth a try.'

And as Ella watched her grandmother's bent head, she smiled to herself. It was almost worth all the discomfort to gain her grandmother's attention for a few precious moments.

The following afternoon as she walked home alone – Janice had gone to the dentist straight after school – she heard the 'whoosh' of tyres on the loose gravel at the side of the lane behind her and turned to see Rob hurtling towards her.

'Seen Jimmy?'

'I think he's keeping out of my way.'

Rob grinned. 'Reckon he can't mek you out.'

'How do you mean?'

'Well, you're different.'

Ella's mouth tightened. 'Don't remind me,' she said grimly.

'Eh?' He looked at her, his eyes wide and then, as he realized what she was thinking, he said, 'Dun't be daft. As if I'd say owt about *that*.'

She was suddenly contrite. No, to be fair, though they sparred with each other and he called her Townie, he had never teased her about the circumstances of her birth. She grinned up at him as he wobbled precariously on his bike trying to slow his pace to match hers. 'Sorry.'

'I should think so, too,' he said, pretending huffiness, but he was smiling too. 'No, what I meant was – before you got so touchy – is that you're such a little spitfire usually, but yesterday, he couldn't believe it when you didn't run home telling tales to your gran, 'cos she'd have caused a rumpus up at Souters,' his grin broadened, 'even if only to get her own back at Mrs Souter for storming to Brumbys' Farm not long back.'

'Oh, you heard about that, then?'

'Jimmy told us.'

They went on in silence, then he said, 'We're off shrimpin' after tea. You coming?'

'If Gran'll let me.' But for once, after yesterday, Ella was sure the answer would be 'yes'.

The nettle stings had settled to a tingling sensation and, as she set off with Rob, armed with her newly repaired shrimping net, she almost forgot about them. As they crested the first line of dunes and her gaze spanned the flat marshland before her, Ella gasped. 'Oh! Oh, isn't it pretty?'

Before her the marsh was a mass of pink and mauve.

'It's sea-lavender.' Rob stood beside her. 'One of the plants that'll grow on a saltmarsh.'

Ella snorted with laughter. 'Pity it's not a crop Gran can grow after the floods. She's still moaning about how long it will take for the land to get back to normal.'

They were quiet for a moment, remembering. Then with a 'Come on,' from Rob they were running down the dune and galloping across the marsh, jumping the rivulets and skirting round the deeper creeks. As they raced down the second line of dunes and on to the beach, Rob shouted, 'There's Janice and Jimmy, look, near the water's edge. Come on, let's go and see what they're up to.'

As they drew closer, she could see the Souters were watching a large cylindrical metal object, rolling about in the shallows, being washed nearer and nearer the beach by the tide. The boys stripped off their shoes and socks and scampered through the shallows to wade into the deeper water.

Ella stood beside Janice. The boys had reached the cylinder and, with the aid of the waves, were pushing it towards the beach. When it came to rest on the sand, though they shoved and heaved, they could move it no further. Jimmy Souter kicked at it with his foot. 'It's bloomin' heavy an' it's all rusty. What do you think it is?'

Janice glanced at Ella. 'Do you think it's treasure off a pirate ship? Y'know, a tin box crammed full with jewels and gold sovereigns.'

Ella was hardly listening. She was staring at it, a slight frown on her forehead. It was pointed at one end and on the other the metal was shaped into fins. It looked vaguely familiar. Now where . . . ?

Suddenly, she was splashing through the water without even taking off her shoes and socks to grab Rob's arm and yell, 'Come away – quick! It's a bomb!'

They stared at her as if she had suddenly gone mad.

'I tell you it's a bomb!' She tugged at Rob's arm.

'Ouch, ya hurting, Ella—'

She gave him an almighty shove towards the beach. 'Come on. You too Jimmy. Quick.' She grasped him, pushing him away, all animosity forgotten in a moment.

'Eh, who are you shovin'?' Jimmy began, but Rob, catching something of the panic in Ella's tone said, 'Do as she ses!'

As they reached the sand, Ella just said, 'Run!' and they all scampered up the beach, their flying feet sending up little showers of sand.

They reached the first line of dunes and jumped into a sandy hollow, where they lay on their stomachs and, breathless, peeped over the top to look back at the bomb, lying deceptively benign, on the sand, the waves running around it from time to time, but not moving it now.

'You're daft, Ella Hilton. 'Ow can that be a bomb?' Jimmy began, but all three were now looking at her questioningly, demanding an explanation for her erratic behaviour.

She sat up and took a deep breath to steady her shaking limbs. She looked at each of them in turn and said quietly, 'My mum was a driver in the WAAFs in the war for a Commanding Officer. She's got – had – a lot of photos. I used to like looking through them. There were some pictures of WAAFs driving a sort of tractor pulling a long trailer with bombs on it. She told me . . .' She bit her lip, the hurt coming back as she was obliged to talk about her mother. 'That was when they were "bombing up" the aircraft.' Ella fell silent for a moment, almost hearing Kate's voice again in her head. 'The WAAFs used to do all sorts in the war, drive the bomb trains out to the aircraft, take the crews out an hour before take-off and meet them again when they came back – if they came back . . .'

'What did you do, Mum?' Ella could hear herself asking again.

'Me? Oh, I had a real cushy number. I was personal driver for the Station Commander.'

'Was he nice?'

Then Kate would look down at her daughter and say softly, 'He was a lovely man, a wonderful man.'

'Go on,' Jimmy's insistent voice dragged her back to the present.

Ella nodded towards the bomb lying innocently on the sand. 'The things on the trailer looked just like that.'

'Oh, heck,' Rob said. 'What ought we to do?'

'Report it, of course,' Ella said, with prompt decisiveness. 'You stay here and watch no one goes near it.' She glanced up and down the beach but, except for a few holiday-makers in the far distance, there was no one. 'Don't go near it yourselves but if anyone looks like coming, tell them to keep away.'

Rob said, 'Shall I come with you?'

'No,' Ella said. 'You stay here and mind they do as I say.' She glanced at the two Souters and then back at Rob as if to say silently, 'I don't trust them to believe me, 'specially Jimmy.'

Solemnly Rob nodded. 'Get me dad, Ella. He'll know for sure.'

She gave him a quick grin. 'Good idea,' and added, pulling her mouth into a quirky smile, 'He'll probably believe me better than Gran will, anyway. Here—' She thrust her shrimping net towards him. 'Look after that for me. I can run faster without it.'

And then she was off, up the dunes, across the pink carpet of sea-lavender, over the westerly dunes and into the lane. On again up the lane towards Rookery Farm.

'Whatever's the matter, love?' Rosie's startled tone greeted her.

'Uncle Danny,' Ella gasped, 'I must find Uncle Danny.'

'He's over at yar gran's, but—'

But Ella was off again, 'Sorry, Aunty Rosie, it's urgent.'

Across the lane, over the stile and through the meadow, straight through the long grass, heedless of the dire warnings that she must not trample down the precious hay crop, through the hole in the hedge, round the corner of the house and – thank goodness – there he was, standing in the middle of the yard with her grandparents.

'Uncle Danny – come quick! There's a bomb on the

beach. Rob – and the Souters – are watching it, but you must come!'

'Steady on, lass. Whatever are you on about?' Danny began.

Her grandmother clicked her tongue against her teeth in exasperation. 'Now what mischief are you into, Missy?'

Ella, red-faced and breathless, was almost weeping now. She took hold of Danny's arm as if to pull him physically after her. 'Please, Uncle Danny!'

'Why do you think it's a bomb?'

'Mum's photos from the war. It's just like them – please!'

The two men, Danny and her grandfather, exchanged a glance. 'She could be right, you know,' Jonathan said seriously. 'There was one washed up further north. I remember reading about it.' There was a sudden expression of fear on his face. 'It – it blew up.'

Turning back to Ella, Danny said, 'Run and ask your aunty Rosie to phone the police.' Since the floods, Rookery Farm now had a telephone. 'Tell her I said so. Come on, Mester, we'll go and see.'

He was limping away as fast as his wounded leg would allow with Jonathan following and Ella running back the way she had just come, leaving Esther standing helplessly in the yard not quite sure just what she ought to do.

It was indeed a bomb and over the next few hours from the comparative safety of a sandy hollow in the dunes, the three children and the two men watched the flurry of excitement as the police arrived to cordon off the area.

'Look, they're building a wall of sandbags round it,' Rob pointed.

'I ought to be getting back to help with the milking,' Jonathan murmured once, but made no move.

'Our mam'll give us heck when we get home,' Janice

remarked, but she too stayed where she was, parting the thick grass to watch.

Jimmy could hardly contain his excitement and kept jumping up only to be dragged down again by one of the others.

A policeman was walking towards them and, as he approached, they stood up but did not move out of the hollow. After taking a few details down in his notebook from the children, he said, 'It turns out it's the responsibility of the Royal Navy being as it's between the high- and low-water mark, and they can't get here until tomorrow.'

'What'll they do?' Jimmy asked. 'Blow it up? Can we watch, Mester?'

'They might defuse it where it is, or they might tow it out a good distance offshore and then blow it up. In the latter case, yes, you could watch from the sandhills. But if they defuse it there . . .' he jerked his thumb over his shoulder and shook his head '. . . no way will you be allowed anywhere along this bit of beach.' The policeman grinned at the disappointed chorus of 'aws' from the youngsters and spread his hands in a gesture of apology to the two men who looked just as put out.

'Well,' he said, putting his notebook back into his pocket. 'Looks like a long night ahead for me and the lads.' With a wave he set off back across the sand.

'Is he going to stand guard all night?' Janice asked.

'I expect so,' Jonathan murmured. 'Come on, we'd better get back home.'

As they came to the gate at Brumbys' Farm, they heard the sound of voices and saw Esther standing talking to two men, waving her hands and saying, 'All this fuss and nonsense. Left here to do the milking on me own—' She broke off as she saw their approach. 'Oh, there you are!'

she said accusingly. 'Fine time to come traipsing home, leaving me here to cope with all the work and now these fellers from the paper—'

The two men, swiftly losing interest in Esther and her ranting, turned. 'We're from the local paper—' One held a notebook in his hand and the other carried a camera. 'Who actually found the bomb?'

The two Souter children both began to speak at once. 'We did – we found it.'

'You gonna tek our picture, Mester, fer the paper?'

'We knew it was a bomb straight away,' Jimmy said, puffing out his chest importantly. 'I've seen pictures.'

Ella, glancing at her grandmother's pursed lips and angry eyes, began to sidle away. If the Souters wanted to take all the credit, she thought, let them. I'll only be in more bother with Gran if I—

But Rob was not going to let the Souters get away with their lies. 'Wait a minute,' he said. 'They found it, yeah, that's true and when me an' Ella got there, it was in the shallows. Jimmy and me started to push it on to the sand, but it was too heavy. Then suddenly, Ella starts shouting that it's a bomb.'

The man with the notebook was writing furiously. 'Which one's Ella?'

Her heart sank as Rob reached out and pulled her forward. 'This is Ella. It was *her* who knew it was a bomb . . .' He cast a glance towards the two Souters that said, contradict me if you dare. 'It was her who'd seen the pictures.'

The reporter was bending towards her. 'What pictures were those, young lady?' He was smiling down encouragingly at her.

'I – er . . .' She glanced towards her grandmother, unsure what she should say. Then she felt her grandpa's hand on her shoulder. 'It's all right, love, you can tell the gentleman.'

So, whilst they all stood and listened and the little man wrote furiously and the other man fiddled with his camera, Ella told them.

'Can we speak to your mum?'

The girl shook her head, suddenly unable to speak.

'Her mother was drowned in the floods,' Jonathan said quietly, and although the reporter said softly, 'Oh, how dreadful,' there was a sudden gleam in his eyes: here was a wonderful, poignant story.

'Where was your mum stationed in the WAAFs, then?'

Ella glanced up at her grandfather for help. Even she wasn't quite sure about that.

'Suddaby,' he said.

'What did she do?'

Here Jonathan turned to Danny who said, 'She was an MT driver.'

Jimmy, determined not to be left out of all the limelight falling on Ella, nudged her and said, 'Is that all? You told us she drove a Commanding Officer about in his big car. I knew you was lying.'

'What's that?' The reporter's trained ears missed nothing. 'She was the CO's driver?'

'Among other duties, yes,' Danny confirmed and Ella felt a surge of pride when she saw the astonished look on Jimmy Souter's face.

'Could we have a picture of the little girl, do you think?' the reporter asked. Ella found herself standing, with Rob and the two Souters ranged behind her, trying to smile into the camera, but her only thought was, 'What is Gran going to say?'

Esther had a lot to say, but for once her chagrin was not directed at Ella. 'Why did you let 'er tell 'em so much,

Jonathan? They'll be back day after day, asking all sorts of awkward questions, digging things up.' She glanced meaningfully at her husband, and Ella, catching the look, knew at once that her grandmother was referring once more to the fact that Ella had no father.

But all her grandpa would say was, 'The child did well, Esther. You should be very proud of her common sense and quick action.'

Esther bristled, 'I am, of course, but . . .'

The following morning found the two adults and the four children once again peering over the side of the hollow watching the proceedings on the beach.

'I reckon they're going to tow it out to sea,' Danny said. 'Look, there's a boat coming.'

Keeping well hidden so that they would not be ordered away from the area they continued to watch until the bomb was towed into the water behind a boat, ploughing a watery furrow through the waves.

'Shall we see it blow up, Mester?' Jimmy wanted to know.

'I don't know,' Jonathan murmured, his gaze on the boat getting smaller and smaller towards the horizon.

'Are you lot going to lie there all day?' came a voice from behind them and, with one accord, they turned to see Esther standing on the edge of the hollow looking down at them. 'Don't you know there's work—'

Something above them caught her attention and whatever she had been going to say ended in her mouth rounding in a surprised 'oh!'

Everyone swivelled back as they heard a dull 'boom' and, out to sea, saw a white plume of water spurting skywards. Jimmy and Janice leapt to their feet and shrieked with delight, but Ella and Rob, catching some of the seriousness on the faces of the adults, just stared.

Jonathan and Danny got to their feet. 'Well, that's it then . . .' Jonathan began, then seeing his wife standing rigidly, still staring out to sea, he added, 'What is it, love?'

She blinked and seemed to shake herself, but Ella felt her glance come to rest on her. 'They could all have been killed,' she murmured. Suddenly, she smiled, her whole face lighting up. She reached out and touched Ella's curly hair. 'Never let it be said I can't give praise when it's due. Ya did well, Missy.'

Ella took a step forward, started to raise her arms to hug her grandmother, but already the older woman was turning away. 'Come on, now. All the excitement's over. There's work to be done.' Esther turned and disappeared up and over the dunes, leaving Ella staring after her not quite knowing whether to be pleased or vaguely disappointed.

The photo and the article were on the front page of the local paper the following Friday.

The heading read, ORPHAN HEROINE SAVES LIVES and the piece went on to give a dramatic account of how the children in the photograph had found the object but that it had been the swift action of one, Ella Hilton, who had recognized it as being a bomb. Although mention was made in a kindly and sympathetic way of Ella's mother, Kate, having been drowned so tragically and so recently, there was nothing said about her father. So Ella breathed a sigh of relief and tucked the newspaper away in the blanket chest on top of her mother's belongings.

The event was talked about by the locals for a few days and even found its way into a national daily newspaper, though only on an inside page; then it was soon forgotten. There was only one other outcome; Mrs Souter arrived once more in the yard of Brumbys' Farm.

Esther stood watching her approach; feet planted firmly apart, hands on hips, her green eyes alight ready to do battle.

'Esther Godfrey, we ain't allus seen eye to eye, you an' me,' the woman began without preamble, 'but Ah've come to thank that little lass o' yourn for what she did.'

'Eh?' Esther gaped and Ella, hiding round the corner of the house, stuffed the back of her hand into her mouth to stifle her giggles.

'If it hadn't been for her, them daft pair of mine might a' been blown sky high. Dick said it could easy 'ave gone off when they was tugging it about. So I reckoned I owed you that much to come and thank you, like.'

''Tain't me you want to thank, Aggie, but I tek it kindly you coming.' Esther smiled. 'Kettle's on the hob. How about a cuppa?'

'Oo ta, Esther. I won't say no.'

Towards the end of July, Peggy arrived unexpectedly to stay a few days at the farm. Ella clung to her and buried her face against the slim woman's smart jacket, breathing in her well-remembered perfume. As soon as they were alone together, she asked at once, 'Can't I come back to live with you, Aunty Peggy?'

'Oh, love, you know you can't. I'm so sorry.' And though she touched Ella's cheek with infinite tenderness and love, there was nothing else she could say.

Peggy seemed anxious and ill-at-ease as if she were

worried about something. Several times during her stay, Ella saw her talking earnestly, almost secretly, to her brother, but never when Esther was present. Whenever someone else approached, they stopped talking. Was Aunty Peggy pleading her cause? the girl wondered. Was she trying to get Jonathan to agree to Ella going back to Lincoln? But when the time came for Peggy to leave, still no word of Ella going back had been mentioned.

She tried once more. 'Can't I go and stay with Aunty Peggy for a week? I can, can't I, Aunty Peggy?' she asked across the tea-table.

Peggy, her cheeks turning a little pink, looked anxiously towards Esther. 'Well, it depends what your gran—'

'We need you here to help with the harvest,' Esther said sharply. 'It's our busiest time and you're old enough now to lend a hand where you can.' She turned to look down at Ella. 'All farmers' children help. Always have done, always will.'

'But I'm not a farmer's child, am I?' Ella glowered, her lower jaw sticking out moodily, the birthmark on her face clearly visible. 'I want to go back to Lincoln. I want to go – home!'

She was aware that Peggy's face was growing redder with embarrassment.

Her grandmother frowned. 'This is your home now, Missy, and you'd better make the best of it.'

'Why can't I even go for a holiday? If I can't go now, what about Christmas or next Easter?'

Ella turned towards Peggy once more for support, but the woman's eyes were downcast towards her plate and she was pushing the food around it as if she had suddenly lost her appetite.

'We'll see,' was the only reply Esther would give. But the girl knew that this time her answer meant 'no'.

When she went with her grandfather to take Peggy to the station the following day, her aunt hugged her closely and whispered. 'Don't fret, love, please. When you're older, maybe she'll let you come then.'

'One day, when I'm older, I *will* go,' Ella vowed, 'and no one – not even *her* – will stop me!'

As the years passed, each school holiday the growing girl, now a pupil at the local grammar school, smart in her dark green and gold uniform, asked if she could go to visit Peggy in Lincoln and every time the answer was the same, 'We need you here,' until in the end, she stopped asking. Her questions about the family, about her own background even, were always silenced with a frown from her grandmother. Everything seemed to be shrouded in mystery, secrets that Esther would not share. Neither would she allow anyone else to tell Ella anything. Occasionally, she would hear her gentle grandfather trying to persuade Esther. 'You ought to tell her, love. Where's the harm? Kate would have explained it all to her by now . . .'

Always, when she asked about Esther's early life, about the Elands or even made tentative remarks about the identity of her own father, her grandmother flew into a temper and, as she grew older, Ella ceased to question. But she never stopped wondering.

As the years flew by, one merging into the next, the days filled with school work, homework and work on the farm, Ella at thirteen, fourteen, fifteen, still felt as if Esther treated her like a child; a child who must be protected and guarded and kept in ignorance.

One day, I'll find out what all the mystery is, Ella promised herself, just as one day I'll go back to Lincoln. One day, I'll go back home.

Part Two

Sixteen

LINCOLNSHIRE, 1958

When the O level results came out in the August of 1958, Rob had not achieved the grades he needed to get into the farm institute.

'I'll have to do retakes,' he told Ella dolefully. 'It means staying on at school another whole year.'

'Poor old Bumpkin!' Ella teased him. 'Never mind, it'll soon go.'

'It's all right for you, Townie!' he grumbled. 'You're a clever-clogs.'

'You'll just have to work harder, that's all. Not so much "gallivanting", as my gran calls it, eh?'

He smiled ruefully. 'That's what me dad ses.'

At sixteen, Rob was several inches taller than Ella, having shot up in the last year so that Rosie despaired of him – for ever growing out of his clothes. 'I reckon he keeps standing in the muck heap,' Danny would tease, 'to mek hissen grow.' Already his son was half a head taller than Danny, but almost as broad shouldered and strong.

'Eh, but he'll brek a few hearts,' Rosie would say fondly, her eyes following her son lovingly. Behind her back, Danny and his mother, Grandma Beth Eland, would exchange a look, but not a word was ever spoken.

'Are they very disappointed?' Ella asked him now.

He shrugged. 'Don't seem to be. I think Mum's quite relieved really that her little boy isn't leaving home yet.'

Despite what Rob said, the autumn term in the fifth

year at the grammar school was hard work for Ella. O levels now loomed for her, too, the following June, and decisions would have to be made about her future. Should she leave school the next summer or stay on to do A levels and maybe go on to university?

'University? Huh!' Her grandmother would sniff each time the subject was raised. 'What good's a fancy education for a girl? Won't help you milk the cows and harvest the corn, will it?'

'But Aunty Lilian went. You didn't stop her,' Ella would argue, standing toe to toe with her grandmother. At almost sixteen, she was now slightly taller than Esther. Still boyishly slim, Ella had changed little in appearance in the five and a half years she had lived at Brumbys' Farm, except to grow taller. Her short hair curled tightly and her skin, tanned to a smooth light brown from helping on the farm, was devoid of the make-up with which her schoolmates experimented. Only the birthmark marred her complexion.

'Aye, an' look what's happened,' her grandmother would fling back. 'Dun't want to know us now, does she?' Her grandmother, too, was little changed: still slim and lithe, a few more grey hairs and another line or two on her face which, she assured Ella, were put there by all the worry the girl caused her.

To her grandmother's bitterness about Lilian, even Ella had no reply for the fact was that Esther's younger daughter was a shadowy, distant figure, who had virtually cut herself off from her family.

Ella would sigh and shake her head. 'I don't think you can blame her going to university for that, Gran.' But her grandmother would carry on muttering dark threats about 'folks getting above theirsens and despising their upbringing'.

It was fortunate for Ella that she was a tough, healthy child, for with the extra homework in preparation for examinations and yet still expected to help on the farm, by the end of the term, even she felt exhausted.

A glowing school report at the end of the autumn term emboldened Ella to ask once more, 'Can I go to Lincoln to see Aunty Peg? After we break up from school?'

She still longed to be in the city again, especially just before Christmas to see all the shops decorated, hear carols sung and get caught up in the excitement of it all. So many of her childhood memories were becoming hazy, she was afraid she would lose them altogether.

'Ya see Peggy when she comes here,' Esther argued.

'Let her go for a night or so, Esther,' Jonathan said, winking across at Ella from behind his newspaper. 'Peg would love to see her.'

'But Peg's at work all day. I dun't like her wandering the streets on her own [illegible]'

'Gran, I'm almost sixteen . . .' She paused and then her blue eyes sparkled. 'How about if I ask Janice to come too? She'd love a trip to the city. I think she'd be able to get time off work. They're not very busy this time of year.'

Janice had left school the previous summer to work in a café in Lynthorpe.

Esther looked from one to another. 'Oh, I see, ganging up on me, are ya?'

Jonathan smiled gently. 'Come on, love. Let the lass have a bit of fun.'

Esther's glance was going from one to the other as if she were considering. Slowly, she said, 'All right, then. Ya can go, but there's one condition.'

Ella's eyes widened in delighted surprise. 'What?'

Then, suddenly, Esther smiled. 'Bring me a present. I

dun't often get a present from the big city.' She put her head on one side, considering, and said slowly, 'D'ya know, never in me whole life have I spent a penny on something that wasn't useful or – or sensible.'

Ella gasped. 'Of course I will.' Leaping up from the supper table, she flung her arms around her grandmother's neck. 'Oh, thank you, Gran, thank you.'

Esther wriggled under Ella's embrace and murmured, 'There's no need for all that,' but when Ella drew back she saw that the older woman's face was pink and she was still smiling.

'I'll write to Peg tonight and ask if it's all right for you and Janice to go,' her grandpa volunteered. 'You could stay two nights.'

On the morning of their trip as she waited in the yard for Janice, Jonathan pressed some money into her hand. 'Get something nice for your gran, something really pretty and frivolous.'

Ella grinned up at him. 'If she chunters at it being a waste of good money, I'll blame you.'

'She'll love it, I promise you. She deserves to be spoilt for once.' He chuckled. 'But I'm sure she wouldn't want us to make a habit of it.'

She tucked the notes safely in her purse with her own spending money as the Souters' car swung in at the gate, Janice's excited face peering out of the passenger window. 'Come on, Ella, we'll miss that bus.'

''Bye Grandpa. See you Thursday night.' Ella ran to climb into the back of Mr Souter's old car, wrinkling her nose at the inevitable smell of chickens and sitting on the edge of the seat to avoid the feathers.

'Hang on to ya hats,' Dick Souter called wheezily from behind the wheel. ''Cos I'll tek ya round corners on two wheels.'

'Oh, Dad,' laughed Janice. 'This car couldn't possibly go fast enough!' But the next minute the two girls found themselves rolling from side to side and hanging on for dear life as Dick Souter, foot pressed to the floor, rocketed them into town to catch the bus.

The journey took two and a quarter hours, but Janice, excited at her first trip to a city, never stopped talking, and Ella was quiet with her own thoughts; every mile was taking her nearer and nearer Lincoln.

After all this time – six long years – she was going home.

They got off the bus in Broadgate and walked along Clasketgate into the High Street and to the large department store where Peggy Godfrey worked.

'Oh, look.' Janice gripped her arm. 'Look at all the – the . . .' her bright eyes flicked from side to side, fearful of missing something '. . . *things*. Oh, isn't it wonderful?' She walked through the departments, touching leather handbags and gloves, leaning over the glass counters displaying jewellery, holding her nose in the air and breathing deeply near the perfume counter and staring in amazement at the range of make-up, lipsticks, eye shadows. 'Oh, look, do look, Ella. I must buy some of this – and this – and oh, look, *blue* mascara.'

They walked up the plush carpeted stairs to the ladies' lingerie where Peggy was now the head of the department.

'Ella!'

Tall and slim, in a navy costume, Peggy seemed to change little through the years: perhaps there were more grey strands in her hair, maybe there were a few more lines on her face, but other than that she looked just the same as Ella always thought of her. She came towards them now with outstretched arms. 'My dear, I think you've grown again since I saw you in the summer. You're as tall as me now.'

Peggy bent forward and kissed Ella's cheek. 'And this is Janice?' She held out her slim, well-manicured hand. 'I'm pleased to meet you, Janice.'

'Hello, Miss Godfrey.' But the girl's eyes were darting everywhere, wide with wonder at the models dressed in flowing satin nightwear and frilly underwear.

Peggy smiled and asked, 'Now, what do you want to do? Do you want the house key to go home, or do you want to leave your overnight cases with me and stay in the town for a while?'

Before Ella could reply, Janice said, 'Ooh, stay in town, Ella, do let's,' and Ella nodded ready agreement.

Peggy laughed. 'Now you've got here at last, you're not going to waste a moment, I can see. I tell you what. You have a look round and I'll meet you both at the High Bridge café at one o'clock for lunch. I only get an hour so you go in and get a table. It'll be packed today with all the last-minute shoppers.'

Ella nodded and handed over the small suitcase that had once been her mother's and Janice's canvas bag into Peggy's safekeeping. 'All right. See you later.'

The city was in festive mood: every shop window was decorated with Christmas trees and festooned with paper chains, red, silver and gold. On a corner near the Stonebow, the Salvation Army band played carols and as they stepped out of the double doors of the department store, they were lost in the bustle of the crowded pavements.

Janice clutched Ella's arm again; it was becoming rapidly bruised with all the girl's excitement. She was staring at a model in one of the huge plate glass windows of the store and watching a window dresser at work.

'Isn't that just the most wonderful dress you've ever seen, Ella?' Janice gasped.

It was a royal blue A-line dress that curved over the model's breast and into her slim waist and then out over flounced petticoats. They stood gazing at it for a long time and then Ella pulled her mesmerized friend away. 'It'll be far too dear for the likes of us. Come on.'

'No, no, look at the ticket. I've brought all me savings to spend. If I . . .' She licked her lips in anticipation. 'If I don't spend so much on presents, I could get it. I'm sure I could.'

Ella shrugged. 'You do what ya like. It's your money,' she said, trying to stop the resentment creeping into her voice as she thought of the meagre few pounds she had to spend on presents for everyone she wanted to buy for; precious little would be left for herself.

Then, giving herself a mental ticking off for such selfish thoughts, Ella grinned, linked her arm through her friend's and laughingly dragged her away from the window. 'Come on, then, let's do all your other shopping and see what you've got left.'

With a lingering last glance at the dress, Janice allowed herself to be led away.

They walked on up the hill and came to a large bookshop. Inside they joined those browsing and Ella ran her eyes along the shelves.

'I ain't never seen so many books in one place,' Janice said, gaping round, ''Cept in a library.' There was a bookshop in Lynthorpe but it was about a quarter of the size of this one.

Rob was top of Ella's list for presents, but she couldn't think what to get him. What did boys of sixteen aiming to go to farming college want? she thought wryly. A book on pig-killing, perhaps!

She came to the section devoted to books for men and ran her eyes along the pictures and titles. There was a book on traction engines which had been built in this very city over the years, with pictures and details. 'That's perfect for Grandpa,' she murmured and picked it up, remembering how he had told her that before coming to Brumbys' Farm he had worked in a factory building such engines. He would love it. Next to it was the ideal gift for Rob; a book about motorbikes. It even gave instructions on how to strip down the engine. He was crazy about them, always talking about the day when he would own one.

About as much chance as Janice buying that dress! Ella thought with amusement, but she bought the book for him all the same.

Then she chose a diary for Uncle Danny but could find nothing she thought suitable in this shop for anyone else. Still, that was three presents bought. She glanced around for Janice to see her friend picking up a magazine on beauty tips.

'Have you bought any presents?'

'Eh?' The girl looked at her in surprise. 'What? Oh no. Plenty of time for that. I can always get them in Lynthorpe.'

Ella gave a click of exasperation. 'But that's why we've come here, isn't it? Christmas shopping? For other people?' she added pointedly.

Janice grinned sheepishly. 'Maybe. Maybe not. Aw, come on, El, I've never been let loose in a place like this before. I'll just get something nice for Rob, I'm not bothered about anyone else.'

'Oh, ta very much,' Ella teased.

Janice gave her a swift grin. 'Well, you know what I mean.' Still holding on to the magazine, she came to Ella. 'Have you got him summat, then?' And as Ella showed her the book on motorcycles, Janice grimaced. 'He'll like that.

Trust you to get there first.' But she said it good-naturedly and together they pondered what Janice could buy Rob for Christmas.

'How about aftershave?'

'Eh? Does he shave yet?'

Ella laughed. 'I think so. Haven't you seen how dark his chin looks some days and then quite pale another. And I saw a little nick on his chin once as if he'd cut himself.'

'Can't say I've noticed,' Janice said airily.

'Thought he was your boyfriend?' Ella said slyly and Janice smiled coyly. 'One of many, young Ella,' she said patting her long hair. 'Keep 'em guessing, that's what I say. Come on, isn't it time we was meeting yar aunty for dinner?'

They walked though the arches of the Stonebow to where the old sixteenth-century half-timbered black and white building straddled the bridge. The smell of real coffee met them even before they stepped into the small shop. They climbed the narrow wooden stairs to the upper floors and found a seat near the window overlooking the High Street and beyond it the river where swans glided up and down. Ella sighed as she sat down and settled her packages at the side of her. The last time she had been in this café, she'd been about nine and her mother had been at her side. But in Janice's company, there was no time for maudlin thoughts. 'Just look down there at all that traffic,' the girl exclaimed, pressing her nose to the small leaded window panes. 'Can them double deckers get through that arch, then?'

Ella nodded.

'There you are,' came Peggy's cheerful voice as she slipped in beside Ella. 'Have you had a good morning?'

'It's wonderful, Miss Godfrey. You're so lucky to live here,' Janice said, and Ella felt a thrill of pride for the city of her birth. She had always loved the place, but to hear Janice in excited raptures added to her pleasure.

They ordered hot soup and steak and kidney pie.

'Now, tell me how they are at home?' Peggy said.

Ella almost said, 'Fleethaven's not my home – Lincoln is,' but for once she bit back the remark. She didn't want Peggy to think she had been unhappy at Brumbys' Farm for the last six years, because she realized with a slight shock, it would not have been true, at least not all of the time. There had been some good times.

'Gran's all right . . .' A mischievous smile quirked her mouth. 'Same as always.' Then a slight frown creased her forehead. 'Grandpa's – all right, I suppose, but, well, he seems to get tired a lot quicker now.'

A look of concern for her brother crossed Peggy's face. 'Well, he is sixty-eight, you know.'

Ella gasped and stared at her. 'Is he really?'

Peggy smiled. 'Trouble with all of us, we're still about twenty inside our heads and still think we can act that age.'

'How old's my gran, then?'

'I'm not absolutely sure. She's certainly two or three years younger than Jonathan.' Peggy paused and then added, 'I should have retired a couple of years ago but, well, my life would be so empty without work that they let me stay on.'

'I don't blame you,' Janice put in. 'I wouldn't want to give up if I worked in such a lovely shop.'

Peggy gave a small smile and sighed. 'I suppose it will have to come to it soon. I'll have to make way for a younger person.' Peggy seemed to shake herself and say, with deliberate cheerfulness, 'What about you two? When do you leave school and what are you going to do?'

'I've already left,' Janice said promptly. 'I'm a bit older than Ella. I work in a café at the moment. It's okay in the summer, but this time of the year, it's dead!' She cast her eyes upwards in a gesture of hopelessness. 'I'd like to get something better some day.'

'I'm sure you will, Janice.' Peggy smiled and then added, 'What about you, Ella?'

She pulled a face. 'Gran wants me to leave school and work on the farm, but I want something more than that.'

'What sort of thing?'

'I don't know, really.' Her voice dropped. 'I still miss the city.'

'What about dressmaking and tailoring like – like your mother?'

'I'm not that good. Oh, I can sew neatly and make things on Mum's sewing machine, Gran's seen to that. But I haven't got Mum's flair for it. I want to get my O levels and then see.'

'Very wise.' Peggy nodded and, getting up, said, 'Well, I'll have to go.'

Downstairs she silenced their protests and insisted on paying for all three meals. 'It's my treat. Come and get the house key from me if you want to go home before I can leave tonight. It'll be after six by the time I get away.'

Ella nodded.

Outside on the pavement, Peggy asked, 'How's the shopping going?'

Ella told her and added, 'I can't think what to buy Grandma Eland and Aunty Rosie, or Gran, though Grandpa's given me some money to buy her something pretty.' She laughed. 'He told me to get her something really frivolous.'

'Why not come back with me? You can wander through all the departments. You might see something that catches your eye.'

'What do you want to do, Janice?'

'What ya like.' Her eyes gleamed. 'I can have another look at that dress.'

As they passed the huge window again, Janice paused and said, 'Do you think they'll let me try it on, Miss Godfrey?'

'Of course, Janice. I'll take you to the dress department and ask Miss Keenes to look after you.'

The warmth enveloped them as they entered the store and as Peggy left them with the rather stern-looking head of the dress department, she said, 'Come up later and I'll help you pick something for your gran.'

The dress fitted Janice perfectly and as she twisted and twirled in front of the full-length mirror, Ella could not help feeling a twmge of envy at her shapely figure, shown off to perfection by the snug lines of the dress.

Janice, her eyes shining, took a deep breath and said, 'I'll take it.'

An hour later, Ella having bought lavender soap for Grandma Eland and hand cream for Rosie, they found their way back to the lingerie department.

'There was a bit of a lull earlier,' Peggy greeted them, 'and I've looked out one or two things.' She glanced around to see that no other customers were waiting to be served before she said, 'Come and have a look.'

Two nightdress and négligé sets were laid out for Ella's inspection, one in peach silk, the other in black satin.

'Can you really see your gran in something like that?' Janice said.

Ella giggled. 'Well, Grandpa said something frivolous and I guess the black one fits that description the best.'

Peggy laughed. 'Men are supposed to like black.'

'Do you think I really dare take her that?'

'She'll clip yar ear, El,' Janice warned, laughing.

Peggy looked worried and said, 'You can blame me if—'

'Oh, I wouldn't do that,' Ella said swiftly. 'I'll take

what's coming.' Silently she added, I always have. Aloud, she said, 'I don't think I've enough money left.'

'Don't worry,' Peggy whispered, so that Janice could not hear. 'I can get it for you on staff discount as you're a relative. Leave it to me.'

When the store closed and the three of them walked back towards home, the two girls were clutching large boxes wrapped in Christmas paper; Janice with her dress and Ella with the frilly black nightdress and négligé for her grandmother. Just what, she wondered, would Esther Godfrey say to it?

As they turned into the long road which led them to the side-street where Peggy lived, a group of students emerged from some buildings on the left.

'Is that a school, Aunty Peg? I'd have thought they'd have broken up by now.'

'Mmm? Oh no. It's the technical college. You can go there after you leave school to do all sorts of courses. Secretarial – that sort of thing.'

'I say, El,' Janice said, glancing back over her shoulder. 'See that good-looking blond lad? He winked at me.'

'Really?' Ella answered absent-mindedly. As they walked on she glanced back to see the students laughing and talking as they walked towards town.

A college, eh? Where you could learn useful skills. And in Lincoln! Now that was worth thinking about.

Their stay in the city seemed to be over far too quickly. On the first evening they sat and talked with Peggy, and then climbed the stairs to share the big double bed in the spare room, giggling and whispering until the early hours.

The following evening Peggy took them to the theatre and they had a fish-and-chip supper afterwards.

'What are you doing for Christmas, Aunty Peg?' Ella asked her as they walked home through the wet streets, hurrying between the circles of light cast by the street lights.

'How – how do you mean?'

'Well, do you go to friends – or what?'

'Er, no. I shall be on my own.'

'Oh, that's awful,' said Janice, whose own home at Christmas was open house to family, friends, anyone who fancied dropping in. 'Rough and ready,' her mother always laughed. 'But ya allus welcome.' Janice couldn't imagine anyone being entirely alone at Christmas.

Horrified too, Ella stood still, and because her arm was firmly linked through Peggy's, the older woman was obliged to stop too. Ella peered at her through the gloom. 'On your own!' Her tone was scandalized.

'Well, yes. I – I have been for the last six years, ever since . . .' She left the words unspoken, but Ella knew exactly what she meant.

'Well, you're not going to be on your own this year. You're to come to us at Fleethaven Point.'

'But will your gran mind? Shouldn't you ask her first?'

'Course she won't mind,' Ella said, quashing any niggling doubts of her own. Besides, she thought, Grandpa would love to see his sister and her grandmother would agree to anything he wanted.

Arriving home she ran at once to find her grandfather. 'Will Gran mind?'

'Of course not. It was a lovely idea of yours. Fancy poor old Peg being on her own every year since . . . I never thought. We should have asked her over long ago.'

Ella doubted, however, that in the early days her grandmother would have agreed; she might have thought

Ella would stow away in Peggy's suitcase to get back to the city.

After her initial surprise, Esther was as enthusiastic as the other two. 'If only we'd known, Jonathan, she could have come every year. I've always liked ya sister, even when . . .' She glanced at him and seemed to bite back the words, adding instead, 'Well – always.'

It was the happiest Christmas Ella could remember since before her mother died. On Christmas morning, she could hardly wait for her grandmother to open her present. Esther's cheeks were pink with pleasure. 'Is this what they wear in the city? It's a mite cold for winter nights in a draughty old farmhouse.' She laughed as she held up the black shimmering nightdress, holding it against herself and swaying to and fro, provocatively.

'It's for special occasions,' Ella heard her grandfather say softly and touched Esther's hand. Ella saw the look which passed between the couple and yet again she felt as if she were outside in the cold, her nose pressed to the window, looking in on a scene of love and warmth and being needed, of belonging.

Once – how long ago it seemed now – she had been loved like that, by her mother.

Was there anyone in the world now who would one day love and need her again?

Seventeen

'Why can't I go? It's only to the pictures, for heaven's sakes.'

'Watch your tongue, Missy!' Her grandmother wagged her finger in Ella's rebellious face. 'You haven't done your homework.'

'Gran, it's Friday night. I've got all weekend to do my homework.'

'Ya grandpa needs some help with the spring sowing at Top End tomorrow. He'll need you to walk behind the drill.'

'I'd sooner drive the tractor,' the girl muttered. 'Besides, I can help him in the daytime and do my homework at night or on Sunday.'

Her grandmother sniffed. "Tis the Lord's day. We dun't work on a Sunday.'

Slyly, Ella said, 'Grandpa does. He mended the tractor last Sunday.'

'That's different.'

'Why is it?'

'Dun't argue with me, Missy. And don't go getting round ya grandpa to let you go. He's not well.'

If there was anything calculated to make Ella give up her planned evening out, it was a reference to her grandfather's lack of strength over the past few weeks. He seemed to be suddenly much older. His hair, now almost completely white, was thin and wispy, and his skin seemed to hang loosely on his frame, which stooped more noticeably. But his eyes twinkled as merrily as ever and his smile still crinkled the lines around his eyes.

Ella eyed her grandmother sharply. She knew the older woman was not above playing on her sympathies, yet loving her grandfather as she did, Ella dare not take the risk of gambling with his well-being.

'All right, Gran,' she said firmly, out-staring Esther. 'You win, but only 'cos of Grandpa.'

'And what's because of Grandpa, might I ask?'

Deep in their argument, neither Esther nor Ella had heard Jonathan step through the back door and come to stand behind them in the kitchen doorway.

They turned to look at him, and Ella noticed, at once, the sweat standing in beads on his forehead, the dark stains under his arms and down the front of his shirt, and yet the early spring day was not that warm. His face looked grey with tiredness.

'I'll make you some tea, Grandpa,' Ella smiled at him and lifted the kettle from the hob and took it out into the scullery to fill it.

'She wants to go gadding out to the pictures tonight with Rob and the Souters,' she heard her grandmother telling him. 'I've said no. There's work to be done.'

The deep rumble of his voice answered her. 'Let the lass have some fun Esther.'

'Fun? Fun, you say. Just 'cos I gave in at Christmas, she reckons it's the high life for her now. Well, she's got another think coming. They don't know the meaning of work, these young 'uns.'

'You'll lose her, Esther. You'll drive her away—'

'Like I drove our Lilian away, I suppose? She never lifted a hand's turn about the farm.'

'You worked her in other ways. Wanted her to better herself.'

'Oh, so it's my fault now she's got so snooty, is it? That she looks down on all of us. We're not good enough for our Lilian the school-marm now, a' we? Never comes near us, does she? We could drop dead in our tracks for all she cares. 'Spect she'll be the same.'

Coming back into the kitchen with the kettle, Ella noticed her grandfather lean his head back wearily against the wooden chair and close his eyes.

'Who's she? The cat's mother?'

'None of your sauce, Missy,' Esther snapped back.

'Don't go on, Gran,' Ella said, forcing a cheeriness, though she was worried now by the sight of her grandfather's fatigue.

'Don't you be so cheeky, Missy, else . . .'

Ella placed the kettle on the fire and turned to face Esther. 'Don't worry, Gran. I'll not go tonight and I'll be up bright and early to help Grandpa tomorrow.'

'You go out tonight, love, if you want to,' he began.

'It's all right, honest, Grandpa. I'll just nip across to Rob's, though, so they don't wait for me.'

She left the kitchen and was about to step out of the back door when she heard her grandfather's voice again. She paused, listening, and then was sorry she had done so for her grandmother's reply brought back all the hurt from years ago.

'You're too hard on the girl, Esther,' he was saying. 'She's a good little lass, willing and helpful.'

And then came the words Ella wished she had not heard. 'She's a right to be,' Esther snapped. 'It's not everyone of my age would take in their daughter's bastard to bring up.'

Ella clutched the door jamb and closed her eyes, screwing them up tightly against the hurt.

'Esther, love,' her grandfather's deep voice came

reproachfully. 'I know you had a rough upbringing under your aunt's harsh ways, but don't do the same thing to Ella. Don't drive her to walk out, like you did.'

Ella moved on out of the back door and walked slowly across the yard. What did her grandpa mean? Don't do the same thing to Ella? What was 'the same thing'?

She was tired of all the hints and innuendos about the past, *her* past. Ever since she had first come here, had been forced by circumstances to stay here, her grandmother had never once answered her probing questions; indeed, often, she had become angry. The words Ella had overheard just now had been like the proverbial 'last straw'. It was time she found out what all the secrets were; high time she started asking questions *and* getting some answers.

But who could she ask?

Biting her lip thoughtfully, she walked round to the front of the house, squeezed through the hole in the hedge and was soon flying round the edge of the field, no longer a meadow but where tomorrow they would plant the spring wheat, and across the plank bridge towards Rookery Farm.

Grandma Eland might know. She'd ask her.

He was driving the tractor into the yard at Rookery Farm.

'Rob,' she called, and waved, shading her eyes against the late afternoon sun dropping low in the western sky. He parked the tractor in the Dutch barn and cut the engine. Then he leapt down and they moved towards each other.

'I can't come tonight,' Ella told him, pulling a face. 'Gran says no.'

She felt him looking at her closely, as he said, 'There's

more to it than that. Her saying no has never stopped you before. You usually come anyway and take what's comin' later. So, come on – tell.'

She pushed her hands into the pockets of her trousers and scuffed at the cobbles on the yard with the toe of her plimsoll.

'She says it's because Grandpa's not too well. He does seem very tired and – and I daren't call her bluff. Not this time.'

'Oh, well, if that's the case, then fair enough. Besides, your gran wouldn't say it just to stop you going.'

Ella glanced at him and smiled to herself. There he went again, sticking up for her grandmother. He'd never altered in his admiration for Esther Godfrey, 'the Missus at Brumbys' Farm', and he wouldn't hear a word said against her. Ella said nothing to disillusion him but she wasn't quite sure she agreed with him; not in this instance anyway.

'So you'll tell Janice and Jimmy?'

'Oh, if you don't come I don't think I'll go either. It's only a war film. I'm not that bothered about it. Besides, it'll come again sometime.'

Ella giggled. 'Janice won't like that,' she murmured.

'Eh?' Rob looked startled. 'What you on about? The film, d'ya mean?'

'No, Bumpkin. The fact that you're not going. Janice has a "thing" about you.'

He stared at her. 'Janice? Don't be daft.'

Her grin widened. 'I'm not. Ever since we were ten, when I first came here.'

'Oh, come off it. At ten? Why, I wasn't giving girls a thought, then.'

'Oh, I know that!' She put her head on one side. 'Changed a bit now, though, eh?'

He had the grace to look sheepish.

'I've always had the feeling,' Ella went on slowly, 'that Janice only befriended me at the start to get closer to you.' She frowned, a half-forgotten memory nudging at her mind. 'I seem to remember her saying something about our families being related. I didn't take a lot of notice at the time. I was too upset about Mum and having to come and live here. I did ask Gran once, but I got my head snapped off – as usual!' Ella lifted her head and looked at him. 'Do you know anything about it?'

'Me?' He looked startled. 'Why should I know? The old 'uns don't tell us much about owt that went on, d'they now?'

'Worse than that,' Ella said wryly. 'They shut up like a clam when you ask them anything.'

'Well, you're such a nosey little blighter. Can you blame them?' Then he paused and frowned more thoughtfully. 'You know, now you mention it, there was something that, well, bothered me for a while . . .'

'What?'

'It was when I first saw your mam and my dad together. They seemed – well – very friendly. *Too friendly*.'

Ella gaped at him. Such a thing had never entered her mind. From childhood she had seen the affection between her mother and Uncle Danny every time he had visited them in Lincoln and she had accepted it as being perfectly natural.

The idea that there was anything wrong in it had never entered her head.

'Mind you,' Rob was saying, 'Me mam didn't seem to bother, so I just thought it must be okay. And then, of course . . .' He left the words unspoken, for they both remembered that only a few days later, Kate had been drowned.

Ella said slowly, 'Your dad was dreadfully upset at her funeral though, wasn't he?'

Rob nodded and his troubled brown gaze met her candid blue eyes.

'I wonder . . . ?' she murmured.

'What?' he prompted.

'If your grandma would tell us?'

He pulled a face and shrugged. 'Ya can ask her, but whether she'll tell you owt, now that's another matter. And I should tread very carefully, if I was you. She gets very agitated if you ask questions. I was asking her about me grandad once. I was only interested 'cos I'm called after him. He was Robert Eland an' all.'

'He was killed in the pub at the Point, wasn't he, when the bomb dropped on it?'

He nodded. 'Yeah, but when I said, "Tell me about me grandad", d'you know, she started crying and I had to leave off.'

'Perhaps it still upsets her to think about him,' Ella suggested. 'Anyway, I'll be careful what I say.'

Grandma Eland was sitting in an easy chair in the living room, dozing in front of a blazing fire. Her large bulk filled the chair, her head lolling against the back. Her mouth was open and her upper false teeth had dropped and were slightly askew in her mouth. She was snoring very gently.

Ella stood uncertainly in the room, debating whether to tiptoe out again without disturbing her. Perhaps, if she waited a few moments, Grandma Eland would wake up. Ella sat down in the chair on the opposite side of the fire, but the heat soon became too much against her cheek and she moved away to the other side of the room and leant against the sideboard.

She glanced around the room; it was a cosy little sitting room where Rob's grandmother spent most of her time now, dozing, knitting or reading. It seemed a dull life to Ella's mind, totally different from that of her own gran who was on the go from six in the morning until ten at night, and yet Grandma Eland seemed contented enough. She had her family close by, all her own belongings around her, her memories. Ella's glance took in the pictures on the wall, the ornaments on the mantelpiece, the shabby furniture that had served a lifetime. Behind her, the carved wooden cuckoo clock whirred as a prelude to striking and then the tiny door flapped open and the bird appeared, 'cuckoo-ed' five times and shot back in again, the door snapping shut. Grandma Eland snored on. Ella smiled and turned to look at the clock standing on its white, lace-edged runner on the sideboard behind her. On either side were framed photographs: one of Uncle Danny in RAF uniform and a family group taken on Danny and Rosie's wedding day. The bride was slim and very pretty, dressed in a costume with a spray of flowers pinned to her lapel and carrying a small bouquet. No white wedding in wartime, Ella thought sympathetically, as she bent to look closer. There were Danny and Rosie in the centre with Grandma Eland to one side. Standing next to her was a serious-looking man, with a full beard covering so much of his face that it was difficult to see his expression. That must be Rob's grandad, she thought, the man he was named after – Robert Eland. She remembered being told that he had been killed only a few days after the wedding, when Danny and Rosie were away on honeymoon. Poor man, Ella thought. When that picture had been taken, he had only a few more days to live. On the other side of the bride and groom in the photograph stood Walter and Enid Maine, Rosie's parents, and behind them . . . Now that was strange, Ella thought, she was sure it was her own gran and grandpa. She scanned the tiny faces in the picture once more, but there was no sign of the one person she had expected to see there – her own mother, Kate. But fancy her gran attending an Eland wedding!

Her gaze flickered over the other pictures and came to rest on a silver-framed one at the very back. The photograph, sepia and faded with age, was of a young man in an old-fashioned uniform, standing very stiffly, his legs bound tightly knee to ankle. The jacket, buttoned up to his throat, looked tight and uncomfortable and in his eyes, staring straight at the camera, there was a strange look; not exactly fear, Ella decided, but certainly apprehension. He was not very tall, but stockily built and, though it was difficult to tell from the faded image, his hair looked to be dark and curling. Although the picture was obviously old, the young man's face staring out at her reminded Ella of Rob.

Ella frowned thoughtfully. The picture was vaguely familiar but she couldn't remember having looked at all Grandma Eland's treasured photographs before and yet . . . Maybe as a child, she had seen them and forgotten. She was turning away, when the door opened and Rosie came in carrying a tray.

'There now, I've brought you both a cup o' tea and a slice of plum bread.' Her glance took in the still-sleeping Grandma Eland. Setting the tray on a small table, she moved towards the old lady.

'Don't disturb her, Aunty Rosie,' Ella said softly, but Rosie only laughed and said, 'It's high time she was awake anyway. It's almost tea time.'

Ella watched as Rosie touched the old woman's shoulder. 'Come on, Grandma. Wakey-wakey. Ella's come to see you.'

As Grandma Eland lifted her head and blinked, Ella thought again how much older she looked than her own grandmother and yet they must be about the same age. Beth Eland's hair was almost completely white, long and pulled back into a bun at the nape of her neck. Her face was round and on her fat cheeks were little red veins. She gasped as she heaved herself upright, straightened her dentures and said, 'Why, Ella love, how nice.'

'I've brought you a cup o' tea,' Rosie said. 'You can sit and have a nice little chat.'

'I can't stay long,' Ella perched on the chair at the side of the fire again and began to pour out the tea, 'I promised Gran, but I just wanted to ask you something.'

She looked across at the old woman. What had they both been like, Esther and Beth, when they'd been young girls? 'I – I just wondered. Did you know my gran when she was young?'

The smile on the round face before her faded; the open, loving look in the dark eyes became wary. Beth's hands, lying in her lap, became suddenly agitated, the fingers twisting together. 'Why – why do you want to know?' Her voice was only a whisper.

Ella shrugged. 'There's something funny. Some sort of – of – mystery.'

She heard the old lady draw in a sharp breath, saw the old eyes widen with a look of fear in their depths.

'I'm sorry. I didn't mean to upset you, but – but I just wondered if you knew what my grannie was like as a young girl. Who brought her up? She sort of – well – hints that she had an unhappy childhood. She seems very bitter, yet when I ask her she shuts up like a clam and won't tell me anything.'

'Oh, that!' The relief on Beth's face was immediately apparent. 'Oh, well, I can't tell you much, love.' The smile was back on her shiny round face, the fear gone from her eyes in an instant. 'All I know is that she'd been brought up by her aunt. Her mam had died when she – ya gran, that is – was born. And, by all accounts, the aunt just used her as a skivvy to help look after her own large family. About seven kids, I think she had; it was a lot anyway. Esther walked out one night when she was about sixteen . . .' Beth was looking at her, but now her eyes had misted over and she seemed to be seeing pictures from the past rather than the young girl sitting in front of her. 'About the age you are now. She came here to find work with old Sam Brumby.'

'Brumby?' Ella said quickly. 'Sam Brumby? Is that why the farm's called Brumbys' Farm?'

'Aye.' Beth nodded. 'His family had been tenants of the old squire's family for generations. But when Sam died there was no one left to carry it on. And Esther wanted that farm. Oh, how Esther Everatt wanted that farm!'

Suddenly there was a flash of fire in the old eyes, a spurt of red anger in her rounded cheeks. 'She didn't care what she did to get it neither . . .' Her hands, the veins standing out sharply on the back, grasped the chair arms. 'Didn't care who she hurt . . .'

'Hurt? What do you mean? Who did she hurt?'

'Eh? Oh . . .' With a start Beth seemed to come back to the present, became aware of exactly what she was saying to Ella. 'Oh – I – er – I shouldn't be telling you all this. It's water under the bridge now, child. It doesn't matter any more.'

Suddenly tired, the old lady leant back in the chair and closed her eyes. 'It doesn't matter any more,' she whispered again. But Ella had the uncomfortable feeling that it still mattered very much – whatever it was. And not only to Beth Eland. The shutters were down once more; Ella could probe no further even though she had not yet asked whether their two families were related somehow.

If all the secrecy and mystery were anything to go by, there were several people around here who were still haunted by the past, events that had shaped their lives and still echoed down the years from generation to generation.

Eighteen

The roaring noise came closer. Ella stood up from where she had been bending over the milking machine and caught her grandfather's glance.

'What on earth . . .?' he began, and then, grimacing a little as he eased his aching limbs into an upright position, they went out of the cowshed together. On the seat of the Ferguson tractor parked near the barn wall, Tibby stood up, his back arched, his fur fluffing out. Ella moved across to him. 'It's all right, Tibs, it won't hurt you.'

Tibby, at six years old, had grown into a large, sleek cat, showing a deceptive idleness that disappeared with the twitch of a whisker at the appearance of a mouse or young rat. Neutered, he displayed a condescending disinterest in the female of the species and seemed to spend his time either relaxing in the sun on summer days, stretched out in the yard in the shade of the pump or, in winter, curled up on the peg rug in front of the range, until shooed out by Esther when he got under her feet.

'Useless, lazy animal,' Esther would mutter, and Ella would smile to herself and tickle Tibby under his chin until he stretched out his neck, closed his eyes and purred blissfully. He spurned the attentions of anyone except Ella; only for her was there ever a welcome. He would walk across the yard to greet her, placing his white-tipped paws carefully one in front of the other as he moved, his tail straight up, but the end crooked like a question mark.

Now, under Ella's touch, his fear subsided and he sat down again, curling his tail around himself and across his paws.

But his huge green eyes were watchful.

The noise was coming closer. Ella shaded her eyes and looked up the lane towards the town. 'It's a motorbike,' she said. 'But who . . .?'

'One of the summer visitors from the town, I expect.' Jonathan was about to turn away to go back into the shed, when the machine came hurtling round the last bend in the lane and into view.

'Oh, no, it isn't,' Ella said, excitedly, 'it's Rob!'

'Rob?' Jonathan turned back, his interest at once re-kindled. 'Rob on a motorbike?'

But Ella was already running towards the farm gate and leaning over it as, the engine throbbing loudly, Rob pulled up and manoeuvred the motorcycle round to stop near the gate. He turned off the ignition and the engine spluttered and died. He was grinning like a Cheshire cat, his white teeth gleaming, his brown eyes sparkling.

Jonathan came and stood beside Ella, resting his arms on the top of the gate. His eyes sparked with mischief as he said, 'And where did you get that from, young feller?'

The young man's grin widened. 'It's mine, Mester Godfrey. I've been saving hard and me dad said he'd put the rest to it for me birthday.' He looked at Ella. 'I've come to take you for a spin.'

She was climbing the gate, not bothering to open it, her leg thrown over the top, when her grandfather said, 'Hold on a minute. You're not supposed to carry anyone else until you've passed your test, are you?' He pointed at the red L plates emblazoned on the front and rear of the machine.

'Well, no, but no one'll see us on these quiet lanes.'

'That's not the point, Rob, and you know it.'

'Oh, Grandpa,' Ella said, 'don't be such a killjoy.' And she jumped down on the other side of the gate and swung her leg over the pillion, and, seating herself comfortably, wrapped her arms around Rob's waist.

'Well, don't say I didn't warn—' her grandfather was saying, but his admonishment was lost as Rob trod hard on the kickstart and the engine leapt into life once more.

The bike roared along the Point road. Ella was exhilarated, sharing the thrill of high speed, the feel of Rob's jacket against her cheek, the warmth of his body close to hers while the wind streamed through their hair, biting their faces. On the outskirts of town, he slowed down and turned in a circle, saying over his shoulder, 'Best not get caught, else ya grandpa'll be proved right.'

Ella laughed, the wind whipping away her words. Back along the Point road, leaning to left and right as the road curved, she followed his lead, fearless even when the bike seemed to drop so low they must surely keel over.

When they came to the junction in the lane, he turned to the right and took the road inland towards Rookery Farm, but they roared past the farm gate and on up the lane towards the Grange.

'Let's go and show the Souters, eh?' he shouted to her.

Behind his back, Ella pulled a face; she was enjoying there being just the two of them, but the boy in the young man wanted to show off his new toy to their friends.

During the last five years, the four of them had gone everywhere together. They had played together, gone to school together and, as time passed, had gone out together, to the cinema and parties, to the funfair on the sea-front in Lynthorpe in the summer, but always in a foursome, never pairing off into two by two. Just lately, however, Ella had the feeling that Janice was once again becoming possessive over Rob. Whereas Ella was still a tomboy, still happiest in trousers and a T-shirt, Janice pored over the fashion magazines and was forever cutting and sewing her clothes in an effort to copy the latest vogue. She still had long hair but twisted it up into all sorts of styles, a different one each day.

They roared along the lane, past Rookery Farm, skirted the deserted Grange and took the road that led south-westwards towards the Souters' Farm.

As he pulled into the yard, a mangy dog began barking.

'Keep that thing away from me,' Ella muttered, as she slid from the pillion seat. 'Else I'll start sneezing my head off.' She looked around her. She rarely came to the Souters' Farm; it always seemed as if Janice and Jimmy came to them, to Rookery Farm or even to Brumbys'. Usually they congregated at Rob's home; Aunty Rosie was much more welcoming than either Mrs Souter or Ella's grandmother.

The place looked just the same as always: the yard of Souters' Farm was littered with all manner of implements and bits of machinery, most of it in rusting heaps. Hens wandered freely about the yard, scratching and pecking and making that call peculiar to the domestic hen which always sounded to Ella as if they were complaining.

Mrs Souter came to the back door. 'Shuddup,' she yelled at the dog, which immediately ceased barking, dropped its head and slunk back towards its dilapidated kennel, casting doleful eyes at the woman.

'Hello, you two. Looking for our Jimmy?' The woman was middle-aged, but looked years older. Her grey hair was lank and greasy-looking and her wrap-around apron was permanently stained around her ribs where she constantly wiped her grimy hands. A cigarette hung from the corner of her mouth and she screwed up her eyes against the drifting smoke.

'Hello, Mrs S,' Rob shouted in greeting. 'Yeah, is he here?'

The woman sniffed, removed the cigarette from her mouth, passed the back of her hand across her nose and then replaced the cigarette. 'Naw. Gone gallivanting into town . . .'

Ella almost giggled aloud. It was what her grandmother might have said too.

'. . . and our Janice. Dolled up to the nines. Be gettin' 'ersen into trouble, that one. I keeps warning her. But does she tek any notice?'

She sniffed again. 'Still,' she added, her glance flitting between them, 'she'll not be the first from these parts, nor the last, I reckon. Though I've telled her if she brings trouble to this door I'll chuck her out.' And now her glance came to rest upon Ella. 'Aye, an' that's been done 'afore, hereabouts.'

'Right you are, Mrs S,' Rob said cheerily, and turned back towards his motorcycle. 'Come on, Ella, we'll see if we can find 'em.'

'If ya do,' the woman's shrill voice came after them, 'ya can tell our Janice to be in by ten, else I'll scutch 'er backside for 'er.'

As the bike throbbed into life again, scattering the hens, Rob called over his shoulder. 'We'll tek the back road to town, but hang on. It's twisty.'

Ella, wrapping her arms tightly around his waist, clung to him as the bike leant over, first to the left then to the right as Rob negotiated the corners of the winding lane.

They were in open countryside with fields on either side, heading towards the main road that would take them into Lynthorpe when, rounding a corner, the machine, leaning heavily over, began to slide on some loose gravel at the edge of the lane. The wheels slipped from under them and they slid helplessly towards the grass verge. When the wheels hit the edge, they were both thrown from the bike, Ella to land on the grass, but Rob towards a gatepost.

Ella heard a thump and a yell and then, as the engine spluttered and died, there was silence.

'Rob – Rob!' Ella scrambled to her feet and rushed to where he lay at the foot of the post, clutching his stomach.

'What happened?' she asked. 'I didn't see.'

For several moments, he could not speak. The breath had been knocked from his body and he was panting and groaning at the same time. At last he gasped, 'I – landed – up against the – gatepost.'

'Oh no!'

He was rolling in agony. But the fact that he was moving was a good sign, she told herself. Practical in an emergency, she said, 'Do you think you've broken anything?'

He shook his head but his face was screwed up with pain. 'No, just ripped me guts to bits.'

She looked down then, half expecting to see blood gushing from his stomach. 'Let's see.'

'No – no,' he stuttered and, still doubled up, tried to roll over on to his knees. He stayed in a kneeling position, but bending forward. 'Are you hurt?'

Ella looked down at herself. 'Only grazed me leg a bit.' She pulled a face and added, 'And a rip in my trousers that'll please Gran no end. I'm all right, it's you. Come on.'

'You – go. Get away.'

'Go? Whatever for? I'm not leaving you here like this.'

He flapped his hand at her. 'If – anyone comes. A policeman – or – or anyone. I'll get done.'

'What for? Having an accident?'

'No – no.' Every word was a gasping agony. 'For 'aving you on the back.'

'Oh,' she said, as realization of what her grandfather had meant dawned and again she said, 'Oh, yes.' Then she thought a bit and added, 'But I'm still not going, so there. If anyone comes along they won't know I was on the back, now will they?'

He groaned. 'Bit obvious, in't it? Out here, miles from anywhere.'

Ella shrugged. 'They couldn't prove it. Come on,' she said, holding out her hand. 'Let's get you up.'

'Ooh-er,' he moaned. 'I don't think I'll ever be able to walk straight again.'

Ella glanced around her. The walls of Rookery Farm blinked white in the sunlight only a couple of fields away but it was over a mile round by the road. 'Shall I fetch your dad? He might bring the car round for you.'

Rob began to laugh and then found it too painful. 'Ouch! No, he won't. He'll only say it serves me right.'

Ella smiled wryly, imagining that her grandmother and possibly even her grandfather too, on this occasion, would say the same.

'Come on, then,' she said. 'We'll have to walk.'

She went towards the bike and pulled it upright, stronger than her thin frame looked. 'I'll push your precious bike for you.'

He snorted and then grimaced with pain. 'Precious? Huh, I don't care if I never see the bloody thing again.'

'It wasn't the bike's fault now, was it?' she chided him reasonably and smiled at him. 'Besides, you'll feel differently in a day or two.'

As he hauled himself gingerly to his feet, gasping with every movement, and began to walk, bent over like an old man of ninety, Ella wondered whether perhaps he really meant what he said.

It took more than a few days for Rob to want to look at his bike. He spent three days in bed and, as they had both predicted, got not a scrap of sympathy from anyone.

'Well, I didn't want him to have a motorbike anyway,' Rosie said. 'They're dangerous. But it was his dad encouraged him. Like a couple of kids, they are, with machines. And your grandad's no better.' Rosie wagged her finger at Ella.

Ella pulled a face but said nothing. This time even her grandad had been stern. 'I told you not to go on the pillion. You hear me, Ella? You keep off that bike till he's passed his test properly.'

Ella hung her head and averted her eyes, but made no promise; she didn't like making promises she had no intention of keeping.

Nineteen

Through the latter half of May and into June came the exams. Rob and Ella sat a few desks away from each other in the school hall, the hot sun streaming through the long windows. Afterwards, they met to discuss the papers and rejoice or commiserate in turn.

'It's a relief to get out at night and into the fields to help with the haymaking,' Rob muttered. 'All this swotting isn't really my scene.'

'You want to go on to college, though, don't you?' Ella teased.

'That's different. That's farming.'

'Oh, you!' she said, and punched him playfully on the shoulder.

A week later, he said, 'We're all off up the coffee bar in town to celebrate the end of exams. You coming?'

'Right then. I'll ask Grandpa.'

Ella was getting crafty now. She had found that if she asked her grandfather first and he said yes then her grandmother, though she might not agree, never countermanded his approval.

Ella put her head on one side and regarded Rob. 'Can I have a lift, though?'

He pulled a face. 'Not right into town. I don't take my test till next week and I don't want to get caught.'

'That's okay. Drop me off at the end of the Point Road and I'll walk the rest.'

He looked doubtful. 'It's a long way right into town even from there.'

She threw back her head and laughed. 'I've got used to it now. It's a long time since I was able to hop on a bus just when I want.'

'See you later, then,' he said, and kick started the motorbike, the engine throbbing in the quietness of the countryside. She leant on the gate and watched him ride away, the noise of the bike's engine audible all the way to Rookery Farm. She smiled fondly and then sighed. Oh, but he was good-looking; with his black hair slicked back now with Brylcreem and the black blazer he wore with shiny brass buttons. Dark brown eyes and always a big grin on his face, he was still the merry, friendly lad he had always been. No wonder all the girls were after him.

She glanced down at herself and sighed. And no wonder the boys weren't after her. She was always dressed in a check shirt and trousers. Her hair, though curly, was still cut very short and she hadn't the money to experiment with make-up like Janice did. But then, Janice was earning. When Ella had suggested that she might take a Saturday job in the summer, helping out in a candy-floss stall in the amusement park on the sea-front, Esther's reply had been the same as always. 'Ya needed here.'

Ella turned from the gate and glanced across the flat expanse of fields towards Rookery Farm remembering what Grandma Eland had told her. 'Ya gran was treated like a skivvy when she was a young lass until she walked out and came here.'

As if on cue her grandmother's voice sounded across the yard. 'Come on, Missy. 'Ave ya nothing better to do than stand there day-dreaming? There's the butter-making to do.'

Ella looked at the woman, still remarkably slim, standing in the doorway. Left home, had she? And at about my age, Ella mused. Just walked out and left her home and family. Ella screwed up her mouth thoughtfully. One day, she thought, I might just do the same.

'I know your little game, Missy. Always asking ya grandpa first so's I can't say no. I weren't born yesterday. Well, ya can go this time but in future you ask me. You hear?'

Ella faced her. 'Why are you so against me having even a bit of fun? It's not as if I'm always asking to go out. Once a week at the most. Rob goes out nearly every night.'

'Then more fool his mam and dad for letting him.'

'Why? Where's the harm?'

'Ya'll come to no good. Staying out till all hours.'

'Ten o'clock? All hours? Oh, Gran, really! Why, Janice Souter stays out till midnight and—'

Esther wagged her finger in Ella's face. 'Dun't give me that. The Souters' way of going on is nowt to be bragging about.'

Ella stared back at her grandmother. 'Well, Mrs Souter tries to stop her, but she can't manage it. Janice stays out anyway.'

'Well, dun't you think you can try that with me, Missy.'

Esther turned away, satisfied to have made her point, complacent that Ella would not dare to disobey her, so she did not see the narrowing of the girl's eyes and the scheming look on her face.

'Where are we going, then?' Ella leant back in her chair and smiled at the other three as they stared at her in amazement.

'Eh?'

'Didn't you ought to be getting home? It's quarter to ten, y'know.' This from Rob whilst Ella saw the slow smile spreading across Janice's face.

'At last!' the girl murmured. 'I wondered just how long it would take you to rebel against the old biddy.'

'What? What are you on about?' Jimmy, confused, glanced from one to the other.

'She's going to stay out – late!' Janice said in a stage-whisper.

'Has ya gran said ya can?' Rob asked.

'No.'

'Then come on,' he said, pushing the empty espresso coffee cup away from him and getting up, 'I'm taking you home.'

Janice laughed. 'Go on, Ella, be a devil and stay out late. Real late. Till at least eleven!'

'Shut it, Janice,' Rob said evenly. 'I'm helping with haymaking at Brumbys'. I dun't want me ears boxed by 'er gran when I get there tomorrow.'

'I reckon you're as frightened of that old witch as she is.'

'I'm not frightened of her,' Ella shot back, 'but I just don't want her stopping me going out altogether.'

'Exactly!' Janice laughed. '*My* mother couldn't stop me if she wanted to. See what I mean?'

'Come on, Ella. Let's go,' Rob said.

'I – I'm not coming.'

'Oh, yes, you are.'

'No, I'm not.'

Janice, a gleeful expression on her face, glanced backwards and forwards from one to the other. 'This is better than a pantomime,' she murmured, whilst Jimmy just muttered, 'I wish someone would tell me what the heck is going on.'

'Look, Ella, dun't be daft,' Rob tried to reason. 'If ya mek ya gran real mad, she'll stop ya coming out at all.'

'I reckon she's going to anyway. She's threatened as much tonight.'

He sat down heavily beside her again and spread his hands trying to reason with her. 'Look, you'll only make matters worse. At the moment ya grandpa's on your side, but if you stay out late, then you'll lose his support an' all.'

'So? If that happens then I'll leave. I'll walk out. Just like *she* did when she was my age.'

'Run away, ya mean?' Jimmy said, catching on at last.

'Where'd you run to?' Janice's tone was disbelieving.

'Back to Lincoln,' Ella said promptly. 'Back to live with my aunty Peggy.'

Janice blinked, nonplussed. She had not expected such a confident answer; one that had obviously already been thought out. 'Well, if ya do go, let me know, 'cos I'll come with ya.'

Slowly Rob shook his head and let out his breath, which he seemed to have been holding. 'Well, it's up to you,' he said, getting up again. 'But I want no part of it. I like ya gran. I always have. And there's no way I'm going to help you upset her. So, night-night, all. I'm off home. See ya.'

'Hey,' Ella called after him, standing up suddenly and knocking the table, causing the coffee still left in the cups to slosh from side to side. 'Wait a minute! How'm I supposed to get home if you go now?'

From the doorway he turned back, raised his hand in farewell and shrugged his broad shoulders. 'That's your problem. If you're such a big girl now that you can defy ya gran and stay out till all hours—'

'You even sound like her!' Ella flared back at him.

He took no notice but went on, 'Then ya big enough to find ya own way home.'

Whistling loudly, he went through the door, letting it swing to behind him, and walked across the pavement to his motorbike propped up near the kerb. She watched as he bent and lifted his crash helmet and gloves from one of the red wooden panniers on either side at the rear of the bike. Pulling them on, he threw his right leg over the bike and eased it up off its stand.

'Oh, damn!' she muttered crossly. 'I'll have to go. I'll get stranded if I don't.'

'I thought you'd give in,' Janice smirked. 'Poor old Cinder-Ella! Even she stayed till the clock struck twelve.'

'He's going, El,' Jimmy put in and Ella snatched up her bag and ran for the door.

'Rob – wait! Rob!'

Someone had put a coin in the juke-box and the voice of Bill Haley reverberated through the coffee bar, drowning her words. She pulled open the door and ran out into the street.

He had been pulling away from the pavement but happened to look back to see her running towards him. His toes touching the road, he balanced the bike as she climbed on to the back. Then he revved the engine and they roared away into the night.

It was a clear, starlit night as they drove along the coast road. The sound of his motorbike could, no doubt, be heard for miles across the flat fields, echoing through the darkness, louder at night in the stillness.

As he pulled into the yard at Brumbys' Farm, he cut the engine and in the silence he said softly, 'I'm glad you decided to come home.'

Morosely, she muttered, 'I didn't have a lot of choice. I suppose you think you've won, don't you?'

'Won? Oh, Ella, it isn't a game, a competition. Ya gran's only trying to take care of you. She cares about you.'

'Huh! Pull the other one. She only took me in out of duty and she never lets me forget it.'

The back door opened and, in the light streaming from the back scullery, the subject of their conversation stood in silhouette.

'Ya late,' was her only greeting. 'It's nearly half past ten.'

The two young people moved forward into the shaft of light.

'It was my fault, Missus,' Rob was going ahead, smiling and apologetic, yet never fawning. 'I'm sorry.'

'Ah, well, that's all right then, Boy. I know *you* wouldn't do it on purpose.' There was a pause, then suddenly, with one of her swift and unexpected changes of mood, Esther smiled and opened the door wider. 'Come in and have a bite, why don't you, Boy? We haven't seen much of you lately. How's ya mam and dad and – er – all?' Even in her most expansive mood, it seemed Esther could still not bring herself to enquire after his grandmother, Beth Eland.

But Rob merely grinned and stepped into the kitchen. 'They're all fine.' He slightly accented the 'all' but not enough to make it pointed. 'Evening, Mester.' He nodded to Jonathan who was sitting in the wooden Windsor chair beside the range, his feet just in their socks resting on the brass fender, wriggling his toes towards the warmth of the fire.

Summer and winter there was always a fire burning in the range grate and most nights would find Jonathan soothing his aches and pains in front of it.

Her fingers cupped round the mug of cocoa, Ella listened to the other three talking, but took no part herself. She was still smarting at having been coerced, tricked almost, into coming home at the time her grandmother stipulated.

'Well, I'd best be off mesen,' Rob said at last. 'I've to be up early in the morning to help me dad cut North Marsh Field and I'll come over in the afternoon and give you a hand here. 'Night.'

'Good night, lad,' Jonathan said, and Esther went with Rob to the back door.

Ella stood up and put her mug on the table and, giving her grandfather a swift peck on his forehead, went towards the door through the living room and to the stairs. As she moved through the adjacent room, she heard Esther come back into the kitchen and say to Jonathan, 'Eh, that lad's so like his grandad, I could almost think it was him standing there. Gives me quite a turn sometimes. Mind you, he ain't got Matthew's dark side . . . '

Ella, livid at Rob for being forced to come home so early and with Janice's teasing still rankling, heard the words but was not really listening. She was still smarting with resentment at what she considered unfair treatment.

If they treat me like a child, then I'll act like one, she thought, the streak of childish rebellion that had always been part of her nature coming to the fore once more. She slammed the door from the living room into the hall, making the china in Esther's cabinet rattle, and then she stamped up the stairs, thumping her feet on every step. She half expected Esther to arrive at the bottom of the stairs, shouting up to her and wagging her finger. But her grandmother did not appear and for once Ella felt cheated of a battle.

Haymaking was well under way and Ella was expected to help as soon as she arrived home from school. Throwing off her dark green school uniform, she was soon dressed in check shirt, trousers and rubber boots and running out to the meadows, waving to her grandpa as she ran towards him.

The tractor was stationary and he was not sitting on the seat but standing on the ground, leaning against the huge wheel, bending over slightly as if he had a pain somewhere.

'Grandpa? Grandpa, what is it?'

As he heard her voice, he straightened up and she saw the sweat glistening on his forehead.

'Nothing, lass. Just a bit of indigestion. I must have eaten my sandwiches your grannie packed up for me a bit too quick.'

Ella glanced to her left. Only a square of uncut grass in the very centre of the field remained. 'You go on back to the house, Grandpa. I can finish this field on my own.'

'Oh no, lass . . .'

'Go on, Grandpa.' She gave him a gentle little push. 'Do as I say.'

He straightened up and stretched and the smile crinkled his eyes, the lines deeply etched into his brown face. 'You sound just like your grannie.'

'Thank you very much!' Ella said in mock dismay, but she was laughing as she said it.

As she reached for the starting handle and inserted it into the front of the tractor, she glanced up to watch her grandfather crossing the field towards the gate. Her hand rested on the cool metal of the handle as she noticed with a shock how he seemed to be hobbling, his tall frame stooping. She sighed heavily. It was only the beginning of the harvesting season; hay was the first crop to be brought in, with the corn in a month or two's time.

Watching him, Ella felt her summer holidays slipping away from her. There would be no point in asking to be allowed to go to Aunty Peggy's in Lincoln; that she was needed to help this year was only too obvious even without her grandmother saying so.

Late into the summer evening as the sun slipped down in the western sky casting long shadows across the field, Ella drove the tractor up and down the field, the square of whispering grass diminishing with each swath cut.

Above the noise of the tractor, she didn't hear Rob until she glanced back at the reaper and saw him following it. He waved his arms and she pressed down the clutch and slipped the engine out of gear. She jumped down and went towards him.

'What are you doing here?'

'Come to see if you need a hand. Only I daren't get in front to catch ya eye. Ya might have run me down.' His white teeth shone through the gathering dusk as he grinned. 'I dun't trust women drivers, not even in a field.'

She slapped his arm and he reached out with his long arms and tickled her just under her ribs. She laughed and squirmed away, then her expression sobered. 'Have you been to the house? Did you see Grandpa?'

'Yeah. Why?' His tone was puzzled.

'I sent him in to rest. He looked harrowed out.'

''Arrered out! My word, Townie, you're even starting to sound like a country girl now,' he teased, then, more seriously, he added, 'He seemed all right. He was seeing to the milking.'

Ella made a noise just like her grandmother's click of exasperation. 'I might have known. Where's Gran? Isn't she making him rest?'

'Didn't see her.'

'Oh,' Ella said, then shrugged and turned away to climb back on to the tractor. 'Well, I'd better get on. If she catches me standing talking to you with the engine still running, I'll be in for it,' and added to herself as she increased the revs on the engine, 'yet again.'

Esther was waiting for her in the yard when Ella drove the tractor through the gate, with Rob perched to one side of her on the mudguard over the huge back wheel. She had unhooked the reaper and left it in the field ready for the following day when the adjacent field would be cut, but Jonathan liked the tractor to be brought back to the yard each night and put under cover in the open-sided barn.

As she walked towards her grandmother, with Rob following, she was struck suddenly by the older woman's stillness. Though she could not see Esther's face in the gathering dusk, Ella was filled with a sudden fear.

'What is it, Gran?' Something was wrong, she could sense it. Her heart began to thump painfully. 'Grandpa? Oh, it's not Grandpa?'

'No – no,' Esther said swiftly, and reached out her hand towards Ella. 'Lass – I'm sorry. It's ya cat, Tibby. Ya grandpa found him when he was takin' the cows back to the field. In the road. He – he'd been knocked down.'

Ella drew in a swift breath. 'Oh no!' Her lovely cat; the tiny kitten that Rob had given her to comfort her in the loss of her mother over six years ago now; the young cat who'd crept under the covers on her bed and nestled against her cold feet, who jumped into her lap, purring and kneading his paws against her legs, and then the grown cat, round and contented, purring a greeting every time he saw her. 'Is he . . . ?'

'No, he's not dead, but he's got a nasty bump on his head and he's hurt here.' She touched her own stomach. 'Ya grandpa thinks mebbe . . .'

First hope, and then dreadful fear, shot through Ella. 'What?'

Her grandmother sighed. 'Perhaps it would be kindest if—'

'No! You're not drowning him in the water butt. Not Tibby. I won't let you.' Ella stared at her grandmother, but in the moment of sudden terror for her pet, she failed to hear the concern in her grandmother's voice, the tenderness. 'Lass, the cat's unconscious. He's badly injured, maybe bleeding inside. We must do what is best.'

I mustn't cry, Ella told herself, at least not in front of her. Esther would despise sentiment over a cat. If she didn't cry at her own daughter's funeral then . . .

Drawing in a deep, shuddering breath, Ella clenched her jaw, and, her voice unnaturally high-pitched, saying, 'Oh well, Gran, it's only an *animal*, isn't it? And a useless, lazy one at that.'

Then the girl turned and ran round the corner of the house, through the orchard towards the hole in the hedge. Squeezing through, she ran pell-mell into the field, tears blinding her now, oblivious to the fact that she was trampling down the ripening wheat. She stumbled, tripped and fell. She gave a groan of anguish, screwed up her face, closed her eyes and gave way to a paroxysm of weeping that had as much to do with six long years of loss as with the anguish over her pet, beloved though the cat was.

She must have lain there for a long time, for when at last she rolled over and sat up, the dusk had deepened into darkness and she saw the beam from a torch wavering a few yards from her.

'Ella? Ella, where are you?'

She sniffled and tried to rub away the tears with the back of her hand. 'Here – over here.'

The corn whispered as he pushed his way through.

Flashing the beam over her just once, he tactfully turned it away and sat down beside her, the night enveloping them in its soft blackness. Without any trace of embarrassment the young man put his arm about her shoulders and hugged her to him.

'Ya shouldn't have said that to ya gran,' Rob said gently. 'She was upset at having to tell ya.'

'She's going to – to kill him.'

'No, she's not.'

She sniffed. 'What? But she said . . .'

'After you rushed off, we went and looked at Tibby again and I said I'd take him to me dad. You know how good he is with animals?'

'And she – she agreed?'

'Course she did.'

'Well, she would, wouldn't she, if it was *you* doing the asking?'

'Now don't be like that, Ella.'

'What did your dad say?'

'He reckons Tibby's stomach is very badly bruised, but there doesn't seem to be anything broken.'

'Really? Then Tibby's going to be all right?'

'Well,' he said slowly, not wanting to promise something that might not, in the end, happen, 'he got a bump on the head too, but me dad bathed it and its only a small cut. He's started to come round, but he's a bit dopey. You'd better come and have a look at him.'

She was scrambling to her feet. 'Where is he?'

'At our place. Me mam's found an old dog basket you can have. Come on, we'll go and fetch him home.'

'I'll stay up all night with him in the barn,' she said determinedly, 'whatever Gran says.'

As they went back to the edge of the field and walked around it towards Rookery Farm, through the stillness of the night, when sounds seemed to echo so plainly for some distance, they heard the sound of shouting and high-pitched laughter coming from the direction of the Point. Then the noise of several motorbike engines being started rent the air.

'Just listen to them fools revving their engines,' Rob muttered in disgust. 'They'll be using the Hump as a ramp and flying over it. Daft beggars!'

'Maybe they're the ones that – that knocked Tibby over.'

'Probably,' Rob said, resentfully, then he sighed and added, 'Though, to be fair, it could have been anyone coming down the lane. He's always hunting on the sand hills, isn't he? It could even have been me.'

'You don't go as fast as that mad lot.'

They listened to the noise of the bikes roaring up the lane towards the town, growing fainter and fainter.

'Well, I've got to admit it, we go at a fair old lick when we get on the straight, don't we?'

He walked all the way back with her to Brumbys' Farm and watched as she settled the basket into the mound of straw in the barn and sat down beside it, gently stroking Tibby's back. The cat opened one eye in a tiny slit and, very softly, there came a few purrs.

Bending over the basket, Ella felt her nose tickle and she sneezed.

Rob laughed. 'That'll be the dog hairs. It's an odd allergy you've got, ain't it?'

'Well, for once, I don't mind putting up with it, as long as Tibby gets better.'

The barn door squeaked open and Esther was standing there holding a lantern high. 'There you are. How is he?'

Rob straightened up and moved towards her. 'Dad reckons he'll be okay.'

Esther nodded and moved closer, holding the light so she could look at the injured animal.

Ella opened her mouth to tell her grandmother she would be staying with Tibby all night, but before she could do so, Esther said quietly, 'Ya can tek the basket up to ya bedroom, just till he's on the mend.' She turned away towards the door, saying over her shoulder, 'But only till then, mind.'

Ella stared after her, watching the swaying light move across the yard. She shook her head and murmured, 'If I live to be a hundred, I'll never understand that woman.'

Rob squeezed her shoulder and said, 'I keep telling you, she's all right, is your gran.' As he went towards the door, he added, 'I'll come over tomorrow and give you a hand to cut yon field.'

She had not expected him to appear the following morning, but when she went out into the yard he was already there with her grandfather, their heads bent together over the engine of the tractor. At the sound of her feet on the cinders in the yard, he glanced up and grinned at her, but as she drew closer she could see his concern for her in his brown eyes.

'Now, then? How is he?'

Her smile was broad. 'A bit better. He's had a tiny drop of milk and he seems content to lie quietly, as if he knows he ought to.'

'Sensible cat.'

'So? Who's driving?'

Rob pulled a face. 'I dun't reckon anyone is yet. We can't get her started.'

'I reckon it's the fuel pump.' Jonathan raised his head. 'I'll have to go into town and see if any of the local garages have a spare.'

'I'll go on me bike, Mester, if ya like.'

'Are you sure, lad? I mean, doesn't your father need your help today? You usually help him on a Saturday, don't you?'

'Oh yes, but I asked him last night if I could give Ella a hand today, so . . .' he grinned cheekily, stood back from the tractor and made an exaggerated, courtly bow towards her, 'I'm at your service, m'lady.'

Jonathan gave a deep chuckle. 'Go on with you, then. And take Ella with you, now you're *legally* permitted to carry a passenger,' he added pointedly.

The two youngsters glanced at each other and smiled, knowing Jonathan had guessed just how often they had broken the law on the quiet back lanes before Rob had passed his test.

'What about Gran?' Ella asked.

He waved his hand at them both, urging them to go. 'I'll see to your gran. Off you go.'

Sitting on the pillion of Rob's bike, her arms tightly around his waist, Ella pressed her body close to the arch of his back. Through the thin summer shirt he wore, she could feel every rippling movement of his muscles, feel the warmth of him.

If only, she thought suddenly, involuntarily tightening her arms about him, he would love me as I love him. Had she always loved him, she wondered. Ever since she had first met him? Even as a child? Or was it only now that she had realized, with a jolt, how she felt about Rob Eland?

For the rest of the day, when they returned from the town and the new part had been fitted to the Ferguson and Rob worked with her in the meadow cutting the grass, Ella couldn't help looking at him differently. She was quiet and guessed Rob would think she was thinking about her pet, and whilst this was, in part, the truth, it was not the sole reason for her reflective mood.

She wasn't sure whether the realization of her feelings for him brought her happiness or sadness. The knowledge that she loved him seemed always to have been there and yet only now did she formulate it into words in her own mind. It was a good feeling, to love someone like Rob, yet there was a tinge of sadness in facing the realization that it was unlikely he would ever love her in the same way. To him, she was the little orphan girl he had protected and taught the ways of the countryside; the 'Townie' he teased, yet never cruelly. She was his friend; that much she knew.

But for Ella, now, it was no longer enough.

Twenty

'Rob's asked if he can take you to a dance next Saturday in the town,' her grandmother said the following week, her tone already indicating that she might agree. Ella's hopes soared.

'A dance? Me?' Ella's wide eyes were incredulous. 'But I can't dance.'

Esther laughed. 'Neither can he, but he ses now it's something called . . . Now what did he call it, Jonathan?'

'Er . . .' Her grandfather wrinkled his forehead thoughtfully. 'Jeeving, was it?'

Ella giggled. 'No, Grandpa, jiving. I've seen it on Janice's telly.'

'Ah yes, that was it. Jiving.' He smiled at her. 'Me and your grannie thought you deserved a bit of fun. You've been a good lass this week, helping . . .' He glanced towards Esther as if willing her to back him up. Ella, too, looked at her grandmother.

'That's right.' Esther nodded. 'Ya've worked hard helping us get the hay in with ya grandpa bein' a bit under the weather.'

Ella smiled, went to her grandmother and kissed her cheek.

'Go on with you, ya daft 'aporth,' Esther said, but she was smiling and the pink tinge on her cheeks showed Ella that her unexpected action had pleased her grandmother.

Then suddenly, Ella's face fell. 'Oh, I can't go. I was forgetting . . .'

The other two looked at her. 'Why? What's the matter?'

'I . . .' she began, and stopped. She had been going to say she had no pretty dress to wear, but such a remark would be tactless after they had been generous enough to give permission, even if, as she suspected, it had been her grandfather who had done the persuading.

'I – er – I'll have to wash my trousers quick, that's all,' she faltered.

'Trousers! You can't go to a dance in trousers for heaven's sakes,' Esther began and then stared at Ella. 'Oh. Oh, I see. You haven't a dress other than ya school dresses, have ya, lass?'

'Well, er, no, Gran.'

Esther looked towards Jonathan, who, standing up, said firmly, 'Then it's high time the girl had, Esther.'

Much to Ella's surprise Esther smiled coquettishly and said, with feigned meekness, 'Yes, Jonathan.'

Ella watched as he crossed the space between himself and his wife, kissed her forehead, patted her behind and went, still chuckling, from the kitchen.

'Well, lass, if we've to mek you a dress afore Saturday night, we'd best get cracking.'

Ella could hardly believe what she was hearing. 'Do you mean it, Gran?'

Esther nodded. 'Get ya mam's sewing machine up on to the table in the living room whilst I go and ferret amongst me bits and pieces upstairs.' She came down a few moments later carrying a length of white nylon and what looked like a roll of fabric. 'This'd make you a pretty blouse, and look . . .' she pulled out the roll and there seemed to be yards and yards '. . . I bought this last summer thinking I'd mek mesen a dress for Sundays. But I've never got round to it. If ya like it, lass, ya can use this.'

The material was iced cotton, roses on a white background.

'It's lovely, Gran. But what about a pattern?'

The look on her grandmother's face was comical. 'Ah, now there you've got me. The only patterns I have are for my age group. Hardly suitable for a sixteen-year-old. Tell you what, you can bike into the town and go and choose a pattern you like. One for a blouse and one for a skirt.'

Excited now, Ella said, 'Can I get one of those that sticks out? She spread her hands round her thighs. 'They're slim at the waist and hips and then sort of puff out in a full skirt. Janice had one on last week. It was lovely.'

'Don't they need some petticoats underneath, though?'

'Oh yes.' Ella's face fell. 'Probably. I never thought of that.'

'Well, have a look on the material counter in Reynolds. When you've chosen your pattern, ask the assistant how much of that stiff net you'd need to make an underskirt with several layers.'

'Can't you come with me, Gran?'

Esther stared at her for a moment and then said slowly, 'Do you know, lass, I think I will.'

Their shopping spree into Lynthorpe was one of the happiest times Ella had ever spent with her grandmother. They returned home loaded with patterns, pink net for an underskirt and black ribbon to bind the rough edges of the net.

'Right then, lass. Ya'd better get to work.'

Though Esther had taught Ella to sew almost from the

time she had come to live at Brumbys' Farm, she had never tackled anything so complicated as this. Under her grandmother's guidance the fabrics were cut and Ella began to sew the pieces together, carefully following the instructions accompanying the paper pattern, assisted – or rather hindered – by a playful Tibby.

'Don't do that, Tibs,' Ella said, when the cat stuck his claws through the thin tissue of the pattern. 'You'll tear it.'

She could not be cross with Tibby for long: she was too thankful to see how quickly he had recovered from his injury.

'What's baste mean, Gran?' Ella asked, poring over the instruction sheet. 'I thought you did that in cooking?'

Esther laughed. 'Big tacking stitches, I think.'

Soon the white nylon blouse, a wrap-over at the front to form a V-neckline, with three-quarter length sleeves, began to take shape. The skirt was a snug-fitting basque over her slim hips and then gathered at about hip level to 'puff out', as Ella put it, into an almost circular skirt at the hem. With the layers of net she made an underskirt, carefully sewing the black ribbon round and round the hem.

'There should be a little gadget that fits on to the machine to help you keep the hems even,' Esther advised. 'Look in the little box at the side of the machine. It might be there.'

Ella took off the metal lid and scrabbled amongst the bobbins and attachments. 'Is it this one?'

'No. That's for putting a zip in.'

Again she poked about and her fingers touched a tiny object at the bottom. She picked it up and, holding it out, asked, 'What's this key for?'

Esther stared at it. 'I don't know. Probably it locks the machine. Leave it in there, anyway.'

So Ella dropped the key back into its hiding place and went on searching for the machine's gadget.

'That's the one.' Esther pointed. 'Now, take the presser-foot off and fit that one. You'll find it much easier to keep a straight line.'

Late that night, Ella was still hand-sewing the hem round the circular skirt. She yawned and rubbed her eyes. Esther came and stood in front of her. 'You go off to bed, lass. I'll finish that for you.'

'Are you sure, Gran? You have to be up early too.' In fact, her grandmother always rose at six every morning, sometimes even earlier in summer.

Esther smiled. 'Go on with you. I'll finish it.' She took the skirt from Ella, sat down and spread it across her knees.

For a moment Ella watched her grandmother's fingers working the tiny, almost invisible, stitches. 'I can see where Mum got her talent for sewing from now,' she murmured and Esther looked up to meet her gaze.

'Aye, well,' she said softly. 'I suppose skills like this get passed down the generations. It was my aunt taught me, though at the time I didn't thank her.' Esther fell silent and bent over her work.

Ella kissed the grey hair on the bowed head and turned swiftly away before either of them should feel embarrassed. 'Night then, Gran – and thank you.'

When at last Ella tried on the finished blouse and skirt and stood before the mirror on Esther's sideboard in the front parlour, standing on tiptoe to see as much of herself as she could, she could hardly recognize her own image. She smoothed her hands down the nylon of the blouse; she was even beginning to get curves in the right places and the full skirt emphasized her tiny waist. She twisted from side to side feeling the skirt and petticoats swish, but her gaze never left the mirror.

Esther said, 'It looks very nice, love. But you'll never be able to go on Rob's motorbike in that.'

'Oh no, Uncle Danny's taking us, Gran, and fetching us home. My golden coach, you know. I shall feel like Cinderella!'

'Well, just like Cinders you'll have to be home by midnight.'

'Midnight! Oh, Gran,' Ella flung her arms around the older woman. '*Thank* you. I didn't think you'd let me stay that late.'

'Well, as you're going with Rob, and Danny's fetching you in the car, I don't mind now and again.'

Ella could hardly believe the sudden change in her grandmother. But then at Esther's next words, the girl understood a little better.

'I got to thinking the other night when I was sewing ya skirt. Mebbe ya grandpa's right and I have been a bit hard on you, lass. That – that because me own childhood was – well – tough, perhaps I don't know how to have fun and I'm stopping you.'

'Oh Gran,' Ella whispered, 'why don't you have some fun too? You could you know.'

'Oh no, not me. I don't need that sort of fun. As long as I've got ya grandpa, that's all I need.'

She hadn't meant it to sound the way it came out, Ella knew, but what her grandmother said was perfectly true; Esther needed no one in her life except the farm and Jonathan. She needed no one else, not even her granddaughter.

Ella, holding her breath, waited for the familiar hurt to come. Strangely, although there was a sense of sadness, the pain was not so acute. Perhaps because the young girl was on the threshold of womanhood and knew, now, what it felt to love a man, just maybe Ella was beginning to understand that one person – the love of one's life – could be enough.

She sighed deeply. If only Rob . . . she dreamed. Ella shook herself and then, just for once, allowed herself a smug smile. At least he was taking *her*, and not Janice Souter, to the dance.

On the Saturday evening, dressed in her finery, Ella tiptoed into her grandparents' bedroom. Her grandfather had gone to bed early.

'Don't fuss, Esther,' he'd said. 'I'm a bit tired, that's all. I just need an early night and I'll be as right as rain in the morning.'

Ella lifted the latch on the door and whispered, 'Grandpa, are you awake?'

'Course I am, love. I'm only resting. Come in and let me have a look at you.'

Though it was not yet quite dark outside, two candles, one on the narrow mantelpiece and one on the dressing table, lit up the room, sending shadows dancing across the ceiling.

'My, you do look pretty, lass. Now, be a good girl and maybe your grannie will let you go again, eh?'

'I will,' Ella said, willingly giving him her promise. As she twirled around to make her skirts swish, she caught sight of the row of silver-framed photographs on the mantelpiece, the light from the candle flickering over them. She stood still and bent to look at the one of her mother in WAAF uniform.

'Do you think . . .' she asked wistfully, 'Mum would think I look – nice?'

Gently, Jonathan's deep voice reassured her, 'She'd think, and quite rightly, that she has a beautiful daughter. Now, no more sad memories, love. Off you go and enjoy yourself. It's what your mum would have wanted.'

She was about to turn away, when she caught sight of a photograph almost hidden at the back of the others. Bending closer she saw it was of a young man with dark curly hair, dressed in an old-fashioned uniform. She almost gasped aloud, but when she turned to look at her grandfather, he was lying back against the pillows with his eyes closed. She glanced back once more at the photograph and then quietly tiptoed from the room, closing the door.

For a moment she stood on the tiny landing at the top of the stairs, her mind in a whirl. Why on earth had her gran got a picture on her bedroom mantelpiece of the same man as Rob's Grandma Eland had on her sideboard? In fact, if she were not mistaken, it was another copy of exactly the same photograph.

From below, she heard her grandmother call, 'Danny's here in the car, Ella.' And as excitement at the thought of the evening ahead claimed her, she ran lightly down the stairs, her new skirt billowing out around her, and promptly forgot all about the mystery.

As he held open the car door for her, she saw the admiring glance Rob gave her. 'Hey, you do look nice. I'd almost forgotten what you look like in a skirt,' he teased, and ducked smartly out of the way as she aimed a playful blow at him. She climbed into the back seat and spread her skirts carefully about her. Rob got into the front seat beside Danny and the car moved out of the yard. Through the back window Ella saw Esther, standing in the doorway to watch them go, still dressed in her apron, sleeves rolled up above her elbows, her day's work not yet finished.

Pushing away a tiny sliver of guilt, Ella smiled and waved and then, deliberately, she turned her thoughts to the evening ahead.

The dance floor felt as if it were vibrating beneath her feet. They had heard the music loud and reverberating, even before they'd climbed the stairs to the upper floor above the café. Ella gasped as the music from the live group hit them, almost physically. Before them was a mass of gyrating bodies, swirling skirts and writhing legs and arms.

'Come on, Townie,' Rob shouted in her ear, 'let's show 'em how.'

Ella swallowed. Janice had been giving her jiving lessons, but the reality seemed so fast.

Rob dragged her into the throng and before she knew what was happening she was twirling round, Rob catching her hand each time and sending her spinning in the opposite direction, jiving just as Janice had taught her. Ella soon forgot to be self-conscious, whirling faster and faster until her head was dizzy, hearing nothing above the blaring music.

'Look out!' Rob suddenly grabbed her arm and pulled her towards him and Ella turned to see, just behind her, a boy flinging his partner over his shoulder in a flurry of petticoats, the sharp stilettos of her shoes slicing a dangerous arc close to where Ella had been dancing.

'Thanks,' she mouthed to Rob and they moved away a little.

'Hey, you aren't bad at this,' he yelled above the noise. 'I'll bring you again if you dance like this.'

Later, breathless, she stood beside him as he bought her a Coke.

'Want a scoop of ice-cream in it?'

'Eh?' Her eyes widened.

'It's ever so nice.' Janice nudged her. 'Go on, try it. I'll have one too, Rob, and then it's time you danced with me for a change.'

From the edge of the dance floor, sipping the Coke with a spoonful of vanilla ice-cream floating on the top, she watched as Janice claimed Rob in a slow number, dancing close together as a singer crooned romantic lyrics.

'You dancing, then?' She heard a voice at her shoulder and turned to see Jimmy standing there, his hands thrust into his pockets. She felt a sudden flash of empathy for Jimmy Souter. With his spiky carroty hair and a face covered with freckles, he hardly ever seemed to get a girlfriend. Girls flocked around Rob's dark good looks, but Jimmy just seemed to tag along in his wake, on the fringe of the action but never quite part of it. Bit like me, Ella thought, and, setting down her glass, she held out her hand. 'Course I am.'

Jimmy danced stiffly, his hand hot against her back through the thin material of her blouse. He held her away from him so that he could look down at his feet, placing them with deliberate care, and she heard him muttering, 'Forward, side, together . . .'

'Don't worry about it, Jimmy. I can't dance either.'

He looked up in surprise. 'Can't you? I saw you dancing with Rob earlier. You looked great together.'

'It's Rob. He's such a good dancer, he makes anyone he dances with look good.'

'Mind you,' Jimmy said, nodding his head so that the hair he had tried to smooth down so meticulously sprang up in untidy tufts, 'our Janice is a smashing dancer. They look good together, don't they?'

Ella was obliged to look across to where Janice and Rob were dancing. They seemed even closer now; Janice's head was snuggled against his shoulder, her arm possessively around his neck. Ella's only consolation as they danced by was that, above Janice's head, Rob gave her a broad wink.

As the dance ended, Rob pushed his way through the crowd to her. 'Phew, I'm melting in here. Let's get out for a bit, El. Have you finished your drink?'

She looked about her. 'I put it down somewhere . . . Oh, there it is. Wait a minute.'

The ice-cream had melted into a white froth on top of the coke and she drank it down. 'Janice is right. It is nice.'

'Somebody's bright idea.' Rob grinned as he grabbed her hand. 'Come on.'

'Rob – Rob . . .' They heard Janice's voice but Rob only gripped Ella's hand tighter and pulled her away, threading their way through the dishevelled dancers queuing for drinks and towards the double doors leading to the stairs.

Outside they breathed deeply in the sharp night air. 'Phew, that's better. That smoke gets on your chest after a bit, doesn't it?'

'I saw Janice smoking earlier.'

He said nothing, but as they walked along the sea-front towards the road leading down to the beach, she felt his arm come around her waist. 'We'll just take a breather and then we'll go back. Okay?'

'Mmm.' Was it okay? she thought to herself and almost giggled aloud. It was what she dreamed about, walking arm in arm with Rob in the moonlight. To think it was really happening.

'Let's go and look at the sea.'

They stood at the edge of the sand where the road gave way on to the beach and listened to the soft lap-lap of the waves, distinct in the night air, the moonlight shimmering on the tip of each wave.

'I love this place, you know, El,' he murmured softly, his eyes gazing out across the vast expanse of silver ocean. 'I don't ever want to leave it.'

For a moment, she laid her head against his shoulder and sighed. If only he were to say the word, she, too, would stay here for ever. Momentarily, his arm tightened about her waist and she raised her head to look into his face. He turned to look at her, but his features were in shadow and she could not read his expression. She felt his breath on her cheek and his face was close to hers.

Her heart began to pound. For a split second, she thought he was going to kiss her, but then, though his voice was not quite steady, he said, 'We'd best be going back. Me dad'll be here to fetch us home soon.' And the moment, a precious moment, was lost.

'Well, did ya enjoy yasen, then?'

'Oh, Gran, it was wonderful.' Ella clasped her hands together and twirled around the kitchen table. 'We danced and danced. Do you know?' She giggled, coming to a stop in front of Esther, and bending forward as if sharing a secret. 'I think all the girls were jealous of me having Rob all to myself nearly all evening, specially Janice. You know she – she likes him, don't you?'

Esther was watching her granddaughter thoughtfully. 'Does she now? And do you like him, Ella?' she asked quietly.

Ella opened her mouth to spill her secret and then

remembered: this was her grandmother she was confiding in.

'Well,' she said carefully, 'of course, I like him. We've been friends ever since I came to – to live here.'

Slowly, Esther nodded. 'He's a good lad. I trust him and there's not many young fellers I'd say that about. You stick with Rob, Ella, and you'll not go far wrong.'

Inwardly, the girl sighed. If only! she was thinking, but aloud she said, 'Yes, Gran. And you shouldn't have waited up for me. Not when you have to get up so early . . .'

Esther gave a wry smile and wagged her finger. 'Well, you'll be up at normal time in the morning, Missy, else I'll want to know the reason why.'

Ella laughed and suddenly put her arms around her grandmother's waist and gave her a swift hug. 'Thank you for letting me go tonight, Gran. I had a lovely time and I will be up in the morning, I promise.'

'Go on with you, Missy,' Esther said, but she was smiling as she reached up to turn down the lamp.

Twenty-One

'We're off to the fun-fair tonight, to celebrate leaving school.' Both Rob and Jimmy Souter were determined to shake the classroom dust from their shoes whatever their results this time. 'I'll pick you up about seven on me bike.'

'Ta very much.' She grinned at him. 'Not so much as a "would you like to come?"'

'Well, ya would, wouldn't ya?'

Of course she wanted to go, she thought. She never missed an opportunity to be with him now if she could help it. 'Who's the "we"?'

'You, me, Jimmy and Janice.'

'Ah.'

He bent closer. 'You and Janice are still friends, aren't ya?'

'Ye-es,' she said slowly, remembering Janice's scathing attitude towards her having to be home at an early hour.

He shrugged. 'Well, she's all right with me. At least she was when we went to the flicks.'

Ella frowned. 'You went to the pictures? Just the two of you?'

'Yeah. Any law against it?'

'When?'

'Oh, ages ago,' he said airily. 'Before exams finished. I'd only got one exam the next day and that was maths. There's not a lot you can revise for maths, is there?'

Ella stared at him. She recalled that had been the night

she'd stayed up late, bogged down with reams of history revision; the only thing that had kept her going had been the thought of Rob working hard too. And all the time he'd been out with Janice Souter.

'Yes, I'll come tonight,' she said, mentally crossing her fingers that her grandmother would grant permission. No way was she going to allow Janice to spend another evening with Rob without her there too.

'Ya can go when the evening milking's done and not afore,' was all Esther said, 'and you be in by ten.'

'Yes, Gran,' Ella said, feigning meekness, though she was fuming inside, but she knew if she argued she probably wouldn't be allowed to go at all and she needed to see for herself just what was going on between Janice and Rob.

They wandered around the fun-fair; ate sticky pink candy floss, tried to crash each other into submission on the dodgems, clung tightly to each other on the Figure Eight and ridiculed themselves in the Hall of Mirrors.

The clock tower on the esplanade showed five to ten when Rob said, 'I'd better run you home, Ella.'

Janice laughed. 'Yeah, go on, take Cinder-Ella home, then you can come back. We'll meet you near the pier when our Jimmy's finished shooting everything in sight.' They turned to watch Jimmy taking shots at a row of moving ducks at the back of a stall.

'Come on, Ella. You'll be late,' Rob said, turning away.

Ella frowned. 'I'm not coming.'

He sighed. 'Now don't start all that again . . .'

She glared at him. 'I'm not going home this early and this time I mean it.'

He stared at her and then his lip curled and she was shocked by the look of disgust on his face.

'You're daft, then,' he said and turned away.

'Rob, where are you going?'

'Well, I'm off home whether you come or not. I've an early start in the morning.'

'Oh, what a good boy am I?' Janice mocked and only laughed when Rob shot her a disdainful glance.

'You're no friend to encourage her. Her gran'll be that worried—'

'No, she won't. She doesn't care about me.'

'If ya think that, then you're more stupid than I thought ya were, Ella Hilton.'

He turned with a gesture of impatience and walked quickly away with long, angry strides.

'Oh dear me,' said Janice mockingly. 'I think we've upset him.'

Ella was staring after him. 'I – I never thought he'd go.'

'Oh, never mind him,' Janice said, tugging at her arm. 'Ya've done it. Ya've really done it. I never thought you would. Come on. We've the whole night in front of us now.'

Ella allowed herself to be led away, but every so often she glanced back over her shoulder half expecting, half hoping Rob would come back.

The three of them wandered through the fun-fair mingling with the crowds. Then Janice spotted a group of youths lounging against a wall, glasses of frothy beer in their hands. She nudged Ella. 'Which one d'ya fancy, then?'

'Eh? What do you mean?' Ella gaped at them.

The boys were dressed in tight-fitting trousers, long jackets and narrow ties as thin as bootlaces. Their thick, crêpe-soled shoes were purple with bright pink socks.

'They're – they're Teddy Boys,' she gasped.

'So? Come on, let's go an' talk to them.'

'But who are they? I mean, do you know them?'

'Course not. They're holiday-makers out for a good time.'

'Oh no, Janice, I don't think—'

'Well, you please yarsen.' The girl flounced away. 'Run home to Grannie, why don't ya?'

'Janice . . .' Ella sighed and trailed after her friend.

On her white high-heeled shoes, Janice swayed as she walked so that her full skirt swirled provocatively around her shapely legs. She was soon surrounded by the five lads, but Ella hung about on the fringe of the group, feeling foolish.

'What d'you want to drink, darlin'?' she heard one of them ask and, raising his voice, added, 'and one for your friend.'

Janice turned and beckoned Ella closer. 'Come on, Ella. Come and meet Mike and Andrew and – er – what did you say your name was?' She turned to another, laughing. The youth put his arm about her waist and whispered something in her ear that made Janice giggle with delight.

'I think I'll—' Ella began, but then one of the group appeared with a tray of drinks.

'Go on, drink it, it won't hurt you,' Janice urged, pushing a glass under her nose.

'What is it?'

'Summat to cheer you up a bit,' Janice said.

The group guffawed. 'That's it, darlin', loosen up a bit . . .' The laughter was louder, more raucous.

'It smells funny—' Ella began.

'Oh, come on, Ella, don't be such a baby. You're showing me up.'

'Oh, sorry, I'm sure,' she flashed and, grabbing the glass, downed the short in one gulp, to the sound of cheering from the youths. One came over to her and put his arm around her shoulders.

'That's better, darlin'.' His breath smelt strongly of beer. ''Ow about you and me going under the pier, eh? Nice and dark there, ain't it?'

'I don't think . . .' Ella began and glanced at Janice, but the other girl was already entwined with another of the youths, his hands running up and down her back and coming to rest on her bottom. Ella gasped as she felt the young man's hand travel down her back to her waist and then begin to move further down, down . . .

She twisted away, 'No, I—' but he caught hold of her wrist and his face, inches from her own, was menacing through the darkness.

'Nar then, don't be like that. Givin' me the come on and then—'

'I never—'

'There's names for girls like you, y'know.' He pulled her to him and thrust his wet lips against her mouth, pressing so hard that his teeth ground against hers. He held her fast with one arm, while he shoved the other hand into the front of her blouse, grabbing her small breast and squeezing it.

'Let me go!' she cried, struggling to free herself from his grasp. Suddenly, she was afraid, very afraid.

'Leave her alone,' came a voice from the shadows.

'Eh?' The lout half turned. 'Wha's it got to do with you?' he began, but found himself swung fully round, forced to release his hold on Ella.

Now her arm was grasped by Rob's firm grip that brooked no argument. But this time she had no intention of arguing; she didn't know when she had last been so pleased to see anyone in her life.

'Aw, want her for yerself, do yer, mate? Well, you've

only to say. Not really my type anyway. Not enough meat in the right places.' He sneered. 'Yer welcome.'

'What – about Janice?' Ella gasped as Rob hustled her through the crowds.

'Never mind Janice Souter. She can tek care of 'ersen.'

'Well, so can I.'

He stopped and swung her round to face him. 'Oh, yeah? It looked like it! You stupid or what, Ella Hilton? Just what do ya think yar grannie's going to say to this?'

There was to be no creeping through the yard into the house and up the stairs for Ella; not with the roar of Rob's motorbike echoing through the stillness of the night.

'Are you determined to wake the whole bloomin' neighbourhood?' she snapped, swinging her leg over the back of his bike and marching towards the back door. As she reached it, it opened and her grandmother, hair down her back and dressed in a long, white cotton nightgown, stood silhouetted in the doorway.

'And what time do you call this, Missy?'

Ella pursed her lips and glowered, remaining mutinously silent, but she knew her face to be red with embarrassment and anger.

Her grandmother swung round now to glare at Rob. 'And I'm surprised at you, Rob Eland. I trusted you to bring her home and what do you do? Keep her out till all hours. Where've ya been, I'd like to know, until gone midnight? Up to no good. Well, ya can forget all ya gallivanting, girl. That's the last time I let you go anywhere. Ya hear me?'

Ella glanced at Rob: his face was bright red, his eyes dark with anguish under the tirade from the woman he so admired and, yes, loved. But he just stood there, taking it all, saying nothing to defend himself because telling the truth would give Ella away.

Ella sighed. 'Gran,' she said, 'it wasn't Rob's fault . . .' and although she saw him shoot her a warning look, she went on, 'it was mine, all mine. He would have brought me home at ten. He tried to, but I wouldn't come.'

Her grandmother was silent for a moment, glancing at first one and then the other. 'That right, Boy?'

Acutely embarrassed, Rob could only nod.

'Then I'm sorry for blaming you. But, as for you . . .' The strong, bony hand came out and gripped her shoulder, 'I've more to say to you in the morning. Ya've not heard the last of this, not by a long way, you 'aven't!'

At half past five the following morning, though she could hardly force her eyes open, her head throbbed and every limb cried out to lie down and rest, Ella dragged herself from her bed, splashed herself with cold water in the bowl on her washstand and crept downstairs. Lifting the latch on the back door, she tiptoed out into the sharp morning air, the sun streaking the sky pale yellow in the east. She stood there a moment, breathing in the fresh air, trying to gather her drowsy senses.

'First job,' she murmured to herself. 'Fetch the cows in.'

She worked until half past eight, until the emptiness in her stomach was a growling void. Her grandpa, who had got on his tractor and headed out of the yard, had not said a word to her and when she went into the kitchen she found the breakfast table cleared and the pots washed. There was no sign of her grandmother.

Ella tipped cereal and milk into a bowl and stood at the sink looking out of the scullery window across the yard. It was very quiet; the only sounds were the hens scratching complainingly and the beasts moving restlessly in the cowshed.

Rinsing her bowl and spoon and leaving them on the draining board, she went back to the cowshed to herd the cows along the coastal road back to North Marsh Field. Returning, she saw her grandfather in the field of wheat examining its ripeness for harvesting.

'Grandpa?' she came up behind him.

'Ella, love. You made me jump. You're up early. Did you have a good time last night?'

She gaped at him, but his head was bent over the waving corn. 'Er, I was late home, Grandpa. Didn't Gran tell you.'

'No, I was asleep. Oh dear. Are you in trouble?'

She nodded. 'Big trouble.' He came towards her and slipped his arm about her shoulders. His blue eyes twinkled down at her. 'Oh dear. I'll have a talk to her.'

Ella smiled wanly and shook her head. 'I don't think even you can help this time, Grandpa.'

To Ella's surprise, Esther said no more on the subject, though in the days that followed she only spoke to Ella to issue orders and kept her busy from the moment she got up in the morning until she fell into bed, exhausted, at night without the desire or the energy to go out anywhere. And for several nights, a sleepy Tibby found himself yanked out of the warm and cosy straw in the barn and carted upstairs to Ella's bed, where his weight sprawled across her feet was her only comfort.

When the corn harvest began, Rob seemed to spend as much time on Brumbys' Farm as he did on his own.

'I'll give you a hand, Ella,' he would say as he appeared most afternoons. 'I've telled ya grandpa to go and rest. He looks done in.'

'I know.' Ella's blue eyes followed the tall figure of her grandfather, his shoulders stooping, as he walked across the stubble towards the gate. 'It's been so hot these last few days. Gran says the heat's getting to him.'

'Mmm.' Rob sounded unconvinced, but added, 'Let's hope that's all it is.'

Ella stared at him. 'Why? Do you think it could be something more serious?'

The young man shrugged. 'I dunno. I'm not a doctor.'

'Well, he won't see one and even Gran won't make him. She still thinks you have to pay to see a doctor.'

Rob chuckled. 'Yeah. The old 'uns seem to live in the past, sometimes, don't they?'

Later, as they sat behind a stook to eat their dinner, Ella said, 'Rob, you know we were talking a bit ago about our families being related?'

'Mmm?' he responded absently, paying more attention to the sandwich he was munching than to her.

'I was in Gran's bedroom yesterday, fetching some washing for her. I'd forgotten all about it, till I saw it again.'

They turned towards each other and their faces were only inches apart, so close she could feel his breath on her face. 'Saw what again?'

'You know that photo your gran has on her sideboard, that real old one of a soldier in uniform?'

He frowned. 'Ye-es.'

'Who is it?'

'I dunno. I thought it were me grandad. Why?'

'Because,' she said slowly, savouring the drama of the moment, '*my* gran's got one exactly the same on the mantelpiece in her bedroom.'

He blinked at her. 'Really?'

Then he turned away and bit into his sandwich. 'Well,'

he mumbled, his mouth full, 'we'll 'ave to ask 'em, then, won't we?'

Later, as they parked the tractor in the yard and jumped down, Rob stretched and yawned. 'Eh, that was some day.' He blinked, his eyes red-rimmed with tiredness. 'I could do with a pint. Pity the pub got bombed in the war. I could just about make it to the old Seagull, but I haven't the energy to traipse into town.'

'I reckon there's some home-made beer in the pantry.'

'No, ya gran'll be mad.'

'She'll never miss it. She'll think Grandpa's had it. I'll meet you in the hayloft. We'll be out of sight there.'

'Ella, don't—' he began, but she was gone.

Moments later she was carrying a flagon of Esther's home-made beer across the yard, into the barn and up the ladder to the hayloft. It was warm and dry, with only the setting sun slanting tiny shafts of light through the ill-fitting boards.

They nestled into the mounds of dry hay, drinking the bitter-sweet liquid.

'When do you start college?' she asked.

'About a month's time, September.'

Ella was silent. She was going to miss him, so much more than she could ever tell him.

'Will you miss me?' she asked, making her tone deliberately flippant.

'Oh, indubitably!'

'By heck, Bumpkin,' she mimicked his dialect, 'that's a big word for you. Getting into being a college boy already? It'll cost us to speak to ya when ya come ho-ame.'

'You!' He set down the flagon and reached out towards her and began to tickle her ribs.

She squealed and squirmed trying to get away from him, but he held her fast. 'No, don't do that. You know I'm ticklish. Don't, Rob, stop it!'

They were laughing and rolling over and over on the hay, legs and arms flailing, romping like two playful puppies.

'What on earth is going on?'

They froze, staring through the gloom at each other, their eyes wide.

'Oh no!' Ella breathed and as Rob rolled off the top of her, they both turned frightened eyes to the top of the ladder to see Esther's head and shoulders.

'Get down here this instant,' she spat at them. 'Both of you.'

'Gran, we're not doing anything . . .'

But Esther had disappeared, climbing down to stand at the bottom, waiting for them.

Rob climbed down first and, her heart thumping, Ella followed, but immediately her feet touched the ground she swung round to face her grandmother boldly. 'I know what you're thinking, but we were only – well – mucking about.'

Before she knew what was happening, Esther had brought her right hand up smartly and dealt a stinging blow to the left side of Ella's face, catching her on her left jawline and making the birthmark redden. 'Hold ya tongue, ya little trollop!' Esther snapped. 'I might have known. It's in the breed, ain't it? Like ya mother – and mine for that matter. Eh, an' I did me best to din it into ya mam, but no, it's in the blood. And now you!'

Then she turned her wrath on Rob. 'And as for you, I expected better of you, Rob Eland.'

Ella rubbed her sore cheek and glanced at Rob. She saw him flinch, his face pale. 'Missus – listen – please. We weren't doing nothing, honest. Just – just playing . . .'

'Oh, aye. 'Spect me to believe that? Ya mun think I were born yesterday. But ya like ya grandad, too, ain't you? A flirt, after anything in skirts!' She leant closer towards him, thrusting her face close to his. 'Get off my farm, Rob Eland, and dun't you set foot on it again. Ya not welcome here and you keep away from her.' She flung her arm out towards Ella. 'Right away. You hear me?'

All colour drained completely from his face.

Ella gave a cry and clung to his arm. 'No, Gran, no. Why won't you believe us? We weren't—'

'I *dun't* believe you.'

For a brief instant, though his eyes were still staring straight into Esther's, Rob touched Ella's hand where she was gripping his arm. She heard him sigh. 'It's no use, Ella. I – I'd better go.'

'Yes, you had,' Esther said.

'Gran, please . . .'

As Rob turned away to leave, Esther grasped Ella by the arm and made to pull her out of the barn and towards the house. 'As for you, Missy, up to ya room till I decide what I'm goin' to do with you.'

With a swift movement, Ella twisted herself from her grandmother's hold. 'No, I won't.'

With Rob gone, they faced each other. 'Ya'll do as ya told, else—'

'Else what, Gran? Else you'll hit me again?' She touched her cheek, still smarting from Esther's hand. 'Else you'll turn me out? Eh? What? What will you do?'

'You little madam!' Esther said through gritted teeth, her mouth set in a hard line. 'Aye, an' I've a good mind to turn you out at that. After all I've done for you, and you do this.'

'Gran, I've done nothing. Rob doesn't think of me like

that anyway, though I wish he did. I wish we *had* done something.'

Again Esther's hand came up, but Ella, half expecting it now, put up her arm to fend her off and the older woman let her own fall. 'Get into the house.'

'No, I won't.' Ella whirled about, grasped the ladder and began to climb back up to the hayloft.

She felt Esther grab her ankle and she kicked out to force her to release her hold. She heard Esther cry out. 'Ouch! Why, you little devil. Kick me, would you?' And she turned to see her grandmother, rubbing a point on her left jawline.

'Well, we're quits now, aren't we, Gran?' and she turned to show Esther where the skin around the birthmark on her own face was glowing bright red.

Ignoring her grandmother's gasp of shock, Ella climbed back up into the loft to collapse on to the hay and bury her face in it, trying to stifle her uncontrollable sobs.

When at last she pulled herself up into a sitting position, sniffed and rubbed the tears away with the back of her hand, it had grown darker in the loft and, outside, dusk was creeping across the farmyard. She heard a rustle in the hay and saw Tibby picking his way towards her. He climbed on to her knee and rubbed his face against her cheek, purring as loudly as he knew how. She hugged him hard to her and buried her face in his soft fur.

It was over, all over. Fresh tears trickled down her cheeks. All her hopes for making Rob love her had been smashed in an instant. And by her grandmother, too. How she hated that woman!

Grandpa! I must find Grandpa and tell him my side. He'll believe me . . .

She had started to scramble up, tipping Tibby unceremoniously into the hay, when she heard shouting in the yard, shrill voices raised in anger. Women's voices.

She crept to the ladder and climbed down. Then she tiptoed to the door of the barn and, keeping hidden behind it, she peeped out.

In the lengthening shadows two figures stood in the centre of the yard. As she might have expected, one was her grandmother, but when Ella recognized the other figure, she gasped with surprise.

Beth Eland stood there, her round body shaking with indignation, her finger wagging only inches from Esther's nose.

'How dare you even think my grandson would be up to no good?'

'Like his grandad, ain't he, Beth? Allus after the women.'

At that moment, Ella saw her grandfather appear out of the cowshed on the other side of the yard. He paused a moment, looking at the two women in surprise, his eyes going from one to the other and back again. Then Ella saw his glance go beyond them and towards the barn where she was standing. She ducked back, but too late; she knew he had seen her. Peeping out again, she saw him coming towards her, skirting the edge of the yard, unobserved by the two women so totally immersed in their quarrel. In a moment he stepped inside the barn and came to stand beside her, putting his arm casually around her shoulders but keeping partially hidden, looking out cautiously just like Ella, as if he, too, wanted to watch what was happening, but not get involved.

'Grandpa?'

'Mmm?' His attention was still on the two women.

'Grandpa – me and Rob – we weren't doing anything, honest.'

For a moment, through the gloom, his keen glance returned her steady gaze. 'I believe you, love. But I'm afraid your grannie never will.' He jerked his head towards the arguing women.

'But why, Grandpa? Why won't she? I've never lied to her in my life. Not even when I've been in trouble. I always owned up, you know I did. And Rob too. He thinks that much of her, he'd cut his right arm off before he'd upset her. She should *know* that.'

Grimly Jonathan said, 'I don't even think such a drastic step as that would convince her. Not in her present mood.'

They fell silent, their attention caught again by the raised voices.

'Ya judge everyone by ya own standards, that's the trouble with you, Esther.' Beth Eland's head nodded vigorously and her fat chins wobbled. 'You think no one else but you can remember things, dun't ya? That only others has done wrong. Well . . .' She thrust her face closer to Esther. 'What 'bout you in the war, eh? Carrying on when ya husband was away fighting?'

Beside her, Ella was sure she felt Jonathan stiffen and she bit her lip. Was Grandma Eland letting out secrets that even he didn't know? Then she frowned. She didn't think her grandpa had been in the last war; he'd been too old. Then what . . .?

'Oh, aye, trust you to rake up all the past. Why, that's years ago.'

'It's you can't let go of the past, Esther Everatt.'

Ella gasped. That name again. She'd heard Grandma Eland refer to her grandmother by that name before, when she'd tried to ask questions about Esther's early life. Shrewdly, Ella guessed it was the name from their young days; the name by which Beth had first known Esther. In her anger, it was the name that came naturally to her lips.

'Ya can't forgive and ya can't forget, can ya? Not ever.'

A memory stirred in Ella's mind; a fleeting picture of her mother and her grandmother . . . But then the argument going on now claimed her attention.

'You're a fine one to talk about not forgiving, Beth. Ya've harboured a grudge agin me all me life nearly, just 'cos you reckon I stole ya sweetheart.'

This was something new. Ella stepped forward, eager to listen, forgetting for a moment just what the quarrel was about. Then she felt her grandfather's warning hand on her shoulder and she glanced up at him.

Did he understand all this? she wondered. Was he being hurt by the words they were flinging at each other? 'Grandpa,' she began, 'didn't you ought to stop them. Maybe . . .'

He was shaking his head, and there was a small smile on his mouth, yet it was tinged with a sadness. 'No, love, leave them be. They've been wanting to have a go at each other for a long time. Years and years this has been building up. We'd better let them get on with it.'

And get on with it they certainly did, though much of what they said was a mystery to the listening girl.

'Well, ya should 'ave kept ya legs crossed,' Esther shouted and Ella gasped at her grandmother's crude remark. If the scene being played out before her hadn't been so awful, it would have been funny.

'Grandpa, what are they on about?'

But Jonathan pretended he had not heard her puzzled question. Round and round the quarrel raged in a maelstrom of emotion, the outpouring of years of bitterness.

'Ya're a mean old beezum, Esther Everatt. Work, work and more work – that's all you've ever known. All ya can think about is ya precious farm. Ya put it before anybody, dun't ya? 'Cept mebbe Jonathan. As for that poor bairn.

Well, me heart fair bleeds for her it does, brought up by you. You've never shown her an ounce of love, 'ave ya? Just 'cos you was born a bastard . . .'

Ella gasped.

'. . . and so was she, ya tek it out on her. 'Tain't *'er* fault, poor scrap, yet ya blame her, dun't ya?'

'Of course I dun't.'

'You, of all people, should understand her better than anyone. You should know how it feels. And yet ya doing the same to her as was done to you. Ya never let her have any fun. Ya keep her here working like a skivvy—'

'Aye, an' what happens when I do give in and let her go out? With *your* grandson?' Esther flung her arm out towards the barn. 'A couple of weeks later, I find 'em rolling in the hayloft. God knows what would have happened if I hadn't heard 'em laughing and squealing like a pair of – a pair of . . .'

'Yeah, yeah go on, like a pair of what? They were hardly up to what you're accusing 'em of if they were meking a racket. Or do you know summat I don't, Esther? Mebbe in ya time, ya've learnt summat I ain't.' Beth dropped her voice a little, but Ella's sharp ears still picked up her words. 'After all, we've both 'ad two fellers, ain't we, Esther Everatt? *An' we've shared one of 'em, ain't we?*'

'Get off my farm, Beth Eland,' Esther shrieked, 'and dun't ever come back!'

Suddenly, Jonathan moved from Ella's side, with a swift, decisive action. He raised his voice. 'That's enough now,' he said firmly, and walked towards the two women.

They turned startled eyes towards him and Beth's hand fluttered to her mouth nervously as if she wished she could bite back her own words.

But Esther only faced her husband squarely. 'Listeners

hear no good of themselves. Where is she? Still skulking in the loft?'

He turned and beckoned to Ella and she moved out of the barn hesitantly and went to stand beside him. As if to demonstrate at once to his wife that he was not taking her part in this quarrel, he put his arm around Ella's shoulders.

Returning Esther's stare steadily, he said quietly, 'Have you ever known Ella, Rob or – since you seem so intent on bringing the past into everything – Kate to lie to you?'

Ella heard her grandmother drag in a shocked breath and Beth, too, gasped.

'That's not fair—' Esther began.

'Oh no? What you two have been slinging at each other in the past few minutes is hardly fair. Raking up things that happened over forty years ago. You could have been friends, the pair of you; *should* have been friends, but no, you go on harbouring bitterness down the years and wrecking other folk's lives too, because of it. What about Kate and Danny all those years ago? If only you'd behaved sensibly and told them the truth from the start then maybe, just maybe, Kate wouldn't have gone off and, well . . .' Ella felt his arm tighten around her '. . . done what she did.'

She looked up at him. This was not the time to ask questions, but she had plenty of questions she wanted to ask now, after what she'd been hearing. And 'by heck', as Rob would say, she was going to ask them.

Twenty-Two

As she had feared, Ella did not see Rob again for days. She heard him, though. Night after night, she heard his motorbike roaring down the lane from Rookery Farm and turning towards the town, the noise echoing through the night air, growing fainter and fainter. Going away from her.

Once, in the pale light of evening, she thought she saw, leaning out of her bedroom window, two figures on his bike, his passenger with long hair blowing out behind her.

In stark contrast to all the heated words, her grandmother now barely spoke to her, only acknowledging her presence by snapping orders for the work she still expected Ella to do.

'Go along with her for a while, Ella love,' her gentle grandfather suggested. 'Do your best to please her.' He sighed. 'You'll have to prove yourself all over again.'

'I'm sorry if I've caused trouble between the two of you,' Ella said in a small voice, genuinely contrite.

Jonathan put his arm about her shoulders as they walked towards the big barn. 'Don't worry yourself about that. I'll be in the dog-house for a few days.' He gave a deep-throated chuckle as if Esther's frostiness really didn't perturb him very much. 'It's not the first time and I don't expect it'll be the last. She'll come around.'

'But what did it all mean, Grandpa? When Gran and

Grandma Eland were quarrelling? They sounded as if they almost hated each other.'

He sighed heavily and murmured, 'It's so long ago now, yet they still harbour bitterness, each about the other.'

'Why? What was it that happened that was so awful?'

He was silent a moment, seeming torn between the desire to answer her questions and yet something still held him back. At his next words she understood.

'It's not my place to tell you everything. Really, it should come from your grannie.'

'She won't tell me anything. You know she won't. It's always been "Don't ask questions that don't concern you, Missy", now hasn't it?'

'I'll tell you a little, if it'll help,' he shook his head slowly, 'but I really don't feel I can tell you it all.' He sat down on a bale of straw and let out such a deep sigh it was almost a groan. 'You do know, don't you, that I'm not your real grandfather, that I was your mother's stepfather?'

Ella's eyes widened in horror. 'Not – my – real – grandfather? But you must be. You've *got* to be!'

He smiled and ruffled her short curly hair as he always had done when she was younger. 'Thanks for the vote of confidence,' he tried to joke, but Ella was not laughing.

'Grandpa?'

'Your gran was married to someone else before me. Matthew Hilton.'

Ella drew in a breath. 'But that's my name.'

'Of course. You – you know your mother was never married, don't you?'

'Yes, but – but I thought the name I'd got was, well, my own father's surname. I never thought it was my mother's maiden name.' There was a pause whilst she continued to stare at him, her young sixteen-year-old mind trying to come to terms with the facts. Facts that everyone else had always known about her, but that she had not fully understood. 'Grandpa, do you know who my father was?'

Jonathan shook his head. 'Your mother would never say. She never did tell us.'

'And this Matthew Hilton?' Now her agile mind was leaping ahead. 'Was he Grandma Eland's sweetheart, then?'

Jonathan nodded and said hoarsely, 'So I understand.'

He got up and for a moment stood looking down at her, sympathy in his eyes. 'I can understand how you feel, love. In your shoes, I'd feel very puzzled and mixed-up too. But it's your grannie who should explain it all to you. I've been trying to persuade her for years to be more open about the past. Not to treat it all as if it's some dark and dreadful secret.'

'And is it?'

He shrugged. 'In her eyes, yes, but in mine, no. It's just, well, life. These things happen, but you can't live in shame for generation after generation.'

'And that's what she's doing? Hiding the truth from me because she's ashamed of what happened?'

He nodded. 'Something like that.' As he moved away, Ella stared after him in disappointment.

'Grandpa, just tell me one more thing – please?' He paused and turned back, waiting for her question.

'This – this secret, whatever it is, is that why Rob's keeping away from me now? Does *he* know?'

'I think, though I'm only guessing, that he's staying away because he doesn't want to make your grannie any madder with him than she already is.'

Ella pulled her mouth into a wry twist. 'Well, I can believe that,' she muttered, remembering his admiration for her grandmother through the years. Esther Godfrey's anger would have hurt him more than anything.

'But as for whether he knows anything, well, maybe his grandma, or even his dad, might have told him something.'

Ella's eyes widened. 'Uncle Danny? Does he know it all?'

Jonathan turned away again, so that she scarcely heard his low-voiced, 'Oh yes, love, Danny knows everything.'

Ella stared after him as he left the barn, his shoulders stooping. She knew she could ask no more of her grandpa. Maybe some of these memories her questioning had evoked were painful for him too. But, just maybe, he had given her a hint of someone she might be able to persuade into revealing some of these dark and dreadful secrets.

Several times during the weeks that followed her conversation with her grandfather, she tried to see Danny, but it seemed that each time she was thwarted in some way; most of the time it was because her grandmother would scarcely let her out of her sight, and on the rare occasions she was able to scamper across the fields to Rookery Farm, Danny was not there.

The rest of her summer holidays were spent in back-breaking labour just to try to please a stubborn old woman who'd never loved her from the very beginning and Ella began to question whether it was really worth the effort.

'You finish the milking and tek the cows back to the field. Me and ya grandpa are going for a walk on the beach.'

Ella stared after them as, hand in hand, the couple walked away from her out of the yard, crossed the lane and disappeared beneath the trees on the sand-dunes. Ella finished the milking, dealt with the milk and cleaned all the machines and equipment. Then she drove the six cows out of the gate, up the lane and into the meadow. Closing the gate she leant on it watching the cows wander further into the field and begin tearing at the grass. What a simple uncomplicated life animals led, she thought. She heard a miaow behind her and turned to see that Tibby had followed her and was stepping daintily through the grass towards her, stopping every few moments to raise his head to listen. She squatted down and he came to her, rubbing his head against her knees and arching his back to be stroked, purring in anticipation.

'Come on, Tibs,' she said, picking him up. 'Let's go and find you some milk.'

She carried him a short way down the lane but suddenly the cat began to struggle. 'Ouch!' she cried as his claws penetrated her thin shirt. She dropped him and the cat, landing on his feet, ran towards the grass verge near the sand-dunes. He squatted low and slunk forward, his tail thrashing wildly. Above him, in the branches of an elder tree, a bird fluttered.

'Oh no, you don't chase birds, m'lad,' Ella said, and went to pick him up again. But Tibby, intent on pursuing his prey, flattened his ears and ran ahead of her under the trees.

'Tibby! Come here this minute, you naughty cat!'

Ducking beneath the trees, she followed him. The bird above them twittered in alarm and fluttered skywards to safety. Tibby swished his tail in annoyance, then playfully, he ran ahead of Ella, stopping every so often to look back at her, and then running again. She emerged at the top of the dunes, to see him half-way down the other side leading on to the marsh.

'Oh, I'm not chasing you any more, you daft animal,' she said smiling fondly. 'You can come home when you're ready.'

She was about to turn back when she caught sight of two figures crossing the marsh, their arms about each other. Her gran and grandpa were walking slowly back towards home, her head resting on his shoulder. Ella guessed they had been out to the end of the Spit, her gran's favourite spot. Echoing across the marsh, she heard her grandmother's laughter; like the laughter of a young girl in love. She saw them pause, saw her grandfather bend his head and kiss her grandmother's upturned face.

Ella turned and stumbled back the way she had come. She had never felt so lonely in her life.

Rob never came to Brumbys' Farm now and Ella didn't particularly want to seek out Janice Souter. Her only escape from the never-ending work was the deserted beach. When she could slip away from the farm, she walked towards the town where the sands were thronged with holiday-makers, children building sand-castles, bathers cavorting in the shallows or swimming further out, their happy laughter making Ella feel even more alone. She walked along the sea bank overlooking the beach and leant on the rail, her gaze scanning the sands.

Then she saw him. Dressed in only a black pair of swimming trunks, running along in the shallows, feet pounding, water splashing. Ahead of him ran a girl dressed in a scanty bathing costume. Every so often, she glanced back over her shoulder towards him, shrieking with laughter as he bent, scooped up a handful of water and splashed her.

It was not Janice, or even a girl she recognized; it was a visitor, a holiday-maker.

Rob was flirting with the summer girls.

She watched him, his black hair gleaming in the sunlight, the water in silver droplets on his body, muscular from the heavy farmwork he did with such ease. Lucky, lucky girl – whoever she was – who now had Rob.

For the past year, they'd been such friends that she had begun to dare to hope that maybe, just maybe . . . But in a few moments, all her dreams had been smashed.

Tears clouded Ella's vision so that the figures blurred. She turned and walked quickly away, back the way she had come towards Fleethaven Point. She kept on walking, right out to the end of the Spit, wishing she could just keep on walking and never stop, right out into the sea.

She stood at the end of the Spit and looked about her. The breeze rippled the surface of the sea and ruffled her hair. She pushed her hands deep into her pockets and stared out moodily across the wide expanse of water.

Was there no one in the world, she asked herself, who loved her? She fingered the birthmark on her jaw. If only she was pretty, perhaps then . . .

She stayed there until, in only her trousers and a thin shirt, she began to feel chilled. She shivered and turned away, retracing her steps along the shingle of the narrow bank of the Spit towards home.

Home! she thought. Huh, that was a laugh. Not even there was she welcome.

'And where have you been, Missy?' was the greeting when she walked back into the yard.

'Just for a walk, Gran,' she said meekly, too distressed by what she had seen on the beach to have the energy to argue today. She sighed heavily and asked, 'What have I done now?'

'There's no need to take that attitude. Go and help yar grandpa with the milking. All them new-fangled machines he's got. I want nowt to do wi' 'em.' And Esther stalked back into the house, her back rigid with disapproval, though not, for once, directed at Ella.

A little later, above the clatter and whirring of the milking machines, Ella heard her name being called and glanced round to see Janice Souter standing in the doorway of the cowshed. Making sure the machines were operating correctly and safely for a few moments, she walked towards the girl and stood leaning against the doorframe.

'Our Jimmy ses you're in jankers on bread and water, El.'

'Something like that,' Ella said, and added pointedly, 'Thought you might have come round sooner. Been too busy out on someone's motorbike, have we?'

'Huh!' Janice tossed back her long hair. 'Once or twice, but he's got his eyes on the summer girls now. Like all the lads round here.' She sniffed. 'Still, two can play at that game. There's some smashing lads down from Leicester. I'm meeting them tonight. A' you game?'

Ella stared at her for a moment, then laughed wryly. 'Even if I was, I'd never get out. Not now.'

'Couldn't you climb down a drainpipe or a tree or summat, like they do in films?'

Ella shrugged. 'It's not worth it. I'm in enough trouble at the moment, without doing anything else.'

'I don't know how you put up with it. I don't know why you don't pack your bags and leave. If it was me, I'd be off.'

'I've been thinking about it,' Ella murmured.

'Oh yeah,' Janice scoffed. 'I bet!'

Ella's eyes narrowed as she thought, Don't you be too sure, Janice Souter. One day I might do just that. But she kept the words unspoken; she wasn't sure how much she could trust Janice.

'I heard there'd been a dust-up,' the other girl was saying, leaning closer, her eyes gleaming. 'Between old Grandma Eland and your gran. What was it all about?'

Ella frowned, remembering again the lashing words. 'I honestly don't know. I – I couldn't understand it all.'

There was a knowing smirk on Janice's face. 'It were about you and Rob getting too *friendly*, weren't it?'

'We weren't. That's what's so unfair. We were only mucking about, but no one will believe us, specially not Gran!'

Janice leant closer and now she whispered, 'Dun't you know *why* she got so upset when she thought you and Rob might be – well – y'know?'

Ella stared at her. Dumbly, she shook her head.

Janice put her mouth closer to Ella's ear. 'Ya can't get friendly with Rob Eland, not *that* way – not ever. Not with ya *brother*!'

Twenty-Three

'Uncle Danny, are you my father?'

In the yard at Rookery Farm, she stood facing him, hands on hips, her feet planted apart, unaware that she was adopting a stance exactly like her grandmother.

The man, coming out of the barn carrying a bale of straw, gawped at her. He turned pale and dropped the bale. As if his legs had suddenly given way, he sat down on it and put his hand to his chest.

'By 'eck, young 'un, ya dun't mince words when ya start, d'ya?' He looked at her hard. 'Ya more like her than you know, Ella.'

'Who? Gran – or my mum?' Her words were laced with an underlying meaning that was not lost on the man in front of her. She could see that she had shocked him and, for a moment, she felt a fleeting concern, but she steeled her heart against compassion.

It was time she had a few answers to all the mystery, to all the funny remarks that had been floating above her head for years now; half-spoken sentences left unfinished when she entered a room and deliberate evasion of her questions. Bright, perceptive and perhaps adult beyond her years in the constant company of the two women in her childhood, her mother and aunt, Ella had been aware of the atmosphere of mystery, but, as a young girl, she had been unable to elicit answers from anyone. Now, at sixteen, and after all the recent quarrels, she was determined to rip away the shroud of secrecy that shadowed her life. She wanted those answers – now.

'Well? Are you?'

Slowly, he shook his head and pulled himself up from the bale as if his limbs were suddenly heavy. He came towards her, his limp more noticeable than ever, and stood looking directly into her eyes. He was not a tall man and Ella's eyes were almost level with his steady gaze. He put both his hands on her shoulders, resting them there. He did not answer her question immediately, but instead asked, 'Ya mean you really don't know, lass? Ya grannie's told you nothing about ya mam and me?'

When she shook her head, he seemed to take a deep breath as if coming to a big decision and said solemnly, 'No, I'm not ya dad. I might have been, I might well have been, but we found out just in time.'

'Found – found out?'

'I am your blood uncle, Ella. Your mam and me, we – we were half-brother and -sister.'

She stared at him and for a moment the only sounds in the farmyard were the hens scratching and complaining.

'Brother and sister? Then – then me and Rob – we're cousins?'

He nodded. 'Well, half-cousins.'

'But there's nothing wrong with cousins marrying, is there?' The words were out before she thought to stop them.

For a moment his expression was almost comical. 'You mean you and Rob are . . .'

'No, no, we're not.' She shook her head in denial, pulled a face and muttered, 'More's the pity . . .'

'Aw, lass, do you like him, I mean, like that?'

She said simply, 'I love him, Uncle Danny. I think I always have.'

'Aw, love.' He pulled her to him now and held her close.

Muffled against him, her face hidden, she found it easier to tell him her secret. 'This year, I thought we were getting closer, that maybe in time he might feel the same. But Gran's put a stop to that. For ever.'

With her ear pressed against his chest, she could hear his heart beating and she heard him sigh deep within himself. As if making up his mind, he eased her away from him and held her by the shoulders. 'It's high time you knew everything, lass. And if no one else is going to tell you, then I will. Tomorrow, Ella, you and me are going to take the day off and go on a little trip.'

'What about Gran?'

Firmly, he said, 'I'll be over to see her tonight. I aren't going to do anything behind her back. That's not my way.'

'Oh, heck!' Ella said and it sounded comical coming from her lips. 'I'll make myself scarce tonight, then.'

'No,' Danny said. 'I want you there. It's high time that grandmother of yours heard a few home truths.'

'I think,' Ella said slowly, 'your mother did a bit of that a few weeks ago.'

'Obviously not enough,' he said, grimly determined, and Ella shuddered to think what was going to happen that evening.

'You'll do no such thing, young Danny!'

They were all standing ranged around the kitchen at Brumbys' Farm: her grandmother on one side of the scrubbed table, Ella, her grandfather and Danny standing in front of the range.

'You're all against me. I never thought you'd turn

against me, Jonathan. Not you. But you're siding with them an' all, aren't ya?'

'Esther love, listen.' The gentle man moved round the table and put his arms about her. She did not push him away but held herself stiffly, as if trying to resist him, yet finding it hard to do so.

'My dearest love, listen to me. I'm always on your side, you know that, but I've never shirked from telling you when I think you're wrong, now have I?'

A ghost of a smile touched her lips, but she remained silent as he went on. 'There's been enough heartache caused over the years by trying to keep things hidden. Let the girl know, then maybe she'll understand better.'

Ella moved towards Esther, reaching out, trying to bridge the gulf between them. 'Gran? Please, Gran. I want to know, to understand. People, even Janice Souter, keep hinting at things to me, things I don't understand and – and that turn out to be untrue anyway.' She glanced at Danny for support.

He nodded and said quietly, 'Janice Souter told Ella that she and Rob are brother and sister. That's why I had to tell her the truth, that part of it anyway.'

'Janice Souter would,' Esther muttered. 'The whole family's nowt but gossips.'

Danny's gaze at Esther was steady, unflinching. 'You know how – how I've always respected you, Missus, and yes, loved you, right from being a young lad. I'm not trying to put all the blame on you.'

'That's very generous of you,' Esther said, her tone laced with sarcasm.

'Esther, love,' Jonathan said softly, tightening his arm around her.

Resolutely, Danny went on, 'Me mam's as much to blame, but the secrets you and she tried so hard to keep hidden very nearly destroyed Kate and me. I won't let the same thing happen to Ella.' His voice was hoarse with emotion as he added, 'If she had still been here, Kate would have told her everything by now. I'm sure of it.'

Esther turned suddenly, pulling herself out of her husband's arms and she rushed towards the door, turning back only to fling out her arm in a gesture of dismissal. 'You say you "respect" me, but you'd have her know all me shame. Go on then, tell her, but she'll get nowt out o' me! Not ever.' Then she ran out through the scullery and across the yard towards the sand-dunes, seeking refuge out in the open at the end of the Spit, but not before Ella had seen the tears in her grandmother's eyes.

The sight shook the girl so that she felt herself turn pale and gripped the edge of the table. 'Oh Grandpa, we've upset her. Maybe we shouldn't . . .'

He smiled and put up his hand to still her words. 'She'll be all right. Don't worry, Ella. You go with Danny tomorrow, then maybe you'll understand your grannie better.'

That night, Ella could hardly sleep. She tossed and turned until her bed was an uncomfortable, tumbled heap and by ten o'clock the next morning when Danny's car pulled into the yard at Brumbys' Farm to pick her up, her eyes were red-rimmed with tiredness and there was a dull ache at the back of her head.

But nothing, she told herself, as she climbed into the passenger seat, was going to stop her going today.

As they drove along the coast road, Ella said, 'Have you told Aunty Rosie and Grandma Eland what we're doing?'

'Yes.'

'And?'

'And what?'

'Do – do they mind?'

Danny grinned. 'My mother's as a'kward as your gran sometimes, but when I explained it all to her, she came around. You see, it's her secret as well. When it all happened, well, it was a shameful thing in them days.' He raised his shoulders. 'We're getting a bit kinder towards such mistakes, but not fast enough to my idea.'

'I still don't understand.'

'All in good time, Ella. All in good time.'

She smiled at him. 'You're enjoying this, Uncle Danny,' she accused. 'Aren't you?'

'Well, it's a day out, a day away from work. And with a pretty girl.' His smile broadened. 'What more could an old feller like me want, eh?'

'Where are we're going?'

'Suddaby.'

The name sounded familiar as if she should know but couldn't just quite remember. 'Where's that?'

'About fifteen miles inland. I'm going to tell you everything from the very beginning, at least the beginning as far as we're all concerned. Then we'll come back to Lynthorpe and, finally, back to Fleethaven . . .' His voice dropped as he said, more to himself than to her, 'Everything comes back to Fleethaven.'

They drove in silence for a while until Danny said suddenly, 'I hope today's not going to upset you too much.'

'Upset me? Why should it?'

'Well, I didn't know if talking about ya mam upsets you.'

She sighed. 'I'd like to talk about her, to know more about her. But no one seems to want to mention her name. It's as if she's a taboo subject. Grandpa will sometimes speak about her, but not for long, and as for Gran, well, I don't think anyone dare say Mum's name in front of her.'

'Mmm.' He was silent for a moment, then he murmured, 'Well, perhaps after today things might become a little clearer for you.'

They were driving through the winding lanes of a village. 'This is Suddaby. Do you remember the very first time you came to Fleethaven Point? To a funeral?'

She nodded. 'Yes. I saw the old man in his coffin.'

Danny glanced at her in surprise. 'Did you? Did you really? Well, that was your great-grandfather, your gran's dad, Will Benson. I think,' he slowed the car down to a crawl past a line of cottages, 'that he lived here somewhere, but I can't be absolutely sure.'

Ella looked at the line of cottages, whitewashed with pretty gardens, their polished windows twinkling in the sun.

The car rounded a corner and they came to the church. Danny pulled on to the grass verge near the gate and they got out. Walking up the curving path, it was peaceful in the churchyard, only the birds fluttering in the tall trees, calling to each other.

Ella suddenly pointed excitedly. 'I do remember now. Rob threw sticks up into that tree. That was at the old man's funeral, wasn't it? I remember it 'cos Mum was walking with you and no one was taking any notice of me. I went galloping across all the graves to get to Rob . . .' She gave a fleeting smile. 'Gran was shouting at me even then.'

Danny said nothing, just nodded. He led her round the corner of the church and amongst the graves until he stopped in front of a row of three identical headstones. Ella felt her pulse quicken. At last, she was going to hear the story from the very beginning, hear all the secrets that had so dogged her life, half whispered snippets that had made no sense to the young child and yet had seemed to affect her life so deeply.

Danny pointed to the headstone in the centre. 'That's your great-grandfather's grave.'

Ella read the inscription. 'In loving memory of William Benson born 20th June 1860 died 23rd January 1953.'

'Goodness, he was ninety-two when he died.'

Danny grinned. 'Look well if your gran teks after him.'

Ella laughed. 'I wouldn't put it past her.' Her glance went to the headstones on either side of Will. One read 'In loving memory of Rebecca Benson, beloved wife of William Benson, departed this life 30th March 1919, aged 62 years. Her reward is in Heaven.'

'So this is Gran's mother, is it?' Ella murmured.

'No,' Danny said quietly at her side. 'No, it isn't. That's the whole point, lass. This . . .' he was pointing to the headstone on the other side of Will '. . . is your gran's mother and your great-grandmother.'

Ella gasped as she leant forward and read the inscription. 'In loving memory of Constance Everatt who fell asleep 9th June 1893, aged nineteen years. The Lord giveth and the Lord taketh away.'

'Everatt? That's the name your mam called my gran when they were rowing that day. Esther Everatt, she called her.' Ella was looking now from one headstone to the other, trying to work it all out.

Danny's voice came softly. 'Will Benson was married to Rebecca. They never had any children and then he fell in love with Connie Everatt, a young lass in the village. She had a bairn, ya gran, but died three days after giving birth.'

Ella gasped. Now the mists of a shameful secret were beginning to clear, floating away to reveal the truth.

'Esther was brought up by her aunt Hannah, Connie's sister. She was an old battle-axe, by all accounts. Never showed ya gran any love and just treated her as a skivvy for her own large family of kids.'

'Did Gran know who her father was all the time?'

Danny shook his head. 'Old Will didn't acknowledge her as his daughter for years, not until after his wife had died, but he always kept a watch over her. I expect everybody in Suddaby village knew, but nothing was said outright. Y'know how it is?'

'So,' Ella murmured, 'her aunt was pretty hard on Gran, was she?'

Danny snorted. 'That's an understatement, lass, from what I've heard. Reckon ya gran might have been happier in the workhouse, and that's saying summat.'

Ella stood for a few moments staring down at the grave of the young nineteen-year-old girl who had died so tragically young and whose early death had left her bastard child to the mercy of a cruel aunt. 'I asked at that funeral who this girl was and it all went deathly silent. No wonder!'

They turned and walked back through the churchyard.

'At sixteen,' Danny went on, 'Esther left the cottage here in the village and walked through the night to Fleethaven Point. Will, on his rounds as a carrier, knew that old Sam Brumby was past managing his farm and needed help, even though the stubborn old goat wouldn't admit it!'

'Is that how Gran came to live there, then? Just like that. Came to work for Sam – and – and stayed?'

Danny smiled, but there was a tinge of sadness in his smile. 'Aye, put simply, that's about it.'

'But there's more?'

He sighed. 'Oh, aye, lass, there's more. A lot more.'

Back at the car they both paused and looked about them. 'I'm sorry I can't tell you exactly where Will lived or where your gran lived as a child with her aunt.'

'It's all right.' She looked up at him. 'I'm surprised you know so much. How come?'

He opened the car door, got in and slammed it shut before he said. 'You'll see.'

They drove slowly out of the village and up a hill. Near the top, he pulled in on to the wide grass verge and switched off the engine. They sat for a few moments looking out over the rolling countryside before them. Below a tractor put-putted its way across the field, stopping every few yards for the stooks to be loaded on to the trailer.

'There's a basket in the back ya aunty Rosie's packed up. Let's have a bite, shall we?'

Suddenly, Ella realized she was very thirsty – and hungry. In her excitement or apprehension that morning, she wasn't sure which, she had eaten very little breakfast.

She got out of the car and climbed into the back seat where she unpacked the basket and handed ham sandwiches wrapped in greaseproof paper to Danny.

'I'll take you to see the old airfield next.'

'Why?' Ella asked, and bit into her sandwich.

'It was an operational bomber station during the war. Ya mam was a WAAF there. Now,' he smiled, 'I know I'm overrunning me tale a bit, but if I tried to tell you everything just in the order it happened, we'd be running round the countryside, backwards and for'ards all day.'

Ella grinned at him. 'It's all right. I think I'll fit all the pieces together when I know them. I always was good at jigsaws.'

Danny guffawed. 'Oh, this is a jigsaw, an' no mistake.'

'I knew Mum was in the WAAFs. Aunty Isobel and

Aunty Mave – they're my godmothers – she met them then.'

'That's right.' Danny nodded.

'I haven't seen them in years. Not since Mum's funeral.' Ella sighed. 'Gran would never let me go back to Lincoln to visit anybody, not even Aunty Peggy. It was always the same, "No, we need you here." I knew it was only an excuse. This last Christmas was the very first time I'd been back in six years.'

'I think,' he said slowly, 'she's always been afraid you wouldn't come back if you once got back to Lincoln.'

Ella laughed wryly. 'She was probably right, too,' her tone sobered and there was a trace of bitterness as she added, 'though I'd have thought she'd have been pleased to see the back of me.'

'Now, now, don't talk like that, young Ella,' he admonished gently, but his understanding smile took away the sting. He, better than anyone perhaps, seemed to understand what her life was like at Brumbys' Farm.

They packed up the basket again and she slid back into the front seat. They drove down the hill and soon came to the derelict airfield, its concrete runways dotted with tufts of grass and broken pieces of rubble, its control tower echoing with ghostly memories, the door squeaking as it swung to and fro in the wind. Danny pulled the car to a halt and switched off the engine. For a few moments he did not seem to be here in the car with Ella, but looking back to the days of the war, hearing again the vibrant noise of the Lancaster bombers as they took off into the night.

'My squadron was posted here, to Suddaby, where Kate was, but on the first mission out of here I was shot down and taken prisoner. I had a bad leg wound, hence the limp.' He glanced at her and grinned swiftly. 'I never got the chance to talk to her much then and I didn't manage to get repatriated until, oh, mid-way through 'forty-three. She'd left the WAAF by then . . .' He turned and looked straight at Ella. 'She'd got you.'

She returned his gaze and said quietly, 'Uncle Danny, do you know who my dad was?'

He did not answer her question immediately but got out of the car and stretched his limbs, his arms above his head. Ella got out too and together they walked on to the deserted airfield and towards the dilapidated control tower before he said, 'No, not really.'

She looked at him, her head slightly on one side. 'Sounds as if you have your suspicions, though.'

'As far as I know, Kate never told a living soul.'

'Not even him?'

Danny sighed and shook his head. 'I don't think so.'

Her heart contracted. She swallowed. 'Do you mean – he was killed – in the war – and she never got the chance?'

'No, no,' Danny said swiftly. 'Not that.' He stopped, but she knew there was more. She bit her lip to stop herself pressing him. He would tell her in his own time, but she knew this was a difficult day – for both of them. So many emotions, so many memories being dragged out and laid bare.

'When Kate told me about you, she said she couldn't marry the father – sorry, your father . . .' his voice dropped to a whisper '. . . because he was already married.'

Her heart felt like a lump of lead in her chest, heavy and cold. 'So,' she said and could hardly keep the tears from her voice, 'he won't want me either.'

Danny put his arm about her. In the cool of the wind that whipped across the flat, desolate airfield, his touch was warm, comforting. 'Don't say that, love. I honestly don't think he even knows of your existence. If he did . . .'

He left the words lying unspoken between them, for in truth, neither knew the real answer.

'Come on, let's take a look around.' He glanced down at her. 'If you want to, that is.'

Ella nodded and her voice was husky as she added, 'Show me where Mum worked. Tell me what she did.'

'She was in the MT Section, Motor Transport. I think,' he steered her in the direction of a square of concrete with buildings around it, 'this was the MT yard. I'm a bit hazy. I wasn't here many minutes,' and he added ruefully, 'literally.'

The buildings were empty and the yard clear except for a heap of rubbish in one corner, an old propeller sticking out the only reminder of the aircraft that had once filled the skies above the airfield. Ella gazed around trying to imagine it alive and humming with activity: huge lorries and jeeps, cars and motorcycles and, of course, the huge, lumbering, magnificent aircraft.

'She drove the CO about, didn't she?'

'Most of the time, yes. But she'd be under the officer in charge of the MT Section. If the CO didn't need her, she'd be detailed for other duties.'

'What?'

'Well, let's think. She used to drive the crew bus, taking the airmen out to the aircraft when they were going on an operation, maybe meet them when they came back – that sort of thing. But she'd never be far from the camp just in case the CO needed her.'

'So . . .' Ella said slowly, thoughtfully, 'she spent most of her time with the CO, did she?'

Danny looked down at her. 'Yes,' he said quietly. 'She did.'

They walked across to the control tower, its windows broken, only shards of glass remaining, the paint peeling;

the glass lookout on the roof had crumbled and lay in a twisted heap of metal.

'Can we go inside?'

Danny glanced about him and shrugged. 'Don't see why not.'

The door, as he pushed it open, scraped on the concrete floor and their footsteps echoed eerily as they went inside. It was gloomy, and a melancholy air hung over the whole place. Upstairs, Danny said, 'This is the control room where Mavis and Isobel worked as R/T Operators. They talked to the aircraft.'

The room was littered with old chairs, desks and wooden shapes that had once held radios now ripped out. On the wall was a huge blackboard with the name SUDDABY painted in white at the top. Underneath was the word RAID and blank spaces for details to be filled in. And the column that seemed, to the wide-eyed girl, the most poignant, RETURN.

How many times had that last column remained heart-rendingly incomplete?

Had her mother sat here watching that board, Ella wondered, waiting through the long hours of darkness for the sound of returning aircraft, her gaze riveted on that last column, waiting for the return of the man she loved?

He must have been on this station, she reasoned. But had he been a pilot, or a member of the ground crew, or maybe an officer? Maybe, just maybe, a very high-ranking officer. Perhaps she was standing in the very place where her father, too, had stood waiting for the sound of Lancaster engines in the night air. Perhaps they, her mother and father, had waited together . . .

Ella felt a shudder run through her. 'Let's go, Uncle Danny.'

They returned to the car and drove in silence for a

while, then, her mind beginning to work again, Ella said, 'You know the day Mum died, the day of the floods?'

'Mmm?'

'She was all excited, I think she was going to meet someone. She'd had a letter. It was waiting for her at Brumbys' Farm.' For a moment hope sprang again, and she turned to look at him. 'Do you think my father could have got in touch and she'd been going to meet him?'

Danny lifted his shoulders. 'I honestly don't know.'

'And you really don't have any idea who he might be?'

'The only people who might be able to make an educated guess are Mavis and Isobel. They were her friends at the time. They're your best bet.'

Ella was thoughtful for a while, then she asked, 'Where are we going now?'

'Back to Lynthorpe. We're – we're going to see ya mam's grave. Now a' ya sure?'

Ella nodded firmly. 'No. I'll be fine. But maybe we could get some flowers on the way, could we?'

He smiled and his voice was husky as he said, 'That's a nice idea, love.'

Now it was Ella who led the way through the churchyard towards the corner where her mother was buried. There was a simple white headstone with the inscription, 'In loving memory of Katharine Hilton, born 4th September 1912. Tragically drowned in the East Coast floods 31st January 1953.'

Ella stood looking down at the grave and then gently laid the flowers on top.

Danny, standing beside her, said softly, 'We fell in love, ya know, ya mam and me.'

Ella stared at him. Fleeting memories filled her mind:

Kate and Danny greeting each other, their fond embrace, the look in their eyes when they looked at each other, their whispered conversations. Now, with his brief words, it was all explained. And she understood, too, why no one else, not even Aunty Rosie, had minded their obvious affection for each other. They had all understood.

'We didn't know then, you see, that we were related. We just thought that all the time your gran was trying to keep us apart, it was because of her feud with my mother. They were so busy trying to keep their own secrets, they never thought about what might happen to us.'

Ella gasped. 'How awful! When did this happen?'

'We were eighteen. When we told both families we wanted to get married, all hell broke loose.' He was silent for a moment, gazing down at the earth where his first love lay. He took a deep breath and pointed to the grave to one side. 'There, see that one? Matthew Hilton?'

Ella stepped to one side and bent forward to read for herself. 'Matthew Hilton, husband of Esther Hilton and father of Katharine, born 20th August 1890, drowned January 1920.'

'He was drowned too,' Ella murmured. 'Like Mum. Funny, I never noticed this grave on the day of her funeral.'

'Hardly surprising,' Danny commented and then went on with his story. 'There was a dreadful storm at the Point. At that time we lived on an old boat on the river bank. It wasn't safe and we came off and went to the Harrises' cottage. But he,' Danny's eyes too were on the Matthews grave, 'he thought we were still on the boat. He came to rescue us, me mam and me.'

She stared at him as, at last, she began to understand. 'He was Gran's first husband, wasn't he? And she's bitter because he was drowned trying to save you and your mother?' Ella felt a moment's empathy for her grandmother. No wonder Esther had been so frantic when Grandpa Godfrey had gone to the Point to rescue Grandma Eland at the time of the floods; she must have been so afraid she might lose Jonathan in exactly the same way.

He nodded and she went on, easing his telling of the story by saying the words for him. 'And he was trying to save *you* and *your* mam because he was your father too.'

Danny nodded. 'Yes, Matthew Hilton was ya mam's dad . . .' he paused and pulled in a deep shuddering breath as he added hoarsely, 'and mine.'

There was a world of sadness and pain in his tone as he went on. 'It was all kept such a dark, dreadful secret that we had no idea. We grew up together, ya mam and me. We were kids together and when we fell in love, well . . .'

Ella looked down again at her mother's grave, imagining how they'd felt, loving each other and yet knowing they could never, ever, be together.

'We were shattered – devastated,' Danny said hoarsely. 'Our whole world was torn apart.' He swallowed and then, more strongly, continued his story. 'Years before, Matthew Hilton lived in the row of cottages at the Point and Beth, my mam, lived next door. They'd been sweethearts, were "walking out together" as they used to call it.'

It was a quaint, old-fashioned phrase, but neither of them were in the mood for smiling just now. Ella remained silent, patiently waiting while Danny explained everything in his own time. She could sense he was finding it difficult to recall the heartbreak of all those years ago and what had caused it; a pain that perhaps he had tried to keep locked away for years. That he was reliving it, for her sake, touched the young girl deeply.

'Matthew was, by all accounts, a bit of a flirt. He had an eye for the girls, y'know? When ya gran arrived at

Fleethaven Point, like I was telling you earlier, well, he made a play for her. But she was having none of him.'

He paused and Ella could not resist asking, 'Then how come she married him?'

'Well, now.' Danny seemed to hesitate. 'This is where it all gets a bit, well, messy. Ya gran, as you now know, was born illegitimate and, I think, because of it, all her life she's been rigid in her views of right and wrong. You know what I mean?'

'Oh, yes,' Ella said bitterly. 'I know what you mean all right. I suppose that's why she wouldn't believe me and Rob.'

'It's been her own moral code. You can't blame her for that, really.'

'I suppose it's understandable when she obviously suffered so much because of the circumstances of her birth and why,' the girl added, as compassion came slowly with the unfolding of the tale, 'she turned against my mum – and – and me.'

His arm tightened about her shoulders.

'So?' she prompted him to continue. 'What happened?'

'Ya gran held out against Matthew, wouldn't give in to him and the more she did that, the more he was mad to have her.'

'But your mother? She did?'

He nodded. 'She didn't see it as wrong if you truly loved someone. And she thought he loved her . . .' Danny turned his dark brown eyes to look into Ella's bright blue gaze. 'I think he did, but he found that out too late.'

'Let me get this straight,' Ella said. 'Matthew and Beth were going out and gran came along and he left your mother when she was expecting you, I take it?'

He nodded, but said swiftly, 'But he didn't know that, not until later. Not till after he'd married Esther.'

'So he left your mother, married Esther and *then* found out your mother was pregnant by him?'

Danny nodded.

Frowning, Ella asked, 'When did your mother marry Robert Eland, then?'

'Soon after Matthew had married Esther and just before I was born. He was a good few years older than her but he'd always loved her and he married her to give me a name. As far as anyone outside Fleethaven Point knows, I'm *his* son. I thought I was too – for years. He was as good a father as anyone could hope to have. That's why we called young Rob after him.'

'So that's what all the family feud is about between your mother and Gran?'

'Er, well, there's a bit more yet.'

'More!' Ella's eyes widened and she sighed with mock exasperation. 'Go on, then.'

'I like to believe that your gran was genuinely fond of Matthew, but there's a lot of folks, my mother included, of course, who think she only married Matthew because she couldn't have the tenancy of Brumbys' Farm in her own name. Squire Marshall wouldn't give it to a woman and when old Sam Brumby died, Esther was in danger of being homeless again. I've heard say that she nursed Sam at home and that it was only because of her devotion the poor old boy was able to die in his own home.' Danny sighed. 'I suppose that's what started all the trouble, really.'

'Sam Brumby dying, you mean?'

'Sort of. When the old man was so ill, Matthew moved into Brumbys' Farm to help Esther look after him and keep the farm going. I don't doubt, though,' Danny added and there was a dry amusement in his voice, 'that mebbe young Matthew had his own reasons for doing so.'

They were silent for a few moments, each busy with their own thoughts.

'Do you mean,' she began hesitantly, not wanting to believe it possible, 'that my gran only agreed to marry Matthew so that she could get Brumbys' Farm?'

Danny wriggled his shoulders uncomfortably. 'That's what folks say, but as I said, I'm not sure I agree with them. I've always admired and respected your gran.'

Ella snorted. 'You and Rob both.'

He grinned. 'Aye, they're great pals.'

'Used to be, you mean. I'm not so sure now.'

'I was very bitter against her for a while when Kate and I found out the truth. If only they'd told us earlier, it would have saved a lot of heartache.' There was such anguish in his voice that Ella slipped her arm through his and hugged it to her side. Trying to draw his thoughts away from his unhappy memories, she asked, 'Where does Grandpa Godfrey fit into all this then?'

'Matthew guessed I was his child, not Robert's, and he was very bitter with ya gran after that, but then she had ya mam – Kate.' His tone softened even when just speaking her name.

'With the outbreak of the war in 'fourteen Matthew volunteered. While he was away ya grandpa happened to come to the Point, met ya gran and they fell in love.'

Ella gasped. 'By heck!' she cried, falling into using Rob's favourite expression. 'She's a fine one to be so high and mighty then.'

'Now, now, don't go judging her, Ella. Jonathan went away again, back to the war, and at that time she had no idea whether he was still alive or not. After the war, it was *Matthew* who came back a broken wreck of a man and she nursed him back to health. She devoted herself to him and gave up any hope she might have had of finding

Jonathan again. She's always had a very strong sense of duty, ya gran. She's never shirked from doing what had to be done.'

'No,' Ella said sadly, 'not even when it came to bringing up her orphaned *bastard* granddaughter.'

'Now, now,' he chided her again gently, but as he squeezed her shoulder again, she knew he understood. 'There's just one more thing I want you to understand, Ella. It's important to *me* that you know and – and . . .' his voice was husky, 'for the sake of your mother's memory.'

She stared at him, waiting. She sensed he was finding it difficult to talk about feelings he had kept buried for so long. 'We – we loved each other very much, but when we found out we were so closely related, we knew we could never be anything but brother and sister. It took us a long time to come to terms with it and I suppose, deep down, we never stopped loving each other in a very special way.'

Ella nodded. 'I know,' she whispered. 'I saw it whenever you both met. Even as a child, I could see.'

He sighed. 'But life moves on. We both found other people to love. Rosie . . .' He smiled fondly as he thought of his wife and said, with modesty, 'Evidently Rosie had always loved me and I found I could love her too. Perhaps not in the same way I once loved Kate. Differently, maybe, but just as much. I'm so lucky,' he murmured, 'that because Rosie loved Kate too, she's always understood.' He paused and then ended softly, 'So now, you know it all.'

Not quite, Ella mused, but she kept her thoughts to herself. I still don't know who *my* father is. As they turned away and, with one last silent farewell to her mother, headed back towards the car, an idea began to form in her mind, growing until it became a pledge.

One day, she vowed, I'll find my dad.

Twenty-Four

When they walked through the back door of Brumbys' Farm and into the kitchen, they found Esther sitting at the kitchen table, her arms resting on the scrubbed surface, gazing into the distance as if she, too, were taking a trip back in time. Slowly she lifted her head and her eyes focused on the present again, on Danny and Ella. They stared at each other for a long time, and, suddenly, the young girl thought she caught a glimpse of a strange expression in the older woman's face; one she had never expected to see. It was fleeting, yet she was sure she had seen it; a silent plea for understanding. It was gone in an instant and the resentment was back.

Danny, trying to warm the icy atmosphere, sat down on the other side of the table. 'Get that kettle singing, Ella lass,' he said, but his gaze never left Esther's face. 'I'm fair parched after all that yakking.'

'Aye, I should think there's been plenty of that!' the older woman said acidly.

Danny reached across and took her wrinkled hands in his. 'I told it fairly, Missus.'

'Ya'd have done better to hold ya tongue altogether, Danny Eland.' There was a pause, then she added with grudging reluctance, 'Still, if she had to be told, then I'd rather it be you do the telling than anyone else.'

As Ella turned away and busied herself over the hob, she heard her grandmother ask softly, 'Did she say owt?'

and Danny, equally quietly, answered, 'Not much. But then, it's a lot to sink in all at once.'

At that moment they all heard the rattle of the back door and Jonathan came into the kitchen, filling the room with his gentleness. He sat down at the table and a few moments later when Ella set cups of tea before them, they were all chatting, the tension lifted by Jonathan's presence.

Ella, sitting down too, listened quietly. No wonder, she thought, Gran had fallen in love with him all those years ago. She felt a sudden stab of sadness at the thought of what she had learnt recently: that this kind, lovable man was not her real grandfather.

Now, having learnt today how that came about, she could not help wondering about the man who overshadowed all their lives, even to this day; her grandfather, Matthew Hilton. Just what had he been like?

That night when Ella went up to bed, she paused on the landing, listened a moment and then, holding her breath, stealthily lifted the latch on the door of her grandparents' bedroom. She tiptoed across the room to the mantelpiece and, holding the candle she carried higher, picked up the photo of the man in the old-fashioned uniform.

In the flickering light she gazed down at the young face. So this was Matthew Hilton. This was her real grandfather and he was Rob's grandfather too. No wonder the photograph had reminded her of Rob.

Ella chewed thoughtfully at her lip. Kate, her mother, had inherited the auburn hair of her own mother, Esther. But she, Ella, was neither dark like her grandfather, nor auburn like her mother and grandmother. So, from whom did she get her blonde hair?

There could only be one answer: from the man who was her father.

Carefully, she replaced the photograph and went into her own bedroom. She stood in the centre of the room and her gaze was drawn towards the huge blanket box in the corner where she knew all her mother's belongings were still stored and had been ever since they had been brought from their home in Lincoln. Almost holding her breath, she tiptoed across the room and lifted the heavy lid. She propped it open with the lift-up bar at one side and, almost with a kind of reverence, she lifted out her mother's handbag. The leather was stained and the fastener was rusty. She forced it open and the fusty smell of sea-water wafted from its interior. The memories crowded into her mind and she swallowed hard. Such a feeling of loneliness and longing flooded through her that Ella felt like the ten-year-old girl she had been then when she had packed her mother's things into this chest. She hadn't opened it since that time, not once. Even now, she still wanted to close the lid and leave the sad memories locked away. But if she wanted to find any clue about her father, then she had to search her mother's papers.

Determined not to be diverted, she took a deep breath, put in her hand and pulled out all the items still resting there. All the personal, intimate things brought her mother's presence suddenly into the room. The girl swayed and clutched at the side of the chest.

'Oh, Mum,' she whispered, 'I still miss you so.'

Resolutely, she steadied herself and spread everything out on her bed. It was the letter that intrigued her: maybe that was the one her mother had received that had made her go off that day? But the crinkled sheets were just a blotchy wash of blue ink; not one word was legible.

She sighed and put everything back into the bag, holding

each item in her hands for a few moments: Kate's lipstick and powder compact, even the keys to Peggy's house in Lincoln; they were all still there just as she had packed them away, undisturbed for six years. She closed the stiff fastener and laid the bag aside.

Next she carefully removed the folded garments, one after another, until she came to a square box. She lifted it out and carried it back to her bed and tried to lift the lid, but the box was locked.

Back at the blanket box she leaned over, scrabbling to the very bottom amongst the clothes, a box of books, a cardboard box in which she found an assortment of baby clothes, but there was nothing in the way of a key which might fit the small box. She leant against the chest and stared at the box on the bed. There was something niggling at the back of her mind. She could remember searching for the key before, and when the police had brought Kate's handbag back, she had been sure that it would be there. She recalled her disappointment when it wasn't. But there was something else, something she ought to know, but Ella just couldn't pull it to the forefront of her mind, and the more she tried, the more elusive the memory seemed to become.

Sighing, she packed all the clothes back into the chest, and, lastly, put the small polished wooden box back, but on the top of all the other items. She closed the huge lid of the chest and began to undress.

Sleep did not come easily. Her mind was too full of all that she had heard from her uncle Danny that day, her head full of pictures of the places they had visited, the memories he had evoked, not only for himself but for her too. Memories of her lovely gentle mother; of life in the little house in Lincoln with Aunty Peggy. There had been just the three of them, cosy and secure in their little world with never, as far as she could recall, a cross word between them. She couldn't remember ever being in trouble then with either her mother or Peggy.

Was it only since she had come to Brumbys' Farm that she had become a wild, rebellious, naughty child, forever in disgrace with her strict grandmother?

She couldn't remember falling asleep, but suddenly she sat bolt upright. The room was in total darkness. The key! She could remember seeing a key and now she knew where: in her mother's sewing machine. In the small box which held bobbins and machine attachments, there had been a tiny key. She remembered seeing it when she had made her blouse and skirt. It was exactly the sort of place her mother would have kept the key to her precious box; close beside her every day as she worked.

Ella slipped out of bed and padded across the floor to the door. Holding her breath she opened it, wincing at every little squeak. She crept down the stairs, pausing to listen every time a stair creaked.

In the living room, she drew aside the heavy blue velvet curtain so that moonlight beamed in. Quietly, she lifted the lid from the machine and took the smaller lid from the box at the side. She scrabbled amongst the clutter there until her fingers closed on the key. Replacing the lid and leaving the machine as she had found it, she sneaked back upstairs. Once in the safety of her bedroom, she breathed easily again and with the door firmly shut she lit her candle, wishing, not for the first time, that her grandmother would agree to have electric light, and went again to the blanket box.

Taking the smaller box back to her bed, she wriggled her cold feet under the covers and, sitting up, rested the box on her knees. Mentally crossing her fingers, she inserted the key into the lock. It fitted, but was stiff to turn through lack of use. Ella found her heart was thumping with excitement as she opened the lid. The box was a vanity case with glass bottles each in their own place. In a small central compartment with a padded lid there was an envelope with the words 'Danielle Hilton, aged three' written on the front. Inside was a photograph of Ella and a curl of strawberry blonde hair wrapped in tissue paper. Ella smiled and laid the envelope to one side on the bed. Next she found her mother's WAAF badges and a photograph of Kate with Mavis and Isobel, all in uniform. In the background, Ella could see the huge shape of an aircraft. There was an old, rather faded, photograph taken in the front garden of the farmhouse of her grandmother and Jonathan standing beside an old man leaning heavily on a stick. That must be Esther's father, Will Benson, Ella thought, the man whose grave she'd seen the previous day.

There was nothing else in the small compartment and Ella felt a stab of disappointment. Surely there must be something else . . . letters, photographs – there *must* be more.

She ran her fingers round the box, feeling its polished smoothness. Then at the side, she noticed two tiny ring handles and pulled them up. The whole of the top of the box lifted out to reveal another, deeper, compartment below and Ella's eyes gleamed. In it lay a bundle of papers and letters. And on the top sat a huge, perfectly formed whelk shell. She picked it up and cradled it on the palm of her hand for a moment. Now why on earth, she pondered, would her mother keep a whelk shell? She placed it beside her on top of the quilt and then, with mounting excitement, Ella began to look carefully through each item.

The first was her own birth certificate, and as she opened the long, stiff paper, she found she was holding her breath.

Now, at last, she might find out . . . But under the heading 'Name and Surname of Father' there was nothing written, only two lines drawn across it. Ella groaned aloud and then clapped her hand over her mouth. For a few moments she stared wide-eyed at her bedroom door and held her breath. But there was no sound of the other door opening and her grandmother's voice demanding, 'Now what are you up to, Missy?'

She looked down again at the long paper in her hands. It gave details of her birth. She hadn't realized before that she'd actually been born in the terraced house in Lincoln, she mused. Then her mother's name, Katharine Hilton. Here was the stark proof that her mother had never married, even though Ella remembered people in Lincoln calling her 'Mrs' Hilton. Somehow until she saw it written plainly before her eyes, there had always been a last vestige of hope that maybe her mother had been secretly married and he'd been killed in the war. Maybe . . .

But no, she thought, she really was what her grandmother called her.

She folded the certificate and laid that to one side too.

Next she lifted out a packet of letters. On the first envelope the address was written in bold, yet neat, handwriting. Ella bit her lip, hesitating a moment, feeling suddenly guilty at prying into all her mother's secrets. Yet she had to know, she had to find out about her father. Surely, her mother wouldn't have minded? Surely by now, as Uncle Danny had suggested, Kate would have told her everything, if only she had still been here to do the telling?

Sighing softly, Ella untied the ribbon holding the letters together and opened the first one.

My Dear Kate

I have settled in well here, but it is not a patch on my previous posting. I hope you are well – I do miss our little chats.

I expect Lincolnshire is looking a little wintry at the moment – no fields of rippling ripe corn. My current driver is not nearly so efficient at changing a wheel in the dark.

I have written twice before, but have not had a reply from you. Perhaps you did not get the letters.

Kate, we must meet. I shall be attending a big meeting in Grantham the week after next. If you're still the new CO's driver, you should be bringing him . . . We could meet on the Wednesday about four, at the station, if you could manage it.

There was nothing in the letter to give any real clues and to Ella's acute disappointment there was not even a name at the end. She knew there had been a lot of difficulty in writing letters in wartime, particularly perhaps for servicemen, but he might have put his name, she thought crossly.

It was the only one from the mystery man; the others were from people she knew. One was from Grandpa to Kate, written to her at the Suddaby station and enclosing another from Aunty Peggy and both letters were dated a few months before Ella's birth.

Her grandfather's letter was short, a mere two lines.

I think, my dear, that the enclosed letter will be the answer for you, at least for the time being . . .

The answer to what?

Ella began to read Peggy's letter,

My dear Jonathan,

Of course Kate can come back to us. We should love to have her – it will be like old times – and she would be company for Mother, who, although still lively in her mind, is increasingly confined to the house and, indeed, to her sofa. As you know, since Father died, Mother has slept downstairs in the living room and so Kate, and her little one when it arrives, could have Mother's bedroom upstairs. I'm still in my own room anyway, so it won't be putting us about at all! And there's still the tiny bedroom Kate had before, when the little one gets older . . .

Ella laid down the letter. So, that was how she had come to be born in Lincoln and why they had continued to live with Aunty Peggy, Jonathan's sister. She read a paragraph again. What did it mean 'Kate can come back to us'? She didn't understand that bit at all. She would have to ask . . . Oh no, she told herself firmly, you can't ask Gran. Now she knew the whole story, or at least most of it, she could sense even from these sparse letters that Kate had gone to live with Peggy because her own mother, Esther, would not have Kate, pregnant and unmarried, at home. Esther Godfrey had turned out her own daughter. That must have been 'the answer' Jonathan referred to; the answer to a problem and a problem caused by her grandmother. That much, at least, Ella could deduce.

In the flickering light from the candles, Ella's mind drifted back to the very first moment she had met her grandmother. What was it she had said? Oh, yes, she remembered now the harsh words between her mother and grandmother.

'I told you ten years ago I didn't want you here, or ya bastard, and I still don't. Nothing's changed.'

And then Kate's forlorn words, 'Can't you ever forget anything or forgive anyone, Mam?'

Remembering the moment vividly now, Ella could hear

their voices in her mind. At last she understood all the resentment and bitterness that lay behind the words. Her mother had not only been referring to the continuing feud between Esther and Beth Eland, but to the unforgiving treatment she herself had received from Esther.

Beneath the letters there were two or three photographs of her mother in uniform. One intrigued Ella; it was of her mother standing beside a huge car with bulbous headlamps covered over and leaving only a slit for the light to shine through. She was holding open the back door of the car and beside her stood a tall man in an officer's uniform. Holding it close to the uncertain light from the candle, Ella strained to see the man in the picture. Her heart began to beat rapidly as she realized that this just might be the first time she had ever seen her father.

Twenty-Five

There was, of course, only one person she could talk to about the things she had found.

All through the following day as she went about the jobs her grandmother had set her, Ella turned over in her mind everything she wanted to ask Uncle Danny and how she should put it to be tactful. But by the time she was free to squeeze through the hole in the hedge and run across the newly cut fields, the sharp stubble crunching under her feet, towards Rookery Farm, all her carefully formed plans were blown away in her eagerness.

Clasped in her hand was something she wanted to show him. As she climbed over the stile and jumped down into the lane near the farm, she heard the familiar roar of the engine of Rob's motorbike revving up in the yard. Her heart gave a leap in her chest and she began to run. The bike came sweeping out of the yard, banking over to the left and as it gathered speed past Ella, he raised his hand in greeting but made no attempt to slow down. Ella stared after him as the bike reached the end of the lane.

Off to see the summer girls, she thought bitterly. Now he won't even stop to speak to me.

But at the junction, Rob turned his motorcycle full circle and came back towards her, pulling up beside her and, cutting the engine, he balanced the machine with his toes touching the ground on either side.

'You all right, El?'

She returned his steady gaze. Today there was no merry grin stretched across his mouth, no teasing laughter, but she could see the concern in his deep brown eyes.

'Why've you been ignoring me?'

He wriggled his shoulders in embarrassment. 'I thought it best. I didn't want to mek ya grannie any madder.'

A spark of resentment flared. 'I see. More bothered about what Gran will say than about me.'

'No – yes – I mean . . .' He was floundering but Ella was in no mood to help him. 'I thought it'd only make things worse for you. I hoped if I stayed away a bit it might all blow over.'

'Blow over?' She snorted. 'No chance!'

'Well, I don't think you an' me dad have helped by going off on your little trip, digging up the past. You're only hurting her more.'

So, she thought, she wasn't the only one who now knew all the secrets. Danny must have told Rob everything too.

'It was their lives, El. It's all so long ago. It doesn't make any difference to us, now does it? Ya gran would have come round if you'd given her time.'

Suddenly she felt more sad than angry. He didn't understand how she felt, how everything that had happened in her grandmother's life, in her mother's life, did indeed still overshadow Ella's own.

'Perhaps it doesn't really affect you, Rob,' she told him quietly, 'but there's still things I have to know.'

She thought she saw the hurt in his eyes, but it was so fleeting that afterwards she wondered if she had imagined it. He stared at her for a moment, a slight frown creasing his forehead. Then looking away, he shrugged. 'Well, it's up to you . . .' He bent forward, twisted a lever and then stamped on the kickstart. The engine noise filled the air, making any more conversation impossible. He wheeled the bike round and, mouthing, 'See ya . . .' at her, he set off down the lane once more, this time turning left at the end, and roared along the coast road towards the town.

Her gaze followed his speeding shape as far as she could see and even when he had disappeared from her view, she could still hear the sound of him.

Her eyes filled with tears but she brushed them aside angrily with the back of her hand and marched with fresh determination towards the gate of Rookery Farm. As she went into the yard, Danny came out of the milking shed. 'Hello, young Ella. You've just missed him. Gone to the pictures, I think. Do you want to go with him? I could run you into town if you like.'

'No!' Her tone was sharper than she had intended. Then she added swiftly as an excuse, 'No thanks, Uncle Danny. I'm not allowed out.'

He sighed. 'I thought ya gran might have calmed down a bit.'

The girl shrugged her shoulders. 'She's still mad about our trip out yesterday.'

'Oh, I'm sorry. I didn't mean to make matters worse.'

'I don't think you could,' she said wryly. 'Anyway, can you spare a minute?'

'Of course.' He paused and then added softly, 'More questions is it, lass?'

She held out her hand. 'Uncle Danny, do you know why Mum would keep this?'

On her open palm lay the large whelk shell; a simple seashore shell, unusual, perhaps, in its size but an ordinary shell none the less, and Ella was totally unprepared for the extraordinary response it evoked in the man who stood looking down at it, mesmerized.

'Where . . .?' he began, his voice hoarse, and she was shocked to see sudden tears in his eyes. 'Now would you believe that?' he murmured, more to himself than to Ella. 'Fancy her keeping that all these years.'

He picked up the shell and held it tenderly, looking back down the years, remembering. 'We were only a couple o' kids when I gave her this. I'd just left school and she was being sent away to boarding school.' He looked up at Ella. 'Ya gran was trying to keep us apart even then, but we didn't know why.'

'Was that when she went to Aunty Peggy's in Lincoln?'

'Eh? Oh, she met them about that time but she didn't go to live with them until later, after we found out that we were brother and sister.'

'Then she went back again to live there when she had me, didn't she?'

He nodded. 'Ya gran tell you that?'

Ella shook her head. 'No, I found some letters and photographs. Uncle Danny, I think one of the men in uniform might – just might – be my father.'

Danny was staring at her, then he nodded slowly. 'It's possible. Probable, I suppose, when you think about it.'

'Uncle Danny, I want to go to Lincoln to see Aunty Peg and, if I can, Mavis. I want to try to find my father.'

'Now, hold on a minute, love. You'll only upset your gran even more.'

Ella's chin was determined. 'Surely she can't object to me wanting to find my father?'

He sighed and fingered the whelk shell, his thoughts still half-way in the past. 'You might be stirring up more trouble and disappointment for yourself. What will happen if your father has a family – children?'

'I'm his child, too.'

'How are you going to prove it, though? Have you got your birth certificate?'

'I – I found it last night amongst Mum's papers.'

'Does it give your father's name?'

She shook her head, unable to speak. She didn't want his reasoning to be right, but she knew it was.

'And don't forget,' Danny said gently, not wanting to say the words but knowing he must, 'I don't think he knows anything about you.'

Her mouth was now set in a decisive line. 'Then it's high time he did know. It seems as if my poor mum took all the shame and he got off scot free.'

Danny smiled pensively. 'Eh, you do sound like ya gran when ya gets a bee in ya bonnet about summat.'

'Well?' Ella said defensively. 'It's true, isn't it?'

He sighed and nodded. 'Yes, I suppose it is. But just remember one thing, Ella. Ya mam must have had her reasons. She loved him very much. That she did tell me. Maybe she loved him so much that she wanted to, well, protect him or not cause him pain. I don't know. As I say, she didn't tell me much. But just – well – tread carefully. Don't do anything hasty that might be totally against what ya mam would have wanted.'

She stared at him for a moment, taking in what he had said, considering it. Slowly, she nodded. 'I promise I'll go carefully, Uncle Danny, but I have to find out *who* he is at least. I have to.'

'I can understand that. But supposing he's still alive? Supposing you do find him, what then? What if he doesn't want to see you, to have anything to do with you? It could be *you* getting hurt then. Ya mam wouldn't have wanted that to happen either.'

'I won't get hurt,' Ella said, and as the picture that still haunted her dreams, of Rob chasing the summer girls along the beach, came into her mind, she added, resolutely, 'Not any more, I won't.'

Now plans were beginning to formulate in her mind,

but she clamped her jaw tightly shut against the temptation to share them with Uncle Danny.

This was something she had to do on her own.

When the O level results came out, Rob had just scraped the grades he needed to go to the farm institute near Lincoln. And Ella's results were good enough for her to be able to choose just whatever she wanted to do: stay on at school to take A levels and try for university or leave now and go to college. The other alternative was to get a job in Lynthorpe, but if she were to suggest that, then she knew what her grandmother would say at once: 'Ya needed here, on the farm.'

Rob came to say goodbye at the end of August. From her bedroom window, Ella saw him climb the stile and walk across the stubble towards Brumbys' Farm; this year the fields between the farms had grown wheat. At the hole in the hedge, he paused, hands shoved deep into his pockets, and glanced up at the house. She stood back from the window, not wanting him to see her watching him.

Her heart turned over. How handsome he looked, the open-necked white shirt dazzling against his tanned skin, his long, lithe body. He seemed to have grown, even, during this last year and now stood a head taller than his own father. He seemed to be standing there trying to decide whether to come through the hedge or not. Black curly hair ruffled by the wind and with a strange, nervous look on his face as he had hovered uncertainly near the hedge, he reminded her so much of the young soldier in the photograph in her grandmother's bedroom, about to go into battle. Then she saw her grandmother come round into the front garden and walk towards him through the few trees left in the orchard. Ella watched as Esther adopted her usual formidable pose: feet planted firmly apart, hands on hips. Through the open window, her voice drifted clearly to the watching girl. 'Well, a' ya coming through or aren't ya?'

She saw Rob grin, push his way through the hedge and walk towards the waiting woman. Closer to each other, their voices not so audible, Ella could not hear the interchange of conversation. They talked for a few moments and then slowly he turned and walked back towards the hedge. He was going and without even coming to find her to say goodbye. He had come to make his peace with her grandmother, but still, he was avoiding Ella. Disappointment, hurt and anger flooded through her. She felt herself clenching her jaw. All right, if that was the way he wanted it, that was the way he could have it! But the lump in her throat threatened to choke her.

The last thing she saw before she turned abruptly away from the window was her grandmother putting her arms around Rob and giving him a swift, affectionate hug; something she had never done to Ella.

An early-morning September mist, with the hint of autumnal sharpness in it, shrouded the farm as Ella let herself quietly out of the back door and tiptoed across the yard. From the direction of the barn, Tibby came towards her, his tail straight up and crooked in a question. She bent and stroked his head. 'Bye, Tibby, old darling,' she whispered. 'I wish I could take you with me, but you wouldn't like it in the city.'

She stood up again and he rubbed himself against her legs, purring loudly. She hitched the bundle to a more comfortable position on her shoulder and continued her way across the yard, the cat following. At the gate, she paused and looked back once at the house, still and silent, awaiting the start of a new day. As dawn crept over the sand-dunes, suddenly, from the chicken house, the cock crowed, a startling shriek in the quiet. 'Stupid bird!' she muttered, and began to hurry along the lane before her grandmother should rise and find her gone.

At the fork in the road, Ella hesitated again, looking towards the white walls of Rookery Farm just glimmering with the first rays of light. She sighed and made a silent apology to those who lived there for going without even saying goodbye. Rob . . . Her mind shied away; she couldn't let herself even think about him.

Tibby gave a miaow and jumped up on to a broad-topped gatepost where he balanced himself and then sat down facing the direction in which she was heading; the only one to watch her leave.

Twenty-Six

'Ella! Whatever are you doing here?'

Peggy's eyes were wide with delighted surprise, but in the next moment filled with concern. 'Why, my dear girl, whatever's wrong? Come in, come in.'

The resolve, the bitter, desperate loneliness that had driven her from Brumbys' Farm, had carried her along the road to town and on to the early morning bus and had sustained her throughout the two-hour journey, finally broke. Ella dissolved into racking sobs, the tears pouring down her face as she put up her arms. 'Oh, Aunty Peg, Aunty Peg.'

The older woman drew her into the house, pushed her gently into a chair in her living room and went through to the small kitchen and plugged in the kettle.

'Now, dear,' she said coming back and sitting down in front of Ella. 'Dry those tears and tell me what this is all about.' There was deep anxiety in her own eyes but she knew she would get no sense out of the girl until she had calmed down.

'I'm sorry,' Ella sniffled, pitifully. 'This isn't like me, is it?'

Peggy shook her head. 'No, it isn't.'

It seemed as if the floodgates of six and a half years' unhappiness were opened at last. She cried for her mother; the loving, gentle mother she had lost. She wept at having been obliged to live in an alien place of wide open spaces and glowering skies and she railed against the woman who had grudgingly taken her in out of a sense of duty. And she cried for Rob.

She told Peggy everything, not sparing herself, right up to the moment when she knew she could take no more.

'I know I've always been difficult, wilful, but – but it's always been as if no one loves me any more . . .'

'Oh, Ella, how can you say that? You know how much I love you.'

'But you weren't there, Aunty Peggy,' she wailed. 'She wouldn't even let me come to see you. Not for six years.'

Peggy sighed. 'But Jonathan loves you.'

Fresh tears welled and flooded down the swollen, blotchy cheeks. 'I know. But – he – he's not my real grandfather, is he?' she whispered.

'Oh.' Peggy blinked. 'So you've been finding out all about the past, have you?' And when Ella nodded, Peggy murmured, 'Your grannie wouldn't like that.'

'She didn't,' the girl said bitterly. 'But Uncle Danny told me, after she was so mad at me and Rob. He took me to Suddaby and then back to Fleethaven. Even Grandpa agreed I ought to be told, but . . .' her face clouded, the feeling of guilt washing over her '. . . he's not very well now. He doesn't seem to have the strength to cope with the rows between me and Gran. I just thought, well, if I left, things might be easier for him too. I mean, she'll look after him. At least, I think she will. He's her whole life – him and the farm.' And the unspoken words hung in the air; that she believed she had no part in her grandmother's life. All she had ever been was a hindrance, an intruder in the couple's life.

Peggy bent forward a little and searched her face, asking perceptively, 'You're not sure, though, are you? I think you're worried about him.'

Ella nodded. 'I – I just wonder if he'll cope with all the work when I'm not there to help. Gran's so strong, she doesn't tolerate weakness in anyone.'

'Not even her beloved Jonathan?' Peggy asked in surprise.

Ella shrugged. 'Oh, I think if anything happened to him, she'd be frantic. It's just . . .' She hesitated, struggling to put into words something that was merely a feeling. 'He never grumbles, you see, never complains that he's tired.'

'And she never notices?'

'Well, sometimes. You know, it was always, "Ella do this, your grandpa's tired," or, "Ella, your grandpa needs help." But if I'm not there . . .'

She left the words hanging in the air, but her unhappy face showed she could not entirely bury her worry for the kind and gentle man she still thought of as her grandfather, never mind the absence of blood ties.

'Do they know you've come here?'

Ella shook her head. 'I – just walked out in the night. Like they say *she* did when she was sixteen. That's how she came to Brumbys' Farm.'

'And you've run away from it,' Peggy murmured and sighed, then added, 'We must let them know you're here, that you're safe.'

'She won't care!'

'Yes, she will,' Peggy said firmly, 'and Jonathan certainly will. You don't want to cause him more worry, now do you?'

Ella pursed her lips against the tears and shook her head.

'Right, then. You drink your tea and I'll just nip up to the phone box at the top of the next street and ring the Elands. Danny will go and tell them. What's his number?'

When Ella had written it on a scrap of paper, Peggy

hurried off to telephone leaving Ella sitting hunched near the fire, her hands cupped around the mug of tea.

It seemed ages before Peggy came back. Sitting down in front of her again, before she even took off her coat, Peggy said, 'I spoke to Danny. He thinks it's perhaps for the best that you've come here for a while. He says there's been nothing but rows for weeks now. But . . .' She paused and stressed her next words. 'He said, "Tell her not to stay away for ever. We all love her."'

Tears filled Ella's eyes but did not fall. She pressed her lips together and shook her head. 'Maybe *they* do, but not Gran. Gran's never loved me – and – and I don't think she ever will.' She raised her tearstained face. 'I'm never going back, Aunty Peg. Never!'

Peggy sighed, but all she said was, 'Never's a long time, love.'

'Aunty Peg, do you know who my real father is?'

'D'you know, I've been waiting for that question ever since you got here.' Peggy smiled.

Ella had been living with Peggy for two weeks.

That first night she had lain awake in the tiny bedroom, listening to the drone of the traffic on the main road passing the top of the street, drifting into sleep and then disturbed by the sudden bang of a door in the adjoining terraced house, the sound of raised voices from the neighbours. She had scrambled out of bed once to peer out of the window to see a drunk weaving his way down the middle of the road, his tuneless singing echoing down the wet street.

She snuggled back into bed but sleep would not come now; the room seemed stifling, the walls so close, the confined space so airless. She got out of bed again and tugged and heaved at the sash window until she could feel a draught of air coming into the room, suddenly with an irrational longing for wide open spaces and freedom. It was so totally unlike the large bedroom at home . . .

Home? Why ever was she calling Brumbys' Farm 'home'? she demanded of herself irritably. *This* was home. Lincoln was home. It always had been, she reminded herself sharply. Never mind what Peggy said, she was not going back to Fleethaven Point. Not ever!

But as sleep had claimed her at last in the early hours of a chill city morning, she imagined she felt the weight of Tibby on her feet and heard the creaking of the timbers in the roof above her head.

She had enrolled for a secretarial course at the Lincoln Technical College and although the term had already started, there was a place because two people had dropped out after the first week. She was interviewed and accepted immediately and hurried along the road each morning to learn shorthand, typing, and book-keeping.

'The teacher makes us type in the dark,' she giggled to Peggy, 'so that we learn to touch-type properly and don't look at the keyboard.'

'How do you know what you're typing?'

'There's a projector and screen and she shows a film of the keyboard and someone's fingers typing and we just watch that and try to do the same.'

'Sounds difficult.'

'Actually, it's fun!' Ella said. 'We type to music too, to learn to keep an even rhythm.'

'I'm glad you're enjoying it, dear.'

'Oh I am, but . . .' It was then that Ella's face clouded and she asked about her father.

Peggy clasped her hands together, her eyes shining. 'It's been on my conscience for years.'

'Whatever do you mean?'

'Let's make a cup of tea,' it seemed as if Peggy always turned to the teapot in times of crisis or with a problem to face, 'and I'll tell you everything.'

'You get the biscuits out and I'll make the tea.' Ella smiled, switched on the kettle and reached for the tea-caddy, though her fingers were trembling. Did Peggy know something that would help her find her father?

'I don't know how much you know or remember,' Peggy began.

Ella shook her head, frowning. 'I don't know anything, except,' her mouth tightened, 'that my mother was never married and that's what caused my gran to be so bitter.' She returned Peggy's gaze steadily. 'I only found out recently exactly why. You see, Gran was a bastard – like me.'

Peggy flinched. 'Then you'd think she'd be a bit more understanding.'

Ella nodded. 'That's what Grandpa's often said. Even when I was young and didn't understand what they were on about, I overheard him say it.'

Peggy took a deep breath. 'Do you remember at your mother's funeral, you saw a man standing under the trees, in the shadows?'

Ella twisted her mouth, struggling to recall that dreadful day. 'I – think so.'

'When we all moved away, he – he went to stand by the grave. None of us took much notice of him at the time. It was only natural, we were all so dreadfully upset. But when we got back to Rookery Farm you asked us, in the kitchen, who he was.' Peggy smiled gently at the memory. 'Gave us quite a shock and threw poor Mavis into a right old dither.'

'Why?'

'They, Mavis and Isobel, guessed it could have been him – your father. And then . . .' Peggy paused, warming to her story, seeming suddenly to be enjoying the drama of the moment. 'He came to see me.'

Ella gasped, 'When? After the funeral? Oh, why didn't you tell me?'

'No, no, it wasn't after the funeral. It was at the time your photograph appeared in a daily paper.'

Ella looked puzzled.

'You remember when you found that bomb on the beach?'

Ella's expression cleared. 'Oh, yes.'

'Well, he saw it. It was all in there – your name, your age, even about your mother having driven the Commanding Officer at Suddaby in the war. He came here to ask about you.'

'Didn't he know about me then?'

'He told me that just after New Year in 1953,' Peggy went on, trying to bring all the strands of the events together, 'he'd written to your mum asking her to meet him again. Evidently, until then, his life had been very difficult and he hadn't been able to contact her. He sent the letter to Fleethaven Point because he knew that was her home.'

Ella nodded excitedly. 'That must have been the letter she received when we got there, to go to the old man's funeral. And,' she paused for effect, 'there was a letter found in her handbag, but it was drenched and the writing absolutely unreadable. So was that why Mum went out in Uncle Danny's car that Saturday?'

Peggy nodded. 'Yes, it was. Your mum went up the coast to meet him. They talked, but she didn't tell him about you. I don't know why. Maybe – if you find him – he can tell you what happened between them.'

Ella whispered, 'So why didn't he come to find me when you told him about me? Why . . .' there was bitterness in her tone now, 'why did he leave me with her?'

Peggy looked uncomfortable for a moment. 'Maybe that's my – well, our – fault. I came to talk it over with your grandfather and he said he thought it would be for the best if you stayed there. You'd only recently lost the most important person in your world. He thought it best that you stayed with people who loved you rather than go to complete strangers.'

Vaguely, she remembered Peggy coming to Brumbys' Farm and talking in secretive whispers to her grandfather. It had not been about Ella going back to Lincoln, as she had hoped at the time, but something even more important.

Ella leaned forward, 'But that was my *father*, for heaven's sake!'

Peggy wriggled. 'Well, I'm sorry, if you think we were wrong. I wanted to tell you when you got older, but whenever I mentioned it to Jonathan – and I did, Ella, believe me, I did – he kept saying, "Wait till she asks. Time enough when she asks." But I can't allow you to blame Jonathan entirely because I agreed with his decision, at least when you were young. I was very tempted to tell you everything when you were here just before Christmas, but then with Janice here . . .' Peggy's voice faltered. Her face creased with guilt, she whispered, 'I'm sorry if you're angry.'

Swiftly Ella smiled, reached out and patted the older woman's hands. Peggy Godfrey had always been so important in her life; whatever she had done, or not done, Ella knew, would have been with the best of intentions. 'Of course I'm not angry with you – or Grandpa, for that matter.' Ella's lips tightened as she added, 'Did *she* know?'

'I presume Jonathan told your grannie, but I don't know for sure.'

'Huh! If she did know, I'm surprised she didn't pack me off to him on the first train.'

Peggy sighed. 'You're incredibly hard on her, you know. I've always been a bit in awe of her, but she's not as bad as you make out, surely?'

Ella snorted wryly. 'Don't you believe it!'

They were silent for a few moments, both busy with their own thoughts.

'So, have you got a name – an address – anything?' Ella persisted.

Peggy nodded and rose to go into the front parlour. 'Wait a minute.'

She came back with a folded paper in her hand. 'He left this and said that if the right time ever came . . .'

Ella unfolded the paper with shaking fingers. The words danced and blurred before her eyes. There was a name, an address in York and even a phone number. She looked up again at Peggy. 'But who is he?'

'The man she drove for in the war, the Station Commander at Suddaby.' Peggy nodded towards the piece of paper trembling in Ella's fingers. 'He's your father. Group Captain Philip Trent.'

Twenty-Seven

'I've got some photos!'

Ella bounced up, dragged open the door and rushed up the narrow stairs, returning moments later with a handful of letters and photographs she had found in her mother's box.

'There,' she demanded, holding one out towards Peggy. 'Is that him? The tall man standing beside Mum near the car?'

Peggy bent over the picture and then nodded. 'Yes, dear. That's him.' She raised her eyes and said, 'That's your father.'

Almost reverently, Ella took the photograph back into her own hands and stared down at it, drinking in the sight of the man, trying to imagine what his voice sounded like, wanting, desperately, to know all about him.

'I tell you who you ought to go and talk to. Mavis.'

'Oh, yes,' Ella murmured, her concentration still on the face in the photograph. 'Uncle Danny said Mavis, or Isobel, might be able to help.'

'She and Isobel were with your mum all the time at Suddaby. I think Isobel's abroad at the moment. But of the two, I would say Mavis was your best bet anyway.' Peggy smiled. 'If anyone knows about him, Mavis will!'

'Oh, Ella, he was a lovely man!' Mavis clapped her fat hands together and beamed delightedly when she had listened to all that Ella had to tell her, about everything that had happened to bring her to this point. 'Are you going to get in touch with him, to see him?'

'Oh, yes,' Ella answered promptly.

'I'm sure he'll be thrilled. Such a kind man, he was. Only . . .' Her face clouded.

'What, Aunty Mave?'

'At the time – in the war, I mean – he was married.'

Ella nodded. 'Well, I'd guessed as much. There had to be more than just the fact that he was a high-ranking officer and she a lowly corporal to stop them getting married. Unless, of course,' she added bitterly, 'it was just a fling and she meant nothing to him.'

Mavis shook her head vehemently until her chin wobbled. 'No, no, he wasn't like that. I mean, he wasn't that sort of man. Very honest, very honourable.'

'It wasn't very honourable to have an affair with a WAAF if he was already married, was it?'

Mavis's eyes were troubled. 'We could never get anything out of your mum. She was incredibly loyal to him. She never actually told us who it was, we just guessed.'

Ella stared at her. 'Then you mean, you don't really know that it was Philip Trent? Not for sure?'

Mavis wriggled her shoulders in embarrassment. 'For a time – we – we thought it was someone else . . .'

'Who?'

'I'd rather not say.'

'Aunty Mave . . .' Ella began warningly.

'Oh, very well,' Mavis said, capitulating at once. 'We thought it was Danny Eland. She was always talking about him, always writing to him, and when he married someone else – I forget her name – well, your mum nearly went berserk.'

'Rosie,' Ella said, almost absently. 'He married Rosie. So you don't know then,' she said slowly, 'just why Danny and my mum didn't marry?'

Mavis shook her head.

Quietly, Ella said, 'They were half-brother and -sister.'

Mavis's face was a picture. 'Brother and sister!' Her huge frame collapsed into a chair, conveniently close.

'*Half*-brother and -sister,' Ella corrected her and then went on to give her the full story.

'Why didn't she ever tell us?'

Ella shrugged. 'Perhaps she thought you wouldn't understand. That it would all sound a bit, well, not quite nice.'

Mavis stared at her. 'Mmm, you could be right. Can't say I blame her, now I think about it. Old Iso could be a bit tart with some of her judgements about people,' Mavis pulled a wry face, 'though by that time we were all pretty good friends.' She was quiet for a moment, perhaps recalling the time the three of them – Kate, Isobel Cartwright and herself – had all been together during the war.

There was the sound of a door opening, a voice and a dog barking. Mavis, levering her bulk up from the low chair, said, 'That'll be my Dave with our Benji. Come into the kitchen and meet them.'

Without waiting for a reply, Mavis went through to greet her husband with a rapturous hug as if he had been gone for a week rather than just to walk the dog. More slowly, Ella followed, fishing in her bag for her handkerchief in readiness.

'Ella's come to see us. This is Dave. We met in the war, too. He was in charge of the control room where I was an R/T operator.'

A grey-haired man with a warm smile was holding out

his hand to her and the dog, a long-haired Old English Sheepdog, shook itself and peered up at her through woolly-covered eyes.

Ella pressed her handkerchief to her nose and, between sneezes, managed to gasp. 'Hello – so pleased – to meet you. I'm so – sorry. I'm allergic to dogs.'

Mavis was standing quite still, staring, open-mouthed, at Ella. 'Well, that settles it, then!'

Ella blinked and dabbed at her streaming eyes.

'You're Philip Trent's daughter all right, Ella, and no mistake. He had an allergy to dogs and horses too!'

'Do you think I should phone or write?'

Back in the terraced house in Lincoln after her trip to Grantham to see Mavis, Ella stood in the middle of the living room biting the side of her thumb in indecision.

'Well, if I were you, I wouldn't phone,' Peggy said, placing a steaming plate of tripe and onions on the table. 'Come and eat and we'll talk about it.' Sitting down, Peggy went on, 'I should write, or you could go to see him. It's half-term next week, isn't it?'

Ella nodded, suddenly nervous. 'He might not be at that address any more. I mean, it is about six years ago . . .'

'But it would be a starting point. You've nothing else to go on, have you? You could stay in a small hotel or a guest house.'

'I haven't any money, Aunty Peg.'

Peggy flapped her hand. 'Don't worry about that.'

'I can't let you do any more,' Ella protested. 'I'm living here free as it is and I feel guilty enough about that already.'

'Well, you shouldn't. I've worked all my life and had no one else to spend it on except myself. Besides,' she smiled to assuage Ella's prickly pride, 'when you get this marvellous job as somebody's secretary, I'll know where to come if I'm short.'

Ella laughed, but touched Peggy's hand as it lay on the table. 'Oh, Aunty Peggy, you are good.'

The older woman blushed, patted Ella's hand and said, 'There's a letter for you behind the clock.'

Ella jumped up and covered the space between the table and the hearth and fished out the letter. 'Is it from . . .?' she began, but her face fell when she recognized Janice Souter's girlish scribble.

She returned to the table more slowly. 'I thought perhaps Grandpa might have written.'

'He will,' Peggy said confidently. 'Don't let your tea go cold.'

Janice's letter covered three pages, the first of which was full of grumbles at Ella:

> *Fancy going off without me and to live in Lincoln as well. Don't you remember? I said to you if you ever left home, I'd go with you. We could take a flat together and have some great fun. What do you say? Have you got a job yet? I expect your Aunty Peg could get you fixed up in that posh store where she works. Do you think she could find me a job too?*

Ella smiled and shook her head. Same old Janice!

She'd write back and explain why she left and tell her that she wasn't working but was still a student. She'd have to be careful how she worded her letter though: she had visions of Janice turning up on Aunty Peggy's doorstep ready to move in too.

*

'Now have you got everything?'

'I think so.'

'Don't forget. Book into a nice small hotel and mind it's clean.'

Ella grinned. 'Yes, Aunty Peg.'

'And ring Rita next door when you get there. You've got their number, haven't you?'

'Yes, Aunty Peg.' Far from being irritated by the older woman's fussing, Ella found it very comforting to feel someone cared enough to worry over her.

'I hope everything goes all right.'

And then the train was pulling out of the station, and in a flurry of 'goodbye' and 'take care', she was on her way to York.

She found a guest house on the long road overlooking the racecourse. The view from her window stretched out over a field dotted with trees to the course itself, the oval white-painted fence of the track and, beyond it, the grandstand in the far distance. To her left as she leant out of the window were the square towers of the Minster, rising proudly above the clustering city.

Ella smiled to herself. It's like having the best of both worlds here, she thought, an open stretch of green before me and, close by, a city.

The food was excellent, the bed comfortable and the room clean, but Ella could not sleep for excitement. What if he'd changed his mind after all this time? What if he didn't believe she was his daughter? A million anxieties crowded her restless mind until she slept uneasily at last, but only to dream of a man standing beneath the trees and weeping over a grave; only the man looked more like Uncle Danny than the face in the wartime snapshot.

After lunch, dressed in an open-necked check shirt, trousers and with a sweater round her shoulders, Ella set off, the precious scrap of paper in her pocket. Armed with a street map she soon found the tree-lined avenue, with detached houses set back a little from the road. She pulled a comical face to herself; just the sort of exclusive houses she would imagine a group captain inhabiting.

She found the number given on the paper and stood staring up at the house for a long time: a double-fronted, white-painted red-brick house with a polished mahogany door and a gleaming brass knocker.

'Oh, heck!' she muttered to herself. 'Now what do I do?'

Her heart was thudding in her chest and her palms were sweaty with excitement. Should she just walk boldly up to the door and knock? But what if his wife answered? How could she ask for Mr Trent? And should she say 'Mister'? Was he still in the RAF or what? Oh dear, this wasn't going to be as easy as she'd thought. She turned and walked a little way down the road and leant against a low wall, watching the house.

She'd better move again, she thought, else someone in this select neighbourhood would begin to think she was 'loitering with intent'.

She was about to wander further down the road again when she had an idea. Could she pretend she was a student from a local college doing research about the last war? About the RAF perhaps? It was worth a try.

She walked back towards the house and hesitated once again at the gate. Then, taking a deep breath, she walked up the driveway and, before her courage could flee, knocked at the door. She waited, balancing on the balls of her feet, ready for flight.

The door opened and an elderly woman stood there. She was at least seventy. Ella's heart sank. She was far too old to be the wife of Philip Trent.

'Not today, thank you,' the woman said crisply, though not unpleasantly. The door was already beginning to close.

'I – I'm not selling anything,' Ella blurted out. 'I'm looking for someone.'

The woman was intimidating. White hair, beautifully set, with every curl in immaculate place, and she wore make-up, though it was skilfully applied and did not look out of place on the wrinkled skin. Her dress was plain but well cut and her nails were long and pointed and painted a delicate pink.

'I don't think there's anyone in this house . . .'

'Please.' Ella started forward, eagerness making her forget her rehearsed speech. 'Philip Trent. He used to live here. Do you know where he went? Where he is now?'

For a brief moment, the woman looked startled. 'What do you want him for?'

'I – do you know him?'

'I might,' the woman said guardedly.

Ella swallowed, the excitement rising in her. Deliberately she tried to keep calm. 'I'm looking for him because – because—' She licked her lips and decided to try to stick to her original story. The woman already looked wary. If she blurted out the truth she had the feeling the door would be slammed in her face.

Ella drew in a deep, steadying breath. 'I understand Mr Trent was a group captain in the RAF in the war. I'm – I'm . . .' The lie did not come easily. 'I'm a student and I'm doing some research for – for a project, and I just wondered if he might be able to help me.'

The woman frowned. 'Who gave you his address?'

'He did.' The words slipped out before she could stop them. 'I mean, he – he gave it to my – my aunt.'

'He knows your family?' The woman's expression lightened.

'Oh, yes.' She almost laughed. This, at least, was true. She could not resist the irony of the moment and added, 'Very well.'

'Oh, well, in that case . . .' She seemed to be mellowing a little but still did not offer to invite Ella inside. 'I'm afraid he's not in at the moment, but I'll tell him you've called. What name did you say? Perhaps you could come back again another time?'

Evading giving her name, Ella said swiftly, 'Yes, of course, I'll call back. This evening, perhaps?'

Now the woman smiled and nodded. 'Yes, about seven thirty, after we've eaten.'

'Thank you. Thank you very much.' Ella turned and began to walk away quickly before the woman could insist on knowing her name. 'I'll see you later.'

As she came to the gate a large green Rover swept in and though the car did not touch her, its sudden appearance startled her so that she stepped backwards, treading heavily half on, half off the edge of the driveway. Her heel sank into the soft earth of a flower border. She lost her balance and felt herself falling backwards. She gave a little scream as her hand caught on a rose-bush and a thorn gouged a deep scratch on the back of her hand.

The car braked, the broad tyres digging deep into the gravel of the drive with a scrunching noise. The driver leapt from his seat and came running towards her, not even bothering to switch off his engine or close the car door behind him.

'I'm so sorry. Are you hurt? Did the car hit you?'

He was kneeling down in front of her, without thought for his light grey trousers and Ella found herself looking up into the bluest pair of eyes she had ever seen, except when she looked in the mirror.

He was helping her to her feet, gently brushing away

the earth and examining her hand, the blood now oozing out down the length of the scratch.

'Please come into the house and bathe that. It's quite deep.'

'Well . . .' She made herself sound deliberately hesitant, as if not wanting to intrude, though she could hardly have planned it better.

The woman was still hovering near the front door. 'Mother,' the man said, 'please show this young lady to the cloakroom and see she has everything she needs while I put the car away.' He turned back to Ella. 'I won't be a moment.'

He was smiling down at her, his blue eyes warm and friendly. He put his hand out to her, not quite touching her, to usher her towards the door into the house.

The woman led the way into a cool hall with a polished parquet floor, a huge circular Chinese rug covering the centre. An enormous arrangement of flowers in a basket on the small side table scented the air as the woman waved a beringed hand and said, 'He will drive in at such a speed. I keep telling him he's not flying a plane now. This way, my dear.'

She opened a door to the left-hand side of the hall and ushered Ella into a cloakroom with a wash basin, toilet and pegs for coats. 'I'll fetch the first-aid box from the bathroom. Just run the cold water over your hand.'

As she bustled away, Ella turned on the tap and let the water run over her hand, washing away the blood and any dirt from the wound.

A knock came at the door and the man popped his head round it. 'Okay?'

She turned, smiled at him and nodded, knowing she was staring at him but unable to tear away her gaze. He squeezed his tall frame into the small room and as his mother came back with a box of first-aid materials he took it from her, set it on a ledge near the basin and said, 'Now then, let's see if I can remember all my first-aid training from my RAF days.'

'That's why this young lady's here,' said the woman from the other side of the half-open door. 'She's a student doing research about the RAF. She says you know her family.'

The head bent over her hand, which its owner was dabbing with antiseptic ointment, slowly came up again and the blue eyes, so close now, were gazing into hers very intently. 'Really?' he said softly. 'And what . . .' he paused and suddenly in the tiny room, the air was vibrant '. . . is your name?'

Ella gazed back at him. Huskily she said, 'I'm called Ella but – but my full name is Danielle Hilton.'

The strong warm hands holding hers trembled, and the breath he released suddenly wafted into her face. 'Oh, my dear girl!' he whispered hoarsely. In the most incongruous place they could have imagined for such a momentous meeting, they stood just staring at each other. 'Do you know who I am?' he said.

'I think so. I think you're . . .' her voice dropped to an almost inaudible whisper that only he would hear '. . . my father.'

He seemed to pull his reeling senses back to reality and dressed her hand, sticking plaster across a wad of lint. 'There. Is that comfortable?'

'Thank you, yes.'

'Come.' He pressed himself to the wall and opened the door for her. 'We have a lot to talk about.'

As she emerged from the cloakroom, she almost giggled nervously at his understatement.

The woman was still hovering in the hall. 'Are you all

right?' Ella nodded and then the woman's glance went to her son. 'Do you know her family, Philip?'

'Oh, yes, Mother. I know her family very well indeed.' As he put his arm about Ella's shoulders, the girl saw the surprise on his mother's face and her glance go swiftly from one to the other and back again.

'We're going to my study and, er, if it won't cause you any trouble, Mother, Ella will be staying for dinner.' He looked down at Ella and smiled, and now there was something else in his eyes, a strange mixture of joy and sadness too. 'Okay?' he asked gently.

She nodded and murmured, 'Okay.'

Was she dreaming? she thought, as he steered her towards a door to the right of the hall and into a book-lined study – a real man's room – and settled her in a leather armchair near a long window looking out over a smooth well-kept lawn.

'I think I need a drink.' He smiled down at her. 'Would you like something?'

She licked her dry lips. 'I wouldn't mind a cup of tea, but if it's any trouble . . .'

'Of course it isn't,' he said, and disappeared from the room briefly, returning a few moments later to sit, drink in hand, in the chair opposite her.

'Is this really happening?' he said, with the same bemused air that she was feeling.

Ella laughed nervously. 'That's just what I was thinking. I used to dream about you, standing under the trees on the day of Mum's funeral . . .' The pain was naked in his eyes and, swiftly, she said, 'Oh, I'm so sorry, that was thoughtless of me.'

'No, no,' he reassured her quickly. 'It's just that all these years I've had no one to talk to about Kate. There's been no one to help me bear the grief, the intolerable loss.' He cleared his throat and, more strongly now, said, 'You saw me there?'

She nodded. 'As we all moved away, I saw you walk across to the grave and just stand there.'

'I was devastated. I'd only just found her again after all that time only to lose her so cruelly.'

Ella leaned forward. 'She met you that day? It was you she came to meet, wasn't it?'

He nodded and said huskily, 'When she was travelling back the floods came. I was on my way home to York when I heard about the flooding. I turned round and went straight back, but I couldn't get through.' His face was pale, reliving that dreadful night. 'I hounded the authorities, but the poor devils were working day and night . . . I couldn't find out anything.' He shook his head. 'At last when I could get through to Lynthorpe and went to the police station . . .' He didn't need to say any more: she knew what he had learned.

Instead, she asked, 'Why didn't she tell you about me?'

A small sad smile appeared as he shook his head. 'We made arrangements that I should come to Lincoln the following week. She – she said she would have something very exciting to tell me, something that would make me very happy, but that first there was something she had to do . . .' He was gazing at her now, drinking in the sight of his daughter.

Ella frowned, puzzled.

'I'm guessing,' he said slowly, 'that she wanted to tell you about me first. You know, to be sure that you understood all that had happened, that you were prepared to meet me.'

'Prepared to meet you?' she exclaimed. 'I've never wanted anything more in my life!'

'Oh, my dear,' he whispered, deeply moved.

'You went to Lincoln to see Aunty Peggy, didn't you, after you saw my picture in the paper that time?'

He nodded. 'She told me all about you. About everything that had happened.'

She studied his face as he talked. He was still a fine-looking man: the fair curly hair she had seen in the photographs was still thick, though grey now, but his kind face was etched with deep lines of sadness.

'You've lived with your grandmother at Fleethaven Point, haven't you? I mean, you've been loved and cared for?'

Ella swallowed. She opened her mouth to tell him, to pour out to him the heartache of those years. How her grandmother had never loved her, how she'd only taken her in – her daughter's bastard – out of a sense of duty, how harshly she'd treated her, how hard she'd worked her, treated her like a skivvy . . .

She almost gasped at the tumult of emotions coursing through her and, to her surprise, like hearing someone else speaking, found herself saying, 'It wasn't always easy. My grandmother is a very strong-minded woman and I . . .' She smiled. 'I am told I'm very like her. We had some battles.'

'But she loved you?' he insisted. It seemed important to him that Ella, his daughter, should have been loved. She could not cause this man, clearly still haunted by the past, yet more pain.

Carefully she said, 'I'm sure she did, in her own way, but – but she's the sort of person who finds it difficult to – to show it. I suppose,' she added, wrinkling her brow reflectively, considering something she had not really thought about before, 'I didn't make it any easier. Even from the start, I always wanted to go back to Lincoln to live with my aunty Peggy.'

He sighed. 'We thought it best, you see, that as your loss was so recent, we shouldn't uproot you, that you should stay with family you knew. But I gave her my address and said that if ever you should ask about me when you were older, then she should give it to you.'

'I'm living with her now,' Ella murmured. Although she didn't elaborate on her reasons for leaving Fleethaven Point or tell him that she had just walked out one night, she did explain that now she was attending a one-year course at the Technical College and hoped to find work in the city and go on living there.

'So, you won't go back to the farm, then?'

She shook her head and dropped her gaze. 'No. I won't ever go back.'

They talked on and on until the shadows lengthened and dusk crept into the room. He wanted to know everything about her and all that she could tell him about her mother. When a smiling Mrs Trent opened the door to say graciously that dinner was ready and would they like to come through to the dining room, Ella and her father were still talking. As they went through to the dining room, he whispered, 'I need a little time to break the news to my mother. She doesn't know anything about you, or even about Kate. Please, could you play along with the student idea, just until I've had time? Tomorrow everything will be all right . . .'

Twenty-Eight

'I don't know how you've got the nerve to show your face again this morning, young woman. You might think you've taken my son in with your lies, but you don't fool me so easily.'

Ella, standing outside the front door again the following morning, gaped at Mrs Trent. Having seemed to accept the fact that her son knew Ella's family in some way and made her welcome, Mrs Trent's obvious hostility was a shock to Ella. The previous evening she had left soon after they had finished dinner, with no further chance to talk to her father alone for his mother had sat with them until she had ushered the girl out into the night, exhorting her to be careful and to go straight back to her hotel; showing, Ella had thought at the time, genuine concern for her.

In the intervening hours, Philip Trent had obviously tried to explain the situation to his mother, only to be met with a blank refusal to believe any part of his story.

The tirade continued. 'I suppose your mother got herself pregnant and made up some cock-and-bull story about her commanding officer being responsible just to make you, and herself, feel good. Do you really imagine that my son, a group captain and a station commander with an exemplary record, would get himself entangled with a silly little WAAF?' The cold blue eyes narrowed. 'What are you up to? Blackmail, is it?'

Ella gasped. 'That's not true,' she said hotly. 'My father—'

'He is not your father!' the woman snapped.

Ella's chin came higher in defiance. 'Oh yes he is – and he knows it.'

'Nothing of the sort,' the woman retorted.

'Hasn't he told you everything?'

The woman waved her hand dismissively. 'Oh, he tried to tell me some romantic nonsense, but it's not true. None of it is true. Why, at the time, he had a wife and a poor, handicapped daughter who died tragically. He was devoted to them both. Your story is a preposterous pack of lies. And,' she added and the threat in her tone was obvious, 'if I see you hanging about here again I'll call the police.'

Tears sprang to Ella's eyes, her disappointment was so acute. Then, blessedly, her spirit, her indomitable spirit, came to her rescue. She held her head high and returned the woman's stare steadfastly.

'Well, *Grandmother*, I am telling the truth. Your son believes I am his daughter, and quite frankly I don't give a damn whether you do or not, just so long as *he* does!'

With that, she turned and marched away down the drive.

Ella found her way to the centre of York where the streets radiated from the Minster, but for once she could take no pleasure in the city, in the shops and squares and old, old buildings. Even the wonderful Minster, though it reminded her of 'her' cathedral, failed to bring her solace.

To have found her father, only to be branded a liar and a trickster by the woman who was, whether she liked it or not, her grandmother, hurt more than she would have believed possible. She took a deep breath and her eyes followed the lines of the towering church above her. Well, she told herself, she'd faced up to a far stronger woman in her time than old Mrs Trent and even at this moment when her heart ached with disappointment she could not help imagining what would happen if her two grandmothers were ever to come face to face. A small smile curved her mouth.

The very thought of Esther Godfrey gave her fresh heart.

She retraced her footsteps back to the road where her father lived. She liked the sound of that; she said it over and over in her mind. Her father. Her father!

There was no green car in the driveway and she did not want to knock at the door again until she was sure he was in the house. Standing behind a tree so that she was obscured from the windows she kept watch. She was still there as the October afternoon turned into evening and dusk crept along the street. Men arrived home from work in cars, or walking, smart-suited men coming home to pretty, house-proud wives and neat, well-behaved children. The street lights came on and a chill wind blew the leaves along the pavement in little, rattling flurries.

And still Ella waited.

At last a car came down the road and she shrank away, hiding from its headlights. It turned into the driveway of the house and drew to a halt outside the front door. The car door slammed and a man's step, quick and eager, bounded across the gravel and to the front door. She reached the gateway and opened her mouth to call his name just as the front door opened and Mrs Trent stood framed in the light streaming out into the darkness.

'Is she here?' She heard his deep voice plainly through the stillness.

'My dear, she never came back. You really must believe me. That girl was a trickster, a con-artist . . .'

As he stepped into the house, the door closed and the light was shut off, leaving Ella shivering in the gloom.

The old beezum! she thought suddenly. That's what Gran would call Mrs Trent; an old beezum.

She marched up the curving driveway, her feet scrunching on the gravel, and lifted the brass knocker and rat-tat-tatted it determinedly.

'Call me a trickster and a con-artist, would she?' the girl muttered, but as the door opened and she found herself staring once more into the cold blue eyes of Mrs Trent, her courage almost deserted her.

'Well, you've got a nerve, I must say.' The woman was speaking in a low voice, hissing the words almost, so that her son would not hear.

Think of Gran, Ella told herself. But not, she thought swiftly and almost giggled at the thought, perhaps exactly what Gran would say; it might be a little too blunt. 'Get out of my way, you old beezum, and let me pass,' were hardly the sort of words that this lady would appreciate.

'Mrs Trent,' Ella said firmly, but respectfully. 'I am here to see my father. I should be obliged if you would allow me to do so.'

The woman gasped. 'Well, really . . .' The door seemed about to be slammed shut in her face when Ella heard footsteps on the hall floor and the door was pulled out of the woman's hand and opened wider.

'Ella, my dear. Come in, come in. You had me worried.'

'I've been waiting – in the road – for you to come home,' she said stepping into the hall.

'You shouldn't have waited out there in the cold. You should have come in.'

Ella smiled at the perplexed woman. 'I didn't know if you'd been able to explain everything. I didn't want to cause your mother any distress.'

His arm was about her shoulders drawing her into the lounge, taking her coat, ushering her towards a chair near the fire.

'We're just having coffee. I'll get another cup.'

As soon as he had left the room, Mrs Trent came close and thrust her face close to Ella's. 'It won't work, young lady. I'll have the police here if you don't leave this instant.'

Ella returned her gaze steadily. 'Please feel free to call them, Grandmother. I have nothing to hide.'

By the time her father returned, Mrs Trent was sitting stiffly in a chair on the opposite side of the fireplace, her back rigid, her mouth pursed.

'Ella,' he began hesitantly as he poured out the coffee. 'This has been quite a shock for my mother. Hasn't it, dear?' He glanced at the older woman.

'Why don't you tell the girl the truth?' she said harshly. 'I don't believe her pack of lies and I never will. When I think of poor little Lizzie – and Grace . . .' The woman dabbed a lace handkerchief at her eyes, but Ella thought the action was rather more for effect than genuine emotion.

Philip Trent's eyes clouded and Ella, though she said nothing, glanced at him questioningly.

'Lizzie was my daughter.' A small smile quirked his mouth. 'My eldest daughter—'

'Your *only* daughter,' his mother interrupted.

Philip sighed but went on, 'She was born very severely handicapped and we were warned she would never reach adulthood. Grace, my wife, devoted herself to the child. She was wonderful, but, well, because of it, we grew apart.'

'That's nonsense. It was the war – the wretched war –

that took you away.' She glanced malevolently at Ella. 'And as for what they used to say about WAAFs – well . . .'

Ella's face burned and Philip said warningly, 'Mother.'

The woman closed her mouth, clamping it shut, but her eyes flashed indignation.

'After Lizzie died, Grace had a breakdown. After all the years of nursing Lizzie and then her loss. She needed me then. I explained everything to Kate . . .' He looked into the fire as if seeing pictures from the past. 'She was marvellous about it. I promised her that one day we would be together, when Grace was strong again, and I meant it. But poor Grace was ill for a very long time – years—'

'And no wonder! The poor dear had much to bear . . .' Mrs Trent put in.

Ignoring his mother, he added softly, 'The last time I saw Kate, in the war, I mean, you must already have been born. How awful it must have been for her not to be able to tell me about you.'

'What happened to your wife?' Ella asked tentatively.

'After several years of treatment and with the love of her family, she made a full recovery. She took a job, carved herself quite a career in the fashion world. She's doing very well and is happier, I think, than she's ever been in her life.'

'Nonsense!' his mother said frostily. 'She was a devoted wife and mother. The marriage break-up was your fault, Philip. I see why now. I see it all now. All that talk about mutual agreement to separate, that you'd stay good friends, indeed. And all because of some silly little WAAF who was no better than she should be . . .'

Philip's face clouded with anger. 'Grace and I married too young, Mother, and only because our families, both forces' families, expected it.'

'Oh, I see, so it's all our fault, is it? Well, really!'

'No, Mother,' he said patiently. 'When Grace was fully recovered we talked and talked as we never had before. We understood each other and have always been, and always will be, very fond of each other.' He turned towards Ella, trying to explain to them both. 'But Grace felt there was something lacking in our marriage. She wanted more out of life and I'm thankful she's found it and is happy.'

'Second best, that's all her career is for her. All she ever wanted was to be your wife and the mother of your children. I've no doubt in my mind that if all this is true – and I don't say I believe it – but if it is, then I've no doubt you broke poor Grace's heart when you told her all about it and that's why she went off and got a job and—'

'Mother,' his voice was clipped, 'I never told Grace anything about Kate. Our separation had nothing to do with that. It was as much Grace's wish as it was mine.'

The woman gasped. 'I don't believe you. Why did you never tell Grace?'

'It would have been cruel and unnecessary.' His voice was husky as he added, 'If things had turned out differently, as I had hoped they would . . .' His eyes, full of a deep sadness, were on Ella. 'Then I would have explained everything to Grace and asked her for a divorce so that I could marry Kate—'

'Then thank goodness things didn't "work out", as you put it,' Mrs Trent said bitterly. 'A divorce in the family? Never!'

Ella gasped and felt the colour drain from her face. How could the woman be so heartless as to be thankful for Kate's death?

Philip at once put out his hand to cover Ella's and, before she could say anything, he turned towards his mother and said, 'That's unkind, Mother. The only reason

I never married Kate was because – because she was drowned in the floods.'

Ella saw momentary shame in the older woman's eyes. 'I'm sorry. I hadn't realized,' she said stiffly, 'but nevertheless, I shall never accept that this girl is my granddaughter. As far as I am concerned, I have only ever had one granddaughter, poor, darling Lizzie . . .'

At that moment there was a knock at the front door. 'Oh, now who can that be at this time of night?' she muttered in exasperation. But she got up and went out of the room.

'Ella, please don't be upset by what my mother says, she—'

The door into the room opened. 'It's Martin from next door. Come in, Martin. Perhaps you can get my son to come to his senses. Come in, come in and bring Tammy. Philip can just sneeze for once.'

Into the room came a tall, thin young man with hair flopping over his eyes and huge thick-lensed spectacles that made his eyes large. 'Sorry, Phil, I didn't mean to barge in . . .'

Following behind him on a lead came a Labrador dog, her pink tongue hanging out, her eyes mischievous and looking for fun. At once Philip stood up and moved to the far side of the room. The dog, however, seemed more interested in the one person in the room who was a stranger to her. She pulled away from her master and came to Ella, rubbing against her leg and panting in her face.

Ella sneezed and began to stand up. 'Oh, I'm sorry . . .' She sneezed again, and scrabbled in her pocket for her handkerchief. She was aware that there was a sudden stillness in the room. The other three people were staring at her while the dog continued to snuffle against Ella's legs giving little barks in greeting.

'Come here, Tammy,' the man called Martin ordered.

Ella sneezed twice and said again, 'I am sorry. I have this allergy, you see . . .'

There was a gasp and Ella looked up to see Mrs Trent, her hand to her bosom, her eyes wide and her mouth open, sinking down on to the settee as if her legs had given way beneath her.

Behind her, Philip began to sneeze in unison with Ella until, laughing between the sneezes, he came across the room to her and put his arm about her shoulders. Turning towards Mrs Trent, he said, 'Now, Mother, not even you . . .' he paused to sneeze again, 'can doubt it now.'

'Well, I'm not sure I agree with you there,' Mrs Trent replied, beginning to recover from the surprise but determined to cling to the last vestige of disbelief. 'Just because the girl has a similar allergy to you doesn't mean . . .' Her voice trailed away as her glance went from her son, to Ella and back to the dog.

'This is Martin Hughes.' Her father now formally introduced the young neighbour who had innocently caused the commotion. Philip smiled down at the dog but made no attempt to touch her. 'And his dog, Tammy. And this . . .' he drew Ella forward, 'is my daughter, Ella.'

The young man's eyes widened. 'I – didn't know you had a daughter – at least . . .'

'Only Lizzie, you mean?' Philip said softly. 'To be truthful, neither did I until about six years ago.'

'Oh. Oh, I see,' Martin said, sitting down and making himself comfortable as if he were prepared to stay there the night, or at least until he had heard the whole story. The dog padded over to the bay window and stretched herself out on the rug, as if she knew she should keep away from Philip.

Mrs Trent rose. 'Well, I don't know about you, but I need a drink. Whisky, Martin?'

'Please.'

As the older woman left the room, Ella said, 'I am sorry all this has upset your mother.'

Philip shook his head. 'It's not your fault. I suppose I rather sprang it on her last night and after you'd tried to be so tactful too, inventing the story about being a student.' He tapped her playfully on the nose with his forefinger.

They smiled at each other as he went on. 'But I was so delighted you'd come at last. I wanted her to share the wonderful news and then, well . . .' he spread his hands, 'she just wouldn't believe me, refused point blank to accept any part of it.' He laughed, a little shamefacedly. 'Wouldn't even believe that I had been "a naughty boy" in the war.'

'She still doesn't believe us,' Ella said in a small voice, unable to keep the longing from her tone. 'Even though we've got the same allergy.'

Philip sighed. 'She's very upset, more, I think, from the point of view that she has been deceived all these years. But I don't really think she has any choice now.'

It was Martin who, brushing back his flop of hair, said, 'Your allergy must be hereditary. Your father had it too, didn't he, Phil?'

Philip nodded.

'Then surely, she *must* believe that I am your daughter,' Ella said.

Philip still seemed unsure. 'She needs a little time, Ella. But she'll come round . . .'

They were the same words which Grandpa Godfrey had used so often about her gran. But Esther had never 'come round'. Would this grandmother, too, be the same?

Twenty-Nine

When the day came for Ella to return to Lincoln to continue her studies, Mrs Trent had still not come to terms with her existence.

'I'm sorry, I should never have come . . .' Ella began, contrite to think she had disrupted a happy household and caused distress to an elderly lady.

'Don't ever say that,' her father said, in mock admonishment but smiling as he added, 'You hear me?'

'But I've upset her.'

'She'll get over it. She's a tough old stick. Now, I want you to promise me that you'll come back for a weekend in a couple of weeks' time, if you can.'

'But . . .'

'No buts,' he said firmly.

She smiled. 'All right.'

'Good,' he said, taking her arm. 'Now I'll take you to the station, though I don't really want to let you go at all.'

As they stood on the platform, he said, 'See you in a fortnight, then? You will come back, won't you, Ella?'

'Of course,' she said, wrapping her arms around him. 'You don't know what it means to me to have found you.'

His voice was hoarse and his arms tightened around her as he said, 'Oh, I think I do, my dear. I think I do.'

She leant out of the carriage window, waving until she could no longer see him.

'Oh, Aunty Peg, Aunty Peg. I've found him!' She flew into Peggy's outstretched arms and hugged her with such enthusiasm that Peggy nearly lost her balance.

'Oh my goodness!' She laughed. 'I don't need to ask if everything went all right.'

Ella pulled a face. 'Well, it did and it didn't, but oh, Aunty Peg, no wonder Mum fell in love with him. He's wonderful! Just like Aunty Mave said he was. Kind and caring and so good-looking, even now.'

They sat up until the early hours for Peggy wanted to hear everything, and some things twice over.

'If only Mrs Trent would accept me.' Ella pulled a wry grimace. 'I seem to have trouble with grandmothers, don't I?'

'Oh, I almost forgot . . .' Peggy said, jumping up and fishing out a letter from behind the clock on the mantelpiece. 'There's a letter from your grandpa. I recognize Jonathan's handwriting.'

The girl took the letter into her hands. With wide eyes, she looked up at Peggy. 'I expect this is a telling-off.'

'Well, you won't know by sitting there holding it,' Peggy said, reasonably. 'Open it and get it over with.'

Ella's eyes scanned the two sheets of paper. 'I can't believe it,' she said at last, staring up at Peggy, the letter falling into her lap. 'He's not even cross. He seems, well, almost to be saying he – he understands. Here,' she held out the pages to Peggy, 'read it. See what you think.'

There was silence in the room, except for the tick-tick of the clock, while Peggy read the letter.

'No, he's not angry. Not at all. A little sad, maybe,

that you've gone. He's missing you dreadfully, that's obvious.'

Ella wriggled and muttered, 'I bet he's the only one who is.'

'Now, now,' Peggy remonstrated gently.

'He – he doesn't mention my gran, does he? He doesn't say what she thinks. There isn't even a message from her.'

Peggy sighed. 'Your gran's like that. When Kate found she was expecting you, your gran threw her out, the real "never darken my door again" bit. Not even Jonathan could bring her round. Until you and your mum went back that time for Will Benson's funeral, she'd never seen Kate, or written to her or even sent her a message. She's doing the same to you, love. It's the way she is. She never forgives and she never forgets. But your grandpa, he'll write regularly. You'll see. And another thing . . .'

'What?'

'He'd want to hear all about how you've found your father. He'll be delighted. You must write back to him. You will, won't you Ella?'

The girl nodded. Even though she now had a new family, had found her father who, she knew already, loved her, the old hurt still remained, could not be washed away.

Why, oh why was it never her gran who loved her?

Peggy had been right. Her Grandpa Godfrey replied at once to her letter saying how delighted he was she had found her father.

'. . . if my little Kate loved him,' he wrote, 'then he must be a fine man . . .'

Ella smiled. What a kind, generous man her grandpa was. Over the following weeks, he wrote regularly; loving, newsy letters about the farm and all the people at Fleethaven.

Rob is doing very well at the Farm Institute. He comes home most weekends. We can hear his motorbike coming nearly five miles away! He and Janice go out together when he's home. We all wonder if one day there'll be wedding bells there.

The knife twisted in the wound and Ella closed her eyes against the pain. Did her grandpa know how much such news would hurt her? Was he trying to prepare her for the inevitable? That one day, Rob would marry someone else.

And still, there was no message from her gran.

'I think I'll write to Uncle Danny and Aunty Rosie,' she said. 'I feel rather bad about just leaving without a word.'

'That's a good idea, love. Your mother wouldn't have wanted any ill-feeling between you and your uncle.'

As she sat down and picked up her pen, Ella thought but did not voice it to Peggy, And I might find out if there's anything really going on between Rob and Janice.

When she returned to York for the promised weekend visit, she was surprised and not a little dismayed to find the door opened by Mrs Trent.

'Come in, Ella.' The woman's voice was expressionless. 'I'll show you to your room.'

She led the way across the hall and made to mount the stairs.

'Please, just a minute . . .'

Mrs Trent, one hand resting on the banister, turned to look down at Ella. She said nothing but merely waited for the girl to speak.

'Look, I don't want to upset you again. I can easily stay in a hotel or somewhere.'

For a long moment they stood staring at each other, then the older woman sighed, turned, and came back down the steps she had just climbed.

In a totally different tone, as if resigned to the inevitable, she said, 'Put your suitcase down there, Ella, and come into the kitchen. I'll make some coffee and we can talk.'

A few minutes later they were sitting on either side of a pine kitchen table, with coffee and biscuits between them.

'I've done a lot of thinking since you were here. And a lot of talking,' her mouth quirked with amusement as she added softly, 'and some listening too.' She took a deep breath. 'I've learnt a lot about my own son that I didn't know.' She was silent a moment, sipping her coffee.

Ella said nothing, though her heart was thudding and her hands felt clammy.

Mrs Trent sighed. 'I suppose what hurt was his deceit, at least what I saw as his deceit. But I've had to come to terms with the fact that he is – and was then – a grown man with a right to live his own life.' Her gaze met Ella's. 'And if that included loving your mother, then – then I must accept it.'

'Their marriage,' she went on, 'his and Grace's – I have to admit, perhaps we were guilty of pushing them together, expecting it of them almost. Her parents and Philip's father and I were all close friends. The men were army officers and we shared married quarters abroad.'

Again there was a silence, then she said suddenly, 'I went to see Grace last week.'

Ella's eyes widened and she gasped.

'Oh, don't worry, my dear. I said nothing about you. If Philip wishes to tell her, then he must do it himself. No, I went because I needed to see if what Philip had said was true.'

'About her being happy now? In her career, you mean?' Ella said.

Mrs Trent nodded.

'And?' Ella prompted gently.

A smile, tentative at first, spread across Mrs Trent's mouth. 'I have to admit, I have never seen her happier. Oh, we talked about Lizzie and cried together a little, but she confirmed what Philip had said. They had come to a mutual understanding to separate. There was one other thing she did say, and it was without any prompting from me.'

Ella waited.

'She said she had wondered if there had ever been anyone else in Philip's life and – and she said if there had been, then she would never blame him.'

'She said that?' For a moment, Ella was incredulous.

Mrs Trent nodded. 'She's a lovely, generous hearted girl who, through her own tragedies, has learnt to be understanding about the needs of others.'

'She must be,' Ella murmured.

'I'm glad I went to see her. She taught me a valuable lesson.' She reached out across the table with a wrinkled, beringed hand that trembled slightly. 'Ella, can we start again? I'd really like to get to know – my granddaughter.'

Tears sprang into Ella's eyes and all she could do was nod her head vigorously.

As often as she could, she travelled to York to be with her 'other family' as she called them. The weeks turned into months and it was early summer again.

'I wonder how it is,' her father remarked on one of her weekend visits, a smile twitching his mouth, 'that every time you're here, Ella, young Martin finds a reason to keep popping in to see us. He doesn't seem to have the same interest when there's just us two old fogies here, does he, Mother?'

Mrs Trent, her blue eyes so like her son's, twinkled. 'No,' she said airily. 'And there I was thinking what a good neighbour he is.'

They all laughed but Ella pulled a wry face. 'I think you've got it wrong, Dad . . .' She still savoured using the name. 'I don't think it's me he comes to see . . .' she touched the birthmark on her jawline, 'not with this!'

Her grandmother leaned forward, squinting at her closely. 'What? What are you talking about, child?'

'Oh, Grandmother.' She laughed. 'Now don't be *kind* about it. I've lived with it all my life. I really don't let it bother me.'

Across the table, her father and grandmother looked at each other. 'I think, Philip, that your daughter needs taking in hand. Tomorrow we begin "Operation Ella". Agreed?'

He nodded, seeming to understand exactly what she was talking about, though Ella stared at each of them in turn completely mystified.

'Agreed,' was all her father said.

Mrs Trent rose from the table. 'Well then, if you will both excuse me, I have some telephoning to do to make arrangements.'

'Are you ready?' It was her father calling up the stairs.

'Coming,' she called back, and ran lightly down. 'Where are we going?'

'You'll see,' was all he would say.

She climbed into the front seat of the green Rover marvelling at the comfortable upholstery and giggling inwardly at the comparison between this luxurious car and the Souters' old banger.

Her grandmother was sitting regally in the back seat as they drove towards the city centre. Parking the car, they walked to one of the largest department stores Ella had ever seen.

'This is like the one where Aunty Peg works in Lincoln, but about twice the size,' she gasped, staring wide-eyed around her.

Grandmother Trent was walking ahead of her, leading the way, nodding to right and left as several of the assistants greeted her by name.

They went up the stairs and came to a part sectioned off; a hairdressing salon and beauty parlour. A middle aged woman came towards them, her fair hair sleek and immaculate, her suit well tailored and smart.

'Good morning, Mrs Trent. Is this your granddaughter?' And Ella found herself shaking the woman's hand. 'Everything's ready.'

'Good.' Mrs Trent nodded and smiled. 'In you go, Ella. Your father and I are going to the restaurant for coffee while we wait for you.'

Ella looked from one to the other, bewildered.

'But what . . .?' she began.

'This way, please, Miss Hilton.'

Miss Hilton indeed! Ella could hardly contain her laughter. What would her gran say if she could see her now?

Ella was led into the hairdressing section where her hair was washed, trimmed and set on huge rollers, her head encased under a drier.

'You've got the prettiest strawberry-blonde hair, dear,' the assistant told her. 'Why don't you grow it longer?'

Ella stared at herself in the mirror. Her hair, combed out into soft waves and curls, framed her face in a style similar to pictures she'd seen of Marilyn Monroe, except that it needed to be longer as the assistant suggested.

The head of department, who had met Ella and her grandmother when they arrived, was at her elbow.

'Now we're going to take you to have a make-up demonstration . . .' and within minutes Ella found herself sitting in a chair, with a girl smearing cream all over her face, talking all the time she worked.

'This is a moisturizer. You use it every day under your make-up base. And this is a blemish concealer, just here and – here . . .'

Ella gasped, stared and leant closer to the mirror. Before her eyes, the birthmark had disappeared. 'Oh,' she said, and again, 'oh! However did you do that?'

The young assistant was smiling down at her. Gently, she said, 'Let me finish the full make-up and then we can cleanse it all off and you can have a go.'

'You mean, I shall be able to do it myself? Every day?'

The assistant laughed. 'Of course.'

'Oh, do show me how – please!'

It was the ardent 'please' that brought tears suddenly to the eyes of the young assistant. By the time Ella stood up from the chair, hardly able to take her eyes off the new image of herself in the mirror, she was scarcely able to recognize the face staring back at her. And, best of all, however she twisted to right and left, lifted or lowered her chin, she could not see the birthmark.

Her escort took her up to the next floor and into the restaurant, leading the way through the diners to a table near the window where her father and grandmother were sitting.

As they turned to look at her, Ella felt a sudden thrill as she saw their mouths drop open and they gasped. 'My dear child. You look absolutely marvellous.' Mrs Trent clapped her hands together.

Her father stood up and held out a chair for her to sit down but not before Ella had seen a sudden moistening of his eyes. He cleared his throat and said strongly, 'Now, shall we order lunch?'

'I don't think I dare eat with this lipstick on.' She laughed, her voice a little unsteady.

'Now, my dear,' Mrs Trent leaned towards her, 'the secret of self-confidence is to take time and trouble with your appearance, but once it's done, forget about it. No one likes to see women constantly fussing with their hair or renewing their lipstick. And you'd better have something to eat. We've a lot of shopping to do yet.'

Philip Trent laughed. 'What a good job I brought my cheque-book.'

By the end of the afternoon, Ella was completely exhausted, but Mrs Trent seemed to be indefatigable. 'Just try this dress on, dear. It'll look wonderful with your tiny waist. Oh, I do wish I could wear these pretty cotton shirt-waisters.'

'But, Grandmother, you've bought me so much already. I can't begin to thank you enough . . .'

'Nonsense, child. I haven't started yet.'

And another dress was folded neatly and placed in a carrier.

'Well now,' Mrs Trent remarked, as they emerged at last from the store, 'I don't know when I last enjoyed myself so much. It's much more fun buying for someone else, and such a pretty young thing too, rather than for an old trout like me.'

There were tears in Ella's eyes as she looked from one to the other. 'You've both been so kind and – and especially about this . . .' She touched her jawline where the cosmetics now covered the birthmark completely.

As they climbed into the car, her father said, 'I had a chat with Doctor Lucas about that and there are operations, you know, but he felt that if it would cover with cosmetics, it would be much more satisfactory.'

'Oh, it's wonderful. I never dreamed . . .'

'Have you never used make-up before, dear?' came Grandmother Trent's voice from the back seat.

Ella could not hold in the smile. 'No, Grandmother. It's not quite the sort of thing Gran would encourage.'

There was a disapproving snort from the back seat, so like Esther Godfrey that Ella almost laughed aloud.

'Just look at all these clothes, Aunty Peg. I feel almost guilty that they've spent so much money on me.'

'Well, don't. They've obviously loved spoiling you. Enjoy it. It's you that isn't used to being spoilt. And I do like your hair like that, Ella. It makes you look older.'

'Oh, good. I've got an interview for a job coming up next week. And now I've got a smart new suit to wear too.' She held up a dark blue jacket and pleated skirt with a soft, pink blouse to go with it.

Peggy looked at the label and nodded approval. 'It's a very good make too.'

'I know.' Ella looked embarrassed again. 'You should have seen some of the prices . . .'

'Now, now, there you go again . . .' Peggy admonished

her, but she was laughing, sharing in the young girl's delight.

Ella gathered up all her new clothes and took them upstairs to put away.

'I can see we shall have to invest in a larger wardrobe soon,' Peggy teased, when she came back downstairs and they sat down to eat.

Ella glanced at the mantelpiece where Peggy always put any letters that arrived for her whilst she was away in York.

The space behind the clock was empty.

'Isn't there a letter from Grandpa?' she asked, and noticed a slight frown on Peggy's forehead.

'No. I can't understand it,' Peggy said and there was no hiding the anxiety in her voice. 'He's always written to me once a month, ever since he married your gran. Never missed, not even all through the war. This is the first time his letter's been late.'

'I'll write after tea and tell him all about my weekend and about all the things they've bought me. Perhaps he's too busy with haymaking to write this week.' Already it was June and Ella could picture the scenes at home. The reaper criss-crossing the field whilst Esther raked and spread the grass, looking up every so often to smile that wonderful smile of hers at her beloved Jonathan. Maybe Rob was there at weekends, helping too, stripped to the waist, standing on top of the haystack, his lithe body glistening in the sunshine. She could picture them laughing together, her grandmother ruffling his black curling hair.

She shook herself, burying the memories. She was back in Lincoln where she had always wanted to be. She'd found a father – and a grandmother – who loved her. She was being spoilt rotten with gifts lavished upon her, and whenever she visited York the ever-attentive Martin Hughes took her out to dinner, to the theatre . . .

Oh, she'd never had it so good, she told herself firmly.

'Grandpa will write soon, Aunty Peg. They're just busy, that's all. You'll see.'

'There you are, you see.' A few days later Ella waved a letter from her grandpa under Peggy's nose. 'They've been busy with the haymaking, just like I said.'

Peggy took the proffered letter from Ella's hand and scanned the pages, a worried frown still creasing her forehead. The letter, full of loving messages, was the same as always and yet, as Ella watched her aunt, she saw that the frown only deepened.

'Well, he *sounds* all right, I'll grant you, but . . .' Peggy bit her lip.

'But what, Aunty Peg?' Ella prompted.

'Oh, nothing. I suppose I'm being silly, but his writing looks, well, not as neat as usual, sort of – shaky.'

Ella looked again at the page. Her grandfather's handwriting was usually a beautiful copperplate, but she had to agree that the breaks between the letters and the occasional untidy slope of the writing was not quite to Jonathan's normal standard. 'I expect he wrote it when he was tired. But if you're really worried, I'll ring Uncle Danny. He'll know if anything's wrong.'

'Wouldn't Danny ring you?'

Ella wrinkled her brow. 'Can't remember if I've ever given him Rita's phone number,' she admitted. Peggy had never had a telephone installed, but relied on being able to use her neighbour's in an emergency.

'I'll nip up to the box on the corner and give them a

quick ring, just to put your mind at rest,' Ella said and privately added, And mine. I couldn't bear it if Grandpa was ill and not telling us, she thought.

'Ella?'

Her heart skipped a beat. She hadn't expected Rob to be at home.

'I've just come home for a few days after finishing exams to help Dad with the haymaking,' he explained when she asked why he was at home.

'How were your exams?'

'Not bad, but I'll be pleased to be home for good. Only another couple of weeks.'

Suddenly an overwhelming longing to be with him, walking along the beach or standing at the end of the Spit or even just harvesting with him, swept through her.

'El? You still there?

Pips sounded in her ear and she scrabbled to insert more money into the slot. 'Yes – yes, I'm here.'

'How's things with you, then?' Was he really interested, or merely being polite, she wondered. With the miles between them and across a crackly telephone wire she couldn't tell.

'Fine. I've a couple more exams then I've finished too. I've an interview for a job soon.'

There was silence at the other end.

'Rob . . .?'

She thought she heard him sigh as he said, 'You're staying there, then? In the city?'

'Well, yes . . .'

The pips sounded again and she pushed in her last coin. 'Rob, listen. The reason I've rung. Is everything all right at home? I mean, at Brumbys' Farm?'

'I think so. Why?'

Now she had to put Peggy's fears into words, it sounded foolish. 'I just wanted to be sure they're all right. Can you take down Rita's phone number and ask your dad to ring me if ever – if ever they need me?'

'Of course.' Suddenly, there was warmth in his voice. 'Wait a minute . . . Right, fire away.'

She told him the number and he repeated it back to make sure he'd got it down correctly. 'Don't forget, Rob. Ask your dad to let me know.'

'You can count on it – and El, when can I . . .'

But the pips sounded once more and the line went dead.

'Oh, damn and blast!' she muttered and slammed the receiver down, then allowed herself a wry grin as she thought of what Gran would say if she could hear her using such language.

Thirty

The year's secretarial course was almost finished and all that remained was for Ella to await the results of the examinations in shorthand, typing and elementary bookkeeping, and find employment.

'You know, I really thought you'd be moving to York once your course had finished,' Peggy said, and then added swiftly, 'Don't get me wrong, I don't want you to go.'

Ella smiled. 'Thanks.' Then she sighed and a small frown furrowed her smooth forehead. 'They have been trying to persuade me to go and live with them in York, but well . . .'

'Well, what?' Peggy prompted.

Ella wriggled her shoulders. 'I don't know. It – it just seems so far away, you know.'

Peggy put her head on one side and regarded the girl thoughtfully. 'No, to be honest, I don't know. York's not so very different from Lincoln, is it?'

Ella shook her head. 'It's not that . . .'

Peggy looked at her keenly. 'You mean, it's a long way from Fleethaven Point, don't you?'

Ella gasped and her eyes widened. 'No! You know I don't care if I never see that place again.'

Peggy laughed and turned away, murmuring something that sounded like, '"The lady doth protest too much, methinks."'

*

'Aunty Peg, Aunty Peg. I've got a job!'

'Oh, Ella, well done. What is it?'

'You remember that interview I had a couple of weeks back?'

'At that firm of solicitors?'

Ella, her eyes shining, nodded. 'Well, they've offered me a three months' trial from July to the end of September and then, if my exam results are reasonable and I've proved myself, they'll make it permanent.'

'How wonderful.' Peggy clapped her hands. 'I'm so pleased. So you've definitely decided not to go to live in York?'

Ella shook her head. 'Well, not yet anyway. Maybe one day. It – it depends . . . You don't mind me staying here?'

Peggy hugged her. 'You know I love having you here, silly.'

Ella put her arms about the older woman and for a moment leant her head against her shoulder.

Peggy Godfrey did not press the matter any further, but shrewdly she guessed that somewhere in the picture now was a young man; but exactly which young man she could not be sure.

'Jonathan's letter's late again,' Peggy said worriedly towards the beginning of September. 'You haven't had word from anyone else at Fleethaven, have you, Ella?'

Ella shook her head. 'No, but Uncle Danny will write or phone if there's something wrong. You know he will.'

Peggy picked up her fork but only toyed with the food on her plate.

Ella leant across the table and touched her hand. 'You're still not convinced though, are you, Aunty Peg?'

'I suppose I'm being silly but . . .' she sighed, hesitating.

'Tell me,' Ella prompted gently.

The words came in a rush then. 'I don't like to say anything against your grannie, you know I don't, but . . .' She stopped as suddenly as she had begun.

Ella finished the sentence for her. 'You mean, you don't think she would let you know if he were ill?'

Miserably, Peggy nodded. 'I know they'll have been busy with the main harvest now, but it's never stopped him writing regularly before.'

Ella thought and then said, 'I could ring Uncle Danny tonight, just to put your mind at rest.'

Peggy's worried brow cleared. 'Oh, thank you, Ella.'

'Ella, love. How lovely to hear you.' Danny's voice came clearly down the wire, so familiar, so warm, that Ella felt the tears spring to her eyes. They had every right, she thought suddenly, to be resentful of the way she had just walked away from them all, and yet there had never been one word of reproach.

Except, of course, that her gran's continued silence was a constant rebuke.

'Uncle Danny, are they all right?'

'Ya gran and grandpa?'

'Yes.'

There was a slight pause and Ella held her breath, her heart thumping suddenly.

'Well, I think so. I saw ya gran yesterday, though I haven't seen ya grandpa for a while.' Again he paused.

'Did she say he was all right?'

'Oh yes, I always ask after him, Ella.' There was another pause and then his words came haltingly, as if he didn't want to make it sound like an accusation. 'Of course, the work's a bit heavy for them now. The farm's not quite as well looked after as it used to be. We try to help out when we can, me an' Rob, but she's a stubborn old goat. Too proud to accept a bit of help, that's her trouble.' He laughed. 'Don't worry, Ella love. I'll keep an eye on them . . .'

At the end of September, when the three months' temporary trial period in the solicitors' office was nearly up, the senior partner called Ella into his office one morning and told her that they would extend her employment for a further three months but only on a temporary basis.

'I don't feel able to make your position permanent yet, Miss Hilton. Although the quality of your work is excellent and you work hard . . .' He paused and steepled his bony fingers together, rocking backwards in his swivel chair. 'I am a little concerned about your, well, your manner towards our clients. You seem a little abrupt at times. You should try to cultivate a more deferential manner towards them. Now, I suggest you take next week off to think things over. If you are prepared to try a little harder, then start back with us, let me see . . . yes, on Monday, the tenth of October.'

Ella stared at the man in front of her and sighed inwardly. She bit back the retort that sprang to her lips. She'd stick it another month, she told herself, but, although she didn't say so, she found the work boring, the staff dull and far too staid and as for the clients, well! She could imagine her gran's comments about some of the complaints and problems that came through the office door.

'A hard day's work'd sort most of 'em out,' she could

imagine being Esther's appraisal. 'Pity they ain't got something better to think about!'

Standing before the joyless face of her employer, Ella had difficulty in keeping the smile from her mouth.

'The old buzzard's given me the week off to "think things over",' she told Peggy, her tone heavy with sarcasm. 'I think I'll go to York on Wednesday until Sunday. Will you be all right?' she added, watching Peggy huddle closer to the fire and pull a shawl around her shoulders.

Peggy sneezed, dabbed at her already bright nose and said, 'Yes, of course I'll be all right. It's only a cold.'

'I know,' Ella said, 'but it is a stinker.'

Peggy smiled weakly. 'That's why I thought I'd better stay off work. Customers get very upset if you breathe germs all over them.'

'I can imagine!'

By the Wednesday, Peggy's cold was no better and she had decided to take the rest of the week off work. 'I've only had about three weeks' illness in all the years I've been there, but I still feel guilty staying away.'

'You've got a nasty cough,' Ella said putting her suitcase down for a moment while she gave Peggy a swift hug. 'You'd be much better keeping warm for another day or two.'

Peggy sniffed miserably. She was hardly ever ill and did not make a good patient.

Ella bit her lip. 'Are you sure you'll be all right. Perhaps I'd better not go . . .'

Peggy flapped her hands at Ella and said again, 'It's only a cold. I'll be fine. You'd better go. You'll miss your train and your father will be meeting you . . .'

'All right, then,' Ella agreed.

Peggy forced a smile and added, 'Have a good time.'

Over dinner that evening she told her father and grandmother about her job in the solicitors' office. 'It's so solemn all the time. I think I'm going to start looking for something else when I get back.'

'Your father will find you a job here in York, won't you, Philip?' her grandmother said across the table, waving her hand as if the fact were already accomplished. 'I'm sure you're owed a few favours. All these committees you're asked to serve on.'

Smiling, he said, 'If it's what Ella would like.'

'Of course it's what she'd like.'

'Now, Mother,' he said gently and winked at Ella, 'no trying to organize the girl's life.'

'As if I would!' she said indignantly, and then turned to Ella. 'Now tomorrow morning we're going shopping. We'll have lunch in town because I've booked you in at the hairdresser's tomorrow afternoon at two. Martin is calling for you at seven and taking you out to dinner. Won't that be nice?'

Ella dared not glance at her father for fear she would laugh aloud. Instead, she said dutifully, 'Yes, Grandmother.'

At seven thirty, Ella found herself being ushered into a smart restaurant by Martin Hughes. She gazed around in amazement at the thick, wall-to-wall carpet, the tables set with pink cloths, a small vase of fresh flowers in the centre of each one. Sparkling crystal chandeliers hung from the ornate ceiling and fancy scalloped drapes covered the windows. A black-suited waiter with a crisp white shirt and black bow tie bowed deferentially and showed them to a secluded corner table for two.

'I thought we'd be more private here,' Martin said. 'There's something I want to ask you.'

'Oh. Really? What?'

Martin was smiling, his eyes large behind the thick lenses of his spectacles. When he looked at her, with her new hair-style and pretty clothes, not to mention the use of make-up to hide the birthmark, Ella could see the admiration in his eyes.

'Not so fast,' he said. 'We'll eat first. Besides, I've got to pluck up courage.'

Ella's eyes widened and she felt a strange fluttering in her stomach. When Martin asked, 'Shall I order for us both?' all she could do was nod.

As they pushed away their empty dessert plates, the hovering wine-waiter filled their glasses.

'Coffee, sir?'

'Yes, please. And two brandies.'

'Certainly, sir.' He gave a little bow and returned in a moment bearing two fat glasses with a measure of amber liquid in each.

Martin picked up his glass and raised it towards Ella. 'To us,' he said.

'Us?'

He nodded and smiled. 'Your grandmother tells me you're coming to live in York. I – er – hope we can see a lot more of each other.'

Ella gaped at him for a moment and then dropped her glance from his earnest gaze. She twirled the brandy glass on the table between fingers that threatened to tremble slightly. She knew he liked her, enjoyed her company, but now he was hinting that he wanted more. She was too honest to let him think she would ever be his girlfriend. He was nice, she liked him, but not in that way; never, ever, could she love Martin. Not while she was still in love with Rob Eland.

She said carefully, 'I am thinking about taking a job here, yes, because I'm not too happy in the one I've got at the moment, but nothing's settled yet . . .'

Martin laughed. 'Oh, I think you can count on it being a *fait accompli*, if your grandmother has anything to do with it.'

Ella felt her jaw tightening, feeling as if her life were being organized for her. She had run away from Fleethaven Point from one autocratic grandmother and now she seemed to have found another.

'Martin, I . . .' she began, but out of the corner of her eye, she caught sight of the waiter hurrying from table to table, bending to ask a question of each of the diners. Answered by a shake of heads, he moved swiftly to the next table and the next. Now he was approaching their table. 'Excuse me, sir . . .' his glance went from Martin to Ella, 'is your name Miss Hilton?'

'Yes.'

'Ah, we've received a telephone call from your father. He asked if you could go home at once.'

Ella was already on her feet and pushing back her chair as the waiter grasped it to pull it back for her. Martin, rising more slowly, asked, 'Did he say why?'

The man shook his head. 'No, sir. But it did sound urgent. I'll get your coat for you, Miss.'

Ella turned fearful eyes to Martin. 'It must be Grandmother. Perhaps she's been taken ill.'

Martin took hold of her arm and steered her between the tables. 'Come on, I'll take you home at once.'

But it was Mrs Trent who opened the front door to

them. 'Your father's in his study, dear. Go in to him. He's on the telephone . . .'

Ella ran across the hall, the carpet in the centre sliding on the polished floor beneath her hurrying feet.

'Dad? What is it?'

He turned to look at her as she opened the door. Then he said into the mouthpiece, 'She's here now. Hold on a moment while I tell her.'

He covered the mouthpiece with his hand and then said, 'Ella, my dear. I've got Danny Eland on the phone . . .'

Ella gave a little cry and her eyes widened. 'No, oh no,' she breathed and reached out with shaking fingers, 'please, let me speak to him.'

Philip handed her the receiver and, with a voice that quavered, she said, 'Uncle Danny, what is it? What's happened? Is it Gran? Or – or Grandpa?' Her questions were tumbling over themselves without giving Danny chance to reply.

'Steady on, lass,' came his calming voice. 'It's not the worst, but ya grandpa's ill.'

'How ill?' Her voice was high-pitched with anxiety and a feeling of dreadful guilt washed over her. Peggy had been right to be worried and Ella had ignored the older woman's intuition. Oh, if something were to happen to Grandpa, she'd never forgive herself. Never . . . She tried to pull her reeling senses together, made herself listen to Danny.

'Ya gran's kept it from us all. She kept telling us they were both fine but then I started to get a bit worried because I never seemed to see ya grandpa; not in the fields nor about the yard. So I went across and tackled her about it. Ella, love, he's been poorly for about a month, but your gran's that stubborn. She's nursing him herself. She won't have the doctor, won't even let any of us near him. We're trying to help out more with the farm work now, but she's still insisting that she doesn't need anyone. Ella, I don't think she's right herself. She's – she's . . .' The words came hesitantly and Ella knew instinctively that even now Danny was reluctant to say anything against Esther. 'She seems sort of – wild.'

'Cross, you mean?' Ella prompted.

The voice on the other end of the wire faded and crackling on the line broke up his words. 'No, no, more that she can't cope . . . Please come home, Ella. They need you, lass. And we – we all miss you . . .'

Tears were rolling down her cheeks, the lump in her throat choking the words. 'I'm coming, Uncle Danny. I'm coming. Right now!'

She caught the first train out of York on the following morning, the Friday. Her father took her to the station.

'I'm sure it won't be as bad as you fear,' he tried to reassure her. 'Come back and see us as soon as you can.'

She'd hugged him fiercely unable to make any promises, unsure just how long it would be before she saw him or her grandmother again.

Mrs Trent had refused to believe that it was anything but a temporary set-back to her plans for Ella. 'Don't forget,' had been her parting words, 'we want you to come and live with us. I've organized the decorators to re-do your bedroom. They're starting tomorrow. Pink, I thought, with curtains and bedspread to match. Yes, a pretty, soft pink . . .'

*

Peggy, still coughing and with her nose sore and peeling, opened the door. Without preamble she said, 'Danny rang Rita and I gave him your father's number.'

Ella nodded. 'I came back as soon as I could. I'm going straight on home . . .' She stared at Peggy, her eyes startled with the realization of what she had just said.

Peggy, though the worry in her eyes had deepened, nodded slowly, and quietly she answered the unspoken question that lay in the air between them. 'My dear girl, although your head has always rebelled against it, in your heart of hearts, you know it is your home.'

Ella flung her arms about her. 'Oh, Aunty Peg, I'm so sorry. I should have listened to you. I should have known there was something wrong.'

'Now, don't be silly and start blaming yourself. How could you possibly have known?' Peggy said sensibly, and hugged the girl warmly.

'*You* seemed to know though, didn't you? That's why you were so worried when his letters were late and when his writing looked funny.'

Peggy sighed. 'I thought I was fussing unnecessarily.'

'Well, you weren't and now I wish I'd taken it more seriously.'

'Never mind that now. Get yourself ready. You're in good time to catch the six o'clock bus out.'

As Ella hurried upstairs to unpack and repack her suitcase, Peggy followed her. 'I wish I could come with you, but this cold's gone on my chest. I went to the doctor this morning and he said on no account must I go out for a few days. Perhaps if I—'

'No,' Ella said firmly. 'I can't do with two of you ill, Aunty Peg. Get yourself better first and then come over if you can. I'll ring Rita first thing tomorrow morning.'

'Promise?'

Ella kissed her cheek. 'I promise. And try not to worry. I'll sort Gran out when I get there. I won't half give her what-for. How dare she not tell us?'

At this moment, in her determination, Ella prepared herself to do battle with Esther Godfrey.

Thirty-One

Ella caught the six o'clock bus out of Lincoln travelling all the way to Lynthorpe. Before leaving, she sat down and scribbled a letter to her employer saying that she would not be returning to them on Monday. On her way to the bus stop she dropped it in the letter box.

The journey seemed to be taking for ever. Ella rubbed the steam from the bus window with her finger-tips and peered out into the blackness of the evening. It was still raining; it would be wet and windy walking the coast road from the bus station in Lynthorpe out to Fleethaven Point. But she didn't care. She'd walk anywhere, even if it took all night, just so long as she was in time. As the bus rocked and swayed along, Ella stared out into the black night watching the grey grass verge and hedges rushing past. The other passengers were chatting, dozing or reading and taking no notice of the girl huddled in her seat.

Her eyes glazed, she no longer saw the other people or heard the prattle around her, or felt the rocking motion of the bus; instead before her mind's eye was the kindly face of her grandpa, in her ears was his deep, gentle voice. She was remembering so many incidents: his outstretched arms enfolding her, carrying her to the hayloft and comforting her tearing grief after the death of her mother; gently explaining about Lady and the ways of farming life; his softly spoken words when he thought her gran too hard on her, 'Oh, let the lass have some fun, Esther.' And even, when all the world had seemed against her, when her grandmother had refused to believe her, even then, Grandpa had had faith in her.

Oh, please let him be all right, she whispered to herself and closed her eyes, willing the bus to go faster, faster . . .

'There's a flood . . .' Dimly, she heard the words and cried out as she lurched forward banging her head. She heard someone scream, 'The sea. It's the sea!' and realized the words had come from her own mouth. Visions of huge waves rolling in, engulfing the land, sweeping away everything in its path – drowning . . . It couldn't be happening again. Was it a punishment for leaving her elderly grandparents to cope alone with all the heavy farmwork? That was it; she was going to be drowned too . . .

'It's not the sea, lass.' A calm voice spoke beside her and she turned frightened eyes towards the man, who touched her elbow gently and pressed her back into her seat. 'It's only the river flooded the roadway. We saw it earlier today on our previous trip. Very swollen, it was. I'm not surprised it's happened, though how we're to get through I don't know.' Ella blinked at him foolishly and looked about her. Then she remembered where she was: in a bus travelling home to Fleethaven Point, though the vehicle was now stationary, the passengers worriedly craning their necks to see out into the darkness.

'But my grandpa – he's ill. I have to get to Lynthorpe. I have to get through.'

'Well, sit tight. I'm just going to have a word with Ron, the driver, and see what he reckons.' The conductor left her and went back to his platform at the rear of the double-decker bus. Holding the handrail, he leaned out of the side, staring ahead into the night.

The passengers clamoured for explanation. 'What is it? What's the matter? What's happening?'

The conductor raised his voice. 'Please keep calm, ladies and gentlemen . . .'

The decision was taken to try to drive through the water to the market place in the centre of the town. Everyone peered out of the window as the bus, moving at a steady rate, drove into the flood, swirling the water aside with its huge wheels, and sluiced a way through.

Now that common sense had reasserted itself after those first frightening moments, when all the horror of seven years earlier had for an instant been so real again, Ella thought, This is daft. First the 'fifty-three floods, and now this. There must be something about me and water.

The bus reached the square and came to a stop on an island of cobbles in the centre of the market place. The driver jumped down from his cab and he and the conductor went towards a policeman. After a few moments' conversation they came back to the bus.

'We can't get any further at present,' the conductor informed his passengers. 'The bridge we normally use has been washed away and the river is still flooding.'

There were cries of disbelief and anxious enquiries. The man spread his hands apologetically. 'I am sorry, ladies and gentlemen. All I can suggest is that you go across to that café over there to wait. The police will let us know . . .'

The market place was busy with people; stranded motorists and rescue services were using the higher ground as a meeting point. Inside the café, Ella perched herself miserably on a stool and sat watching the figures rushing to and fro outside.

'Here, love, have a cup of tea.' She looked up to see a young man holding out a cup towards her.

'That's very kind of you. Thanks,' she said, and suddenly realized how dry her mouth was.

'Looks like we might be stuck here for a while,' the young man said, quite cheerfully, sitting down beside her.

'I hope not,' Ella said anxiously. 'I'm trying to get home to Fleethaven Point. My grandpa's ill.'

'Oh, that's tough luck. Will they be expecting you?'

Ella shook her head. 'No,' she said, and her voice was only a whisper. 'They don't know I'm coming.'

'Oh well, at least they won't be worried about you.'

No, she thought sadly, they won't be worried at all. Her gran hadn't even bothered to let her know her grandpa was ill. They didn't know – none of them would know – that she was caught in the floods, just like her mother all those years ago. She gazed out of the café window into the night, watching the black water lapping at the cobbles of the market place, shining wet in the lights streaming from the café window.

'I'll put the wireless on,' the café owner said in a loud, hearty voice. 'Cheer us all up a bit, eh?'

He twiddled the knobs on a brown bakelite radio on a shelf behind the service counter and the deep tones of a male singer softly bade her to hurry home to his waiting arms, aching to hold her . . .

Ella groaned inwardly and closed her eyes against the tears that suddenly threatened.

Two hours later, a policeman in wellingtons came into the café. 'Right, ladies and gentlemen. You'll be pleased to know we've got a single-decker bus that's going to take you out by another route . . .' Voices clamoured and, once everyone had decided whether to board the bus or not, they set off. Steadily the driver inched the vehicle through the water and, taking a left-hand turn instead of right over the bridge, they left the market town and drove up out of the flood and into the countryside.

'Do you know where we are?' Ella asked peering out. All she could see were hedgerows, the rain still slashing against the window. Completely lost and utterly dependent upon the man at the wheel, Ella stared forlornly into the black void.

'Haven't a clue,' the young man said airily, his nose now buried in a book. 'Long as he gets us to Lynthorpe this side of tomorrow morning, I don't much care.'

The bus must have doubled back and joined its normal route, for they came to a stop Ella recognized and three passengers alighted, calling out a cheery 'goodnight' to those left on board. Eventually, after what seemed a lifetime of anxiety, the driver called out, 'Next stop Lynthorpe,' and Ella sent up a silent prayer of thankfulness.

It was well after midnight when Ella alighted at the bus station and by now she knew everyone would be in bed and asleep at Rookery Farm. It wouldn't be fair to phone Uncle Danny and ask him to come and pick her up at this time of night. Hitching her rucksack into a more comfortable position on her shoulders, she set off to walk to Fleethaven Point.

With every step of the way along the road running beside the sand-dunes, the wind whipping across the flat fields and clouds scudding across the moon, the words were running through her mind.

I'm coming, Grandpa. Hold on, I'm coming home.

She found she was holding her breath as she tiptoed into the farmyard. Somewhere an owl hooted and the barn door creaked to and fro, swinging in the wind on rusty hinges. The house, as she had expected, was in darkness.

She heard a soft 'miaow' and, straining her eyes through the blackness, saw a dark shape walking towards her and felt it rubbing against her legs. She reached down and touched the soft fur. 'Tibby, oh, Tibby.'

She picked him up. He seemed lighter and, as her hands felt him, thinner than she remembered, but he rubbed his face against her chin and purred as ecstatically as always, digging his claws into her shoulder.

'Well, at least someone's pleased to see me,' she murmured into his pointed ear. She glanced again at the house: there was no sign of anyone being awake. She would not startle them by knocking on the door now; she would wait until morning. Feeling her way into the barn, she climbed carefully up the ladder and into the hayloft, remembering wryly the last time she had been up here with Rob.

Nestling into the dry hay with Tibby snuggled up to her, Ella dozed fitfully, for cold and fear of what she would find in the morning made restful sleep elusive.

'Oh, please let him be alive . . .'

Thirty-Two

A door banged and Ella jumped awake. 'Gran . . .' she said aloud and scrambled to her feet, shaking off bits of hay as she climbed stiffly down the ladder and pulled open the barn door.

She gasped in surprise at the sight before her.

The yard was littered with hay and straw; she had never seen it so untidy. The tractor, parked near the barn, was not sheeted down properly and had only a piece of old sacking slung over its engine. The cockerel, about to open its beak to herald the morning, stood on the seat of the tractor. Scrawny-looking hens wandered freely around, scratching and complaining. Bewildered, Ella stepped out into the yard. There was no clattering of churns, no sound at all of the early-morning work under way. She went towards the cowshed and peered in. The floor was filthy, and in the far corner the milking machine looked dusty and unused; indeed, there was no sign that it was in daily use for milking at all now.

Brumbys' Farm? This was not Brumbys' Farm; at least not how she knew it, not how she remembered it. Souters', yes, but not the farm belonging to Esther Godfrey!

Frowning, Ella turned away. She went to the pump in the middle of the yard. The handle squeaked protestingly as she worked it up and down, but clear water gushed out and she bent and sluiced the tiredness from her eyes. She heard a noise and slowly straightened up to see a figure standing in the open doorway of the farmhouse.

The water still dripping from her face, Ella stared, her mouth hanging open.

An old woman stood there: her white hair stuck out in unkempt wisps, her blouse was dirty grey and her black skirt was stained and torn at the hem. Shocked, Ella moved forward.

'Gran?' The word was a horrified whisper; a disbelieving question. Surely, surely this was not her gran? This haggard old witch was not, could not possibly be, Esther Godfrey. As she drew closer, she could see that even the green eyes were dull, almost lifeless.

'Be off with ya.' The voice was cracked, feeble and querulous.

'Gran, it's me. Ella . . .'

The eyes squinted and stared. Then the woman sniffed. 'Go away. Go back where ya came from. I don't need you. I can manage.'

Stung to retort, Ella said, 'Aye, an' it looks like it an' all.' She swept her arm behind her to encompass the untidy yard, the neglected machinery, the empty cowshed. Her heart contracted now in fear. 'Grandpa?' she began.

'We don't need you. We don't need anyone. As long as we've got each other . . .'

Hope soared. Then he wasn't dead. Not unless . . .

But the woman standing before her was so altered, so changed, almost as if she had lost her reason, her will to live. Then was he . . .?

Ella took a deep breath. With her feet, dusty from the night's walk, planted firmly apart and hands on hips, she faced the old woman. 'Well, Gran. I'm here and I'm staying, whether you like it or not.'

For a brief instant the old eyes flickered. For a fleeting

moment the fire sparked. 'Huh, what d'you think you can do, eh? A townie! It's a strong farmer's lad I need. Not a townie – and a girl!' She sniffed and turned away, back into the kitchen.

Ella stepped into the house. In the scullery, the draining board was littered with dirty pots, the sink stained brown. In the kitchen, no fire burned in the grate and there was no sign of food on the table.

Her grandmother shuffled towards the wooden Windsor chair by the cold range and sat down. Closer now, Ella could see that the skin on her hands was wrinkled and mottled, her nails cracked and broken. She was thinner and her shoulders sagged dejectedly.

For a moment Ella gaped in horror at her grandmother, the sight of the pathetic old woman tearing at her conscience. 'Oh, Gran. If only I'd known. I should never have gone. I should never have left you . . .'

Tears blurred her vision, but now, panic-stricken, she brushed them aside and went towards the living room, into the hall and up the stairs. She felt sick with fear. He was dead; she was sure he was dead. He must be; that was the reason her gran looked like she did.

Holding her breath, she pushed open their bedroom door and peered round it, knowing she must look, but afraid of what she would see.

Her grandfather was propped up in the bed against three pillows, his eyes closed, his breathing laboured. His face was strained and white, uneven stubble covering the lower half. She moved to the bedside and bent over him. 'Grandpa . . .?' When he did not respond, did not even open his eyes, she touched his hand. His skin was cold and slightly clammy to her touch and she almost recoiled in panic.

Then she was running, down the stairs, through the

living room and back into the kitchen. She stood before her gran, leant over her as she sat in the chair.

'I'm going to phone for the doctor. I won't be long.'

'Don't need no doctor. Can't do no good.'

'Well, I'm going . . .'

The old woman flapped her hands. 'Aye, go. You go. Just let him die in peace . . . an' me an' all!'

'He's not going to die. I won't let him.' Ella felt like shaking the old woman. 'Nor you either, ya daft old beezum!'

There was the ghost of a smile on Esther's mouth, a spark in the green eyes that had seemed so dead. And the words, when she spoke, were an echo from the past; a past the old woman was trying desperately to cling on to. 'I'll have none of your chelp, Missy!'

'You'll have a lot more of my chelp before I'm finished, Gran.'

The old woman leant her head back against the chair and closed her eyes as if even that brief exertion had exhausted her.

Ella was running again, out of the house, through the hole in the hedge, across the field where the corn had never been cut and lay in flattened waste.

'Oh, Gran,' she sobbed as she ran. 'Oh, Gran, what have I done to you?' Where had that strong, resilient, feisty woman gone, with the bright hair and flashing green eyes; the woman who took on the world, fearless and independent? Where, oh where had she gone? It was like looking at a ghost, a shadow of the woman she had been. As she ran, panting painfully, memories haunted Ella. Esther taking her hand at Kate's funeral, 'You're coming home with me.' She hadn't been obliged to take the girl into her home. How many women of sixty-odd would have done so? Esther teaching her to sew, to cook and bake. Oh, yes, at the time, it had all seemed like hard work, drudgery; as if she were being used as no more than a skivvy. But mentally Ella ticked off all the skills she had learned under Esther's watchful eye: she could milk cows, she could drive a tractor, she knew when the bloom on the grass meant it was ready for cutting, she knew when to harvest wheat, barley, oats. She could 'put away' a pig; she could pluck and draw chickens, turkeys, even skin and draw rabbits . . .

And then she remembered other times; her grandmother smoothing crushed dock leaves on to the nettle stings; her greying head bent over the tiny stitching, sitting up far into the night to finish making Ella's skirt for her to go out dancing . . .

'Oh, Gran, I'm so sorry,' she wept.

'Uncle Danny, Uncle Danny,' she cried, breathless and red in the face, as she reached the yard at Rookery Farm. But it was Rob who emerged from the cowshed. She stopped, shocked by the thrill of joy that ran through her even in this desperate moment. She felt the urge to run to him, this friend of her childhood, and yet, perversely, she was suddenly shy. He had been a boy when she left, but now, before her, stood a man. The year at college, and his return home to farm the land he loved side by side, an equal, with his father, had turned Rob from a good-looking, though gangly, youth into a handsome man. His black hair glistened in the pale October morning light and beneath his open-necked shirt, his shoulders were broad and muscular. He seemed to have grown taller too. The very sight of him caught at her breath. He was staring at her, gaping almost, as if he too were taking in the changes the year's absence had wrought in her. They had not seen each other in all that time. They had spoken once, but only on the phone, and now there was no time to talk, not even time to greet him properly . . .

'Can I use your phone? It's urgent.'

'Course ya can. Come on.' As they walked quickly towards the back door he said, 'Dad said you were coming. When did you get here?'

She pulled a face. 'Middle of the night. There were floods at Horncastle. We got trapped there for hours . . .'

'Ya kidding?'

She shook her head. 'Ironic, isn't it?'

'I'll say . . .' He opened the door and raised his voice. 'Mam, it's Ella. She needs the phone – quick.'

'Oh, Ella, love.' Rosie was hugging her quickly, but catching some of the anxiety in Ella's face led her at once into the hall and to their telephone.

'Do you know the doctor's number?' and when Rosie flipped open a notepad, Ella lifted the receiver.

Minutes later she put down the phone. 'He's coming straight away.'

'You'd better get back, then. Come back later, when you can, and see us.' Rosie kissed her cheek again, squeezed her arm and whispered, 'I'm so glad you've come home, Ella.'

'I'll pop back tonight. I must ring Peggy, if you don't mind, Aunty Rosie.'

'You know we don't, love.'

'I'll come back with you,' Rob volunteered, and Ella nodded gratefully.

As they jogged back across the fields, Rob told her, between breaths, what had been happening.

'We had no idea what was going on, El. Me dad's blaming himself now, saying he should have done something sooner, but every time we went to the farm, all ya gran said was, "He's resting," or "He'll be all right in a day or two," and to be honest, for a time, we believed her. We tried to help with the work. Cut some of her hay and stacked it. Some of the corn, an' all, though we didn't get to this one . . .' He waved his hand to indicate the field through which they were running. 'Shame it's gone to waste. Then the day before yesterday me dad insisted on seeing ya grandpa. And then he got a right shock, I can tell you. That's when he tried to ring you.'

'And I was in York,' she murmured, feeling a fresh wave of guilt.

'Dad tried to get the doctor in yesterday, but ya gran seemed to get real – well – odd. Ranting and raving at us to mind our own business and let her mind hers. Even my grandma went across, but she couldn't get any sense out of your gran either. She came back mumbling to herself about stubborn old women who ought to let bygones be bygones. Your gran had shaken her fist at her shouting, "You keep away Beth Eland," and saying she didn't need any help, specially not hers. That they'd all gone and left her, Kate, Lilian – and you. But she didn't need anyone. She could manage. She'd look after him, she said. And when I went last night . . .' He paused as they negotiated the narrow plank bridge and ran on. 'She gave me a right turn. D'you know what she said to me?'

Ella shook her head.

'"I don't need you here, Matthew Hilton, I can look after Sam . . ."'

Ella stopped in her tracks and stared at him. 'She had gone a bit funny, then. Gone back into the past. Matthew was your – our – grandfather, wasn't he?'

Rob nodded. 'Aye, and he came to the farm to help her nurse old Sam Brumby when he was dying. That's when all the trouble started . . .'

Ella nodded grimly. 'Yes, and we've got trouble again now. Come on . . .'

*

The doctor arrived within half an hour and examined both Jonathan Godfrey and, though much to her disgust, Esther too.

'They're both undernourished. They've been neglecting themselves, Ella. I really ought to have them removed to hospital. Your grandfather might have had a slight heart attack, but I can't be sure unless I can do some proper tests.'

Ella shook her head. 'I think it would finish them off, Doctor. As long as you tell me what to do, I'll look after them.'

'Right then . . .' He dusted a chair and sat down at the kitchen table. 'I hope you're ready for this, lass,' he said in his bluff but kindly way, 'because it's not going to be easy.'

'I could come and stay here to help,' Rob, hovering in the background, volunteered and Ella looked up to meet his steady, concerned gaze.

Suddenly, time seemed to tilt, and ghostly shadows shifted in the dusty corners.

'Full circle,' she murmured, though only for Rob to hear. 'We've come full circle.'

In the days that followed, Ella didn't think she had ever worked so hard in her life; not even as a child under her grandmother's bidding. And yet, as she worked, it was as if Esther's voice followed her everywhere, 'Scrub it, Missy. Get some elbow grease into it,' even though now the woman herself was a sick, weak old lady confined to her bed.

Without the willing help of Rob Eland and the rest of his family, Ella doubted she would have coped.

'What happened to her cows?' she asked as she

scrubbed, black-leaded and relit the kitchen range, the warmth filling the cold, dank kitchen, rekindling life.

'There's only two left,' Rob told her. 'The others died. We've got 'em with our herd and we bring her the milk across each day.'

Ella glanced up. 'And a bit more besides, I reckon.'

Rob grinned. 'Well, it's the least we can do,' he said as he banged at an upholstered chair and raised a cloud of dust.

'I don't know how this place has got like this in such a short time,' Ella muttered.

Rob did not answer and when she looked up, she found him looking at her strangely.

'What?' she asked. 'What is it?'

'It's not been a short time, Ella, now has it?' he said quietly. 'Only none of us knew. Me dad reckons they must have been struggling to cope for months, maybe ever since you left, if truth be known. But they never said anything. I should've come across more often when I was home at weekends but, well . . .' His voice faded away and his glance avoided her eyes.

Out every night on his motorbike, with the girls, she thought grimly. But it was only a fleeting pang of jealousy. He was here with her now, helping her when she most needed a friend and she was grateful for that.

'But Grandpa used to write to me,' Ella countered. 'He said they were fine. It . . .' She hesitated again feeling the guilt because she had brushed aside Peggy's intuitive concern. 'It was only recently his letters were late and – and different.'

'Of course he kept writing to you.' A note of impatience was creeping into Rob's tone now. 'He wouldn't want you to feel obliged to come back. He knew you hated it here, had always hated it; that all you'd ever wanted was to get back to the town. And from your letters he knew you were happy, specially when you'd found your father and had a new family.'

'But Gran? I mean, she didn't care about me that much . . .'

Rob stared at her and then said roughly, 'Well, if that's what you think, Ella Hilton, then you ain't got the sense you were born with.' And with that parting shot, he marched out into the yard carrying an armchair and began banging it with the cane carpet beater until he had to stop as clouds of dust set him coughing.

Ella bent over the range once more, pondering on his words. They certainly didn't help to ease the weight of guilt she already felt.

Not one bit.

The following day she found clean sheets in the huge blanket chest in the bedroom that had once been hers, but where her grandmother was now in the bed.

'I thought they might be better sleeping separately for a bit,' she had told Rob. 'One's disturbing the other at the moment.'

After warming the bed-linen on the clothes-airer in the kitchen for a few hours, she changed all three beds. She was sleeping in the tiny room with the sloping ceiling leaving the doors open between the rooms so that she could listen out through the night.

Carrying the bundle of dirty laundry out to the wash-house, a musty, unclean smell assailed her nostrils as she opened the door and once again her heart contracted to think that Esther Godfrey – proud, defiant Esther – had come to this.

Oh, Gran, her heart moaned again, and guilt swept through her afresh.

Rob stayed at Brumbys' Farm sleeping on an old settee in the best parlour.

'She'd have a double duck fit, ya gran, if she could see me sleeping here on her best chaise-longy thing.' He laughed as he folded the blankets.

Ella giggled. 'I don't think she'll mind as long as you're down here and I'm safely upstairs in the little bedroom with her between us.'

Playfully, Rob adopted a suggestive leer. 'Afraid I'll have my wicked way with you, is she?' Then suddenly his expression sobered and in his dark brown eyes there was something more, a look that made Ella catch her breath and her heart start to thump.

But he turned away and bent over the settee, snatching up the pile of blankets and sheets and placing them in a neat pile on a nearby chair. When he turned round again, he avoided looking at her directly. 'Ya grandpa needs shaving,' he said brusquely. 'That beard of his looks awful.'

'Oh, er, yes,' Ella said, swallowing hard. 'D'you think you could have a go?'

'Ooh, I dunno. I'll ask me dad to come over. He'll not mind.'

And when Danny had come and shaved him, although Jonathan still looked thin and tired, he looked so much better. Ella kissed his wrinkled cheek. 'That's more like my grandpa.'

His hand reached out and touched hers. 'I'm glad you came back, love. Don't go away, lass, will you? Not till we're both well again.'

Ella leant forward and whispered something in her grandfather's ear. The old man's eyes watered and he clasped her hand in his and held it to his cheek, before he sank back against the pillows with a huge sigh, closed his eyes and slept.

'What did you say to him?' Rob asked as they crept downstairs.

'Never you mind,' Ella answered, but she was smiling as she said it.

Rob grinned back. 'Well, whatever it was, it seemed to work.'

'Yes,' Ella whispered, and her smile was pensive for a moment. 'It did, didn't it?

Thirty-Three

In the tiny bedroom with its sloping ceiling only inches above her head, Ella lay awake. Though she was tired and every limb ached from a day spent cooking, cleaning and washing, she found sleep elusive. She was aware, so vibrantly aware, of Rob sleeping downstairs, only feet away.

She stared into the blackness, listening to the creaking of the timbers in the roof, the wind rattling the loose catch on the small window. Had she imagined that special look in his eyes because she *wanted to see it there*? Oh, how she wanted Rob to look at her like he looked at other girls, like young men looked at the girl they were falling in love with. With a groan she buried her face in her pillow. No, it wasn't possible. She must stop being so foolish, building up her hopes. He was here to help her because it was her *gran* he'd always admired and loved. Soon, she told herself fiercely, he'd be off again on his motorbike with Janice, not her, on the pillion.

In the grey light of early morning, when Ella emerged, yawning, from her tiny bedroom into the larger room where her grandmother was sleeping, she stopped and stared at the bed. The rumpled covers were pushed back and the bed was empty.

She gave a click of exasperation and, crossing the

landing, poked her head round the door of the bedroom where, for the moment, her grandpa was alone. He was still asleep, his mouth slightly open.

Ella hurried downstairs: there was no one in the kitchen and the back door stood wide open, the late October morning blowing coolly into the house. Her glance raked the yard and she listened.

There was neither sight nor sound of her grandmother.

Ella sped back through the house and almost fell through the door into the front parlour where Rob was sleeping. Dragging open the curtains to let in the pale light, she turned to see Rob sprawled on the couch, his arms flung wide, snoring gently.

'Rob! Rob! Wake up. Gran's gone from her bed . . .'

'Eh? What?' He was awake in an instant and throwing back the covers. Startled, Ella gave a shriek and turned away. Rob was completely naked. As she hurried from the room she heard his low chuckle.

In the kitchen she shook the fire into a glow.

'Where d'you think she's gone?' Rob asked, buckling his belt as he came up behind her. He grabbed his boots from under the scullery table and began pulling them on.

'I don't know.' Ella bit her lip. 'You go and look in all the sheds and the barn. I'll go round the front of the house.'

Checking first that Esther was not in the lavatory, Ella ran round the corner of the house, past the pond, through the orchard and squeezed through the hole in the hedge. Early-morning mist clung to the hedges and shrouded the fields.

'Gran,' she called, and her voice echoed in the stillness.

She ran back into the yard to see Rob emerging from the barn. 'She's not here.'

'Did you check the loft?'

When he nodded, Ella bit her lip. 'Where can she be? Where would she go?'

They stared at each other and then together said, 'The Spit!'

They were running side by side, over the westerly dunes, across the marsh to the eastern dunes, along the beach and out to the promontory, Rob's long legs taking him ahead of Ella. He called back, 'She's there! I can see her.'

Breathless, dragging cold air into her lungs, Ella looked up to see the solitary figure, standing at the very end of the sand-bank jutting out into the sea, the water lapping all around her. Her white night-gown flapping round her bare feet, a shawl pulled around her shoulders, Esther stood there motionless, just staring at the water. Rob had slowed his pace so that he did not come upon her suddenly and startle her and Ella was able to catch up with him.

'Gran,' she said gently, but the breeze whipped away her words and tossed them into the sea. Nearer, she said again, 'Gran . . .' but it wasn't until she touched the old woman's shoulder, making her jump, that Esther was aware of their presence.

'Gran, whatever . . .?' Ella began, but Rob touched Ella's arm and said softly, 'Be gentle with her Ella. Summat's caused this. Go easy.'

Ella put her arm about the thin body and turned Esther round, gently steering her away from the water's edge and back along the Spit. Still Esther's gaze was upon the lapping waves, mesmerized by the water.

'He drowned here, y'know,' she said suddenly and, turning, gripped Rob's arm in a surprisingly strong grasp for one who had become so frail. 'Then Kate drowned too. They've all gone now. I don't want to live. I don't want to go on wi'out him. There's no one left now he's gone an all. And Ella too – gone, all gone. I've lived too long . . .' She was staring up at Rob, seemingly oblivious to the fact that Ella was there too.

'Come on, Missus,' Rob said kindly. 'Let's get you home. Ya'll catch ya death out here.'

She tried to pull away, tried to turn back towards the water and, afraid she meant to plunge into its depths, the two youngsters clung on to her. Struggling, swaying from side to side on the narrow bank of sand and shingle, in danger any minute of toppling into the water, the three of them staggered back towards the beach. When the sand bank widened out and they reached safety, Ella and Rob glanced at each other with relief.

'Oh, Gran, your feet are bleeding!'

'Come on, Missus,' Rob said again firmly and, putting one arm under hers and around her back, the other under her knees, he swung her up into his arms and carried her.

'I'll run ahead and get some bricks into her bed. I keep some in the oven all the time now, for Grandpa . . .' Her eyes widened. 'Oh, heck! I didn't go back in to see to him this morning, what with all this . . .'

She was running ahead of them, like the wind across the marsh, panting up the dunes, slipping and sliding down amongst the elder trees, sobbing now with relief at having found her gran, but weeping too with the sadness of it all.

Poor Gran. She had lost her reason. To remember her as she had been and to see her now, like this, was breaking Ella's heart.

Wrapping three hot bricks from the oven in the range in pieces of blanket she staggered upstairs with them and put them into Esther's bed. Downstairs again, she put the kettle on the fire and found, at the back of the cupboard, a bottle of whisky. Vividly, the memory came back of how her grandmother had put whisky in some hot milk to warm her, chilled as she had been when the cold waters of the North Sea had invaded their home.

At that moment, Rob manoeuvred his way through the door and, without stopping, carried Esther straight upstairs and laid her in the bed. Esther closed her eyes and lay back against the pillows.

From the other room, they heard Jonathan's voice. 'Ella? That you Ella, lass?'

Ella hurried to the other bedroom and lifted the latch. 'I'm sorry, Grandpa. It's all right now, but Gran—'

'Ella! Come here!' It was Rob shouting from the other room and, fear rising in her throat, Ella rushed back again to see her grandmother struggling to get out of the bed again and Rob valiantly trying to stop her.

'Oh dear. What is the matter with her?'

'Let – me – go,' Esther was shouting, suddenly amazingly strong again. 'It's him – I want to see . . .'

'I think she wants to see your grandpa,' Rob said, and released his hold. 'We'd better let her.'

Ella put her arm about her grandmother. 'Come on then, Gran. Let's take you.'

They went out of the room, across the tiny landing and into the bedroom where Jonathan lay, his eyes turned towards the door. Her white hair dishevelled, her eyes wide, Esther peered, almost fearfully, round the door. Then she stood just staring at him and Ella felt a shudder run through the frail body.

'Esther, my dear. There you are.' He held out his hand to her.

Trembling Esther reached out with her own. 'I thought you were – dead!' she whispered.

Ella gasped and above her grandmother's head she stared back at Rob who had followed them.

'That explains what she was rambling on about,' he muttered.

'Come on, get in here with me,' Jonathan was saying, pulling back the bedclothes. 'This is where you belong.' With a whimper, like a lost, frightened child, Esther scrambled into the bed and snuggled up to him. She laid her head on his chest and he wrapped his arms about her and stroked her hair. 'There, there. It's all right,' he said, and though he still sounded tired, he was smiling happily.

Ella, tears blurring her vision, stumbled from the room and quietly pulled the door closed behind her.

'Come on, I reckon I need a drink more than she does.'

Downstairs in the kitchen, Ella sat at the table, resting her arms on the scrubbed surface, staring into the distance, whilst Rob mashed a cup of tea and tipped a measure of whisky into it.

'I shouldn't have separated them,' she said, contrite. 'I shouldn't have put her in the other room. She thought I'd done it because he'd died.'

Rob nodded. 'Well, he's a lot better now, isn't he? Surely, she could move back into her own bed now.'

Ella nodded, and murmured, 'It's the only place she wants to be.'

When Ella told him what had happened, the doctor said, 'It must have preyed on her mind as to why you'd moved her. Perhaps she'd been dreaming that he was dead and woke up believing it, became disorientated and wandered off. It wasn't your fault, my dear. You were only trying to do what you thought was best to give them both some rest.' The kindly man's eyes were comforting rather than reproachful. Then he added, 'I understand the Spit has had special significance for Esther all her life?'

Rob, standing beside Ella, said, 'Me dad says she often went out to stand at the very end of it, specially when she was unhappy. It was where her first husband's body was washed up when he was drowned.'

'Poor woman,' the doctor murmured as, carrying his medical bag, he followed Ella up the stairs. When she opened the bedroom door and they stepped into the room, it was to see the two old people, still wrapped in each other's arms, soundly asleep.

The doctor stood watching them for several moments, observing with his trained, experienced eyes. 'Tender loving care,' he murmured softly. 'I don't think I've anything in here,' he tapped his bag, 'to beat that, Ella. Let's leave them be.'

Downstairs, he said, 'I think you should get your grandfather up each day, just into a chair in the bedroom at first. I'll call again tomorrow and give them both a thorough check. He looks more himself already. He's a much better colour.'

'And Gran? Will she be all right? I mean . . .' Ella asked anxiously, '. . . her mind?'

The doctor smiled. 'I'm sure your grandmother will be fine. She's still weak and exhausted. Once her husband's well again, you'll see, she'll be back to her old self, ordering everyone about.'

Ella smiled, wanting desperately to believe him. 'I never thought I'd be saying it, but I hope so. Oh, I do hope so.'

With each day, Ella could see her grandparents improving steadily and, reassured by the kindly doctor who still visited every other day, without being asked to do so, Ella took time to write a long and loving letter to her father and her grandmother in York to explain how things were at home – her pen hesitated over the word but she left it as her first instinct had written it – home at Fleethaven Point.

Grandpa Godfrey is very ill and weak and Gran cannot cope alone. I rather think she is ill too, possibly just exhausted, but they do need my help.

She paused in her writing and looked out of the kitchen window across the fields, seeing not, as there should have been, row upon row of neat brown furrows, but uncut corn left to rot, or stubble where Uncle Danny had managed to harvest the field for Esther.

As soon as they're better, I'll make a start, she promised silently, as she bent her head again to begin another letter, this time to her former employers in Lincoln. She wrote apologizing for the swiftness of her departure, explaining the reason, and was surprised to receive by return of post a courteous letter from the man she had thought rather cold and pompous.

If you should decide to return to office work, please do not hesitate to contact us, when we should be happy to reconsider your employment with ourselves.

Ella smiled wryly, wondering whether the condescending tone was deliberate or not. Perhaps he could not help writing in that vein. Ella folded away the letter and went out to clean out the grate under the copper in the wash-house.

'Bit late in the day to be starting washing, ain't it?'

Ella looked up, her face grey with ash. 'Hello, Gran, what are you doing out here?' Esther was still in her nightgown, with a shawl around her shoulders and her feet stuffed into her wellingtons.

The old woman sniffed. 'Grannie,' she said automatically. 'I've spent long enough in me bed. Time I was up and doin'.'

Ella stood up. 'About time an' all!' She grinned back.

'Less of your cheek, Missy.' Esther pulled the shawl closer around her shoulders. The fire in the reprimand was missing, and Ella was surprised how sad the realization made her feel.

Ella dusted her hands and went towards her grandmother. 'Come on,' she said gently. 'Let's go and find you your clothes and you can get dressed and come and sit downstairs in the kitchen, if you're feeling better.'

Mumbling, Esther allowed herself to be taken back into the house and, seated in the Windsor chair beside a now blazing fire in the range, Ella removed her boots.

'There now. I'll fetch your clothes and you can dress yourself here in front of the fire.'

'Where's Rob?'

'Oh, he's out in the fields. There's no one to see you and I'll turn my back if you're bashful,' Ella teased her gently.

'He's been staying here, ain't he?' The old eyes were suddenly bright with suspicion.

Ella met her gaze squarely. 'Yes,' she said quietly.

'Where's he bin sleeping, then?'

Ella took a deep breath. 'Downstairs and before you say anything, Gran, I've been upstairs in the little bedroom, so don't start . . .'

The smile was tentative at first and then it twitched the corners of the wrinkled mouth and spread, creasing her thin cheeks, spreading up into her green eyes and giving them a glimmer of life. 'I weren't going to, lass. I weren't going to,' she said softly.

Ella went to the shelf at the far side of the kitchen and reached down two bowls. Then she ladled a thick soup from the pan on the fire.

'I'm just taking some of this up to Grandpa. I'm going to get him up to sit in a chair for a while this afternoon. Doctor said I could. I don't want him lying in that bed till he takes root.' She lifted the tray. 'And don't go wandering outside again in your nightie. I'll bring your clothes down and when you've got dressed you can sit there and peel the 'taties for dinner,' and lapsing deliberately into the dialect so strong in her grandmother's speech, Ella grinned mischievously and added, 'Time you were mekin yasen useful, an' all!'

'None o' your chelp, Missy!'

As Ella climbed the stairs, the smile was still on her lips. She let out a sigh of thankfulness: the sparkle was back in Esther Godfrey's eyes.

Thirty-Four

Peggy arrived the following day.

'I couldn't stay away any longer, Ella. I've still got a bit of a cough, but I'm much better. How are they?'

Ella hugged her aunt. 'Much better, thank goodness. Oh, but I'm so glad to see you.'

'I could stay a day or two if it would help,' Peggy offered.

Ella glanced at Rob. 'Rob's staying here with me at the moment.' Suddenly, she was shy. 'I couldn't have managed without him.'

He laughed, his eyes crinkling with good humour. He winked cheekily at Peggy. 'At last! She's finally admitted it.'

Peggy smiled too. 'I'm glad you're here with her, Rob,' she said, 'but I take it there's no room for me.'

'You could stay at our place, Miss Godfrey. Me mam would love to have you.'

Peggy laughed. 'Now, now, young Rob. Don't go making offers on your mother's behalf before you've even asked her.'

But Rob was right. Rosie was delighted to have Peggy stay a couple of nights with them, though the fact that Rob arranged this and made no mention of moving back home himself now that Esther and Jonathan were improving quite surprised Ella.

'I've brought a letter for you from your father,' Peggy

said that first evening, handing a long white envelope to her. 'He enclosed it in a letter to me saying he was sending it care of me just in case, well, anything awful had happened and would I pass it on to you if everything was all right. He seems a very thoughtful man.'

Ella nodded and her voice was husky as she answered simply, 'He is. I have written, but our letters must have crossed in the post.'

Inside were two letters: the one from her father, as she might have expected, was loving, concerned and supportive and he promised to come to see her at Fleethaven as soon as she sent word that her grandparents were well enough for visitors. The other was from her grandmother Trent, who, though she asked politely after Ella's grandparents, went on immediately with all the plans she was making for Ella's return to York. Ella let the pink pages fall on to the table and sat staring at it for a few moments.

'Want you back, do they?' came Rob's voice from the other side of the table, and she looked up to see him watching her, a wary, almost defensive look deep in his brown eyes.

'Well, yes, but . . .'

Before she had time to say any more, he turned swiftly and left the kitchen, banging the back door behind him so violently that the house seemed to shake.

'Now what on earth was that about?' Peggy remarked.

'I don't know,' Ella murmured slowly, staring towards the door. 'I really don't know.'

'There's no need for you to sleep here any longer, Rob.'

'Oh, I see. Served me usefulness and cast aside like an old shoe, eh?'

'It's not like that and you know it,' she began hotly and

then she saw his wide grin. 'Oh, you,' she said and punched his shoulder.

'Ouch! You don't half pack a punch for a townie.'

'I've been grateful for your help. You know I have. I couldn't have coped without you . . .'

'Glad you realize it.'

She began to giggle. 'But I reckon Gran keeps hopping out of bed several times a night to see that I'm sleeping upstairs and you're safely downstairs.'

His eyes widened. 'Has she said anything?'

Ella nodded.

He laughed. 'Right you are, then. I must admit I'm quite looking forward to getting back to me own bed. That thing in her parlour isn't as comfortable as it looks.'

Impulsively, she put out her hand and touched his bare arm. The feel of his skin beneath her fingers sent such a pulse of longing through her that she blushed and stuttered. 'I – I mean it, Rob. You've been great.'

He stood close to her, looking into her eyes, his gaze boring into hers as if he would read into its depths. 'I've been glad to help yar gran – and yar grandpa too, of course. You – you must know how I feel about . . .'

Swiftly, Ella nodded. 'Oh yes, I know,' and there was bitterness in her tone as she added, 'I know exactly how you feel.'

She turned away and hurried from the room, leaving him to gather his things together. If only it wasn't always her grandmother he felt so deeply about, she mourned inwardly, choking back tears that threatened suddenly.

When he came out of the front room, carrying his belongings, she went with him to the hole in the hedge and watched him walk away from her, his bundle of clothes slung over his shoulder.

Oh, Rob, her heart was crying silently. Don't go. Don't

leave me. But she made no sound and, whistling, Rob walked on.

The day Grandpa Godfrey came downstairs for the first time was like Christmas.

'Aah,' he said, giving a big sigh as he sat down in the Windsor chair at the side of the range, 'it's nice to be back in the land of the living.'

Esther stood beside him, put her hand on his shoulder and kissed the top of his head. 'You'll soon be out tinkering with your tractor and doing the ploughing.'

'Oh no, he won't,' Ella said. 'A bit of tinkering, maybe. But the ploughing – oh no!' Then realizing she might have sounded too harsh, added, 'Well, not this year anyway. You're just going to sit and watch me out the window and tell me off when I get the furrows crooked.'

Esther, still standing with her hand resting on Jonathan's shoulder, stared at her granddaughter. 'But I thought, now we're better, you'd . . .' she began, and then fell silent.

'What? What did you think?'

'Oh, nothing,' Esther murmured, stroking her husband's hair.

Unseen by her grandmother, Ella winked broadly at her grandpa and was rewarded by his knowing smile. 'Now you're both up and about,' Ella went on, 'I'll have to tackle the outside work and the ploughing's first on the list. Well?' She glanced from one to the other. 'It won't do itsen, will it?'

She heard her grandfather's deep chuckle and saw him reach up and pat Esther's hand where it still lay on his shoulder. 'I reckon you've met your match at last, Esther Godfrey.' And still chortling, he leant his head back against the wooden back of the chair and closed his eyes. 'Met your match at last!'

'It's Grandpa's birthday two weeks before Christmas, isn't it?' Ella remarked towards the end of November.

Esther wiped the vestiges of the sticky pastry she was making from her hands. 'Yes. Why?'

'How old is he?'

Her grandmother wrinkled her forehead. 'Seventy.'

'I thought he might be.' Ella nodded. 'Do you think he's well enough for us to have a bit of a party for him?'

The green eyes were wary. 'Who're you going to invite?'

Ella hid her smile and put her head on one side and said, deliberately casual, 'Well, Peggy, of course. And then there's all our friends from round about . . .'

The suspicion deepened. 'Friends?' came the clipped reply. 'What friends?'

'Well, there's the Maines and the Harris boys from the Point.' Ella ticked them off on her fingers. 'The Souters . . .'

Esther pulled a face.

'. . . and, of course, the Elands.'

Her grandmother's head shot up. 'Oh no!'

'Now, Gran. It's time to bury the hatchet. Surely? While you and Grandpa were ill, I couldn't have managed without their help.'

'Well, Rob was good, I'll grant you that, but . . .'

'And who do you think's looked after your two cows and brought the milk across every day?'

'Well . . .'

'And where did all those lovely soups and jellies and blancmanges to try and tempt Grandpa's appetite come from, do you think? 'Cos I didn't have time to make them.'

Esther stared at Ella and then blinked. 'Oh,' she said,

and stirred the knife in her pastry thoughtfully. 'I hadn't realized . . .'

'No, Gran. I don't think you had. But it's time you did and high time you thought about it. I nipped across there one day to phone Peggy and there was Grandma Eland and Rosie with their heads together trying to think what they could bake that you'd both enjoy and that would "perk you up a bit", as Grandma Eland said herself.'

'Did she? Did she really?'

Ella nodded and added quietly, 'She came before, too, didn't she? Before I came home, to try and help you?'

Esther's eyes were downcast. 'I dun't remember.'

Ella wasn't sure whether or not she believed her, but she let it go.

Now there was silence in the kitchen, whilst Ella waited, leaning against the door frame with her arms folded, watching her grandmother rolling the pastry over and over.

'So,' Esther said at last, without looking up. 'What do you want me to bake for this 'ere party, then?'

On the day of the party, the first Saturday in December, the weather was unusually kind. A bright winter sun and a light breeze seemed determined to smile benignly on all Ella's efforts. She had worked tirelessly the previous week, scrubbing and cleaning until the whole house shone, baking and cooking, and early on the Saturday morning, she was outside feeding the hens and sweeping the yard.

''Tain't Royalty coming, is it?'

Ella looked up to see her gran standing in the doorway, hands on hips surveying her farmyard. Ella stared at her for a moment and sent up a silent prayer of thanks: her gran was almost her old self again, just as the doctor had promised, although she got tired a little quicker than Ella remembered. Her hair, pure white now, was neatly cut and shaped and washed to shining health. Her face had filled out and the awful gaunt, haggard look had gone. There were a few more lines on her face, but the green eyes flashed fire once more when something didn't suit her.

But this morning, she was smiling.

'Not quite Gran . . .'

'Grannie . . .' she corrected automatically, but absently.

'But just as important – to me, anyway.'

Esther moved closer. 'Young Rob, y'mean?' She spoke so quietly that Ella almost missed the words. She looked up sharply, staring at her grandmother.

'How . . .?' she began and felt her face colouring.

Esther smiled gently. 'Aw, lass. I'm not blind, even if he is.' Then her smile took on a sadness. 'I'm sorry – if he doesn't – well – feel the same about you.'

Ella leant on her broom and sighed. 'I've lived with it a long time now. It didn't hurt quite so much when I was away. But back here, well, it's more difficult seeing him so much. I have to remember not to let it show.'

'Maybe you shouldn't try so hard to hide it.'

Ella laughed. 'Oh, Gran, he doesn't know I exist. He's after the girls all right, but all the pretty ones.'

'He's like his grandad,' Esther murmured and her eyes misted over, looking back down the years.

'Matthew Hilton, you mean?'

She nodded. 'He looks like him, spittin' image of him, he is. When I was ill there – I – I got confused. I thought he was Matthew.' She drew her hand across her forehead and shook her head as if to clear it, to banish such memories for ever. 'Matthew was a flirt an' all. After anything in skirts!'

Ella sighed. 'I don't think Rob means any harm. He just – well – likes a bit of fun.'

Esther nodded. 'He's not got a dark side like Matthew had. Ah well, it's all a long time ago now, and Beth's coming today – thanks to you.' She cast a comical look at Ella. 'So I'll have to be on me best behaviour, won't I, else I'll have your grandpa after me, an' all.'

'And I'd better get a move on, or I'll never be ready.'

'Ready, Missy? We've been ready a week.' Laughing, Esther disappeared into the house.

At two o'clock when the first guests were expected, they were ready. Ella had put on one of her dresses Grandmother Trent had bought her and used a little make-up, carefully concealing the birthmark on her jawline. She had washed her hair and, longer now, it framed her face, falling in cascading curls and waves to her shoulders.

'Oh Ella, you look a picture,' Grandpa greeted her, looking resplendent himself, if still a little thin, in his best suit, whilst Esther had on a new royal blue dress. They were waiting, a little self-consciously it seemed to Ella, in the living room when she came downstairs. Ella saw her grandmother looking keenly at her face, at the place on her jaw where usually the birthmark was plainly visible, but she said nothing as Ella turned away, saying brightly, 'They should be here soon . . .' and went to the back door.

A car was turning into the drive; a huge, dark green car with soft leather upholstery.

'Oh!' Ella cried.

'What?' asked her grandmother, coming up behind her.

'It's my dad!' and Ella flew across the yard towards the tall man unfolding himself from the driver's seat and flung herself against him.

From the back seat of the car, Peggy and Mrs Trent emerged.

'This is your grandpa's doing.' Peggy was laughing. 'He asked me to write to your father and invite him and Mrs Trent to come to the party you were planning for him.'

'It's wonderful to see you.' Ella hugged first Peggy and then Mrs Trent. 'Oh, how I've missed you all.' Then she ran back to Jonathan, who was standing near the back door, his arm about Esther's shoulders, reached up and kissed his cheek. 'Thank you, Grandpa.'

From the boot of the car, Philip was lifting a huge bouquet of flowers and, as Ella made the introductions, he said, 'I know it's really Mr Godfrey's day, but I thought he wouldn't mind . . .' And he laid the flowers in Esther's arms.

'For – for me?' she stuttered, her face pink. Ella watched her gran look up into the face of the tall man as he said softly, 'We meet again, Mrs Godfrey.'

For a moment, Esther looked puzzled. Then she gasped. 'You! It is – was – you. Kate brought you here in the war, didn't she?'

Philip Trent nodded. 'Yes.'

Ella watched Esther struggling with conflicting emotions, whilst Philip took her hand in his and said softly, 'I loved Kate very much, Mrs Godfrey. Whatever you think of me, I want you to believe that.'

Esther looked deep into his eyes for what seemed, to those watching, a long time, then suddenly she smiled, and though there was still a tinge of sadness in her face at the memories this man's presence evoked, she said, 'I do. I can see it in your eyes.'

Then to everyone's surprise, not least Esther's, Philip bent and kissed her cheek. 'And now,' he said, straightening up, 'I'd like you to meet Ella's other grandmother.' He held out his arm to draw his mother forward and Ella held her breath as the two women from such different backgrounds regarded each other.

Mrs Trent, stepping carefully across the cobbles of the yard in her high-heeled court shoes, adjusted the grey fox fur about her shoulders and held out her gloved hand. Esther, in a daze, shook it and opened her mouth, but whatever she had been going to say was never spoken for, in a flurry of noise and excited chatter, the Eland family arrived and the party began.

She was so busy looking after all the guests that it was some time before Ella had time to talk to anyone.

'So when are you coming back to York?' Grandmother Trent's voice could be heard clearly above the muted chatter in the living room. 'Your room's all ready now. We've even bought new furniture for it, haven't we, Philip?'

There seemed, to Ella, to be a sudden silence, as if everyone in the room was listening and waiting for her answer.

'Now, Mother,' Philip's calm voice came to Ella's rescue, 'she'll come when she can.'

'Maybe so, Philip, but that job you've found for her won't stay open for ever. Have you told her about it?'

'Not yet. We're here for a party, a birthday party,' he went on. 'And I think it's high time we had a toast.'

'Wait a minute. There's something else . . . Rob, can you help me a minute?' Ella said, and disappeared into the pantry, where she whispered, 'I've made Grandpa a cake. It's a surprise.'

Rob, his eyes dark, was not smiling. 'It's not the only surprise we've 'ad today, is it?' he muttered.

'What are you talking about?'

'Oh, nothing,' he said, but his tone was morose.

'Come on, help me light the candles.'

'Candles?' he repeated. 'You ain't put seventy candles on a cake?'

She giggled. 'No, just seven. One for each decade.'

From a tin, she carefully lifted the cake, white-iced and decorated with pink roses. Together, they lit the spindly candles and Rob carried it into the living room.

'Oh, isn't it lovely?' Rosie clapped her hands. 'Did you make it, Missus?'

Esther shook her head, her glance catching and holding Ella's. 'I didn't know anything about it.'

Grandma Eland heaved herself up from the low armchair and waddled to the table to inspect the cake. 'It's beautiful, Ella love. She's a credit to you, Esther.'

Esther sniffed. 'It *looks* very nice, I grant you. But the proof of the pudding . . .'

Ella laughed. 'Come on, Grandpa, and cut this cake. Gran wants to try a piece and give her verdict.'

As Jonathan took up the huge knife and cut the cake, Philip raised his glass and led everyone in singing 'Happy Birthday'. Slices were handed round and Mrs Trent cut hers into delicate squares. 'My dear Ella, it tastes wonderful. I really wouldn't know where to start. I don't think I've ever made a cake in my life. We've always employed a cook.'

Ella, catching sight of the astounded expression on Esther Godfrey's face, was obliged to turn away quickly, almost choking on the crumbs as she stifled her laughter.

'Well,' Ella heard Esther saying indignantly, 'she'd be no granddaughter of *mine* if she couldn't bake a cake.'

The air in the room crackled as the two women glared at each other. Everyone else held their breath, watching and waiting. Ella moved swiftly to Esther's side and put her arm around her waist. Laughing she said, 'And milk a cow, put a pig away, to say nothing of driving a tractor, eh, Gran?'

'There's nowt to be ashamed of in being able to turn yar hand to a good day's work, Missy.'

'Oh, I'm not ashamed, Gran, I promise you. In fact, I'm quite proud of the fact.'

Esther's glance swivelled and she was looking directly into Ella's eyes, their faces so close. The defensive expression in Esther's green eyes softened as she said, quietly now so that the others in the room scarcely heard, 'Aye, lass, and I'm proud of you an' all.'

Tears welled in Ella's eyes, but before she could say any more, Mrs Trent's voice came again. 'It's a little different from the job your father has in mind for you, Ella. If you won't tell her, Philip, then I will. Ella, one of Philip's friends is the managing director of quite a large company and he's looking for a secretary. You'd have your own office. Now, what do you say to that, my dear?' And Mrs Trent beamed as if she personally had created the job for her granddaughter.

Ella smiled, 'It sounds wonderful, Grandmother, but—'

'No "buts" Ella.' Mrs Trent waved aside any obstacle. 'Opportunities like that for someone of your age don't come very often.'

Beneath her arm, still around Esther's waist, Ella felt her gran stiffen, then she pulled away from Ella and went towards Jonathan, her wrinkled hands stretched out towards him.

It wasn't until they were almost ready to leave just after six o'clock that her father drew Ella outside into the cool evening.

'Dad, there's something I ought to tell you . . .'

'You don't have to, my dear. You're going to stay here, aren't you?'

She looked up at him through the dusk. 'How did you know?'

'You belong here,' he said simply and suddenly she knew it was the truth. Though she may have rebelled against it for years, refusing to acknowledge it, this *was* her home.

'I'm not staying out of a sense of duty, only because I really want to.'

'I know that.' His arm was round her and his deep voice just above her head. 'But you will come to see us whenever you can?'

'Of course I will,' she promised. 'Whenever I can. I feel awfully guilty about all the money you must have spent on the bedroom for me and this marvellous job Grandmother says you've fixed up for me . . .'

He laughed aloud. 'Don't give either of them another thought, my dear. Besides, your room will be there for you whenever you can come to see us. There is just one thing, though. What about young Martin Hughes? He's forever asking about you.'

Haltingly, she said, 'He's nice, but there could never be anything more than friendship between us.'

'Not on your side, maybe, but I'm not so sure about his feelings for you,' Philip said.

'I'll write to him,' she promised.

'Well, let him down gently, my dear.'

She put her arms round him and hugged him. He was such a kind man, thinking of the feelings of others, and she loved him for it. For a moment his arms were around her fiercely as if, now he had found her, he never wanted to let her go. When they released each other and turned back towards the house, her father's arm resting on her shoulders, they saw Esther standing in the doorway watching them.

'Gran . . .?' Ella began, but without a word Esther turned away and went back inside the house.

Thirty-Five

'So, when are ya going?'

'Eh?' Startled, Ella stared at her grandmother, pausing mid-way between kitchen and pantry as she cleared away all the food after the party. All the guests had gone, and Grandpa Godfrey had been dispatched to bed early. He had kissed Ella on the forehead. 'My dear girl, I don't know when we last had such fun. Thank you for everything.' And Ella knew he was not referring to this day alone.

'I don't know what you mean, Gran,' she said. 'Wait a minute till I've put these cakes away.'

'Now,' Ella said, coming back into the kitchen and standing on the hearthrug in front of her grandmother sitting in the straight-backed wooden chair. 'What are you talking about? Where am I supposed to be going?'

'Back to Lincoln – or mebbe even to – them!'

The old eyes would not meet Ella's gaze, but the girl noticed that Esther's hands were gripping the arms of the chair until her knuckles showed white.

'Gran,' she said softly, 'I'm not going anywhere. Not back to Lincoln, nor to live with my father. I'm staying here—'

'But for how long? Eh?' Esther's head snapped up, her eyes sparking with resentment. 'Tell me that! Ya'll soon get fed up and be off again. Off to ya dad and ya fancy grandmother with her posh clothes and . . .'

Ella's blue eyes were holding the green, belligerent gaze. Slowly she shook her head. 'No, Gran. This is my home. I'm staying here – for good!'

The old eyes stared up at her and then, to Ella's shock, they filled with tears; tears that overflowed and trickled down the soft wrinkles of Esther's face.

'Grannie – oh, Grannie – don't!'

Her arms were round the old woman, and she bent over her, resting her cheek against the silky white hair. Esther's hands loosened their grip upon the chair and came round Ella's waist, clinging, beseeching. 'Don't – leave us – again – Ella. We – need you.'

'Oh, Grannie, I love you so much. I won't leave you again. I promise.'

They were sitting together in the deepening dusk, the only light coming from the glow of the coals in the range. Ella sat on the rug, her head resting against her grannie's knee, the old hands stroking her hair.

'There's something I want to ask you, lass.' Esther's voice was strangely hesitant.

'Mmm?'

'That mark on ya face. What've ya done? Where – where's it gone?'

Ella twisted her head and looked up at her, meeting her eyes, dark in the shadows.

'It's just make-up.' She laughed. 'It's good, isn't it? Covers it completely.'

Esther was biting her lower lip.

'What is it, Grannie?' Ella prompted gently.

'I always felt so guilty about it.'

'Guilty? Why? I don't understand.'

'It was my fault you got it.'

Ella shook her head, mystified. 'How could it be?'

'When Kate came to tell us she was pregnant I was so angry, I lashed out at her. After all I'd taught her. Never to give 'ersen to a man till she had a wedding band on her finger. Never to bring a bastard into the world . . .'

Understanding now fully what lay behind the old lady's unbending attitude, knowing the heartache of her early years that had caused her to be so bitter, Ella squeezed her hand.

'I hit her, Ella, right on her cheek and – and when you were born, you had that little birthmark . . .' she swallowed, and Ella knew instinctively that Esther was not finding her confession easy, '. . . right where my fingers left their mark on Kate's face.'

Ella knelt up and put her arms about her grandmother. 'Oh, Grannie. That's all a load of old wives' tales. It was just coincidence. Nothing more.'

'I ain't so sure . . .' the voice quavered, vulnerable at the telling of a long-buried guilt.

'Well, I am,' the young girl said confidently. 'It's all a lot of nonsense. You're not to think of it any more.'

She kissed Esther's cheek and found herself once more clasped in a fierce bear-hug.

The words were muffled against her hair, but she heard them. 'Oh, Ella, I do love you. Really, I do. I always have.'

Much later when her grannie had gone up to bed and Ella had washed every plate and cup and saucer that Esther seemed to possess, she went outside to shut the hens up for the night, calling softly to her cat. 'Tibby? Come on.

They've all gone now.' But there was no sign of him. She smiled to herself. I expect he's mousing in the field, she thought.

It was a beautiful night, crisp and clear, the moon and stars bathing the countryside in their silvery glow. She stood and breathed in the air, listened to the distant sound of the sea, so much clearer in the darkness. She strolled amongst the trees in the orchard and then pushed her way through the hole in the hedge.

'Tibby? Where are you?' she called again. Even in the moonlight she could see the flattened wheat and sighed. She really would have to tackle this field soon, but she wasn't quite sure what to do and she didn't want to worry her grandparents. Maybe she would walk over to Rookery Farm tomorrow and ask Uncle Danny for his advice.

She heard Rob's whistling through the darkness long before she heard the rustle of his footsteps through the corn coming towards the hole in the hedge.

'And what brings you out so late, Bumpkin?' she called.

'By heck. Ya made me jump.' He laughed and, as he came closer, said, 'I might ask the same of you, Townie.'

'I'm looking for that stupid cat of mine. I reckon he took fright at all the visitors.'

'Oh, he'll come back when he's good and ready.'

They stood together listening to the sounds of the night. The soft hoot of an owl and a rustling in the hedgerows as the night creatures came awake.

'The old 'uns all right?' he enquired.

In the darkness, she smiled. 'Fine. Tired, but I think they've enjoyed it.'

Again there was a long silence and she heard him shuffling his boot on the ground.

Then through the darkness came the same words her grandmother had asked, 'When are you going, then?'

Epilogue

On 19 September, 1964, the marriage between Robert Eland and Danielle Hilton took place in the local church, the bride walking proudly down the aisle on the arm of her father. As the bridal party came out of the church into the blustery sunlight, the two grandmothers, Esther and Beth, walked side by side, their arms linked, beaming proudly. The bride paused as she walked down the path and, lifting her long white gown, she moved amongst the gravestones to lay her bouquet on the grave of her mother, Kate. Then she stooped and from the bouquet she plucked a single red rose and laid it on the grave of Matthew Hilton, the grandfather both she and her new husband shared.

Mr Arthur Marshall, still the owner of the Grange and all the surrounding farmland, save that belonging to Esther Godfrey and Brumbys' Farm, was delighted to sell the crumbling, derelict house that had once been his family's home to the young Mr and Mrs Eland, and though he still retained the ownership of the land surrounding it, he granted them the tenancy to farm the land too.

So Rob and Ella painted and decorated and rebuilt their new home and moved into the Grange where Rob had always vowed he would one day live.

Two years later, Ella was able to say, 'And now we're a family,' as she laid Rob's son in his arms, the two old ladies hovering impatiently in the background for a sight of their first great-grandchild.

Two more boys were born to Ella and Rob and then a little girl with bright red curls and a smile like the sun appearing after storm clouds; a little girl they named Esther Elizabeth.

Peggy retired from her job in Lincoln and came to live in her own rooms in the Grange, becoming self-appointed nanny to Ella's growing family, and Philip Trent was a regular and frequent visitor, bringing his mother, too, whenever her failing health permitted.

In the winter of 1975, Jonathan Godfrey died peacefully in his sleep and four weeks later, losing the will to live without him, Esther faded, withered and died. At her bedside, Beth Eland sat holding her hand until the end.

They're all buried in the small churchyard now: Esther and Jonathan, alongside their beloved Kate; Beth beside her husband, Robert Eland; and only a few feet away from them all, lies Matthew Hilton.

Danny and Rosie still live at Rookery Farm, although now, Danny's working day is more in the capacity of foreman.

And Brumbys' Farm? Of course, it now belongs to Ella and forms part of the land which Rob and she farm together. But the house lies empty, waiting to love and be loved once more.

Though it is not entirely forgotten, for on summer days Ella will walk down the lane, over the stile and across the fields to squeeze through the hole in the hedge. She wanders through the empty rooms, pauses in a shaft of dusty sunlight, and hearing ghostly voices from the past, whispers in reply, 'I'm here, Grannie, I'm still here.'

All Pan Books are available at your local bookshop or newsagent, or can be ordered direct from the publisher. Indicate the number of copies required and fill in the form below.

Send to: Macmillan General Books C.S.
Book Service By Post
PO Box 29, Douglas I-O-M
IM99 1BQ

or phone: 01624 675137, quoting title, author and credit card number.

or fax: 01624 670923, quoting title, author, and credit card number.

or Internet: http://www.bookpost.co.uk

Please enclose a remittance* to the value of the cover price plus 75 pence per book for post and packing. Overseas customers please allow £1.00 per copy for post and packing.

*Payment may be made in sterling by UK personal cheque, Eurocheque, postal order, sterling draft or international money order, made payable to Book Service By Post.

Alternatively by Access/Visa/MasterCard

Card No. ☐☐☐☐☐☐☐☐☐☐☐☐☐☐☐☐

Expiry Date ☐☐☐☐☐☐☐☐☐☐☐☐☐☐☐☐

Signature ____________________

Applicable only in the UK and BFPO addresses.

While every effort is made to keep prices low, it is sometimes necessary to increase prices at short notice. Pan Books reserve the right to show on covers and charge new retail prices which may differ from those advertised in the text or elsewhere.

NAME AND ADDRESS IN BLOCK CAPITAL LETTERS PLEASE

Name ____________________

Address ____________________

____

____

____

8/95

Please allow 28 days for delivery.
Please tick box if you do not wish to receive any additional information. ☐

Dear Reader:

Toward the end of summer, with its hot, sticky days, I like to bring some of my garden inside. Daisies and di[illegible] [illegible] hesitate—it seems a shame to snip them. [illegible], rainy day, or one where the heat blasts me back indoors, it's a lovely thing to have flowers I've helped grow keeping me com[illegible] around the house.

If I am outside, and the weeding and deadheading is do[illegible] the day, I can sit in the shade, on bench or garden wal[illegible] just enjoy. Or I can take my granddaughter for a walk, [illegible] her the flowers, tell her their names as my mother and [illegible] did for me. I like to think I'm helping instill this love of [illegible]ing things in her—and will do the same for my grandso[illegible] as my parents instilled it in me, and as I passed that love [illegible] boys. My family is another passion for me, another [illegible] full of color and bloom and unlimited potential.

Every year, from spring planting through summer [illegible] through fall when my zinnias and mums give me flow[illegible] the trees begin to flame, I'm given the gift of seasons. Through the long, cold winter while my gardens sleep, I think of what they'll give me when they wake in spring, and what I'll give them. When the first crocus pops its brave head out of the frosty ground, I know soon I'll be digging up rocks, chasing deer, pulling weeds, wandering through my gardening center to see what I can't resist this year. And watching life renew, watching hope flower, even while I plant.

In the garden is joy and beauty, work and reward. I hope you make your own.

NORA ROBERTS

Nora Roberts is the *New York Times* bestselling author of more than one hundred fifty novels. Under the pen name J. D. Robb, she is author of the *New York Times* bestselling futuristic suspense series, which features Lieutenant Eve Dallas and Roarke. There are more than 280 million copies of her books in print, and she has had more than one hundred *New York Times* bestsellers.

Visit her website at www.noraroberts.com

Other titles by Nora Roberts:

Homeport
The Reef
River's End
Carolina Moon
The Villa
Midnight Bayou
Three Fates
Birthright
Northern Lights
Blue Smoke

Three Sisters Island Trilogy:
Dance Upon the Air
Heaven and Earth
Face the Fire

Chesapeake Bay Quartet:
Sea Swept
Rising Tides
Inner Harbour
Chesapeake Blue

The Key Trilogy:
Key of Light
Key of Knowledge
Key of Valour

In the Garden Trilogy:
Blue Dahlia
Black Rose
Red Lily

As J.D. Robb:

Naked in Death
Glory in Death
Immortal in Death
Rapture in Death
Ceremony in Death
Vengeance in Death
Holiday in Death
Conspiracy in Death
Loyalty in Death
Witness in Death
Judgement in Death
Betrayal in Death
Seduction in Death
Reunion in Death
Purity in Death
Portrait in Death
Imitation in Death
Divided in Death
Visions in Death
Survivor in Death
Origin in Death

By Nora Roberts and J.D. Robb
Remember When

Red Lily

NORA ROBERTS

Red Lily

PIATKUS

All the characters in this book are fictitious and any resemblance to real persons, living or dead, is entirely coincidental.

This edition published in Great Britain in 2005 by
Piatkus Books Ltd of
5 Windmill Street, London W1T 2JA
email: info@piatkus.co.uk

Reprinted 2006

First published in the United States in 2005 by the Berkley Publishing Group, a division of Penguin Group (USA) Inc., New York.

The moral right of the author has been asserted

A catalogue record for this book is available from the British Library

ISBN 0 7499 3614 2

Printed and bound in Great Britain by
Mackays of Chatham, Chatham, Kent

To Kayla, child of my child,
and all those lights who've yet to shine
when this was written.

Grafting and budding involve joining two separate plants so that they function as one, creating a strong, healthy plant that has only the best characteristics as its two parents.

American Horticulture Society
Plant Propagation

Youth fades; love droops, the leaves of friendship fall;
A mother's secret hope outlives them all.

Oliver Wendell Holmes

Red Lily

PROLOGUE

Memphis
January 1893

SHE WAS DESPERATE, DESTITUTE, AND DEMENTED.

Once she'd been a beautiful woman, a clever woman with one towering ambition. Luxury. She'd achieved it, using her body to seduce and her mind to calculate. She became the mistress of one of the wealthiest and most powerful men in Tennessee.

Her house had been a showplace, decorated at her whim—and with Reginald's money. There'd been servants to do her bidding, a wardrobe to rival the most sought-after courtesan in Paris. Jewelry, amusing friends, a carriage of her own.

She'd given gay parties. She'd been envied and desired.

She, the daughter of a biddable housemaid, had all her avaricious heart had desired.

She'd had a son.

It had changed her, that life she hadn't wanted to carry

inside her. It had become the center of her world, the single thing she loved more than herself. She planned for her son, dreamed of him. Sang to him while he lay sleeping in her womb.

She delivered him into the world with pain, such pain, but with joy, too. The joy of knowing when the pain was done, she would hold her precious son in her arms.

They told her she delivered a girl child. They told her the baby was stillborn.

They lied.

She'd known it even then, even when she was wild with grief, even when she sank into the pit of despair. Even when she went mad, she knew it for a lie. Her son lived.

They'd stolen her baby from her. Held him for ransom. How could it be otherwise when she could *feel* his heart beat as truly as she felt her own?

But it hadn't been the midwife and doctor who'd taken her child. Reginald had taken what was hers, using his money to buy the silence of those who served him.

How she remembered the way he'd stood in her parlor, coming to her only after her months of grief and worry. Done with her, she thought as she buttoned the gray dress with trembling fingers. Finished now that he had what he had wanted. A son, an heir. The one thing his cold-blooded wife hadn't been able to provide.

He'd used her, then taken her single treasure, as if he had the *right*. Offering her money and a voyage to England in exchange.

He would pay, he would pay, he would pay, her mind repeated as she groomed herself. But not with money. Oh no. Not with money.

She was all but penniless now, but she would find a way. Of course she would find a way, once she had her darling James back in her arms.

The servants—rats and sinking ships—had stolen some of her jewelry. She *knew* it. She'd had to sell most of the rest, and had been cheated in the price. But what could she expect from the thin-lipped scarecrow of a jeweler? He was a man, after all.

Liars and cheats and thieves. Every one of them.

They would *all* pay before she was finished.

She couldn't find the rubies—the ruby and diamond bracelet, heart-shaped stones, blood and ice, that Reginald had given her as a token when he'd learned she was pregnant.

It was a trinket, really. Too delicate, too *small* for her tastes. But she *wanted* it, and tore through the messy maze of her bedroom and dressing area in search.

Wept like a child when she found a sapphire brooch instead. As the tears dried, as her fingers closed around the pin, she forgot the bracelet and her desperate desire for it. Forgot that she'd been searching for it. Now she smiled at the sparkle of rich blue stones. It would be enough to provide a start for her and James. She would take him away, to the country perhaps. Until she felt well again, strong again.

It was all very simple, really, she decided with a ghastly smile as she studied herself in the glass. The gray dress was quiet, dignified—the proper tone for a mother. If it hung on her, drooping at the bodice, it couldn't be helped. She had no servants now, no dressmakers to fuss with alterations. She would get her figure back once she and James found their pretty country cottage.

She'd dressed her blond hair in top curls and, with considerable regret, eschewed rouge. A quiet look was better, she concluded. A quiet look was soothing to a child.

She would simply go get him now. Go to Harper House and take back what was hers.

The drive out of the city to the grand Harper mansion was long, cold, and costly. She no longer had a carriage of her own, and soon, very soon, Reginald's agents would come back to the house and remove her as they'd threatened already.

But it was worth the price of a private carriage. How else could she bring her James back to Memphis, where she would carry him up the stairs to his nursery, lay him tenderly in his crib, and sing him to sleep?

"Lavender's blue, dilly dilly," she song softly, twisting her thin fingers together as she stared out at the winter trees that lined the road.

She'd brought the blanket she'd ordered him from Paris, and the sweet little blue cap and booties. In her mind he was a newborn still. In her shattered mind the six months since his birth didn't exist.

The carriage rolled down the long drive, and Harper House, in all its glory, stood commanding the view.

The yellow stone, the white trim were warm and graceful against the harsh gray sky. Its three stories were proud and strong, accented by trees and shrubs, a rolling lawn.

She'd heard that peacocks had once wandered the estate, flashing their jeweled tails. But Reginald hadn't cared for their screaming calls, and had done away with them when he'd become master.

He ruled like a king. And she'd given him his prince. One day, one day, her son would usurp the father. She would rule Harper House with James. Her sweet, sweet James.

Though the windows of the great house were blank and glazed by the sun—secret eyes staring out at her—she imagined living there with her James. Saw herself tending him there, taking him for walks in the gardens, hearing his laughter ring in the halls.

One day, of course, that's how it would be. The house

was his, so in turn, the house was hers. They would live there, happily, only the two of them. As it was meant to be.

She climbed out of the carriage, a pale, thin woman in an ill-fitting gray dress, and walked slowly toward the front entrance.

Her heart thudded at the base of her throat. James was waiting for her.

She knocked, and because her hands refused to be still, folded them tightly at her waist.

The man who answered wore dignified black, and though his gaze swept over her, his face revealed nothing.

"Madam, may I assist you?"

"I've come for James."

His left eyebrow lifted, the barest fraction. "I'm sorry, Madam, there is no James in residence. If you're inquiring about a servant, the entrance is in the rear."

"James is not a servant." How *dare* he? "He is my son. He is your master. I've come for him." She stepped defiantly through the doorway. "Fetch him immediately."

"I believe you have the wrong house, Madam. Perhaps—"

"You won't keep him from me. James! James! Mama is here." She dashed toward the steps, scratched and bit when the butler took her arm.

"Danby, what is the problem here?" A woman, again in servant black, bustled down the wide hall.

"This . . . woman. She's overwrought."

"To say the least. Miss? Please, Miss, I'm Havers, the housekeeper. You must calm yourself, and tell me what is the matter."

"I've come for James." Her hands trembled as she lifted them to smooth her curls. "You must bring him to me this instant. It's time for his nap."

Havers had a kind face, and added a gentle smile. "I see. Perhaps you could sit for a moment and compose yourself."

"Then you'll bring James? You'll give me my son."

"In the parlor? There's a nice fire. It's cold today, isn't it?" The look she gave Danby had him releasing his hold. "Here now, let me show you in."

"It's a trick. Another trick." Amelia bolted for the stairs, screaming for James as she ran. She made it to the second floor before she collapsed on weak legs.

A door opened, and the mistress of Harper House stepped out. She knew it was Reginald's wife. Beatrice. She'd seen her at the theater once, and in the shops.

She was beautiful, sternly so, with eyes like chips of blue ice, a slender blade of a nose, and plump lips that were curled now in disgust. She wore a morning dress of deep rose silk, with a high collar and tightly cinched waist.

"Who is this creature?"

"I'm sorry, ma'am." Havers, swifter of foot than the butler, reached the door of the sitting room first. "She didn't give her name." Instinctively, she knelt to drape an arm around Amelia's shoulders. "She seems to be in some distress and chilled right through."

"James." Amelia reached up, and Beatrice deliberately swept her skirts aside. "I've come for James. My son."

There was a flicker over Beatrice's face before her lips clamped into a tight line. "Bring her in here." She turned, strode back into the sitting room. "And wait."

"Miss." Havers spoke quietly as she helped the trembling woman to her feet. "Don't be afraid now, no one's going to hurt you."

"Please get my baby." Her eyes pleaded as she gripped Havers's hand. "Please bring him to me."

"There now, go on in, talk to Mrs. Harper. Ma'am, shall I serve tea?"

"Certainly not," Beatrice snapped. "Shut the door."

She walked to a pretty granite hearth and turned so the

fire smoldered behind her, and her eyes stayed cold when the door shut quietly.

"You are—were," she corrected with a curl of her lips, "one of my husband's whores."

"I'm Amelia Connor. I've come—"

"I didn't ask your name. It holds no interest for me, nor do you. I had assumed that women of your ilk, those who consider themselves mistresses rather than common trollops, had enough wit and style not to step their foot into the home of what they like to call their protector."

"Reginald. Is Reginald here?" She looked around, dazedly taking in the beautiful room with its painted lamps and velvet cushions. She couldn't quite remember how she came to be here. All the frenzy and fury had drained out of her, leaving her cold and confused.

"He is not at home, and you should consider yourself fortunate. I'm fully aware of your . . . relationship, and fully aware he terminated that relationship, and that you were handsomely recompensed."

"Reginald?" She saw him, in her fractured mind, standing in front of a hearth—not this one, no not this one. Her hearth, her parlor.

Did you think I'd allow someone like you to raise my son?

Son. Her son. James. "James. My son. I've come for James. I have his blanket in the carriage. I'll take him home now."

"If you think I'll give you money to ensure your silence on this unseemly matter, you're very mistaken."

"I . . . I came for James." A smile trembled on her lips as she stepped forward, arms outstretched. "He needs his mama."

"The bastard you bore, and that was forced on me is called Reginald, after his father."

"No, I named him James. They said he was dead, but I

hear him crying." Concern covered her face as she looked around the room. "Do you hear him crying? I need to find him, sing him to sleep."

"You belong in an asylum. I could almost pity you." Beatrice stood, the fire snapping at her back. "You have no more choice in this matter than I. But I, at least, am innocent. I am his *wife.* I have borne his children, children born within the bounds of marriage. I have suffered the loss of children, and my behavior has been above reproach. I have turned a blind eye, a deaf ear on the affairs of my husband, and given him not one cause for complaint. But I gave him no son, and that, *that* is my mortal sin."

Color rushed into her cheeks now, all fury. "Do you think I want your brat foisted on me? The bastard son of a whore who will call me mother? Who will inherit this?" She threw her hands out. "All of this. I wish he had died in your womb, and you with him."

"Give him to me, give him back to me. I have his blanket." She looked down at her empty hands. "I have his blanket. I'll take him away."

"It's done. We're prisoners in the same trap, but at least you deserve the punishment. I've done nothing."

"You can't keep him; you don't want him. You can't have him." She rushed forward, eyes wild, lips peeled. And the blow cracked across her cheek, knocking her back and to the floor.

"You will leave this house." Beatrice spoke quietly, calmly, as though giving a servant some minor duty. "You will never speak of this, or I will see to it that you're put in the madhouse. My reputation will not be smeared by your ravings, I promise you. You will never come back here, never set foot in Harper House or on Harper property. You will never see the child—that will be your punishment, though it can never be enough in my mind."

"James. I will live here with James."

"You are mad," Beatrice said with the faintest hint of amusement. "Go back to your whoring. I'm sure you'll find a man who'll be happy to plant another bastard in your belly."

She strode to the door, flung it open. "Havers!" She waited, ignoring the wailing sobs behind her. "Have Danby remove this thing from the house."

BUT SHE DID COME BACK. THEY CARRIED HER OUT, ordered the driver to take her away. But she came back, in the cold night. Her mind was broken to pieces, but she managed the trip this last time, driving in a stolen wagon, her hair drenched from the rain, her white nightdress clinging to her.

She wanted to kill them. Kill them all. Slash them to ribbons, hack them to pieces. She could carry her James away then, in her bloody hands.

But they would never let her. She would never take her baby into her arms. Never see his sweet face.

Unless, unless.

She left the wagon while shadows and moonlight slid over Harper House, while the black windows gleamed and all inside slept.

The rain had stopped; the sky had cleared. Mists twined over the ground, gray snakes that parted for her bare, frozen feet. The hem of her gown trailed over the wet and mud as she wandered. Humming, singing.

They would pay. They would pay dearly.

She had been to the voodoo woman, and knew what had to be done. Knew what would be done to secure all she wanted, forever. For always.

She walked through the gardens, brittle with winter, and to the carriage house to find what she needed.

She was singing as she carried it with her, as she walked in the damp air toward the grand house with its yellow stones alit with moonlight.

"Lavender's blue," she sang. "Lavender's green."

ONE

Harper House
July 2005

TIRED DOWN THROUGH THE MARROW, HAYLEY YAWNED until her jaw cracked. Lily's head was heavy on her shoulder, but every time she stopped rocking, the baby would squirm and whimper, and those little fingers would clutch at the cotton tank Hayley was sleeping in.

Trying to sleep in, Hayley corrected and murmured hushing noises as she sent the rocker creaking again.

She knew it was somewhere in the vicinity of four in the morning, and she'd already been up twice before to rock and soothe her fretful daughter.

She'd tried—at about the two A.M. mark to snuggle the baby into bed with her so they'd both get some sleep. But Lily would have nothing but the rocker.

So Hayley rocked and dosed, rocked and yawned, and wondered if she'd ever get eight straight again in this lifetime.

She didn't know how people did it. Especially single mothers. How did they cope? How did they stand up under all the demands on heart, mind, body—wallet?

How would she have managed it all if she'd been completely on her own with Lily? What kind of life would they have had if she had no one to help with the worry, the sheer drudgery, the fun and the foolishness? It was terrifying to think of it.

She'd been so ridiculously optimistic and confident, and *stupid,* she thought now.

Sailing along, she remembered, nearly six months pregnant, quitting her job, selling most of her things and packing up that rattletrap car to head out.

God, if she'd known then what she knew now, she'd never have done it.

So maybe it was good she hadn't known. Because she wasn't alone. Closing her eyes, she rested her cheek on Lily's soft, dark hair. She had friends—no, family—people who cared about her and Lily and were willing to help.

They didn't just have a roof over their heads, but the gorgeous roof of Harper House. She had Roz, distant cousin and then only through marriage, who'd offered her a home, a job, a chance. She had Stella, her best friend in the world to talk to, bitch to, learn from.

Both Roz and Stella had been single parents—and they'd coped, she reminded herself. They'd better than coped, and Stella had had two young boys to raise alone. Roz *three*.

And here she was wondering how she'd ever manage one, even with all the help only an offer away.

There was David, running the house, cooking the meals. And just being wonderfully David. What if she had to cook every night after work? What if she had to do all the shopping, the cleaning, the hauling, the *everything* in addition to holding up her end at her job and caring for a fourteen-month-old baby?

Thank God she didn't have to find out.

There was Logan, Stella's gorgeous new husband, who was willing to tinker around with her car when it acted up. And Stella's little guys, Gavin and Luke, who not only liked to play with Lily but were giving Hayley a hint of the sort of things she had coming in the next few years.

There was Mitch, so smart and sweet, who liked to scoop Lily up and cart her around on his shoulders while she laughed. He'd be officially here all the time now, she thought, once he and Roz got back from their honeymoon.

It had been so nice, so much fun, to watch both Stella and Roz fall in love. She'd felt a part of it all—the excitement, the changes, the expansion of her new family circle.

Of course, Roz's marriage meant Hayley'd have to stop dragging her feet on finding a place of her own. Newlyweds were entitled to privacy.

She wished there was a place close by. Even on the estate. Like the carriage house. Harper's house. She sighed a little as she rubbed a hand over Lily's back.

Harper Ashby. Rosalind Harper Ashby's firstborn, and one delicious piece of eye candy. Of course she didn't think about him that way. Much. He was a friend, a co-worker, and her baby girl's first crush. From all appearances, that love affair was mutual.

She yawned again, lulled like the baby by the rhythm of the rocking and the early-morning quiet.

Harper was, well, just flat-out amazing with Lily. Patient and funny, easy and loving. Secretly she thought of him as Lily's surrogate father—without the benefits of smoochies with Lily's mother.

Sometimes she played pretend—and what was the harm in that?—and the surrogate part of father didn't apply. The smoochies did. After all, what red-blooded American girl—currently very sex-deprived girl—wouldn't fantasize now and again about the tall, dark, and ridiculously handsome type, especially when he came with a killer grin, heart-melting brown eyes, and a pinchable butt?

Not that she'd ever pinched it. But in theory.

Plus he was completely smart. He knew everything there was to know about plants and flowers. She loved to watch him working in the grafting house at In the Garden. The way his hands held a knife or tied raffia.

He was teaching her, and she appreciated it. Appreciated it too much to indulge herself and take a nice hungry bite out of him.

But imagining doing it didn't hurt a thing.

She eased the rocker to a stop, held her breath and waited. Lily's back continued to rise and fall steadily under her hand.

Thank God.

She got up slowly, moving toward the crib with the stealth and purpose of a woman making a prison break. With her arms aching, her head fuzzy with fatigue, she leaned over the crib and gently, inch by inch laid Lily on the mattress.

Even as she draped the blanket over her, Lily began to stir. Her head popped up, and she began wailing.

"Oh, Lily, please, come on, baby." Hayley patted, rubbed, swaying on her feet. "Ssh now, come on. Give your mama a little break."

The patting seemed to work—as long as she kept her hand on Lily's back, the little head stayed down. So Hayley sank to the floor, stuck her arm through the crib slats. And patted. And patted.

And drifted off to sleep.

* * *

IT WAS THE SINGING THAT WOKE HER. HER ARM WAS asleep, and stayed that way when her eyes opened. The room was cold; the section of the floor where she sat beside the crib a square of ice. Her arm prickled from shoulder to fingertip as she shifted to keep a protective hand on Lily's back.

The figure in the gray dress sat in the rocker, softly singing the old fashioned lullaby. Her eyes met Hayley's, but she continued to sing, continued to rock.

The jolt of shock cleared the fuzziness from Hayley's head, and had her heart taking one hard leap into her throat.

Just what did you say to a ghost you hadn't seen for several weeks? she wondered. Hey, how are you? Welcome home? Just what was the proper response, especially when the ghost in question was totally whacked?

Hayley's skin was slicked with cold when she pushed slowly to her feet so she could stand between the rocker and the crib. Just in case. Because it felt as if a few thousand needles were lodged in her arm, she cradled it against her body, rubbing it briskly.

Note all the details, she reminded herself. Mitch would want all the details.

She looked pretty calm for a psychotic ghost, Hayley decided. Calm and sad, the way she had the first time she'd seen her. But she'd also seen her with crazed, bulging eyes.

"Um. She had to get some shots today. Inoculations. She's always fussy the night after she gets them. But I think she's settled down now. In time to get up again in a couple of hours, so she'll probably be cranky for the babysitter until she gets her nap. But . . . but she should sleep now, so you could go."

The figure faded away seconds before the singing.

* * *

DAVID FIXED HER BLUEBERRY PANCAKES FOR BREAKfast. She'd told him not to cook for her or Lily while Roz and Mitch were gone, but he always did. Since he looked so cute fussing in the kitchen, she didn't try very hard to discourage him.

Besides, the pancakes were awesome.

"You've been looking a little peaky." David gave her cheek a pinch; then repeated the gesture on Lily to make her giggle.

"Haven't been sleeping much lately. Had a visitor last night."

She shook her head when his eyebrows rose, and his mouth curved into a leer. "Not a man—too sad for my bad luck. Amelia."

Amusement faded immediately, replaced by concern as he slid into the breakfast nook across from her. "Was there trouble? Are you all right?"

"She was just sitting in the rocker, singing. And when I told her Lily was fine, that she could go, she did. It was completely benign."

"Maybe she's settled down again. We can hope. Have you been worried about that?" He took a careful study of her face, noted the smudges under the soft blue eyes, the pallor beneath the carefully applied blush on her cheeks. "Is that why you haven't been sleeping?"

"Some, I guess. Things were pretty wild around here for a few months. Our gooses were constantly getting bumped. Now this lull. It's almost creepier."

"You've got Daddy David right down here." He reached over to pat her hand, his long, concert pianist's fingers giving it a little extra rub. "And Roz and Mitch will be back today. The house won't feel so big and empty."

She let out a long breath, relieved. "You felt that way, too. I didn't want to say, didn't want you to feel like you weren't enough company or something. 'Cause you are."

"You, too, my treasure. But we've gotten spoiled, haven't we? Had a houseful for a year around here." He glanced toward the empty seats at the table. "I miss those kids."

"Aw, you softie. We still see them, everybody, all the time, but it's weird, having everything so quiet."

As if she understood, Lily launched her sip-cup so that it slapped the center island and thudded on the floor.

"Atta girl," David told her.

"And you know what else?" Hayley rose to retrieve the cup. She was tall and lanky, and much to her disappointment, her breasts had reverted to their pre-pregnancy size. She thought of them as an A-minus cup. "I think I'm getting in some sort of mood. I don't mean rut, exactly, because I love working at the nursery, and I was just thinking last night—when Lily woke up for the millionth time—how lucky I am to be here, to be able to have all these people in our lives."

She spread her arms, let them fall. "But, I don't know, David, I feel sort of . . . blah."

"Need shopping therapy."

She grinned and got a washcloth to wipe Lily's syrupy face. "It is the number-one cure for almost everything. But I think I want a change. Something bigger than new shoes."

Deliberately, he widened his eyes, let his jaw go slack. "There's something bigger?"

"I think I'm going to cut my hair. Do you think I should cut my hair?"

"Hmm." He cocked his head, studied her with his handsome blue eyes. "It's gorgeous hair, that glossy Mahogany. But I absolutely loved it the way you wore it when you first moved here."

"Really?"

"All those different lengths. Tousled, casual, kicky. Sexy."

"Well . . ." She ran her hand down it. She'd grown it out, nearly to her shoulders. An easy length to pull back for work or motherhood. And maybe that was just the problem. She'd started taking the easy way because she'd stopped finding the time or making the effort to worry about how she looked.

She wiped Lily off, freed her from the highchair so she could wander around the kitchen. "Maybe I will then. Maybe."

"And toss in the new shoes, sweetie. They never fail."

IN HIGH SUMMER BUSINESS SLOWED AT THE GARDEN center. It never trickled down too far at In the Garden, but in July, the heady late winter through spring rush was long over. Wet heat smothered west Tennessee, and only the most avid of gardeners would suffer through it to pump new life into their beds.

Taking advantage of it, and her mood, Hayley wheedled a salon appointment, and an extra hour off from Stella.

When she drove back into work after her extended lunch break, it was with a new do, *two* new pair of shoes, and a much happier attitude.

Trust David, she decided.

She loved In the Garden. Most days, she didn't feel as if she was going to work at all. There couldn't be a better quality in a job than that, in her opinion.

She enjoyed just looking at the pretty white building that looked more like someone's well-tended home than a business, with the seasonal beds spreading out from its porch, and the pots full of colorful blooms by its door.

She liked the industry across the wide gravel lot—the

stacks of peat and mulch, the pavers and landscape timbers. The greenhouses that were full of plants and promises, the storage buildings.

When it was busy with customers, winding along the paths, pulling wagons or flatbeds full of plants and pots—everyone full of news or plans—it was more like a small village than a retail space.

And she was a part of it all.

She stepped in, and did a turn for Ruby, the white-haired clerk who manned the counter.

"Don't you look sassy," Ruby commented.

"I feel sassy." She ran her fingers through her short shaggy hair, then let it fall again. "I haven't done anything new with my hair in a *year*. More. I almost forgot what it was like to sit in a beauty parlor and have somebody do me."

"Things do slide with a new baby. How's our best girl doing?"

"Fussy last night after her shots. But she bounced back this morning. My butt was dragging. Pumped now though." To prove it, she flexed her arms to show little bumps of biceps.

"Good thing. Stella wants everything watered, and I do mean everything. And we're waiting on a big delivery of new planters. They'll need to be stickered and shelved once they come in."

"I'm your girl."

She started outside in the thick, drowsy heat, soaking the bedding plants, the annuals and perennials who'd yet to find a home. They made her think of those awkward kids in school who never got picked for the team. As a result, she had a soft spot for them and wished she had a place where she could dig them into the soil, let them bloom, let them find their potential.

One day she would have a place. She'd plant gardens,

take what she'd learned here and put it to use. Make something beautiful, something special. There would have to be lilies, naturally. Red lilies, like the ones Harper brought to her when she was in labor with Lily. A big, splashy pool of red lilies, bold and fragrant that would come back year after year and remind her how lucky she was.

Sweat trickled down the back of her neck, and water dampened her canvas skids. The gentle spray annoyed the gang of bees covering the sedum. So, come back when I'm finished, she thought as they flew off with an annoyed buzz. We're all after the same thing here.

She moved slowly, half dreaming, down the tables holding the picked-over stock.

And if one day she had a garden, and there was Lily playing on the grass. With a puppy, she decided. There should be a puppy, all fat and soft and frisky. If she was able to have all that, couldn't she add a man? Someone who loved her and Lily, someone funny and smart who made her heart beat just a little faster when he looked at her?

He could be handsome. What was the point of a fantasy if the guy wasn't great-looking? Tall, he would be tall, with good shoulders and long legs. Brown eyes, deep delicious brown, and lots of thick dark hair she could get her hands into. Good cheekbones, the kind you just wanted to nibble your way along until you got to that strong, sexy mouth. And then—

"Jesus, Hayley, you're drowning that coreopsis."

She jerked, whipping the sprayer, then on a little yip of distress whipped it back again. But not before the water hit Harper dead-on.

Gut shot, she thought, torn between embarrassment and inappropriate giggles. He looked down at his soaked shirt, his jeans with a kind of grim resignation.

"Got a license for that thing?"

"I'm sorry! I'm so sorry. But you shouldn't sneak up behind me that way."

"I didn't sneak anywhere. I walked."

His voice was aggravated, but so Memphian, she thought, where she knew hers hit twang when she was excited or upset. "Well, walk louder next time. I really am sorry though. I guess my mind was wandering."

"This kind of heat, it's easy for the mind to wander then lie down to take a nap." He pulled the wet shirt away from his belly. His eyes crinkled at the corners when he narrowed them. "What did you do to your hair?"

"What?" Instinctively she reached up, pulled her fingers through it. "I had it cut. Don't you like it?"

"Yeah, sure. It's fine."

Her finger itched on the trigger of the sprayer. "Please, stop. That kind of flattery'll just go to my head."

He smiled at her. He had such a great smile—sort of slow, so that it shifted the angles of his face and lit up in those deep, dark brown eyes—she nearly forgave him.

"I'm heading home, for a bit anyway. Mama's back."

"They're back? How are they? Did they have a good time? And you don't know yet because you haven't been home. Tell them I can't wait to see them, and that everything's fine over here, and Roz shouldn't worry and come over and start in working when she's barely walked in the door. And—"

He cocked his hip, hooked a thumb in the front pocket of his ancient jeans. "Should I be writing any of this down?"

"Oh, go on then." But she laughed as she waved him away. "I'll tell them myself."

"See you later."

He walked off, the man of her daydreams, dripping a little.

She really had to get her mind off Harper, she warned herself. Get it off and keep it off. He wasn't for her, and she knew it. She walked over to give the potted shrubs and climbers a good soak.

She wasn't even sure she wanted anybody to be for her—right now, anyway. Lily was number one priority, and after Lily came her job. She wanted her baby happy, healthy and secure. And she wanted to learn more, do more at the nursery. The more she learned, the less it would be a job, and the more it would be a career.

Pulling her weight was fine, but she wanted to do more.

After Lily, her work and the family she'd made here, came the fascinating and spooky task of identifying Amelia, the Harper Bride—and laying her to rest.

Most of that fell to Mitch. He was the genealogist, and along with Stella the most organized mind of the bunch. And wasn't it cool that he and Roz had found each other, fallen in love, after Roz had hired him to research the family tree to try to find where Amelia fit in? Not that Amelia had cared for the falling-in-love part. Boy, she'd been a stone bitch about it.

She might get mean again, too, Hayley thought. Now that they were married and Mitch was living at Harper House. She'd been quiet for a while, but it didn't mean she'd stay quiet.

If and when the whirlwind resumed, Hayley intended to be ready for it.

two

HAYLEY WALKED INTO HARPER HOUSE—AH, THE blessed *cool*—with Lily on her hip. She set Lily on her feet, then dumped her purse and the diaper bag on the bottom step so they'd be handy for her to carry up. Up's where she wanted to go. She wanted to shower for, oh, two or three days ought to do it, then drink an ice cold beer, straight down.

But before she did anything, she wanted Roz.

Even as she thought it, Roz came out of the parlor. She and Lily gave mutual cries of delight. Lily changed direction, and as she headed toward Roz, Roz closed the distance and scooped her up.

"There's my sweet potato." She gave Lily a fierce hug, nuzzled her neck, then with a grin for Hayley, looked back at the baby and listened with amazement to the excited and incomprehensible babbling. "Why, I can't believe all that happened in just one week! Don't know what I'd do if you weren't here to catch me up on all the local gossip." She grinned at Hayley again. "And how's your mama?"

"I'm fine. I'm great." Hayley dashed over to lock them both in a hug. "Welcome home. We missed you."

"Good. I like being missed. And look at this." She flipped her fingers over Hayley's hair.

"I just did it. Just today. Woke up with a bug up my butt. Oh, you look so beautiful."

"Listen to you."

But it was true, always true. And now a weeklong honeymoon in the Caribbean had added a dewy glow to innate beauty. Sun had turned the creamy skin pale gold so that Roz's long, dark eyes seemed even deeper. The short, straight hair capped a face with the sort of classic, timeless beauty Hayley knew she could only envy.

"I like that cut," Roz commented. "It looks so young and easy."

"Gave my morale a boost. Lily and I had a rough night. She got her shots yesterday."

"Mmm." Roz gave Lily an extra hug. "No fun there. Let's see if we can make up for it. Come on in here, baby girl," Roz said, snuggling Lily again as she went back in the parlor. "See what we got you."

The first thing Hayley saw was a life-sized doll with a mop of red hair and a sweet and foolish smile.

"Oh, she's so cute! And almost as big as Lily."

"That was the idea. Mitch spotted her before I did, and nothing would do but we bring her home to Lily. What do you think, sweetie?"

Lily poked the doll in the eye a couple of times, pulled its hair, then was happy to sit on the floor and get acquainted.

"It's the kind of doll she'll name in a year or so, then keep in her room till college. Thank you, Roz."

"We're not done. There was this little shop, and they had the most adorable dresses." She began to pull them out of the bag while Hayley goggled. Soft smocked cotton, ruched lace, embroidered denim. "And look at these rompers. Who could resist?"

"They're wonderful. They're beautiful. You'll spoil her."

"Well, of course."

"I don't know what to . . . She doesn't have any grand—anybody to spoil her like this."

Roz arched a brow, folded a romper. "You can say the G word, Hayley. I won't faint in horror. I like to think of myself as her honorary grandmother."

"I'm so lucky, We're so lucky."

"Then why are you tearing up?"

"I don't know. All this stuff's been going on in my head lately." She sniffled, heeled a hand under her eyes to rub away the dampness. "Where I am, how I got here, how it might've been for us if I'd been on my own with Lily the way I thought I'd be."

"Might've beens don't get you very far."

"I know. I'm just so glad I came to you. I was thinking last night that I should start looking for a place."

"A place to what?"

"Live."

"Something wrong with this place?"

"It's the most beautiful house I've ever seen." And here she was, Hayley Phillips from Little Rock, living in it, living in a house that had a parlor furnished with beautiful antiques and deep rich cushions, with generous windows that opened up to acres of more beauty.

"I was thinking I should look for a place, but I don't want to. At least, well, not right now." She looked down, watched Lily struggle to carry the doll around the room. "But I want you to tell me, and I know we're good enough friends that you will, when you want me to start looking."

"All right. That settled then?"

"Sure."

"Don't you want to see what we brought you?"

"I got something, too?" Hayley's lake blue eyes went bright with anticipation. "I *love* presents. I'm not ashamed to say it."

"I hope you like this one." She took a box out of the bag, offered it.

Wasting no time, Hayley took off the top. "Oh, oh! They're gorgeous."

"I thought the red coral would suit you best."

"I *love* them!" She took the earrings out of the box and holding them to her ears rushed to one of the antique mirrors on the wall to study how they looked. The trios of delicate and exotic red balls swayed from a glittery triangle of silver. "They're wonderful. God, I have something from Aruba. I can't believe it."

She dashed back to give a chuckling Roz a hug. "They're just beautiful. Thank you, thank you. I can hardly wait to wear them."

"You can give them a test drive tonight if you want. Stella, Logan, and the boys will be over. David tells me we're having a welcome-home dinner."

"Oh, but you'll be tired."

"Tired? What am I, eighty? I just got back from vacation."

"Honeymoon," Hayley corrected with a smirk. "Bet you didn't get a lot of rest either."

"We slept in every morning, you smart-ass."

"In that case, we'll party. Lily and I'll go upstairs and get ourselves all clean and pretty."

"I'll give you a hand up with all these things."

"Thanks. Roz?" Everything inside her had settled down to a glow. "I'm really glad you're home."

* * *

IT WAS SO MUCH FUN TO PUT ON HER NEW EARRINGS, to dress Lily in one of her pretty new outfits, to fuss a little over both herself and her daughter. She shook her head just for the pleasure of feeling the way her hair fell and her earrings swung.

There now, she thought, not feeling dull and blah anymore. Since she was feeling celebrational, she capped it off with new shoes. The thin-heeled strappy black sandals were impractical and unnecessary. Which made them perfect.

"And they were on sale," she told Lily. "Gotta say, they've got to be more fun than Prozac or whatever."

It felt great to wear a dress—with a short skirt—and sexy shoes. A new haircut. Red lipstick.

She gave a turn for the mirror and struck a pose. Maybe she had a skinny build, but there was nothing much she could do about that. Still, she wore clothes pretty well, if she did say so. Kind of like a clothes hanger. Add new hair, new earrings, new shoes, and you had something.

"Ladies and gentlemen, I do believe I'm back."

DOWNSTAIRS, HARPER WAS SPRAWLED IN A CHAIR, sipping a beer and watching the way Mitch touched his mother—her hair, her arm—while they related some of the highlights of their trip for Logan and Stella and the boys.

He'd heard some of it already when he'd buzzed home for an hour that afternoon. He wasn't really listening. He was just watching, and thinking it was good, it was time his mother had someone so obviously besotted with her.

He was happy for her—and relieved. No matter how

well his mother could take care of herself, and God knew she could do just that, it was a comfort to know she had a smart, able man at her side.

After what had happened last spring, if Mitch hadn't moved in, he'd have done so himself. And that might've been a little sticky with Hayley living there.

It was more . . . comfortable, he decided, for everybody, if he continued to live in the carriage house. It might not have been much distance geographically, but psychologically it did the job.

"I told him he was crazy," Roz continued, gesturing with her wine with one hand, patting the other on Mitch's thigh. "Windsurfing? Why in God's name would we want to teeter around on a little hunk of wood with a sail attached? But he just had to try it."

"I tried it once." Stella sat, her curling mass of red hair spilling over her shoulders. "Spring break in college. It was fun once I got the hang of it."

"So I hear." Mitch's mutter had Roz grinning.

"He'd get up on the thing, and in two seconds, splash. Get up, and wait, I think he's got it. Splash."

"I had a defective board," Mitch claimed, and poked Roz in the ribs.

"Of course you did." Roz rolled her eyes. "One thing you can say about our Mitchell is he's game. I don't know how many times he hauled himself out of the drink and back on that board."

"Six hundred and fifty-two."

"How about you?" Logan, big and built and rugged beside Stella, gestured toward Roz with his beer.

"Oh, well, I don't like to brag," Roz said and examined her fingernails.

"Yes, she does." Mitch gulped down club soda, stretched out his long, long legs. "Oh, yes, she does."

"But, I enjoyed the experience quite a lot."

"She just . . ." Mitch sailed his hand through the air to illustrate. "Sailed off as if she'd been born on one of the damn things."

"We Harpers do tend to have excellent athletic abilities and superior balance."

"But she doesn't like to brag," Mitch pointed out, then glanced over at the click of heels on hardwood.

Harper did the same, and felt his reputed superior balance falter.

She looked frigging amazing. The skinny little red dress, the mile-high shoes combined to make her legs look endless. The sort of legs a man could imagine cruising over for miles, and miles. Her hair was so damn sexy that way, and her mouth was all hot and red.

She had a baby on her hip, he reminded himself. He shouldn't be thinking about what he'd like to do to that mouth, that body when she was carrying Lily. It had to be wrong.

Across the room, Logan let out a long, low whistle that had Hayley's face lighting up.

"Hello, beautiful. You look good enough to eat. You look good, too, Hayley."

At that, she gave one of those husky rolls of laughter, and hip-swayed over to drop Lily in Logan's lap. "Just for that."

"How about some wine?" Roz offered.

"To tell you the truth, I've been wanting a cold beer."

"I'll get it." Harper all but sprang out of his chair, and was heading out of the parlor before she could respond. He hoped the trip to the kitchen and back would bring his blood pressure back to normal.

She was a cousin, sort of, he reminded himself. And an employee. His mother's houseguest. A mother. Any one of those reasons meant hands-off. Tally them up, and it put Hayley way off-limits. Added to that, she didn't think of him that way, not even close.

A guy made a move on a woman under those circumstances, he was just asking to screw up a nice, pleasant friendship.

He got out a beer, got out a pilsner. As he was pouring, he heard the squeal, and the rapid clip of heels on wood. He glanced over and spotted Lily running, with Hayley scrambling behind her.

"She want a beer, too?"

With a laugh, Hayley started to scoop Lily up, only to have her baby girl go red in the face and arch away. "You. Like always."

"That's my girl." He hoisted her up, gave her a toss. The mutinous little face went sugar sweet and bright with smiles. Pretending to pout, Hayley finished pouring her beer.

"Shows where I am in her pecking order."

"You got the beer, I got the kid."

Lily wrapped an arm around Harper's neck, dipped her head to rest it on his cheek. Hayley nodded, lifted her glass. "Looks like."

IT WAS WONDERFUL TO HAVE EVERYONE AROUND THE table again, the whole Harper House family, as Hayley thought of them, sitting together, diving into David's honey-glazed ham.

She'd missed having a big family. Growing up, it had been just Hayley and her father. Not that she'd felt deprived, she thought, not in any way. She and her father had been a team, a unit, and he was—had been—the kindest, funniest, warmest man she'd ever known.

But she'd missed having meals like this, a full table, lots

of voices—even the arguments and drama that went hand-in-hand in her mind with big families.

Lily would grow up with that, because Roz had welcomed them. So Lily would have a lifetime of meals like this one, full of aunts and uncles and cousins. Grandparents, she thought, stealing a glance toward Roz and Mitch. And when Roz's other sons, or Mitch's son, came to visit, it would just add to the rich family stew.

One day, Roz's sons, and Mitch's Josh, would get married. Probably have a herd of kids between them.

She shifted her gaze toward Harper and ordered herself to ignore the little ache that came from thinking of him married, making babies with some woman whose face she couldn't see.

Of course, she'd be beautiful, that was a given. Probably blonde and built and blue-blooded. The bitch.

Whoever she turned out to be, whatever she looked like or *was* like, Hayley determined she'd make friends. Even if it killed her.

"Something wrong with the potatoes?" David murmured beside her.

"Hmm. No. They're awesome."

"Just wondered why you looked like you were forcing down some bad-tasting medicine, sugar."

"Oh, just thought about something I'm going to have to do, and won't like. Life's full of them. But that doesn't include eating these potatoes. If fact, I was wondering if you could show me how to cook some things. I can cook pretty good. Daddy and I split that chore, and we were both okay with the basics—I could even get a little fancy now and then. But Lily's growing up on your cooking, so I ought to be able to fix it for her myself when need be."

"Hmm, a kitchen apprentice. One I can mold into my own likeness. Love to."

When Lily began to drop the bits of food still on her tray delicately to the floor, Hayley popped up. "Guess who's done."

"Gavin, why don't you and Luke take Lily outside and play awhile?"

"Oh." Hayley shook her head at Stella's suggestion. "I don't want them to have to mind her."

"We can do it," Gavin piped up. "She likes to chase the ball and the Frisbee."

"Well . . ." At nearly ten, Gavin was tall for his age. And at just-turned-eight, Luke was right behind him. They could—and had—handled Lily at play on the backyard grass. "I don't mind if you don't, and she'd love it. But when you're tired of her, you just bring her back."

"And as a reward, ice cream sundaes later."

David's announcement got a couple of cheers.

When playtime was over, the sundaes devoured, Hayley carried Lily up to get her ready for bed, and Stella brought the boys up to the sitting room they'd once shared to watch television.

"Roz and Mitch want an Amelia talk," Stella told her. "I didn't know if you'd gotten the word."

"No, but that's fine. I'll be down as soon as she is."

"Need any help?"

"Not this time, but thanks. Her eyes are already drooping."

It was nice, she thought, to hear the muted crash and boom of some sort of space war on the sitting room television and the bright chatter of the boys' commentary on the action. She'd missed those noises since Stella had gotten married.

She settled Lily in for the night—hopefully—checked the monitor and the night-light. Then left the door ajar as she returned downstairs.

She found the adults in the library, the most usual meeting spot for ghost talk. The sun had yet to set, so the room was washed with light that was just hinting of pink. Through the glass, the summer gardens were ripe, sumptuous, spears of lavender foxglove dancing over pools of white impatiens, brightened with elegant drips of hot-pink fuschia.

She spotted the soft, fuzzy green of betony, the waxy charm of begonias, the inverted cups of purple coneflowers with their prickly brown heads.

She'd missed her evening walk with Lily, she remembered, and promised herself she'd take her daughter out for a stroll through the gardens the next day.

Out of habit, she crossed to the table where a baby monitor stood beside a vase of poppy-red lilies.

Once she was assured it was on, she tuned in to the rest of the room.

"Now that we're all here," Mitch began, "I thought I should bring you up-to-date."

"You're not going to break my heart and tell us you researched during your honeymoon," David put in.

"Your heart's safe, but we did manage to find some time to discuss various theories here and there. The thing is, I had a couple of e-mails from our contact in Boston. The descendant of the Harper housekeeper during Reginald and Beatrice's reign here."

"She find something?" Harper had chosen the floor rather than one of the seats, and now folded himself from prone to sitting.

"I've been feeding her what we know, and told her what we found in Beatrice Harper's journal, regarding your great-grandfather, Harper. The fact that he wasn't her son, but in fact Reginald's son with his mistress—whom we have to assume was Amelia. She hasn't had any luck, yet, digging up any letters or diaries from Mary Havers—the housekeeper. She has found photographs, and is getting us copies."

Hayley looked toward the second level of the library, to the table loaded with books, Mitch's laptop. And the board beside it that was full of photos and copies of letters and journal entries. "What will that do for us?"

"The more visuals, the better," he said. "She's also been talking to her grandmother, who's not doing very well, although she does has some lucid moments. The grandmother claims to recall her mother and a cousin who also worked here at the time, talk about their days at Harper House. Lots of talk about the parties and the work. She also recalls her cousin talking about the young master, that's how she referred to Reginald Jr. And saying the stork got rich delivering that one. That her mother told her to hush, that blood money and curses aside, the child was innocent. When she asked what she meant, her mother wouldn't speak of it, except to say she'd done her duty by the Harper family, and would have to live with it. But the happiest day of her life had been when she'd walked out the door of this house for the last time."

"She knew my grandfather had been taken from his mother." Roz reached down, touched a hand to Harper's shoulder. "And if this woman is remembering correctly, it sounds as though Amelia wasn't willing to give him up."

"Blood money and curses," Stella repeated. "Who was paid, and what was cursed."

"There would have been a doctor or a midwife, perhaps both, attending Amelia during the birth." Mitch spread his hands. "Almost certainly they'd have been paid off. Some of the servants here might have been bribed."

"I know that's awful," Hayley said. "But you wouldn't call that blood money, would you? Hush money more like."

"Bull's-eye," Mitch told her. "If there was blood money, where was the blood?"

"Amelia's death." Logan shifted, leaned forward. "She haunts here, so she died here. You haven't been able to find any record of that, so we have to assume it was covered up. Easiest way to cover something up is money."

"I agree." Stella nodded. "But how did she get here? There's no mention of Amelia in any of Beatrice's journals. No mention of Reginald's mistress by name, or of her coming to Harper House. She wrote about the baby, and how she felt about Reginald bringing him here, expecting her to pretend she'd given birth to him. Wouldn't she have been just as outraged, and written of that, if he'd established Amelia in the house?"

"He wouldn't have." Hayley spoke quietly. "From everything we've learned about him, he wouldn't have brought a woman of her class, one he considered a convenience, a means to an end, into the house he was so proud of. He wouldn't have wanted her around his son—the one he was passing as legitimate. It'd be a constant reminder."

"That's a good point." Harper stretched out his legs, crossed them at the ankles. "But if we believe she died here, then we have to believe she *was* here."

"Maybe she passed as a servant," Stella suggested. She gestured, and her wedding ring glinted gold in the softening light. "If Beatrice didn't know her, what she looked like, Amelia might have managed to get a position in the house, so she'd be close to her son. She sings to the children of the house, she's obsessed with the children here, in her way. Wouldn't she have been even more so with her own child?"

"It's a possibility," Mitch commented. "We haven't found her through the household records, but it's a possibility."

"Or she came here to try to get him." Roz looked at Stella, at Hayley. "A mother, frantic, desperate, and not completely balanced. She sure as hell didn't go crazy after she died. I'm not willing to stretch credulity that far. Doesn't it play that she would have come here, and something went terribly wrong? We have to consider that if she came here, she might have been murdered. Blood money to cover up the crime."

"So the house is cursed." Harper lifted a shoulder. "And she haunts it until, what, she's avenged? How?"

"Maybe just recognized," Hayley corrected. "Given her due, I guess. You're her blood," she said to Harper. "Maybe it's going to take Harper blood to put her to rest."

"I have to say that sounds logical." David gave a little shudder. "And creepy."

"We're a bunch of rational adults sitting around talking about a ghost," Stella reminded him. "It doesn't get much more creepy."

"I saw her last night."

At Hayley's statement all eyes turned to her. "And you didn't tell us?" Harper demanded.

"I told David this morning," she shot back. "And I'm telling everybody now. I didn't want to say anything in front of the kids."

"Let's get this on record." Mitch rose to go to the table for his tape recorder.

"It wasn't that much of a big."

"We agreed last spring after the last two violent apparitions, that everything goes on the record." He came back to sit again, and set the recorder on the table. "Tell us."

Talking on tape made her feel self-conscious, but she related everything.

"I hear her singing sometimes, but usually when I go in to check, she's gone. You know she's been there. Sometimes I hear her in the boys' room—Gavin's and Luke's old room. Sometimes she's crying. And once I thought . . ."

"Thought what?" Mitch prompted.

"I thought I might've seen her walking outside. The night y'all left on your honeymoon, after we had the wedding party here? I woke up—had a little more wine than I should, I guess—and I had a little headache. So I took some aspirin, checked on Lily. I thought I saw someone, out the window. There was enough moonlight that I could make out the blond hair, the white dress. It appeared like she was going toward the carriage house. But when I opened the doors, to go out on the terrace and get a better look, she was gone."

"Didn't we have an agreement, starting after Mama finally decided to clue us in about nearly being drowned in the bathtub that we put everything on record?" Anger simmered in Harper's voice. "We don't wait a damn week to make an announcement."

"Harper," Roz said dryly. "That horse is dead. Don't start beating it again."

"We had an agreement."

"I didn't know for sure." Hayley's back went up, and reflected in her tone as she glared down at Harper. "I still don't. Just because I thought I saw a woman walking toward your place didn't mean she was a ghost. Could just as likely—more likely—have been flesh and blood. What was I supposed to do, Harper, call you over at the carriage house and ask if you were getting a bootie call?"

"Jesus Christ."

"Well, there you are." Pleased, she nodded decisively. "It's not like you never have female company over there."

"Fine, fine. Just FYI, I didn't have female company—flesh and blood variety—that night. Next time, follow through."

"Class," Mitch said mildly, and gave a professorial tap of pencil on notebook. "Can you tell us any more about what you saw, Hayley?"

"Honestly, it was only a few seconds. I was just standing there, hoping the aspirin would kick in before morning, and I caught a movement. I saw a woman—a lot of blond or light hair, and she was wearing white. My first thought was Harper got lucky."

"Oh, man," was Harper's muttered comment.

"Then I thought about Amelia, but when I went out to see better, she was gone. I only mention it because if it was her, and I guess it was, that's twice I've seen her in about a week. And that's a lot for me."

"You were the only woman in the house during that week," Logan pointed out. "She's been more likely to show herself to women."

"That makes sense." And made her feel better.

"Added to that, it was the night after Mitch and I were married," Roz said. "She'd have been miffed."

"And it's the second time we've got a firsthand report of her walking toward the carriage house. There's something there," Mitch said to Harper.

"She's not letting me know about it. So far."

"Meanwhile we keep looking. We believe she lived in this area, so our best bet is Reginald kept her in one of his properties." Mitch lifted his hands. "I'm still pursuing that avenue."

"If we find out her name, her whole name," Hayley asked him, "would you be able to research her the way you did the Harper family?"

"It'd give me a start."

"Maybe she'll tell us, if we just find the right way to ask. Maybe . . ." She trailed off when singing came through the monitor. "She's with Lily, and she's early tonight. I'm just going to go up and check."

"I'll go with you." Harper got to his feet.

She didn't argue. Even after more than a year, the sound of that sad voice sent a chill up her spine. As was her habit, she'd flicked lights on in her wing so she wouldn't have to come back up in the dark. They reassured her now, as the sun was nearly set, as did the sounds of Luke and Gavin playing in the sitting room.

"You know, if you're uneasy being over here alone, you could move into the other wing, closer to Mama and Mitch."

"Just what the newly married couple need. Me and a baby as chaperones. Anyway, I'm mostly used to it. She's not stopping." She dropped her voice to a whisper. "She almost always stops before I get to the door."

Instinctively she reached for Harper's hand as she eased open the door she always left off the latch.

It was cold, but she'd expected that. Even after Amelia was gone, the chill would linger. Yet Lily was never disturbed by it. Her breath puffed out, a little startled cloud when she heard the distinctive creak of the rocker.

That was a new one, Hayley thought. Oh boy.

She sat in the rocker, wearing her gray dress. Her hands lay quiet in her lap as she sang. Her voice was pretty, unschooled but light and tuneful. Comforting, as a voice singing lullabies should be.

But when she turned her head, when she looked toward the door, Hayley's blood ran as cold as the air in the room.

It wasn't a smile on her face, but a grimace. Her eyes bulged, and were rimmed with violent red.

This is what they do. This is what they give.

As she spoke—thought—the form began to disintegrate. Flesh melted away to bone until what sat in the chair was a skeleton that rocked in rags.

Then even that was gone.

"Please tell me you saw that." Hayley's voice trembled. "Heard that."

"Yeah." With his hand firm on hers, he drew Hayley across the room to the crib. "Warmer here. Feel it? It's warm around the crib."

"She's never done anything to scare Lily. Still, I don't want to leave, go down again. I'd just feel better if I stayed close tonight. You can tell the others what happened?"

"I can bunk up here tonight. Take one of the guest rooms."

"It's all right." She arranged Lily's blanket more securely. "We'll be all right."

He tugged her hand, gestured so that she went back out into the hall with him. "That was a first, right?"

"A definite first for me. It's going to give me nightmares."

"You sure you're going to be okay?" He touched his hand to her cheek, and it flitted through her mind that was another first. They were standing close, her hand in his, his fingers on her cheek.

All she had to do was say, no. Stay with me.

And then what? She could start something, and ruin everything.

"Yeah. It's not like she's mad at me or anything. No reason to be. We're good, we're fine. You'd better go down, fill the others in."

"You get spooked in the night, call. I'll come."

"Good to know. Thanks."

She slid her hand out of his, eased back, and slipped into her own room.

No, Amelia had no reason to be mad at her, Hayley considered. She had no boyfriend, no husband, no lover. The only man she wanted was off-limits.

"So you can relax," she murmured. "Looks like I'll be going solo for the next little while.

THREE

HE HUNTED HER UP THE NEXT DAY, MID-MORNING. But he had to be sly about it. He knew her well enough to be sure if she thought he was trying to help, to get her mind off things, to give her any sort of break, she'd brush him off.

Hayley Phillips was the original I'm-fine-don't-worry-about-me girl.

Nothing wrong with that, Harper thought. In her place, a lot of women would have been happy to take advantage of his mother's generosity, or at least to take that generosity for granted. Hayley did neither, and he respected that. He could admire her stand—to a point. But plenty of times, to his mind, that point tripped over into just mule-headed stubborn.

So he kept it casual, even when he had to poke into two greenhouses, work his way to the main building before he found her setting up a new display of houseplants.

She was wearing one of the nursery's bib aprons over black camp shorts and a V-necked tank. There was damp soil on the apron, and on her forearm. Only repressed lust could be responsible for him finding it so absurdly sexy.

"Hey, how's it going?"

"Not too bad. Had ourselves a little run on dish gardens. Customer just came in and bagged five as centerpieces for her sorority reunion lunch. And I talked her into taking the sago palm for her own sunroom."

"Nice going. Guess you're busy then."

She glanced over her shoulder. "Not too. Stella wants to make up more dish gardens, but she's tied up with Logan, which isn't as sexy as it sounds. Big job came in, and she's locked him in the office until she gets all the details for the contract. Last I walked by, he wasn't all that happy about it."

"Ought to be at it for a while then. I was going to do some chip-budding. Could use some help, but—"

"Really? Can I do it? I can take one of the two-ways in case Ruby or Stella need me."

"I could use another pair of hands."

"Mine'll be right back. Hold on."

She dashed through the double glass doors, and was back in thirty seconds, shed of the apron and hitching a two-way to her waistband. And giving him a quick peek at smooth belly skin.

"I read up some, but I can't remember which is the chip-budding."

"It's an old method," he told her as they started out. "More widely used now than it used to be. What we're going to do is work some of the field stock, some of the ornamentals. Mid-summer's the time for it."

Heat hit like a wet wall. "This sure is mid-summer."

"We'll start on magnolias." He picked up a bucket of

water he'd left outside the door. "They never stop being popular."

They walked over gravel, between greenhouses, and headed out to the fields. "Things stay quiet last night?"

"Not a peep after that little show we were treated to. I'm hoping she doesn't plan an encore of that trick. Gross, you know?"

"She sure knows how to get your attention anyway. Okay, here's what we do first." He stopped in front of a tall, leafy magnolia. "I'm going to pick some ripe shoots, this season's wood. You want one not much thicker than a pencil with well-developed buds. See this one?"

With an ungloved hand, he reached up, gently drew a shoot down.

"Okay, then what?"

"I clip it off." He drew pruners out of his tool bag. "See here, where the base is starting to go woody? That's what we're looking for. You don't want green shoots, they're too weak yet."

After he'd cut it, Harper put the shoot in the water bucket. "We keep it wet. If it dries out, it won't unite. Now you pick one."

She started to move around the tree, but he caught her hand. "No, it's better to work on the sunny side of the tree."

"Okay." She rolled her bottom lip between her teeth as she searched, selected. "How about this one?"

"Good. Here, make the cut."

She took the pruners, and since he was close he could smell the scent she wore—always light with a surprising kick—along with the garden green.

"How many are you doing?"

"About a dozen." He stuck his hands in his pockets as he leaned in to watch her, smell her. And told himself he was suffering for a good cause. "Go ahead, pick another."

"I don't get out in the field much." She drew down another shoot, looked toward Harper and got his nod. "It's different out here. Different than selling and displaying, talking to customers."

"You're good at that."

"Yeah, I am, but being out here, it's getting your hands into the thing. Stella knows all this stuff, and Roz, she knows everything. I like to learn. You sell better the more you know."

"I'd rather ram that shoot in my eye than have to sell every day."

She smiled as she worked. "But you're a loner at heart, aren't you? I'd go crazy holed up in the grafting house day after day like you. I like seeing people, and having them talk to me about what they're looking for and why. I like selling, too. 'Here, you take this pretty thing, and give me the money.' "

She laughed as she put another shoot in the bucket. "That's why you and Roz need somebody like me, so you can squirrel away in your caves and work with the plants for hours, and I can sell them."

"Seems to be working."

"That's a dozen, even. What next?"

"Over here, what we've got is rooted shoots I got from stool-grown stock plants."

"Stooling, I know what that is." She stared down at the nursery bed and its line of straight, slim shoots. "Um, you hill the ground up to stimulate rooting, and cut them back hard in the winter, then you take the roots from the whatdoyoucallit, parent plant, and plant them out."

"You have been reading up."

"I like to learn."

"Shows." And was just one more click for him. He'd never found a woman who'd interested him physically, emotionally, who shared his love of gardening. "Okay. We use a sharp, clean knife. We're going to trim off all the leaves from the budstick—the shoots we just cut. But we'll leave just a little stub, just about an eighth of an inch of the petiole—the leaf stalk."

"I know what a petiole is," she muttered, and watched Harper demonstrate before she took her turn.

Good hands, she thought. Quick, skilled, sure. Despite—or maybe because of the nicks and calluses—they were elegantly male.

She thought they reflected who he was perfectly, that combination of privileged background and working-class.

"Cut the soft tip from the top, see? Now watch." He angled around so she could see, and their heads bent close together. "We want the first bud at the base, that's where we're going to cut into the stem, just a little below there. See how you have to angle the cut, going down, then another above, behind the bud toward that first cut. And . . ." Gently, holding the chip by the leaf stalk, he held it out.

"I can do that."

"Go ahead." He slipped the bud chip into a plastic bag, and watched her work.

She was careful, which was a relief to him, and he heard her whispering his instructions to herself with every move.

"I did it!"

"Nice job. Let's get the rest."

He did seven in the time it took her to do three, but she didn't mind. He showed her how to stand astride the root-stock to remove the sideshoots and leaves from the bottom twelve inches.

She knew it was a maneuver, and really, she'd probably feel guilty about it later, but she deliberately fumbled her first attempt.

"No, you need to position it between your legs, more like this."

As she'd hoped, he came over to stand behind her, in a nice vertical spoon, his arms coming around, making her belly dance as his hands closed over her wrists.

"Bend down a little, loosen at the knees. That's it. Now . . ." He guided her hand for the cut. "Just a sliver of the bark," he murmured, and his breath breezed along her ear. "See, there's the cambium. You want to leave a lip at the base where the chip will layer."

He smelled like the trees, sort of hot and earthy. His body felt so firm pressed against hers. She wished she could turn around, just turn so they were pressed front to front. She'd only have to rise up on her toes for their mouths to line up.

It was a maneuver, and *shame* on her, but she looked over her shoulder, looked dead into his eyes. And smiled. "Is that better?"

"Yeah. Better. A lot."

As she'd hoped, his gaze skimmed down, lingered on her mouth. Classic move, she thought. Classic results.

"I'll . . . show you how to do the rest."

He looked blank for a moment, like a man who'd forgotten what he was doing in the middle of a task. She couldn't have been more delighted.

Then he stepped back, reached in his tool bag for the grafting tape.

That had been so nice, she mused. Line to line, heat to heat, for just a few seconds. Of course now she was all churned up, but it felt good, felt fine to have everything swimming around inside her.

But as penance for her calculation, she behaved herself, played the eager student as she positioned the bud chip on the stock so the cambium layers met as snugly as her body had met Harper's.

She bound the chip to stock using the tape; around and over the bud as instructed.

"Good. Perfect." He still felt a little breathless, and the palms of his hands were damp enough that he wiped them on the knees of his jeans. "In six weeks, maybe two months, the chip will have united, and we'll take off the tape. Late next winter, we'll cut the top of the stock, just above this bud, and during the spring the grafted bud will send out a shoot, and we're off and running."

"It's fun, isn't it? How you can take a little something from one, a little something from another, put them together and make more."

"That's the plan."

"Will you show me some of the other techniques sometime? Like what you do in the grafting house?" Her body was angled, her head bent over the next rootstock. "Roz and Stella showed me some of the propagation techniques. I've done some flats by myself. I'd like to try something in the grafting house."

Alone with her there, in all that moist heat. He'd probably drown in a pool of his own lust.

"Sure, sure. No problem."

"Harper?" She knelt to join chip bud with rootstock. "Did you ever think, when your mama started this place, it'd be what it is?"

He had to focus, on her words, on the work and ignore—or at least suffer through—his body's reaction to her.

Lily's mama, he reminded himself. A guest in his home. An employee. Could it be any more complicated?

Jesus, God. Help.

"Harper?"

"Sorry." He wrapped grafting tape. "I did." When he looked up, looked around, beyond the fields and nursery beds, to the greenhouses, and sheds, he calmed. "I guess I could see it because it was what I wanted, too. And I know when Mama puts her mind to something, puts her back into it, she's going to make it work."

"What if she hadn't wanted it, or put her mind to it? What would you be doing?"

"Just what I'm doing. If she hadn't decided on this I'd've started it myself. And because I wanted it, she'd've got on board, so I guess we'd have pretty much what we have here."

"She's the best, isn't she? It's good that you know that, that you understand how lucky you are. I see that between you. You don't take each other for granted. I hope Lily and I have that one day."

"Seems like you already do."

She smiled at that, and rose to go to the next rootstock. "Do you think you and Roz are the way you are with each other, to each other—and your brothers, too—because you didn't have a daddy most of your life? I mean, I think I was closer to my own daddy because it was just the two of us than I might've been otherwise. I've wondered about that."

"Maybe." His hair, a thick tangle of black, fell forward as he worked. He shook it back, momentarily annoyed he'd forgotten a hat. "I remember her and my father, how they were together. It was special. She's got something like that with Mitch—not the same. I guess it's never the same, not supposed to be. But they've got something good and special. That's what she deserves."

"Do you ever think about finding somebody? Somebody good and special?"

"Me?" His head whipped up, and he narrowly missed slicing his own finger with the knife. "No. No. Well, eventually. Why? Do you?"

He heard her sigh as she moved down the nursery bed. "Eventually."

* * *

WHEN THEY WERE FINISHED, AND SHE HAD GONE, Harper walked back to the pond. He emptied out his pockets, tossed his sunglasses on the grass. Then dived in.

It had been something he'd done—with or without clothes—since childhood. There was nothing like a quick dip into the pond to cool you down on a sticky summer day.

He'd been on the point of kissing her. More than, he admitted, and sank under the surface, along the lily pads and yellow flags. It had been more than a kiss—even a hot and greedy one—that had run through his mind when he'd had his hands on her.

He had to put that aside—well off to the side—as he had been for more than a year now. She looked to him for friendship. God help him, she probably thought of him as a kind of brother.

So he'd just have to keep tamping down his less than brotherly feelings until he beat out the last of the sparks. Or burned up.

Best thing for him to do was get himself back into circulation. He was spending too much time at home, and too much of that time alone. Maybe he'd go into the city tonight, make some calls, meet some friends. Better yet, make a date. Have dinner, listen to music. Charm himself into some willing female's bed.

The trouble was, he couldn't think of any particular female he wanted to be with, over dinner, with music, or in the bed. That right there, it seemed to him, illustrated his pitiful state of affairs. Or lack of them.

He just wasn't in the mood to do the dance that ended up between the sheets. He couldn't bring himself to call another woman, put on the show, go through the pretense, when the woman he wanted was sleeping in his own house.

And as far out of his reach as the moon.

He pulled himself out of the water, shook like a dog. Maybe he'd go into town though. He picked up the rest of his things, shoving them in his dripping pockets. See if any of his unattached friends felt like catching a movie, eating some barbecue, hitting a club. Something, anything, to take his mind somewhere else for a night.

BUT WHEN HE GOT HOME, HE WASN'T IN THE MOOD TO go out. He made excuses to himself: It was too hot, he was too tired, he didn't feel like the drive. What he really wanted was a cool shower and a cold beer. He was pretty sure there was a frozen pizza buried with the leftovers David was always giving him. There was a ballgame on TV.

What else did he need?

A long warm body with miles of leg and smooth skin. Luscious lips and big blue eyes.

Since that wasn't on the menu, he decided to drop the temperature of the shower to cold.

His hair was still dripping and he wore nothing but ancient cutoffs when he wandered into the kitchen for that beer.

Like the rest of the house, it was small-scale. He didn't need big, he'd grown up in big. And he liked the charm and convenience of his little rooms. He thought of the converted two-story carriage house as a kind of country cottage. The way it sat away from the main house, surrounded by the gardens with their curving paths, shaded by old trees, gave it the kind of solitude and privacy that suited him. And kept him close enough to the main house that he could be on hand if his mother needed him.

If he wanted company, all he had to do was stroll over. If he didn't, he stayed put. More often than not, he admitted, he stayed put.

He remembered when he'd decided to move in, and his biggest decorating plan had been to paint all the walls white and be done with it. Both his mother and David had been all over him like white on rice for that one.

They'd been right, he had to admit it. He liked the silvery sage walls in his kitchen and the stone gray counters, the distressed wood of the cabinets. He supposed the color had inspired him to juice the place up a little with the pieces of old pottery or china sitting around, the herbs growing on the windowsill.

It was a nice space, even if he was just eating a sandwich over the sink. He liked standing here, looking out at his own little greenhouse, and the explosion of the summer gardens.

The hydrangeas were as big as soccerballs this year, he noted, and the infusion of iron he'd given them turned them a strong, unearthly blue. Maybe he'd cut a few, plunk them down somewhere in the house.

Butterflies were massing around the garden he and his mother had planted to lure them. A flurry of colorful wings flashed over the welcoming bloom of purple coneflower, the sunny coreopsis, fragrant verbena, and the reliable asters. Backing them was the elegant dance of daylilies.

Maybe he'd cut a few of those, too, and take them over to the house so Lily could have them in her room. She liked flowers, liked when he took her walking in the gardens so she could touch them.

And her eyes, blue like her mama's, got so big and serious when he recited the names. Just like she was taking it all in, filing it away.

Christ, who'd have thought he'd be so gone on a kid?

But it was so cool the way she'd march along with her little hand in his, then stop and reach up, that pretty face turned to his, that pretty face full of light because she knew he'd swing her up. Then the way she'd hook her arm around his neck, or pat his hair. It just killed him.

It was amazing to love, to be loved in that open, uncomplicated way.

He took a pull of the beer, then opened the freezer to look for the pizza. He heard the quick knock on the front door seconds before it opened.

"Hope I'm interrupting an orgy," David called out. He strolled in, cocked his head at Harper. "What, no dancing girls?"

"They just left."

"I see they ripped your clothes off first."

"You know how it is with dancing girls. Wanna beer?"

"Tempting, but no. I'm saving myself for an exceptional Grey Goose martini. Night off, heading into Memphis to meet some people. Why don't you cover up that manly chest and come along?"

"Too hot."

"I'm driving, got AC. Go on, put on some dancing shoes. We're going to check out some clubs."

Harper pointed his beer toward his friend. "Every time I check out some clubs with you, somebody hits on me. And they're not always female."

"You heartbreaker. I'll protect you, throw myself bodily on anyone who tries to pat your ass. What're you going to do, Harp, stew around here with a beer and Kraft's mac and cheese."

"Kraft's mac and cheese is the packaged dinner of champions. But I'm going with frozen pizza tonight. Besides, there's a game on."

"You *are* breaking my heart. Harper, we're young, we're hot. You're straight, I'm gay, which means we cover all available ground and double our chances of getting lucky. Between us we can cut a mighty swath down Beale Street. Don't you remember, Harp?" He took Harper by the shoulders, gave him a dramatic shake. "Don't you remember how once we ruled?"

He had to grin. "Those were the days."

"These are still the days."

"Don't you remember how once we puked our guts up in the gutter?"

"Sweet, sweet memories." David hitched himself up to sit on the counter, took Harper's beer for one sip. "Should I be worried about you?"

"No. Why?"

"When's the last time you had your pipes cleaned?"

"Jesus, David." He took a gulp of beer.

"Used to be a time when the nubiles were lined up three deep on the path to your door. Now the closest you come to a bang is nuking Kraft's in the mike."

It was too close to the truth for comfort. "I'm on sabbatical. I guess I got tired of it," he said with a shrug. "Besides, things have been pretty busy and intense around here for a while. The business with the Bride, especially finding out she was like my great-great-grandmother. Somebody screwed with her, messed her up. Careless, you know, callous, the way it's playing out. I don't want to be careless anymore."

"You never were." Soberly now, David boosted himself down. "How long have we been friends? Almost for fucking ever. I've never known you to be careless with anyone. If you're talking sex, you're the only person I know who stays friendly with a lover once the heat blows off. You're not careless with people, Harper. And just because Reginald was a bastard—most likely—doesn't mean you're doomed to be."

"No, I know. I'm not obsessing about it or anything. Just

sort of taking stock. Just chilling awhile until I figure out what I want for the next phase."

"You want company, I can take you up on that beer and whip up something considerably less revolting than frozen pizza."

"I like frozen pizza." He'd do it, Harper thought. He'd blow off his plans, just to hang, to be a pal. "Go, there's a martini with your name on it." He slapped a hand on David's shoulder to lead him to the front door. "Eat, drink, make Barry."

"Got my cell phone if you change your mind."

"Thanks." He opened the door, leaned on the jamb. "But while you're steaming along Beale, I'm going to be sitting in the cool, watching the Braves trounce the Mariners."

"Pitiful, son, just pitiful."

"And drinking beer in my underwear, which cannot be overstated." He broke off, felt the punch straight to the belly when Hayley and Lily came around a turn of the garden.

"Now that's a pretty sight."

"Yeah. They look good." The baby wore some sort of romper thing, pink and white stripes, with a little pink bow in her hair—dark hair, like her mother's. She looked sweet as a candy stick.

And Mama—tiny blue shorts, a yard of leg, bare feet. Some skinny little white top and wraparound shades. A different kind of candy altogether. Maybe it was sweet, but it was sure as hell hot.

He tipped up the beer to cool his throat, and Lily spotted them. She let out something between a yell and a squeals—all delight—and pulling away from Hayley made a beeline toward the carriage house as fast as her little legs could manage.

"Slow down, sweet potato." David moved forward to

scoop her up, give her a toss. She patted his face with both of her hands, gabbled at him, then reached for Harper.

"As always, I'm day-old paté when you're around."

"Hand her over," Harper hitched her onto his hip where she kicked her legs with joy and beamed at him. "Hey, pretty girl."

In response, she tilted her head to lay it on his shoulder.

"What a flirt," Hayley commented as she walked up. "Here we are having a nice walk, having a little girl-talk, she spots a couple of handsome men, and blows me off."

"Why don't you leave her with Harper, put on a party dress and drive on into Memphis with me?"

"Oh, I—"

"Sure." Harper kept his voice carefully neutral as he jiggled Lily. "She can hang with me. You can bring that Portacrib thing over and I'll put her down when she's tired."

"That's nice, I appreciate it. But it's been a long day. I don't think I'm up for a trip to Memphis."

"Fuds and duds, Lily." David leaned over to kiss her. "I'm surrounded by fuds and duds. I'm flying solo then, and I better get started. See y'all."

"I don't mind watching her if you want to get out awhile."

"No. I'm going to put her down pretty soon, then curl on up myself. Why aren't you going?"

"Too hot," he said, decided it was the easiest catchall excuse.

"Isn't it? And you're letting all the cool out. Come on, Lily."

But when she tried to take the baby, Lily squirmed away and clung to Harper like ivy to a tree. The sound she made was distinctly *da-da.*

The flush glowed on Hayley's cheeks even as she gave a weak laugh. "She doesn't mean anything. Those D sounds are the easiest to make, is all. Lots of things are da-da these days. Come on, Lily."

This time her arms circled Harper's neck like a noose, and she started to wail.

"You want to come in for a while?"

"No, no." She spoke quickly now, a tumble of words. "We were just taking a little walk, nearly done with it, and she has to have a bath before bedtime."

"I'll walk back with you." He turned his head, kissed Lily's cheek then whispered in her ear so she laughed and snuggled against him.

"She can't have everything she wants."

"She'll have to learn that soon enough." He reached behind him, and shut the door.

SHE MANAGED BATH AND BEDTIME, KEPT HERSELF distracted with Lily's needs until the baby was asleep.

She tried to read, she tried TV. Too restless for either, she plugged in a yoga tape she'd bought at the mall and gave it a spin. She went down for cookies. She put on music, then turned it off.

By midnight, she was still edgy and unsettled, so gave up and went out on the terrace to take in the warm night.

The lights were on in the carriage house. His bedroom light, she assumed. She'd never been up to the second floor, or what he called the loft. Where he slept. Where he was probably in bed right now, reading a book. Naked.

She should never have walked that way with Lily. All those directions to take, and she'd headed straight toward the carriage house. As besotted as her daughter.

God, she'd nearly melted at the knees when she'd come around that turn in the path and seen him.

Leaning against the doorjamb, wearing nothing but those ragged old cutoffs. Hard chest, golden tan, his hair all curly and damp. That lazy smile on his face as he'd taken a sip from a bottle of beer.

He'd looked so sexy—a freaking billboard for sexy, framed in that cottage doorway, surrounded by flowers, sultry in the heat. She'd been amazed she'd been able to get reasonable words out of her throat when she'd been tingling the whole time, inside and out, while they'd stood there.

And she had no business tingling around Harper. It really had to stop. Why couldn't it go back to the way it used to be? When she'd been pregnant, she'd felt comfortable around him. Even the first months after Lily's birth she'd been easy in his company. When had it started to change on her?

She didn't know, she couldn't pinpoint it. It just was.

And couldn't be. Lily wasn't the only one who couldn't have everything she wanted.

four

SHE FELT ODD AND OUT OF SORTS AT WORK. AS IF HER skin was too small, her head too heavy. Too much yoga for the novice, she decided. Too much work, not enough sleep. Maybe she should take a little vacation. She could get the time off, and she could afford a few days. She could drive back to Little Rock, visit some of her old friends and co-workers. Show Lily off.

But it would eke into the vacation fund she'd started to take Lily to DisneyWorld for her third birthday. Still, how much would it cost, really? A few hundred dollars, and the change of scene might do her good.

She swiped the back of her hand over her forehead. The air in the greenhouse felt too close, too thick. Her fingers as she tried to arrange dish gardens were too fat and clumsy. She didn't see why she got stuck with this job. Stella could've done it, or Ruby. Then she could work the counter—a monkey could work the counter this time of year, she thought irritably.

She should have had the day off. It wasn't as if they needed her. She should have been home, in the cool, relaxing for a damn change. But here she was, sweating and dirty, stuffing plants into bowls because Stella said so. Orders, orders, orders. When was she going to be able to do what she wanted, when she wanted?

They looked down on her because she didn't have the bloodline, she didn't have the education, she didn't have the fancy background that made them all so *important*. But she was just as good as they were. Better. She was better because she'd made her own way. She'd clawed her way up from nothing because—

"Hey, hey! You're breaking the roots on that ludisia."

"What?" She stared down at the plant, and her fingers went limp as Stella snatched it from them. "I'm sorry. Did I kill it? I don't know what I was thinking."

"It's okay. You looked upset. What's wrong?"

"Nothing. I don't know." She shook herself, and flushed with the shame of her own thoughts. "The heat's making me irritable, headachy, I guess. I'm sorry I haven't got these done. I can't seem to concentrate."

"It's okay. I came back to give you a hand anyway."

"I can do it. You don't have to take the time."

"Hayley, you know how I like to play in the dirt when I can. Here." She reached into the cooler under the workbench, took out two bottles of water. "Take five."

What had she been thinking before? she wondered as she took a long pull from the bottle. Nasty, petty thoughts. She didn't understand why her mind would have come up with such mean things. She didn't feel that way. But for a minute or two she had, and it made her feel ugly now.

"I don't know what's wrong with me, Stella."

Frowning, Stella laid her hand on Hayley's brow in the classic mother's gesture. "Maybe you're coming down with a summer cold."

"No, I think it's more the blahs. Not even the blues, just the blahs. They keep sneaking up on me, and I don't know why. I've got the most beautiful baby in the world. I love my job. I've got good friends."

"You can have all that, and still get the blahs." Stella took an apron off a hook, studying Hayley as she tied it on. "You haven't dated in more than a year."

"Closer to two." And that called for another long drink of water. "I've thought about it. I've been asked out a few times. You know Mrs. Bentley's son, Wyatt? He was in a few weeks ago, buying her a hanging basket for her birthday, and he was flirting pretty hard. Asked me if I'd like to have dinner sometime."

"He's pretty cute."

"Yeah, he's got that sexy jock thing going for him, and I thought about it, then I just didn't want to go to all the bother, and I edged back."

"I seem to remember you pushing me out the door when I talked about not wanting to go to all the bother when Logan first asked me out."

"I did, didn't I?" She smiled a little. "I've got such a big mouth."

Before Stella selected plants, she tightened the band that held her mass of curling red hair into a tail. "Maybe you're just a little nervous on the board? You know, taking that dive into the dating pool again."

"I've never been nervous about dating. It's one of my primary skills. I like going out. And I know if I wanted to, you or Roz, or David would take care of Lily." The knowledge brought on another stab of guilt for the resentful thoughts that had wormed into her mind. "I know she'd be fine, so that's no excuse. I just can't seem to get myself in gear."

"Maybe you just haven't met somebody who makes you want to oil the gears and get them moving again."

"I guess . . . maybe." She took another long drink, braced herself. "The thing is, Stella . . ."

When the silence dragged on, Stella glanced up from the pot she was building. "What's the thing?"

"First you gotta promise, *swear* that you won't tell anybody. Even Logan. You can't say anything."

"All right."

"You absolutely swear?"

"I'm not going to spit in my palm, Hayley. You'll have to take my word for it."

"Okay. Okay." She walked down the aisle between tables, then back again. "The thing is, I like Harper."

Stella nodded encouragement. "Sure. So do I."

"No!" Frustrated, mortified to hear herself say it out loud, Hayley set the water down and clamped her hands over her face. "God."

It took her a minute for the light to shine. "Oh," Stella said with her eyes going wide. "Oh. Oh," she repeated drawing out the syllable. Then she pursed her lips. "Oh."

"If that's the best you can do, I'm going to have to hit you."

"I'm trying to take it in. Absorb it."

"It's crazy. I know it's crazy." Hayley dropped her hands. "I know it's not right, it's not even on the table. But I . . . forget I said anything. Just highlight and hit delete."

"I didn't say it was crazy, it's just unexpected. As far as not being right, I don't follow you."

"He's Roz's son. Roz, the woman who took me in off the street."

"Oh, you mean when you were penniless, naked, and

suffering from some rare, debilitating disease? It was saintly of her to take you in, clothe you and spoon-feed you broth night after night."

"I'm allowed to exaggerate when I'm being a fool," Hayley snapped. "She did take me in, she gave me a job. She gave me and Lily a home, and here I am imagining how I can get naked and sweaty with her firstborn."

"If you're attracted to Harper—"

"I want to bite his ass. I want to pour honey all over his body then lick it off an inch at a time. I want to—"

"Okay, okay." Stella held out one hand, laid the other on her heart. "Please don't put any more of those images in my head. We'll just agree you've got the hots for him."

"Major hots. And I can't do anything about it because we're friends. Look how screwed up things got for Ross and Rachel. Of course Monica and Chandler's a different story, but—"

"Hayley."

"And I know this isn't a television show," she muttered over Stella's roll of laughter. "But you know how life imitates art? Besides, he doesn't think about me that way."

"The honey-licking way?"

Hayley's eyes went blurry. "Oh God, now I've got that image in my head."

"Serves you right. Anyway, are you sure he doesn't think of you that way?"

"He hasn't made a move, has he? It's not like there haven't been opportunities. And what if I made a move on him, and he was just, like, horrified or something?"

"What if he wasn't?"

"That could be even worse. We'd have ourselves some wild jungle sex, then after we'd both be . . ." She lifted her hands into the air, waved them wildly. "Oh God, what've I done, and all awkward with each other. And I'd have to take Lily and move to Georgia or somewhere. And Roz would never want to speak to me again."

"Hayley." Stella patted her on the shoulder. "This is just my impression, just my opinion, but I'm fairly sure Roz knows Harper has sex."

"You know what I mean. It's different when he's having sex with women she doesn't know."

"Oh yes, I'm sure she's perfectly delighted that her son has sex with strangers. Strangers to her, anyway," she added with a laugh. "And naturally she'd be appalled to learn that he might be intimate with a woman she knows and loves. Yes, that would be a real knife in the heart."

"It's a kind of betrayal."

"It's no kind of betrayal. He's a grown man, Hayley, and his choices in relationships are his own business. Roz would be the first to say so, and the first—without a doubt—to tell you she doesn't want to be one of the angles in this triangle you've formed."

"Well, maybe, but—"

"Maybe, maybe, but, but." Stella waved them all aside with such enthusiasm, Hayley had to duck and blink. "If you're interested in Harper, you should let him know. See what happens. Besides, I think he's had a crush on you from the get-go."

"He has not."

Stella shrugged. "Just my opinion, just my impression."

"Really?" The quick bump under her heart at the idea was painful and nice. "I don't know. I think if he has a crush on anybody, it's Lily. But I could think about maybe giving it a little push, see what happens."

"Positive thinking. Now, let's get these dish gardens done."

"Stella." Hayley poked a finger in the dirt. "You swear you won't say anything about this to Roz."

"Oh, for God's sake." Stella held out her palm and, mimicking the sacred rite she'd seen her sons perform, spat in it.

When offered the hand Stella held out, Hayley stared at it, and said: "Eeuuww."

IT MADE HER FEEL BETTER. HAVING SOMEBODY ELSE know what she was thinking and feeling took a weight off. Especially when that somebody else was Stella. Who hadn't been shocked, Hayley reminded herself. Surprised, sure, but not shocked, so that was good.

Just as it was good to take a couple of days and think about it. In fact, she was thinking about it, a little dreamily, when with Lily down for the night, she stretched out on the sitting room couch to unwind with some TV.

Idly, she channel surfed and decided how nice it was to have nothing to do for an hour. Still, reruns, repeats, and other summer dreck, she decided, wasn't what she wanted for a lazy hour of entertainment.

She flipped to an old black-and-white movie, something she didn't recognize. It seemed like some kind of romantic drama, where everyone wore gorgeous clothes and went dancing every night at elaborate clubs where they had orchestras and voluptuous girl singers.

Everybody drank highballs.

Why did they call them highballs? she wondered, yawning as she snuggled down. Because the glasses were tall, okay, but why were the glasses called balls? She should look it up sometime.

What would it be like to wear those incredible gowns and glide around a dance floor with everything all Art Deco and glittering? He'd be wearing a tuxedo, of course. She bet Harper looked awesome in a tux.

And what if they'd both come with someone else, but then they saw each other. Through all that silk and shine, their eyes met. And they just knew.

They'd dance, and everything else would wash away. That's the way it was in black-and-white. It didn't have to be complicated; whatever separated you could be vanquished or overcome. Then it all washed away except the two of you together as the end music swelled.

And when it did, you'd be in each other's arms, your face tipped up to his as your lips came together in that movie-perfect kiss. The kind you felt all the way down to the soles of your feet, the kind that meant you'd love each other forever.

Soft, soft kiss, so tender as his hand brushed over your hair, then deepening, heating just a bit when your arms locked around his neck. Up on your toes so your body leaned to his.

Line, angle, curve, all beautifully fitted.

Then after it faded to black, his hands moved over you, touching where it tingled and ached. Stroking over silk and skin so that your mouths met now with little gasps and moans.

The taste of that kiss was so potent, so powerful, the flavor of it streamed through your whole system, woke everything up, made everything swell.

And everywhere you'd felt cold and tired warmed again because you wanted, and were wanted.

Candles were flickering. Smoke and shadows. Flowers scented the room. Lilies, it had to be lilies. The flowers he'd brought her, bold and red and passionate. His eyes, deep brown, depthless brown, told her everything she wanted. That she was beautiful to him, and precious.

When they undressed each other, her gown melted away into a pool of glittery white against the black of his jacket.

Skin to skin, at last. Smooth and soft. Gold dust and milk. His shoulders under her hands, the length of his back, so she could feel those muscles tense as she aroused him.

The way he touched her, with such need, filled her with excitement so that when he gathered her up in his arms—oh—she was quivering for him. He laid her on the bed, the big white bed with sheets as soft as water, then sank into it with her.

His lips skimmed her throat, captured her breast so appetites quickened, and the tug, that long, liquid pull in her belly made her moan out his name.

Candlelight. Firelight. Flowers. Not lilies, but roses. His hands were smooth—a gentleman's hands. Rich hands. She stretched under them, arched, adding throaty purrs. Men liked their whores to make noise. She stroked her hand along the length of him. Ready, more than ready, she thought. But she'd tease him a bit longer. It was wives who lay passive, who let men do what they willed, to have done with it.

That's why they came to her, why they needed her. Why they paid.

She brought her shoulders off the mound of pillows, so her curling mane of golden hair spilled back. And she rolled with him, lush breasts and hips to entice, rolled him over on the bed to slither her way down, to nip and lick her way down his body to do what his cold-blooded, prim-mouthed wife would never do.

His grunts and gasps were her satisfaction.

His hands were in her hair now, gripping, twisting while she pleasured him. His body was trim, and she could gain some enjoyment from it, but had he been fat as a pig she'd have convinced him he was a god to her. It was so easy.

When she straddled him, looked down at his handsome face, saw the greedy desperation in his eyes, she smiled.

She took him into her, fast and hard and thought that nothing fit so well inside her as did a rich man's cock.

Hayley bolted up from the sofa as if she'd been shot out of a cannon. Her heart clanged, hammer to anvil, in her chest. Her breasts felt heavy as if, oh God, as if they'd been fondled. Her lips tingled. Panicked, she grabbed at her hair and nearly wept with relief when she felt her own.

Someone laughed, and had her stumbling back, rapping up against the couch and nearly spilling onto it again. The television, she saw as she crossed her arms protectively over her breasts. Just the television, sophisticated drama in black-and-white.

And oh, God, what had happened to her?

Not a dream, or not just a dream. It couldn't have been.

She dashed out of the room to check on Lily. Her baby slept, snuggled with her stuffed dog.

Ordering herself to calm, she went downstairs. But when she reached the library, she hesitated. Mitch sat at the library table, tapping away at the keyboard of his laptop. She didn't want to disturb him, but she had to check. She had to be sure. Waiting until morning just wasn't in the cards.

She stepped inside. "Mitch?"

"Hmm? What? Where?" He looked up, blinked behind his hornrims. "Hi."

"I'm sorry. You're working."

"Just some e-mail. Do you need something?"

"I just wanted to . . ." She wasn't shy, and she wasn't prudish, but she wasn't sure how to comfortably relate what she'd just experienced to her employer's husband. "Um, do you think Roz is busy?"

"Why don't I call up and see?"

"I don't want to bother her if . . . Yes, yes, I do. Could you ask her to come down?"

"All right." He reached for the phone to dial the bedroom extension. "Something happened."

"Yeah. Sort of. Maybe." To settle one point, she walked to the second level, behind the table and studied the pictures on Mitch's work board.

She stared at the copy of the photograph of a man in formal dress—strong features, dark hair, cool eyes.

"This is Reginald Harper, right? The first one."

"That's right. Roz, can you come down to the library. Hayley's here. She needs to talk to you. Right." He hung up. "She'll be right down. Do you want something—some water, some coffee?"

She shook her head. "No, thanks. I'm okay, just feeling a little weirded out. Ah, when Stella first came here, when she was living here, she had dreams. That's when it really started, right? I mean, before that there were . . . incidents. Sightings. But nothing much ever happened—at least not that Roz heard of—that was dangerous. Regarding The Bride, I mean."

"That seems to be the case. There's been a kind of escalation, which seemed to start when Stella moved in with her boys."

"And I came a few weeks after. So it was the three of us here, living in Harper House." Her skin still felt chilled. She rubbed her bare arms and wished for a sweatshirt. "I was pregnant, Stella had the boys, and Roz, well, Roz is bloodline."

He nodded. "Keep going."

"Stella had the dreams. Intense dreams, which we have to believe were somehow plugged into her subconscious by Amelia. That's not a very scientific way of putting it, but—"

"It's good enough."

"And when Stella and Logan—" She broke off as Roz came in. "I'm sorry I dragged you down here."

"It's all right. What happened?"

"Finish your thought out first," Mitch suggested. "Line it up."

"Okay, well, Stella and Logan got involved, and Amelia didn't like it. Stella's dreams got more disturbing, more pointed, and there were violent incidents, culminating in how she blocked us all out of the boys' room that night—that first night you came here, Mitch."

"I'll never forget it."

"She told us her name that night," Roz commented. "Stella got through to her, and she gave us her first name."

"Yeah. Wouldn't you say she's left Stella be pretty much since then? She'd have told us if she had dreams still, or if anything happened to her directly."

"The focus transferred to Roz," Mitch said.

"Yeah." Pleased they seemed to be traveling the same road, Hayley nodded. "And it was even more intense, right? Like waking dreams, Roz?"

"Yes, and an escalation of violent behavior."

"The closer you got to Mitch, the crazier she got. That's the kind of thing that pisses her off. She nearly killed you. She rode to the rescue, you could say, when you were in trouble, when push came to shove, but before that she attacked you. But since then, since you and Mitch got engaged, got married, she's backed off."

"Apparently, at least for the moment." Roz stepped over, ran a hand down Hayley's arm. "She's moving on you now, isn't she?"

"I think so. I think that the three of us being in the house—you and Stella and me—maybe that pushed her out of pattern." She looked toward Mitch, lifting her hands. "I don't know how to put it, exactly, but things really got rolling then, and the ball seems to pick up bulk and speed, if you get me."

"I do, and it's interesting. The three of you—three women at varying stages of life—all unattached at the point you came together. Your connection made a connection to her, we could say. And as Stella, then Roz became emotionally, romantically involved, it caused Amelia's behavior to deteriorate."

"Honey, did she hurt you?"

"No." Hayley pressed her lips together, then looked from Roz to Mitch. "I know we're supposed to, like, report anything, so Mitch has it on record. I just don't know how to say all this. At least not delicately. It's a little bit embarrassing."

"You want me to step out?" Mitch asked her. "So you can talk to Roz about it?"

"No, that's just dumb—of me, I mean. She'll just tell you anyway." To brace herself, Hayley blew out a long breath. "Okay, so I was taking an hour to relax, watch some TV upstairs in the sitting room. And there was this old movie on, and I was daydreaming, I guess. All those fabulous clothes, you know, and the beautiful lighting, and the fancy clubs where people went out to dance and all. I was imagining what it would be like, how I'd be all dressed up, and I'd see someone."

She trailed off a moment. She didn't have to say the someone was Harper. That didn't have to be relevant.

"Anyway, we'd dance, and fall in love, and have that big movie kiss? You know what I mean."

Roz smiled. "Absolutely."

"Well, then I guess I was drifting off some, and I was thinking about what happens after The End? Thinking about sex, I guess," she said and cleared her throat. "Just a fantasy thing, candlelight and flowers and a big white bed, being in love. Making love." She lowered her head, put it in her hands. "This is mortifying."

"Don't be silly. Healthy girl like you didn't think about

sex, I'd be worried." Roz gave her shoulder a little shake.

"It was nice. Romantic and exciting. Then, it changed. Or I changed. And it was calculating. I was thinking about how I'd do these things. I could feel, the skin and the form and the heat. There were roses. I could smell roses, but I had lilies in the fantasy, and now there were roses, and fire-light. And his hands were different—soft and smooth. Rich, that's what I thought. And I thought the guy's wife wouldn't do what I'd do, and that's why he came to me. How he'd pay. And I felt my hair, and I could see it. Long and blond and curly. I saw it when it fell over my face, not like I was watching, but like I was there. It *was* me. And I saw him. His face."

She turned to the board and pointed at Reginald. "His face. He was inside me, and I saw his face."

She let out another long breath. "So."

After a moment of silence, Roz spoke. "I don't think it would be that unusual for your mind to weave that sort of thing together, Hayley. We all spend a lot of time thinking about these people, trying to put it all together. We know she was his mistress, we know she bore him a child, so we know they had sex. And for her, we can assume or at least speculate that it was, at least in part, a kind of business arrangement."

"You know how your body feels when you've been fooling around? Physically. Not just the buzz you get from a sex dream, but how you feel physically when you've been with a guy. Maybe I haven't been with one since before Lily was born, but you don't forget how it feels. And that's where I was when I woke up, or came out of it. Roz, I smelled those roses. I know how his body was shaped."

She had to take a breath, had to swallow hard. "I felt him inside me. Inside her, I guess, but it was like being her while it was happening. She liked being with someone handsome and skilled. It wouldn't have mattered if he'd been ugly as homemade sin and a dud in bed, but this was like a bonus. Rich was the bottom line—the rest was icing. I know that, because I was right inside her head. Or she was in mine. I didn't imagine it."

"I believe you," Mitch told her.

"We believe you," Roz corrected. "You're the closest to her age when she died, at least the age we think she was. Maybe she's relating to that, to you, and trying to go through you to tell us what it was like for her."

"Possibly." Mitch tipped back in the chair when Roz arched her brows at him. "It could give us more insight on her, on what happened and why. What else can you tell us about her?"

"Well, I don't think she got that much of a rush out of sex—from the power, the control, yeah, but not the rest of it. It's just what she did, and from his, um, response, she was good at what she did. Her body was a lot better than mine."

With a sheepish smile, she held her hands in front of her breasts to mime someone well-endowed. "And she was cold inside. The whole time they were doing it, she was thinking about what she'd get out of him. There was a derision—that's the best way to describe it—for the wives of men like him. I guess that's about it."

"Hardly her best side. Or maybe it is, from her point of view," Mitch considered. "She was in charge, doing what she'd chosen to do. Young, beautiful, desired by a powerful man and controlling that man through sex. Interesting."

"Creepy's what it was. And if I get to have sex, I'd like to have it with my own body. But anyway, I feel better, getting all that out. I think I'll go back up, maybe do some yoga. I don't think she's going to bother me while I'm trying to twist myself into the warrior position or whatever. Thanks for hearing me out."

"Anything else happens, I want to hear it," Roz told her.

"That's a promise."

Roz waited until Hayley was gone, then turned to Mitch. "We're going to have to worry about her, aren't we?"

"Let's not skip straight to worry." He took her hand. "Let's start with we'll keep an eye out for her."

five

From Stella's kitchen window, Hayley could see the spread of the back gardens, the patio, the arbor, the treehouse Logan and the boys had built snugged into the branches of a sycamore.

She watched Logan push Lily on a red swing that hung from another branch while the boys tossed an old ball for Parker to chase.

It was, she thought, a kind of moving portrait of summer evening. The sort of lazy contentment that only comes on breathless summer days right before the kids are called in for supper and the porch light goes on. Yellow glows to chase the moths away and to shine a circle that says: We're home.

She remembered, so clearly, what it was to be a child in August, to love the heat, to rush through it to snatch every drop of the sun before it went down.

Now, she hoped, she was learning what it was to be a mother. To be on the other side of the screen door. To be the one who turned on the porch light.

"Do you get used to it, or do you still look out sometimes like this, and think 'I'm the luckiest woman in the world.' "

Stella moved over to the window, smiled. "Both. You want to sit out on the patio with this lemonade?"

"In a minute. I didn't want to talk about this at work. Not just because it's at work, but because it's still on the Harper estate. And she's on the estate. She can't come here."

"Roz told me what happened." Stella laid a hand on Hayley's shoulder.

"I didn't tell her that it was Harper. I mean when I was fantasizing, I was with Harper. I'm just not going to tell her I was fantasizing about getting naked with her son."

"I think that's a judicious edit at this point. Has anything happened since?"

"No, nothing. And I don't know whether to hope something does or something doesn't." She watched Logan field the mangled slobbery ball that rolled his way, then toss it, sending dog and boys on a mad chase while Lily bounced in the swing and clapped her hands.

"I can tell you this, if I have to star in someone's life and times, I'd rather take a turn in yours."

"I believe in being a good and true friend, Hayley, but I'm not letting you have sex with Logan."

Hayley snorted out a laugh, then gave Stella an elbow nudge. "Spoilsport, and though I wasn't going there, I bet—wow."

Stella's smile was lazy as a cat's. "You bet right."

"Anyway. I was just thinking how it would be to have someone as crazy about me as Logan is about you. Toss in a couple of great kids, a beautiful home you've made together, and who needs fantasies?"

"You'll have what you're looking for one day, too."

"Listen to me, you'd think I was the redheaded stepchild. I don't know what's wrong with me lately." She rolled her shoulders as if shrugging off a weight. "I keep catching myself doing a poor-me routine. It's not like me, Stella. I'm happy. And even when I'm not, I look for a way to make myself happy. I don't brood and bitch. Or hardly."

"No, you don't."

"Maybe I've got a thing for Harper, but a little frustration's not enough to bring me down. Next time you hear me feeling sorry for myself, give me a good smack."

"Sure. What are friends for?"

SHE MEANT IT, TOO. SHE WASN'T THE TYPE TO SIT around ticking off the negatives of her life to see if she could make them outweigh the positives. If something was wrong, something was missing, she acted. Fix the problem and move ahead. Or if the problem couldn't be fixed, she found the best way to live with it.

When her mother had left, she'd been sad and scared and hurt. But there'd been nothing she could do to bring her back. So she'd done without—and done pretty damn well, Hayley thought as she drove back to Harper House.

She'd learned how to help make a home, and she and her father had had a good life. They'd been happy; she'd been loved. And she'd been useful.

She'd done well in school. She'd gotten a job to help with expenses. She knew how to work, and how to enjoy the work. She liked to learn, and to sell people things that made them happy.

If she'd stayed in Little Rock, at the bookstore, she'd have made manager. She'd have earned it.

Then her father had died. That had blasted a hole in the foundation of her life, and had shaken her like nothing before or since. He'd been her rock, as she'd been his. Nothing had felt steady or sure when he'd died, and her grief had been a constant raw ache.

So she'd turned to a friend—that's all he'd been really, she admitted as she turned down the drive to Harper House. A nice boy, a comfort.

Lily had come from that, and she wasn't ashamed of it. Maybe comfort wasn't love, but it was a positive act, a giving one. How could she have paid that kindness back by pushing the boy into marriage, or responsibility when he'd already moved on by the time she'd realized she was pregnant?

She hadn't wallowed—or hardly. She hadn't cursed God or man, for long. She'd accepted responsibility for her own actions, as she'd been taught, and had made the choice that was right for her.

To keep the child, and raise the child on her own.

Hadn't worked out quite that way, though, she thought with a smile as she parked. Little Rock, the bookstore, the house she'd shared with her father had no longer been her comfort zones once she'd started to show. Once the looks and the questions and the murmurs had begun.

So, fresh start.

She climbed out of the car, rounded it to open the back door and unhook Lily from her car seat.

Sell everything that could be sold, pack up the rest. Positive, move forward. All she'd expected by coming here to Roz was the possibility of a job. What she'd been given was family.

Just more proof, to her mind, that good things happened

when you took steps, when you worked for them—and when you were lucky enough to find people who'd give you a chance to do your best.

"That's what we are, Lily." She hoisted Lily up, covered her face with kisses. "We're a couple of lucky girls."

She swung the diaper bag over her shoulder, bumped the car door shut with her hip. But as she started toward the house an idea bloomed.

Maybe it was time to try her luck again.

Sit around waiting for things to happen and nothing much did. But act, you either failed or succeeded. Either was better than standing still.

She strolled around the house, taking her time, just to see if she could talk herself out of it. But the idea was planted now, and she couldn't find a good enough reason to uproot it.

Maybe he'd be shocked or stunned or even appalled. Well, that would be his problem. At least she'd know *something* and stop wondering all the damn time.

As she rounded the curve in the path, she set Lily down, and let her little girl trot toward Harper's front door.

Maybe he wasn't home, out with some woman. Or worse, had some woman in *his* home. Okay, that would be bad, but she'd deal with it.

It was time she dealt with it.

Though the dark wasn't deep yet, the path lights were glowing, those pretty soft green lanterns speared at the edges of the brick to guide the way. A few early lightning bugs blinked on and off, on and off over the heads of flowers, and out beyond to the roll of grass to lose themselves in the shadows of the woods.

She drew in the perfume of heliotrope, sweet peas, roses, and the more pungent aroma of earth. All of those scents, along with the different tones of growing green would forever make her think of Harper, and this place.

She caught up with Lily, knocked. On impulse she stepped back and to the side, leaving her little girl clapping her hands at Harper's front door. Where the porch light was on, a glowing circle of yellow.

When the door opened, she heard Lily give her greeting—something between hi and hey and a cry of pleasure.

"Look what I found at my front door."

From her vantage point, Hayley could see Lily's arms go up; and Harper's come down. When he scooped her up, Lily was already babbling in her excited and incomprehensible language.

"Is that right? Just thought you'd drop by to say hi? Maybe you ought to come in and have a cookie, but we'd better find your mama first."

"She's right here." Laughing, Hayley stepped over to the door. "Sorry, but it was so cute. You know she can't walk by your place without wanting to see you, so I thought I'd knock and let her stand there on her own."

She reached out, but as usual when Harper was involved, Lily shook her head and wrapped herself around her favorite man.

"I mentioned the C word. Why don't you come in and I'll dig one out for her."

"You're not busy?"

"No. Was just thinking about getting a beer and doing some paperwork. Just as soon postpone the paperwork part of it."

"I always like coming in here." She glanced around the living room as he carried Lily back toward the kitchen. "You're pretty tidy, too, for a single straight guy."

"Comes from living with Mama, I guess." With Lily on his hip, he reached in a cupboard and got out the box of animal crackers he kept on hand for her. "Now how'd these get here?"

He opened the box, let her dig one out. "Want a beer?"

"I wouldn't mind. I stopped off at Stella's after work. Ended up having burgers on the grill, but I passed on the wine. I don't like sipping when I'm driving, even just a little when I've got Lily in the car."

He offered her a beer, got one for himself. "How you doing?" When she only angled her head, he shrugged. "Word spreads. I heard about what happened. In any case, it's something we're all involved in, so word should spread."

"It's a little embarrassing to have word of my sex dreams spreading."

"It wasn't like that. Besides, nothing wrong with a good sex dream."

"I'd as soon the next one I have be all my own idea." She tipped back the beer, watching him. "You look a little like him, you know."

"Sorry?"

"Reginald, especially now that I've seen him in what you could call a more intimate situation. Something more personal than an old photograph. You've got the same coloring, and the same shape to your face—your mouth. His build's not as good as yours."

"Oh. Well." He lifted his beer, drank deep.

"He was slim, but soft. Like his hands. And he was older than you, a little gray in the hair. And some hard lines coming in around the mouth, out from the eyes. But still, very handsome, very virile."

She got Lily's sip-cup of juice and her music cube out of the diaper bag. Bribing her, she lifted her away from Harper and set her on the floor.

"You got better shoulders, and no pudge right here." She poked her finger into his belly.

"Okay."

Lily sat down with her music cube, playing with it so it switched from "This Old Man" to "Bingo."

"I noticed all that," Hayley said, "seeing as we were all naked and sweaty."

"I bet."

"I especially noticed the resemblance—the similarities and the differences because when I started out fantasizing—my own part of it—it was with you."

"It was . . . what?"

Okay, a little shocked, but more confused, she decided, and moved in. "It started with you, something like this."

She slid a hand around to the back of his neck, rose up on her toes. She stopped, her lips a whisper from his, to savor that instant when the breath catches and the heart stumbles. Then she closed the distance.

Soft, as she'd imagined it would be soft. And warm. His hair was a silky weight on the back of her hand, and his body such a pleasure to press against.

He'd gone so still, but for his heart that slammed against hers. Then she felt his hand on her back, the fist he made as he gathered her shirt in his fingers.

On the floor, Lily's music cube was a jubilant crash of sound.

She made herself ease back. One step at a time, she reminded herself. Though her belly was quivering, she did her best to take a casual sip of beer while he stared at her with those dark eyes.

"So, what do you think?"

He lifted a hand, then dropped it again. "I appear to have lost the capability for rational thought."

"When you get it back, you'll have to let me know."

She turned to gather the baby's things.

"Hayley." He reached out, grabbed her by the waistband of her jeans and tugged. "Uh-uh."

Her belly jumped, joyfully. She glanced over her shoulder. "Which means?"

"The short way of saying you don't walk in here, kiss me like that, then walk out again. Question. Was that a demonstration to catch me up with what's happening with Amelia, or was it something else?"

"I've been wondering what it would be like, so I decided to find out."

"Okay." He turned her around, glanced down to be sure Lily was still occupied, then backed her into the counter.

His hands were at her hips when his mouth met hers. As his tongue dipped in, an intimate taste, those hands slid up, cruising over her, setting off little charges under her skin.

Then he stepped back, rubbed a thumb over her tingling lips. "I've been wondering what it would be like, too. So I guess we both know."

"Looks like," she managed.

Since Lily came over to tug at his pants, Harper boosted her up on his hip. "I guess it's complicated."

"Yeah, it is. Very. We'll need to take it slow, think it all the way through."

"Sure. Or we can say screw that and I can come to your room later tonight."

"I . . . I want to say yes. I'm thinking yes," she said on a rush. "Yes is screaming inside my head and I don't know why yes isn't coming out of my mouth. It's exactly what I want."

"But." He nodded. "It's okay. We should give it a little time. Be sure."

"Be sure," she repeated, and hurried to pick up Lily's things. "I need to go, or I'll forget about a little time and being sure, because, *man,* you sure can kiss. And I need to get Lily ready for bed. I don't want to mess things up, Harper. I so don't want to mess things up."

"We won't."

"We can't." She took Lily, though the baby cried pitifully at being pried away from Harper. "I'll see you at work."

"Sure, but I can walk you back."

"No." She hurried toward the door with Lily struggling and crying in her arms. "She'll be okay."

The crying escalated into a full-blown temper tantrum with kicking legs, stiffly arched back and ear-piercing shrieks. "For God's sake, Lily, you'll see him again tomorrow. It's not like he's going off to war."

The diaper bag slipped off her shoulder to weigh like an anchor on her arm while her sweet baby morphed into a red-faced demon from hell. Tiny, hard-toed walking shoes punched bruises into her hip, her belly, her thighs as she struggled to cart twenty pounds of fury through the dragging summer heat.

"I'd like to've stayed, too, you know." Frustration sharpened her voice. "But we can't, that's just the way it is, so you're going to have to deal."

Sweat dripped into her eyes, blurred her vision so that for a moment, the grand old house seemed to be floating like a mirage. An illusion she'd never reach.

It would just keep swimming farther away, because it wasn't real. Not for her. She'd never really belong there. It would be better, smarter, easier if she packed up, moved on. The house and Harper were one in the same—things that could never be hers. As long as she stayed here, *she* was the illusion.

"Well, what's all this?"

She saw Roz through the shimmer of heat, the daze of

twilight, and felt her own body sway as everything snapped back into focus. A sly tongue of nausea curled in her stomach. Then Lily, tears streaming, all but launched herself out of her arms and into Roz's.

"She's mad at me," Hayley said weakly, and tears stung her own eyes as Lily wrapped her arms around Roz's neck and wept into her shoulder.

"Won't be the last time." Roz rubbed Lily's back, going into that instinctive side-to-side rocking motion as she studied Hayley's face. "What set her off?"

"She saw Harper. She wanted to stay with him."

"It's hard leaving your best guy."

"She needs a bath and bed. Should've had them already. I'm sorry we bothered you. I guess they could hear her screaming clear down to Memphis."

"You didn't bother me. She's not the first baby I've heard in a temper, and she won't be the last."

"I'll take her up."

"I got her." Roz turned to take the steps up to the second floor. "You frazzled each other out. That's what happens when babies want one thing and their mama knows they need something different. Then you end up feeling guilty because they act like it's the end of their world, and you're the one who pulled the rug out."

A tear spilled over, and Hayley rubbed it away. "I hate letting her down."

"And how did you let her down by doing what's best for her? This baby's tired," Roz said as she opened the door to the nursery, turned on the lamp. "And sweaty. She needs her bath, a nightie, and a little quiet time. Go on, get her bath started. I'll get her clothes off."

"That's all right, I can—"

"Honey, you've got to learn to share."

Since Roz was already carrying a now calm Lily away,

Hayley moved into the bathroom. She ran the water, adding the bubbles Lily liked to splash in, the rubber duck and frogs. And caught herself swallowing back tears a half dozen times.

"I got myself a naked baby," she heard Roz say. "Yes, I do. And look at that belly, just calling out to be tickled."

Lily's laughter had Hayley sniffling back more tears as Roz stepped in.

"Why don't you go have yourself a shower? You're hot and you're blue. Lily and I'll have some fun in the tub."

"I don't want you to have to do all this."

"You've been around long enough to know I don't offer to do something if I don't want to do it. Go on. Clean up, cool down."

"All right." Since she feared she'd burst into tears at any moment, she fled.

SHE WAS CLEANER, AND SHE WAS COOLER, IF NOT A great deal steadier when she came back to find Roz putting a little cotton nightgown on a sleepy Lily.

The nursery smelled like powder and sweet soap, and her baby was calm.

"And here's your mama come to give you good night kisses." She lifted Lily, and the baby stretched out her arms to Hayley. "Come on over to the sitting room when you're done putting her down."

"Okay." She held Lily close, breathing in her hair, her skin. "Thanks, Roz."

She stood where she was, holding her little girl, letting the embrace center her. "Mama's sorry, baby. I'd give you the world if I could. The whole wide world and a silver box to put it in."

There were kisses, and quiet murmurs as she laid Lily

down in the crib with her little dog to cuddle. Leaving a low light burning, she slipped out of the room and down the hall to the sitting room.

"I got us some bottled water out of your stash." Roz held one out. "That do for you?"

"Perfect. Oh, Roz, I feel so stupid. I don't know what I'd do without you."

"You'd do fine. Better with me, but then everybody does." Roz sat, stretched out her legs. Her feet were bare tonight, and her toes painted a gumdrop pink. "You keep beating yourself up because your child had herself a tantrum, you're going to be permanently black and blue before you're thirty."

"I knew she was tired. I should've brought her straight into the house instead of letting her visit Harper."

"And I bet she enjoyed the visit as much as he did. Now she's sleeping peaceful in her crib, and no harm done."

"I'm not a terrible mother, am I?"

"You're certainly not anything of the sort. That baby is happy and healthy and loved. She has a sweet disposition. She also knows what she wants when she wants it, and that's a sign of character in my opinion. She's got a right to a temper, hasn't she, same as anybody else?"

"Boy, she's sure got one. I don't know what's wrong with me, Roz." Hayley set the bottle down without drinking. "I'm emotional and bitchy one minute, on top of the world the next. You'd think I was pregnant again, except there's no possibility of that unless the Second Coming's scheduled some time soon."

"That might be your answer right there. You're young and healthy. You've got needs, and they're not being met. Sex is important."

"Maybe, but it's not easily, or safely come by for somebody in my situation."

"I know what that's like, too. You know if you're interested in dating again, you have all manner of willing baby-sitters."

"I know."

"Actually, Hayley, I think sex might be one of the keys to Amelia."

"I'm sorry, Roz, I'd do most anything to help, but I have to draw the line at having sex with Amelia. Ghost, female, psycho. That's a full three strikes."

"There's our girl," Roz said with a laugh. "Mitch and I were talking about what happened to you the other evening, sort of expanding on our theories. Sex is what Amelia used to get what she wanted in life. It was her commodity. In any case, that's our conclusion: She was Reginald's mistress. And it was how, obviously, she conceived a child."

"Well, maybe she loved him. Amelia. It's possible she was seduced by him, in love with him. We really only have Beatrice's viewpoint of her from the journals, and she wouldn't be an objective source."

"Good point, and yes, possible." Roz took a thoughtful sip of water. "But that still points to sex. Even if she was in love and being used, it came down to sex. Reginald went to her for his pleasure, and his purposes. To conceive a male heir. It's not far-fetched to assume Amelia's view of sex is far from healthy."

"Okay."

"Then we come into it, the three of us, living together in this house. Stella hears her, sees her—not that unusual as there were children involved. But there's Logan, and not just an emotional spark between them, but a sexual one. And the episodes begin to escalate. We move to me and Mitch, another sexual contact, and more escalation. Now you."

"I'm not having sex." Yet, she thought. Oh boy.

"You're thinking about it. You're considering it. As Stella was. As I was."

"So . . . you think her focus is on me, the sexual energy kind of thing being the magnet. And things will escalate again."

"I think that may be, and particularly if that sexual energy becomes tied together with genuine affection. With love."

"If I got involved with someone, emotionally, sexually, she could hurt them. Or Lily. She could—"

"Now wait." Roz laid a hand over Hayley's. "She's never hurt a child. Never in all these years. There's absolutely no reason to think she might cause Lily any harm. But you're another matter."

"She could hurt me, or try. I get that." Hayley let out a shaky breath. "So I have to make sure she doesn't. She could hurt someone else, too. You or Mitch, David, any of us. And if there was someone I cared about, someone I wanted, he'd be the most likely target, wouldn't he?"

"Maybe. But I know you can't live your life on maybes. You have a right to your life. Hayley, I don't want you to feel obligated to stay here, or to keep working at In the Garden."

"You want me to leave?"

"I don't." Roz's hand gripped tighter. "On a purely selfish level, I want you here. You're the daughter I never had, that's the God's truth. And that child in the other room is one of the brightest lights of my life. It's because of what you mean to me I'm telling you to go."

Hayley took a deep breath as she rose, first to cross to the window. To look out over the summer gardens, so bold and bright in the hazy dark. And beyond them, to the carriage house, with the porch light glowing.

"My mama left us. Daddy and I weren't enough to keep her. She didn't love us enough. When he died, I didn't even know where to write and tell her. She'll never see her granddaughter. That's a shame for her, I think. But not for Lily. Lily has you. I've got you. I'll go if you tell me to. I'll get another place, get another job. And I'll stay away from Harper House for as long as it takes. But you need to tell me something first, and I know you'll tell me the truth because that's what you do."

"All right."

She turned back, met Roz's eyes. "If you were standing here where I am, having to decide whether to leave people you love—especially when you might be able to help—to leave a place you love, work you love. And you had to decide that because maybe something might happen. Maybe you might have trouble, have to face something hard along the way. What would you do, Roz?"

Roz got to her feet. "I guess you're staying."

"I guess I am."

"David made peach pie."

"Oh my God."

Roz held out a hand. "Let's go have a big sinful slice, and I'll tell you about the flower shop I'm thinking of adding on next year."

IN THE CARRIAGE HOUSE, HARPER RAIDED HIS STASH of leftovers. And thought of Hayley while he ate some of David's fried chicken.

She'd gone and changed the playing field, and he wasn't quite sure what to do with the ball. He'd spent the last year and a half suppressing his feelings and urges when it came to Hayley, and assuming—from her attitude, from every damn signal—that she considered him a friend. Even, God help him, a kind of surrogate brother.

He'd done his best to fill that role.

Now she'd come waltzing in, and put the moves on him. Kissed the brains right out of his head, to the tune of—what the hell was it?—"Bingo."

He was never going to be able to hear that ridiculous song again without getting hot.

What the hell was he supposed to do now, ask her out? He was good at asking women out. It was normal, but there was nothing normal about all of this, not when he'd convinced himself she wasn't interested that way. That he shouldn't be.

Add that they worked together. That she lived in the main house with his mother, for God's sake. Then there was Lily to consider. It sliced him in two, the way she'd cried for him when Hayley had taken her home. What if he and Hayley got together, and something went wrong? Would it spill over onto Lily?

He'd have to make certain it didn't, that's all. He'd have to be careful, take it slow and easy.

Which crossed out any idea brewing in the back of his mind about going over to Hayley's room after dark and letting nature take its course.

He cleaned up the kitchen, as was his habit, then went up to the loft that held his bedroom, a bath, and a small room he used as an office. He spent an hour on paperwork, ordering his mind back to the business at hand every time it drifted toward Hayley.

He switched on ESPN, picked up a book, and indulged in one of his favorite solo evening activities. Reading between innings. Somewhere in the eighth, with Boston down two and the Yankees with a runner on second, he drifted off.

He dreamed that he and Hayley were making love in Fenway Park, rolling naked over the infield grass while the game played on around them. Somehow he knew the batter had a count of three and two, even as Hayley locked those long legs around him, as he sank into her. Into that heat, into those soft blue eyes.

The crash woke him, and his dreaming mind heard the joyful crack of ball on bat. He thought home run even as he sat up, shaking his head to toss off sleep.

Jesus! He rubbed his hands over his face. Weird, very weird, even if it did combine two of his favorite activities. Sports and sex. Amused at himself, he started to toss the book aside.

Thc crash from downstairs was like a bullet shot, and no dream.

He was on his feet in a fingersnap, and grabbing the Louisville Slugger he'd had since his twelfth birthday as he rushed out of the room.

His first thought was that Bryce Clerk, his mother's ex-husband, had gotten out of jail and was back to cause more trouble. He'd be sorry for it, Harper thought grimly as he gripped the bat. His blood was up as he charged toward the fury of crashing and banging.

He slapped on the lights in time to see a plate come winging toward him. Instinct had him swinging for the fences. The plate shattered, shooting out shards.

Then there was utter silence.

The room he'd washed up before going upstairs looked as though it had been set upon by a particularly destructive gang of vandals. Broken dishes littered the floor along with spilled beer and the jagged remains of the bottles it had come from. His refrigerator door hung open, with all the contents pulled out. His counters and walls were covered with what looked like a nasty mix of ketchup and mustard.

There was no one there but himself. And he could see his own breath in the chill that had yet to fade out of the air.

"Son of a bitch." He scooped a hand through his hair. "Son of a goddamn bitch."

She'd used ketchup—at least he hoped it was that benign condiment rather than the blood it resembled—to write her message on the wall.

I will not rest

He studied the mess. "You're not the only one."

SIX

MITCH ADJUSTED HIS GLASSES AND LOOKED MORE closely at the photographs. Harper had been thorough, he thought, getting pictures from every angle, taking close-ups and wide angles.

The boy had a steady hand and a cool head.

But . . .

"You should've called us when this happened."

"It was one in the morning. What was the point? This is what it looked like."

"What it looks like is you pissed her off. Any ideas?"

"No."

Mitch spread the photos out, adjusting their order, while David looked over his shoulder. "You clean that shit up?" David asked Harper.

"Yeah." Temper seemed to vibrate off the blades of his tensed shoulders. "She got every damn dish in the place."

"No great loss there. They were ugly anyway. What are those?" David snatched one of the pictures up. "Twinkies? What are you, twelve? Harper." His face a picture of pity, David shook his head. "I worry about you."

"I happen to like Twinkies."

Mitch held up a hand. "Snack choices aside—"

"Twinkies are bombs of sugar and fat and preservatives." Interrupting Mitch, David tried for a pinch at Harper's waist.

"Cut it out." But the move, as designed, pushed a little humor through the wall of Harper's temper.

"Girls," Mitch said mildly. "To get back to the matter at hand. This is another change of pattern. She's never, to your knowledge, come into the carriage house, or caused you any particular trouble." He looked to Harper for confirmation.

"No." A glance at the photos he'd taken brought back the shock, the fury, and the *time* it had taken to deal with the destruction. "And this is a hell of a debut."

"Your mother's going to have to know about this."

"Yeah, yeah." Still steaming, Harper paced to the back door, scowled out at the morning haze. He'd waited, deliberately, until he'd seen his mother head out for her morning run. "I value my life, don't I? But I wanted us to go over this first, before we bring her into it." He glanced up at the ceiling, where he imagined Hayley was getting started on the day. "Or any of them."

"Strategizing to protect the womenfolk?" David said in an exaggerated drawl. "Not that I don't agree, son, but Roz isn't going to care for that." He jerked a thumb toward the ceiling. "She won't either."

"I don't want them going postal over it, that's all. If we could downplay it some. It was just dishes and kitchen crap."

"A personal attack, Harper, not on you but on your property, in your home. That's how it is, and that's how they'll see it." Mitch waved a hand at him before he could speak. "We've dealt with worse, all of us, and we'll deal with this. The important thing is to figure out why it happened."

"Maybe it's because she's crazy," Harper snapped back. "That might be a small, contributing factor."

"Takes after his mama when he's riled up," David offered. "Mean and stubborn."

"I've noticed. She's been seen walking in the direction of the carriage house in the past." Mitch leaned a hip on the table. "You saw her yourselves when you were kids. We can assume she did, at some point in her life, go there. We can assume it was after Reginald Harper brought their love child here to pass him off as his legitimate heir."

"And we can assume she was crazy as a crack monkey," David added. "From the way she looked."

"Yet, from what we know she's never bothered with the place since Harper's lived there. How long?"

"Shit, I don't know." He shrugged, drummed his fingers on the thighs of his ragged work pants. "Since college. Six, seven years."

"But she goes in now, destructively. She may be crazy, but there's a reason. Everything she's done has a root and a reason. Have you brought anything in there recently? Anything new?"

"Ah, no." But the idea made him pause and consider instead of stew. "Plants. I rotate plants, but I've done that for years. And the usual stuff, you know, groceries, CDs, clothes. Nothing particular or unusual."

"Anyone?"

"Sorry?"

"Have you had anyone over who hasn't been there before? A woman?"

"No."

"Now that's just sad." David swung an arm around Harper's shoulders. "Losing your touch?"

"My touch is still gold. Just been a little busy."

"And before it happened, you were?"

"Watching the game upstairs in the bedroom, reading. Zonked out, and the next I know it's crash, boom, bang."

He heard Lily's happy call and winced. "Damn it, here they come. Mitch, let's put those away, put this all away until—"

He broke off, cursing himself for not moving faster, when Lily ran in just ahead of Hayley. She zipped straight for him, all grins and upstretched arms.

"She heard your voice," Hayley said as he picked Lily up. "Her face just lit."

"His touch is gold," David said dryly, "with toddlers."

"It's sure her favorite way to start the morning." She went to the refrigerator for juice, and when she turned with the bottle and Lily's cup in her hands, spotted the photographs. "What's all this?"

"It's nothing. Just a little late-night adventure."

"Good God, what a mess! You have a party and not invite us?" Then she blinked, and paled as she leaned closer. "Oh. Oh, Amelia. Are you all right? Are you hurt?" She dropped Lily's cup as she swung toward him. "Harper, did she hurt you?"

"No. No." He patted the hand she was running over his face, his arm. "It's just dishes."

David bent to retrieve the plastic cup, wiggled his eyebrows at Mitch on the way up, and said, "Aha," under his breath.

"But look at your things." She snatched up a photo. "Your sweet little kitchen. What is *wrong* with her? Why does she have to be so damn mean?"

"Being dead probably ticks her off some. I think Lily wants her juice."

"All right, all right. If it's not one thing it's six others with her—Amelia, not Lily. I'm getting fed up." She poured the juice, secured the lid, then handed it to Lily. "There you are, baby. Just what are we going to do about this?" she demanded as she rounded on Mitch.

"Innocent bystander," he reminded her and held up his hands.

"We all are, aren't we? But that doesn't mean a damn to her, apparently. Bitch." She sat down, folded her arms.

"Feel better?" David asked her, and poured her some coffee.

"I don't know what I feel."

"Just dishes." Harper settled Lily in her highchair. "And according to David, ugly ones."

Hayley worked up a smile. "They weren't too ugly. I'm sorry, Harper." She touched his hand. "I'm so sorry."

"Sorry about what?" Roz asked as she came in.

"There's the bell for round two." David gestured with the coffeepot. "I think I'll make crepes."

SHE COULDN'T CONCENTRATE. HAYLEY WENT THROUGH the routine of waiting on customers, ringing up sales on automatic. When she didn't think she could stand making inane chat with another living soul, she went into Stella's office to throw herself on her mercy.

"Give me some manual labor, will you? Something hot and sweaty. Get me off the counter, please. I keep feeling this bitch attack coming on, and I don't want one to spew onto the customers."

Stella pushed back in her chair to give Hayley the once-over. "Why don't you take a break instead?"

"I stop doing, I'll start thinking. Then I'll start seeing those pictures of Harper's kitchen in my head again."

"I know it's upsetting, Hayley, but—"

"It's my fault."

"How is Harper's kitchen getting trashed your fault? And did you have anything to do with the broken vase in my living room, because no one in my house is taking responsibility. At the moment, I Dunno is taking the rap."

"I Dunno is the classic whipping boy."

"Between him and Not Me, nothing is safe, nothing is sacred."

Blowing out a breath, Hayley dropped into a chair. "All right, I will take a break, just for a minute. Can you take one, too, talk to me?"

"Sure." Stella swung away from the spreadsheet on her computer monitor.

"When I left your place last night I went to Harper's. I talked myself into taking some action, making a move, going up a step, you know? He wants to think of me as Cousin Hayley, or Lily's mama, or whatever the hell he thinks, fine. But I'll give him a taste and see what he thinks of that."

"Woo-hoo. And?"

"I laid one on him. Standing right there in his kitchen, moved in and gave him one of those here's-what-you're-missing-so-why-don't-you-come-get-it kisses."

Stella's lips quivered up into a smile. "And did he? Come and get it?"

"You could say. The kiss he gave me back was more of the since-you-opened-the-gate-I'm-galloping-right-on-in variety. He's got a really amazing mouth. I sort of figured he did, but having a couple of good samples made me realize I'd underestimated. Considerably."

"That's good, isn't it? It's what you wanted."

"It's not about what I want. Or maybe it is." She pushed back to her feet, but there was nowhere to pace in the tiny office. "Maybe that's just the point. In his kitchen, Stella. I kissed him in his kitchen, and a few hours later, she's in there wrecking the place. It doesn't take a math whiz to put that two and two together. I opened the gate, all right, but she's the one who came in."

"You're mixing metaphors. I'm not saying you're entirely wrong," she added, and stretched out from the chair to open her little cooler for bottled water. "But I am going to say it's not your fault. She's a volatile presence, Hayley, and none of us is responsible for her actions, or what happened to her."

"No, but try telling her that. Thanks," she said when Stella handed her one of the bottles.

"What we're doing is trying to find out, maybe to make it as right as it can be made, but we have to live our lives while we do."

"It's about sexual energy and emotional attachments. That's what Roz thinks, and I think she's on to something."

"You told Roz about you and Harper."

She took a long, deep drink. "No, no, I mean in general. And there isn't any 'me and Harper,' not really. Roz and Mitch think it's the sexual buzz and the developing emotions that get her stirred up, at least in part. So I've got to work off some of this buzz and these feelings."

"Even if you could, you're not taking Harper's buzz or feelings into account."

"I can take care of that. It's when they're directed at me. Otherwise, she'd've slapped at him before." Her fingers tightened on the bottle, but she caught herself before the gesture pushed water over the lip. "You can bet he's done more than kiss a woman in his kitchen in that house before last night, and she didn't get bent out of shape."

"Again, no argument. But if it does connect to you and Harper, then it must mean something. Maybe something important. The way Logan and I, the way Mitch and Roz mean something important to each other."

"I can't think about that. Not now. I just want to work off this edge. Give me something physical."

"I want all the excess stock cleared out of greenhouse one, brought around front for a display. One table for annuals, one for perennials, and marked thirty percent off."

"I'll get right on it. Thanks."

"Be sure to remember you thanked me when you collapse from heat exhaustion," Stella called out.

SHE LOADED FLATS AND POTS ON A FLATBED CART AND hauled them around the front of the building. It took her four trips. She muscled over the tables she wanted, positioning them where they'd be most likely to catch the eye of someone driving by. Possible impulse sales, she decided.

She still had to stop from time to time, talk to customers or direct them, but for the most part, she was blessedly left alone.

The air was close and heavy, the sort that brewed itself into thunderstorms. She hoped it did. She'd relish a bitching good storm. It would suit her mood exactly.

Still, the work kept her mind busy. She played the game of identifying and reciting the name of each specimen as she unloaded. Pretty soon she might be as good as Roz or Stella at recognizing plants. And she was pretty sure by the time she finished the work, she'd be too worn out to think about anything.

"Hayley. Been looking for you." Harper's brows drew together as he got closer. "What the hell are you doing?"

"Working." She swiped a forearm over her sweaty brow. "That's what I do around here."

"It's too hot for this kind of work, and the air quality's in the toilet today. Get inside."

"You're not my boss."

"Technically I am as I'm part owner of this place."

She was a little breathless, and the damn sweat kept dribbling into her eyes. It only made her more irritable. "Stella told me to set this up, and I'm setting it up. She's my immediate supervisor."

"Of all the stupid—" He broke off, strode inside.

And straight into Stella's office. "What the hell's wrong with you, sending Hayley out in this heat hauling stock around?"

"Good God, is she still at it?" Alarmed, she pushed back from her desk. "I had no idea she'd—"

"Give me a goddamn bottle of water."

Stella grabbed one out of her cooler. "Harper, I never thought she'd—"

But he held up a hand to cut her off. "Don't. Just don't."

He marched out again, stormed outside, straight to Hayley. She took a swat at him when he grabbed her arm, but he pulled her away from the front of the building.

"Let go. What do you think you're doing?"

"Getting you into the shade for a start." He propelled her around the back, through tables and potted shrubs, between greenhouses, until he came to the shaded banks of the pond.

"Sit. Drink."

"I don't like you this way."

"Right back at you. Now drink that water, and consider yourself lucky I don't just toss you in the pond to cool you off. I expected better of Stella," he said when Hayley glugged down water. "But the fact is, even though this is her second summer, she's a Yankee. You were born and raised down here. You know what this kind of heat can do."

"And I know how to handle it. And don't you blame Stella for anything." But she had to admit, now that she'd stopped, she felt a little queasy and light-headed. Giving in, she stretched out flat on the grass. "Maybe I overdid it. I got caught up, is all." She turned her head, looked over at him. "But I don't like being pushed around, Harper."

"I don't like pushing people around, but sometimes they need it." He pulled off his fielder's cap and waved it at her face to stir the air and cool. "And since your color's several shades under fire engine now, I'd say you did."

It was hard to argue when it felt so good to stretch out on the grass, and so sweet to have him fanning her with his sweaty old cap.

The sun was behind him, but filtered through the high, thickly leaved branches so that it dappled over him, made him look romantic and handsome sitting in the summer shade.

All that dark hair, curling a bit at the ends from the heat and humidity. And those long, chocolate brown eyes were so . . . delicious. The blades of his cheekbones, the full, sexy shape of his mouth.

She could lie here, she thought, for hours just looking at him. The idea was foolish enough to make her smile.

"You get away with it, this once. I had a lot on my mind, and good, sweaty work helps me deal with it."

"I got another way to deal with it." He leaned down, then stopped, cocked his head when she brought her hand up between them.

"We're on the clock here."

"I thought we were on a break."

"Work environment." The work, however draining, had done the trick. She'd made her decision. It wasn't about what she wanted, but about what was right. "Besides, I realized that sort of thing isn't a good idea."

"What sort of thing?"

"The you and me sort." She sat up, shook her hair back and made sure she smiled at him. It would drop the base out of her world if they stopped being friends. "I like you, Harper. You mean a lot to me, to Lily, and I want to stay friends. We add sex to that, sure, it'd be nice for a while, but then it'd just get awkward and sticky."

"It doesn't have to."

"Odds are." She touched his knee, gave it a brisk rub. "I was just in a mood yesterday. I liked kissing you. It was nice."

"Nice?"

"Sure." Because she knew that expression on his face—or rather the lack of expression—meant he was angry and fighting it back, she bumped up the smile several degrees. "Kissing a good-looking guy's always nice. But I've got to think beyond that kind of thing, and the best thing for me is to leave things just the way they are."

"Things aren't the way they were. You already changed that."

"Harper, a couple of smoochies between friends isn't such a big." She patted his hand, started to get up, but he clamped his fingers around her wrist.

"It was more than that."

His temper was winning, she could see it. And from the few times she'd watched it fly, she knew it was formidable. Better he was mad, she thought quickly. Better for him that he was mad or disgusted or even hurt for the short term.

"Harper, I know you're probably not used to having a woman put on the brakes, but I'm not going to sit here and argue about whether I'm going to have sex with you."

"It's more than that."

More. And that single word had her heart trembling. "It isn't. And I don't want it to be."

"What's this, some kind of game? You came to me, you moved on me. And now it's that was nice, but I'm not interested?"

"That's the nutshell. I've got to get back to work."

His voice stayed calm and cool; a dangerous sign. "I know what you felt when I had my hands on you."

"Well, for God's sake, Harper, of course I felt something. I haven't had any action in months."

His fingers tightened, then released. Let her go. "So, you were just cruising for a fuck buddy."

It wasn't her heart that bumped this time, but her belly. "I did something on impulse I realized I shouldn't have done. You want to make it crude, go ahead."

Her vision wavered, so she seemed to be looking at him through a rippling wave of heat. The anger inside her spiked up, so acute it all but scored her throat. "Men always take it down to fucking, lying and cheating and buying their way to it. And once they have, the woman's no more than a whore to be used again or tossed away. It's men who are the whores, plotting and planning their way to the next rut."

Her eyes had changed. He couldn't say how, but he knew he wasn't looking at her through them. The heat of his temper froze in fear. "Hayley—"

"Is this what you want, Master Harper?" With a sly smile, she cupped her breasts, caressed them. "And this?" She slid a hand between her legs. "What will you pay?"

He took her shoulders, gave her a quick shake. "Hayley. Stop it."

"Do you want me to play the lady? I'm so good at it. Good enough to be used to breed."

"No." He needed to stay calm, though he could feel his own fingers tremble. "I want you exactly the way you are.

Hayley." He gripped her chin, kept his eyes focused on hers. "I'm talking to you. We've got things to do around here, then you've got to go get Lily. You don't want to be late picking up Lily."

"What? Hey." Frowning, she pushed at his hand. "I said I didn't . . ."

"What did you say?" He moved his hands back to her shoulders, rubbed them gently up and down. "Tell me what you just said to me."

"I said . . . I said I did something on impulse. I said— Oh God." The color drained out of her face. "I didn't. I didn't mean—"

"Do you remember?"

"I don't know. I don't feel right." She pressed a clammy hand to her belly as nausea rolled. "I feel a little sick."

"Okay. I'm going to get you home."

"I didn't mean those things, Harper. I was upset." Her knees wobbled when he helped her to her feet. "I say stupid things when I'm upset, but I didn't mean them. I don't know where that came from."

"That's all right." His tone was grim as he took her weight to walk her around the front. "I do."

"I don't understand." She wanted to lie on the grass again, lie in the shade until her head stopped spinning.

"We'll get you home first, then we'll talk about it."

"I have to tell Stella—"

"I'll tell her. I didn't bring my car. Where are your keys?"

"Um. In my purse, behind the counter. Harper, I really feel . . . off."

"In the car." He opened the door, nudged her in. "I'll get your purse."

Stella was behind the counter when he hurried in. "Hayley's purse. I'm taking her home."

"Oh, Harper, is she sick? I'm so sorry. I—"

"It's not that. I'll explain later." He snatched the purse out of Stella's hand. "Tell Mama, tell her to come. Tell her I need her home."

Though she protested she was feeling better, he all but carried her in the house, then jerked his chin at David. "Get her something. Tea."

"What's the matter with our girl?"

"Just get the tea, David. And Mitch. Get Mitch. Come on, lie down in here."

"Harper, I'm not sick. Exactly. I just got overheated or something." But it was hard to argue with a man who plopped you down on a sofa.

"It's the 'or something' part that worries me. You're still pale." He ran his knuckles down her cheek.

"It could be because I'm completely embarrassed by what came out of my mouth. I shouldn't have said those things, Harper, even if I was mad."

"You weren't that mad." He looked around as Mitch came into the room.

"What's going on?"

"We had . . . a thing."

"Hey, baby, what's the matter?" Mitch walked to the sofa, crouched down.

"Just the heat." The sick weakness was passing, and let her work up an embarrassed smile. "Made me a little crazy."

"It wasn't the heat," Harper corrected. "And you're not the one who's crazy. Mama's on her way. We're going to wait for her."

"You didn't drag Roz away from work over this? Just how bad do you want me to feel?"

"Quiet down," Harper ordered.

"Look, I don't blame you for being mad at me, but I'm not going to lie here and—"

"Yes, you are. Lily doesn't have to be fetched for a couple hours. One of us will go get her."

Since her only response was a dropped jaw, he turned as David brought a tea tray into the room. "You can get Lily from the sitter's, can't you?"

"No problem."

"Since she's my daughter, I'm the one who picks her up, or delegates," Hayley snapped.

"Color's coming back," Harper observed. "Drink your tea."

"I don't want any damn tea."

"There now, sugar, it's nice green tea." David soothed as he set the tray down and poured. "Be a good girl now."

"I wish y'all would stop fussing and making me feel like an idiot." She sulked, but took the cup. "But since you ask, David, I will." She continued to sulk as she sipped, then cursed under her breath when she heard Roz come through the front door.

"What's the matter? What happened?"

"Harper's on some sort of rampage," Hayley said.

"Harper, you rampaging again?" Roz rubbed her hand over his arm as she brushed by him to study Hayley. "When are you going to grow out of these things?"

"Roz, I'm sorry for all this trouble," Hayley began. "I got a little overheated and wonky, is all. I'll put in extra time tomorrow to make up for today."

"Oh good, then I won't have to fire you. Now somebody tell me what the hell's going on?"

"First, she was working herself up to a good case of heat exhaustion," Harper told her.

"I overdid just a little, which isn't the same as—"

"Didn't I tell you to quiet down once already?"

She set the cup down with a snap of china on china. "I

don't know where you get off taking that tone with me."

The glance he sent her was as mild, and as formidable as his tone. "Since it's not working, I'll just tell you to shut the hell up. I got her into the shade, got some water in her," he continued. "We talked a couple minutes, then we had an argument. In the middle of it, it wasn't her talking anymore. It was Amelia."

"No. Just because I said things I shouldn't have—"

"Hayley, it wasn't you saying them. She sounded different," he told Mitch. "Different tonal quality, you could say. And the accent was pure Memphis. Not a trace of Arkansas in it. And her eyes, I don't know how to explain it exactly. They were older. Colder."

Everything inside Hayley sank and shivered. "It's not possible."

"You know it is. You know it happened."

"All right." Roz sat beside Hayley. "What did happen, Hayley, from your point of view?"

"I wasn't feeling quite right—the heat. Then Harper and I got into an argument. He just pushed my buttons, that's all, and I slapped back. I said things. I said . . ."

Her hand shook, groped for Roz's. "Oh God, oh God. I felt—away, detached. I don't know how to say it. And at the same time, I was filled with all this rage. I didn't know what I was saying. It was like I stopped saying anything. Then he was saying my name, and I was irritated. For a minute I couldn't remember. My—my brain felt a little dull, like it does when you first wake up from a nap. And I felt a little queasy."

"Hayley." Mitch spoke gently. "Has this happened before?"

"No. I don't know. Maybe." She closed her eyes a moment. "I've been having these thoughts, these moods, that don't seem like me. A lot of bitchiness, but it just seemed like I was feeling bitchy, that's all. God, what am I going to do?"

"Stay calm," Harper advised. "And we'll figure it out."

"Easy for you to say," she shot back. "You're not possessed by a psychopathic ghost."

seven

"A little like old times," Stella commented as she settled down in the upstairs sitting room with Roz and Hayley. And a bottle of cool white wine.

"I should be getting Lily her supper."

Roz poured the wine, then chose one of the sugared green grapes from the platter David had put together. "Hayley, you not only know she'll be fed, but that she'll handle all those men just fine."

"And it's good practice for Logan. We're thinking maybe we'll try to have a baby."

"Really?" For the first time in hours Hayley felt pure pleasure. "I think that's great. You'll make a beautiful baby, and Gavin and Luke would just love having another brother or a sister."

"Still in the talking stage, but we're leaning toward the acting on it stage."

"Feeling better?" Roz asked Hayley.

"Yeah. A lot. Sorry I cracked on you."

"I think we can make allowances. And give you some leeway. You didn't want to talk about what Mitch called the trigger—what you and Harper were arguing about. You needed your panic time and your weepy time, and you've had them."

"And then some. Nothing clears men out of the room faster than female hysterics."

"Which, I believe, was something you wanted anyway." Roz raised her brows and popped another grape. "You didn't want to discuss this with Mitch. Not what you argued about, or what you said to Harper—or rather what Amelia said."

Rather than meet Roz's eyes, Hayley kept hers fixed on the platter as if the cure for cancer was coded in among the glossy grapes and strawberry flowers. "I don't see what's important about what was said. The important thing is it happened. I think we should all—"

"That's enough nonsense." Roz's voice was mild as May. "Everything's important, every detail. I haven't pushed Harper on this, but I will. I'd prefer to hear it from you and it's been each one of us most intimately involved with this thing. So suck up your pride or whatever it is, Hayley, and spill it."

"I'm sorry. I took advantage of you."

"And how did you do that?"

Hayley took a bracing gulp of wine. "I hit on Harper."

"And?"

"And?" That stumped her for a minute. "You took me into your home, me and Lily. You treat us like family. More than. You—"

"And don't make me regret it by putting strings around it that I never tied on. Harper's a grown man, and makes his own decisions about a number of things, including the women in his life. If you hit on him I have no doubt he knew how to block or hit back."

As Hayley remained silent, Roz settled back with her wine, tucked her legs up, sipped. "And unless I don't know or understand my son as well as I think, I'd bet on the latter."

"It happened in the kitchen. I made it happen. Just kissing," Hayley said quickly when she realized how it sounded. "I mean Lily was right there and it was the first time . . ."

"The kitchen," Roz murmured.

"Yes, yes. You see?" She shuddered. "And that same night, she tore his kitchen apart. So I realized this wasn't something that could happen just because I've got the . . . because I'm attracted to Harper. I told him that I wasn't interested after all, and I probably hurt his feelings. But it's better his feelings get hurt than something else happen."

"Mmm-hmm." Roz nodded as she watched Hayley over the rim of her glass. "I don't imagine he took it well."

"Not exactly, so I was like, what's the big deal." She set her glass down so she could gesture freely with both hands. "Then he said something deliberately crude, and it upset me. Because it wasn't like that. It was just a kiss—well, two," she corrected. "But it wasn't like we stripped down naked and had monkey sex on the kitchen floor."

"Difficult when Lily was there," Roz commented.

"Yeah, but even so, I'm not like that, even though I got pregnant with Lily the way I did. And it might seem like I'm I big ho, but—"

"It doesn't seem," Stella cut in. "Not for a minute. We all know what it is to need someone. Whether for the moment, or for more. Personally, I don't care to hear you talking about a friend of mine that way, or to intimate that I would."

Roz smiled, stirred herself to lean forward and tap her glass to Stella's. "Nice."

"Thanks."

"I forgot where I was," Hayley said after a moment.

"You were arguing with Harper," Stella said helpfully. "You big ho."

It made her laugh, settled her down. "Right. We were arguing, then it happened, the way I said. I sort of faded back, and there were these things coming out of my mouth I didn't put there. About how men are all liars and cheats, and just want to fuck you, and treat you like a whore. It was ugly, and it wasn't true. Especially not about Harper."

"The first thing you have to remember is it wasn't you saying it," Stella reminded her. "And the second is, it fits with what we know of her, and the pattern of her behavior. Men are the enemy, and sex is a trigger."

"During the argument, before Amelia's participation, Harper said something to make you feel cheap."

Hayley picked up her glass again, looked at Roz. "He didn't mean it the way I took it."

"Don't make excuses for my boy." Roz angled her head. "If he was perfect, he wouldn't be mine. The point is, you felt that way, and she moved in."

"Roz, I want you to know, I'm not going to pursue this thing with Harper. This personal thing."

"Is that so?" Roz raised her eyebrows. "What's wrong with him?"

"Nothing." Blinking, Hayley looked to Stella for support and got a smile and a shrug. "Nothing's wrong with him."

"So you're attracted to him, nothing's wrong with you, but you've dumped him before things really got started. Why is that?"

"Well, because he's . . ."

"Mine?" Roz finished. "Then what's wrong with me?"

"Nothing!" At her wit's end, Hayley spread a hand over her face. "I can't even believe how embarrassing this is."

"I expect you and Harper to work this out, and to leave me entirely out of the equation. I will make one observation, as his mother. If he knew you were showing him the door in order to protect him from possible future harm, he'd turn right back around and kick that door in. And I'd applaud the action."

"You won't tell him."

"It's not my place to tell him. It's yours." She pushed to her feet. "Now I'm going downstairs, and I'll discuss this with Mitch over our dinner. Meanwhile, I think you have another hour coming—for sulking time. After that, I expect you to straighten up."

Stella gestured with her glass as Roz walked out, then took a slow, satisfying sip. "She's just frigging terrific, isn't she?"

"You weren't a lot of help," Hayley complained.

"Actually, I was. I agreed with everything she said there at the end, but I didn't mention it. Seems to me, keeping my mouth shut was helpful. Hey, you're doing really well with this sulking hour," she added. "And you're only a couple minutes into it."

"Maybe you should shut up again."

"I love you, Hayley."

"Oh, shit."

"And I'm worried about you. We all are. So we're going to figure this out. Go team and all that. In the meantime you've got to decide what's best for you in regards to Harper. You can't let Amelia drive the train."

"It's tough when she's already highjacked it and put on the engineer's hat. She was inside me, Stella. Somehow."

Stella got up, moved to the couch to sit beside Hayley, to drape her arm over her friend's shoulders.

"I am seriously freaked," Hayley whispered.

"Me, too."

SHE FELT LIKE SHE WAS TIPTOEING ON EGGSHELLS. Only the eggshells were sharp as razor blades. She questioned everything she did or thought or said.

It all seemed like her, she decided as she undressed for bed. She'd tasted the pasta salad, the garden-fresh tomatoes at dinner. It was her head that had throbbed with a tension headache, and her hands that had tucked Lily into the crib.

But just how long could she go on being so hyper-aware of every single action, every breath she took without going a little loopy herself?

There were things she could do, and she was going to start doing them the next day. The first order of business was to weigh down her credit card with the purchase of a laptop. The Internet was probably full of information on possession.

That's what they'd call what had happened to her. Possession.

What she knew about it came out of books, novels mostly. To think she'd enjoyed having her spine tingled with those kind of stories once. Maybe she could take some of the things she'd read and apply it to her situation. Though the one that came first to her mind was Stephen King's *Christine*. She was a woman not a classic car, and come to think of it, the solution of smashing the car to bits didn't seem very practical. Besides, it hadn't really worked anyway.

There was *The Exorcist,* but she wasn't Catholic—and that dealt with demons. Still, she'd be willing to try a priest if things got any worse. In fact, the minute her head spun a three-sixty, she was heading for the nearest church.

She was probably overreacting, she decided, and slipped on a tank and cotton shorts. Just because it happened once didn't mean it would happen again. Especially now that she was aware. She could stop it from happening, probably. Willpower, strength of self.

She needed to do more yoga. Who knew that yoga wasn't the cure for possession?

No, what she was going to do was get some air. The thunderstorm she'd wanted was just starting to lash. The wind was up, and shimmers of lightning were buzzing light against the windows. She'd throw open the terrace doors, let the wind pour in. Then she'd read something light, a nice romantic comedy, and turn her head off for sleep.

She walked to the doors, gave them a big, dramatic yank.

And screamed.

"Jesus! Jesus!" Harper grabbed her before she could let out the next peal. "I'm not an ax murderer. Chill."

"Chill? Chill? You're skulking around, scare my hair white, and I'm supposed to chill?"

"I wasn't skulking. I was just about to knock when you opened the doors. I think you may have cracked my eardrum."

"I hope I did. What are you doing out there? It's just about to storm."

"A couple of things. The first was I saw your light and wanted to see if you were okay."

"Well, I was before you gave me a damn heart attack."

"Good." His gaze drifted down, up again. "Nice outfit."

"Oh stop." Annoyed, she folded her arms over her chest. "It's no less than I might wear running around the yard with the kids."

"Yeah, I've noticed you running around the yard. The second is I was thinking about what happened this afternoon."

"Harper, I haven't been able to think about anything

else for hours." Weary of it, she pushed a hand through her hair, then pressed it to her temple. "I just don't think I *can* think about it any more tonight."

"You don't have to, you just have to answer a question." When he started to step inside, she gave him a good, solid shove back.

"I didn't ask you in. And I don't think it's a good idea for you to be in here when I'm not really dressed."

His eyebrows lifted as he leaned comfortably on the doorjamb. Like he owned the place, she thought. Which, of course, he did.

"Let me point out that you've been here for about a year and a half. During that time I've somehow managed to restrain myself from jumping you. I think I can continue that policy for another few minutes."

"You're feeling pretty snarky, aren't you?"

"I'd say what I'm feeling is pissed off. Especially if you're going to be a drama queen and insist we have this conversation with me standing out here and you standing in there."

The first fat drops began to fall, and he lifted his eyebrows again. Exactly the way his mother did.

"Oh, all right, come in then. No point in you standing out there getting soaked like an idiot."

"Gee, thanks so much."

"And leave those doors open." She jabbed a finger at them because the gesture made her feel more in charge. "Because you're not staying."

"Fine." The wind whipped in through them, chased by a charge of thunder. And he stood, thumbs hooked in the front pockets of ratty jeans, his hip cocked.

She wondered, even through the irritation, why she didn't drool.

"You know," he began, "after I more or less—mostly

less—calmed down about everything, replayed it in my head some, the way you do, something interesting occurred to me."

"You going to make a speech or ask your question?"

He inclined his head, an action that managed to look regal despite the jeans, T-shirt and bare feet. "You've done a lot of swiping at me since you came here. I've tolerated it pretty well, for certain reasons. I'm about done with that now. But to get back to my point. The interesting thing that occurred to me was timing. Here's how it plays for me. You come over, make your move, I make one back. We have a moment, a couple of them. You want to take it slow, I get that. Then the next time we're together, you're all about now you're not really interested after all, it was just an impulse, no big, and let's just be pals."

"That's right. And if your question is have I changed my mind—"

"It's not. Between those two interludes, I get a visit from our resident crazy, who happens to decide to trash my place. My kitchen to be exact, the scene of interlude one. So my question is, how much did that event play into your role in interlude two?"

"I don't know what you're talking about."

"Well now you're just lying, straight to my face."

Her expression went to pitiful. She could actually feel it move across her face and settle in. "I wish you'd go away, Harper. I'm tired, and I have a headache. It hasn't been the easiest day for me."

"You pulled back because you figured she didn't like us together. Enough that she fired what we could call a warning shot."

"I pulled back because I pulled back. And that should be enough."

"It would be, would have to be, if that were true. If that

was all. I'm not going to push myself on you, on any woman who doesn't want me. I've got too much pride for that, and I was raised better."

He straightened, took another step toward her. "And those are the exact same reasons I don't walk away from a fight anymore than I let somebody stand in front of me if there's trouble."

He angled his head again, rocked on his heels. "So don't even think about getting in my way on this, Hayley, about stepping aside from something to protect me from her."

She cupped her elbows. "You say you won't push, but I feel pushed, so—"

"I've wanted you since the first minute I saw you."

Her arms went limp, simply fell to her sides. "You have not."

"The first moment—it was like being blasted with light. Went straight through me." With his eyes on hers, he tapped a fist on his chest. "I think I stuttered. I could hardly speak."

"Oh God." She pressed a hand to her heart, hoping that would hold it in place. "That's a lousy thing to say to me."

"Maybe." His lips twitched, his eyes warmed. "I'll just follow it up with some lousy behavior then." He reached out, drew her against him.

"Harper, this really isn't something we should—" It was some move, or so she would think when she could think again. With a subtle shift, a tiny bump, they were fitted together. Angle to angle, line to line so that every inch of her body felt the jolt.

"Oh," she murmured. "Uh-oh."

A smile flickered at the corners of his mouth, then that mouth was on hers. Hot and warm and sweet, like liquid sugar. The kiss was a slow, irresistible seduction, a drugging of the senses, as his hands cruised over her, a light and lazy touch. A touch, she thought mistily, of a man confident enough to take his time—sure enough that he had plenty of it.

And his lips rubbed silkily over hers until she'd have sworn she felt her own shimmer.

It was like being gradually, skillfully, thoroughly melted, body and will, heart and mind, until what choice was there really, but surrender?

She moaned for him, that soft, helplessly pleasured sound. And she yielded, degree by erotic degree, until the fingers that had gripped his shoulders went lax.

When he eased back, her eyes were blurred, her lips parted.

"Hayley?"

"Mmm."

"That's not the response of a woman who isn't interested."

She managed to get her hand on his shoulder again, but it wasn't much of a push. "That wasn't really fair."

"Why not?"

"Because . . . that mouth." She couldn't stop her gaze from dropping down to it. "You should need a license to kiss that way."

"Who says I haven't got one?"

"Well, in that case. Do it again, would you?"

"Was planning on it."

It was the same rush with the wind spewing in through the door, and his mouth lighting small, sparkling fires inside her. Little tongues of heat, she thought, that were going to lick their way through her until she simply dissolved.

"Harper." She said it with the kiss, shuddering at the sensation of their lips moving together.

"Hmm?"

"We really have to stop this." She couldn't resist nipping that sexy bottom lip of his, just a little. "Sometime."

"Later is good. Let's say next week."

She had to laugh, but it came out shaky, then ended on a gasp as his mouth slid from hers to find some magic point just under her ear.

"That's good, that's . . . exceptional. But I really think we need to wait, just a . . . Oh." She let her head fall back as his cruising mouth found yet another magical spot. "That's so . . ."

She turned her head to give him better access, and her heavy eyes blinked clear. Widened. "Harper."

When she jerked in his arms, he just shifted his grip. "What? It's not next week yet."

"Harper. Oh God, stop. Look."

Amelia stood in the doorway, the storm raging at her back. Behind her, *through* her, Hayley could see trees whipping in the wind and the bruised fists of clouds that smothered the sky.

Her hair was matted and wild, her white gown streaked with mud that dripped, it seemed to drip, into a filthy pool over her bare and bloodied feet. She carried a long, curved blade in one hand, a rope in the other. And her face was a mask of bitter rage.

"You see her, don't you? You see her." Hayley shuddered now from fear and cold.

"Yeah, I see her." In one easy move, he changed his stance so Hayley was behind him. "You're going to have to get over it," he said to Amelia. "You're dead. We're not."

The force of the blow lifted him off his feet, shot him back five feet to slam against the wall. He tasted blood in his mouth even as he shoved clear again.

"Stop! Stop!" Hayley shouted. Force of will and fear had her pushing against the freezing wind toward Harper.

"He's your grandbaby. He comes out of you. You sang to him when he was a boy. You can't hurt him now."

She started forward, with no clear idea what she would do if she reached Amelia. Before Harper could yank her back, a gust of wind knocked her off her feet and sent her sprawling. She thought she heard someone scream, in rage or grief. Then there was nothing but the sound of the storm.

"Are you crazy?" Harper dropped down beside her to prop her up.

"No, are you? You're the one whose mouth's bleeding."

He swiped the side of his hand over it. "You hurt?"

"No. She's gone. At least she's gone. Christ, Harper, she had a knife."

"Sickle. And yeah, that's a new one."

"It can't be real, right? I mean, she's not corporeal, so the rest of it isn't real either. She couldn't slice us up with it. You think?"

"No." But he wondered if she could make you imagine you were cut, or do yourself some kind of harm defending yourself.

She stayed on the floor, getting her breath back, leaning on him as she stared through the open doors. "When I first came here, when I was pregnant, she'd come to my room sometimes. It was a little spooky, sure, but there was something comforting, too. The way it seemed she was just looking in on me, seeing if I was okay. And this sense I got, this wistfulness, from her. And now she's—"

She was on her feet and running the instant she heard the singing come through the baby monitor.

She was fast; Harper was faster and got to Lily's door two strides ahead of her. Quick enough to throw out an arm and block her. "It's okay, it's all right. Let's not wake her up."

Lily slept in the crib, curled under her blanket with her stuffed dog. In the rocking chair, Amelia sang. She wore her gray dress, her hair in neat coils, and her face was calm and quiet.

"It's so cold."

"It's not bothering the baby. It never bothered me as a kid. I don't know why."

In her chair, Amelia turned her head to look over. There was sorrow on her face, grief, and, Hayley thought, regret. She continued to sing, low and sweet, but her gaze was on Harper now.

When the song was done, she faded away.

"She was singing to you," Hayley told him. "Some part of her remembers, some part of her knows, and she's sorry. What must it be like, to be insane for a hundred years?"

Together, they crossed to the crib where Hayley fussed with the blanket.

"She's okay, Hayley. Lily's just fine. Come on."

"Sometimes I don't know if I can take it, this roller-coaster ride through the haunted house." She pushed at her hair as they walked back to Hayley's bedroom. "One minute she's knocking us around, and the next, she's singing lullabies."

"Dead lunatic," he pointed out. "Still, maybe it's a way of telling us she might come after you or me, but she won't hurt Lily."

"What if I do? What if she does what she did at the pond, and makes me hurt Lily, or someone else?"

"You won't let that happen. Sit down a minute. You want something? Water or something?"

"No."

He eased her down so they sat on the side of the bed. "She never hurt anybody in this house. Maybe she wanted to. Maybe she even tried, but she never did." He took her hand, and because it still felt chilled, rubbed it between both of his. "That's one thing that would've gotten passed down. A crazy woman attacking a Harper, or even a servant. It would've been reported, and she'd have been taken away, put in jail or an asylum."

"Maybe. What about the sickle, and the rope? That says: I'm gonna tie somebody up and slice them to ribbons."

"Nobody ever got sliced to ribbons in Harper House." He rose to move over and close her terrace doors.

"That you know about."

"Okay, that I know about." He sat again. "We'll pass this on to Mitch. He can look into police records maybe. It's an avenue."

"You've got this calm surface," she said after a moment. "It's deceptive, seeing as there are all these little hot pockets under it. Shows me I don't know you as well as I thought. I did."

"Back at you."

She sighed, looked down at her hands as they sat on the side of her bed together. "I can't just sleep with you. I thought I could—at first. Then I thought, I can't go jumping on that. I do and he's going to get hurt. She's going to hurt him." She looked up. "You were right about that."

He only smiled. "Duh."

She gave his arm a swat. "Think you're so clever and smart."

"Only because I am. You can ask my mama, when she's in a good mood."

"You're easy to be around, except when you're not." She studied him, trying to take in all the new things she was learning. "I like that, I guess, finding all those under-the-surface pockets. And God knows you're nice to look at."

"How big a fall are you building me up for?"

"It's not—" She shook her head, rose to wander the room. "I've got all these feelings stored up, and all these needs. It'd be so easy to set them loose on you."

"I don't recall putting up a fight."

"I didn't know you looked at me, not that way. Knowing you did, you do, just adds to everything. I've never been kissed like that in my life, and I've been kissed pretty good now and then. If she hadn't come in here when she did, it's likely we'd be in bed right now, going where that kiss was leading."

"That's no way to make me feel fonder of my great-great-grandmother."

"I'm not feeling so fond of her myself. But it gave me time to think instead of just want." Ordering herself to be sensible, for both of them, she sat on the arm of a chair. "I'm not shy about sex, and I think if you and I were somewhere else, in some other sort of situation, we could be lovers without all these extra complications."

"Why do people always think being lovers shouldn't be complicated?"

She frowned, then shook her head. "Well, that's a question. A good one. I don't know."

"Seems to me," he began, crossing to her. "That there are flings, and that's uncomplicated by design. Nothing wrong with it. But being lovers, going into it thinking about more than a night or two, that should have weight. You've got weight, you've got some complications."

"You're right, I can't say you're not. But there's a lot to consider before we take a step like this. I think we need to be sure it's the right thing for both of us before we take that step. There are things we don't know about each other, and maybe we should."

"How about dinner?"

She stared up at him. "You're hungry?"

"Not now, Hayley. I'm asking you for a date. Have dinner with me. We'll go into the city, have a meal, listen to some music."

Her shoulders relaxed and the tight coil in her belly loosened. "That'd be good."

"Tomorrow?" he said as he drew her to her feet.

"If your mama or Stella can mind Lily, tomorrow's fine. Ah, we'll need to tell them about what happened. About Amelia."

"In the morning."

"It's a little awkward, explaining how you were in here, and what we were doing when—"

"No." He took her face in his hands, laid his lips on hers. "It's not. You going to be all right now?"

"Yeah." She looked over his shoulder to the doors he'd shut. "Storm's passing, you should go now, in case it decides to rain some more."

"I'll bunk in Stella's old room."

"You don't have to do that."

"We'll both sleep easier that way."

SHE DID FEEL BETTER, EVEN THOUGH IT DIDN'T EXactly cajole sleep to imagine him just down the hall. Or to imagine how easy it would be to tiptoe down there, slide into bed beside him.

She had no doubt they'd both sleep a lot easier *that* way.

It was hell being responsible and mature.

Even a bigger hell to realize she cared about him more than she'd bargained for. But that was good, wasn't it? she thought as she tossed and turned. She wasn't a slut who hopped into bed with a guy just because he was good-looking and sexy.

Some people might think differently, because of Lily, but it hadn't been that way. She'd cared for Lily's father. She'd liked him. Maybe she'd been careless, but it hadn't been cheap.

And she'd wanted the baby. Maybe not at first, she admitted. But after the panic and pity, the anger and denial, she'd wanted the baby. She'd never wanted anything in her life as much.

Her beautiful baby.

She'd taken nothing from the father, had she? The spineless, selfish bastard who'd used her grief to have his way. That hadn't been stupid. She'd been smart not to tell him, to go away, keep her child to herself. Only hers. Always.

But she could have more, couldn't she? She was thinking about this all the wrong way. Why should she work? Sweat and slave, settle for a room in the great house. She could have it all. Her child would have it all.

He wanted her. She could play this well. Oh yes, who knew better how to play a man. He would come begging before she was done, and she would bind him to her.

When it was done, Harper House would be hers, hers and her child's.

At last.

eight

IN THE PROPAGATION HOUSE, HAYLEY WATCHED ROZ set a ceanothus cutting in a rockwood plug. "Are you sure you don't mind watching Lily?"

"Why would I mind? Mitch and I will spend the evening spoiling her rotten while you aren't around to run interference."

"She loves being with you. Roz, I feel so weird about everything."

"I don't know why you'd feel weird about going out on a date with Harper. He's a handsome, charming young man."

"Your young man."

"Yes." Roz smiled as she dipped another cutting in rooting compound. "Aren't I lucky? I also have two other handsome, charming young men, and wouldn't be the least surprised if they had dates, tonight."

"It's different with Harper. He's your first, he's your partner. I'm working for you."

"We've been over this, Hayley."

"I know." Just as she knew that impatient tone. "I'm not able to wind myself through it as easy as you, I guess."

"You might if you'd relax, go out, and have a good time." Roz glanced up before sliding the cutting into the plug. "Wouldn't hurt to try to catch a quick nap beforehand, either. See if you can deal with those circles under your eyes."

"I didn't sleep well."

"Not surprising, considering."

The music in the propagation house today was some sort of complicated piano, drenched in romance. Hayley had more skill identifying plants than classical composers, so she just let the music drift around her as she worked.

"I kept having weird dreams, at least I think I did. I can't remember any of them clearly. Roz, are you afraid?"

"Concerned. Here, you do the next one." She stepped back so Hayley could take over. "And angry, too. Nobody slaps at my boy—except me. And if I get the opportunity, I'll tell her so, in no uncertain terms. That's good," she said with a nod as Hayley worked. "This kind of hardwood cutting needs a dry rooting medium or you get rot."

"She may have gotten that sickle and the rope out of the carriage house. I mean all those years ago. Maybe she tried to use them and someone stopped her."

"There are a lot of maybes, Hayley. Since Beatrice didn't mention Amelia again in any of her journals, we may never know all of it."

"And if we don't we may never get her out. Roz, there are people, paranormal experts, who you can hire to clean houses." She glanced up, knitted her brows. "I don't know why you smile at that. It's not such a strange idea."

"I just had an image of a bunch of people running around the house armed with buckets and brooms, and that ray gun sort of thing Bill Murray used in *Ghostbusters*."

"Proton streams—and I have no idea why I know that. But really, Roz, it's a fringe science and all that, but there are serious and legitimate studies. Maybe we need outside help."

"If it comes to that, we'll see about it."

"I looked up some sites on the Internet."

"Hayley."

"I know, I know, just a contingency."

They both looked over as the door opened. Mitch came in, and something about the look on his face had Hayley holding her breath.

"I think I found her. How soon can you wrap things up here and come home?"

"An hour," Roz decided. "But for God's sake, Mitchell, don't leave it at that. Who was she?"

"Her name was Amelia Connor. Amelia Ellen Connor, born in Memphis May 12, 1868. No death certificate on record."

"How did you—"

"I'll get into all that at home." He flashed her a wide-grin. "Rally your troops, Rosalind. See you there."

"Well, for heaven's sake," she muttered when he walked out. "Isn't that just like a man? I'll finish up here, Hayley. You go tell Harper and Stella to finish up whatever they're doing. Let me think," she said as she pressed fingers to her temple. "Stella can get in touch with Logan if she wants him there, and she'll need to leave Ruby in charge, see that she closes today. Looks like we're taking off a couple hours early."

* * *

AMELIA ELLEN CONNOR. HAYLEY CLOSED HER EYES and thought the name as she stood just inside the foyer of Harper House. Nothing happened, no ghostly revelations or appearances, no sweep of sudden knowledge. She felt a little foolish because she'd been sure *something* would happen if she concentrated on the name while standing inside the house.

She tried saying it out loud, quietly, but got the same results. She'd wanted to be found, Hayley thought. She'd wanted to be acknowledged. All right then.

"Amelia Ellen Connor," she said aloud. "I'm acknowledging you as the mother of Reginald Edward Harper."

But there was nothing but silencc in answer, and the scent of David's lemon oil and Roz's summer roses.

Deciding she'd keep the failed experiment to herself, she headed to the library.

Roz and Mitch were already there, with Mitch hammering away at his laptop.

"Says he wants to get some things down while they're fresh in his mind," Roz told her with some exasperation whipping around the edges of her voice. "Stella's in the kitchen with David. Her boys are with their grandparents today. Logan'll be along when he's along. I imagine the same goes for Harper."

"He said he'd come. He just had to finish . . ." She lifted her shoulder. "Whatever."

"Have a seat." Roz waved a hand. "Dr. Carnegie seems determined to keep us in suspense."

"Iced tea and lemon cookies," David announced and he wheeled in a cart just ahead of Stella. "You cracked him yet?" he nodded toward Mitch.

"No, but it's not going to take much more to push me to do just that. Mitch!"

"Five minutes."

"It's such a simple name, isn't it?" Hayley shrugged when Roz looked at her. "Sorry, I was just thinking. Amelia, that's sort of flowy and feminine. But the rest. Ellen Connor. It's solid and simple. You sort of expect the rest to be flowy, too, or a little exotic. Then again, Amelia means industrious—I looked it up."

"Of course you did," Roz said fondly.

"It doesn't sound like that's what it should mean. I think Ellen's a derivative of Helen, and makes me think Helen of Troy, so it's actually more sort of feminine and exotic when you come down to it. And none of that's important."

"Interesting, as always though, to see how your mind works. And here's the rest of our happy few."

"Ran into Harper out front." Logan walked over to kiss Stella. "Sweaty, sorry. Came straight from the job." He picked up a glass of iced tea David had poured and drank every drop.

"So what's the deal?" Harper zeroed in on the cookies, took three, then plopped into a chair. "We've got her name, so what, drum roll?"

"It's pretty impressive Mitch could find her name with the little we had to go on," Hayley shot back.

"Not saying otherwise, just wondering what we do with it."

"First, I'd like to know how he came by it. Mitchell," Roz said with growing impatience. "Don't make me hurt you in front of the children."

"So." Mitch pushed back from the keyboard, took off his glasses to polish them on his shirt. "Reginald Harper owned several properties, including houses. Here in Shelby County, and outside it. Some were rented, of course, investment properties, income. I did find a few, through the old ledgers, that were listed as tenanted through certain periods, but generated no income."

"Cooking the books?" Harper suggested.

"Possibly. Or these residences might have been where he installed mistresses."

"Plural?" Logan took another glass of tea. "Busy boy."

"Beatrice's journal speaks of women, not woman, so it follows. It also follows, as we find him a shrewd, goal-oriented type that as he wanted a son, whatever the cost, he maintained more than one candidate until he got what he was after. But the journals also indicate Amelia was local, so I concentrated on the local properties."

"I doubt he'd list a mistress as a tenant," Roz said.

"No. Meanwhile, I've been scouring the census lists. A lot of names, a lot of years to cover. Then a little lightbulb goes off, and I narrowed it to the years Reginald held those local properties, and before 1892. Still a lot to cull through, but I hit in the 1890 census."

His gaze scanned the room, landed on the cart. "Are those cookies?"

"Jesus, David, get the man some cookies before I have to kill him. What did you hit in 1890?"

"Amelia Ellen Connor, resident of one of Reginald's Memphis houses. One that generated no income from the later half of that year, through March of 1893. One, in fact, he'd listed as untenanted during that period."

"Almost certainly has to be her," Stella said. "It's too neat and tidy not to be."

"She knows her neat and tidy," Logan commented. "In spades."

"If it's not our Amelia, it's one hell of a coincidence." Mitch tossed his glasses onto the table. "Reginald's very careful bookkeeper noted on Reginald's books a number of expenses incurred during the period the property was supposedly empty, and Amelia Connor listed it as her residence on the census. In February of 1893, considerably more expenses were noted dealing with refurbishing in preparation for new tenants, paying tenants. The house was sold, if you're interested, in 1899."

"So we know she lived in Memphis," Hayley began, "at least until a few months after the baby was born."

"More than that. Amelia Ellen Connor." He slipped his glasses back on and read his notes. "Born 1868 to Thomas Edward Connor and Mary Kathleen Connor née Bingham. Though Amelia listed both her parents as deceased, that was only true of her father, who died in 1886. Her mother was alive, and very possibly well, until her death in 1897. She was employed by the Lucerne family as a housemaid at a home on the river, called—"

"The Willows," Roz finished. "I know that house. It's older than this one. It's a bed-and-breakfast now, a very lovely one. It was bought and restored oh, twenty years ago at least."

"Mary Connor worked there," Mitch continued, "and though she listed no children for the census, a check of vital records shows she had a daughter—Amelia Ellen."

"Estranged, I suppose," Stella said.

"Enough that the daughter considered her mother dead, and the mother didn't acknowledge the daughter. There's another interesting bit. There's no record of Amelia having a child, just as there's no record of her death."

"Money can grease wheels or muddy them up," Hayley added.

"What's next?" Logan wondered.

"I'm going to go back over old newspapers, again, keep looking for any mention of her death—unidentified female, that sort of thing. And we'll keep trying to find information through the descendants of servants. I'll see if the people who own The Willows now will let me have a look at any documents or papers from that time."

"I'll smooth the way." Roz offered. "Old family names grease wheels, too."

SHE WAS OUT ON A DATE FOR THE FIRST TIME IN . . . it was really too sad to think about how long. And she looked pretty good, if she did say so herself. The little red top showed off her arms and shoulders, which were nicely toned between hauling Lily, yoga, and digging in the dirt.

There was a great-looking guy sitting across from her in a noisy, energetic Beale Street restaurant. And she couldn't keep her mind on the moment.

"We'll talk about it," Harper said, then picked up the glass of wine she'd ignored and handed it to her. "You'll feel better getting it out than working so hard not to say anything."

"I can't stop thinking about it. Her. I mean she had his baby, Harper, and he just took it. It's not so hard to see why she'd have this hard-on about men."

"Devil's advocate? She sold herself."

"But, Harper—"

"Hold on. She came from a working-class family. Instead of opting to work, she opted to be kept. Her choice, and I got no problem with it. But she traded sex for a house and servants."

"Which gives him the right to take her child?"

"Not saying that, by a long shot. I'm saying it's unlikely she was a rosy-cheeked innocent. She lived in that house, as his mistress, for what, more than a year before she got pregnant."

She wasn't ready to have it all taken down to its lowest level. "Maybe she loved him."

"Maybe she loved the life." He jerked a shoulder.

"I didn't know you were so cynical."

He only smiled. "I didn't know you were so romantic. More than likely, the truth of it hits somewhere in the middle of cynicism and romance, so we'll split the difference."

"Seems fair. I don't always like being fair though."

"Either way it falls, we know this is one screwed-up individual, Hayley. It's pretty likely she was screwed up before this happened. That doesn't mean she deserved it, but I'm betting on a hard edge. It takes one, doesn't it, to list your own mother as dead when she's living a few miles away?"

"Yeah. It doesn't paint a nice picture. I guess part of me wants to see her as a victim, like the heroine, when it's just not that cut and dried."

Deliberately she sipped her wine. "Okay, that's enough. That's all she gets for tonight."

"Fine with me."

"I just have to do one thing."

Harper reached in his pocket. "Here, use my phone."

Laughing, she took it. "I know she's fine with Roz and Mitch. I just want to check."

SHE ATE CATFISH AND HUSH PUPPIES AND DRANK TWO glasses of wine. It was amazing how liberating it was to sit as long as she liked, to talk about whatever came to mind.

"I forgot what this was like." Simply because she could, Hayley lounged back in her chair. "Eating a whole meal without interruptions. I'm glad you finally asked me out."

"Finally?"

"You've had plenty of time," she pointed out. "Then I wouldn't have had to make the first move."

"I liked your first move." He reached over, took her hand.

"It was one of my better ones. Harper." Relaxed, she eased forward, her eyes on his. "Were you really thinking about me that way all this time?"

"I put a lot of effort into not thinking about you that way. It worked some of the time."

"Why did you? Put a lot of effort into it, I mean."

"It seemed . . . rude," was the best he could think of, "to imagine seducing a houseguest, especially a pregnant one. I helped you out of the car once—the day of your baby shower."

"Oh God, I remember." It made her laugh even as she covered her face with her free hand. "I was so awful to you. I felt so hot and fat and miserable."

"You looked amazing. Vital. That was my first impression of you. Light and energy, and well, sex, but I tried to tramp that one out. But that day, when I helped you out, the baby moved. I felt it move. It was . . ."

"Scary?"

"Powerful, and yeah, a little scary. I watched you give birth."

She went still, and flushed to the tips of her ears. "Oh, oh God, I forgot about that." She squeezed her eyes shut. "Oh no."

He grabbed her hands, pulled them toward him to kiss. "It was impossible to describe. After I got over the get-me-the-hell-out-of-here stage, it was just staggering. I saw her born. I've been in love with her ever since."

"I know." Embarrassment faded as her heart swam up into her eyes. "That I know. You never ask about her father."

"It's not my business."

"If we take this any further, it should be. You should at least know. Could we maybe take a walk?"

"Sure."

THEY TURNED AWAY FROM THE LIGHTS AND ACTION of Beale Street and wandered toward the river. Tourists flocked there as well, to stroll through the park or stand and watch the water, but the relative quiet made it easier for her to go back in her mind, and take him with her.

"I didn't love him. I want to say that right off because some people still like to think poor girl, some guy got her in trouble then didn't stand by her. And they think your heart's been broken by some asshole. It wasn't like that."

"Good. It'd be a shame if Lily's father was an asshole."

The laugh bubbled up, made her shake her head. "You're going to make this easier. You've got a way of doing that. He was a nice guy, a grad student I met when I was working at the bookstore back home. We'd flirt with each other, and we hit it off, went out a couple of times. Then my father died."

They crossed the little bridge over the replica of the river, wandered past the couples sitting at stone tables. "I was so lost, so sad."

He slid his arm around her shoulder. "I think if anything happened to my mother, it would be like being blinded. I've got my brothers to hold on to, but I can't imagine the world without her."

"It's like that, like you just can't see. What to do next, what to say next. No matter how kind people are—and they were, Harper, a lot of kind people—you're in the dark. People loved my father, you just had to. So there were neighbors and family and friends, the people I worked with, that he worked with. But still, he was so much the center of my life, I felt alone, just isolated in this void of grief."

"I was a lot younger when my father died, and I guess in some ways it's easier. But I know there's a stage you have to go through, the one where you can't believe anything's ever going to be right again, or solid again."

"Yes, exactly. And when you get through it, start to feel again, it hurts. This guy, he was there for me. He was very sweet, very comforting, and that's how one thing led to another."

She tilted her head to meet his eyes. "Still, we were never more than friends. But it wasn't a fling, it was—"

"Healing."

Her heart warmed. "Yes. He went back to school, and I got on. I didn't realize I was pregnant at first. The signs didn't filter through my head. And when I did . . ."

"You were scared."

She shook her head. "I was *pissed*. I was so mad. Why the hell had this happened to me? Didn't I have enough to deal with? It wasn't like I'd slept around, it wasn't like I hadn't been responsible, so what the hell was this? A joke? God, Harper, I wasn't all soft and shivery. I was enraged. I got around to panic at some point, but I bounced back pretty quick to mad."

"It was a tough spot, Hayley. You were alone."

"Don't pretty it up. I didn't want to be pregnant. I didn't want a baby. I had to work, I had to grieve, and it was about damn time somebody up there gave me a freaking break."

They moved toward the river, and she kept her voice down as she looked out toward the water. "Now I was going to have to get an abortion, and that meant I'd have to figure out how to get some time off work, and pay for it."

"But you didn't."

"I got the literature, and I found a clinic, and then I started thinking maybe it'd be better if I had it then gave it up for adoption. Signed up with one of those agencies. You read so much about these infertile couples pining for a baby. I thought maybe that would be something positive I could do."

He brushed a hand down her hair, spoke softly. "But you didn't do that either."

"I got literature on that kind of thing, started researching. And all the time I was going back and forth, cursing God and so on, I was wondering why this guy wasn't coming back in the store, or calling me. Part of my thinking when I was a little calmer was that I had to tell him, he had to know. I didn't get pregnant by myself, and he'd better take some responsibility, too. Somewhere in all that thinking, it got real. I was going to have a baby. If I had a baby, I wouldn't be alone. That was selfish thinking, and the first time I realized I was leaning toward keeping it. For me."

She breathed deep and faced him. "I decided to keep the baby because I was lonely. That, then, was the heaviest weight on the scale."

He didn't say anything for a moment. "And the grad student?"

"I went to see him, to tell him. Tracked him down at college, all ready to say, oops, look what happened, and here's what I've decided to do so step on up."

A breeze fluttered her hair, and she let it go. Let the damp warm air breathe over her face. "He was glad to see me, a little embarrassed, I think, that he hadn't kept in touch. The thing was, he'd fallen in love with somebody. Big sunbursts of love," she said, throwing her arms out to illustrate. "He was so happy and excited, and when he talked about her he just sent off waves of love."

"So you didn't tell him."

"I didn't tell him. What was I supposed to do? Say, gee, that's nice, glad you found someone who makes your world complete. How do you think she'll feel about the fact that you knocked me up? Too bad you screwed up the rest of your life because you were being a friend to me when I needed one. On top of that, I didn't want him. I didn't want to marry him or anything, so what was the point?"

"He doesn't know about Lily?"

"Another selfish decision, maybe with a little unselfish

best-for-him worked in. I wrestled with it later, when the pregnancy got more real, when I started to show and feel the baby kick around inside me. But I stuck with what I'd done."

She paused a moment. It was harder than she'd known it could be to finish it out, to go on when he was quiet, when the quality of his listening was so complete.

"I know he has a right to know. But that's what I did, and what I'd do again. I heard he married that girl in April, and they moved up to Virginia where his people are from. I think, whatever the reasons were, I did the right thing for all of us. Maybe he'd love Lily, or maybe she'd just be a mistake to him. I don't want to know. Because she was a mistake for me for those first few months, and I hate knowing that. I didn't start to love her, really love her, until I was about five months gone, and then it was like . . . oh, it was like everything in me opened up, and she was filling it. That's when I knew I had to leave home. Give us both a new start, clean slate."

"It was brave, and it was right."

It was so simple, his response, and nothing like what she'd prepared for. "It was crazy."

"Brave," he repeated. He stopped, by deliberate design, next to a patch of small yellow lilies. "And right."

"Turned out right. I was going to name her Eliza. That was the name I had picked out for a girl. Then you brought those red lilies into the room, and they were so beautiful, so bright. When she was born, I thought, she's so beautiful, so bright. She's Lily. So . . ." She let out a long breath. "That's the big circle, from the beginning around to the end."

He leaned down, touched his lips to hers. "The thing about circles? You can keep widening them."

"Is that a way of saying you weren't so bored by my personal soap opera you might want to do this again?"

"One thing you've never done is bore me." He linked his hand with hers so they could continue walking. "And yeah, I'd like to do this again."

"Away from the house. Away from her."

"We can do that. The thing is, Hayley, we live there. We work there. We can't avoid her."

TOO TRUE, HAYLEY THOUGHT WHEN SHE WALKED INTO her bedroom. All the drawers on her dresser hung open. Her clothes from there, from the closet, were all heaped on the bed. She crossed over, lifted a shirt, a pair of jeans. No damage, she noted, so that was something.

There'd been nothing amiss in Lily's room when she'd checked, and that was even more important. Curious, she walked to the bathroom. All of her toiletries had been shoved into a pile on the counter.

"Your way of reminding me this isn't really my place?" she wondered. "That I may be told to pack up and go any time? Maybe you're right. If and when, I'll handle it, so all you managed to do was give me an hour's annoying work before I go to bed."

She began to put away the creams and colognes, the lipsticks and mascaras. Discount brands mostly, with a couple of splurges tossed in. And maybe she did wish she could afford better, just for the fun of it.

The same went for the clothes, she admitted as she went into the bedroom to deal with them. What was wrong with wishing she could afford really good fabrics or designer labels?

It wasn't like she was obsessed with it.

Still, wouldn't it be wonderful to be hanging up fabulous dresses instead of knockoffs and discount rack. Silks and cashmere. It would feel so good against her skin.

Roz had all those incredible clothes, and walked around in old shirts half the time. More than. What was the point in having so much, then taking it for granted? Leaving it hanging when someone else could use it. Use it better, too. Someone younger who knew how to live. Who deserved it, who'd *earned* it instead of just having everything handed to her.

And all those jewels, just going to waste, sitting in a safe when they'd look so beautiful around her throat. Sparkling.

She should just take them, take a few pieces here and there. Who'd know the difference?

Everything she wanted was right here for the taking, so why not . . .

She dropped the shirt she'd been holding. Holding, she realized in front of her the way a woman holds some lovely gown. Swaying in front of the mirror. And thinking of theft.

Not me. Shaking, she stared at her own reflection.

"Not me," she said aloud. "I don't need what you need. I don't want what you want. Maybe you can get inside me, but you can't make me do something like that. You can't."

She dumped the rest of her clothes in a chair, then lay down on the bed fully dressed. And slept with the lights on.

NINE

SHE WAS GLAD TO BE WORKING THE COUNTER, GRATEful to the steady trickle of customers who kept her busy. Amelia didn't appear to be interested in her when she was working. At least not so far.

She'd made a list, documenting every incident she remembered clearly for Mitch's files. She'd noted down the locations: the pond, her bedroom, the nursery. She wasn't absolutely sure, but she thought there had been other times her thoughts weren't really hers. In the garden at Harper House, when she'd been daydreaming at work.

Once it was down on paper, she decided, it didn't seem that enormous.

At least not during the day, when people were around.

She looked over as a new customer came in. Young, good shoes, good haircut. Healthy disposable income, Hayley decided, and hoped to help her dispose of some.

" 'Morning. Can I help you find something today?"

"Well, I . . . I'm sorry, I think I've forgotten your name."

"It's Hayley." She narrowed her focus while keeping her expression pleasant. Swingy, streaky blond hair, narrow face, pretty eyes. A little bit shy.

Then her own eyes popped wide. "Jane? Roz's cousin Jane? Holy cow, look at you."

The woman flushed. "I . . . got my hair cut," she told her, and fluffed a hand over the flattering swing.

"I'll say. You look great, totally great."

The last time she'd seen Jane, she'd helped Roz and Stella move the woman's few possessions out of the overstuffed, overheated city apartment ruled by Clarissa Harper. The woman they'd smuggled out—along with journals Clarissa had nipped out of Harper House—had been dull and dowdy, like a pencil sketch that barely showed up on the paper.

Now her plain, dishwater blond hair had been lightened, highlighted, and shortened to a sassy length that didn't drag down her long, thin face.

Her clothes were simple, but the cotton shirt and breezy cropped pants were a far cry from the dumpy skirt she'd been wearing when she'd made her escape.

"I've gotta say: Wow. You look like you've been on one of those makeover shows. You know, like *What Not to Wear*. And oh boy, what just came out of my mouth was really rude."

"No, it's okay." Her smile spread even as her blush deepened. "I guess I feel made over. Jolene—you know Jolene, Stella's stepmother?"

"Yeah, she's terrific."

"She helped me get the job at the gallery, and the day before I started, she came to my new apartment. She just . . . highjacked me. She said she was my fairy godmother for the day. Before I knew it, I was getting my hair cut, and they were putting aluminum foil in what was left of it. I was too terrified to say no."

"Bet you're glad you didn't."

"I was in a daze. She dragged me out of there to the mall, and said she was going to start me off with three outfits, top to toe. After that, she expected me to fill out the rest of my wardrobe in a like manner."

Her smile wreathed from ear to ear even as her eyes went damp. "It was the most wonderful day of my life."

"That's the sweetest story." Hayley teared up as Jane did. "You deserved a fairy godmother after being kicked around by that wicked witch. You know, historically fairy tales were women's stories, passed orally in a time when women didn't have many rights."

"Um. Oh?"

"Sorry, trivia head. It's just that this is all such a girl thing, I guess. I've got to get Stella."

"I didn't want to interrupt anything. I just hoped to see Cousin Rosalind, and thank her."

"We'll get her, too." Hayley hurried over to Stella's office door. "But Stella's really going to want to see this." She poked her head in without knocking. "You've got to come out here a minute."

"Is there a problem?"

"No, just take my word and come out here."

"Hayley, I've still got half a dozen calls to make before I . . ." She trailed off, automatically putting on her greeting-the-public face when she spotted Jane. "Sorry. Is there something—Oh my God. It's Jane."

"New and improved," Hayley said, then winced. "Sorry."

"Don't be. That's just how I feel."

"Jolene said she'd given you the Jo Special." Delighted,

Stella walked a circle around Jane. "Boy, didn't she just. I love your hair."

"So do I. Your stepmother, she's been so good to me."

"She's enjoyed every minute of it. I've had reports, but I have to say, a picture's worth a thousand. I hope you're doing as well as you look."

"I love my job. I love my apartment. I really love feeling pretty."

"Oh." Stella's eyes filled.

"Same thing happened to me," Hayley said as she got a two-way from behind the counter. "Roz," she said into it, "we need you at checkout."

She clicked it off on Roz's staticky complaint about being busy.

"I don't want to drag her away from her work."

"She'll want to see you. And I want to see her see you. God, this is fun!"

"Tell us what else you've been up to," Stella said.

"Work's number one. I really love it, and I'm learning so much. I've made a couple of friends there."

"Male types?" Hayley wondered.

"I'm not ready for that yet. But there is this man in my building. He's very nice."

"Is he cute? Shoot, customer," Hayley grumbled as one came in through the back with a loaded cart. "Don't talk about anything sexy while I'm busy."

"I thought I'd be embarrassed to see the two of you again." Jane turned to Stella as Hayley waited on the customer.

"Why?"

"That time, when I met you, I was so whiny and horrible."

"You were not, you were scared and upset. For good reason. You were taking a big step, letting us in so Roz could get those journals."

"They belonged to her. Clarissa didn't have the right to take them from Harper House."

"No, she didn't. But it was still a big step for you, to let Roz get them back, to move out, start a new job, a new life. I know how scary that is. So does Hayley."

Jane glanced over her shoulder to where Hayley rang up sales and chatted with her customer. "She doesn't look like she'd be scared of anything. That's what I thought when I met her, and you. That the two of you would never be afraid to stand up for yourselves, never let yourselves get pushed around like I did."

"We all get scared, and we don't always do something so radical and positive about it."

Roz came in, the only sign of irritation the slap of her gardening gloves on her thigh. "Is there a problem?"

"Absolutely not." Stella gestured. "Jane wanted to see you."

Roz's brows lifted, and her smile spread slowly. "Well, well, well. Jolene is a woman of her word. Aren't you just blooming." She stuck her gloves in her back pocket, then lost her breath as Jane threw arms around her. "I'm glad to see you, too."

"Thank you. Thank you so much. I'll never be able to tell you."

"You're welcome."

"I'm so happy."

"I can see that. Feel it, too."

"Sorry." Sniffling, Jane released her. "I didn't intend to do that. I wanted to come, to tell you, to thank you, and to tell you I'm doing a good job at work. I got a raise already, and I'm making something of myself."

"I can see that, too. I don't have to ask if you've been well. I'm happy for you. And, however small it might be of me, I'm downright delighted to see you looking so pretty, so excited about your life because that must just burn Cousin Rissa's bony ass."

Jane gave a watery laugh. "It does. It has. She came to see me."

"What'd I miss, what'd I miss?" Hayley demanded as she hurried over. "Go back and repeat all the good stuff."

"I think we're just getting to it." Roz angled her head. "So Rissa got her broom out of storage and came to see you?"

"In my apartment. I guess my mother gave her my address, even though I asked her not to. It was about a month ago. I looked through the peephole and saw her. I almost didn't answer the door."

"Who could blame you?" In support, Hayley patted Jane's back.

"But I thought, I can't just sit here like a rabbit hiding in my own apartment. So I opened the door, and don't you know she walked right in, sniffed the air, ordered me to fetch her some sweet tea, then sat down."

"Bless her heart," Roz drawled. "Her ego never withers."

"What floor's that apartment on again?" Hayley squinted as she tried to remember. "Third or fourth, as I recall. She'd've made a nice splat if you'd tossed her out the window."

"I wish I could say I did, but I went and got the tea. I was just quaking. When I came back with it, she said I was an ungrateful, wicked girl, and I could cut off my hair, get myself into some rathole of an apartment, fool some brainless ninny into giving me a job I was certainly unqualified to handle, but it didn't change what I was. She said a number of uncomplimentary things about you, Roz."

"Oh, tell."

"Well, um. Scheming harlot for one."

"I always wanted to be called a harlot. People just don't use the word enough these days."

"That's what started getting my back up. I thought maybe she was entitled to call me ungrateful, because I was." Jane fisted her hands on her hips, jutted her chin in the air. "My apartment's not a rathole, it's just sweet, but with her tastes it might seem like it, and she didn't know Carrie—my boss?—so she might think she's brainless to give me a chance. But she had some nerve calling you names when she's the one who stole from you."

Jane squared her shoulders, gave a decisive nod. "And I said so."

"To her face." Hooting out a laugh, Roz framed Jane's face in her hands. "I couldn't be more proud."

"Her eyes almost bugged out of her head. I don't know where the words came from. I don't have much of a temper, but I was so *mad*. I just cut loose on her, said all the things I hadn't hardly let myself think when I was living with her, and waiting on her hand and foot. How she was mean and spiteful and no one had an ounce of affection for her. How she was a thief and a liar, and she was lucky you hadn't called the police on her."

"Get you." Hayley gave her an elbow nudge. "That's better than tossing her out the window."

"And I wasn't even done."

"Keep right on going," Hayley prompted.

"I said I'd beg on the street before I'd come back and be her whipping girl. Then I told her to get out of my apartment." Jane threw out an arm and pointed. "I gestured, just like this? Sort of over the top, I guess, but I was wound up. She said I'd regret it. I think she might've said I'd rue the day, but I was so stirred up I didn't pay much mind. And she left."

She blew out a breath, waved a hand in front of her face. "Whew."

"Why, Jane, you're a Trojan." Roz took her hand, gave it a squeeze. "Who'd have thought?"

"It didn't end there, exactly. She tried to have me fired."

"That bitch." Hayley's face darkened. "What did she do?"

"She went to Carrie, told her I was a woman of loose morals, how I'd had an affair with a married man, and that I'd stolen from her when she'd graciously taken me into her home. Said she felt it was her Christian duty to warn Carrie about me."

"I've always thought there were special front row seats in hell for Christians such as Clarissa," Roz commented.

"When Carrie called me into her office and told me she'd been there, what she'd said, I was sure I was going to be fired. Instead she asked me how I'd stood living with that horrible old crow. That's what she called her. And the fact that I had told her I had a lot of patience and fortitude, which she thought were good qualities in an employee. Since I had them and had proven I was willing to work hard and learned fast, she was giving me a raise."

"I like Carrie," Hayley decided. "I'd like to buy her a drink."

"THERE'S NOTHING BETTER THAN A HAPPY ENDING." Unless, Hayley decided, it was sitting in the shade on the glider, sipping a cold drink while Lily played on the grass. And Harper swung beside her.

"It's always a happy ending when Cousin Clarissa gets the heave-ho. She used to terrorize me when I was a kid, whenever she came around. Before Mama booted her out."

"Know what Jane said she called your mama?"

"No." The relaxed expression on his face settled into cold stone. "What?"

"A harlot."

"A . . ." The stone broke into a huge, rolling laugh that

had Lily clapping her hands. "A harlot. God, Mama would *love* that."

"She did. You really know her, don't you? It was just such a good morning. Pushed all the bad stuff away awhile. Seeing somebody who'd discovered themselves the way Jane has, or is, I guess. The one time I met her before? She was practically invisible. Now's she's, well, she's pretty hot."

"Yeah? How hot?"

She laughed, elbowed him. "Never you mind. One cousin at a time."

"Exactly what kind of cousins are we anyway? I've never figured it out."

"I think your daddy and mine were third cousins, which makes us fifth. At least, I think. Maybe we're fourth cousins once removed. It could be third cousins, twice removed. I can never get it just right in my head. And there's half blood in there, too with my great-grandmother's second marriage—"

It was probably just as well he stopped her mouth with his. "Kissing cousins covers it," he decided.

"Works for me." Because it did, she leaned in to take his mouth again.

Lily interrupted with a few squawks and babbles, tugging on Harper's legs until he hauled her up. Curling her arm around his neck, she pushed Hayley back.

"Well, I guess that shows me." Amused, Hayley leaned in again, and Lily pushed her back and wrapped tighter to Harper.

"Girls are always fighting over me," he said. "It's a curse."

"I bet. That one you were with last New Year's Eve looked like she could scratch and bite."

He smiled at Lily. "I don't know what she's talking about."

"Oh, yes, you do. The blonde with about a yard of hair and perfect Victoria's Secret breasts."

"Yeah, the breasts are coming back to me."

"That's a terrible thing to say!"

"You started it. Amber," he said with a chuckle as he lifted the baby high over his head to make her laugh.

"Of course. She looked like an Amber."

"She's a corporate lawyer."

"She is not."

"God's truth." He held up a hand like a man taking an oath. "Beautiful doesn't have to mean bimbo, of which you are living proof."

"Good save. Were you serious—and forget that spilled out. I hate when women, or men for that matter, poke into past relationships."

"You showed me yours. Not serious. She didn't want serious, neither did I. She's focused on her career right now."

"You ever been serious?"

"I've approached the parameter of serious a few times. Never crossed over into the zone." He sat Lily between them, snugging her in so she could swing.

Better leave it at that, Hayley told herself. Leave it comfortable with the three of them lazing on the glider with the bees humming in the hazy heat and the flowers bursting through it with bold summer colors.

"This is the best part of summer," she told him. "Evening shade. It seems like you could sit where you are for hours, without a single important thing to do."

"Don't want to get away from here awhile?"

"Not tonight. I wouldn't want to leave Lily two nights running."

"I was thinking we could take her to get some ice cream after dinner."

Surprised, she looked over. Then wondered why she'd

been surprised he'd suggest it. "She'd love that. So would I."

"Then it's a date. In fact, why don't we go out, get a burger and finish it off with ice cream?"

"Even better."

STEAMY JULY MELTED INTO SWELTERING AUGUST, days of white skies and breathless nights. It seemed almost normal, almost peaceful as day blended into day.

"I'm starting to wonder if just finding out her name was enough." Hayley potted up pink and yellow pentas. "Maybe the fact we worked to find it, and how she's Roz's great-grandmother's satisfied her, calmed her down."

"You think she's done?" Stella asked her.

"I still hear her singing in Lily's room, almost every night. But she hasn't done anything mean. Every once in a while I feel something, or sense something, but it fades away. I haven't done anything weird lately, have I?"

"You were listening to Pink the other day, and talking about getting a tattoo."

"That's not weird. I think we should both get tattoos—a flower theme. I'd get a red lily, and you could get a blue dahlia. I bet Logan would think it was wicked sexy."

"Then let him get the tattoo."

"Just a little one. A girly one."

"I think girly tattoo is an oxymoron."

"Absolutely not," Hayley protested. "Flowers, butterflies, unicorns, that kind of thing. I bet I could talk Roz into getting one."

The idea had Stella tossing back her red curls and laughing. "Tell you what, you talk Roz into getting a tattoo and . . . Nope, I still won't join the party."

"Historically, tattoos are ancient art forms, back to the Egyptians. And they were often used to control the supernatural. Since we've got some heavy supernatural going on, it would be like a talisman, *and* a personal statement."

"My personal statement will be refusing to let some guy named Tank carve a symbol—girly or otherwise—into my flesh. Just call me fussy. Those look good, Hayley. Very sweet."

"Customer wanted sweet, and the yellow and pink are her daughter's wedding colors. These'll make nice centerpieces for the wedding shower. I think I'd shoot for something a little bolder, a little punchier myself. Maybe jewel tones."

"Something you're not telling me?"

"Hmm?"

"Bride colors on your mind?"

"Oh, no." She laughed and set a completed pot aside. "No, nothing like that. We're just, Harper and me, we're just taking it slow. Really, really slow," she added with a huff of breath.

"Isn't that what you wanted?"

"Yeah, I did. I do. I don't know." She blew out another breath, fluttering her bangs. "It's smarter. It's more sensible to take things really easy. There's a lot at stake most people don't have to consider. Like our friendship, and the work, and our connection to Roz. We can't just jump into the sack because I've—we've got an itch."

"But you want to jump into the sack."

Hayley slid her eyes over to Stella's. "I was thinking more dive in, headfirst."

"Why don't you just tell him, Hayley?"

"I made the first move. He's got to make this one. I sure as hell hope he picks up speed pretty soon."

"I'M TRYING NOT TO RUSH HER." IN THE KITCHEN, Harper drained the better part of a can of Coke. He rarely broke for lunch, but early afternoon meant there would be no one in the house but David.

"You've known her going on two years, Harp. That's not just not rushing, that's standing still."

"It was different before. We've only just starting seeing each other this way. She said she wanted slow. I think it's killing me."

"I don't think people actually die from sexual frustration."

"Good. I'll be the first. I'll be written up in medical journals posthumously."

"And I'll be able to say I knew him when. Here, eat."

Dubiously, Harper poked at the sandwich David set in front of him. "What is this?"

"Delicious."

Without much interest, Harper picked up the sandwich. "What is this?" he asked again after a sampling bite. "Lamb? Cold lamb?"

"With a touch of nectarine chutney."

"That's . . . pretty damn good. Where do you come up with—no, no, stay on target." He took another bite. "I'm good at reading women, but I can't get a handle on her, on this. It's never been important before—not this way—so I keep clutching."

With his own sandwich, David slid across from him. "It is good you came to me, young student, for I am the master."

"I know. I thought about just walking over one night, maybe with a bottle of wine, knock on her terrace door. The direct approach."

"It's a classic for a reason."

"But she's nervous about Amelia, about having any sort of, you know, encounter, in the house. At least that's my take."

"Is encounter code for hot sex?"

"Damn you, you're too clever for my pitiful ruses. Anyway, I could have her and Lily over for dinner, and after the baby was asleep—a little wine, a little music." He shrugged and felt he was riding around the same circle again.

"There's also a reason why fine hotels have room service and Do Not Disturb signs."

"Room service?"

"Work with me, Harp. You take her out to dinner—fancy dinner. Let's try the Peabody. They have lovely rooms, lovely service, fine food—in-room dining."

Chewing thoughtfully, Harper played it out in his head. "I take her out to dinner—in a hotel room? Don't you think that's a little . . . brilliant," he decided after a moment.

"Yes, I do. Wine, candles, music, the works, all in the elegant privacy of a hotel suite. You'll be bringing her breakfast in bed the next morning."

Harper licked chutney off his thumb. "I'd need a two-bedroom suite for that. Lily."

"Your mama, Mitch, and I would be more than happy to entertain the charming Lily for a night. And to show your amazing forethought—or mine—I'll pack an overnight bag for Hayley. You'll just have to get the room, take her things in, arrange the service, set the scene. Then sweep her up there and off her feet.

"This is a good idea, David. I should've thought of it myself, which just shows how messed up in the head she's got me. I've got to get back, talk Stella into juggling the schedule so I can pull this off. Thanks."

"I'm always here to serve the course of true love, or at least hot hotel sex."

SHE WORE HER RED DRESS. IT WAS THE NICEST SHE had, and she liked the way it looked on her. But she wished he'd given her time to go out and get something new. All their other dates had been casual.

He'd seen her in this dress. The fact was, he'd seen her in everything she owned.

Still, she had great shoes. Roz's cast-off Jimmy Choo's that probably cost three times what the dress did. And worth every penny, Hayley decided as she turned in front of the full-length mirror. Just look what they did for her legs. Sexy instead of skinny, she decided.

Maybe she should wear her hair up. Lips pursed, she scooped it off her neck, angling her head this way and that to check the effect.

"What do you think?" she asked Lily, who was sitting on the floor busily putting a pile of little toys in Hayley's oldest purse. "Up or down? I think I can pull the up-do off, if I keep it sort of tousled. Then I could wear those cool earrings. Let's try it."

When a man said he wanted to take you out to a special dinner, she decided as she pinned and re-pinned, the least you could do was pull out all the stops, appearance-wise.

Right down to the underwear. At least that was new—and purchased recently with the idea that eventually he'd see her in it.

Maybe tonight, if they could extend the evening a little. He could come back here with her. She'd just have to block Amelia out of her mind. Block the idea that Harper's mama was right in the other wing. That her own daughter was in the next room.

Why the hell did it have to be so complicated?

She wanted him. They were both young, free, unattached, healthy. It should be simple.

Becoming lovers should have weight. She remembered Harper's words. Well, the situation had weight. It was time she started thinking of that as a plus instead of a minus.

"I'm the one making it weird, Lily. I can't seem to help it. But I'm going to try."

She put on the earrings, long, flashy gold dangles, considered a necklace and rejected it. The earrings made the show. "Well." She stepped back to do a little turn for her daughter. "What do you think? Does Mama look pretty?"

Lily's response was a mile-wide grin as she dumped everything out of the purse.

"I'll take that as a yes," Hayley said, then turned back to the mirror for one last check.

The breath left her body so fast her head went light.

She wore a red dress, but not the thin-strapped, short-skirted number she'd had for more than two years.

It was long and elaborate, cut low so that her breasts rose up to be framed by the silk with a cascade of rubies and diamonds spilling down over the exposed flesh.

Her hair was piled high in an elaborate confection of shining gold curls with a few arranged to frame a striking face with lush red lips and smoldering gray eyes.

"I'm not you," she whispered. "I'm not."

She turned deliberately away, crouched to pick up scattered toys with trembling fingers. "I know who I am. I know who she is. We aren't the same. We aren't alike."

Chilled with a sudden panic, she spun back again, more than half afraid she'd see Amelia step out of the glass, and become flesh and blood. But she saw only herself now, with her eyes too wide and dark against her pale cheeks.

"Come on, baby." She grabbed Lily, and at the baby's wail of protest, snatched up the old purse, then her own evening bag.

She made herself walk at a reasonable pace, and slowed even that as she approached the stairs. Roz would see the shock on her face, and she didn't want to talk about it. Just for one night she wanted to continue the illusion of normal.

So she took her time, got her breath back, got her features under control. She strolled into the main parlor with Lily on her hip and a smile on her face.

ten

HEAT LIGHTNING SIZZLED IN THE SKY, BROODY BURSTS, as they drove into Memphis. The traffic was as sulky as the night, but Harper seemed immune to it. They might have limped into the city, but the air was cool in the car, and Coldplay simmered out of the speakers.

Every so often he'd take his hand off the wheel to lay it over hers. A casually intimate gesture that made her heart sigh.

She'd been right to say nothing of that vision, or apparition, whatever it had been, in her bedroom mirror. Tomorrow was soon enough.

"I've never had dinner here," she said when he pulled into the hotel's lot. "I bet it's wonderful."

"One of Memphis's finest jewels."

"I've been in the lobby. You can't come to Memphis

without seeing the Peabody's duck walk. It'd be like not seeing Graceland or Beale Street."

"You forgot Sun Records."

"Oh! Isn't that the coolest place." She shot him a stern look. "And don't think I don't know you're laughing at me."

"Maybe a chuckle. Not an outright laugh."

"Well, anyway, the Peabody's got an awesome lobby. You know they've been doing that duck walk for over seventy-five years."

"Is that a fact?"

She gave him a little shove as they walked toward the hotel. "I guess you know all there is to know about the place, being a native."

"Finding out more all the time." He led her into the lobby.

"Maybe we could have a drink in here before dinner, by the fountain." She imagined something cool and sophisticated to mirror the way she was feeling. A champagne cocktail or a cosmopolitan. "Is there time?"

"We could, but I think you'll like what I have in mind even better." He walked with her toward the elevators.

She glanced back over her shoulder with some regret. All that gorgeous marble and colored glass. "Is there a dining room upstairs? They don't have one on the roof, do they? I've always thought roof-top dining was so elegant. Unless it rains. Or it's windy. Or it's too hot," she added with a laugh. "I think roof-top dining's really elegant in the movies."

He only smiled, nudged her inside ahead of him. "Did I tell you that you look beautiful tonight?"

"You did, but I don't mind certain kinds of repetition."

"You look beautiful." He touched his lips to hers. "You should always wear red."

"And look at you," She ran her fingers down the lapels

of his dark jacket. "All duded up in a suit. The rest of the women in the restaurant won't be able to eat for envying me my good luck."

"If that's the case, we might just have to give them a break." He took her hand as the doors opened, then led her into the hallway. "Come with me."

"What's going on?"

"Something I hope you'll like." He stopped at a door, took out a key. He unlocked the door, opened it, gestured. "After you."

She stepped inside, her breath catching as she saw the spacious room. Her hand fluttered up to her throat as she crossed the black and white checkerboard tiles into a parlor where candles flickered, and red lilies speared lavishly out of glass vases.

The colors were deep and rich, long windows adding the sparkling lights of the city. In front of one, a table was set for two, and a bottle of champagne sat in a gleaming silver bucket.

There was music playing, slow, soft Memphis blues. Stunned, she turned a circle, saw the spiral staircase that led to a second level.

"You . . . you did this?"

"I wanted to be alone with you."

Her heart was still in her throat as she turned to face him. "You did this for me?"

"For both of us."

"This beautiful room—just for us. Flowers and candles, and God, champagne. I'm overwhelmed."

"I want you to be." He stepped to her, took both her hands. "I want tonight to be special, memorable." And brought them to his lips. "Perfect."

"It's sure off to a good start. Harper, no one's ever gone to so much trouble for me. I've never felt more special."

"It's just the start. I ordered dinner already. It'll be up in about fifteen minutes. Plenty of time for us to have that drink. How do you feel about champagne?"

"I feel like I couldn't settle for anything less right now. Thank you." She leaned to him, took his mouth for a long, warm kiss.

"I'd better open that bottle, or I'll forget the lineup of events."

"There's a lineup?"

"More or less." He walked over to lift the bottle from the bucket. "And just so you can relax, I gave Mama the number here. She's got that, your cell, mine, and I made her promise to call if Lily so much as hiccups."

He popped the cork as she laughed. "All right. I'll trust Roz to keep it all under control."

She did a little spin, just couldn't help herself. "I feel like Cinderella. Minus the evil stepsisters, and well, the pumpkin. But other than that, me and Cindy, we're practically twins."

"If the shoe fits."

"I'm going to wallow in this, Harper, I may as well just tell you that. I don't know how sophisticated I can be when I just want to jump up and down, go racing around to look at everything. I bet the bathrooms are amazing. Do you think that fireplace works? I know it's too hot for a fire, but I don't care."

"We'll light it. Here." He handed her a glass, tapped his to it. "To memorable moments."

She held the moment, the glow of it. "And to men who make them happen. Oh, wow," she said after the first sip. "This is really good. Maybe I'm dreaming."

"If you are, I am, too."

"That's all right then."

He touched her, skimming his fingers over the back of

her neck, exposed by her upswept hair. Then with the lightest of pressure eased her toward him. The knock on the door brought on a wry grin.

"Prompt service. I'll get it. Once they've set up dinner, we'll be completely alone."

HE MADE IT ALL HAPPEN, SHE MUSED. THE BIG PICture, the tiny details so the evening unfolded for her like the pages of a storybook. And because of him, she was sitting in an elegant suite, sipping champagne with the romance of candlelight, the shimmer of firelight. Flowers scented the air. There was a lovely meal she could barely taste through the anticipation bubbling in her throat.

Tonight, they would make love.

"Tell me what it was like for you, growing up," she asked him.

"I liked having brothers, even when they pissed me off."

"You're close. I can see that whenever they come to visit. Even though they live away from Memphis, the three of you are like a team."

He topped off her glass. "Did you wish for sibs when you were a kid?"

"I did. I had friends and cousins to play with, but I did. A sister especially. Somebody to tell secrets to in the middle of the night, or even to fight with. You had all that."

"As kids, it was like having a personal gang, especially when David came along."

"Bet the four of you drove Roz crazy."

He grinned, lifted his glass. "We did our best. Summers were long, the way they're supposed to be when you're a kid. Long, hot days, and the yard, the woods, they were the whole world. I remember how it smelled, all green and thick. And this time of year, how you'd hear the cicadas all night."

"I used to leave my window open a little ways at night so I could hear them better. I bet y'all got in plenty of trouble."

"Probably more than our share. You couldn't slip much by Mama. She had this radar, it was a little scary. I remember how she'd be in the garden, or in the house doing something, and I'd come around and she'd just know I'd been doing something I shouldn't've been doing."

She propped an elbow on the table, cupped her chin in her hand. "Name something."

"The most baffling, at least at the time, was when I was with a girl the first time." He drenched one of the strawberries in whipped cream, held it out for her to bite. "I came home having had my first sample of paradise in the backseat of my much-loved Camaro, about six months after my sixteenth birthday. She came into my room the next morning, and put a box of Trojans on my dresser."

With a shake of his head, he polished off the berry. "She said, and I remember this very well, that we'd already talked about sex and responsibility, about being safe and smart and careful, so she assumed that I had used protection, and would continue to do so. Then she asked if I had any questions or comments."

"What did you say?"

"I said, 'No ma'am.' And when she walked out the door, I pulled the covers up over my head and asked God how the hell my mama came to know I'd had sex with Jenny Proctor in my Camaro. It was both mystifying and humiliating."

"I hope I'm like that."

His eyebrows lifted as he coated another berry. "Mystified and humiliated?"

"No. As smart as your mama. As wise as that with Lily."

"Lily's not allowed to have sex until she's thirty, and married a couple of years."

"Goes without saying." She bit into the berry he offered,

mmm'd over it. "What happened to Jenny Proctor?"

"Jenny?" He got a look on his face, a kind of half smile that told her he was looking back. "Why, she just pined away for me. She was forced to go to California to college, and stay out there and marry a screenwriter."

"Poor thing. I shouldn't have any more," she said when he topped off her glass again. "I'm already half buzzed."

"No point in doing things halfway."

Angling her head, she sent him a deliberately provocative look. "Is part of the lineup you talked about getting me loose on champagne so you can have your way with me?"

"It was on the schedule."

"Thank God. Is that event coming up soon, because I don't think I can sit here and look at you much longer without having you touch me."

His eyes darkened as he rose, held out a hand for hers. "Here was my plan. I was going to ask you to dance, so I could get my arms around you, something like this."

She slid into them. "I haven't found a single flaw in your plan so far."

"Then I was going to kiss you, here." He brushed his lips over her temple. "And here." Her cheek. "And here." And her mouth, sinking in slowly and deeply until that meeting of lips was the center of the world.

"I want you so much." She pressed against him, burrowed in. "It takes me over. Take me over, Harper. I'll go crazy if you don't."

He circled her toward the steps, stopped at the base and looked into her eyes. "Come upstairs, and be with me."

With her hand in his, she started up, then let out a breathless laugh. "My knees are shaking. I can't even tell if it's from nerves or excitement. I've imagined myself with you so many times, but I never imagined I'd be nervous."

"We'll go slow. No rush."

Her heart was beginning to trip and stumble, but there was one more thing. "Um, I'm using something—birth control—but I think we should . . . I didn't bring any of those Trojans."

"I'll take care of it."

"Should've figured you'd thought of everything."

"Be prepared."

"Were you a Boy Scout?"

"No, but I dated a few former Girl Scouts."

It made her chuckle, and nearly relax again. "I think . . ."

She trailed off as she stepped into the bedroom. There were candles waiting to be lit, and the lamp on low. The bed was already turned down, with a single red lily resting on the pillow.

The romance of it saturated her.

"Oh, Harper."

"Wait." He walked around the room to light the candles, to turn off the lamp. Then he picked up the flower and offered it. "I brought you these because it's how I think of you, how I've thought of you since the beginning. I've never thought of anyone else the same way."

She stroked the petals over her cheek, breathed in their fragrance, then set the lily aside. "Undress me."

He lifted a hand, nudged the thin strap from her shoulder, laid his lips there. In turn, with her heart beating thickly, she slid the jacket off his.

Then her mouth found his as her fingers opened the buttons of his shirt, as his drew down the zipper at the back of her dress. His hands cruised over her back, and hers spread over his chest. When her dress slithered to the floor, she stepped out of it—then held her breath as he eased back and just looked at her.

She wore flimsy scraps of red that shimmered in the candlelight against her smooth pale skin. And high, high heels with long, long legs. Desire, already impossibly strong, clutched at his belly.

"You're amazing."

"I'm skinny. All angles, no curves."

He shook his head, reached out to trace a finger over the subtle curve of her breast. "Delicate, like a lily stem. Would you take your hair down?"

With her eyes on his, she reached up to pull out the pins, then skimmed her fingers through it. And waited.

"Amazing," he repeated. Taking her hand, he drew her to the bed. "Just sit," he said, then knelt in front of her to slip off her shoes.

His lips trailed up her calf and had her clutching the edge of the bed. "Oh God."

"Let me do the things I've thought about doing." His teeth grazed the back of her knee. "All of them."

There was no thought to deny him, and no words that could surface through the flood of sensation. His tongue slid along her thigh, that mouth burning tiny brands into her flesh even as his hands traveled up, tracing her breasts with his fingers until they ached over her thundering heart.

She shuddered out his name, falling back on the bed as he came to her.

She could hold him close now, touch as she was touched. Taste as she was tasted. The pleasure filled her—the glide of his hands, the heat of his lips, the catch of his breath as they rolled together to find more.

No rush, he'd told her, but he couldn't slow his hands. They wanted to take, and take more. Her breasts in his hands, in his mouth, small and firm and satin smooth, and when he feasted on them she bowed up, exposing the long, slender line of her throat.

At last, she was his.

Her nails bit into his back, scraped down his hips. Tiny

thrilling pains. Then she was over him, her mouth as greedy as his, and her quick, gasping breaths roaring in his head like a storm.

Candlelight sheened over her skin, skin going damp with the heat they fueled through each other. The gold of those flickering lights glowed in the deepening blue of her eyes as he slid his hand over her, found her hot. Found her wet.

The orgasm was like a burst of light, a stunning flash that blinded her, set her body on fire then left it to glow. She felt herself slide toward oblivion, then come back into the bright, bright world of swimming sensations. Her body was awake, alive.

Then his mouth found her and sent her spinning beyond pleasure. It was a roiling heat that built and built, then gushed through her so that she was weak and wavery when he dragged her to her knees.

He looked at her, into her it seemed, so deep she thought he must see everything she was. And his mouth took hers in a kiss that made her heart tremble.

So this was love, she thought. This utter trust and surrender of self. This complete gift of heart that left you open, defenseless. And full of joy.

She touched her hand to his cheek, her lips curving as she shifted, as she wrapped her legs around him. "Yes," she said, and took him into her. "Yes," then arched back with a moan as the beauty swamped her.

He lowered his brow to her shoulder, barely able to breathe as she closed around him. But he drew her back to him, heart against heart. Not close enough, he thought. It could never be close enough.

Her arms locked around him, her mouth found his as they rocked themselves toward the edge, and over.

* * *

THERE WAS PROBABLY SOMETHING MORE RELAXING than sprawling on a big bed, limbs tangled with your lover's after mind-melting sex. But Hayley figured it was probably illegal.

In any case, she'd take this shimmery afterglow.

As far as romantic nights, this one left everything else she'd experienced in the dust. Gliding on it, she curled her body a little closer to his, and smiled dreamily when his hand stroked over her back.

"That was wonderful," she murmured. "You're wonderful. Everything's wonderful. I feel like if I stepped outside right now, this light inside me would blind the entire population of Memphis."

"If you stepped outside right now, you'd be arrested." His hand slipped lower. "Better just stay right here with me."

"You're probably right. Mmm, I feel so loose." She stretched like a cat. "I guess I was pretty blocked up, you know? Self-servicing isn't nearly as satisfying as . . . Oh God, I can't believe I said that."

His shoulders were already shaking as he snorted out a laugh. And hooked an arm firmly around her before she could roll away. "Happy to be . . . at your service."

She buried her face against his shoulder. "Things just jump out of my mouth sometimes. It's not like I'm a sex maniac or anything."

"Well, now you've shattered my dreams."

She cuddled closer, tipped her head up. "It's nice being here like this. I mean just like this," she said, and feathered her fingers through his hair. "All soft and warm, snuggled up in bed. I wish we could just stay, and tonight would just go on and on."

"We can stay, and when tonight stops going on, we can have breakfast right here in bed."

"That sounds amazing, but you know I can't. Lily—"

"Is sound asleep in the Portacrib we moved into my mother's sitting room earlier today." When her eyes widened, he pressed a kiss to her forehead. "Mama was practically rubbing her hands together with glee at the prospect of keeping her overnight."

"Your mama . . ." She pushed up on her elbow. "God, did everybody know about this but me?"

"Pretty much."

"Roz knows we're . . . that's just very strange. But I don't think I should—"

"Mama said to remind you she managed to raise three boys, keep them all alive and out of jail."

"But . . . I'm a terrible mother. I want to stay."

"You're not a terrible mother. You're an awesome mother." He sat up as she did, took her shoulders. "You know Lily's fine, and you know Mama loves having her."

"I do. I do know that, but . . . what if she wakes up and wants me? Okay," she said with a sigh when he just lifted his eyebrows. "If she wakes up, Roz'll handle it. And Lily loves spending time with her, and Mitch. I'm being a cliché."

"But you're such a pretty one."

She looked around the room. Beautiful, sumptuous—absolute freedom. "We can really just stay?"

"I'm hoping you will."

She bit her lip. "I don't have any . . . things, you know? Not even a toothbrush. A hairbrush. I don't have my—"

"David packed you a bag."

"David . . . well, that's all right then. He'd know what I'd want." She felt giddy little bubbles rising up in her throat. "We're just staying?"

"That's the plan. If it's okay with you."

"If it's okay with me?" she repeated, and a gleam came into her eyes as she launched herself at him. "Let me show you what I think about that."

* * *

LATER, SHE CAME RUSHING OUT OF THE BATHROOM. "Harper, did you see these robes? They're so big and soft." She stood rubbing a sleeve against her cheek. "There are two of them, one for each of us."

Lazily, he opened one eye. The woman, he thought, was proving to be insatiable. Praise Jesus. "Nice."

"Everything in here is wonderful."

"Romeo and Juliet suite," he murmured, almost drifting.

"What?"

"The suite. It's the Romeo and Juliet suite."

"Really, but that's . . ." Her brows drew together. "Well, if you think about it, they were a couple of teenage suicides."

On a laugh, he opened his eyes. "Trust you."

"I never saw it as being romantic. Tragic is what it was—and plain stupid. Not the play," she corrected, turning a circle to swirl the robe. "It's brilliant, but those two? Oops, she's dead, I'll drink this poison. Oops, he's dead, I'll stab myself in the heart. I mean, *Jesus,* and I'm babbling."

"What you are," he said, staring at her, "is fascinating."

"I get pretty opinionated about books. But whoever it's named for, the suite's downright awesome. It just makes me want to dance all around it, buck-ass naked."

"I knew I should've brought a camera."

"I wouldn't mind." Holding the robe up like a cape, she swirled once more. "I think it'd be sexy if we took naked pictures of each other. Then when I'm old, and all brittle and wrinkled up, I'd look at myself and remember being young."

She bounced onto the bed. "You got any naked pictures of yourself?"

"Not so far."

"Look at you." She tickled his knee. "You're embarrassed."

"Not entirely." Oh yeah, he thought, she was fascinating. "You got any?"

"Never trusted anybody enough before. And I've got this bony build. But you didn't seem to mind it."

"I think you're beautiful."

He meant it, and wasn't that a miracle? She could see it in his eyes. She'd felt it in his touch. "I feel beautiful tonight." She rose, wrapping the white robe around her. "All plush and lush and decadent."

"Let's order dessert."

She stopped twirling. "Dessert? But it's almost two in the morning."

"They have this amazing invention called twenty-four-hour room service."

"All night? I'm such a rube. But I don't care." She plopped back down on the bed. "Can we eat it up here? In bed?"

"The rules attached to twenty-four-hour room service are if you order after midnight, you're required to eat in bed. Naked."

She grinned wickedly. "Rules are rules."

They lay belly-down, facing each other, with a plate of chocolate-soaked cake between them.

"Probably going to be sick," she said as she ate another mouthful. "But it's so good."

"Here." He stretched out an arm, managed to grab one of the glasses on the floor. "Wash it down."

"I can't believe you ordered another bottle of champagne."

"You can't do naked chocolate cake without champagne. It's declassé."

"If you say so." She drank, then forked up more cake and held it out for him. "You know . . ." She wagged the fork at him. "On the date-o-meter you're going to have to go a ways to top this one. I don't think I can settle for anything less than, oh, a wild weekend in Paris or maybe a quick jet to Tuscany to make love in a vineyard."

"How about a sun-and-sex-soaked sojourn to Bimini."

"Sex-soaked sojourn." She gave a tipsy giggle. "Say that five times fast." On a moan, she rolled over to her back. "If I eat another bite, I believe I'll regret it for the rest of my life."

"Can't have that." He set the plate aside. Then easing forward, closed his mouth over hers in a lingering upside-down kiss.

"Mmm." She rubbed her lips together when he lifted his head. "You taste very potent."

"Got a nice chocolate high going here."

She smiled as he slid down to her, as his hands trailed over her breasts, her torso, her belly. Then gasped when his lips nibbled away.

"Oh my God, Harper."

"I forgot to mention this part of late-night dessert." He shifted, reached out. Swirling a finger through cream and chocolate, he smeared it lightly onto her breast. "Oops. I'd better get that off."

SHE FELT SO SMUG AND COSMOPOLITAN, STEPPING OUT of the elevator into the lobby with her overnight bag. It was nearly noon, and she was just wandering into the day. She'd had breakfast in bed. The fact was, she thought, she'd had about everything in bed that was available in the State of Tennessee.

She imagined even her toenails were glowing as a result.

"I'm going to check out." He nipped a little kiss on her lips. "Why don't you sit down?"

"I'm going to walk around. Look at everything. And I want to pick up a few things in the gift shop."

"Be right back."

She let out a happy sigh. She wanted to remember everything. The people, the fountain, the tidy bellmen, the shiny displays of art and jewelry.

She bought a little quacking duck for Lily, and a silver frame as a thank-you gift for Roz. Then there were the sweet duck-shaped soaps, and the pretty yellow cap that would look so cute on Lily. And . . .

"No man in his right mind turns his back on a woman in a gift shop," Harper said from behind her.

"I can't help it. Everything's so pretty. No," she said when she saw him reach for his wallet. "I'm getting these." She set all her items on the counter, then picked up a canister once it was rung up. "This is for you."

"Duck soap?"

She inclined her head. "To commemorate our stay. We had the best time," she told the clerk.

"I'm glad you enjoyed the hotel. Are you here on business or pleasure?"

"Just pleasure." Hayley gathered the bag. "Just lots and lots of pleasure." She tucked her free hand into Harper's as they strolled back into the lobby. "We'd better get home before Lily forgets what I look like and . . . oh man, just *look* at that bracelet."

The display showcasing a local jeweler glittered and shone, but all Hayley could see was the delicate bracelet with sizzling white diamonds framing gleaming ruby hearts.

"It's drop dead, isn't it? I mean it's elegant, even delicate, and the heart shapes make it romantic, but something about it just says: Hey, I'm an important piece. Maybe because it's an estate piece. Antique jewelry has such a—what's the word I want. Panache," she decided.

"Nice."

"Nice," she said and rolled her eyes at him. "Such a guy. What it is, is stunning. Some of the other pieces in there have bigger stones, more diamonds, whatever, but this is the one that stands out. To me, anyway."

He scanned the name and address of the store. "Let's go get it."

"Sure." She laughed up at him. "Why don't we pick up a new car on the way, too?"

"I like my car. It would suit you. Rubies would be your stone."

"Harper, paste is my stone."

She tugged his hand, but he continued to study the bracelet. The longer he looked at it, the more clearly he could see it on her. "I'll just talk to the concierge."

"Harper." Distressed now, she stepped back. "I was just looking. That's what we girls do—we look in shop windows."

"I want to buy it for you."

It was more than distress now, and closer to panic. "You can't buy me something like that. It probably costs—I can't even guess."

"Then let's find out."

"Harper, just wait. Just . . . I don't expect you to buy me expensive jewelry. I don't expect you to do things like this." She gestured to encompass the hotel. "It was the most incredible night of my life, but it's not why—Harper, it's not why I'm with you."

"Hayley, if it was why you were with me, you wouldn't be. Last night was for us, and it meant every bit as much to me as it did to you. I've got enough of my mother in me that you should know if I do something like this, it's because I want to. I want to buy this for you, and if it's not out of my range, that's what I'm going to do." He kissed her forehead. "Just hang here a minute."

Speechless, she watched him walk to the concierge desk.

And on the drive home, she continued to be speechless at the way the ruby hearts in their diamond frames glittered on her wrist.

eLeveN

SHE FRETTED FOR THE REST OF THE AFTERNOON, AND lavished attention on Lily. It was a strange and, she imagined, strictly maternal sort of juggling act to balance the fact that she'd missed her baby girl with the fact that she'd had the most wonderful time without her.

Guilt, she thought, came in many forms. By the time Roz got in from work, Hayley had built up a sputtering head of guilt.

"Welcome home." Roz stretched her back, eyed Hayley who stood in the foyer. "Did you have a good time?"

"Yes. Wonderful. Beyond wonderful. I should start out saying you raised the most incredible man."

"That was the goal."

"Roz, I can't thank you enough for keeping Lily that way." Unconsciously, she covered the bracelet on her wrist with her other hand. "It was more than I could expect."

"I enjoyed it. We all did. Where is she?"

"I wore her out," Hayley said with a weak smile. "All but kissed the skin off her bones. She's taking a quick nap. I got you a gift."

"Isn't that sweet." Taking the box, Roz strolled into the parlor to open it. And beamed when she found the frame, already spotlighting a picture of her with Lily. "I love this shot. I'm going to put this on the desk in my sitting room."

"I hope she didn't give you any trouble last night."

"Not a bit. We had ourselves a fine time."

"I—we—Harper. Hell. Can we sit down a minute?"

Obligingly, Roz sat on the sofa, propped her feet on the table. "I wonder if David's made any lemonade? I could drink a gallon."

"I'll go get you some."

Roz waved toward a seat. "I'll get my own in a minute. Tell me what's on your mind."

Hayley sat, stiff-backed, her hands folded in her lap. "I got to know the mothers of some of the guys I dated. We always got along okay. But I never . . . it's so surreal to be good friends with the mother of a man I'm . . . romantically intimate with."

"I'd think, all in all, that would be a bonus."

"It's not that it isn't. I suppose it would be less surreal if I'd gotten to know you, gotten to be friends with you *after* things became—"

"Romantically intimate."

"Yeah. I don't know how to talk to you about it, exactly, because the relationships are all tangled together. But I wanted to say, to tell you, that you raised an amazing individual. I know I did that, but I want to say it again. Harper went to so much trouble, took such care to give me something special. There aren't many like that, at least in my experience."

"He's a very special man. I'm glad you see that, and appreciate it."

"I do. He had this beautiful suite, and flowers and candles. Champagne. No one's ever done anything like that for me. I don't just mean the lavishness, you know? I'd've been fine with a plate of ribs and a motel room. And how crude is that," she muttered, closing her eyes.

"Not crude. Honest. And refreshing."

"What I mean to say is no one's ever taken that time, that care to plan a whole evening with me in mind."

"It's a disconcerting thrill to be swept off your feet."

"Yes." Relief poured through her. "Yes, exactly. My head's still spinning. I wanted you to know that I'd never take advantage of his nature, his consideration."

"He bought you that bracelet."

Hayley jolted, clamped a hand over it. "Yes. Roz—"

"I've been admiring it since I came in. And watching you rub your hand over it, guiltily. As if you'd stolen it."

"I feel like I did."

"Oh, don't be ridiculous." Roz's eyebrows drew together as she waved a hand. "You'll irritate me."

"I didn't ask for it. I told him not to. All I did was admire it in the window, and the next thing you know he's making arrangements with the concierge and the jewelry store. He wouldn't tell me how much it cost."

"I should hope not," she said staunchly. "I raised him better."

"Roz, these are real stones. It's an antique. It's a real antique."

"I've been on my feet most of today. Don't make me get up to get a closer look at it."

Emotions in turmoil, Hayley stepped over, held out her wrist. Roz simply tugged her down on the sofa. "That is a beauty, and certainly suits you. How many ruby hearts are there?"

"I wouldn't count them," she began, then lowered her head at Roz's bland stare. "Fourteen," she confessed. "With ten little diamonds around here, and two between each heart. God, I'm crass."

"No, you're a girl. And one with excellent taste. Don't wear that to work, no matter how much you want to. You'll get it dirty."

"You're not upset?"

"Harper is free to spend his money as he sees fit, and has the good sense to spend it with some discrimination. He gave you a lovely gift. Why don't you just enjoy it?"

"I thought you'd be mad."

"Then you underestimate me."

"I don't. I don't." Tears swam into her eyes as she burrowed against Roz. "I love you. I'm sorry, I'm so twisted up. I'm so happy. I'm so scared. I'm in love with him. I'm in love with Harper."

"Yes, honey." Roz curled an arm around Hayley, and patted gently. "I know."

"You know." Sniffling, Hayley reared back.

"Look at you." Smiling a little, Roz brushed Hayley's hair away from her damp cheeks. "Sitting here crying, happy, scared tears. The kind a woman sheds over some man she's realized she's crazy about, and doesn't know quite how the hell it happened to her."

"I didn't really know until last night. I knew I liked him, that I cared about him, but mostly I thought I wanted to bang him. Then . . . Oh God, oh God, I actually said that." Mortified, she pressed the heels of her hands against her eyes and rubbed. "See why this is surreal? I just told Harper's mother I wanted to bang him."

"I admit, the situation is a bit unique. But I think my sensibilities can handle it."

"It all just opened up inside me last night, everything opened up and poured through. I've never felt like that." Hayley pressed a hand to her heart, and the rubies glittered. "I've never been in love before, not all the way in love. And I thought, when it happened, that this is it, this is how it feels when you fall. Don't tell him." She gripped Roz's hand. "Please don't tell him."

"It's not for me to tell him. It's for you, when you're ready. Love's a gift, Hayley, to be taken and received freely."

"Love's a lie, an illusion created by weak women and conniving men. An excuse for the middle class to breed and their betters to ignore so they can marry within their own station and build more wealth."

Roz felt the shudder run through her, and her breath back up in her lungs. But she straightened, continued to look in the eyes that were no longer only Hayley's. "Is that how you justified the choices you made?"

"I lived very well on my choices." She lifted her arm, smiled as she trailed a finger over the bracelet. "Very well. Better than those I came from. She was content to serve on her knees. I preferred serving on my back. I could have lived here."

She rose, wandering the room. "I should have. So now I am here. Always."

"But you're not happy. What happened? Why are you here, and so unhappy?"

"I made life." She whirled, cupping a hand over her belly. "You know the power of that. Life grew in me, came from me. And he took it. My son." She looked around, those eyes darting. "My son. I came for my son."

"He's gone now, too." Roz rose slowly. "Long ago. My grandfather. He was a good man."

"A baby. My baby. Little boy, sweet, small. Mine. Men, men are liars, thieves, cheats. I should have killed him."

"The child?"

Those eyes glittered, bright and hard as the diamonds on her wrist. "The father. I should have found a way to kill him, all of them. Burned the house to the ground around them, and sent us all to hell."

There was a chill, and the pity Roz had once felt couldn't chip through the ice of it. "What did you do?"

"I came, I came in the night. Quiet as a mouse." She tapped a finger to her lips, then began to laugh. "Gone." She turned a circle, holding her arm high so the rubies and diamonds flashed. "All gone, everything gone. Nothing left for me." Her head cocked, her gaze turned to the monitor, and Lily's waking cries.

"The baby. The baby's crying."

Her head lolled as she slid to the floor.

"Mitch! David!" Roz rushed across the room to drop down beside Hayley.

"Got a little dizzy," Hayley murmured, passing a hand over her face. Then she looked around, groped for Roz's hand. "What? What?"

"It's all right. Just stay down a minute. David." Roz glanced over her shoulder when both men hurried into the room. "Get us some water and the brandy."

"What happened?" Mitch demanded.

"She had a spell, an episode."

"Lily. Lily's crying."

"I'll get her." Mitch, touched Hayley's shoulder. "I'll go get her."

"I remember. I think. Sort of. My head hurts."

"All right, sweetie. Let's get you onto the couch."

"Little queasy," Hayley managed when Roz helped her to her feet. "I'didn't feel it coming, Roz. Then it was . . . it was stronger that time. It was more."

David brought both water and brandy, and sitting on Hayley's other side, put a glass of water in her hand. "Here now, baby doll, sip some water."

"Thanks. I'm okay, feeling better. Just a little shaky."

"You're not the only one," Roz said.

"You talked to her."

"We had quite the conversation."

"You asked her questions. I don't know how you held it together like that."

"Have a little brandy," Roz suggested, but Hayley wrinkled her nose.

"I don't like it. I feel better, honest."

"Then I'll have your share." Roz picked up the snifter and took a healthy swallow as Mitch came in with Lily.

"She'll want her juice. She likes a little juice when she gets up from a nap."

"I'll get her some," Mitch told Hayley.

"No, I'll take her in. I'd like to do something normal for a few minutes." She got to her feet, reaching for Lily as Lily reached for her. "There's my baby girl. We'll be right back."

Roz got to her feet when Hayley left the room. "I'm going to call Harper. He'll want to know about this."

"I'd like to know about this myself," Mitch reminded her.

"You'll want your notebook and tape recorder."

"WE WERE JUST SITTING THERE TALKING. I WAS TELLING Roz what a wonderful time I'd had last night, and showing her the bracelet. And—sorry Harper—but I was telling her I felt guilty about you buying it for me. And I guess I got emotional." She sent a pleading look at Roz, clearly begging confidence. "And then she was just there. Like a bang. I'm a little bit vague on it. It was like hearing a conversation—like when you hold a glass to a wall to hear what people are saying in the next room. All sort of tinny and echoing."

"She was amused, in my opinion, in a nasty sort of way," Roz began, and took them through it.

"She was accustomed to receiving gifts for sex." Mitch scribbled in his notebook. "So that's how she'd equate the bracelet Hayley's wearing. She wouldn't understand," he continued, hearing the quiet sound of distress she made, "generosity, or the pleasure of giving for the sake of the gift. When something was given to her, it was an exchange. Never a token of affection."

Hayley nodded and continued to sit on the floor with Lily.

"She came here," he continued. "By her own words she came here at night. She wanted to cause harm to Reginald, perhaps the entire household. Maybe even planned to. But she didn't. We could assume harm came to her here. She said she was here, always."

"Died here." Hayley nodded. "Remains here. Yes. It felt like that. Like I could almost, almost, see what was in her head while it was happening. And that's what it felt like. She died here, and she stays here. And she thinks of the child she had as a baby still. She's the way she was then, and in her mind—I think—so is her son."

"So she relates to, is drawn to, children," Harper finished. "Once they grow up, they're no real substitute for hers. Especially if they happen to grow up into men."

"She came to help me when I needed it," Roz pointed out. "She recognizes the blood connection. Acknowledges it, at least when it suits her. Hayley's heightened emotions brought her out. But then she answered questions, she spoke intelligently."

"So I'm a kind of conduit." Hayley fought back another shudder. "But why me?"

"Maybe because you're a young mother," Mitch suggested. "Close to the age she was when she died, raising a child—something that was denied her. She made life. It was stolen from her. When life is stolen, what's left?"

"Death," Hayley said with a shudder. She stayed where she was when Lily ran over to Harper and lifted her arms to be held. "She's getting stronger, that's how it felt. She likes having a body around her, having her say. She'd like more. She'd like . . ."

She caught herself twisting the bracelet, and stared down at it. "I forgot," she whispered. "Oh God, I forgot. Last night, when I was dressing, checking myself out in the mirror. She was there."

"You had one of these experiences last night?" Harper demanded.

"No. Or not like this one. She was there, instead of me, in the mirror. I wasn't—" She shook her head impatiently. "I was me, all the way, but the reflection was her. I didn't say anything because I just didn't want to go around about it last night. I just wanted to get out awhile, then everything . . . it went out of my mind until now. She wasn't like we've seen her before."

"What do you mean?" Mitch sat, pencil poised.

"She was all dressed up. A red dress, but not like what I was wearing. Fancy gown, low-cut, off the shoulders. Ball gown, I'd guess. She wore a lot of jewels. Rubies and diamonds. The necklace was . . ." She trailed off to stare at the bracelet in speechless shock.

"Rubies and diamonds," she repeated. "She was wearing this. This bracelet. I'm sure of it. When I saw it at the hotel, I was so pulled toward it. I couldn't see anything else in the display. She was wearing this, on her right wrist. It was hers. This was hers."

Mitch left his seat to crouch on the floor by Hayley and examine the bracelet. "I don't know anything about dating jewelry, about eras along this avenue. Harper, did the jeweler give you a history?"

"Circa 1890," he said tightly. "I never thought twice about it."

"Maybe she pushed you to buy it for me." Hayley shoved to her feet. "If she—"

"No. I wanted to give you something. It's as simple as that. If it makes you uncomfortable to have it, or weirds you out, we can keep it in the safe."

Utter trust, she remembered. That was love. "No. It wasn't an exchange, it was a gift." She crossed to him, kissed him lightly on the lips. "So screw her."

"That's my girl."

Lily batted her hand on his cheek until he turned his face to hers, then she bumped her mouth to his.

"Or one of them," he added.

BY EVENING, SHE WAS CALM AGAIN. CALMER STILL when she settled down in the rocking chair with Lily. She prized these moments, when the room was quiet and she could rock her baby to sleep. Sing to her, and though her voice was no prize, Lily seemed to like it.

This was what Amelia craved, maybe what she craved most under the madness. Just these moments of unity and peace, a mother rocking her child to sleep with a lullaby.

She would try to remember that, Hayley promised herself, whenever she got too frightened or too angry. She would try to remember what Amelia had lost, what had been stolen from her.

She tried "Hush, Little Baby," because it pleased her she knew all the words. And Lily's head was usually heavy on her shoulder by the time the song was finished.

She was nearly there when a movement at the doorway had her heart bumping her ribs. Then it stilled when Harper smiled in at her. In the same rusty, sing-song voice she was using for the lullabye, she warned him.

"She won't go down if she sees you in here."

He nodded, lingered another moment, then slipped away.

Humming, she rose to walk to the crib, tucking Lily in with her stuffed dog within cuddling reach. "When you're three, Mama'll get you a real puppy. Okay, when you're two, but that's my final offer. 'Night, baby."

Leaving the night-light glowing, she left the baby sleeping. Harper turned from the terrace doors when she came in.

"That was a pretty picture, you and Lily rocking in the chair. Mama says she used to rock me and my brothers to sleep in that chair."

"It's why it feels so good. A lot of love's sat in that rocker."

"It's cooler tonight, at least a little cooler. Maybe we could sit out for a while."

"All right." She picked up her bedside monitor, and went with him.

In front of the rail, there was a trio of huge copper pots, greening softly in the weather. She'd been charged with selecting and planting the flowers in them this year, and was always thrilled to see the thriving mix of color, shape, and texture.

"I don't mind the heat, not this time of day anyway." She leaned down to sniff a purple bloom. "The sun goes down a little more, the lightning bugs'll come out, and the cicadas'll start singing."

"Gave me a scare when Mama called earlier."

"Guess so."

"So here's the thing." He ran a hand absently along her arm. "You shouldn't stay here after tonight. You can move on over to Logan's tomorrow. Take some time off," he continued as she turned to stare at him.

"Time off?"

"The nursery's the same as Harper House, as far as this goes. Best you steer clear of both for a while. Mitch and I'll see what we can do about tracing the bracelet, for what that's worth."

"Just pack up and move to Stella's, quit work."

"I didn't say quit. Take some time off."

There was such patience in his voice, the sort of patience that raised her hackles like fingernails on a blackboard.

"Some time."

"Yeah. I talked to Mama about that, and to Stella about you staying with them for a while."

"You did? You talked to them about it."

He knew how a woman sounded when she was getting ready to tear a strip out of him. "No point getting your back up. This is the sensible thing to do."

"So you figure the *sensible* thing is for you to make decisions for me, talk them over with other people, then present them to me on a platter?" Deliberately she took a step back, as if to illustrate she stood on her own feet. "You don't tell me what to do, Harper, and I don't leave this house unless Roz shows me the door."

"No one's kicking you out. What's the damn big deal about staying with a friend for a while?"

It sounded so reasonable. It was infuriating. "Because

this is my home now. This is where I live, and the nursery is where I work."

"And it'll still be your home, still be where you live and where you work. For Christ's sake, don't be so pigheaded."

The lash of temper delighted her. It meant she could lash right back. "Don't you swear at me and call me names."

"I'm not—" He bit off the rest of the words, rammed his hands in his pockets to stride up and down the terrace while he fought with his temper. "You said she was getting stronger. Why the hell would you stay here, risk what happens to you, when all you have to do is move a couple miles away? Temporarily."

"How temporarily? Have you figured that out, too? I'm supposed to just sit around at Stella's, twiddling my thumbs until you decide I can come back?"

"Till it's safe."

"How do you know when it'll be safe, if it'll ever be safe. And if you're so damn worried, why aren't you packing up?"

"Because I . . ." He cleared his throat, turned to glare out at the gardens.

"That was a wise move. Choking back any comment that resembled because you're a man. But I saw it on your face." She gave him a hard shove. "Don't think I didn't see what almost came out of your mouth."

"Don't tell me what almost came out of my mouth, and don't put words into it. I want you somewhere I don't have to worry about you."

"Nobody's asking you to worry. I've been taking care of myself for a lot of years now. I'm not so stupid, or so *pig-headed* that I'm not concerned about what's been going on. But I'm also smart enough to consider that maybe I'm the last push. Maybe I'm what's going to finish this. Roz *talked* to her, Harper. Next time maybe there'll be answers that tell us just what happened, and what needs to be done to make it right."

"Next time? Listen to yourself. I don't want her touching you."

"It's not your decision, and I'm no quitter. Do you know me so little you'd think I'd just say, yes, Harper, and trot along like a nice little puppy?"

"I'm not trying to run your life, goddamn it, Hayley. I'm just trying to protect you."

Of course, he was. And he looked so aggrieved, so frustrated, she had to sympathize. A little. "You can't. Not this way. And the only thing that you're going to accomplish by making plans around me that don't include talking to me first is piss me off."

"There's a news flash. Just give me a week then. Just do this for a week and let me try to—"

"Harper, they took her child away. They drove her mad. Maybe she was heading there anyway, but they sure as hell gave her the last push over the edge. I've been part of this for over a year now. I can't walk away from it."

She lifted her hand, stroked the bracelet she continued to wear. "She showed me this. Somehow. I'm wearing what was hers. You gave it to me. It means something. I have to find out what that is. And I, very much, need to stay here with you." She softened enough to touch his cheek. "You had to know I'd stay. What did your mother say when you said you were going to tell me to go to Stella's?"

He shrugged, walked back to the terrace rail.

"Figured that. And Stella, I imagine said the same."

"Logan agreed with me."

"I bet he did." She moved to him now, wrapped her arms around him, rested her cheek on his back.

He had a good, strong back. Working man, prince of the

castle. What a fascinating combination of both he was. "I appreciate the thought, if not the method. That help any?"

"Not so much."

"How about it's nice that you care enough about me to try to boss me around?"

"It's not bossing you around to—" He broke off with a curse and a sigh when he turned to see her grinning at him. "You're not going to budge."

"Not an inch. I think some of the Ashby blood, even as diluted as it is in me must have stubborn corpuscles. And I want to be a part of finding the answers to all this, Harper. It's important to me, maybe more important now that I've shared a kind of consciousness with her. Boy, that sounds pretty woo-woo, but I don't know how else to say it."

"How about she invades you?"

Her face sobered. "All right, that's fair. You're still mad, and that's fair, too. I guess I don't mind knowing you're worried enough about me to be mad."

"If you're going to be reasonable about this, it's just going to piss me off more." He laid his hands on her shoulders, rubbed. "I do care about you, Hayley, and I am worried."

"I know. Just remember I care about me, too, and worry enough to be as careful as I can be."

"I'm going to stay with you tonight. I'm not budging about that."

"Good thing that's just where I want you. You know . . ." She slid her hands up his chest, linked them around his neck. "If we start fooling around, she might do something. So I think we ought to test that." She rose on her toes, played her lips over his. "Like an experiment."

"In my line of work I live for experiments."

"Come on inside." She stepped back, caught both his hands in hers. "We'll set up the lab."

* * *

LATER, WHEN THEY LAY TURNED TOWARD EACH OTHER in the dark, she brushed at his hair. "She didn't seem to be interested this time."

"You can't predict a ghost who should be haunting an asylum."

"Guess not." She snuggled closer. "You're a kind of scientist, right?"

"Kind of."

"When scientists are experimenting, they usually have to try more than once, maybe with some slight varieties, over a course of time. I've heard."

"Absolutely."

"So." She closed her eyes, all but purring at the stroke of his hand. "We'll just have to try this again, at some opportunity. Don't you think?"

"I do. And I think I hear opportunity knocking right now."

She opened her eyes, laughed into his. "They don't call that opportunity where I come from."

twelve

DAVID TURNED THE MAP UPSIDE DOWN, AND RAN A fingertip down a line of road. "We're like detectives. Like Batman and Robin."

"They weren't detectives," Harper corrected. "They were crime fighters."

"Picky, picky. All right, like Nick and Nora Charles."

"Just tell me where I turn, Nora."

"Should be a right in about two miles." David let the map lay on his lap and shifted to enjoy the scenery. "Now that we're so hot on the trail of the mysterious jewels, just what are we going to do if and when we find out where the bracelet originally came from?"

"Knowledge is power." Harper shrugged. "Something like that. And I've had enough of sitting around waiting for something to happen. The jeweler said it came from the Hopkins estate."

"Cream cheese."

"What? You're hungry?"

"Cream cheese," David repeated. "You spread it on smooth and thick. 'My girlfriend really loved the bracelet. She's got a birthday coming up soon, and since it was such a hit with her, I wondered if you had any matching pieces. Something from the same estate? That's the Kent estate, isn't it?' Guy practically fell over himself to give you the information, even if he did try to sell you a couple of gaudy rings. Ethel Hopkins did not have flawless taste. You should've sprung for the earrings, though. Hayley would love them."

"I just bought her a bracelet. Earrings are overkill at this point."

"Your right's coming up. Earrings are never overkill," he added when Harper made the turn. "About a half mile down this road. Should be on the left."

He pulled into a double drive beside a late-model Town Car, then sat tapping his fingers on the steering wheel as he studied the lay of the land.

The house was large and well-kept in an old, well-to-do neighborhood. It was a two-story English Tudor with a good selection of foundation plants, an old oak and a nicely shaped dogwood in the front. The lawn was trimmed and lushly green, which meant lawn service or automatic sprinklers.

"Okay, what have we got here?" he queried. "Established, upper middle class."

"Ethel's only surviving daughter, Mae Hopkins Ives Fitzpatrick," David read from the notes he'd taken from the courthouse records. "She's seventy-six. Twice married, twice widowed. And you can thank me for digging that up so quickly due to my brilliant observation of Mitch's methods."

"Let's see if we can charm our way in, then get her to tell us if she remembers when her mother came by the bracelet."

They went to the door, rang the bell, and waited in the thick heat.

The woman who opened the door had a short, sleek cap of brown hair, and faded blue eyes behind the lenses of fashionable gold-framed glasses. She was tiny, maybe an inch over five feet, and workout trim in a pair of blue cotton pants and a crisp white camp shirt. There were pearls around her throat, a whopping sapphire on the ring fingers of either hand and delicate gold hoops in her ears.

"You don't look like salesmen to me." She spoke in a raspy voice and kept a hand on the handle of the screened door.

"No, ma'am." Harper warmed up his smile. "I'm Harper Ashby, and this is my friend David Wentworth. We'd like to speak with Mae Fitzpatrick."

"That's what you're doing."

Genetic good luck or, more likely, a skilled plastic surgeon, Harper thought, had shaved a good ten years off her seventy-six. "I'm pleased to meet you, Miz Fitzpatrick. I realize this is an odd sort of intrusion, but I wonder if we might come in and have a word with you?"

The color of her eyes might have been faded, but the expression of them was sharp as a scalpel. "Do I look like the simpleminded sort of woman who lets strange men into her house?"

"No, ma'am." But he had to wonder why a woman who claimed good sense would believe a screened door was any sort of barrier. "If you wouldn't mind then, if I could just ask you a few questions regarding a—"

"Ashby, you said?"

"Yes, ma'am."

"Any relation to Miriam Norwood Ashby?"

"Yes, ma'am. She was my paternal grandmother."

"I knew her a little."

"I can't really claim the same."

"Don't expect so, as she's been dead some time now. You'd be Rosalind Harper's boy then."

"Yes, ma'am, her oldest."

"I've met her a time or two. First time being at her wedding to John Ashby. You have the look of her, don't you?"

"I do. Yes, ma'am."

She slid her eyes toward David. "This isn't your brother."

"A family friend, Miz Fitzpatrick," David said with a full-wattage smile. "I live at Harper House, and work for Rosalind. Perhaps you'd feel more at ease if you contacted Miz Harper before you speak to us. We'd be happy to give you a number where you can reach her, and wait but here while you do."

Instead she opened the screen. "I don't believe Miriam Ashby's grandson is going to knock me unconscious and rob me. Y'all come in."

"Thank you."

The house was as neat and well-tended as its mistress, with polished oak floors and muted green walls. She let them into a generous living room that was furnished in a contemporary, almost minimalistic style.

"I suppose you boys could use a cold drink."

"We don't want to put you to any trouble, Miz Fitzpatrick," Harper told her.

"Sweet tea's simple enough. Have a seat. I'll be with you in a minute."

"Classy," David commented when she left the room. "A bit pared down, but classy."

"The place, or her?"

"Both." He took a seat on the sofa. "Ashby-Harper is a very slick entree. Charm wouldn't have worked on her."

"Interesting she knew my grandmother—she's some younger—and that she was invited to my mother's wedding. All these little intersections. I wonder if one of her ancestors knew Reginald or Beatrice."

"Coincidence is only coincidence if you don't have an open mind."

"Living with a ghost tends to leave it gaping." Harper got to his feet as Mae came back with a tray of glasses. "Let me get that for you. We very much appreciate your time, Miz Fitzpatrick." He set the tray on the coffee table. "I'll try not to take up too much of it."

"Your grandmother was a kindhearted woman. While I didn't know her intimately, your grandfather and my first husband had a small business venture together many years ago. A real estate venture," she added, "that was satisfactorily profitable for all involved. Now, why has her grandson come knocking on my door?"

"It has to do with a bracelet from your mother's estate."

She angled her head with polite interest. "My mother's estate."

"Yes, ma'am. It happens that I bought this bracelet from the jeweler who acquired it from the estate."

"And is there something wrong with the bracelet?"

"No. No, ma'am. I'm hoping you might remember some of the history of it, as I'm very interested in its origins. I'm told it was made sometime around 1890. It's made up of ruby hearts framed in diamonds."

"Yes, I know the piece. I sold it and several others recently as they weren't to my taste and saw no reason to have them sitting in a safety deposit box as they had been since my mother's death some years ago." She sipped her tea as she watched him. "You're curious about its history?"

"Yes, ma'am, I am."

"But not forthcoming with your reasons."

"Oddly enough, I have reason to believe it—or one very like it—was in my family. When I discovered that, I found it interesting and thought satisfying my curiosity would be worth a little time in trying to trace it back."

"Is that so? Now, that I find interesting. The bracelet was given by my grandfather to my grandmother in 1893, as an anniversary gift. It's possible that there was more than one made, in that same design, at the time."

"Yes, possibly."

"There is, however, a story behind it, if you'd like to hear it."

"I really would."

She held out the plate of cookies she'd brought out with the tea, waited until each of the men had taken one. Then she settled back with a hint of a smile on her face. "My grandparents did not have a happy marriage, my grandfather being somewhat of a scoundrel. He enjoyed gambling and shady deals and the company of loose women—according to my grandmother, who lived to the ripe age of ninety-eight, so I knew her quite well."

Rising, she walked to an étagère and took down a photo framed in slim silver.

"My grandparents," she said, passing the photo to Harper. "A formal portrait taken in 1891. You can see, scoundrel or not, he was quite handsome."

"Both are." And, Harper noted, the style of dress, hair, even the photographic tone was similar to the copies of photographs Mitch had pinned to his workboard.

"She's a beauty." David glanced up. "You favor her."

"So I've been told. Physically, and in temperament." Obviously pleased, she took the photo, replaced it. "My grandmother claimed two of the happiest days of her life were her wedding day, when she was too young and foolish to know what she was getting into, and the day she became a widow—some twelve years later, and could enjoy life without the burden of a man who couldn't be trusted."

She sat again, picked up her tea. "A handsome man, as you saw for yourselves. A charming man, by all accounts, and one who had considerable success with the gambling and the shady deals. But my grandmother was a moral sort of woman. One who managed to bend those morals, just enough to enjoy the results of her husband's successes, even as she decried them."

She set down her tea, sat back, obviously relishing her role. "She told the story, often, of discovering—during one of my grandfather's drunken confessions that the anniversary gift—the ruby hearts—had come from a somewhat less than reputable source. He had acquired it in a payoff of a gambling debt from a man who bought jewelry and so forth on the cheap from those unfortunate or desperate enough to have to sell their possessions quickly. Often, more likely, from those who had stolen those possessions and used him as a fence."

She smiled broadly now, no doubt relishing the thought. "It had belonged to a wealthy man's mistress, and was stolen from her by one of the servants after she had been cut off by him. The story, as my grandmother claimed it was told to her, was that the woman had gone raving mad, and had subsequently vanished."

She reached for her tea, sipped. "I always wondered if that story was true."

HARPER WENT TO HIS MOTHER FIRST, AND KNELT DOWN beside her in the gardens at home. Absently, he began to help her weed.

"I heard you took some time off today," she began.

"I had something I wanted to do. Why aren't you wearing a hat?"

"I forgot it. I was only going to come out for a minute, then I got started."

He pulled off the ballcap he wore, tugged it down over her head. "Do you remember how so many times after school, if I was working out here when you came home, you'd sit down beside me, help me weed or plant and tell me your troubles, or your triumphs of the day?"

"I remember you were always here to listen. To me, to Austin and Mason. Sometimes to all three of us at once. How'd you do that?"

"A mother's got an ear for the voices of her children. Like a conductor for each separate instrument in his orchestra, even in the middle of a symphony. What are your troubles, baby boy?"

"You were right about Hayley."

"I make being right a policy. What was I right about exactly?"

"That she wouldn't move over to Logan's because I asked her to."

Under the bill, Roz's eyebrows arched. "Asked her?"

"Asked her, told her." He shrugged. "What's the difference when you've got the person's welfare in mind?"

She let out a husky laugh, patted her dirty hands on his cheeks. "Such a man."

"A minute ago I was your baby boy."

"My baby boy is such a man. I don't see that as a flaw. An amusement sometimes—such as now—a puzzlement now and then, and on rare occasions a damned irritation. Are you fighting? It didn't seem to me you were at odds when you came down to breakfast together this morning."

"No, we're all right. If you don't like me sleeping with her in the house, I get that."

"So you'll respect the sanctity of our home and sleep with her elsewhere?"

"Yeah."

"I slept with men I wasn't married to in Harper House. It's not a cathedral, it's a home. Yours as much as mine. If you're having sex with Hayley, you might as well have it comfortably. And safely," she added with a direct look.

Even after all these years, it made his shoulders hunch. "I buy my own condoms these days."

"I'm glad to hear it."

"And that isn't what I wanted to get into. I traced the bracelet back to Amelia."

Those eyes widened as she sat back on her heels. "You did? That was fast work."

"Fast work, coincidence, lucky break. I'm not sure where it falls. It came from the estate of an Esther Hopkins. She's been dead a few years now, apparently, and her daughter decided to go ahead and sell some of the things she didn't like, or care to keep. Mae Fitzpatrick. She said she knew you."

"Mae Fitzpatrick." Roz closed her eyes and tried to flip through the vast mental files of acquaintances. "I'm sorry, it doesn't seem familiar."

"She was married before. Wait a minute . . . Ives?"

"Mae Ives doesn't ring bells either."

"Well, she said she'd only met you a couple of times. Once was when you married Daddy. She was at your wedding."

"Is that a fact? Well, that's interesting, but not all that surprising. I think between my mama and John's we had everybody in Shelby County and most of Tennessee at the wedding."

"She knew Grandma Ashby."

He sat on the garden path with her and told her of the conversation he'd had with Mae Fitzpatrick.

"Amazing, isn't it," she mused. "All those little angles and curls, and how they fit together."

"I know. Mama, she had it figured. Too well-bred to say it right out, but she put it together, about Reginald Harper being the wealthy protector who'd cast his mistress off. She's likely to talk about it."

"And you think that bothers me? Honey, the fact that my great-grandfather had mistresses, that he kept women, tossed them aside, and lived a life generally rife with infidelity isn't a reflection on me, or you. His behavior isn't our responsibility, which is something I sincerely wish Amelia would realize."

She dug out more weeds. "As to the rest of his behavior, which is beyond deplorable, it's not our fault either. Mitch is writing about it. Unless you and your brothers feel strongly that all of this should be kept as closely within the family as possible, I want him to do this book."

"Why?"

"It's not our fault, it's not our responsibility. That's all true," she said as she sat back to look at him. "But I feel that airing all of this, is somehow giving her her due. It's a way to acknowledge an ancestor who, no matter what she did, what she became, was treated shabbily at best, monstrously at worst."

She lifted her hand, pressed her soil-streaked palm to his. "She's our blood."

"Does that make me heartless because I want her gone, I want her ended for what she nearly did to you, for what she's doing now to Hayley?"

"No. It means Hayley and I are closer to your heart. That's enough for today." She swiped her hands on the thighs of her gardening pants. "We're going to boil in this wet heat if we stay out much longer. Come on inside with me. Let's sit in the cool and have a beer."

"Tell me something." He studied the house as they walked down the path. "How did you know that Daddy was the one?"

"Stars in my eyes." She laughed, and despite the heat hooked an arm through his. "I swear, stars in my eyes. I was so young, and he put stars in my eyes. But that was infatuation. I think I knew that he was mine when we talked for hours one night. I snuck out of the house to meet him. God, my daddy would have skinned him alive. But all we did was talk, hour after hour, under a willow tree. He was just a boy, but I knew I'd love him all of my life. And I have. I knew because we sat there, almost till dawn, and he made me laugh, and made me think and dream and tremble. I never thought I'd love again. But I do. It takes nothing away from your father, Harper."

"Mama. I know." He closed a hand over hers. "How did you know with Mitch?"

"I guess I was too cynical for those stars, at least at first. It was slower, and scarier. He makes me laugh and think and dream and tremble. And there was a time during that longer, slower climb that I looked at him, and my heart warmed again. I'd forgotten what it was like to feel that warmth inside the heart."

"He's a good man. He loves you. He watches you when you come into a room, when you walk out of one. I'm glad you found him."

"So am I."

"With Daddy? What willow was it?"

"Oh, it was a big, beautiful old tree, way back, beyond the old stables." She paused, looked toward the ruin, gestured. "John was going to come back sometime soon after, carve our initials in the trunk. But that next night lightning struck it, split it right in two, and—Oh my God."

"Amelia," he said softly.

"It had to be. It never occurred to me before this, but I remember there hadn't been a storm. The servants were talking about the tree and the lightning hitting it when there hadn't been a storm."

"So even then," he said, "she took her shots."

"How mean, how petty of her. I cried over that tree. I fell in love under it, and cried when I watched the groundskeepers clear away the wood and pull the trunk out."

"Don't you wonder if there were other things? Small, violent acts we passed off as nature or some strange quirk, all while we thought of her as benevolent?"

He studied the house now, thought of what it was to him—and what had walked there long before he was born. "She's never been benevolent, not really."

"All that hate and anger stored up. Trapped."

"Leaking now and again, like water through a crack in a dam. It's coming faster and harder now. And we can't put it back in, Mama. What we have to do is empty it out, draw out every drop."

"How?"

"I think we're going to have to break the dam, while we're the ones holding the hammer."

IT WAS TWILIGHT WHEN HAYLEY WANDERED THROUGH the gardens. The baby was asleep, and Roz and Mitch were taking monitor duty. Harper's car was there, so he was *somewhere*. Not in the carriage house, because she'd knocked, then poked her head in and called.

It wasn't as if they were joined at the hip, she reminded herself. But he hadn't stayed for dinner. He'd said he'd had something to do, that he'd be back before dark.

Well, it was nearly dark, and she was just wondering.

Besides, she liked walking in the gardens, in the gloaming. Even under the circumstances. It was soothing, and she could use a little soothing after running the story he'd told her about the bracelet over and over in her head.

They were getting closer to the answers, she was sure of it. But she was no longer sure it would all end quietly once they had them.

Amelia might not be content to give up her last links with this world and pass on—she supposed that was the term—to the next.

She liked inhabiting a body. If you could call it inhabiting. Sharing one? Sliding through one? Whatever it was, Amelia liked it, of that Hayley was sure. Just as she was sure it was something as new for Amelia as it was for herself.

If it happened again—*when,* she corrected, ordering herself to face facts. When it happened again, she was going to fight to stay more aware, to find more control.

And wasn't that what she was doing out here alone, in the half light? No point in pretending to herself this wasn't a deliberate move. A sort of dare. *Come on, bitch.* She wanted to see what she could handle, and how she would handle it when no one else was around to run interference. Or be hurt.

But nothing was happening. She felt completely normal, completely herself.

And was completely herself when sounds out of the shadows made her jump. She stopped, caught in the crosshairs of fight or flight, ears straining. The rhythmic, repetitive sound made her frown as she inched forward.

It sounded . . . but it couldn't be. Still her heart beat like wings as she crept closer, envisioning a ghostly figure digging a grave.

Amelia's grave. It could be. This could be the answer, at last. Reginald had murdered her, then buried her here on the property. She was going to be shown the grave—on unconsecrated ground. They could have it blessed or marked or—well, she'd look up what was done in cases like this.

Then the haunting of Harper House would be over.

She picked her way quietly around the ruins of the stables, edging as close to the building as she dared. Her palms sprang damp, and her breath seemed to rattle in her throat.

She turned the corner of the building, following the sound, prepared to be terrified and amazed.

And saw Harper, his T-shirt stripped off and tossed to the ground, digging a hole.

The letdown had the breath expelling from her lungs in a frantic whoosh.

"Harper, for Christ's sake, you scared me brainless. What are you doing?"

He continued to spear the blade of the shovel into the ground, tossing the dirt into the pile beside it. Though she was still jittery, she cast her eyes skyward, then marched to him.

"I said—" He jumped a clean foot off the ground when she poked a finger in his back. And even as she yelped in response, he whirled, cocking the shovel over his shoulder like a bat. He managed to check his swing, cursed a blue streak as she stumbled back and fell hard on her ass.

"Jesus, God almighty!" He dragged the headset down to his shoulders. "What the hell are you doing, sneaking around in the dark?"

"I didn't sneak, I called you. If you didn't play that headset so loud you could hear a person when they said something. I thought you were going to brain me with that shovel. I thought . . ."

She began to giggle, tried to snuff it back. "You

should've seen your face. Your eyes were this big." She held up her hands, curling her fingers into wide balls, then dissolved into laughter when he snarled at her.

"Oh, oh, I'm going to wet my pants. Wait." She squeezed her eyes, bounced quickly in place while more giggles bubbled. "Okay, okay, back in control. The least you could do is help me up after you knocked me down."

"I didn't knock you down. Damn near though." He offered a hand, pulled her up.

"I thought you were Reginald, digging Amelia's untimely grave."

Shaking his head, he leaned on the shovel and stared at her. "So you came on around to what, give him a hand?"

"Well, I had to see, didn't I? What in the world are you doing, digging a hole out here in the dark?"

"It's not dark."

"You said it was dark when you yelled at me. What are you doing?"

"Playing third base for the Atlanta Braves."

"I don't see why you're being pissy. I'm the one who fell down and nearly wet her pants."

"Sorry. Did you hurt yourself?"

"No. You planting that tree?" She finally focused in on the slim, young willow. "Why are you planting a tree, Harper, back here and at this time of night?"

"It's for Mama. She told me this story today, about how she snuck out of the house to meet my father one night, and that they sat under a willow that used to be back here, and talked. That's when she fell in love with him. The next day it got hit by lightning. Amelia," he said and dug out another shovelful of dirt. "She didn't put it together before, but you've got to figure the odds. So I'm putting one in for her."

She stood silently for a moment while he eyeballed the hole, then the rootball, then dug some more.

"That's the sweetest thing. That just coats my heart with sweetness, Harper. Can I help, or is it something you want to do alone?"

"Hole's about right. You can help me put it in."

"I never planted a tree before."

"See, you want the hole about three times as wide as the rootball, but no deeper. Get the sides of the hole loose so the roots have room to spread."

He picked up the tree, set it in the hole. "How's that look to you?"

"It looks right, like you said."

"Now you peel the burlap back, from the main stem, then we'll see the original soil line, at least we will if you turn on that flashlight over there, because it is getting dark. Took me a while to get everything I needed for this."

She turned it on, crouched down and aimed. "How's that?"

"Good. See?" He tapped a finger on the mark at the base. "That's the soil line, and we've got the right depth here. We've just got a little bit of roots that need pruning off. Hand me those."

She got the clippers, passed them to him. "You know digging a hole for a tree sounds the same as digging a grave."

He flicked her a look. "Have you ever heard anybody digging a grave?"

"In movies."

"Right. We're going to fill the hole, but we do it little by little and firm the soil down as we do. I don't have any spare gloves. Here."

"No." She waved him back when he started to pull off his work gloves. "A little dirt won't hurt me. Am I doing this right?"

"Yeah, that's good. You just keep filling and firming,

hilling it up toward the base and leaving a kind of shallow moat around the edge of the hole."

"I like the way it feels. The dirt."

"I know what you mean." When they'd finished to his satisfaction, he took out his knife, trimmed off the exposed burlap, then pushed to his feet. "We'll give it plenty of water, pour it into the rim around the mound, see?"

He hauled up one of the buckets he'd filled, nodded when she lifted the other.

"There, you planted a tree."

"Helped plant one anyway." She stepped back, reached out a hand for his. "It looks lovely, Harper. It'll mean a lot to her that you thought to do this."

"It meant something to me to do it." He gave her hand a squeeze, then bent to pick up his tools. "Probably should've waited until next spring, but I wanted to do it now. A kind of nose-thumbing. Go ahead and knock them down, we'll just put them back up. I wanted to do it now."

"You're so angry with her."

"I'm not a kid, charmed by lullabies anymore. I've seen her for what she is."

Hayley shook her head, shivered a little in the close evening air. "I don't think any of us have seen her for what she is. Not yet."

thirteen

THE GRAFTING HOUSE WAS MORE THAN A WORK SPACE for Harper. It was also part playhouse, part sanctuary, and part lab. He could, and often did, lose himself for hours inside its warm, music-filled air, working, experimenting, or just reveling in being the only human among the plants.

A lot of times he preferred the plants to humans. Though he wasn't altogether sure what that said about him, he wasn't all that concerned about it.

He'd found his passion in life, and considered himself fortunate that he could make a living doing something that made him completely happy.

His brothers had to leave home to find theirs. It was the bonus round for him that he'd been able to stay where he loved, and do what he loved.

He had his home, his work, his family. Throughout his adult life he'd had women he'd liked and enjoyed. But none of them had ever made him think, had ever nudged him to consider the next step on the rung of what he'd thought of vaguely as The Future.

He hadn't worried about that either. His vision of marriage was reflected in what he knew his parents had together. Love, dedication, respect, and tempering it all, like an alloy in steel, an unwavering friendship.

He understood his mother had found that a second time, with Mitch. Not so much lightning striking twice as a true and perfect graft that united to make a new and healthy plant.

In his mind, nothing less strong, less important was worth the time or risk.

So he'd enjoyed the women who'd passed through his life, and had never pictured any of them as The One.

Until Hayley.

Now, so much of his world had changed, while other parts of it remained, comfortably, the same.

He'd flipped on Chopin for his plants' enjoyment today. And had P.O.D rocking the party on his headset.

The space might not appear efficient with its groupings of plants in various stages of growth, the buckets of gravel or wood chips, the scatter of tapes and twine, clothespins and labels. There were scraps of burlap, piles of pots, bags of soil, tangles of rubber bands. Trays of knives and clippers. But he knew where to find what he wanted when he needed it.

There might have been times he couldn't put his hands on a pair of matching socks, but he could always put them on the tool he needed.

He walked along, airing the tents and cases that housed his plants, as he did every morning. A few minutes without their covers would dry off any surface moisture that might have condensed on his rootstocks. Fungal disease was always a worry. Still, too much air might dry out the union.

As he aired them, he checked specimens for progress, for any signs of disease or rot. He was particularly pleased with the camellia he'd cleft-grafted over the winter. His specimens would take another year, perhaps two to flower, but he believed they'd be worth the wait.

The work required his passion, but it also required his patience, and his faith.

He made notes to be transcribed to his computer files. There was active, steady growth in the astrophytum seedlings he had protected under a bottle cloche, and the nurse grafts of his clematis looked strong and healthy.

Making the rounds once more, he retented the plants. He'd need to check the pond later to study the water lilies and irises he'd hybridized. A side and personal experiment he hoped would prove rewarding.

Plus, it would give him an excuse to take a cooling dip in the heat of the day.

But for now, he had several cultivars to see to.

He gathered the tools he'd need, then selected a healthy rootstock from his pot-grown lantana, made the oblique cut, then matched it with a scion of viburnum. The girths were similar enough that he was able to use the simple slant of each cut to place them together so the cambiums on each side met truly.

Using elastic bands, he kept the pressure light and even as he bound them together. Judging the graft good, he used grafting wax to seal the joining. He set it in a seed tray, covered the roots and graft with moist soil—his mother's mix—then labeled.

Once he'd repeated the process several times, he tented the tray, and swiveled to his computer to log in the work.

Before he started on the next house specimens, he switched his music to Michelle Branch and pulled a Coke from his cooler.

By the time he'd finished, Michelle had played through and his morning's work was completed.

He gathered a bag of tools and supplies, left his headset behind, and went out to check his field-grown and water plants.

There were a few customers wandering around, scouting out the discounted stock under shade screens or poking into the public greenhouses. He knew if he didn't make his escape quickly, one of them might catch him.

He didn't mind talking plants or directing a customer toward what they were looking for. He just preferred keeping his mind in the game, and right now that game was checking his field plants.

He made it past the portulaca before someone called his name. Should've kept the headset on, he thought, but turned, readying up his customer smile.

The brunette had a curvy little body, which he'd had occasion to see naked several times. At the moment, she was showing it off in belly-baring shorts and a brief top designed to make a man give thanks for August heat.

With a delighted laugh, she bounced up on her toes, clamped her arms around his neck and gave him a loud smack of a kiss. She still tasted of bing cherries, and brought back a flood of equally sweet memories.

Instinctively he gave her a hard hug before stepping back to get a better view. "Dory, what're you doing in town? How've you been?"

"I've been terrific, and I just moved back. Just a couple weeks ago. Got a job with a PR firm here. I got tired of Miami, missed being home, too, I guess."

She'd probably changed her hair from the last time he'd seen her. Women were forever changing their hair. But since he wasn't absolutely sure, he fell back on the standard: "You look great."

"Feel the same. And look at you, all buff and tan. I was going to call you but I wasn't sure you were still living in that sweet little house."

"Yeah, still there."

"I was hoping. I always loved that place. How's your mama, and David, and your brothers, and oh, just everybody." She gave a bubbling laugh, threw out her arms. "I feel like I've been living on Mars for the past three years."

"Everybody's good. Mama got married a few weeks ago."

"I heard. My mama caught me up with some of the local news. I heard you haven't."

"Haven't what? Oh, no."

"I was thinking you and I could do some catching up." Dory trailed a finger down his chest. "I'd love to see your place again. I could pick up some Chinese, a bottle of wine. Like the old days."

"Ah, well . . ."

"A kind of welcome-home and thank-you for you helping me pick out some houseplants for my new place. You'll do that, won't you, Harper? I'd like a few nice ones."

"Sure. I mean, sure I'll help you pick out some plants. But—"

"Why don't we go inside, out of this heat. You can tell me what you've been up to while you help me out. But save some of the good stuff for later."

She took his hand, squeezing it as she tugged him with her. "I've missed seeing you," she continued. "We barely had a chance to talk when I was up for a few days last year. I was going out with that photographer then, remember? I told you."

"Yeah." Vaguely. "And I'm—"

"Well, that is so over. I don't know why I wasted a year of my life on a man so self-centered. It was always about him, you know what I mean? What made me think I wanted to hook up with the artistic, broody type?"

"I—"

"So I shook him and the sand out of my shoes, and here I am."

Inside, she turned and slid her hands in the back pockets of his jeans. An old habit of hers that brought on another memory flash. "I really have missed the hell right out of you. You're glad to see me, aren't you, Harper?"

"Sure. Sure, I am. The thing is, Dory, I'm seeing somebody."

"Oh." Her full bottom lip pouted. "Some serious somebody?"

"Yeah."

"Oh well." She left her hands in his pockets another moment, then drew them out. Gave his ass a little pat. "I guess I figured it would take a lot of luck on my part for you to be flying solo. How long have you been seeing her?"

"Depends. What I mean is, I've known her awhile, but we've only started . . . we've only been involved recently."

"Looks like I should've gotten here sooner. We're still friends, right? Good friends."

"We always were."

"That's what I remembered, and I guess what I missed with Justin, the photographer. We never managed to be friends, and we sure as hell weren't anything close to friends when it fell apart. You, on the other hand. I was telling another friend of mine not long ago how I've never been dumped as sweetly as I was with you."

She laughed, rose on her toes to kiss him lightly. "You're a rare one, Harper."

She stepped back, and seconds later, Hayley came through the glass doors. "I'm sorry, am I interrupting? Is there something I can help you with?"

"No, thanks. Harper's giving me a hand." Dory patted

hers on his arm. "I'm clueless about plants, so I came to the expert."

"Hayley, this is Dory. We went to college together."

"Is that right?" She smiled, widely. "I don't think I've seen you in here before."

"I haven't been, for a long time. I've just moved back from Miami. New job, fresh start, you know how it goes."

"Don't I just," Hayley purred with that wide smile still in place.

"I decided I'd come see Harper, and catch up, and get a few plants to liven up my new apartment. Wait till you see it, Harper, it's a big step up from the hole I rented off-campus back in the day."

"Anything would be. I hope you got rid of that futon."

"I burned it. Harper hated that thing," she said to Hayley. "Even offered to buy me a bed, but all I had was this tiny little place—just one room. If I had three people over, we were so crammed together we were halfway to an orgy."

"Those were the days," Harper said, and made Dory laugh.

"Weren't they? Well, you'd better show me what I'm going to need, or I'll keep you talking the rest of the day."

"I'll just leave y'all alone." Hayley backed out the doors.

She got back to work, but made certain she wasn't on checkout duty when Dory was ready to pay for the plants Harper selected for her. But she could hear Dory laugh—a particularly grating laugh, in her opinion—as she stocked shelves across the room.

Harper leaned on the counter through the process, she noted out of the corner of her eye. And just look how he wore that lazy smile of his while they talked about mutual friends and the good old days.

And damn if that Dory didn't keep touching him. Little pats and pokes in between her hair flips. The steam began to rise from her belly up to her throat as Harper pulled the cart of potted plants out to Dory's car.

Hayley decided she really needed to check the stock of the shelves by the window. And if a person happened to look out while they were working, it wasn't spying. It was glancing.

Enough of a glance that she saw Harper lean down and exchange a liplock with his college buddy.

Bastard.

Then he waved her off before strolling around the side of the building like he wasn't a low-life cheating scum. Worse, the sort that did his low-life cheating right in front of her face.

You'd think he'd have the courtesy, the good breeding, to at least do it behind her back.

Well, that was just fine. She wasn't going to let it matter. She wasn't going to give a single wrinkled, balled-up damn.

And she wasn't going outside to kick him in his two-timing balls either. She was just going out to see if any customers needed her assistance.

That's what she got paid for. Not for flirting, not for spending half the day reminiscing. And certainly not for kissing customers before she waved bye-bye.

She was nearly to the grafting house when she saw him out in the field. He was already crouched down, examining grafts on the magnolias she'd helped him graft and plant weeks before.

He flicked her a glance and a smile as she approached. "Take a look. These are coming along. Couple of weeks we can remove the tape."

"If you say so."

"Yeah, they're looking good. I need to check some of the other ornamentals. I think we're going to have some nice weeping pears and cherries for next season. Have I shown you the fruiting pears I did? The dwarfs?"

"No. Did your friend get what she was after?"

"Hmm. Yeah." He rose, walked across to check the balance of the canopies on his weepers. "Kept it simple," he said absently as he studied the tree. "Low maintenance. What I did here was use *pyrus communis* for stock—three-year-olds, and grafted three pendulas. You gotta make sure you get the spacing right, so you produce a nice shape."

"And you know all about shapes."

"Yeah. I like chip-budding these. I did these two springs ago, and these this spring. See how they develop?"

"I see how a lot of things develop. I was surprised you didn't go with her, carry the plants to her door."

"Who? Oh, Dory?" He flipped Hayley an absent look as sarcasm sailed, visibly, over his head. "She'll be able to handle it. A couple trips."

He continued to walk, continued to examine.

"Here? For these weeping cherries, I used a semi-dwarfing rootstock. Should make a nice specimen tree for smaller spaces. 'Round October, I'm going to take some ripe shoots from the Colt stock. What you do is bundle them, and drop them root-end down in a trench in the nursery bed, and hill 'em up so they're about three-quarters buried. Then next spring, we'll lift the bundles, plant the cuttings, and by summer they'll be ready to use for rootstocks."

"That's all just fascinating, Harper. Did you spend all that time with Dory lecturing her on how to make a damn rootstock?"

"Huh." His distraction was evident on his face as he glanced around. "She's not interested in this kind of work. She's in public relations."

"Private ones from what I saw."

"What?"

"I was about to come back and suggest the two of you get a room. You ought to know better than to make out in one of the retail areas."

This time his mouth dropped open. "*What?* We weren't. We were just—"

"Those doors are glass, Harper, in case you've forgotten. I saw you, and you ought to have more respect for your workplace than to fool around in one of the public areas during working hours. But as you're the boss, I guess you can do what the hell you like."

"My mother's the boss, and I wasn't fooling around anywhere. Dory and I are old friends. We were just—"

"Kissing, touching, flirting, making dates. It's unprofessional, in my opinion, to do that during work hours. But it's downright rude to do it in front of me."

"Behind your back would be better?"

Because it echoed her own nasty thoughts, her eyes went hot, searing like suns. "Let me just say, fuck you, Harper."

Since it was as good an exit line as she could think of when her brain was ready to explode, she turned on her heel. And spun right back when he grabbed her arm.

He didn't look distracted now, she noted. He looked ice-cold mad. "I wasn't flirting or making dates."

"Just kissing and touching then."

"I kissed her because she's a friend, a good one, who I haven't seen in a while. I kissed her the way you kiss a friend. Which is nothing like this, for instance."

He gave her a yank that threw her off balance so her body collided with his. Then was scooped up, pulled in. He got a fistful of her hair, gave it a quick tug. And had his mouth crushed to hers.

Not sweetly, not warmly, but with the stark heat of raw temper. She struggled, shocked that she was clamped so hard and tight she couldn't fight her way free. A thread of fear snaked through her anger, and began to tighten just before he let her go.

"That's how I kiss women I don't feel friendly toward."

"You think you have the right to treat me that way?"

"As much as you do to accuse me of doing something, of being something I'm not. I don't cheat and I don't lie, and I'm not going to apologize for my behavior. If you want to know something about my relationship with Dory, or anyone else, past or present, then ask. But don't come tearing into me with accusations."

"I saw—"

"Maybe you saw what you were ready to see. That's on you, Hayley. Now I've got work. If you've got any more to say about this, then say it after hours."

He strode off toward the pond, leaving her no choice, as she saw it, but to storm away in the opposite direction.

"THEN HE HAD THE NERVE, THE *NERVE* TO SNAP AT ME and act like I was in the wrong." Hayley paced back and forth on Stella's front porch while Lily raced over the lawn after Parker. "Acting like I've got a dirty mind or that I'm some crazy jealous witch because I have a reasonable and legitimate complaint about him slobbering all over another woman. And in front of my face."

"Before you said she was slobbering over him."

"It was mutual slobbering. And when I walked in on them, after seeing all this going on through the door, he acts like it's nothing. He doesn't even have the grace to look embarrassed or nervous."

"So you said." Twice, Stella thought, but she understood the nature of female friendship and didn't mention the repetition. "Sweetie, we've both known Harper for some time now. Don't you think he would've looked embarrassed if he'd been caught doing something he shouldn't?"

"I guess I just don't mean enough to him for it to embarrass him."

"Now stop. That's not true."

"It feels true." Hayley slumped to the steps. "It feels awful."

"I know." Sitting beside her, Stella wrapped her arm around her shoulders. "I know it does. I'm so sorry you were hurt."

"He doesn't even care."

"Yes, he does. Maybe what you saw hit you wrong because of the way you feel about him."

"Stella, he *kissed* her."

"He's kissed me, too."

"It's not the same."

"If you hadn't met me before, and you saw him kiss me, what would you think?"

"Before or after I mentally ripped your lungs out through your nose?"

"Ouch. I'm not saying it didn't look bad, but that you might have, possibly, misinterpreted. I'm saying that because I know Harper, and because of his reaction."

"You're saying I overreacted."

"I'm saying, if I were you, I'd want to find out for sure."

"He slept with her. Okay, okay," she muttered when Stella stared at her. "Before, and before is before, blah blah. But she was so pretty. She had a great body, and those dark, exotic eyes. And this sheen, you know, this polish. Oh, hell."

"You're going to go talk to him."

"I guess."

"Want me to keep Lily while you do?"

"No." Hayley let out a long sigh. "She needs her supper

soon, and besides, if I take her with me we're not as likely to yell at each other."

"All right. You can call me if you want, let me know how it goes. Or you can just come back over. I'll break out the Ben and Jerry's."

"Way I'm feeling, I'll need a full quart."

SHE HAD LILY'S HAND IN HERS WHEN SHE KNOCKED on the door of the carriage house. He hadn't been long out of the shower, she noted when he answered. His hair was still damp. But if the grim set of his face was any barometer, it hadn't cooled him off.

"I'd like to talk to you." She said it briskly. "If you have the time."

He simply bent down to pick up Lily who'd already wrapped her arms around his leg. He turned, without a word for Hayley, and carried the baby back toward the kitchen. "Hey, pretty girl. Look what we got here."

One-handed, he opened a cupboard, took out a couple of plastic bowls, then rooted through a drawer for a big plastic spoon. He set them, and Lily, on the floor where she immediately went to town banging.

"Want a drink?" he said to Hayley.

"No, no, I don't. I want to ask you—"

"I'm having a beer. You want any milk or juice for Lily?"

"I didn't bring her sippy cup."

"I have one."

"Oh." The fact that he did threw her off, made her heart start to melt. "She could have a little juice. You have to dilute it."

"I've seen the routine." He fixed the juice, handed it to Lily, then got out a beer. "So?" He took a long gulp.

"I wanted to ask—No, I wanted to say that I know we

haven't made any sort of commitment to each other. But sleeping with someone is a form of commitment to me, enough of one that it's insulting to see the person I'm sleeping with kissing and flirting with another woman. And I don't find that unreasonable."

He took another pull, slowly, thoughtfully. "You know if you'd put it that way to begin with, you wouldn't have insulted me, or pissed me off. I'm going to repeat that I was flirting with Dory, but not the way you mean."

"If you come on to all women the way—"

"Or coming on to her. And be careful or you'll piss me off again. If you want to know what was going on, why don't you ask?"

"I don't like being in this position."

"Well, neither do I. If that's the way you want to leave it, I need to throw something together for dinner. I missed lunch."

"Fine." She started to bend down for Lily, then stopped. "Why are you so hard?"

"Why are you so mistrustful?"

"I *saw* you. She had her arms around you. She put her hands in your damn pockets and felt your ass. You weren't exactly fighting her off, Harper."

"Okay, you've got a point. It was something she used to do, and I didn't think much about it when she did it today. I was thinking more how I was going to tell her I couldn't pick things up with her, couldn't see her beyond the friendship thing because I was with somebody else."

"How long does it take to say that?"

"A little longer than it might otherwise if a woman's got her hands on your ass." She opened her mouth, but the way his eyebrows shot up had her closing it again, and waiting. "Right or wrong, Hayley. But I did tell her, before you came through the door."

"Before? But . . . you didn't even miss a beat, Harper. And the two of you were all . . ." She waved a hand, trying to find the phrase. "Touchy. And you kissed her when you went out to the car."

His eyes narrowed. "You were watching us."

"No. Yes. So what?"

"Too bad you didn't manage to slip a listening device on me, then this conversation wouldn't be necessary."

She folded her arms and met his insult straight-on. "I'm not apologizing for my behavior either."

"Fine. First, why should I have missed a beat? I wasn't doing anything to feel guilty about. Next, Dory's a touchy kind of person. She makes contact with people, which is probably why she's good in PR. And yeah, I kissed her before she left. I'll probably kiss her next time I see her. I like her. We have a history. We met in high school, ended up in college together—and ended up being an item for about a year. In college, Hayley, for Christ's sake. When we stopped being an item, we stayed friends. If you can manage to whip some of the green out of your vision, you'd probably end up being friends with her, too."

"I don't like being jealous. I've never really been jealous before, and I don't like it."

"If you'd heard our conversation out by her car, you'd have heard her tell me that she hoped you and I would come into the city, have drinks, so she could get to know you. She said it was good to see me, and good to see me happy. I said pretty much the same, and I kissed her goodbye."

"It's just . . . you looked like a couple."

"We're not. That's what you and I are. That's what I feel," he said when she only stared at him. "That's what I want. I don't know what I've done to make you doubt me, or that."

"You've never actually said . . ."

He stepped to her, caught her face in his hands. "I don't want to be with anyone but you. You're the only one, Hayley. Is that clear enough?"

"Yeah." She laid her hand on his, turned her head so that her lips pressed to his palm.

"So we're good now?"

"It looks like. Um, you told her you were seeing me. I mean me?"

"I didn't have to. When you walked back out, she punched me in the arm. She said, 'She's taller than me, she's thinner than me and she's got better hair.' What is it about your breed and hair?"

"Never mind that. What else did she say?"

"That it was bad enough I was blowing her off, but it had to be over somebody who looked like you. I figured it for some sort of twisted girl compliment."

"A nice one. Now I feel guilty. I bet I would like her, and that's just a little bit irritating." She brooded a minute, then beamed. "But I'll get over it. I'm not going to apologize, exactly, because—hey, hands on your ass. But I'll offer to cook you dinner."

"Sold," he said without hesitation.

"Got anything in mind?"

"Nothing. Surprise me. Us," he corrected and scooped Lily up to hang her upside down. "I'll get shortie here out of your hair. We have some havoc to wreak in the other room."

And just like that, she thought, her life was back on level. With the sounds of growling from Harper, and wild giggles from Lily rolling out of the living room, Hayley opened the refrigerator to examine the contents.

Pitiful, she decided. A total guy assortment of beer, soft drinks, bottled water, what appeared to be an ancient fried chicken leg, two eggs, a stick of butter and a small, moldy hunk of cheese.

She opened the freezer, and hit the payload. Several carefully labeled containers of leftovers. David to the rescue. But it was a shame she couldn't actually cook something, impress Harper.

Who's pitiful? He flaunts another woman in your face and you grovel. Now cooking for him, like a servant. Women are nothing but servants to men. Their conveniences.

He lies as all men lie, and you believe because you're weak and foolish.

Make him pay. They should all pay.

"No." She said it softly when she found herself standing in front of the open freezer door. "No. Those weren't my thoughts. And I won't have them in my head."

"You say something?" Harper called out.

"No. No," she said more calmly.

There was nothing to say. Nothing to think. She would put a meal together and they'd eat. Like a couple. Or even, just a little bit, like a family.

The three of them. Only the three of them.

fourteen

FEELING SO SETTLED WAS JUST A LITTLE SPOOKY TO Harper's mind. They'd taken to having dinner together in the evenings. Sitting together in the kitchen, Lily strapped in the highchair he'd carted over from the main house, he and Hayley at the table with a meal, and conversation seemed so easy it made him nervous.

They were drifting into something solid, like a boat sailing toward shore in a light wind. He wasn't sure whether when they hit it, they'd end up bruised and battered or safe and sound.

Did she seem edgy, too, under the casual? he wondered. Or was he projecting his own jitters?

It was all so normal, this eating together at the end of the day, talking about work or Lily's latest accomplishment. Yet twined through the respite was an intensity, a feeling. A here we are, and here we'll stay—at least for the night.

How much did he, did both of them, want to keep the "at least" in the mix?

"I was thinking," he began, "that if things are slow inside tomorrow, I could show you how to hybridize."

"I know a little. Roz walked me through a snapdragon."

"I was thinking a lily. They're a good specimen for it, and we could try one. I was thinking we could try for a mini, something in a kind of candy pink. And name it for Lily."

Her face switched on to glow. "Really? Like create a new specimen, for her? Oh, Harper, that would be so awesome."

"I thought pink—but a strong pink—and we could try for a hint of red blushing the petals. Red's your color, so it'd be like Hayley's Lily. I was thinking."

"You're going to make me cry."

"Spend some time hand-pollinating and you might just cry. It's not an instant-gratification deal."

"I'd really like to try."

"Then we'll work on it. What do you think of that, shortie?" he asked Lily. "Want your own flower?"

She picked up a green bean with two delicate fingers and dropped it with some care on the floor.

"I bet she likes the flower more than her vegetables. That's her signal she's done." Hayley rose. "I'll clean her up."

"I could do it. Give her a bath."

With a laugh, Hayley removed the highchair tray. "Ever given a toddler a bath?"

"No, but I've had a few. Just fill up the tub, dump her in, hand her the soap. Then go back and dry her off after I've had another beer. Just kidding," he said when Hayley's eyes bugged out. He unstrapped Lily, hitched her up. "Your mama thinks I'm a bath moron. We'll show her."

"Oh, but—"

"Stay with her at all times. Don't even turn your back.

Warm water, not hot. Blah, blah, blah," he continued as he walked away. Over his shoulder, Lily happily waved bye-bye.

She checked on them three times, but tried to be subtle about it.

By the time she'd finished dealing with the kitchen, Lily was running around, all pink and powdered and wearing nothing but her Huggies. Some men, she decided, were natural with children. Harper seemed to be one of them.

"What's next on her agenda?"

"I usually let her play for another hour or so, tires her out. Then maybe we'll read a book—or part of one—if she'll sit still long enough. Harper, don't you want to get rid of us?"

"No. I'm hoping you'll stay. I can set that portable deal up in the spare room. We'll hear her if she wakes up. Then you could be with me." He took Hayley's hands, leaned in to take her lips. "I want you to be with me tonight."

"Harper . . ." She eased away, then hurried after Lily. "Wait," she said, and stopped in the living room when Lily made a beeline for a pile of plastic trucks and cars. "Where'd they come from?"

"They were mine. Some things you keep."

She imagined Harper as a little boy, playing with his trucks and making engine noises, much as her baby was doing now. "Harper, this is so hard."

"What's hard?"

"Not falling dead stupid in love with you."

He said nothing for a moment, then turned her around to face him. "What if you did?"

"That's what I don't know. See, that's what I don't know." Her voice hitched, and she swallowed to even it out. "There's a lot tangled up in this. We only started being with each other a few weeks ago, and there's all this stuff happening. I don't know what you want, what you're looking for."

"I'm still figuring it out."

"That's fine for you, Harper. I mean it really is, it's just fine. But what if I love you? I love you, and you figure out what you want is a trip to Belize and six months bumming on the beach? I've got Lily to consider. I can't—"

"Hayley, if I wanted to be a beach bum, I think I'd know it by now."

"You know what I'm talking about."

"Okay, yeah. What if I fall for you, what if I love you and you decide you want to go back to Little Rock with Lily and open your own nursery?"

"I couldn't—"

He held up a hand. "Sure you could. It's the kind of risk people take when they get involved this way. Maybe you'll fall, and maybe the other person won't want what you're looking for."

"So we're sensible? Take it a day at a time."

"We could. We could do that."

"What if I don't want to be sensible?" she fired back. "What if I want to stand here right now and tell you I'm in love with you? What are you going to do about it?"

"I'm not sure since it's pissing you off."

"Of course, I'm pissed off." She threw up her arms. "I'm in love with you, damn it, Harper, and you want to be sensible, take it a day at a time. And from where I'm standing your way just sucks sideways."

He considered himself a fairly laid-back sort of man, albeit one with a dangerous temper, which he was careful to control most of the time. How, he wondered, had he fallen so completely for a women whose moods tended to bounce around like a pinball?

Proved, he supposed, that there was no logic in love.

"Instead of going off, you should listen. I said we could be sensible. We could take it a day at a time. But since I'm in love with you right back, I'm not so crazy about that idea either."

"You go around doing romantic stuff, movie-time romantic stuff. And then the sweet things like giving my little girl a bath, and I'm supposed to stay sensible? I mean, what do you expect, Harper, what do you expect when you . . ."

She caught her breath, then took a long one while he just looked at her, that lazy half smile on his face. "What was that part after how I should listen?"

"I said I was in love with you right back."

"Oh. Oh." She crouched when Lily brought her one of the trucks. "That's nice, honey. Why don't you go get it?" She rolled the truck across the room, got back up. "You're not saying that because I'm being bitchy."

"Generally, my policy doesn't include telling a woman I'm in love with her when she's being bitchy. Fact is, I haven't said it to anyone before, because it's the kind of thing that has weight. Should have weight. So you're the first."

"It's not because you're so stuck on Lily?"

He cast his eyes to heaven. "For Christ's sake."

"I'm picking it apart." She held her hands up, wagged them. "I hear myself. I'm just breathless. You make me so happy I've been miserable."

"Yeah, I can see how that works. Completely not."

"I've been so scared." On a laugh, she threw her arms around him. "I was so scared that I'd fall for you, then we'd end up being friends like that woman who came into the nursery the other day. I'm not going to be friends with you, Harper, if this doesn't work out." She reared back, then pressed her mouth hard to his. "I'm going to hate you forever."

"Good. I think."

She sighed, long and deep, as she laid her cheek to his. "What do we do now?"

"Since it's a first for me, I'd like to ride on it awhile. It's some pretty heady stuff. More immediately, I'd say we'll play with Lily. Tire her out good, so that after you put her to bed I can take you to mine."

"I like that plan."

BY THE TIME SHE'D SETTLED LILY DOWN, HARPER HAD music on. She knew he was rarely without it. Though it was just dusk, he had candles flickering in his bedroom. And flowers—a touch she'd rarely seen in another man, but had come to expect from him.

"She okay?" he asked her.

"Fine. She goes down pretty easy, doesn't always stay that way through the night though."

"Then we should take advantage of the quiet." He slid his hands down her arms, then back up the sides of her body. "I love making love with you. Touching you. Watching you when I touch you. The way your body moves with mine."

"Maybe we're just in lust."

"I've been in lust." His lips cruised over her jaw. "Is that what this feels like to you?"

"No." She turned her head so their lips could meet. "Not just."

"I think about you. How you look, how you sound, how you feel. And here we are."

She linked her arms around his neck as he lowered her to the bed. His hands glided down, up, then palmed over her breast.

"You are perfect. Perfect, perfect." He nibbled his way down, then nipped lightly at her nipple through her shirt until she quivered under him.

Then he tugged her shirt down, and took flesh.

More than arousal, she thought even as her body bowed up in response. There was joy fizzing through the excitement, like the bubbles in champagne. He loved her. Harper with the patient hands and ripping temper loved her.

Whatever happened, she was loved. And the love that rose so full and strong inside her was welcomed. There was no gift she treasured more.

To show him, and how she needed to show him, she poured herself into a kiss on a flood of that love.

She surrounded him with it so he felt his heart ache from the brilliance. He loved. It had never come to him before, this stunning surge of emotion that filled heart and soul, gut and mind. This woman, the one who moved with him, merged with him, was the one who sparked it.

He savored the scent and flavor of her skin as the sky deepened to night and a whippoorwill began to sing in the apple tree outside his window.

Inside, the air went soft and thick, throbbing with the sounds of sighs. He felt her rise, tremble, and tremble on the peak, then float down on a moan that was his name. Her skin quivered where he touched and his own warmed as her hands glided over him.

Her lips. He could sink into them until pleasure swirled and shimmered in his mind like mists.

When she rolled over him, rose over him, he could see her face in the candlelight. The glow of it framed by her dark hair, the delicate blue of her eyes deepened with passion.

Her lips reclaimed his, soft, soft even as the kiss deepened. Then the throaty hum as she took him into her. He closed his eyes, riding the sensation as she closed around him.

"This is what you want," she whispered. "What you all want."

The change was like a finger snap, the cold like a sheath of ice. He looked at her, and everything inside him stilled.

"No."

"To penetrate. To bury yourself."

"Stop." Even as she rocked, arousal mixing with horror, he gripped her hips to hold her still.

"Tell her anything. Love. Promises. Lies. As long as you get between her legs." Her thighs clamped him, long, lean vises. Hayley's body, he knew, but not Hayley. Revulsion rose in his throat.

"Stop." He reached up, and what was inside her laughed.

"Shall I make you come? Shall I ride you like a pony until you—"

He shoved her back, and she continued to laugh, sprawled naked in the flickering light.

"Leave her alone." He hauled her back. "You've got no right to her."

"As much as you. More. We're the same, she and I. The same."

"No. You're not. She doesn't look for the easy way. She's warm and strong and honest."

"I could have been." Something else came into her eyes then. Regret, grief, need. "I can be. And I know better than she does what can be done with this body." She pressed it to his, began to whisper erotic suggestions in his ear.

With sick panic burning in his belly, he shook her. "Hayley. Damn it, Hayley. You're stronger than her. Don't let her do this." And though it was still something else that looked at him, though her lips were cold, so cold, he kissed her. Gently. "I love you. Hayley, I love you. Come back to me."

He knew when she did, the instant. And gathered her hard and close while she shivered. "Harper."

"Ssh. It's okay."

"She was—Oh God. It wasn't me. I didn't mean those things. Harper—"

Comfort, he thought, wasn't the answer, not here, not now. "It's you I want." His lips skimmed over her face, and his hands began to stroke her warm once more. "Just you, just me. We won't let her touch this. Look at me."

He gripped her hands in his, and plunged into her. "Look at me," he repeated. "Stay with me."

The cold became heat, the horror became joy. She stayed with him. Linked.

SHE COULDN'T SPEAK, EVEN WHEN HIS HEAD WAS pillowed on her belly and the whippoorwill had given way to the cicadas. So much churned inside her she couldn't separate the shock from the fear, the fear from the shame.

He brushed a kiss over her flesh, then rose.

"I'm going to get us some water, and I'll look in on Lily."

She had to choke back words now. Please that he not leave her alone, even for a moment. But that was foolish, and impossible. She couldn't be watched every minute. More, she couldn't bear the idea that he might feel he had to watch her, waiting for Amelia to use her again.

She sat up, drawing her knees up to rest her brow on them.

She stayed that way when he came back, sat on the bed beside her.

"Harper. I don't know what to say."

"It wasn't your fault, let's just get that out of the way. And you pushed her out, or pushed through her, whatever the hell."

"I don't know how you could stand to touch me after."

"You think I'd let her win? You think I'd let her beat us?"

The barely restrained fury in his voice had her lifting

her head. "You . . . you were inside me when she—It's so creepy."

"Here." He nudged the water on her. "Creepy for both of us," he agreed. "And a little incestuous for me. Jesus. Nothing like getting really close to your great-great-grandmother."

"She wasn't thinking of you that way. I don't know if that helps." Fighting off a shudder, she handed the water back to him. "She was . . . I felt like she was seeing him. Reginald. She was—I was—all turned on, you know, then it was like this spit of rage spewing up through that. But the kind that makes it more, sort of more exciting. Darker. Then it was all blurred together. Her and me, him and you. And I was so wound up I couldn't get a grip on anything. Then you said you loved me, you kissed me and I could hold on to that."

"She tried to use us. We didn't let her." He set the water aside before easing her back so he could lie beside her and draw her close. "It's going to be okay."

But even lying beside him, held firm and safe in his arms, she couldn't quite believe it.

IT WAS AWKWARD, BUT HARPER FELT MITCH SHOULD know about any incident involving Amelia. Even if that incident had happened in bed with Hayley.

At least it was a man-to-man sort of thing. If his mother had to have the information, Harper would just as soon have it filtered through his stepfather.

"How long did it last?" Mitch asked.

"Maybe a couple of minutes. Seemed longer, considering the situation, but probably around that."

"She wasn't violent."

"No. But you know . . ." He had to pause a moment and

give his attention fully to the work board in the library. "Rape's not always violent, but it's still . . . Anyway, that's what it felt like, to me. Like a kind of rape. Like a power thing. Got you by the dick, so I'm in charge."

"It fits the kind of personality profile we've been building. She wouldn't get that while what's between you and Hayley is sexual, sex for the sake of sex isn't the driving force. Must've shaken you up."

Harper only nodded. There was still a coating of that raw sickness in his belly. "How much more do we need to know before we can stop this?"

"I wish I could tell you. We have her name, her circumstance. We know your bloodline comes down through her. We know her baby was taken, and we're assuming without her consent. Or that after she gave it, she changed her mind. We know she came here, to Harper House, and we have to believe she died here. Maybe if we find out how, but that's no guarantee."

He'd never counted on guarantees, not in his life or in his work. His father had died when he'd been seven, which had put paid to any sort of traditional family warranty. His work was a series of experiments, calculated risks, learned skills, and sheer luck. None of those guaranteed success.

Harper considered failure a postponement at worst, and another step in the process at best.

But things were considerably different when it involved the woman he loved, and her welfare, her well-being.

He was reminded of that when he found her watering flats.

She wore the cotton shorts and tank that was a kind of summer uniform around the nursery. Her feet were tucked into thin, backless canvas shoes that could take a soaking, and her face was shaded by the bill of one of the nursery's gimme caps.

She looked entirely too sad and thoughtful. The thoughtful part was proven right when she jumped nearly a foot off the ground when he said, "Hey."

"God, you scared me."

"That's what you get for taking side-trips when you're on the clock. Speaking of which, I'm going to start that hybridizing, and could use an assist."

"You still want to do that?"

"Why wouldn't I?"

"I thought maybe when you thought things through, you'd want to keep your distance for a while."

He simply stepped up to her, cautiously nudging the watering wand aside and kissed her. "Guess you're wrong."

"Guess I am. Lucky for me."

"Just come on over when you're done. I already let Stella know I was stealing you for a while."

He spent the time setting up for the work, lining up the tools, the plants he wanted to use. He logged the species, the cultivar, the name and characteristics of the desired plant in his files.

Since headphones wouldn't be an option as he wouldn't be working alone, he switched Beethoven for Loreena McKennitt. He figured his plants would like it fine, and he'd be a lot happier.

When Hayley came in, he was digging out a Coke, so he pulled out two.

"This is pretty exciting."

He handed her the can. "Tell me what you know about hybridizing first."

"Well, it's like you have a mama and a daddy, the parents. Two different plants—they can be the same type or two different . . . What is it?"

"Genera."

"Right. So you want ones with stable characteristics and

you cross them by hand-pollinating. Like pollen from one, seed from the other—like sex."

"Not bad. We're going to use this miniature I've been screening as a parent plant. And this variegated will be the other, the seed parent. See I've had it protected with a bag—that keeps insect pollinators from messing with it, and we're going to remove the stamens now, before it can self-pollinate. I potted these up, brought them in last winter so they could develop."

"You've been thinking about doing this for a while."

"Yeah, since she was born, more or less. Anyway, we work with the pollen parent today. You know how?"

"Roz did it before. I really just watched."

"This time, you try it. I cut this one already, just above the node, see? It's been in water and it's fully open now. See how the anthers are split? They're ready for pollen."

"So, you did the foreplay."

"One of my little skills."

She gave an exaggerated roll of her eyes. "Tell me about it."

"You go next."

"Oh man. I have to pull the petals off, right?"

"Quick, gentle twists, work inward until you see the anthers."

"Here goes."

"That's good," he said as he watched her. "Just be careful to leave the anthers intact. Yeah, nice work, good hands."

"I'm nervous. I hate screwing up."

"You're not." Her fingers were quick and precise as they twisted the petals away. "And if you do, we'll pick another."

"Is that right? Is that okay?"

"What do you see?"

She bit her lip. "The little anthers are all naked."

"Next step." He picked up a clean camel-hair brush.

"You need to collect the pollen. Use this, brush it over the anthers. We'll store it in this dish, keep it dry. See, it's fluffy, so it's ripe. I'll label the dish."

"This is fun. You wouldn't believe how totally I sucked in high school chemistry."

"Just needed a better lab partner. All mine aced. Now we're going to prep the seed parent. See this?" He held up the lily he'd chosen. "We don't want her fully open. We're looking for well-developed but with immature anthers—before self-pollination can happen. We take petals and anthers off her."

"Strip her right down."

"So to speak. No fragments left, they can cause rot fungi, then you're screwed. What we're after is nice exposed stigmas."

"You do that part. Then it's like a team."

"Okay." He twisted off the petals, then reached for his tweezers, skillfully plucking out the anthers. "Now she waits until tomorrow for the pollen. That gives her stigmas time to get sticky. Then we'll transfer the ripe pollen onto the stigmas. You can use a brush, but I like using my finger. There."

He stepped back.

"That's it?"

"That's the first one. Let's do the next. We've got a good dozen seed parents on here. I think we'll try a couple of pollen parents on her. See what we get."

They took turns with the steps. A nice, companionable rhythm, Hayley thought, and a satisfying one. "How did you pick the plants to work with?"

"I've been scoping them out awhile, tracking growth habits and form, color patterns."

"Since she was born."

"Yeah, pretty much."

"Harper, you know how I said if things don't work out with us, I'll hate you for the rest of my life?"

"Yeah, I got that."

"Well, I will, but I'll suck it in—mostly—because I know you love her. You really do."

"She's got me wrapped. I gotta admit. Tomorrow, we'll pollinate, label, log. Then we'll keep an eye on her. Probably take about a week before we see the ovary swelling, if we're successful here."

"Swelling ovaries. Takes me back."

He grinned, kept working. "Couple weeks more, the pod should be formed, then it takes about a month more for the seed to ripen. We'll know it has when the top begins to split."

"Yeah, déjà vu."

"Cut it out. That's just weird."

He moved to his computer, his long fingers tapping keys as he input data. "What we'll do is take the seeds, dry them and plant them late fall. I like to do it that way so it won't germinate until spring."

"We plant them outside."

"No, in here. Mama's potting soil, four-inch pots, then we put them out. When they're big enough, we'll put them in nursery beds. It'll take another year before they bloom and we see what we've really got."

"Fortunately, I know nothing about a two-year pregnancy."

"Yeah, women get by with nine little months. Blink of an eye."

"You try it, pal."

"I'm a fan of the way things work. So. I've got the records logged, and if things work out, we should eventually see some new flowers, and some of them should have characteristics of each parent." He glanced over the work, nodded. "We'll get what we're after, or if not exactly, hopefully something close enough that we can do another generation, or try a different parent."

"In other words, this could take years."

"Serious hybridizing isn't for weenies."

"I like it. And I like that it's not an overnight kind of deal. You have all this anticipation. And maybe you won't get exactly what you had in mind, but something else. Something, not necessarily better, but just as beautiful."

"Now you're talking the talk."

"I feel good." She stepped back from the worktable. "I was having such a bad day. I kept thinking about what happened last night, circling around and around it, and just feeling sick about the whole thing."

"It wasn't your fault."

"I know—in my head. But somewhere in there I wondered if we'd be able to be easy together again—or at least this soon. If you'd be, I don't know, uncomfortable and I'd be jittery. It seemed like the chance we had to just be in love might've been spoiled."

"Nothing's changed for me."

"I know." They stood side-by-side at the workbench and she tilted her head onto his shoulder. "And I feel calmer knowing it."

"I better let you know I told Mitch what happened."

"Oh." She sucked in a breath, winced. "I guess it had to be done, and better you than me. Was it awful?"

"No. Just a little weird. We spent a lot of time talking about it without making any eye contact."

"I'm not going to think about it," Hayley decided. "I'm just not." She turned just enough to kiss him. "I'd better get on with the work I really get paid for. I'll see you back home."

* * *

AS SHE HUMMED HER WAY THROUGH THE REST OF THE day, Stella passed by, then stopped to put her hands on her hips. "Hybridizing certainly agrees with you."

"Feel great. Step two tomorrow."

"Well, good. You looked a little draggy this morning."

"Didn't sleep very well, but I've got my second wind, and then some." She glanced around to be sure no one was within hearing distance. "We're in love." Grinning, she used the index fingers of both hands to draw a heart in the air. "Me and Harper. Together."

"Wow. News flash."

With a laugh, Hayley continued hauling bags of potting soil from cart to shelf. "I mean really in love. So we said the L word to each other."

"I'm happy for you." She gave Hayley a hug. "Seriously."

"I'm happy for me, too. But there's this . . . I have to tell you about this thing that happened." Cautious, Hayley took another look around, and related the incident to Stella in undertones.

"My God. Are you all right?"

"It was awful, so awful, it still makes my stomach churn. I didn't know how we'd get past it. That was almost worse than the experience itself. But we have. We did. I can't imagine how he must've felt, but he didn't pull back from me."

"He loves you."

"He does. He really does." Miracles everywhere, she thought. "Stella, I always believed I'd fall in love one day, but I never knew it could be like this. Now that I know, I can't imagine not keeping it. You know?"

"I do. You should be happy. You should know this other thing is separate from that. And you and Harper should enjoy this bliss stage because it's very precious."

"I feel like everything in my life has been leading up to

this, to him. The good and the bad. I can take the bad because I know we've found something in each other that really matters. I guess that sounds lame, but—"

"It does not. It sounds happy."

fifteen

THE SECONDHAND LAPTOP WAS A GOOD BUY, AND USing it made Hayley feel she was doing something active. An hour or two in research mode may not have garnered her a great deal of new information, at least as applied to her situation, but it assured her she wasn't alone.

There were a lot of people out there who at least believed they'd had experience with ghosts and hauntings. She was already documenting an essential piece of advice from every website she'd visited. But at least with the computer she could type her reports instead of scrawling them in a notebook.

And it was fun to be able to e-mail friends back in Little Rock.

Of course she got caught up in surfing the web, much as she got caught up when scanning books. There was just so much information, so many interesting things. And one invariably led to another so that if she wasn't careful, she'd be up past midnight hunched over the keyboard.

She had her chin propped on her elbow, her mind focused on an on-line report from Toronto of a ghost baby crying when a hand brushed her shoulder.

She didn't jump, held back a scream. Instead she closed her eyes and spoke in a nearly normal tone. "Please tell me that's a real hand."

"I hope it is as it's attached to my wrist."

"Roz." Hayley let out her breath slowly. "Points for me, right, for not jumping up to cling to the ceiling like a cartoon cat."

"That might've been entertaining." She narrowed her eyes to read the screen. "Ghosthunters dot com?"

"One of many," Hayley told her. "And really, there's some pretty cool stuff. Did you know that one of the traditional ways to discourage ghosts from coming into a room was to stick pins or hammer iron nails around the door? It's like they'd get caught on them and couldn't get in. Of course, if you did it while they were already in, then they couldn't get out."

"I catch you nailing anything into my woodwork, I'll skin you."

"Already figured that. Plus I don't see how it could work." She scooted around, away from the screen. "They say you should talk to the ghost, politely, just ask it to leave. Like: Hey, sorry about your bad luck being dead and all that, but this is my house now and you're disturbing me, so I wonder if you'd mind just moving on."

"I'd say we've tried variations of that."

"Yeah, no go." When Roz sat on the sofa in the sitting room, Hayley understood she hadn't come by just to chat about Amelia. Nerves began to drum. "Of course, they say you should document everything, but Mitch already has us doing that. And take photographs. You can hire a ghost hunter, but I don't guess you want a bunch of strangers in the house."

"You guess right."

"Or you can ask a minister or a priest to bless the house. That couldn't hurt."

"You're afraid."

"More than I was, yeah. But I know this stuff"—she tapped the screen—"isn't really helpful because what we're doing, what we always planned to do was find out who, what, why. And if we did manage just to boot her out, we wouldn't know it all. But I like, well, harvesting information."

"You and Mitch, peas in a pod. Have you documented what happened the other night, with you and Harper?"

"Yes." Heat burned her cheeks. "I haven't, ah, given it to Mitch yet."

"It's very personal. I wouldn't like sharing that sort of personal experience with an outsider."

"You're not. I mean, he's not. Neither of you."

"Anyone, no matter how you love them, is an outsider when it comes to the bed, Hayley. I want you to know I understand that. I also want you to know you've got no need to walk on eggshells with me about this. I waited a couple of days, hoping it wouldn't be quite as touchy a subject."

"I know Harper went to Mitch about it, and I knew Mitch would tell you. I just couldn't, Roz. If it'd been anybody but Harper—not that I'd be with anybody but Harper . . . And I'm already messing this up."

"You're not."

"It's . . . Harper's yours."

"Yes, he is." She propped her feet on the table, her most habitual position. "I knew when he fell in love with you, though you didn't know, and I doubt he did."

"I think maybe it was the night we stayed at the Peabody."

Roz shook her head. "That's romance, and valuable. But that wasn't when. Who held your hand when Lily was born?"

"Oh." Hayley lifted a hand to her throat as it filled. "He did. Harper did, and I think he was almost as scared as I was."

"When I saw, and I understood, my heart ached. Just for a moment. You'll know what I mean when it's Lily's turn. And if you're lucky, as I'm lucky, you'll watch your child fall in love with someone you can love, and respect and admire, be amused by, feel close to. So when your heart aches, it's with happiness, and gratitude."

Tears spilled down her cheeks. "I don't know how I could get any luckier than I already am. You've been so good to me. No, please don't brush it off," she said when Roz shook her head. "It means so much to me. When I came here, I thought I was so smart and strong, so ready. If she kicks me out, I thought, I'll just keep going. I'll find a job, get an apartment, have this baby. I'll be fine. If I'd known what it takes—not just the hours, the effort, but the love and the worry that just fills you up when you have a child, I'd've thrown myself at your feet and begged for help. But all I had to do was ask."

"I gave you a job and a place to stay because you're family, and because of the situation you were in. But that's not why you're still here. You earned your place at In the Garden, and your place in this house. Make no mistake, if you hadn't, I'd have shown you the door."

"I know." And knowing it made Hayley grin. "I wanted to prove myself to you, and I'm proud that I did. But, Roz, because I have Lily, I know what Harper means to you. And part of the reason I'm scared, more scared than I was, is I'm afraid The Bride might hurt him."

"Why do you think that?"

"She saw Reginald in him. Maybe one of the reasons she's moved on to me is because of the feelings that I developed for Harper. When I first met him, I remember thinking, wow, if I was in the market, I'd be all over that one."

When Roz laughed, Hayley flushed. "See what comes out of my mouth?" she demanded. "Jesus, you're his *mother.*"

"Forget that a minute. Keep going."

"Well, see I wasn't in a place in my head, or anywhere else, where I could think seriously about a man, a relationship. I just thought he was hot, then as I got to know him, sweet and funny and smart. I liked him a lot, and I got irritated now and then that he was so cute and I was pregnant and cranky and not at my best. After Lily, I tried to think of him as kind of a brother, or a cousin. Well, he is a cousin, but you know what I mean."

"The way you think of David or Logan, or my other sons."

"Yeah. I really tried to put Harper in that same slot. And there was so much to do and learn, that it was easy to ignore that little low tickle that was going on inside me. You know the one."

"Thank God I do," Roz said with feeling.

"Then it wasn't so easy, and the feelings for him kept getting stronger. It seems to me, when I started to admit them to myself, started to imagine how it could be with him, that's when Amelia started slipping in."

"And the stronger your feelings, the stronger and more demonstrative her objections."

"I'm worried that she'll hurt him, through me. Not seeing Harper, but Reginald. I'm worried I won't be able to stop her."

Roz frowned. "Seems that you're not giving Harper enough credit for being able to handle himself."

"Maybe not. But she's awful strong, Roz. Stronger than she was, I think." Remembering the sensation of having her *self* pushed aside, Hayley inhaled, exhaled, deeply. "And it seems to me she's had a lot of time to think about payback."

"Harper's stronger than she thinks. And so are you."

SHE HOPED ROZ WAS RIGHT. AS SHE LAY SLEEPLESS, with Harper beside her, she hoped she had the grit and the brains to combat the vengeance of a vindictive spirit. Worse, one she felt some sympathy for.

But Harper wasn't responsible for what had happened to her. No one who lived at Harper House now was responsible. There had to be a way, some way, for her to make Amelia understand that. To show her that Harper was not only the child she'd once sung to, but a good, caring man. And nothing like Reginald.

What had he been like, really? Reginald Harper. A man so obsessed with having a son, he would deliberately impregnate a woman not his wife. Whether or not Amelia had consented—and that they couldn't know—it had been a selfish and hurtful act on his part. Then to take the child, to force his own wife to accept it as her own. He couldn't have loved. Not his wife, not Amelia, certainly not the child.

It was no wonder Amelia despised him, and with her spirit or mind, or heart, shattered, that she'd grouped all men along with him.

What had it been like for her? For Amelia?

SHE SAT AT HER DRESSING TABLE, CAREFULLY ROUGING her cheeks by gaslight. Pregnancy had stolen her color. Just one more indignity, after the horrible sickness morning after morning, the widening of her waist, the incessant fatigue.

And yet, there were benefits. So many she hadn't counted

on. She smiled as she added color to her lips. How could she have known Reginald would be so pleased? Or so generous.

She lifted her arm to study the ruby and diamond hearts that circled her wrist. A bit delicate for her taste, really, but you couldn't fault the glimmer.

And he'd hired another maid, given her carte blanche for a new wardrobe to accommodate her changing body. More jewels. More attention.

He visited her three times a week now, and never came empty-handed. Even if it was only to bring her chocolates or candied fruit when she mentioned craving sweets.

How fascinating to know that the prospect of a child could make a man so biddable.

She imagined he'd been very solicitous of his wife, in turn. But then she'd plagued him with girls rather than the son he coveted.

She would give him a son. And in giving, would reap the benefits for the rest of her life.

A bigger house to start, she decided. Clothes, jewels, furs, a new carriage—perhaps a small country house as well. He could afford it. Reginald Harper would spare no expense for his son, even his bastard son, she was sure.

As the mother of that son, she would never have to seek out another protector, never have to flirt and seduce and bargain with the men of wealth and position, offering sex and comfort in exchange for the mode of life she craved. Deserved. Earned.

She rose from the dressing table, and hair shining gold, jewels glittering white and red, gown sweeping silver, she turned in the chevel glass.

This was her exchange now. This bulge of the belly. Look how odd and awkward, how fat and unfashionable she looked, despite the gown. And yet, Reginald doted. He would stroke that bulge, even during passion. And in passion, he was kinder, gentler than she'd ever known him to be. She could almost love him during those times, when his hands were tender instead of demanding. Almost.

But love was not part of the game, and a game was all it was. This bartering pleasure for style. How could she love what was so weak, so deceitful, so arrogant? A ridiculous notion, as ridiculous as feeling pity for the wives they betrayed with her. Women who folded their thin lips and pretended not to know. Who passed her on the street with their noses in the air. Or women like her mother who slaved for them for pennies.

She was meant for bigger things, she thought, and lifted a heavy crystal decanter to stroke scent on her throat. She was meant for silks and diamonds.

When Reginald arrived, she would pout, just a little. And tell him of the diamond broach she'd seen that afternoon. How she would pine without it.

Pining wasn't good for the child. She imagined the broach would be hers within a day.

She gave a light laugh, a little turn.

Then stopped, went still. Her hand trembled as she lifted it to press over her belly.

It had moved.

Inside her a flutter, a stretch. Little wings beating.

The glass reflected her as she stood in her shimmering gown, her fingers spread over the slight bulge as if she would guard what was inside.

Inside her. Alive. Her son.

Hers.

HAYLEY REMEMBERED IT VIVIDLY. EVEN IN THE morning there was nothing of the fragmented or misty quality of a dream.

"It was, I think it was, a kind of a bid for sympathy. More for empathy." She held her cup in both hands as she sipped coffee in the breakfast nook.

"How so?" Mitch had his tape recorder and notebook as she'd requested. "Did she speak directly to you at some point?"

"No, because it wasn't her, it was me. Or it was both of us. I wasn't dreaming so much as I was there. I felt, I saw, I thought. She wasn't just showing me, but reliving. If that makes sense."

"Eat your eggs, sweetie-pie," David urged her. "You look peaked."

She scooped some up obediently. "She was beautiful. Not like the way we've seen her, really. Vibrant and drop-dead—excuse the term. There was so much going through her head—my head—I don't know. Irritation about the changes in her body, the inconvenience, plots and plans to get more out of Reginald, surprise at his reaction to her condition, disgust for men like him, for their wives, envy, greed. It all just kept rolling around in a big mass."

She paused, breathed. "I think she was already a little bit crazy."

"And how was that a bid for sympathy?" Harper asked her. "Why would you feel sorry for someone like that?"

"It was the change. It was feeling the baby move. I felt it, too. That shock of feeling, the sudden realization that there's life inside you. And there's this wave of love along with it. In that moment, the baby was hers. Not a ploy or an inconvenience, but her child, and she loved it." She looked at Roz.

"Yes."

"So she was showing me. I loved my child, wanted it. And the man, the kind of man who'd use a woman like me, took it from me. She was wearing the bracelet. The heart bracelet. And I did feel for her. I don't think she was a good person, certainly not a nice one, and even then, before the rest happened, I don't think she was balanced. But she loved the child, wanted it. I think what she showed me was real, and she showed me because I'd understand it more than anyone else. Yeah, I felt sorry for her."

"Sympathy is fine," Mitch said. "But you can't let down your guard. She's using you, Hayley."

"I know, and I won't. I can feel for her, but I don't have to trust her."

DAYS PASSED, AND SHE WAITED FOR THE NEXT MOVE, the next experience, but August boiled quietly toward September. The most wrenching experience was having her ancient car break down between work and the sitter's, and finally having to accept it was time to replace it.

"It's not just the money," she told Harper as she strolled Lily through the used-car lot. "It's one of my last links to childhood, I guess. My daddy bought that car, secondhand. I learned to drive with it."

"It'll go to a good home."

"Hell, Harper, it's going on the scrap heap, and we both know it. Poor, pitiful old thing. I know I've got to be sensible, too. I can't be hauling Lily around in an unreliable car. I'll be lucky if that salesman who took it off for appraisal doesn't come back and say I owe him just for dumping it on him."

"Just let me handle it."

"I will not." She stopped by a hatchback, kicked its tires. "You know what I hate? I hate that a lot of car salesmen and mechanics and that whole breed treat women who come in like brainless bimbos just because they don't have a penis. Like all the automotive data and know-it-all is stored in their dicks."

"Jesus, Hayley." He had to laugh, even as he winced.

"It's true. So, I've done my research. I know what I want and how much I should have to pay. He doesn't want to deal with me, then I'll just take my business elsewhere."

She stopped by a sedan, braced one hand on the fender and waved the other in front of her face. "God almighty, it's hot. Feel like every fluid in my body's boiled away."

"You look a little pale. Why don't we go inside, sit down for a minute?"

"I'm okay. Just not resting well. Even when I sleep, I feel like I'm on alert, like the first few weeks after Lily was born. Makes me draggy and irritable. So if I end up snapping at you, try to bear with me."

He rubbed the small of her back. "Don't worry about it."

"I appreciate you coming with me today, I really do. But don't feel like you've got to step in."

"Ever bought a car?"

She sent him a sidelong, annoyed look as she continued to push Lily's stroller. "Just because I haven't, doesn't mean I'm some rube down from the hills. I've bought lots of other things, and I can guarantee I know more about negotiating prices than you. Rich boy."

He grinned. "I'm just a working gardener."

"You may work for a living, but you've got a few silver spoons tucked away for rainy days. Now here's what I'm after."

She stopped to study a sturdy-looking five-door Chevy. "It's got plenty of room, but it's not big and bulky, and it's clean. It's bound to get better mileage than my old car and it's not flashy."

She frowned over the listed price. "I'll just get him to come down a bit, and it'll be in my range. Sort of."

"Don't tell him you—"

"Harper."

"Backing off." He shook his head, stuck his hands in his pockets.

And had to saw his tongue in half when the salesman came out, big smiles, and announced the meager offer on the trade-in.

"Oh, is that all?" Hayley widened her baby blues and fluttered her lashes. "I guess sentiment doesn't count, does it? But maybe, maybe you could just ease that up, a little bit, depending on what I buy. This one's pretty. I like the color."

Playing him, Harper realized, noting how she'd bumped up her accent. He went along for the ride as the salesman steered her toward a couple of pricier options, watched her chew her lip, flash her smile, and steer him right back to what she wanted.

Guy's toast, he decided as she finagled the price down, took Lily out of the stroller to sit with her behind the wheel. Harper concluded nobody could resist the pair of them.

Two hours later, they were driving off the lot with Lily dozing in her carseat and Hayley beaming behind the wheel.

" 'Oh, Mr. Tanner, I just don't know a thing about cars. You're so sweet to help me out this way.' " Harper shook his head. "When we were sitting in there doing the paperwork I wanted to warn him to lift up his feet. It was sure getting deep."

"He made a nice sale, got his commission and I got what I went in for. That's what counts." But she let out a hoot of laughter. "I liked when he tried to bring you into it, showed you under the hood and you just scratched your head like you were looking at a cruise missile or something. I think we made him feel good, like he was giving me what I needed for the price I could pay. And that counts, too. Next time I have to buy, I'd go right back to Mr. Tanner."

"Didn't hurt for you to tear up a couple times."

"That was real. I was sad to sell that old heap—and don't think these car payments aren't going to sting some." More, she thought, it had put an ache in her throat when Mr. Tanner had assumed they were a family.

"If you need some help—"

"Don't go there, Harper." But she reached over to pat his hand, to show she appreciated the offer. "We'll be fine, Lily and me."

"Why don't I take you out to lunch to celebrate then?"

"That's a deal. I'm starving."

They had looked like a family, she thought. A normal young family buying a secondhand car, having lunch in a diner, treating the baby to a cup of ice cream.

But putting them there was rushing it, for all of them. They were a man and a single mother who were romantically involved. Not a unit.

At home, she decided to take advantage of the rest of her day off by curling up with Lily for an afternoon nap.

"We're all right, aren't we, baby?" she murmured as Lily played with her mother's hair, her big eyes heavy, her pretty mouth going slack. "I'm doing right by you? I'm sure trying."

She snuggled down a little closer. "I'm so tired. Got a million things I ought to be doing, but I'm so tired. I'll get them all done sooner or later, right?"

She closed her eyes, started to calculate her finances in her head, juggling funds, changing weekly deposits. But her brain wouldn't focus.

It drifted back to the used-car lot, and Mr. Tanner shaking hands with her before she drove off. How he'd smiled at her and wished her and her charming family well.

Drifted to sitting out on her terrace with Harper, drinking cold wine in the heat-soaked night.

Dancing with him in the shimmering romance of the suite at the Peabody.

Working with him in the grafting house.

Watching him lift Lily onto his shoulders.

It should be easier to be in love, she thought sleepily. It should be simpler. It shouldn't make you want more when love was everything.

She sighed once, and told herself to enjoy what she had, and let the rest come.

And the pain was like knives in the belly, shocking, sharp, and horrid. Her whole body fought against them, and she screamed at the sensation of being ripped in two.

The heat, the pain. Unbearable. How could something so loved, so desired, punish her this way? She would die from it, surely she would die. And never see her son.

Sweat streamed off her, and the utter weariness was nearly as severe as the pain.

Blood and sweat and agony. All for her child, her son. Her world. No price too dear to pay for giving him life.

And as the pain sliced her, sent her tumbling toward the dark, she heard the thin cry of birth.

Hayley woke drenched in sweat, her body still radiating from the pain. And her own child blissfully asleep in the protective crook of her arm.

She eased free, fumbled for the bedside phone.

"Harper? Can you come?"

"Where are you?"

"In my room. Lily's sleeping right here. I can't leave her. We're all right," she said quickly. "We're fine, but something just happened. Please can you come?"

"Two minutes."

She made a wall of pillows around the baby, but knew even then she couldn't leave the room. Lily might roll off somehow, or certainly climb over and fall. But she could pace, even on her weakened legs she could pace.

She flung open the doors even as Harper ran up the steps.

"They told her it was stillborn." She swayed, and her knees nearly folded. "They told her her baby was dead."

SIXTEEN

In the parlor where the light was soft through gauzy curtains and the air was sweet with roses, Harper stood by the front window with his fists balled in his pockets.

"She was wrecked," he said with his back to the room. "She just sort of folded up when I got there, and even when she pulled it together, she looked sick."

"She wasn't hurt." Mitch held up a hand when Harper whirled. "I know how you feel. I do. But she wasn't physically harmed, and that's important."

"This time," he shot back. "It's out of hand. All of this is fucking out of hand."

"Only more reason for us to stick together, and stay calm."

"I'll be calm when she's out of the house."

"Amelia," Logan asked, "or Hayley?"

"Right now? Both."

"You know she can stay with us. And if I were in your shoes, I'd want to pack her up and haul her out. But from what I gather, you tried that once and it didn't work. If you think you've got a better shot at it now, I'll carry her suitcase."

"She won't budge. What the hell is wrong with these women?"

"They feel connected." David spread his hands. "Even when they see Amelia at her worst, they feel attached. Engaged. Right or wrong, Harp, there's a kind of solidarity."

"And it's her home," Mitch added. "As much as yours now, or mine. She won't walk out of it and leave this undone. Any more than you, or I, or any or us." He glanced around the room. "So we finish it."

Logic, even truth, didn't settle Harper's anger, or his worry. "You didn't see her after it happened."

"No, but I've got the gist from what you told me. She matters to me, too, Harper. To all of us."

"All for one, great. I'm for it." His gaze shifted to the parlor doors, and his mind traveled upstairs, to Hayley. "But she's the one on the line."

"Agreed." Mitch leaned forward in his chair to draw Harper's attention back to him. "Let's look at what happened for a minute. Hayley was taken through childbirth, and a traumatic aftermath when Amelia was told the baby was dead. And she went through this while she was napping with Lily. But Lily wasn't disturbed. That tells me that there's no intent to harm or even frighten the baby. If there were, how long do you think it would take Hayley to head out that door?"

"That may be true, but to get whatever it is she wants, Amelia's going to keep using Hayley, and using her hard."

"I agree." Mitch nodded. "Because it works. Because

this way she's feeding us information we might not ever be able to find. We know now that not only was her child taken from her, but that she was told, cruelly, that it was dead. It's hardly a wonder that her mind, which already seemed to be somewhat imbalanced, shattered."

"We can assume she came here for him," Logan suggested. "And died here."

"Well, the kid's dead, too. Dead as she is, dead as disco." Harper slumped into a chair. "She's not going to find him here."

UPSTAIRS, HAYLEY WOKE FROM A LIGHT DOZE. THE curtains were pulled so the light was dim but for a thin chink. She saw Roz sitting, reading a book in that narrow spear of light.

"Lily."

Roz set the book aside and rose. "Stella has her. She took her and the boys over to the other wing to play so you'd have some quiet. How are you feeling?"

"Exhausted. A little raw inside yet." But she sighed, comforted when Roz sat and stroked her hair. "It was harder than when I had Lily, rougher and longer. I know it was only a few minutes, really, but it seemed like hours. Hours and hours of pain and heat. Then this awful muzzy feeling toward the end. They gave her something, and it made her kind of float away, but it was almost worse."

"Laudanum, I imagine. Nothing like a shot of opiate."

"I heard the baby cry." Struggling to relax, Hayley curled on her side, tilting her head up to keep Roz in her line of sight. "You know how it is, no matter what's gone on in those hours before, everything inside you rising up when you hear your baby cry the first time."

"Hers." Roz took Hayley's hand. "Not yours."

"I know, I know, but for that instant he was mine. And that horrible tearing grief, that crazy disbelief when the doctor said it was stillborn, that was mine, too."

"I've never lost a child," Roz told her. "I can't even imagine the pain of it."

"They lied to her, Roz. I guess he paid them, too. They lied, but she knew. She heard the baby cry, and she *knew.* It drove her crazy."

Roz shifted on the bed, angling so she could rest Hayley's head on her lap. And sat in silence, staring at that thin lance of light through the curtains.

"She didn't deserve it," Hayley started.

"No. She didn't deserve it."

"Whatever she was, whatever she did, she didn't deserve to be treated that way. She loved the baby, but . . ."

"But what?"

"It wasn't right, the way she loved it. It wasn't a healthy sort of thing. She wouldn't have been a good mother."

"How do you know?"

"I felt . . ." Obsession, she thought, hunger. Impossible to describe the vastness of it. "It had to be a boy, you see? A girl wouldn't have mattered to her. A girl wouldn't have been just a disappointment, but an outrage. And if she'd had the boy and kept it, she would've twisted it. Not on purpose, but he wouldn't have been the man he was. He wouldn't have been the one who loved his dog and buried it with a marker, and loved your grandmother. And none of this would be the way it is."

She turned her head so that she could look up at Roz. "You, Harper. Nothing would be the same. But it doesn't make it right. It still doesn't make what happened right."

"Wouldn't it be nice if everything balanced in the

world? If right came out on top and wrong was punished. It sure would be simple."

Hayley's lips curved. "Then Justin Terrell, who cheated on me in tenth grade, would be fat and bald and asking people if they want fries with that instead of being part owner of a successful sport's bar and bearing a strong resemblance to Toby McGuire."

"Isn't that just the way?"

"Then again, maybe I'd go to hell for not telling Lily's biological father about her."

"Your motives were pure."

"Mostly. I guess doing what's best isn't always doing what's right. It was best for that baby to be raised here, at Harper House."

"Not the same thing, Hayley. No one's motives were pure, or even mostly, in that case. Lies and deceit, cold cruelty, and selfishness. I shudder to think what might have become of that child had it been a girl. You feeling better now?"

"Lots."

"Why don't I go down, fix you something to eat? I'll bring you food on a tray."

"I'll go down. I know Mitch wants to record all this. I know Harper's probably told him by now, but it's better if I give it to him firsthand. And I think I'll feel better yet when I do."

"If you're sure."

She nodded as she pushed herself up on the bed. "Thanks for sitting with me. It felt good knowing you were here while I slept."

She glanced in the mirror, winced. "I'm going to put on some makeup first. I may be possessed by a ghost, but I don't have to look like one."

"That's my girl. I'll go let Stella know you're up and around."

HAYLEY FIGURED SHE OWED ROZ ANOTHER ONE WHEN she realized everything had been arranged so that just she and Mitch would sit in the library to document the experience.

It was easier, somehow, to talk only to him. He was so smart and scholarly, in a studly kind of way. Sort of Harrison Fordish, in hornrims she decided.

With the leading edge of the fatigue and the shock dulled by a little sleep and a lot of TLC, she felt steadier, and more in control.

In any case, she loved this room. All the books, all those stories, all those words. Gardens outside the windows, big cozy chairs inside.

When she'd first come to Harper House she'd sometimes tiptoe down at night, just to sit in this room—her favorite of all of them—and marvel.

And she liked the way Mitch approached the whole Amelia project. With his work boards, his computer, his files and notes, he made it all rational, doable, grounded.

She studied the board now, with its long lists and columns that comprised Harper's family tree.

"Do you think, after all this is over, you could do a family tree for me?"

"Hmm?"

"Sorry." She glanced back at him, waved a hand. "Mind's wandering."

"It's okay, you've got a lot on it." He put down his notebook, focused his attention on her. "Sure I can do that. You give me the basics you know—father's full name, date and place of birth, your mother's, and we're off and running."

"I'd really like that. It'd be interesting. Harper and I cross a couple generations back, sort of over to the side. Is he awful mad at me?"

"No, honey. Why would he be?"

"He was upset. He wanted to scoop me and Lily right up and haul us to Stella's. I wouldn't go. I can't."

Mitch doodled on a pad. "If I could've gotten Roz out of this house a few months ago, I'd have done it—even if it had taken dynamite."

"Did you fight about it?"

"Not really." Amusement danced in his eyes. "But then I'm older, wiser, and more in tune with the limitations a man faces when dealing with a stubborn woman."

"Am I wrong?"

"That's not for me to say."

"It is if I'm asking you."

"Rock and hard place, kid. That's where you've shoved me." He pushed back, took off his glasses. "I understand exactly how Harper feels and why, and he's not wrong. I respect how you feel and why, and you're not wrong either. How's that?"

She managed a wry smile. "Smart—and no help at all."

"Just another benefit of that older and wiser phase of life. But I'm going to add one thing as a potentially overprotective male. I don't think you should spend a lot of time alone."

"Good thing I like people." When his cell phone rang, she rose. "I'll go on, let you get that."

Because she'd seen Harper outside, she went out the side door. She hoped Stella wouldn't mind a little more time on Lily patrol. She wandered the path toward where he worked in the cutting garden.

Summer still had her world in its sweaty clutches, but the heat was strong and vital. Real. She'd take all the reality she could get. Mammoth blue balls of hydrangeas weighed down the bushes, daylilies speared up with their elegant cheer, and passionflowers twined their arbor in bursts of purple.

The air was thick with fragrance and birdsong, and through it rode the frantic wings of butterflies.

Around the curve Harper stood, legs spread, body slightly bent as his quick, skilled fingers twisted off deadheads, then dropped them in a bag knotted to his belt. At his feet was a small, shallow basket where daisies and snapdragons, larkspur and cosmos already lay.

It was, somehow, so sweepingly romantic—the man, the evening, the sea of flowers—that her heart floated up to her throat and ached there.

A hummingbird, a sapphire and emerald whir, arrowed past him to hover over the feathery cup of a deep red blossom of monarda and drink.

She saw him pause to watch it, going still with his hand on a stem and his other holding a seed head. And she wished she could paint. All those vivid colors of late summer, bold and strong, and the man so still, so patient, stopping his work to share his flowers with a bird.

Love saturated her.

The bird flew off, a small, electric jewel. He watched it, as she watched him.

"Harper."

"The hummingbirds like the bee balm," he said, then took his sheers and clipped a monarda. "But there's enough for all of us. It's a good spreader."

"Harper," she said again and walked up to slide her arms around him, press her cheek to his back. "I know you're worried, and I won't ask you not to be. But please don't be mad."

"I'm not. I came out here to cool off. It usually works. I'm down to irritated and worried."

"I was set to come out here, argue with you." She rubbed her cheek over his shirt. She could smell soap and sweat, both healthy and male. "Then I saw you, and I just don't want to argue. I just don't want to fight. I can't do what you want when everything inside me pulls the other way. Even if it's wrong, I can't."

"I don't have any choice about that." He clipped more flowers for the basket, deadheaded others. "And you don't have any say about this. I'm moving in. I'd rather you and Lily shift over to my place, but it makes more sense for me to move into your room for now since there are two of you and one of me. When this is over, we'll reevaluate."

"Reevaluate."

"That's right." He'd yet to look at her, really look, and now moved off a few paces to cut more blooms. "It's a little hard to figure out where we're going, what we're doing under the circumstances."

"So you figure we'll live together, under the circumstances, and when those circumstances change, we'll take another look at the picture."

"That's right."

Maybe she did feel like arguing. "Ever heard of asking?"

"Heard of it. Not doing it. At the nursery, you work with Stella, Mama or me, at all times."

"Who suddenly made you the boss of me?"

With steady hands, unerring eye, he just kept working. "One of us will drive back and forth with you."

"One of you coming with me every time I have to pee?"

"If necessary. You've got your mind set on staying, those are the terms."

The hummingbird whizzed back, but this time she wasn't caught by its charm. "Terms? Somebody die and make you king? Listen, Harper—"

"No. This is how it's going to be. You're determined to

stay, see this through. I'm just as determined you'll be looked after. I love you, so that's the end of it."

She opened her mouth, closed it again, and took a calming breath. "If you'd said that—the I love you part—right off, I might've been more open to discussion."

"There is no discussion."

Her eyes narrowed. He'd yet to stop what he was doing and face her fully. "You sure can be a hard-ass when you put your mind to it."

"This didn't take much effort." He reached down, gathered the flowers in the basket, tucking their stems into a casual bouquet. Now he turned, and those long brown eyes met hers. "Here."

She took them, frowned at him over them. "Did you cut these for me?"

The slow, lazy smile moved over his face. "Who else?"

She blew out a breath. He'd added nicotiana to the bouquet, and when she inhaled, she drew in its rich perfume. "It's exasperating, I swear, how you can be pushy one minute and sweet the next. They're really pretty."

"So are you."

"You know, another man might've started off with the flowers, the flattery, and the I-love-yous to soften me up for the rest. But you go at it ass-backwards."

His gaze stayed on hers, steady. "I wasn't worried about softening you up."

"I get that. You're not waiting for me to say, all right, Harper, we'll do this your way. You're just going to make sure I do."

"See how quick you catch on?"

She had to laugh, and clutching the flowers in one hand gave in and linked her arms around his neck. "In case you're interested, I'm glad you're going to be staying with me. Next time I have my spine tingled, I'd as soon you be there."

"I will be."

"If you've got more work to do out here—"

She broke off when Logan strode down the path. "Sorry. Something's up," he said. "Better come on back in."

HAYLEY FELT THE EXCITEMENT, LIKE A HUM IN THE AIR when they stepped back into the library. She took a quick scan first, saw Lily playing cars with Gavin and Luke on the floor by the fireplace David had filled with flowers for the summer months.

Spotting her mother, Lily began to jabber and interrupted her game to come over and show off her dump truck. But the minute Hayley lifted her, Lily stretched out her arms for Harper.

"Everybody's second choice when you're around," Hayley commented as she passed her over.

"She understands I know the fine points of Fisher-Price. It's all right," he added. "I've got her. What's up?" he asked his mother.

"I'm going to let Mitch explain. Ah, David, we can always count on you."

He wheeled in a cart with cold drinks, and finger food for the kids. "Gotta keep body and soul together." He winked at the boys. "Especially around this house."

"Y'all get what you want," Roz ordered. "And let's get settled."

While the wine looked tempting, Hayley opted for the iced tea. Her stomach wasn't quite a hundred percent yet. "Thanks for looking out for my girl," she said to Stella.

"You know I love it. It always amazes me how well the

boys play with her." Stella brushed a hand down Hayley's arm. "How're you feeling?"

"A little off yet, but okay. You know what this is about?"

"Not even a glimmer. Go on and sit. You look worn out."

As she did, Hayley grinned. "You're getting a little southern in your accent. Yankee southern, but it's starting to creep in. Kinda cute."

"Must come from being outnumbered." Because she was concerned with how pale Hayley looked still, she sat on the arm of the chair.

"How long you going to keep us dangling?" Logan complained, and Mitch stood in front of the library table.

Like a teacher, Hayley thought. Sometimes she forgot he'd been one.

"Y'all know I've been in contact for several months with a descendant of the housekeeper who worked here during Reginald and Beatrice Harper's time."

"The Boston lawyer," Harper said and sat on the floor with Lily and her truck.

Mitch nodded. "Her interest has been piqued, and the more she's looked for information, the more people she's spoken with, the more invested she's become."

"Added to that Mitch has been doing a genealogy for her—gratis." Roz added.

"Tit for tat," he said. "And we needed some of the information anyway. Up till now she hasn't been able to find a great deal that applied to us. But today, she got a hit."

"You're killing us here," Stella commented.

"A letter, written by the housekeeper in question. Roni—Veronica, my contact, found a box full of letters in the attic of one of her great-aunts. It's considerable to sort through, to read through. But today, she found one written by Mary Havers to a cousin. The letter was dated January 12, 1893."

"A few months after the baby was born," Hayley added.

"That's right. Most of the letter deals with family business, or the sort of casual conversational observations that you'd expect—particularly in an era when people still wrote conversational letters. But in the body of the letter . . ." He held up papers. "She faxed me copies. I'm going to read the pertinent parts."

"Mom!" Luke's aggrieved voice wailed out. "Gavin's looking at me with the *face*."

"Gavin, not now. I mean it. Sorry," Stella apologized. She took a deep breath and determined to ignore the whispered argument from behind her. "Keep going."

"Just hold on one minute." Logan rose, walked over to crouch and have a conversation with the boys. There was a cheer, then they scrambled up.

"We're going to take Lily out to play," Gavin announced, and puffed out his chest. "Come on Lily. Wanna go outside?"

Clutching her truck, she deserted Harper, waved bye-bye, and took Gavin's hand. Logan closed the door behind them. "We're going out for ice cream later," he said to Stella as he walked back to his seat.

"Bribery. Good thinking. Sorry, Mitch."

"No problem. This was written to Mary Havers's cousin, Lucille.

Leaning back on the library table, Mitch adjusted his glasses, and read.

" 'I should not be writing of this, but I am so troubled in my heart and in my mind. I wrote to you last summer of the birth of my employers' baby boy. He is a beautiful child, Master Reginald, with such a sweet nature. The nurse Mister Harper hired is very competent and seems both gentle with him and quite attached. To my knowledge, the mistress has never entered the nursery. The nurse reports to Mister Harper, and only Mister Harper. Belowstairs Alice, the nurse, tends to chatter, as girls often do. More than once I have heard her comment that the mistress never sees the child, has never held him, has never asked of his welfare.' "

"Cold bitch," Roz said quietly. "I'm glad she's not a blood ancestor. I'd rather have crazy than cruel." Then she lifted a hand. "Sorry, Mitchell. I shouldn't interrupt."

"It's okay. I've already read this through a couple times, and tend to agree with you. Mary Havers continues," he said.

" 'It is not my place to criticize, of course. However, it would seem unnatural that a mother show no interest in her child, particularly the son who was so desired in this house. It cannot be said that the mistress is a warm woman, or naturally maternal, yet with her girls she is somewhat involved in their daily activities. I cannot count the number of nurses and governesses who have come and gone over the last few years. Mrs. Harper is very particular. Yet, she has never once given Alice instructions on what she expects regarding Master Reginald.

" 'I tell you this, Lucy, because while we both know that often those abovestairs take little interest in the details of the household, unless there is an inconvenience, I suspect there is something troubling in this matter, and I must tell someone my thoughts, my fears.' "

"She knew something wasn't right," Hayley interrupted. "Sorry," she added with a glance around the room. "But you can hear it, even in what she doesn't say."

"She's fond of the baby, too." Stella turned her wineglass around and around in her hands. "Concerned for him. You can hear that, too. Go on, Mitch."

"She writes, 'While I told you of the baby's birth, I did not mention in previous correspondence that there was no sign in the months before that Mrs. Harper was expecting. Her activities, her appearance remained as ever. We who serve are privy to the intimate details of a household and those who live in it. It is unavoidable. There was no preparation for this child. No talk of nursemaids, of layettes, there was no lying-in for Mrs. Harper, no visits from the doctor. The baby was simply here one morning, as if, indeed, the stork had delivered him. While there was some talk belowstairs, I did not allow it to continue, at least in my presence. It is not our place to question such matters.

" 'Yet, Lucille, she has been so separate from this child it breaks the heart. So, yes, I have wondered. There can be little doubt who fathered the boy as he is the image of Mister Harper. His maternity, however, was another matter, at least in my mind.' "

"So they knew." Harper turned to his mother. "She knew, this Havers, and the household knew. And nothing was done."

"What could they do?" Hayley asked, and her voice was thick with emotion. "They were servants, employees. Even if they'd made noise about it, who would listen? They'd have been fired and kicked out, and nothing would have changed here."

"You're right." Mitch sipped from his glass of mineral water. "Nothing would have changed. Nothing did. She wrote more."

He set down his glass, turned the next page. " 'Earlier today a woman came to Harper House. So pale, so thin was she, and in her eyes, Lucy, was something not only desperate but not quite sane. Danby—' That was the butler at the time," Mitch explained. " 'Danby mistook her for someone looking for employment, but she pushed into the house by the front door, something wild in her. She claimed to have come for the baby, for her baby. For her son she called James. She said she heard him crying for her. Even if the child had cried, no one could hear in the entrance hall as he was tucked up in the nursery. I could not turn her away, could not wrest her away as she ran wildly up the stairs, calling for her son. I do not know what I might have done, but the mistress appeared and bade me show the woman up to her sitting room. This poor creature trembled as I led her in. The mistress would allow me to bring no refreshment. I should not have done what I did next, what I have never done in all my years of employment. I listened at the door.' "

"So she did come here." There was pity in Stella's voice as she laid a hand on Hayley's shoulder. "She did come for her baby, Poor Amelia."

" 'I heard the cruel things the mistress said to this unfortunate woman,' " Mitch continued. " 'I heard the cold things she said about the child. Wishing him dead, Lucy, God's pity, wishing him and this desperate woman dead even as she, who called herself Amelia Connor, asked to have the child returned to her. She was refused. She was threatened. She was dismissed. I know now that the master got this child, this son he craved, with this poor woman, his lightskirt, and took the baby from her to foist it on his wife, to raise the boy here as his heir. I understand that the doctor and the midwife who attended this woman were ordered to tell her the child, a girl child, was stillborn.

" 'I have known Mister Harper to be coldly determined in his business, in his private affairs. I have not seen affection between him and his wife, or from him for his daughters. Yet I would not have deemed him capable of such a monstrous act. I would not have believed his wife capable of aligning herself with him. Miss Connor, in her ill-fitting gray dress and shattered eyes, was ordered away, was threatened with the police should she ever come back, ever speak of what was spoken of in that room. I did my duty, Lucille, and showed her from the house. I watched her carriage drive away. I have not been easy in my mind since.

" 'I feel I should try to help her, but what can I do? Is it not my Christian duty to offer some assistance, or comfort at the very least, to this woman? Yet my duty to my employers, those who provide the roof over my head, the food I eat, the money which keeps me independent, is to remain silent. To remember my place.

" 'I will pray that I come to know what is right. I will pray for this young woman who came for the child she birthed, and was turned away.' "

Mitch set the pages down. And there was silence.

Tears slid down Hayley's cheeks. Her head was lowered, as it had been during the last page of Mitch's recital. Now she lifted it, and with her eyes shining with tears, smiled.

"But I came back."

seventeen

"HAYLEY."

"Don't." Mitch stepped forward as Harper sprang off the floor. "Wait."

"I came back," Hayley repeated, "for what was mine."

"But you weren't able to get to the child," Mitch said.

"Wasn't I? Didn't I?" In the chair Hayley lifted her arms, held her palms up. "Aren't I here? Didn't I watch him, didn't I sing him to sleep, night after night? And all the others who came after? They were never rid of me."

"But that's not enough now."

"I want what' s mine! I want my due. I want . . ." Her eyes darted around the room. "Where are the children? Where are they?"

"Outside." Roz spoke quietly. "Playing outside."

"I like the children," Hayley said dreamily. "Who would have guessed? Such messy, selfish creatures. But so sweet, so soft and sweet when they sleep. I like them best when they sleep. I would have shown him the world, my James. The world. And he would never have left me. Do you think I want her pity?" she said in a sudden rage. "A housekeeper? A *servant*? Do you think I want pity from her? Damn her and the rest of them. I should have killed them in their sleep."

"Why didn't you?"

Her gaze shifted, latched on Harper. "There are other ways to damn. So handsome. You are so like him."

"I'm not. I'm yours. The son of the son, of your son."

Her eyes clouded, and her fingers plucked at the thighs of her pants. "James? My James? I watched you. Sweet baby. Pretty little boy. I came to you."

"I remember. What do you want?"

"Find me. I'm lost."

"What happened to you?"

"You know! You did it. You're damned for it. Cursed with my last breath. I will have what's *mine*." Hayley's head fell back, and her hand clutched at her belly before her body shuddered. "God." She breathed out audibly. "Intense."

Harper grabbed her hands, knelt in front of her. "Hayley."

"Yeah." Her eyes were blurred, her face white as paper. "Can I have some water?"

He brought her hands up, pressed his face into them. "You can't keep doing this."

"Just as soon not. She was pissed. Thanks," she said to David as he handed her a glass of water. She drank it down like a woman dying of thirst. "Pissed, then sad, then pissed again—all sort of over the top on the emotional scale. The letter got to her. Well, it got to me."

She turned to Mitch with her hands still caught in Harper's. "I felt so sorry for her, and for the housekeeper. I could see it. You know, how you do when you're reading a book. The house, the people. I could imagine what it would be like if somebody had Lily, and I couldn't do anything to get her back. 'Course the first thing I'd've done was clock Beatrice. The bitch. I guess I was getting pretty worked up, in my head, and she just sort of slid in."

Her fingers tightened on Harper's. "She's twisted up about you. Mostly, she's just twisted altogether, but she remembers you as a baby, as a little boy, she feels love for you because you're her blood. But you're his, too. And you resemble him, sort of. At least that's how it seems to me. It's confusing when it happens."

"You're stronger than she is," Harper told her.

"Saner anyhow. Way."

"You did great." Mitch set his tape recorder aside. "And I'd say you've had enough for today."

"It's been a busy one." She worked up a smile as she looked around the room. "Did I wig everybody out?"

"You could say that. Look, why don't you go up, stretch out," Stella suggested. "Logan will go out, check on the kids. Right?"

"Sure." He stepped over to Hayley first, gave her head a pat. "Go on up, beautiful, take a load off."

"I think I will, thanks." Harper straightened, took her hand to bring her to her feet. "I don't know what I'd do without you guys, I really don't."

Roz waited until they were out of the room. "This is wearing on her. I've never seen her look so tired. Hayley's a bundle of energy most times. Hell, she wears me out just watching her."

"We've got to finish this." Logan walked to the door, opened it. "And soon," he said before he went outside.

"What can we do?" Stella spread her hands. "Waiting and watching doesn't seem like enough. I don't know about the rest of you, but seeing that happen, seeing it, shook me right down to the bone."

"I could go to Boston, help Veronica sort through the papers." Mitch shook his head. "But I'm just not comfortable leaving right now."

"Safety in numbers?" Roz reached out a hand for his, squeezed. "I feel the same. To tell the truth, at this point I don't like David spending so much time alone in the house."

"She doesn't bother me." He'd poured a glass of wine and lifted it now in a half toast. "Maybe because I'm not a blood-related male. Add gay to that and I'm not of much interest to her. You can factor in that she'd see me as a servant. That puts me bottom of the feeding chain."

"A lot she knows," Roz replied. "But that's logical, from her point of view, and does a lot to relieve my mind. Find her. She's said that before."

"Her grave," Mitch put in.

"I think we're all agreed on that." Roz walked over, helped herself to a sip of David's wine. "And how the hell are we supposed to do that?"

LATER, WHEN THE HOUSE WAS QUIET AND LILY SLEEPing in her crib, Hayley couldn't settle. "One minute I'm ready to drop, and the next I'm all revved up. I must be really annoying."

"Now that you mention it." With a grin, Harper pulled her down on the sofa beside him. "Why don't we watch the game. I'll raid the kitchen for junk food."

"You want me to sit here and watch baseball?"

"I thought you liked baseball."

"Yeah, but not enough to zone out in front of the TV."

"Okay." He heaved an exaggerated sigh. "I'm about to

make the ultimate sacrifice for my breed. Pick a DVD. We'll watch a movie, even if it's a chick flick."

She eased back. "Really?"

"But you have to make the popcorn."

"You mean you'll sit here and watch a girlie movie without making snide comments."

"I don't remember agreeing to the second part."

"You know, I like action flicks."

"Now we're talking."

"But I'd love to watch something romancey, with a couple of good weep scenes. Thanks!" She pressed her lips noisily to his, then jumped up. "I'm loading the popcorn with butter." At the door, she stopped and beamed back at him. "I feel better already."

SHE'D NEVER HAD SO MANY UPS AND DOWNS IN HER moods in all of her life. From manic energy to exhaustion, from joy to despair. She ran the gamut, it seemed, every day. And under the swings, the spurts and the tumbles was an edgy anticipation of what happens next. And when.

When she spiraled down, she struggled to remind herself of what she had. A beautiful child, a wonderful man who loved her, friends, family, a good interesting job. And still, once the spiral began, she couldn't seem to control the fall.

She worried there was something physically wrong with her. A chemical imbalance, a brain tumor. Maybe she was going as crazy as The Bride.

Feeling harassed and overtired, she swung into Wal-Mart on her morning off to pick up diapers, shampoo, a few other basics. She could only thank God to be able to snatch this little window of alone-time. Or alone with Lily time, she corrected, as she strapped her daughter in the shopping cart.

At least nobody felt they were obliged to watch her when she was away from Harper House or work. And watching was what they did. Like hawks.

She understood why, God knew she appreciated the concern and care. But that didn't stop her from feeling smothered. She could barely start to brush her teeth without whoever was hovering offering to spread the paste on the brush for her.

She wandered down aisles, listlessly picking up what she needed. Then detoured into cosmetics, thinking a new lipstick might cheer her up. But the shades seemed too dark or too light, too bold or too dull. Nothing suited her.

She looked so pale and wan these days, she decided if she put anything bright on her lips they'd look as though they walked into the room a foot ahead of her.

New perfume maybe. But every tester she sniffed made her feel slightly queasy.

"Just forget it," she muttered, and glanced back at Lily who was trying to stretch out her arm to reach a spin rack of mascaras and eye pencils.

"Not for a long time yet, young lady. It's fun being a girl though, you'll see. All these toys we get to play with." She chose one of the mascaras herself, tossed it in the cart. "I just can't seem to gear myself up for it right now. We'll just go on, get your diapers. And maybe if you're good, a new board book."

She turned down another aisle, reluctant to leave. Once she did, she'd need to take Lily to the sitter's, go to work. Where somebody would be attached to her hip for the rest of the day.

She wanted to do something normal, damn it. More she wanted to *feel* like doing something. Anything.

And an absent glance to her right stopped her in her tracks.

Something that was both panic and nausea, with a helping of dull realization spurted into her belly. It continued to rise as she did hasty calculations in her head.

While everything inside her sank, Hayley closed her eyes. She opened them again, looked into Lily's happy face. And reached for the home pregnancy test.

SHE DROPPED LILY OFF, KEPT A SMILE PLASTERED ON her face until she walked out the door to her car. Afraid to do otherwise, she kept her mind blank while she drove home. She wouldn't think, she wouldn't project. She would just go home, take the test. Twice. When it came out negative, which of course it would, she'd hide the packages somewhere until she could dispose of them without anyone knowing she'd had a panic attack.

She wasn't pregnant again. She absolutely couldn't be pregnant again.

She parked, and made certain the boxes were buried at the bottom of her bag and well hidden. But she'd taken two steps into the house when David appeared like some magic genie.

"Hi, sugar, want a hand with that?"

"No." She gripped the bag to her chest like a cache of gold. "No," she repeated more calmly. "I'm just going to take these things up. And I have to pee, if that's all the same to you."

"It is. I often have to pee myself."

Knowing her tone had been nasty, she rubbed a hand over her face. "I'm sorry. I'm in a mood."

"Something else I often have." He pulled an open tube of Life Savers from his pocket, thumbed out a cherry circle. "Open up."

She smiled, obeyed.

"Let's see if that sweetens your mood," he said as he popped the candy into her mouth. "Can't help worrying about you, honey."

"I know. If I'm not back down in fifteen minutes, you can call out the cavalry. Deal?"

"Deal."

She hurried up, then dumped the contents of the bag on her bed—for God's sake, she'd forgotten the diapers. Cursing, she snatched both pregnancy tests and bolted to the bathroom.

For a moment she was afraid she wouldn't be able to pee. Wouldn't that just be her luck? She ordered herself to calm down, took several long breaths. Added a prayer.

Moments later, with the sweetness of cherry candy still on her tongue, she was staring at the stick with PREGNANT reading clear as day in its window.

"No." She gripped the stick, shook it as if it were a thermometer and the action would drop things back down to normal. "No, no, no, no! What *is* this? What are you?" She looked down at herself, rapped a fist lightly below her navel. "Some kind of sperm magnet?"

Undone, she sat on the toilet lid, buried her face in her hands.

THOUGH SHE MIGHT HAVE PREFERRED TO CRAWL INTO the cabinet under the sink, curl up in the dark, and stay there for the next nine months, she didn't have much time to indulge in a pity fest. She washed her face, slapping on cold water to eradicate the signs of her bathroom crying jag.

"Yeah, crying's going to make a difference," she berated herself. "That'll do the trick, all right. It'll change everything so when you look at that *stupid* test again the damn stick will read: Why no, Hayley, you're not pregnant.

You just needed to sit on the toilet and bawl for ten minutes. Idiot."

She sniffled back what felt like another flood of tears and faced herself in the mirror. "You played, now you pay. Deal with it."

A quick makeup session helped. The sunglasses she grabbed out of her purse helped more.

She buried the home pregnancy test boxes in the bottom of her underwear drawer, jumpy as a drug addict hiding his stash.

When she went out, David was already halfway up the stairs.

"I was about to get my bugle."

She stared at him. "What?"

"To call the cavalry, honey. You were longer than fifteen."

"Sorry. I got . . . Sorry."

He started to smile and brush it off, then shook his head. "Nope, not going to pretend I don't know you've been crying. What's the matter?"

"I can't." Even on those two words her voice shook, broke. "I'm going to be late for work."

"Somehow the world will keep turning. What you're going to do, is sit right down here in my office." Taking her hand, he tugged until she sat on the steps with him. "And tell Uncle David your troubles."

"I don't have troubles. I'm *in* trouble." She didn't mean to tell him, to tell anyone. Not until she had time to think, to deal. To bury her head in the sand for a few days. But he draped an arm around her shoulders to hug her, and the words leaped out of her mouth.

"I'm pregnant."

"Oh." His hand stroked up and down her arm. "Well, that's something my secret horde of super chocolate truffles won't fix."

She turned her head, pressed her face to his shoulder. "I'm like some sort of fertility bomb, David. What am I going to do? What the hell am I going to do?"

"What's right for you. You're sure now?"

Sniffling, she boosted her butt off the steps, tugged the stick out of her pocket. "What's that say in there?"

"Mmm. The eagle has landed." Gently, he caught her chin in his hand, lifted her face. "How are you feeling?"

"Sick, scared. Stupid! So damn stupid. We used protection, David. It's not like we were a couple of lust-crazed teenagers in the back of a Chevy. I think I have some sort of *über*eggs or something, and they just spit on barriers and *suck* the sperm in."

He laughed, then gave her another squeeze. "Sorry. I know it's not funny to you. Let's calm down here and take a look at the big picture. You're in love with Harper."

"Of course I am, but—"

"He's in love with you."

"Yes, but—Oh, David, we're just getting started on that. On being in love, on being together. Maybe I let myself imagine how it might be down the road some. But we haven't made any plans about the long-term. We haven't talked about it at all."

"That's why sooner comes before later, honey. You'll talk now."

"How can any man in the world not feel trapped when a woman comes up and tells him she's pregnant?"

"You manage to get that way all by yourself?"

"That's not the point."

"Hayley." He drew back, tipped her sunglasses down her nose so he could look into her eyes. "That's exactly the point. With Lily, you did what was right for you, and what you felt in your heart was right for the father, and for the baby. Right or wrong—and personally I think it was right—but either way, I think it was brave. Now you've got to be brave again, do what's right for everybody concerned. You've got to tell Harper."

"I don't know how. I get sick thinking about it."

"Then you might love him, but you're not giving him credit for being the man he is."

"I am, that's the trouble." She stared back down at the stick and the word in that window seemed to scream in her head. "He'll stand up. How will I know if he did because he loves me, or because he feels responsible?"

David leaned over, kissed her temple. "Because you will."

IT ALL SOUNDED GOOD. IT SOUNDED REASONABLE, logical, and adult. But it didn't make it any easier to do what she was about to do.

She wished she could delay it, just ignore it all for a few days. Even pretend it would go away. And that was small and selfish and childish.

When she reached the nursery, she slipped into one of the employee bathrooms to take the second test. She glugged down most of a pint of water, turned the spigot on for good measure. She started to cross her fingers, but told herself not to be a complete ass.

Still, she read the results with eyes squinted half shut.

It didn't change the results.

Well, still pregnant, she thought. There was no crying this time, no cursing fate. She simply tucked the stick back in her pocket, opened the door, and prepared to do what needed to be done next. She had to tell Harper.

Why? Why did he have to know? She could go away now, she thought. Pack up and go. The baby was *hers*.

He was rich, he was powerful. He would take the child

and toss her aside. Take her son. For the glory of the great Harper name he would use her like a vessel, then rip away what grew in her.

He had no right to what was hers. No right to what she carried inside her.

"Hayley."

"What." She jolted like a thief, then blinked at Stella.

She was standing among the shade plants, surrounded by hostas green as Ireland. Yards away from the restroom.

How long had she been standing there, thinking thoughts not her own?

"Are you all right?"

"A little turned around." She drew in a long breath. "I'm sorry I'm late."

"It's all right."

"I'll make it up. But I need . . . I have to talk to Harper. Before I get started I need to talk to him."

"In the grafting house. He wanted to know when you got in. Hayley, I wish you'd tell me what's wrong."

"I need to talk to Harper first." Before she lost her nerve, or her mind.

She hurried away, walking quickly between the tables of plants, across the asphalt skirt, past the greenhouses. Business was picking up, she noted, after the high summer slump. Temperatures were easing off, just a little, and made people think about their fall plantings. Stella's boys were going back to school. Days were getting shorter.

The world didn't stop just because she had a crisis on her hands.

She hesitated outside of the grafting house, struck by the fact that her mind—so full a moment before—was now a complete blank.

There was only one thing to do, she decided. That was to go in.

The house was warm and full of music. It so well suited him, full of plants in various stages of growth and development, smelling of soil and green.

She didn't know the music that played, something with harps and flutes. But she knew whatever it was wouldn't be playing through his headphones.

He was down at the far end, and it seemed like the longest walk of her life. Even when he turned, saw her, and flashed a grin.

"Hey, just who I wanted to see." He made a come-ahead gesture with one hand as he drew his headset off with the other. "Take a look."

"At what?"

"Our babies."

Since he shifted to the plants, he didn't see her jerk of response. "They're right on schedule," he continued. "See, the ovary sections have already swelled."

"They're not the only ones," she mumbled, but moved forward to stand beside him and study the plants they'd grafted a few weeks before.

"See? The pods are fully formed. We give them another three, four weeks for the seeds to ripen. The top'll split. We'll gather the seeds, plant them in pots. Keep 'em outdoors, exposed. And in the spring, they'll germinate. Once they're about three inches, we'll plant them out in nursery beds."

It wasn't procrastinating to stand there talking about a mutual project. It was . . . polite. "Then what?"

"Usually we'll get blooms the second season. Then we'll study and record the differences, the likenesses, the characteristics. What we're hoping for is at least one—and I'm banking on more—mini with a strong pink color, and that blush of red. We get that, we've got Hayley's Lily."

"If we don't."

"Pessimism isn't the gardener's friend, but if we don't, we'll have something else cool. And we'll try again. Anyway, I thought you might want to work with me on a rose, for my mother."

"Oh, um . . ." If it was a girl, should they name her Rose? "That'd be nice. Sweet of you."

"Well, it's Mitch's idea, but the guy couldn't grow a Chia Pet. He wants to try for a black. Nobody's ever managed a true black rose, but I thought we could play around and see what we came up with. It's the right time of year—time to wash down, disinfect, air and dry out this place. Hygiene's a big for this kind of work, and roses are pretty fussy. They're time-consuming, too, but it'd be fun."

He looked so excited, she thought, at the idea of starting something new. Just how would he look when she told him they already had?

"Um, when you do all this, you pick the parents—the pollen plant, the seed plant. Deliberate selection, for specific characteristics."

Her blue eyes, Harper's brown. His patience, her impulse. What would you get?

"Right. You're trying to cross them, to create something with the best—or at least the desired characteristics—of both."

His temper, her stubbornness. Oh God. "People don't work that way."

"Hmm." He turned to his computer, keying data into a file. "No, guess not."

"And with people, they can't always—or don't always—plan it all out like this. They don't always get together and say, hey, let's hybridize."

He shot a laugh over his shoulder. "Now that's a line I never thought to use in a bar, picking up a girl. I'd put it in the file, but since I've already got a girl, it'd be wasted."

"You never used a line on me," she told him. "Anyway, hybridizing's about creating something, a separate something. Not just about the fun and games."

"Hmm. Hey, did I show you the viburnum? Suckering's been a problem, but I'm pretty happy with how it's coming along."

"Harper." Tears wanted to spurt and spill again. "Harper, I'm sorry."

"It's not a big," he said absently. "I know how to deal with suckering."

"I'm pregnant."

There, she thought. She said it. Fast and clean. Like ripping a bandage off a wound.

"You said what?" He stopped typing, slowly swiveled on his stool.

She didn't know how to read his face. Maybe it was because her own vision seemed blurry and half blind. She couldn't read the tone of his voice, not with the roaring going on in her ears.

"I should've known. I should have. I've been so tired, and I missed my period—I just forgot about it—and I've been queasy on and off, and so damn moody. I thought, I didn't think. I thought it was what was happening with Amelia. I didn't put it together. I'm sorry."

The entire burst came out in a disjointed ramble that she could barely comprehend herself. She dropped into silence when he held up a hand.

"Pregnant. You said you were pregnant."

"God, do I have to spell the word out for you?" Not sure if she wanted to weep or rage, she yanked the test stick out of her pocket. "There, read it yourself. P-R-E—"

"Hold it." He took the stick from her, stared at it. "When did you find out?"

"Just today, now. A little while ago. I was in Wal-Mart, getting some things. I forgot Lily's diapers and bought mascara. What kind of a mother am I?"

"Quiet down." He rose, took her shoulders and nudged her onto the stool. "You're all right? I mean it doesn't hurt or anything."

"Of course it doesn't hurt. For Christ's sake."

"Look, don't crawl up my ass." He scrubbed a hand over the back of his neck as he studied her. Much, she thought, as he did his plants-in-progress. "It's my first day on the job. How much are you pregnant?"

"Pretty much all the way."

"Damn it, Hayley, I mean how far along, or whatever you call it?"

"I think about six weeks. Five or six."

"How big is it in there?"

She dragged a hand through her hair. "I don't know. About as big as a kernel of rice."

"Wow." He stared at her belly, laid a hand on it. "Wow. When does it start to move around? When does it get, like, fingers or toes?"

"Harper, can we focus here?"

"I don't know any of this stuff. I want to know. You need to go to the doctor, right?" He grabbed her hand. "We should go now."

"I don't need to go to the doctor now. Harper, what are we going to do?"

"What do you mean what are we going to do. We're going to have a baby. Holy shit!" He plucked her right off the stool and a half a foot off the ground. The face he tilted up to hers was split with a dazzled grin. "We're going to have a baby."

She had to brace her hands on his shoulders. "You're not mad."

"Why would I be mad?"

Now she felt dizzy, overwhelmed, shaken to the core. "Because. Because."

He lowered her, slowly, back onto the stool. And now his voice was careful and cool. "You don't want the baby."

"I don't know. How can I think about what I want? How can I think at all?"

"Pregnancy affects brain waves. Interesting."

"I—"

"But, okay, I'll do the thinking. You go to the doctor so we're sure everything's okay in there. We get married. And next spring we have a baby."

"Married? Harper, people shouldn't get married just because—"

Though he leaned back against the worktable, he still managed to hedge her in. "In my world, where the sky's blue, people who love each other and are having babies get married all the time. Maybe this is a little ahead of our regularly scheduled program, but it's the kind of bulletin you pay attention to."

"We had a regularly scheduled program?"

"I did." He reached over to tuck her hair behind her ears, then tugged gently at the ends. "I want you, you know I do. I want the baby. We're going to do this right, and that's the way it's going to be."

"So you're ordering me to marry you."

"I had planned to charm you into it, at some point a little farther down the road. But since the timing's changed—and pregnancy's jammed your power of thought—we're going this way."

"You're not even upset."

"No, I'm not upset." He paused a moment as if taking stock. "A little scared, a lot awed. Man, Lily's going to love this. Baby brother or sister to torment. Wait till I tell my brothers they're going to be uncles. What till I tell Mama she's going to be a . . ."

"Grandmother," Hayley finished and nodded, subversively pleased to see a flicker of doubt in his eyes at last. "Just how do you think she's going to feel about that?"

"I guess I'll find out."

"I can't—just can't take all this in." She pressed the heels of her hands to her temples as if it would stop her head from spinning. "I don't even know what I'm feeling." Dropping her hands in her lap, she stared at him. "Harper, you don't think this is a mistake?"

"Our baby's not a mistake." He gathered her in, felt her breath give a hitch as she struggled with tears. "But it's one hell of a surprise."

eighteen

HE WENT IN AND OUT OF A DAZE FOR THE REST OF THE day. There was a lot to be considered, worked out, planned. The initial steps were crystal to him, as clear and precise as the initial steps in any graft.

They would get Hayley into the doctor, get her and the baby checked out. He'd start reading up on baby stuff—womb stuff—so that he understood the process, got sharper images in his head of what was going on in there.

They'd get married as soon as possible, but not so fast it had to be something rushed and cold and practical. He didn't want that for Hayley, or when he thought it through, for himself.

He wanted to get married at Harper House. In the gardens he helped tend, in the shadow of the house where he'd grown up. He wanted to make his promises to Hayley there, and he realized, to make them to Lily there, and to this new child who was now the size of a grain of rice.

This was what he wanted, what he had, somehow, been moving toward all of his life. It was something he'd never thought about before, and knew now as surely as he knew his own name.

Hayley and Lily would move into the carriage house. He'd speak to his mother about adding on to it, giving it more space while staying true to the heart and the traditional style.

More space for their children, he thought, so that they, too, could grow up in Harper House, with its gardens, its woods, its history that would be theirs as it was his.

He could see all of that, he could *know* all of that. But what he couldn't see was the child. The child he'd helped create.

A grain of rice? How could something so small be so huge? And already be so loved?

But now there was a step that had to be taken before the others.

He found his mother in the garden, adding a few asters and mums to one of her beds.

She wore thin cotton gloves, soiled with seasons of work. Cropped cotton pants, the color of bluebonnets that were already smudged with the greens and browns of the task she performed. Her feet were bare, and he could see the backless slides she'd stepped out of before she'd knelt at the border.

When he'd been a child, he'd believed her to be invincible, almost supernatural. She knew everything whether you wanted her to or not. She'd had the answers when he'd needed them, had given him hugs—and the occasional licks. Some of which he'd still like to dispute.

Most of all she'd been there, unfailingly been there. In the best times, in the worst, and all the times between.

Now, it would be his turn.

She tilted her head up as he approached, absently brushed the back of her hand over her brow. It struck him how beautiful she was, her hat tipped over her eyes, her face serene.

"Had a good day," she said. "Thought I'd extend it and fluff up this bed. Gonna rain tonight."

"Yeah." Automatically he glanced up at the sky. "Hoping for a nice soaker."

"Your mouth, God's ear." She squinted against the sun as she studied him. "My, don't you have your serious face on. You gonna sit down here so I don't get a crick in my neck?"

He crouched. "I need to talk to you."

"You usually do when you have your serious face on."

"Hayley's pregnant."

"Well." She set down her trowel, very carefully. "Well, well, well."

"She just found out today. She thinks about six weeks. She got the symptoms—I guess you call them symptoms—mixed up with everything else that's going on."

"I can see how that might happen, Is she all right?"

"A little upset, a little scared, I guess."

She reached up, took off his sunglasses, looked into his eyes. "How about you?"

"I've been taking it in. I love her, Mama."

"I know you do. Are you happy, Harper?"

"I'm a lot of things. Happy's one of them. I know this isn't how you'd hoped I do things."

"Harper, it doesn't matter what I hoped or want." Carefully she selected a blue aster, set it in the hole she'd already dug. Her hands worked, tucking it in, patting the earth as she spoke. "What matters is what you and Hayley want. What matters is that little girl, and the child you've started."

"I want Lily. I want to marry Hayley and make Lily

mine, legally. I want this baby. And I know it might seem like I've just dropped a pill into a glass of water. Pow, instant family, but . . . Don't cry. Please don't cry."

"I'm entitled to cry when my firstborn tells me he's making me a grandmother. I'm damn well entitled to a few tears. Where the hell is my bandanna?"

He pulled it out of her back pocket, handed it to her.

"I've got to sit all the way down a minute." She plopped down on her butt, wiped her eyes, blew her nose. "You know this day's going to come. From the moment you hold your child in your arms, you know. It's not your first thought, even a conscious one, but it's there, this knowledge that the thread's spinning out. Life cycles. Women know them. And gardeners. Harper."

She opened her arms to him. "You're going to be a daddy."

"Yeah." Because he could, he always could, he pressed his face to the strong line of her neck.

"And I'm going to be a grandmama. Two for one." She drew back, kissed his cheeks. "I love that little girl. She's already ours. I want you and Hayley to know I feel that way. That I'm happy for you. Even if you did manage to do this so the new baby arrives during our busiest season."

"Oops. Didn't think of that."

"I forgive you." She laughed, then pulled off her gloves so she could take his hands, flesh to flesh. "You asked her to marry you?"

"Sort of. Mostly I told her she was going to. And don't give me that look."

Her eyebrows stayed raised, her eyes steely. "It's exactly the look you deserve."

"I'm going to take care of it." He looked down at their joined hands, then lifted hers, one by one, to his lips. "I love you, Mama. You set the bar high."

"What bar is that?"

He looked back up, into her eyes. "I couldn't settle for anybody I loved or respected less than I love and respect you."

Tears swam again. "I'm going to need more than that bandanna in a minute."

"I'm going to give her the best I've got. And to start, I'd like to have Grandmama's rings. Grandmama Harper's engagement and wedding rings. You said once when I got married—"

"That's my boy." With hers curved, she kissed him lightly on the lips. "That's the man I raised. I'll get them for you."

ONE OF THE OTHER THINGS HE'D NEVER IMAGINED was how he'd propose to a woman. To *the* woman. A fancy dinner and wine? A lazy picnic? A giant WILL YOU MARRY ME? on the scoreboard screen at a game.

How weak was that?

The best, he decided, was the place and the tone that suited them both.

So he took her for a walk in the gardens at twilight.

"I don't feel right about your mother riding herd on Lily again. I'm pregnant, not handicapped."

"She wanted to. And I wanted an hour alone with you. Don't—don't go there. God, it's getting so I can see what's going on in your head. I'm crazy about Lily, and I'm not going to spend time telling you what's so damn obvious."

"I know. I know you are. I just can't settle into all this. It's not like I went jumping into bed all over two states. But here I am, for the second time."

"No, this time is different. This is the first time. See that flowering plum?"

"I can only tell—or tell sometimes—when they're blooming."

"This one." He stopped, reached up to touch one of the glossy green leaves. "My parents planted this right after I was born. We'll plant one for Lily, and we'll plant one for this baby. But see this one? It's got nearly thirty years on it now, and they planted it for me. I always felt good about that. Always felt this was one of my places, right here. We'll be making other places, you and me, but we'll start here, with one that already is."

He took the box out of his pocket, watched her lips tremble open, her gaze shoot up to his face. "Oh my God."

"I'm not getting down on one knee. I'm not going to feel like an ass when I do this."

"I think it had something to do with him pledging his loyalty. I mean that's why guys started the one-knee thing."

"You'll just have to take my word on mine. I want this life we've started. Not just the baby, but what we've started together. You and me, and Lily, and now this baby. I want to live that life with you. You're the first woman I've loved. You'll be the last."

"Harper, you—you really do take my breath away."

He opened the box, smiled a little when he saw her eyes widen. "This was my grandmother's. Kind of an old-fashioned setting, I guess."

"I—" She had to swallow. "I prefer the word *classic*, or *heirloom*. Or let's get real, woo-hoo. Harper, Roz must—"

"It was promised to me. Given to me to give to you, to the woman I want to spend my life with. I want you to wear it. Marry me, Hayley."

"It's beautiful, Harper. You're beautiful."

"I'm not done."

"Oh." She gave a nervous laugh. "I can't imagine there's more."

"I want you to take my name. I want Lily to take my name. I want the whole package. I can't settle for less."

"Do you know what you're saying?" She laid a hand on his cheek. "What you're doing?"

"Exactly. And you better answer me soon, because I'd hate to spoil this romantic moment by wrestling you to the ground and shoving this ring on your finger."

"It's not going to come to that." She closed her eyes for a moment, thought of flowering plums, of generations of tradition. "I knew you'd ask me to marry you when I told you I was pregnant. You're built that way, to do what's right. What's honorable."

"This isn't—"

"You had your say." She shook her head fiercely. "I'm having mine. I knew you'd ask, and part of the reason I felt sick about all this was because I was afraid I wouldn't know for sure. That you'd ask because you felt it was what you had to do. But I do know, and that's not why. I'll marry you, Harper, and take your name. So will Lily. We'll love you all of our lives."

He took the ring out of the box, slid it on her finger.

"It's too big," he murmured as he lifted her hand to kiss.

"You're not getting it back."

He closed his hand over hers to hold the ring in place. "Just long enough to have it sized."

She managed a nod, then threw herself into his arms. "I love you. I love you, I love you."

With a laugh, he tipped back her head to kiss her. "I was hoping you'd say that."

* * *

SHE FELT A LITTLE AWKWARD GOING IN WITH HARPER to make the announcement to his mother and Mitch, to have David serving champagne. She was allowed half a glass, and had to make do with that for both toasts.

One on the engagement, and one for the baby.

Roz gathered her into a hug, and whispered in her ear. "You and I have to talk. Soon."

"Oh. I guess so."

"How about now? Harper, I'm going to steal your girl for a few minutes. There's something I want to show her."

Without waiting for a response, Roz hooked an arm through Hayley's and led her out of the room and toward the stairs.

"You giving any thought to the sort of wedding you want?"

"I—no. It's so much."

"I'm sure it is."

"Harper . . . he said something about getting married here."

"I was hoping. We could use the ballroom if you want something splashy. Or the gardens and terrace if you want something more intimate. Y'all discuss it and let me know. I'm dying to dive in, and I plan to be very opinionated, so you'll have to watch me like a hawk."

"You're not mad."

"I'm surprised you'd say such a thing to me."

"I'm trying to put myself in your place," Hayley said as they climbed the stairs. "And I can't quite get there."

"That's because you've got your own place. I like having mine to myself." She turned toward her wing.

"I didn't get pregnant on purpose."

At the entrance to her bedroom, Roz paused, looked Hayley squarely in her swimming eyes. "Is that what's going on in your head? Me thinking this is calculated on your part."

"No—not exactly. A lot of people would."

"I'm pleased to say I'm not a lot of people. I'm also a superior judge of character, with only one major stumble in my illustrious career. If I thought less of you, Hayley, you wouldn't be living in my home."

"I thought . . . when you said we had to talk."

"Oh, that's about enough of this business out of you." Roz walked over to the bed, opened the box that sat on it. She lifted out what looked like a pale blue cloud.

"This was Harper's blanket, what I had made for him right after he was born. I had one made for each of my boys, and they're one of the things I saved to pass on. If you have a girl, you'll use something of Lily's or want something new and feminine. But I hope, if you have boy, you'll use this. In either case, you should have this now."

"It's beautiful."

Roz held it against her cheek a moment. "Yes, it is. Harper is one of the great loves of my life. There's nothing I want more on this earth than his happiness. You make him happy. That's more than enough for me."

"I'll be a good wife to him."

"You damn well better be. Are we going to sit down and have a cry now?"

"Oh yeah. Yeah, that'd be good."

WHEN SHE LAY BESIDE HIM IN THE DARK, SHE LIStened to the steady, drumming rain.

"I don't know how I can be so happy and so scared at the same time."

"I'm right there with you."

"This morning, it felt like everything crashed down on my head, like a whole bookcase, and every book smacked me with the hard edge. Now it turns out it was flowers falling, and I'm covered in all these soft petals and perfume."

He took her hand, the left, the one where her thumb kept rubbing along her third finger. The ring was in its box on the dresser. "I'll get it to the jeweler tomorrow."

"I don't know how I'm going to feel about being married to somebody who reads my mind." Then she rolled over onto him, tossed back her hair. "I think I can read yours, too. And it goes something like this."

She lowered her lips to his.

Soft and smooth, that's how she felt with him. Lovely and loose. And most of all, loved. Whatever tried to darken her heart, whatever brewed in the night, she could, she would, hold off and have this time with him.

Safe, secure. Seduced.

She could trust him to hold her, as he did now, with their bodies warm, their lips tender. She could trust herself to be strong with the taste of him teasing her tongue.

They moved together, slow and easy, while the rain drummed musically on the stones of the terrace. Her heart drummed, too. Pleasure and anticipation. She knew him so well. Friend and partner, now lover. Husband.

Overcome, she laid her cheek on his. "I love you, Harper. It seems like I've already loved you forever."

"We've still got forever."

He brushed his fingers over her face, her cheeks, her temples, into her hair. He could see her in the gloomy dark, the shape of her, the gleam of her eyes. Witchy and mysterious in this storm light, but nonetheless his. He could look at her and see the long roll of the future. Touch her, and know the simple beauty of the now.

He sampled her lips, skin, the long line of her throat, the subtle curve of her breast. Her heart beat under it, steady as the rain. And quickened as his mouth possessed.

Slowly, guided by her sighs, he took his hands and lips over her. The narrow torso, so white, so delicate in the dim light, and the jump of muscles as he passed, the quivers, told him she was roused.

He laid his lips, gently, so gently, on her belly, and laid his cheek there just a moment, in wonder of what grew in her. Her hand brushed over his hair, stroked.

"Its middle name has to be Harper," she murmured. "Boy or girl, whatever we choose for the first name, it's important we pass the Harper name on."

He turned his head to press another kiss over their child. "How about Cletis? Cletis Harper Ashby."

He fought to keep his lips from curving against her skin when her hand stilled. "That's a joke, right?"

"Little Cletis, or Hermione, if it's a girl. You just don't see enough Hermiones these days."

He kissed his way back up until his lips hovered over hers.

"You'd be sorry if I fell in love with those names and insisted on them. Wouldn't be so funny then, would it?"

"Maybe Clemm." He dropped little kisses at the corners of her mouth. "Or Gertrude."

Her fingers drilled into his ribs. "Looks like I'm going to have to be sure I'm the one filling out the birth certificate. "Especially since I'm thinking we'll stick with flower names. Begonia's my personal favorite."

"But what if it's a girl?"

She grabbed both of his ears and pulled, then gave up on a laugh.

And was laughing when he slipped inside her.

* * *

SHE WAS SO WARM, SO CONTENT, SNUGGLED UP BESIDE him, drifting off to sleep. The patter of rain was music, a lullabye to float away to dreams on.

She imagined herself walking toward him, her long white dress shimmering in the sunlight, lilies, bold and red lying in the crook of her arm, like a child. He would wait for her, wait to take her hand, to make promises. Take the vows that meant forever.

Till death do you part.

No. She shifted with the quiver under her heart. She wanted no mention of death on the day they married. No promises tied to it.

Death brought shadows, and shadows blocked the sun.

Empty promises. Words spoken by rote and never meant to be kept. Clouds over the sun, and the rain turning her white gown to dull, dingy gray.

It was cold, bleak. But there was such heat in her. Hate was a furnace, rage the fire that stoked it.

How strange, how extraordinary that she should feel so alive, so viciously *alive* at last.

The house was dark. A tomb. They were all dead inside. Only her child lived, and would always, ever. Endless. She and her son would live forever, be together until the end of days while the rest rotted.

This was her vengeance. Her only task now.

She had given life. She had grown it inside her own body, had pushed it into the world with a pain akin to madness. It would not be stolen from her. It was hers to keep.

She would bide in that house with her son. And she would be the true mistress of Harper House.

After this night, she and James would never be parted again.

The rain drenched her as she walked, humming her tune as the hem of her soaked nightdress waded through mud.

They would play in the gardens in the bright spring. How he would laugh. Flowers blooming, birds singing, only for them. Tea and cakes, yes, tea and cakes for her precious boy.

Soon, very soon now, an endless spring for them.

She walked through the rain, wading through the crawl of fog. Now and then she thought she heard some sound—voices, laughter, weeping, shouting.

Now and then, she thought she saw some movement out of the corner of her eye. Children playing, an old woman sleeping in a chair, a young man planting flowers.

But they were not of her world, not of the world she sought.

In her world, they would be the shadows.

She walked the paths, or trod over the winter beds, her feet bare and filthy. Her eyes mad moonbeams.

She saw the silhouette of the stables. What she needed would be there, but so would others. Servants, rutting stablehands, dirty grooms.

Instead, she tapped a finger on her lips, as if for silence, but a rolling laugh escaped. Maybe she should burn the stables, set a fire that would rise up in the sky. Oh, how the horses would scream and the men run.

A toasty blaze on an ice-cold night.

She felt that she could light fires with a thought. And thinking, whirled to face Harper House. She could burn it to ash with her mind. Every room bursting with heat. And he, the great Reginald Harper, and all who had betrayed her would perish in the hell she created.

But not the child. No, no, not the child. She pressed both hands to her mouth, banished the thought before the spark flew. It was not the way for her son.

He must come with her. Be with her.

She walked toward the carriage house. Her hair, tangled around her face, dripped into her eyes, but she walked unhurried.

No locks here, she thought at the wide doors. Who would dare trespass on Harper land?

She would.

The door creaked as she pulled it open. Even in the gloom, she could see the shine of the carriages. No dull wheels for the great master. Big, glossy carriages to carry him and his whore-wife, his mewling daughters, wherever they chose to go.

While the mother of his son, the creator of *life,* drove in a stolen wagon.

Oh, he would pay.

She stood in the open doorway, swaying as her mind rolled in circles, buzzing rings of rage and confusion and terrible love. She forgot where she was, what she was, why. Then the purpose looped around once more.

Could she risk a light? Dare she? She must, she must. She couldn't see in the dark.

Not yet.

Though her fingers shook with cold as she lighted a lamp, she didn't feel it. The heat still burned through her, and made her smile as she saw the hank of rope.

There now, that would do, that would do nicely.

She left the lamp burning, the door open as she walked back out into the rain.

WHEN HARPER TURNED, REACHED FOR HER, SHE wasn't there. He half woke, stretching his arm out farther, expecting to meet her skin.

"Hayley?"

He murmured her name, pushed onto his elbow. His first

thought was that she'd gone into Lily, but he heard nothing from the bedside monitor.

It took him a few seconds longer to realize what he did hear.

The rain was too loud. Pushing up quickly he saw the terrace doors were open. He rolled out, grabbing his jeans.

"Hayley!" He dragged on his jeans, bolted for the door. He saw nothing but the rain and the dark.

Rain pelted him, his heart constricted to an ice chip in his chest. On a panicked oath, he rushed back inside, and into Lily's room.

The baby slept, peacefully. Her mother wasn't there.

He strode back to the bedroom, grabbed the monitor, and shoving it in his back pocket went out to find her.

Calling for her, he bolted down the steps. The carriage house, he thought. He'd always believed Amelia had gone there. The night he'd seen her in the garden when he'd been a child, he'd been sure that's where she'd been going.

Her gown had been wet and muddy, he remembered as he ran. As if she'd been in the rain.

He knew his way, even in the dark. There was no turn of the path that wasn't familiar to him. He saw his front door hanging open, felt a trip of relief.

"Hayley!" He slapped on the light as he rushed in.

The floor was wet, and muddy footprints crossed the room, into the kitchen. He knew the house was empty even before he called for her again, before he ran through it, heart thundering, looking for her.

This time he grabbed the phone, speed-dialing as he ran back out.

"Mama, Hayley's gone. She went outside. I can't find her. She's—oh Jesus, I see her. Third floor. She's on the third floor terrace."

He tossed the phone aside and kept running.

She didn't turn when he shouted her name, but continued to cross the terrace like a wraith. His feet skidded on wet stone, and flowers were crushed as he leaped off the path into beds to cut to the stairs leading up.

Lungs burning, heart screaming, he bounded up.

He reached the third level as she flung open a door.

She hesitated when he called out to her, and slowly turned her head to face him. And smiled. "Death for life."

"No."

He made the last leap, grabbed her arm and jerked her inside out of the rain. "No," he said again, and wrapped his arms around her. "Feel me. You know who I am. You know who you are. Feel me."

He tightened his grip when she struggled. Held her close and warm even as her head whipped from side to side and her teeth snapped like a wild dog's.

"I will have my son!"

"You have a daughter. You have Lily. Lily's sleeping. Hayley, stay with us."

And swept her up in his arms when her body sagged.

"I'm cold. Harper, I'm cold."

"It's all right. You're all right." He carried her across the wide ballroom with its ghostly dust sheets as rain lashed windows.

Before he reached the door, Mitch shoved it open. After one quick glance, Mitch let out a breath. "Your mother went to check on Lily. What happened?"

"Not now." With Hayley shivering in his arms, Harper moved by Mitch. "We'll deal with it later. She needs to get warm and dry. The rest will have to wait."

NINeteeN

HE HAD HER BUNDLED IN A BLANKET FROM NECK TO toe, and sat behind her on the bed drying her hair with a towel.

"I don't remember getting up. I don't remember going out."

"Are you warm enough?"

"Yeah." Except for the sheen of ice inside her bones. She wondered if any heat would ever reach that deep in her again. "I don't know how long I was out there."

"You're back now."

She reached back, laid a hand over his. He needed warmth and comfort as much as she did. "You found me."

He pressed a kiss to her damp hair. "I always will."

"You took Lily's monitor." And that, she thought, meant even more. "You remembered to take it. You didn't leave her alone."

"Hayley." He wrapped his arms around her, pressed his cheek to hers. "I won't leave either of you alone." Then laid a hand on her belly. "Any of you. I swear it."

"I know. She doesn't believe in promises, or faith, or love. I do. I believe in us, with everything I've got." She turned her head so her lips could brush his. "I didn't always, but I do now. I have everything. She has nothing."

"You can feel sorry for her? After this? After everything?"

"I don't know what I feel for her. Or about her." It felt so wonderful to be able to lean her head back, rest it on his good, strong shoulder. "I thought I understood her, at least a little. We were both in a kind of similar situation. I mean, getting pregnant, and not wanting the baby at first."

"You're nothing alike."

"Harper, erase the personalities, and your feelings for just a minute. Look at it objectively, like you do at work. Look at the situation. We were both unmarried and pregnant. Not loving the father, not wanting to see our lives changed, burdened even. Then coming to want the baby. In different ways, for different reasons, but coming to want the baby so much."

"Different ways and different reasons," he repeated. "But all right, I can see that, on the surface, there's a pattern."

The door opened. Roz came in with a tray. "I'm not going to disturb you. Harper, you see that she drinks this." After setting the tray at the foot of the bed, Roz skirted around to the side. She took Hayley's face in her hand, kissed her cheek. "You get some rest."

Harper reached out, took Roz's hand for a moment. "Thanks, Mama."

"You need anything, you call."

"She didn't have anyone to take care of her," Hayley said quietly when the door closed behind Roz. "No one to care about her."

"Who did she care about? Who did she care for? Obsession isn't caring," he added before Hayley could speak. He eased away to get up, pour the tea. "What was done to her sucked big-time. No argument, no debate. But you know what? There aren't any heroes in her sad story."

"There should be. There should always be heroes. But no." She took the tea. "She wasn't heroic. Not even tragic, like Juliet. She's just sad. And bitter."

"Calculating," he added. "And crazy."

"That, too. She wouldn't have understood you. I think I know her well enough now to be sure of that. She wouldn't have understood your heart, or your honesty. That's sad, too."

He walked to the doors. He was getting the soaker he'd wished for and could stand there, watch the earth drink in the rain.

"She was always sad." He reached inside, beyond his anger and found the pity. "I could see it even when I was a kid, and she'd be in my room, singing. Sad and lost. Still I felt safe with her, the way you do when you're with someone you know cares about you. She cared, on some level, for me, for my brothers. I guess that has to count for something."

"She still cares, I feel that. She just gets confused. Harper, I can't remember."

She lowered the cup, and emotion swam into her eyes. "Not like I could the other times it happened. I could see, at least a part of me could. I don't know how to explain. But this time, it's mixed up, and I can't see. Not all of it. Why was she going into the ballroom? What did she do there?"

He wanted to tell her to relax, not to think. But how could she? Instead he came back, sat by her. "You went to the carriage house. You must have. The door was open, and I could see where you'd walked back to the kitchen. The floor was wet."

"That's where she went that night, the night she died here. She had to have died here that night. Nothing else makes sense. We saw her that time, you and me. Standing out on the terrace, wet and muddy. She had a rope."

"There could've been rope in the carriage house. Probably was."

"Why would she need a rope to get the baby? To tie up the nursemaid?"

"I don't think that's why she wanted rope."

"She had that sickle thing, too." Bright and gleaming, she remembered. Sharp. "Maybe she was going to kill anyone who tried to stop her. But the rope. What would she do with rope besides tie somebody up?"

Her eyes widened and she set the cup down with a rattle when she read the look in his eyes.

"Oh my God. To kill herself? To hang herself, is that what you're thinking? But why? Why would she come all the way out here? Why would she drag herself through the rain, and hang herself in the ballroom?"

"The nursery was on the third floor back then."

What little color had come back into her cheeks drained again. "The nursery."

No, she thought as the image played in her mind, she might never be truly warm again.

ON HER DAYS OFF, HAYLEY WAS USED TO THE HOURS flying by. The time was so crowded with chores—shopping, laundry, organizing what had gotten disorganized during workdays, caring for Lily and the myriad tasks that turned up—she barely remembered what it was like to have what those who didn't have full-time jobs and a toddler called free time.

Who knew she liked it that way?

Finding herself with time on her hands left her feeling broody and restless. But when the boss ordered you to take the day off, there was no arguing. At least not when the boss was Rosalind Harper.

She'd been banished to Stella's house for the day without even Lily as a distraction. She'd been told to rest, and she'd tried. Really she had. But her usual delight in reading didn't satisfy her; the stack of DVDs Stella had handed her didn't entertain, and the quiet, empty house kept her counting the minutes rather than lulling her into a nap.

She passed some of the time roaming the rooms, rooms she'd helped paint. Stella and Logan had turned it into a home, mixing Stella's flair for detail and style with Logan's sense of space. And the boys, of course, she thought as she paused outside of the room Gavin and Luke shared with its bunk beds and shelves loaded with comic books and trucks. It was a home created with children in mind, lots of light and color, the big yard that bumped right up to kiss the woods. Even with the elegance of gardens—and how could the landscaping be anything but beautiful here—it was a yard where kids and a dog could romp around.

She picked up Parker—the dog had been her only company through the day—and nuzzled him as she walked back downstairs.

Would she be as clever as Stella with a home and family? As loving and smart and sane?

She'd never planned it this way. Stella was the one for plans. She'd just cruised along, happy enough with her job at the bookstore, helping her father tend the little house they shared. Now and again she'd thought about taking a few extra classes in business—to prepare for the vague dream of opening her own bookstore. One day.

She'd thought about falling in love—one day. Most girls did, she imagined. But she hadn't been in any hurry for it, for the big love, and what followed. Permanency, home, kids. The whole minivan, soccer-mom routine had been distant as the moon in her head. Years off. Light-years off.

But things had happened that had pushed her in directions she'd never expected to go. So here she was, not yet twenty-six, pregnant with her second child, working in a field she'd known next to nothing about two years before.

And so stupidly in love she was all but breathing valentines.

Just to ice that cake, a cryptic and certainly psychopathic spirit had decided to borrow her body from time to time.

When Parker wiggled, she set him down, then followed him into the kitchen where he parked himself by the back door and stared holes through it.

"Okay, okay, out you go. Guess I'm not the most sparkling company today."

She let him out, and he pranced across the yard, into the woods as if he had an appointment to keep.

She wandered out herself. It was a pretty day. The rain had freshened things, cooled the air a little. She could take a walk, do some weeding. Or she could stretch out on the patio chaise and see if being outdoors was more conducive to napping.

Without much hope, she cocked the chair back, thought about going back in for a book. And was asleep in minutes.

SHE WOKE A LITTLE FUZZY IN THE BRAIN TO THE SOUND of snoring. Baffled, she pressed a hand to her mouth, but the sound continued. There was a light cotton throw tossed over her, and the table umbrella had been cocked to shade her.

The snoring came from Parker who was flopped on his back beside her chaise, his feet straight up in the air so he looked like a toy dog that had been knocked off its perch.

Her life might've been strange at the moment, but she didn't think a dog could have moved the umbrella or brought her a blanket.

Even as she cleared sleep from her throat and pushed herself up, Stella came out the back door bearing two glasses of iced tea.

"Nice nap?" she asked.

"I don't know. I slept through it. Thanks," she added as she took a glass of tea. "What time . . . Wow." She blinked at her own watch. "I was out for almost two hours."

"Glad to hear it. You look better."

"I hope to God. Where are the kids?"

"Logan picked them up after school. They like going to jobs with him. Gorgeous out, isn't it? The perfect day for drinking tea on the patio."

"Everything okay at the nursery? This kind of weather brings people in."

"And it did. We were busy. Look at those crepe myrtles. I love this yard," she said with a sigh.

"You and Logan have done an amazing job. I was thinking that before. What a good team you are."

"Turns out. Who'd have thought a cranky disorganized know-it-all and an anal-retentive overachiever could find true love and happiness?"

"I did. Right from the start."

"I suppose you did. Smartie. Have you eaten?"

"I wasn't really hungry."

Stella wagged a finger. "Somebody in there might be. I'm going to fix you a sandwich."

"Don't fuss, Stella."

"PB and J?"

With a shake of her head, Hayley gave in. "No fair. You know my weaknesses."

"Sit right there. The fresh air's good for you. I'll be back in a minute."

True to her word, Stella was back not only with the sandwich, but a sprig of purple grapes, bite-size wedges of cheese. And a half a dozen Milano cookies.

Hayley looked at the plate on her lap, then up at Stella. "Will you be my mommy?"

With a laugh, Stella sat on the chaise at Hayley's feet. And began to rub them in a way that had every muscle in Hayley's body sighing in relief. "One of my favorite things about being pregnant was getting pampered once in a while."

"Missed that the first few months the first time out."

"So, you'll make up for it with this one." Stella patted Hayley's leg. "How you feeling—gestating-wise?"

"Good. Tired, you know, and up and down on the emotional scale, but pretty good. Better now," she added after another bite of the sandwich. "And I hate admitting that—a long nap, comfort food, it's doing the job. I'm going to take care of myself, Stella, I promise. I was careful carrying Lily, and I'll be careful this time, too."

"I know you will. Besides, nobody's going to give you a choice."

"I get . . ." She moved her shoulders restlessly. "Funny when everybody's worried about me."

"Then you'll have to get funny, because we can't help it. Not with everything that's going on."

"Last night, it was so . . . I've used all the words before. Strong, strange, bizarre, intense. But this was the most of all of them. Stella, I didn't tell Harper everything. I couldn't."

"What do you mean?"

"I didn't tell him what I felt. He'd wig, the way guys do. I'm counting on you not to."

"Tell me what's going on."

"It's a feeling—and I don't know if it's just stress or if it's real. But I feel. Stella, she wants the baby. This baby." Hayley pressed a hand to her belly.

"How—"

"She can't. No power on this earth, no power anywhere, is strong enough to push me aside. You know, because you've had a child inside you. Harper, he'd freak."

"Explain this to me, so I don't."

"She gets mixed up is the best way I can explain it. From the here and now, to back in her own time. She wavers back and forth. When she's in the now, she wants what I have. This child, the life, the body. Even more, wealth and privilege. She wants the sensations and the payoff. Do you understand?"

"All right, yes."

"She's much more frightening, much more selfish when her mind's in the now. When it's back, when she's caught up in what happened to her, it's like it *is* happening. Then she's just angry and vindictive, so she wants someone to pay for what happened to her. Or she's sad, and pitiable, and she just wants it all to stop. She's tired. Harper thinks she committed suicide."

"I know. We talked a little."

"He thinks she hanged herself in the nursery. Right there while the baby slept. She could've done it. She was lost and crazy enough to have done it."

"I know that, too." Stella rose, walked to the edge of the patio to look out over the yard. "I've been having dreams again."

"What? When?"

"Not here, not at night. Daydreams, you could say. At

work. On Harper ground. Images like before of the dahlia. The blue dahlia. Only it's monstrous. That's how she wants me to see it. Petals like razors, waiting to slice your fingers to ribbons if you touch it. It's not growing out of a garden this time." She turned back; met Hayley's eyes. "But out of a grave. Unmarked, black dirt. The dahlia is the only thing that grows there."

"When did they start?"

"A few days ago."

"Do you think Roz has had them, too?"

"We'll need to ask her."

"Stella, we have to go up to the old nursery."

"Yes." She walked back, took the hand Hayley held out to her. "We will."

IT WAS EASY TO TALK WITHOUT MEN WHEN THE ANnounced activity was wedding planning. Men, Hayley noted, scattered like ants when terms like guest lists and color schemes were mentioned.

So they were able to sit on Stella's patio in the balm of the evening with Lily being passed from one pair of arms to another, or playing in the grass with Parker.

"I didn't think it would be so easy to chase Harper off," Hayley complained. "You'd think he'd want some input into the wedding plans. He's getting married, too."

Roz and Stella exchanged amused looks before Roz reached over, patted Hayley's hand. "Sweet, foolish child."

"I guess it doesn't matter, since that's not what we're doing. But still." Annoyed with herself, Hayley waved her hands. "Anyway. Amelia's been messing with you, too."

"Twice," Roz confirmed. "Both times when I was alone in the propagation house. I'd be working, and then I'd be somewhere else. It's dark, too dark to tell where, and cold.

Very cold. I'm standing over an open grave. When I look down I see her, looking back at me. Her hands are clasped over the stem of a black rose. Or it looks black in the dark."

"Why didn't you tell us?" Stella demanded.

"The same could be asked of you. I intended to tell you, and did tell Mitch. But we've had a few major distractions."

Hayley hauled Lily onto her lap and admired the thick plastic bracelet she played with. "I know that when this first started and I suggested a seance everybody thought it was a joke. But maybe we should try it. The three of us have this connection to her. Maybe if we tried, really tried to communicate, she'd tell us what she wants."

"I'm not pulling out the turban and crystal ball anytime soon," Roz said, definitely. "In any case, I don't think she knows. By that, I mean she wants to be found—and I think she means her grave, or her remains. But she doesn't know where it is."

"We can't be a hundred percent certain it's on Harper property," Stella put in.

"No, we can't. Mitch is doing all he can to find death records, burial records. We don't think there are any for her."

"A secret burial." Hayley nodded. "But she always wants us to know what happened to her. It still pisses her off." She shrugged, smiled a little. "It's one of the things I get, pretty loud and clear. If she was killed, or killed herself, in the house, we need to find out."

"The nursery," Roz stated. "It was still in use when I was born."

"You stayed up there when you were a baby?" Hayley asked.

"So I'm told. At least for the first few months, with the nursemaid. My grandmother didn't approve, Grandmama Harper. Apparently she'd only used it when they were entertaining. She used her considerable influence on my parents until they moved me to a room on the second floor. I never used it for my boys."

"Why?"

Roz pursed her lips and thought over Hayley's question. "First, I didn't want them that far away from me. And yes, I didn't like the feel of the room. Something I couldn't explain, and didn't think about that much at the time."

"The furniture in Lily's room came from there."

"Yes. Once Mason was out of the crib, I had everything taken back up. I took to storing the boys' things in there when they outgrew them. We don't use the third floor as a rule. It's too costly to maintain, and more space than we can practically use. Though I have had parties in the ballroom in the past."

"I'd never been up there," Hayley commented. "Which is strange now that I think about it, because I like going through houses, seeing how they look, picturing them the way they were, that kind of thing. But I never even thought of going up there in all the time I've lived in the house. Stella?"

"No, and you're right, it is odd. The boys had the run of the house for more than a year. You'd think I'd have had to chase them down from there at some point. But I don't think they ever went up either. Even if they did it in secret, Luke would've spilled. He always does."

"I think we should." Hayley looked from one to the other. "I think we have to."

"Tonight?" Stella asked.

"I don't think I can stand to wait. It's driving me crazy."

"If that's what we're going to do, we'll all do it together. The six of us," Roz said. "Not the children. David can keep them downstairs. You have to be sure, Hayley. At this point it seems, of all of us, you're the closest to her."

"I am sure. But not just me, which is something else I

wanted to bring up. Harper. Her feelings for him, about him." A little chilled, Hayley rubbed her arms. "They're awfully mixed, and potent. She loves him—the child of the child of the child sort of thing. And she hates him—a man, a Harper man, Reginald's blood."

She looked at Stella, at Roz. "That combination of feelings, it's powerful. I think maybe more powerful because of the way Harper and I feel about each other."

"Love, sex, kinship, vengeance, grief." Roz nodded. "And insanity."

"His feelings about her are pretty mixed, too." Hayley let out a breath. "I don't know if that matters, but I think all of it, at this point, everything's important. I think we must be getting close to the end of it."

"Hallelujah," Stella announced.

"I know. I want this over. I want to really plan a wedding, and plan for this baby. I want to sit here with the two of you and talk about flowers and music and the kind of dress I'm going to wear."

Roz covered Hayley's hand with hers. "We will."

"Last night, before it happened, it was like I was imagining it, seeing myself in a long white dress and the flowers . . . But I guess that's out." She gave a half shrug as she patted her belly. "I don't guess I'm entitled to a long white dress."

"Honey." Roz gave Hayley's hand a quick squeeze. "Every bride's entitled to a long white dress."

FOOD CAME FIRST, A FAMILY MEAL, THE KIND OF RITUAL that brought them all together where flowers were set and children chattered. Roz had said such things were important, and Hayley could see the purpose of it.

This is who we are, it seemed to say. What we are and

what we'll be regardless of trouble. Maybe because of it.

She'd been given this, this family. A mother, a sister, a lover, brothers and friends. A child who was loved by them, and another child to come.

Whatever it took to keep it whole and safe, she would do.

So she ate. She talked and listened, helped wipe up spills, and buried her nerves under the treasure of normality.

There was talk of flowers and books, of school and books. And here was the talk of wedding plans she'd pined for.

"I guess Hayley told you we'd like to get married here, if that suits you, Mama."

"That's what I like to hear." Roz set her fork aside. "In the gardens? We'll insist the weather stay fine, and have tents as a backup. I intend to roll up my sleeves regarding the flowers. I insist you give me my head there. You'll want lilies, I expect."

"Yes. I want to carry red lilies."

"Bold colors then, toss the pastels. I can work with that. I know you don't want anything too formal, and since we've had two weddings already this year, I think we can iron out the details without much pain and suffering."

"Step away now," Logan advised Harper. "Save yourself. Just say, 'That sounds fine.' And if they give you two choices in anything, don't fall into the trap. Just say, 'They're both great,' and tell her to pick."

"He thinks he's being funny," Stella said dryly. "I'm not kicking him under the table because he's right."

"How come everybody's getting married?" Gavin demanded. "How come we always have to wear ties?"

"Because they like to torture us," Logan told him. "It's the way of women."

"They should have to wear ties, too."

"I'll wear a tie," Stella offered. "You wear high heels."

"I know why people get married," Luke piped up. "So they can sleep in the same bed and make babies. Did you and Mitch make a baby yet?" he asked Roz.

"We already made our quota some time ago. And on that note." Roz pushed away from the table. "I think it's time for you boys to help David clear this up so you can have ice cream in the kitchen."

"All right, troops. Fall in. You, too, Private." Before Hayley could deal with it herself, David moved over to take Lily out of the high chair. "Just because you're short, doesn't mean you can skate out of KP. She likes to help me load the dishwasher," he said to Hayley. "We're fine."

"I just need to talk to you for one minute in the kitchen."

"Clear and stack, gentlemen," he ordered, then carried Lily out of the dining room. "We got this end covered," he said to Hayley. "You don't need to worry."

"No, that's not it. I know Lily's fine with you. It's about the wedding. I need to ask you for something."

He set Lily down, gave her a pot and a spoon to bang. "What do you need?"

"I know this might sound sort of strange, but I think you get to tailor a day like your wedding day to suit you best, don't you?"

"If not that day, what day?"

"That's right. So I was wondering, I was hoping, you'd give me away."

"What?" David's face went utterly blank. "Me?"

"I know you're not old enough to be my daddy, or anything. But I wasn't thinking about it that way. I was thinking how you're one of my best friends, and Harper's, too. How we're like family. And how a day like that's about family. I don't have my daddy, or any blood kin I love the way I love you. So I want you to walk me down the aisle—so to speak—and give me to Harper. It would mean a lot to me."

His eyes went misty as he wrapped his arms around her. "That's the sweetest thing," he crooned. "The damnedest sweetest thing."

"Will you?"

He drew back. "I would be honored." Taking both her hands, he turned them over, kissed her palms. "Extremely."

"Whew. I thought you might think it was silly."

"Not even close. I'm so proud, and touched. And, honey, if you don't go on now, I'm going to embarrass myself in front of my troops."

"Me, too." She sniffled. "Okay. We'll talk about all of it later on." She crouched down to kiss Lily's head, and was largely ignored. "You be good, baby girl."

"Hayley." David drew a breath as she stopped at the door. "Your daddy? He'd be proud, too."

The best she could manage was a nod as she left him.

She brushed away tears as she followed the voices in the parlor, then paused when she heard the temper in Harper's.

"I don't like this idea, not one bit. And I like less the fact that the three of you were off plotting this on your own."

"We womenfolk," Roz said with a sarcasm that dripped so heavy Hayley could feel its weight outside the room.

"The fact that you are women isn't any of my doing," he shot back. "But the fact that *my* woman is pregnant is. I don't take chances on this."

"All right, you have a valid point. But what do you intend to do with her for the next seven, eight months, honey?"

"Protect her."

"You do make it hard to argue."

"Arguing isn't going to help." Mitch's voice of reason cut between them. "We can discuss and debate, and we're unlikely to be in full agreement on all points. But we do have to come to some decisions."

Hayley straightened her spine, and stepped into the room. "I'm sorry. Hard not to overhear. Harper, I was going to ask if we could go outside so I could talk to you, but I think what I have to say needs to be said here, to everyone."

"I've got some things to say you might rather hear in private."

She only smiled. "There'll be plenty of time for you to yell at me in private. A lifetime of it. I know you kept it buttoned till now because of the kids. But I'd like you to hear me out before you say anything more."

She cleared her throat and moved farther into the room. "Earlier today, when I was alone, I was wondering how I'd gotten here. I'd never figured on moving away from where I grew up, having a couple of kids before I figured out where I really wanted to go, really wanted to do. Getting married, having babies, that was going to be later, after I'd made something of myself, had some fun. Here I am, living in another state. I've got a daughter not yet two and another baby on the way. I'm getting married. I'm working in a field I never thought about being in before. How'd I get here? What am I doing here?"

"If you're not happy—"

"Please, just listen. I asked myself that. I've still got choices. There are always choices. So I asked myself, is this what I want, is this where I want to be, what I want to do? And it is. I love you. I didn't know I had all this in me."

She kept her eyes on Harper's, only on Harper's and crossed her hands over her heart. "I didn't know I could love a child the way I do Lily. I didn't know I could love a man the way I love you. If I had every choice in the world, this is the one I'd pick. Being with you, with our children, in this place. Because you see that's one more thing, Harper. I love this house, I love this place. As much as you do. What it is, what it stands for, what it'll be to our children, and theirs."

"I know. My mind traveled that same road. That's why you're the one for me.

"I can't walk away from here. Please don't ask me to do that. I can't walk away from this house, this family, the work I've come to love. The only way I can stay is to try to do this thing, to settle this. Right a wrong, or at least understand it. Maybe I was meant to. Maybe we found each other because *we* were meant to. I don't know if I can do it if you're not with me." She scanned the room. "All of you."

Then she looked at Harper. "Be with me, Harper. Trust me to do what's right. Trust us to do it."

He stepped to her, rested his brow on hers. "I am with you."

twenty

"THERE'S NO GUARANTEE ANYTHING WILL HAPPEN." Mitch slipped a spare tape in his pocket.

"I think I can make it happen. What I mean . . ." Hayley moistened her lips. "I think I can draw her. She wants this—a part of her does, and has for a century."

"And the other part?" Harper asked.

"Wants revenge. When it comes down to it, she'll probably be more inclined to hurt you than me."

"And she can hurt us," Roz pointed out. "We've seen that."

"So we go up there armed with cameras and tape recorders." Logan shook his head.

"We happy few," Mitch stated.

"Well, she's raised the stakes." Logan took Stella's hand. "Since none of us are willing to fold, let's ante up."

"We stay together," Roz said as they started up the

stairs. "No matter what. We've never really confronted her as a group before. I think there's strength in that."

"She always had the upper hand, she always moved first." Harper nodded. "Yeah, we stay together."

When they reached the third floor, Roz turned toward the ballroom. Going with instinct, she stepped forward, pushed the double pocket doors open.

"There were lovely parties here. I remember creeping up at night to watch the dancing."

She reached in to switch on the light. It showered down on the shrouded furniture, and the lovely pattern of the maple floor. "I nearly sold those chandeliers once." She looked up at the dazzling trio of them dripping down from ornate plaster medallions. "Couldn't bring myself to do it, even though it would've made day-to-day living easier. I gave my own parties here, once upon a time. I believe it's time I did so again."

"She came in this way, that night. I'm sure of it." Though her hand was already in Harper's, Hayley tightened her grip. "Don't let go."

"Not a chance."

"She came in the terrace doors. They weren't locked. She could've broken the glass if they had been. She came in, and oh . . . Gilt and crystal, the smell of beeswax and lemon oil. The rain dripping, dripping from the gutters. Turn on the lights."

"I have," Roz said quietly.

"No, she turns on the light. Harper."

"Right here."

"I can see it. I can see it."

The fog rolled in the doors behind her, smoking damp over the glossy floors. Her feet were caked with mud, with blood where she'd trod on stones, and left streaks of that mud, of that blood, where she walked.

Alive still. Heart beating blood.

This, this is how they lived at Harper House. Grand rooms lit by sparkling chandeliers, gilt mirrors on the walls, long, polished tables and potted palms so lush they smelled of the tropics.

She had never been to the tropics. She and James would go one day, one day they'd go and stroll on sugar sand by warm blue water.

But no, but no, their lives were here, in Harper House. They had cast her out, but she would be here. Always here. To dance in this ballroom, lit by crystal drops.

She swayed, a partnerless waltz, her head tilted up flirtatiously. The blade in her hand shooting light from its keen edge.

She would dance here, night after night if she chose. Drink champagne, wear fine jewels. She would teach James to waltz with her. How handsome he would be, wrapped in his soft blue blanket. How sweet a picture they would make. Mother and son.

She must go to him now, go to James, so they could always be together.

She wandered out. Where would the nursery be? In the other wing, of course. Of course. Children and those who tended them didn't belong near grand ballrooms, elegant withdrawing rooms. Smell the house! How rich its perfume. Her son's home. And hers now.

The carpet was soft as fur on her feet. And even so late, even when the house was in bed, the gaslights glowed on low.

Spare no expense! she thought. Money to burn.

Oh, she should burn them all.

At the stairs she paused. They would be sleeping down there, the bastard and his whore. The sleep of the rich and the privileged. She could go down, kill them. Hack them to pieces, bathe in their blood.

Idly, she rubbed her thumb over the curved blade of the sickle, had blood welling red. Would their blood run blue? Harper blood. It would be so lovely to see it, spilling out of their white throats, pooling regally blue on their linen sheets.

But someone might hear. One of the servants could hear, and stop her before her duty was done.

So quiet. She tapped a finger to her cheek, stifled a laugh. Quiet as a mouse.

Quiet as a ghost.

She walked to the other wing, easing doors open if they were closed. Peeking inside.

She knew—it was her mother's heart speaking, she thought—as her trembling hand reached for the latch on the next door. She knew her James slept inside.

A low light burned, and with it she could see the shelves of toys and books, the rocking chair, the small bureaus and the chests.

And there, the crib.

Tears spilled out of her eyes as she crossed to it. There he lay sleeping, her precious son, his dark hair clean and sweet, his plump cheeks rosy with health.

Never had there been a more beautiful baby than her James. So pretty and soft in his crib. He needed to be tended, and rocked, and sung to. Sweet songs for her sweet son.

She'd forgotten his blanket! How could she have forgotten his blanket? Now she would have to use what another had bought him when it came time to carry him off with her.

Gently, so gently, she brushed her fingers over his soft hair and sang his lullaby.

"We'll be together always, James. Nothing will ever part us again."

Sitting on the floor, she went to work.

She used the blade to hack through the rope. It was difficult to form the noose, but she thought she did well. Well enough. Discarding the sickle, she carried a chair, positioned it under the ceiling lamp. And sang softly as she tied the rope to the arms of the lamp.

It held on a strong, testing pull and made her smile.

She pulled out the gris-gris she had in a bag looped around her neck by a ribbon. She'd memorized the chant the voodoo queen had sold her, but she struggled with the words now as she sprinkled the gris-gris in a circle around the chair.

She used the blade to slice open her own palm. And let the blood from her hand drip over the gris-gris, to bind the work.

Her blood. Amelia Ellen Connor. The same blood that ran in her child. A mother's blood, potent magic.

Her hands shook, but she continued to croon as she went to the crib. For the first time since he'd been born, she lifted her child into her arms.

Bloodied his blanket, and his rosy cheek.

Ah, so warm, so sweet! Weeping with joy she cuddled the child against her damp and filthy gown. When he stirred and whimpered, she hugged him only closer.

Hush, hush, my precious. Mama is here now. Mama will never leave you again. His head moved, his mouth sucking as if in search of a nipple. But when with a sob of joy, she tugged her gown below her breast, pressed him there, he arched and let out a cry.

Hush, hush, hush. Don't cry, don't fret. Sweet, sweet baby boy. Sawing her arms back and forth to rock him, she moved to the chair. Mama has you now. She'll never, never let you go. Come with Mama, my darling James. Come with Mama now where you will never know pain or grief. Where we will waltz in the ballroom, have tea and cake in the garden.

She climbed, awkward with his weight, with his wiggles, onto the chair. Even as he wailed, she smiled down at him, and slipped the noose around her neck. Softly singing, she slipped the smaller noose around his.

Now, we're together.

The connecting door opened, a spill of light that had her turning her head, baring her teeth like a tiger protecting her cub.

The sleepy-eyed nursemaid shrieked, her hands flying to her face at the sight of the woman in the filthy white gown, and the baby in her arms, screaming with fear and angry hunger, with a rope around his neck.

"He's mine!"

As she kicked the chair away, the nursemaid sprang forward.

Screams gave way to the cold, and the dark.

Hayley sat on the floor of what had been the nursery, weeping in Harper's arms.

SHE WAS STILL ICY, EVEN IN THE PARLOR WITH A BLANKET over her legs, and the unseasonable fire Mitch had set to blaze in the hearth.

"She was going to kill him," she told them. "She was going to kill the baby. My God, my God, she meant to hang her own child."

"To keep him." Roz stood, staring at the fire. "That's more than madness."

"If the nurse hadn't come in when she did. If she hadn't heard him crying and come in quickly, she would've done it."

"Selfish woman."

"I know, I know." Hayley lifted her hands, rubbed her shoulders. "But she didn't do it to hurt him. She believed they'd be together, and happy, and, oh Jesus. She was broken, in every possible way. Then at the end, when she lost again . . ." Hayley shook her head. "She keeps waiting for him. I think she must see him in every child who comes to Harper House."

"A kind of hell isn't it?" Stella asked. "For madness."

She'd never forget it, Hayley thought. Never. "The nurse, she saved the baby."

"I haven't been able to trace her," Mitch put in. "They had more than one nursemaid during his babyhood, but the timing of this points to a girl named Alice Jameson—which also jibes with Mary Havers's letter to Lucille. Alice left the Harper employ in February of 1893, and I haven't found anything more on her."

"They sent her away." Stella closed her eyes. "That's what they'd have done. Paid her maybe, or just as likely threatened her."

"Both would be my guess," Logan said.

"I'll push on it, do what I can to find her," Mitch promised, and Roz turned to smile at him.

"I'd appreciate it. I wouldn't be here without her, nor would my sons."

"It wasn't what she wanted us to know," Hayley said quietly. "Or not all of it. She doesn't know where she is. Where she's buried. What they did with her. She won't be able to leave, to rest, to pass over, whatever it is, until we find her."

"How?" Stella spread her hands.

"I have an idea on that." Roz scanned faces. "One I think's going to hit this group about fifty-fifty."

"What's the point?" Harper objected. "So Hayley can see her try to hang a baby again?"

"So she, or one of us, can see what happened next. Hopefully. And by we, I mean myself, Hayley and Stella."

For the first time since they'd started upstairs, Harper released Hayley's hand. He shoved off the couch. "That's a damn stupid idea."

"Don't take that tone with me, Harper."

"It's the only tone I've got when my mother goes crazy. Did you see what just happened up there? The way Hayley walked from the ballroom to the old nursery? The way she talked as if she was watching it happen, and like she was part of what was happening?"

"I saw perfectly well. That's why we have to go back."

"I've got to side with Harper on this, Roz." Logan gave an apologetic shrug. "I don't see sitting down here while three women go up there alone. I don't give a rat's ass if it's sexist."

"I expected as much. Mitch?" Her eyebrows winged up when he sat, frowning at her. "Well, you're about to surprise me again."

"You can't seriously agree with her on this?" Harper whirled around to his stepfather.

"The hell of it, Harper, is that I am. I don't like it, but I see where she's going, and why. And before you take my head off, consider this: They'll do it later, at some point when none of us is around."

"What happened to staying together?"

"It's a man who used her, abused her, stole her child, cast her off. She's been poking at me and Stella again. She won't trust you. Maybe we can convince her to trust us."

"And maybe she'll toss you off the third floor terrace."

"Harper." Roz crossed to him, her smile as thin as a blade. "Anybody gets tossed out of this house, it's going to be her. That's a stone promise. My sympathy for her is at an end. You still have it." She looked over at Hayley. "And that's fine, probably an advantage. But mine is over. What she would have done if not for intervention is unforgivable to me. I will have her out of this house. Can you go back?" she asked Hayley.

"Yes, I can. I want it done. I don't think I'll ever have another easy moment until it is."

"You're asking me to risk you."

"No." Hayley rose to go to Harper. "To believe in me."

"YOU KNOW HOW, IN THE MOVIES, THE STUPID, USUally scantily clad blonde, goes down in the basement alone when she hears a noise, especially if there's a slasher-type killer running around?"

Roz laughed at Hayley as they stood on the third floor landing. "We're not stupid."

"And none of us are blond," Stella added. "Ready?"

They clasped hands and started down the hall.

"The problem with this," Hayley began in a voice that sounded tinny to her ears, "is that if she doesn't know what happened to her after, how will we?"

"One step at a time." Roz gave Hayley's hand a squeeze. "How are you feeling?"

"My heart's beating a mile a minute. Roz, when this is over, can we open this room again? Make it, I don't know, a playroom maybe. Something with light and color."

"A wonderful idea."

"And here we go," Stella declared. They walked in together.

"How did it look before, Hayley?" Roz asked her.

"Um. The crib was over there." She gestured with her chin. "Against the wall. The lights were on low. Gaslights, like in that movie with Ingrid Bergman. The one where Charles Boyer tries to drive her crazy. There was a rocking chair over there, and another, straight-backed chair—the one she used—over there. Shelves here," she pointed, "with toys and books on them. And a . . ."

Her head snapped back, her eyes rolled up white. As she began to choke, her legs buckled.

She heard, through the storm surge in her ears, Roz shout to get her out. But she shook her head wildly.

"Wait, wait. God it *burns*! The baby's screaming, and the maid, the nurse. Don't let go of me."

"We're taking you out," Roz said.

"No, no. Just don't let go. She's dying—it's horrible—and she's so angry." Hayley let her head fall onto Roz's shoulder. "It's dark. It's dark where she is. Was. No light, no air, no hope. She lost. They took him again, and now she's alone. She'll always be alone. She can't see, she can't feel. Everything seems so far away. Very cold, very dark. There are voices, but she can't hear them, only echoes. It's so empty. She's going down, down, so heavy. She can only see the dark. She doesn't know where she is. She just floats away."

She sighed, left her head on Roz's shoulder. "I can't help it, even in this room, I feel sorry for her. She was cold and selfish, calculating. A whore, certainly, in the lowest sense of the word. But she's paid for it, hasn't she? More than a hundred years of being lost, of watching over other people's children and never having more than that one mad moment with her own. She's paid."

"Maybe she has. Are you all right?"

Hayley nodded. "It wasn't like before, not the way I could feel her pulling at me. I was stronger. I need life more than she does. I think she's tired. Almost as tired as we are."

"That may be, too. But you don't let your guard down." Stella looked up where once had hung an armed gaslight chandelier. "Not for a minute."

"Let's go back." Stella rose, helped Hayley to her feet. "You did what you could. We all have."

"It doesn't seem like enough. It was a brutal death. It wasn't quick, and she saw the maid run out with the baby. She reached out her arms for him, even when she was strangling."

"That's not a mother's love, whatever she thought," Roz said.

"No, it's not. It wasn't. But it was all she had." Hayley moistened her lips, wished desperately for water. "She cursed him—Reginald. Cursed all them—the Harpers. She . . . she willed herself to stay here. But she's tired. Part of her, the part that sings lullabies, is so tired and lost."

She let out a sigh, then smiled when she saw Harper pacing the landing. "We've all got so much more than she did. We're fine." She left the other women to go to him. "I guess we didn't get what we were after, but we're fine."

"What happened?"

"I saw her die, and I felt her in the dark. Awful. Dark and cold and alone. Lost." She leaned against him, let him lead her downstairs. "I don't know what happened to her, what they did with her. She was going down in the dark, in the dark and cold."

"Buried?"

"I don't know. It was more . . . floating away in the dark, drifting down where she couldn't see or hear, or find her way out." Unconsciously, she rubbed a hand over her throat, remembering the sensation of the rope biting in. "Maybe it was a soul thing—you know the opposite of the tunnel of light."

"Floating, drifting?" Harper's eyes went sharp. "How about sinking?"

"Ah . . . yeah. I guess."

"The pond," he said and looked at her. "We never thought of the pond."

"THIS IS CRAZY." IN THE HAZY LIGHT OF DAWN, HAYley stood on the bank of the pond. "It could take hours, more. He should have help. We could get other people. Search-and-rescue people."

Roz slid an arm over her shoulders. "He wants to do this. He needs to." She watched while Harper pulled on flippers. "It's time for us to step back, let them do."

The pond looked so dark and deep with the skim of fog rising over its surface. The floating lilies, the spears of cattails and iris greens that had always seemed so charming to her were ominous now, fairy-tale foreign and frightening.

But she remembered how he'd paced the landing while she'd gone up the stairs into the nursery.

"He trusted me," Hayley said quietly. "Now I have to trust him."

Mitch crouched beside Harper, handed him an underwater lamp. "Got everything you need?"

"Yeah. Been a while since I scuba'd." He took deep, steady breaths to expand his lungs. "But it's like sex, you don't forget the moves."

"I can get some students, some friends of my son's who know the moves, too." Like Hayley, Mitch studied the wide, misty surface of the water. "It's a big pond for one man to cover."

"Whatever else she was, she was mine, so it's for me to do. What Hayley said last night about maybe she'd been meant to help find her. I'm feeling the same about this."

Mitch braced a hand on his shoulder. "You keep an eye

on your watch, surface every thirty minutes. Otherwise, your mama's going to toss me in after you."

"Got it." He looked over at Hayley, shot her a grin.

"Hey." She stepped to him, crouched down. With a hand on his cheek she touched her mouth to his. "For luck."

"Take all I can get. Don't worry. I've been swimming in this pond . . ." He glanced up at his mother, and vague memories of his own tiny hands slapping at the water while she held him flashed into his mind. "Well, longer than I can remember."

"I'm not worried."

He kissed her again, tested his mouthpiece. Then, adjusting his mask, slid into the pond.

He'd swum here countless times, he thought as he dived, following the beam of the light through the water. Cooling off on hot summer afternoons, or taking an impulsive dip before work in the morning.

Or bringing a girl back after a date and talking her into a moonlight skinny dip.

He'd splashed with his brothers in this pond, he remembered, playing his light over the muddy bottom before he checked his watch, his compass. His mother had taught them each how to swim here, and he remembered the laughter, the shrieks, and the cool, quiet moments.

Had all that happened over the grave of Amelia?

Mentally, he cut the pond into wedges, like a pie, and methodically began to search each slice.

At thirty minutes, then an hour, he surfaced.

He sat on the edge, feet dangling in while Logan helped him change his tank. "I've covered nearly half. Found some beer cans, soft drink bottles." He tilted his face toward his mother. "And don't look at me, I got more respect."

She reached down, skimmed a hand over his dripping hair. "I should think."

"Somebody'd get me a bag, I'd clean up as I go."

"We'll worry about it later."

"It's not deep, maybe eighteen feet at the deepest point, but the rain's stirred up the mud some, so it's a little murky."

Hayley sat beside him, but he noted she was careful not to dip her toes in the water. "I wish I could go in with you."

"Maybe next year I'll teach you how to scuba." He patted her belly. "Stay up here and take care of Hermione."

He rolled back into the water.

It was tedious work, without any of the adventure or thrill he'd experienced when he'd strapped on tanks on vacations. The strain of peering through the water, training his gaze on the circle of light had a headache brewing.

The sound of nothing but his own breath, sucking in oxygen from the tank was monotonous and increasingly annoying. He wished it was done, over, and he was sitting in the dry, warm kitchen drinking coffee instead of swimming around in the damn, dark water looking for the remains of a woman who, at this point, just pissed him off.

He was tired, sick and tired of having so much of his life focused on a suicidal crazy woman—one who would have, if left to her own devices, killed her own child.

Maybe Reginald wasn't so much the villain of the piece after all. Maybe he'd taken the kid to protect him. Maybe . . .

There was a burn in his belly, not sickness so much as a hot ball of fury. The sort, Harper realized, that could make a man forget he was fifteen feet or so underwater.

So he rechecked his watch, deliberately, paid more attention to his breathing, and followed the path of his light.

What the hell was the matter with him? Reginald had been a son of a bitch, no question about it. Just as Amelia had been self-centered and whacked. But what had come from that selfish union had been good and strong. Loving. What had come from it mattered.

So this mattered. Finding Amelia mattered.

She was probably buried out in the woods, he decided. But hell, why dig a hole in the ground in winter when you've got a private pond handy? It seemed right, so right he wondered they hadn't thought of it before.

Then again, maybe they hadn't thought of it before because it was lame. People used the pond, even back then. To swim, to fish. Bodies that got dumped in water often resurfaced.

Why risk it?

He moved to another area, skimmed his light.

Nearly another hour passed in the murk, in the wet. He'd have to finish for the day, he decided. Get his tanks refilled and continue tomorrow. Customers would be coming in soon, and nothing put off retail like hearing that some guy was looking for human remains.

He trailed his light through the roots of his water lilies, thought fleetingly that he might try to hybridize a red one. Something that really snapped. He studied the roots, pleased with the health and progress of what he'd begun. And decided to surface.

His light caught something below, and slightly south. He checked his watch, noted he was approaching borrowed time, but he kicked, dived, scanned.

And he saw her, what was left of her. Bones, filthy with mud, tangled with growth. Weighed down, he saw, with a stirring of pity, by bricks and stones, tied to those bones, hands, legs, waist by the rope he imagined she'd hanged herself with.

The rope she'd meant to use on her son.

Still, shouldn't she have surfaced at some point? Why hadn't the rope rotted, those weights shifted? It was basic physics, wasn't it?

But basic physics didn't take ghosts and curses into account.

He paddled a hand in the water, moving closer to her.

The blow knocked him back, sent him somersaulting and ripped the light from his hand.

He was in the dark, with the dead, and running out of air.

He fought not to panic, to let his body go loose and limp so that he would drop to the bottom, and be able to spring off to the surface.

But another wave bowled him over.

He saw her, gliding through the water, her white gown billowing, her hair floating out in tangled ropes. Her eyes were wide with lunacy, and her hand reaching out, curled like claws.

He felt them close around his neck, squeeze, though he could see her still, feet away, suspended in the water over her own bones.

He struck out, but there was nothing to fight. He clawed toward the surface, but she held him down as inevitably as the bricks and stones that had carried her to the bottom.

She was killing him, as she'd planned to kill her own child. Maybe that had been the plan all along, he thought dimly. To take a Harper with her.

He thought of Hayley, waiting for him on the surface, of the child she carried. Of the daughter she'd already given him.

He wouldn't give them up.

He looked back down at the bones, tried to find a glimmer of that pity. And he looked at Amelia, eternally mad.

I remember you. He thought it with all his will. *Singing to me. I knew you'd never hurt me. Remember me. The child that came from your child.*

He groped for his diving knife, sliced his palm with the

blade. As she had once sliced hers in madness. His blood dripped and clouded in the murky water between them, and drifted down toward the filthy bones.

That's your blood in me. Connor blood as much as Harper. Amelia to James, James to Robert, Robert to Rosalind, and Rosalind to me. That's why I found you. Let me go. Let me take you home. You don't have to be alone or lost anymore.

When the pressure on his throat released, he fought the urge to kick straight for the surface. He could still see her, and wondered how it was he could see tears flow down her cheeks.

I'll come back for you. I swear it.

He pushed up, and he thought he heard her singing, the light, sweet voice of his childhood. When he looked back, he saw the beam of his light spear out from the bottom, arrow to her so she was illuminated in its shaft.

And watched her fade away like a dream.

Breaking the surface, he ripped his mouthpiece away, sucked in air that burned his scored throat. Sunlight sparkled in his eyes, dazzling them, and through the roaring in his ears there were voices calling his name.

Through the dazzle, found Hayley standing on the verge, a hand pressed to her belly. On the wrist of that hand, ruby hearts glittered like hope.

He swam through the lilies toward her, swam away from death toward life. Logan and Mitch helped pull him out of the water where he lay on his back, drawing in air, looking into Hayley's eyes.

"I found her."

epilogue

THE SUN FILTERED THROUGH THE LEAVES OF SYCA-mores and oaks and cast pretty patterns of light and shadows on the green of the grass. On the branches birds sang, filling the balmy air with music.

Gravestones stood, marble white, granite gray, carved to mark the dead. On some, flowers lay, petals fading, petals fluttering in the light breeze. Tributes to those who'd passed before.

Harper stood between his mother and Hayley, holding their hands as the casket was lowered.

"I don't feel sad," Hayley declared. "Not anymore. This feels right. More than right, it feels kind."

"She earned the right to be here. Beside her son." Roz looked at the graves, the names. Reginald and Beatrice, Reginald and Elizabeth.

And there, her parents. There aunts and uncles, cousins,

all links in the long chain of Harpers. "In the spring," she said, "we'll put a marker for her. Amelia Ellen Connor."

"You already have, in a way." Mitch turned his head to kiss her hair. "Burying her son's rattle with her, his picture. Hayley's right. It's kind."

"Without her, I'm not. Without her, Harper, Austin, Mason are not. Nor are the children who come from them. She deserves her place."

"Whatever she did, she deserved better than what was done to her." Stella sighed. "I'm proud I was part of this, of giving her back her name, and I hope, giving her peace." She smiled at Logan, then over at David and all the others. "We were all part of it."

"Tossed in the pond. Discarded." Logan rubbed a hand over the small of Stella's back. "All to protect, what? Reputation."

"She's found now," David added. "You did good, Roz, pushing through the system to have her buried here."

"The Harper name still has the weight to shove the bureaucrats. Truth be told I wanted to give her this nearly as much as I wanted her out of my house, away from what and who I love." She rose up to peck Harper's cheek. "My boy. My brave boy. She owes you most of all."

"I don't think so," he disagreed.

"You went back." Hayley pressed her lips together. "Even after she tried to hurt you, you went back to help bring her out."

"I told her I would. Ashbys keep their word as well as Harpers. I'm both." He picked up a fist of earth, held it over the grave, let it sift through his fingers. "Now it's done."

"What can we say about Amelia?" Roz lifted a red rose. "She was mad—let's be honest. She died badly, and didn't live much better. But she sang to me, and to my children.

Her life gave me mine. So rest now, Great-grandmama." She dropped the rose onto the casket.

In turn the others sent a rose into the grave, and stepped back. "Let's give them a minute alone," Roz said, nodding toward Harper and Hayley.

"She's gone." Hayley closed her eyes, settled her mind. "I can feel it. I knew she was gone before you came up. Knew you'd found her before you told us. It was like the rope tying me to her was cut."

"Happiest day of my life. So far."

"Whatever she needed, she has." She stared down at the casket, at the flowers that lay on it. "I was so afraid, when you were in the pond, that you wouldn't come back to me."

"I wasn't finished with you. Not nearly." He took her shoulders, turned her away from the grave, toward him, toward the sunlight. "We've got a life to live. It's our time now."

He took the ring out of his pocket, slipped it onto her finger. "Fits now. It's yours now." He lowered his lips to hers. "Let's go get married."

"I think that's a great idea."

With their hands clasped, they walked away from death, into love, and life.

In Harper House, the wide halls and gracious rooms were quiet, full of sun, full of memories. Full of past, open to tomorrow.

No one sang there.

But its gardens bloomed.

Turn the page for a look at

BLUE SMOKE

by

Nora Roberts

one

baltimore, 2005

For better or worse, it was done. Reena's heart was pounding, her throat bone dry, and at the base of her belly was a little tickle that could have been panic or excitement.

She'd bought herself a house.

She stood on the white marble steps, the keys in her clammy hand. Settlement was over, the papers were signed. She had a mortgage.

And a bank loan, she thought, that stretched out so long she'd be ready for retirement when it was paid off.

Did the math, didn't you? she reminded herself. You can make this work. It was time she owned property. Oh God, she was a property owner.

And hadn't she fallen in love with this house? It was so like home. What that said about her, she wasn't entirely sure, but it had been love at first sight. Everything about it had called to her.

The location, the familiarity, even the slightly tired interior that just begged her to liven it up, her way. It even had a backyard—maybe it was narrow enough to spit from line to line, but it was an actual yard with actual grass. It even had a tree.

Which meant she'd have to mow grass and rake leaves, which meant buying a lawn mower. And a rake. But for a woman who'd lived in apartments for the last ten years, it was heady stuff.

So, here she was, moving into a three-story row, three short blocks from the house where her parents still lived.

Still in the neighborhood, she thought. And as distant as the moon.

But it was good. It was all good. Hadn't the uncles, along with her father, inspected the place top to bottom? There'd been no stopping them. Needed a little fixing up, sure. And more furniture than she could currently claim.

But that would all come.

All she had to do was put the key in the lock and walk through the door, and she'd be standing in her own house.

Instead, she turned around, sat on the steps and waited to get her breath back.

She'd taken a big bite of her savings, plus the generous lump of dough her grandparents had given her—and the rest of the grands.

Now look what I've done. Gone into debt. And didn't a house keep siphoning away money? Insurance, taxes, repairs, upkeep. She'd managed to avoid all that up till now. Those pesky details had gone from being her parents' problem to her landlords' problem.

Never hers.

Managed to avoid all that, she thought, and most every

other kind of commitment. She had the job and her family, friends she'd kept from childhood.

But she was the only unmarried Hale. The only child of Gibson and Bianca Hale yet to go forth and multiply. Not enough time, that's what she told her family if they teased or pressed the matter. Haven't found the right man.

True, all true. But how many times had she retreated from—or just sidestepped—a potential relationship in the last few years?

Dating was fine, sex was good, but don't ask me to form an attachment. Xander said she thought like a man. Maybe it was true.

And maybe she'd bought this house as a kind of compensation, the way some singles or no-children couples bought a puppy.

See! I can make a commitment when I want to. I bought a house.

A house, she admitted, she couldn't seem to make herself enter now that everything was signed and sealed.

Maybe she could just turn it over. Give it a slap of paint, fix it up here and there, then resell it. There was no law that said she had to keep it for thirty years.

Thirty years. She pressed a hand to her belly. What had she done?

She was thirty-one years old, damn it. She was a cop with a decade on the job. She could walk into a stupid house without having a crisis. Besides, some portion of her family was bound to descend before much longer, and she didn't want to be caught sitting on the stairs having a neurotic attack.

She stood up, unlocked the door and walked deliberately inside.

Instantly, as if she'd popped a cork on a bottle labeled Stress, the tension drained out.

The hell with mortgages and loans and the terror of

picking out paint colors. This is what she'd wanted. This big, old, high-ceilinged place with its carved trim, its hardwood floors.

Of course it was too much room for one person. She didn't care. She'd use one of the bedrooms for storage, once she had enough to store. She'd make another into an office space, another into a home gym, and keep the last spare for a guest room.

Ignoring the echoes, the emptiness, she strolled into the living room. Maybe she'd take the various offers from various relatives on hand-me-down furniture. At least for now. Put some of Mama's drawings on the walls. Make this a cozy, comfortable space.

And the smaller parlor, that was going to be her library. Then she'd need a big table for the dining room. Lots of chairs for when she had family over.

The kitchen was good, she thought as she took a tour of the first floor. It was one of the points that had cemented her decision. The previous owners had outfitted it well with glossy black appliances that had a lot of years left in them. Lots of smooth, sand colored counters and honey-toned cabinets. She might get around to having a few of the doors replaced with glass. Stained glass maybe, or some fancy ripply glass.

She'd enjoy cooking here. Bella was the only one of the lot who'd apparently escaped the love of making food. There were nice, generous windows over the sink and they opened up to a view of the skinny backyard.

The lilacs were blooming. *Her* lilacs were blooming. She could talk to Uncle Sal about putting in a little postage stamp patio, and pick Bella's brain about designing a small garden.

Of course it had been years since she'd planted anything other than a geranium in a windowsill pot. Years, she recalled, since she and Gina had planted tomatoes and peppers and cosmos in the yard of the group house they'd shared in college.

But it seemed to her—at least with the sweetened distance of memory—that she'd enjoyed the digging and weeding.

Probably stick with flowers this time, she decided, and keep it low-maintenance. Yes, Bella would be the one to ask what would work best.

For flowers, fashion, and the right place to be seen, Bella was your girl.

She thought about heading upstairs, to tour the second floor, to mentally arrange furniture. But decided to finish off the first-level walk-through by stepping out in her backyard.

She wanted to walk on her own grass.

The yard was bordered on both sides by a chain link fence. Her neighbor to the right had some sort of spreading bushes planted along the line. Nice touch, she mused. She'd think about something like that. It wasn't just pretty, but added an illusion of privacy.

And to the left . . .

Well, well, well, she thought. She couldn't say much about the yard, but its occupant was worth the price of a ticket.

Fortunately for her, there were no bushes to obstruct the view.

The man had his back to her, and the rear view was very promising. Mid-May temperatures hadn't dissuaded him from taking off his shirt. But maybe whatever he was doing with the lumber and the power tools heated him up.

His jeans ran low on the hips, and the tool belt lower yet. But he managed to avoid the butt crack reveal, which racked up points. He wore a ball cap backward, which may or may not deduct points from the total score, and there seemed to be a lot of wavy black hair under the cap.

She might make a pass at him right there as he was working. She caught music from the boom box beside his sawhorses and gave him additional points for keeping it at a reasonable volume. She could barely catch Sugar Ray.

Six-two, she judged. About one-eighty of good, toned muscle. She didn't want to guess his age until she saw his face. But so far, as next-door neighbors went, he looked like a nice perk.

The realtor had mentioned the carpenter next door, in case she wanted to get any bids on work. But the realtor had failed to mention the carpenter next door had an excellent ass.

His grass was mowed, and he appeared to know what he was doing with the big, sexy tool. No rings on good, strong-looking hands. No visible tattoos or piercings.

Possibilities went up.

His house was similar to hers, though he already had that postage stamp patio in some sort of stone. No flowers—too bad on that as she considered it showed flair and responsibility to pot and tend flowers. Still, the patio looked clean and boasted a muscular barbecue grill.

If the rest of him lived up to the rear view, she might wangle her way to an invite for grilled steak.

He paused, set aside what she was pretty sure was a nail gun. The noise from the compressor shut down, and she heard Sugar Ray more clearly as Carpenter Guy reached for a big bottle of water and aimed it toward his mouth.

He stepped back from his work as he did, and she made out his profile. Good nose, strong mouth—smart enough to wear safety glasses, and cool enough to make them sexy. It looked like the face was going to live up to the rest of the package.

Early thirties, she decided. And wasn't that handy?

When he turned his head and glanced her way, she lifted a hand in what she considered a friendly, hi-new-neighbor salute.

He seemed to freeze, more like she'd aimed her weapon at him rather than a casual wave. He reached up, slowly, drew off his glasses. She couldn't make out the color of his eyes, but she felt the intensity of the stare.

The grin seemed to explode on his face. He tossed the glasses on the ground, strode straight to the fence and vaulted over.

Moved well—quick and agile. Green, she noted. His eyes were a misty green—and lit up a little too manically at the moment for comfort.

"There you are," he said. "Son of a bitch. There you are."

"Yeah, here I am." She gave him a cautious smile. He smelled of sawdust and sweat—which would have been appealing if he wasn't looking at her like he was prepared to gobble her up in one bite. "Catarina Hale." She offered her hand. "I just bought the house."

"Catarina Hale." He took her hand and held it, just held it with his calloused one. "Dream Girl."

"Uh-huh." His score plummeted. "Well, it's nice to meet you. I've got to get back inside."

"All this time." He continued to stare at her. "All these years. You're better than I remembered. How about that?"

"How about that?" She tugged her hand free, backed up.

"I can't believe it. You're just here. Boom. Or maybe I'm having a hallucination."

He grabbed for her hand again, and she slapped hers on his chest. "Maybe you are. Maybe you've had a little too much sun. Better go back to your corner now, Carpenter Boy."

"No, wait. You don't get it. You were there, then you weren't. Then the other time, and then again. And you keep getting away before I can catch up. And now you're right here, talking to me. I'm talking to you."

"Not anymore." Nobody had mentioned the carpenter next door was a lunatic. Shouldn't there have been full disclosure? "Go home. Lie down. Seek help."

She turned, started back to the door.

"Wait, wait, wait." He lunged after her.

In response she spun around, caught his arm, tipped him off balance and jerked his arm behind his back. "Don't make me arrest you, for God's sake. I haven't even moved in yet."

"The cop. The cop." He laughed, twisted his head around to grin at her. "I forgot they said a cop was moving in. You're a cop. That's so cool."

"You're one second away from serious trouble."

"And you smell really good."

"That's it." She pushed him up against the back wall of her house. "Spread 'em."

"Okay, okay, hold on." He was laughing and tapping his forehead against the wall. "If I sound like a crazy person, it's just the shock. Um, oh, shit. Don't cuff me—at least until we know each other better. College Park, May 1992. A party—crap, I don't know whose house it was. Group house, off campus. Jill, Jessie—no Jan. I think Jan somebody lived in the house."

Reena hesitated, the cuffs still in her hand. "Keep going."

"I saw you. I didn't know anybody. Came with a friend, and I saw you across the room. You were wearing this little pink top—your hair was longer, just past your shoulders. I like the way you're wearing it now. Sort of exploding to the jaw."

"I'll tell my hairdresser you approve. I met you at a party in College Park?"

"No. I never got to you. The music stopped. It was a moment for me. Can I turn around?"

He didn't sound crazy—exactly. And she was intrigued. She stepped back. "Hands to yourself."

"No problem." He held them up, palms out, then lowered them to hook his thumbs on his tool belt. "I saw you, and I was . . . Pow." He punched a fist to his heart. "But by the time I got across the room—place was packed—you were gone. I looked everywhere. Upstairs, outside, everywhere."

"You saw me over ten years ago, across the room at a college party, and you remember what I was wearing?"

"It was like . . . for a minute, it was just you. Sounds weird, but there it is. Then this other time? A pal dragged me to the stupid mall on a Saturday, and I saw you up a level. Just there, and I went running around looking for the damn stairs. But by the time I got up, you'd Houdini'd again. Wow. Wow."

He grinned like a mental patient, shoved his hat farther back on his head. "Then winter of '99? I'm stuck in traffic coming from a client's place. Got The Boss on the radio. 'Growin' Up.' And I look over, and I see you in the car beside me. You're tapping out the beat on the wheel. You're just there. And I—"

"Oh my God. Weird Guy."

"Sorry."

"The weird guy who goggle-eyed me on my way to the mall."

His grin spread again, but this time seemed more amused than manic. "That would be me. Half the time I thought I made you up. But I didn't. You're right here."

"Doesn't mean you're not still Weird Guy."

"Not criminally. We could talk. You could ask me in for coffee."

"I don't have any coffee. I don't have anything yet."

"You could come to my place for coffee—except I don't have any either. See, it's right next door. You could come over for a beer, or a Coke. Or the rest of your life."

"I think I'll pass."

"Why don't I make you dinner? Take you to dinner. Take you to Aruba."

Laughter trembled up her throat but she swallowed it back down. "I'll take Aruba under advisement. As for dinner, it's one in the afternoon."

"Lunch." He laughed, pulled off the ball cap and stuffed it in his back pocket, raked long fingers through his dense black hair. "I can't believe how completely I'm screwing this up. I didn't expect to see Dream Girl next door. Let me start over, sort of. Bo. Bowen Goodnight."

She accepted the hand. She liked the strength of it; she liked the calloused roughness of the palm. "Bo."

"I'm thirty-three, single, no criminal record. Got thumbs-up my last physical. I run my own business. Goodnight's Custom Carpentry. And I've got this real estate thing with a partner. The pal I came to that party with. I can get you references, medical reports, financial statements. Please don't disappear again."

"How do you know I'm not married with three kids?"

His face went blank. It actually paled. "You can't be. There is no God so cruel."

Enjoying him now, she angled her head. "I could be a lesbian."

"I've done nothing in my life to earn such a vicious slap by Fate. Catarina, it's been thirteen years. Give me a break."

"I'll think about it. It's Reena," she added. "Friends

generally call me Reena. I've got to go. I've got people coming over."

"Don't disappear."

"Not until my mortgage is paid off. It's been interesting meeting you, Bo."

She slipped back inside, left him standing there.

THEY BROUGHT FOOD, OF COURSE. AND WINE. AND flowers. And most of her furniture.

Since they were moving her in, Reena decided she'd better get in the spirit. She made trips back to the apartment over Sirico's for boxes, for suitcases packed with clothes. For a last goodbye.

She'd been comfortable here, she thought. Maybe too comfortable. Comfort could become rut if you didn't keep an eye out. But she'd miss being able to dash downstairs for a meal, or just to chat. She'd miss the easy routine of strolling up the block and stepping into her parents' home.

"You'd think I was moving to Montana instead of a few blocks away." She turned to her mother, saw the tears swimming. "Oh, Mama."

"It's silly. I'm so lucky to have all my children close. But I liked having you right here. I'm proud that you bought a house. It's a good, smart thing to do. But I'll miss knowing you're right here."

"I'm still right here." She lifted the last box. "Part of me worries that I've taken on more than I can handle."

"There's nothing my girl can't handle."

"Hope you're right. And remind me of that the first time I have to call the plumber."

"You call your cousin Frank. And you should talk to your cousin Matthew about the painting."

"Bases covered." Reena walked to the door, waited for

her mother to open it. "And I've got a handyman right next door."

"You don't hire somebody to work in your house if you don't know him."

"Turns out I do—or he knows me."

She told Bianca the story as they finished loading the car and started the short drive to the new house.

"He sees you once at a party when you're in college? And he's smitten."

"I don't know about smitten. He remembered me. And he's very cute."

"Hmmm."

"He took it well when I threatened to cuff him."

"So, maybe he's used to it. Maybe he's a criminal. Or he enjoys bondage."

"Mama! Maybe he's just a cute, slightly strange guy with a great butt and power tools. Mama, I'm a big girl. And I carry a gun."

"Don't remind me." Bianca waved it away. "What kind of name is Goodnight?"

"It's not Italian," Reena murmured. She pulled up, then watched the door of the house next door open. "Well, it looks like you're going to get the chance to judge for yourself."

"That's him?"

"Um-hmm."

"Good looking," Bianca commented, then stepped out of the car.

He'd cleaned up, Reena noted. His hair was still a bit damp, and he'd put on a fresh shirt—ditched the tool belt.

"Saw you hauling stuff in. Thought maybe you could use a hand. Can I get this out of the way?" he said to Bianca. "Wow, beautiful women run in the family. I'm Bo, from next door."

"Yes, my daughter told me about you."

"She thinks I'm crazy—because I gave her pretty good reason. I'm generally less bizarre."

"So, you're harmless."

"God, I hope not."

It made her smile. "Bianca Hale, Catarina's mother."

"It's nice to meet you."

"You've lived here long?"

"No, actually, only about five months."

"Five months. I don't remember seeing you in Sirico's."

"Sirico's? Best pizza in Baltimore. I get delivery all the time. The spaghetti and meatballs is incredible."

"My parents own Sirico's," Reena said as she popped the trunk.

"Get out. Seriously?"

"Why don't you come in," Bianca said, "have a meal?"

"I will. It's just I've been working pretty much round the clock the past couple months, and—Here let me get those." He nudged Reena aside to pull out boxes while he addressed her mother. "I haven't been seeing anyone—dating—just recently. I don't like eating alone in a restaurant."

"What's wrong with you?" Bianca asked. "Young, good-looking. Why don't you date?"

"I do—I mean, did. Will. But I've had a lot of work, and I'm working on this place in my spare."

"Have you been married before?"

"Mama."

"We're having a conversation."

"It's not a conversation. It's an inquisition."

"I don't mind. No, ma'am, no marriages, no engagements. I've been waiting for Reena."

"Stop it," Reena ordered.

"We're having a conversation," he reminded her. "Do you believe in love at first sight, Mrs. Hale?"

"I'm Italian. Of course I do. And call me Bianca. Come in, meet the family."

"I'd love to."

"Slick," Reena muttered as he stepped aside for Bianca to enter.

"Desperate," he corrected.

"Just put that down there."

"I can take it where it goes."

"For now, it goes there." She pointed to the base of the steps, closed the door.

"Okay. I like your mother."

"Why shouldn't you?" She took off her sunglasses, tapped them against her palm as she studied him. "You might as well come on back—and remember, you asked for it."

She walked back toward the kitchen, avoiding a couple of her nephews who raced in the opposite direction. In the kitchen, sauce was simmering on the stove, wine was being poured, and several arguments were taking place at once.

"This is Bo," Bianca announced, and silence fell. "He lives next door. He's a carpenter and has a crush on Reena."

"Actually, I'm pretty sure she's the love of my life."

"Will you stop." But Reena laughed as she shook her head. "This is my father, Gib, my sister Fran, her husband, Jack, one of the kids running out of here was their son Anthony. This is my sister Bella—the other one streaking by was her son Dom, her other kids, Vinny, Sophia and Louisa are around somewhere. My brother Xander, and his wife, An; their baby is Dillon."

"It's nice to meet you." Fran offered him a smile. "Can I get you a glass of wine?"

"Sure, thanks."

"Fran and Jack manage the restaurant for my parents.

Bella's husband couldn't make it by today. Xander and An are doctors, and work at the neighborhood clinic."

"It's nice to meet everyone."

She knew what he saw. The tall, handsome man at the stove giving him a careful measure. Lovely, pregnant Fran pouring wine, while redheaded Jack gave their redheaded daughter a piggyback ride. Bella leaning against the counter in her designer shoes and country club hair. Xander sipping wine and standing beside his gorgeous golden-skinned wife as she burped their six-week old infant.

Of course the questions came popping out from all directions, but he fielded them easily enough. And didn't seem surprised to see the Italian, Irish, Chinese mix in the kitchen of a nearly empty row house.

He slid into the flow so easily, she was surprised to hear him say he was an only child when asked about his family.

"My parents split when I was a kid. I grew up in PG County. My mother lives in North Carolina now. My father's out in Arizona. I guess my partner's like my brother. We've known each other forever. Maybe you remember him," he said to Reena. "He dated a girl who knew Jan, went to Maryland. I think her name was Cammie."

"No, sorry. I didn't socialize all that much in college."

"She spent most of her time studying," Bella put in, with the slightest smirk. "Then she had her heart broken by tragedy."

"Bella." Bianca's voice was sharp as a whip.

"Oh, for God's sake, it was years ago. If she's not over it, she ought to be."

"When someone dies, they stay dead no matter how many years pass."

"I'm sorry." Bo turned to Reena.

"You don't have anything to apologize for," she said with a long look at her sister. "Here, have some antipasto."

She picked up a platter. "Until I get a dining room table, we'll be eating standing up or sitting on the floor."

"I could make you one."

"One what? A table?"

"Yeah. It's one of the things I do. Actually, my favorite thing. Building furniture. Give me an idea what you want, and I'll make you a table. Ah, like a housewarming deal."

"You can't just make me a table."

"Hush." Bianca moved in. "You do good work?"

"I do exceptional work. I offered her references before. Maybe you know Mr. and Mrs. Baccho, over on Fawn Street?"

Bianca's eyes narrowed. "I know them. Dave and Mary Teresa. You're the boy who did their china cabinets."

"The oak and glass built-ins. Yeah, that's my work."

"It's good work." Her gaze slid toward her husband. "I'd like something like those. Come in here, look at the dining room."

"Mama."

"It doesn't hurt to have him look," Bianca called back, and drew Bo away.

An passed the baby to Xander. She was a tiny thing, barely five feet with a glossy wedge of coal black hair and deep black eyes. She plucked a stuffed mushroom from the platter Reena held. "He's hot," she murmured. "Serious hotness factor."

"I haven't moved in yet, and she's got me dating the boy next door."

"Hey, worst you can do is get a free table out of it." She grinned around the mushroom. "And the guy looks like he can swing a hammer to me."

"I heard that innuendo," Xander called out.

"I'm going to go separate them." Reena handed the platter to An and walked quickly to the dining room.

Her mother was gesturing, holding her hands apart, talking about necessary seating.

Bo looked over, patted a hand on his heart. "She just walks into the room and my head spins."

Reena arched her eyebrows. "You're going to want to take that down a few levels."

"It's my first day, so you need to cut me some slack. We're thinking drop leaf. That way, you'd have the smaller size, and the extension for dinner parties and family meals without the bother of the leaves."

"I don't know what I want yet." About tables, she thought, about you. About anything but the job. "I can't just say."

"I'll make you up a few designs. Get the ball rolling. It's the same setup I've got next door, so I can use my space for measurements. Lots of potential here." He smiled at her. "Unlimited potential. I'd better go."

"You should stay," Bianca objected. "Eat."

"Thanks, I'll take a rain check. You need anything," he said to Reena, "I'm right next door. I wrote down my number." He pulled a card out of his pocket. "Cell's printed on there, home number's on the back. You need anything, just call."

"All right. I'll walk you out."

He handed her his wineglass. "That's okay. I know the way. You stay with your family. I'll be in for that meal, Bianca."

"See that you are."

Bianca waited until she was sure he was out of earshot. "He has good manners. He has good eyes. You should give him a chance."

"I've got his number." Reena stuffed it in her pocket. "I'll think about it."